Inheritors of the Storm

". . . *we'll have revolution in the countryside in less than twelve months.*"

— Edward A. O'Neil, President
American Farm Bureau Federation
(February 1933)

"*We are at the end of our string. There is nothing more we can do.*"

— Herbert Hoover
(Midnight, March 3, 1933)

Inheritors
OF THE
Storm

Victor Sondheim

Dell Publishing Co., Inc.   New York

Published by
Dell Publishing Co., Inc.
1 Dag Hammarskjold Plaza
New York, New York 10017

Dell edition produced by Book Creations, Inc.
Executive Producer: Lyle Kenyon Engel

Dell ® TM 681510, Dell Publishing Co., Inc.

Printed in the United States of America

Book I

Patrimony

March–June 1933

1

He was a big man, with a jutting jaw and ruddy complexion. He looked robust and confident as he stood, hatless in the raw March wind, among all the frightened men on the flag-draped platform. Looking at him, you'd never have guessed that he was propped up on steel braces, that the powerful shoulders had been developed by years of pushing himself around in a wheelchair.

The crowd was unusually quiet. There were forty acres of them jammed into the open spaces in front of the Capitol, overflowing onto rooftops, sitting in the bare branches of trees. They stood patiently in their damp uncomfortable clothes, hushed as if awaiting salvation. Perhaps they were. The flags over the Senate and House office buildings were at half-mast, and there were men with machine guns, incongruous amidst the festive bunting.

He raised a large freckled hand to take the oath. Other presidents had contented themselves with saying, "I do." This one broke precedent by repeating it, phrase by phrase, in a clear firm voice—"like a bridegroom at the altar," a news magazine was to say later.

The instant he finished he swung round to face the crowd. He ignored an attempt to applaud him. The big jaw was thrust out, the affable smile gone. "My friends," he began grimly. "This is a day of national consecration. . . ."

Below, to one side of the podium with its garlanded eagle, cameras flashed and shivering reporters scribbled in their notebooks. A battery of network microphones trembled in their spring-mounted frames, carrying the sound of the voice across an exhausted land; scratching it with static, flattening its vibrant overtones, turning the resonance to tin, but carrying it all the same.

Bradford Sinclair, Sr., hesitated a bare moment before pulling down the window shade. As he stood there with the cord in his hand, it occurred to him that someone out there might wonder why he had drawn a shade in the middle of the day. Then he decided he didn't care. There were plenty of drawn shades in Beulah, Iowa, these days.

He took a last look at Elm Street. Beyond the brown unawakened lawn and the ornamental iron fence that enclosed it, the broad avenue was quiet and peaceful. The rows of sixty-year-old elms, their branches still bare, met to form a skeleton archway against a dull gray sky, not quite shutting out a glimpse of rolling prairie at the end of the street. A milkman's horse clop-clopped down the pavement. A Dodge roadster, low and sleek, went by, its tires hissing against the wet asphalt.

He jerked the shade down savagely and turned to his desk at the other end of the study. He realized he'd been holding his breath and let it out. The papers were still there, of course, in neat compulsive stacks on the desktop. They lay in a pool of yellow light cast by the green-shaded desk lamp, just as he'd left them.

He sighed and went over to sit in the deep leather chair. He picked up the first paper, but did not look at it. Instead he lifted his fine patrician head and listened to the sounds of the house.

Sinclair was a distinguished-looking man with a long-jawed scholarly face and neat sparse white hair. He bore a marked resemblance to Woodrow Wilson that nobody had ever dared to comment on in his presence. Even in his own study, his tie remained unloosened, his vest buttoned to the top, the gold watch chain meticulously draped. He looked altogether sober and trustworthy, as a banker should. He was only in his middle fifties, but the events of the last three years had made him look older.

A faint clatter of dishes came from the kitchen. That was Mrs. Hansen, getting the roast prepared; Mary's brother Elroy would be here for noon dinner. From upstairs came the annoying whine of a Hoover: Helga, the maid, vacuum sweeping the hall rugs. She was staying away from the bedroom door. Mary was taking one of her naps.

The house seemed emptier with Jeremy and Brad junior away at school. The other children were never home these days. Gordon had gulped a glass of milk for breakfast and gone off with his friend Freddie Mueller, promising to do his Saturday chores when he got back. Lord knew where the girls were; Mary was much too lax with them.

He forced his eyes to the paper he held. It was all listed there in his neat, spidery hand. Everything he owned. Everything he owed. And everything he'd stolen.

How had it happened? Sinclair passed a hand over his face and discovered that his eyes were wet. He put the paper down and polished his eyeglasses industriously.

The fat years had fooled him, just as they had fooled everybody else. He could see Thayer Chadwick's round smooth face saying to him: "There's nothing wrong with trading in your own bank's stock. I'm doing it, the rest of the board is doing it, the chairman of National City Bank in New York is doing it. It's a way of showing confidence. If you can't have confidence in your bank, who can, tell me that? Listen, Sinclair, you've been crackerjack, absolutely crackerjack, and the directors and I want to show our appreciation. Five thousand shares of Beulah Trust stock at preferential prices—the first time anybody outside the family's ever been allowed to own more than five percent." He'd waved a chubby, expansive hand. "And you can pay in installments, off your profits. Don't *worry* about it! Everything's going up, up!"

But things hadn't gone up. They'd gone down, that black season of twenty-nine, and Beulah Trust shares had gone down along with everything else. Everything except his repayments to Chadwick and his board. They'd gone on and on.

He'd been three years paying the money back, stripping his other investments, what was left of them after the Crash. The slight rally in 1931 had fooled him. He'd plunged again, bought too much on margin.

But he'd managed to juggle. Oh, yes! And if it hadn't been for that fellow Roosevelt withholding his help to the outgoing Hoover administration these four strange months of interregnum, he might have made it work.

The country had been going down the drain since election day. The government was paralyzed. The banking system was in collapse. Panicky depositors started a run on the banks—but in the entire country the banks had only about six billion dollars to meet forty billion in deposits. Michigan's banks had closed three weeks ago, and the bank panic was on in earnest. By inauguration eve, the governors of seventeen states had declared bank holidays.

But the Beulah Trust had managed to keep its doors open. There wasn't much of a cash flow, with loans suspended and all the farm mortgages being foreclosed, but there was enough. Enough to keep a bank president named Bradford Sinclair, Sr., from going to jail.

And now, as of Saturday morning, March 4, 1933, there were no more balls left for him to juggle.

The phone call had come before dawn. It had roused him from dreams of spiders and dark places and sticky threads that clung to his legs while a hairy snuffling thing that wore the face of Thayer Chadwick emerged from the shadows. For a moment, heart pounding, he hadn't known where he was. Then he'd slipped out of bed quickly, so as not to awaken Mary, and hurried downstairs in the frigid dark without bothering to find robe or slippers.

It was Chadwick, and he hadn't awakened from the dream after all.

"I just got a call from the governor. It's all over, Sinclair. Everything's gone smash. The whole country. New York and Illinois declared bank holidays during the night. It won't be in the morning papers. The public'll find out when they try to get their money out this morning. That Roosevelt fellow's had his men on the phone all night, calling the governors. And the bastard isn't even President yet! Governor Herring had no choice but to go along. He told me he's closing the banks here in Iowa, too. His assistants are drafting the proclamation now."

Sinclair had stood there stupidly. "What . . ." he began.

"Don't bother to come in today," Chadwick rushed on. "There'll be mobs—you wouldn't be able to get through anyway. I've asked the police chief to guard the building. I'm calling a directors' meeting for Monday. We'll have to reorganize. The examiners will be in next week. Sinclair, are you there? Are you hearing this?"

"What . . . yes . . ." he'd managed.

"All right, then. I'll see you after the directors' meeting."

He'd hung up, leaving Sinclair shivering in the dark hall. There was no point in going back to bed. He'd dressed in the bathroom, as quietly as possible, in his best suit—the dark gray wool one he'd bought during his last trip to Chicago. A silver predawn light was filtering through the windows by then, and he heard the rattle of grates and the squeaking of dampers as the ancient coal furnace came to life. That was Gordon's job; the boy must have gotten up early this morning. But by the time he'd gotten downstairs again, Gordon was gone.

Mrs. Hansen was already bustling about the kitchen, ready with his coffee and the newspaper. She'd looked at him with frightened eyes, as if she knew, but probably she was only frightened about her job, the way all the servants in Beulah who hadn't been fired yet were worried.

Chadwick had been right. There was nothing in the paper about the bank closings in New York or Illinois, and nothing about Iowa. The news was still about yesterday's rush on the banks, and about preparations for the inauguration. In Germany they were preparing for the Sunday elections that were expected to put the party of the new Chancellor, Hitler, firmly in power.

He'd taken his coffee into the study, locked the door, and told Mrs. Hansen he didn't want to be disturbed. She was obviously wondering why he wasn't going to the bank this Saturday morning, but she didn't dare ask why. He remembered that one of the farmers he'd had to refuse a loan to that week had been named Hansen. He wondered if it had been a relative. The man had lost control of himself and started to weep. It had been embarrassing.

He'd spent the whole morning poring over his records, over and over again, knowing it was hopeless. The worthless stock certificates, saved since that October day in 1929, were tied in neat little bundles. Steel, chemicals, aeronautics, tobacco, railroads. There were more of them in his own safe at the bank. Some of them had never been traded again after the debacle. There wasn't enough in the lot of them to cover his deficiencies.

Reluctantly he got out the insurance policy the bank had taken out on him when he became president. ". . . *within three years from the Date of Issue . . . incontestable . . . risk not assumed . . . but in such event . . .*" The words swam before his eyes.

The bank would reopen. There would be enough for that. His honor would be saved. They wouldn't be cursing his name in Beulah, Iowa, for years to come. There would be a little money left over. Mary and the children would have to tighten their belts for a while. The servants would have to go, of course. The boys would have to leave school for a year or two and work. But they were go-getters. They were Sinclairs. And he'd always told them to hang on to the stocks. Some day, surely, they would be worth something again.

He wrote a note in his painstaking hand, leaving nothing out. He weighted it down on the desk with the gold watch the bank had given him. Brad junior had always wanted that watch.

He cocked his head. The Hoover was silent. There were no sounds of anyone moving about the house.

He unlocked the bottom drawer of his desk and slid it open. He took out the big, heavy government model Colt .45 automatic and weighed it in his hand. It smelled of oil and cold metal. It was funny. He'd carried it all through the war and never used it. It was the men he commanded who'd done all the firing. Once, during the mop-up operations near . . . what was the name of that little French village in the Argonne? . . . Something-sur-Meuse . . . he'd come upon a wounded German officer, lying there with his life bubbling away through a ghastly hole in his throat. All around, through the shattered trees, was the sound of desultory small arms fire as the advancing First finished off wounded Jerries. He'd drawn his pistol and put it up against the man's head, very close. The German's eyes had flown open and he'd looked at Sinclair's uniform, his gaze falling on the silver captain's bars. He'd opened his mouth, but nothing came out but a rush of blood. He'd stared at Sinclair with mute appeal, waiting. He expected to be shot. He wanted to be shot. Sinclair had released the thumb safety and started to squeeze the grip and trigger. But he couldn't do it. He'd simply walked away, the gun dangling against his breeches. Afterward, he realized he'd been foolish. The German officer might have had a gun and still been able to use it to put a bullet in his back as he walked away.

He pushed back the heavy leather chair and stood up. He walked to the door, unlocked it, and looked out into the hall. No one was there. From the kitchen he could hear the sound of the radio. Mrs. Hansen was listening to the inaugural ceremonies, like almost everybody else in the country.

". . . nor need we shrink from honestly facing conditions in our country today," the rich, mellow voice was saying through a hail of static. "This great nation will endure as it has endured, will revive . . ."

There was a flash of the old irritation at the sound of the voice, then he shrugged, tired of it all. Let the fellow have his chance, he thought. We've reached bottom. Maybe he can do something after all.

Slowly, walking stiffly, the gun at his side at full cock the way he'd held it that time in the Argonne, he mounted the carpeted stairs. He walked into the bathroom and closed the door behind him. It was all polished mahogany and shiny yellow paint in here, smelling of ammonia from Helga's morning cleaning.

He could still hear the radio. Mrs. Hansen must have turned it up. ". . . the only thing we have to fear is fear itself," the new President was saying. "Nameless, unreasoning, unjustified terror . . ."

He knelt carefully by the tub, bending his head over it so as not to leave a mess for Mrs. Hansen. He turned on the water and blew out his brains all over the spotless porcelain.

2

Gordon Sinclair didn't like the looks of the crowd. They were milling around in the hardpacked cleared area in front of Dutch Hansen's big red cattle barn, grim purposeful farmers with faces like old harness leather and necks like cracked baked clay. They shivered in their patched bib overalls with blue gooseflesh showing through the rents in the cloth, the luckier among them wearing shapeless castoff suit jackets or mended overcoats over the work clothes. They kept forming in small, sullen groups, talking in low voices. There were a couple of hundred of them so far, the wrong crowd for a farm auction, and more were arriving every minute in battered flivvers and broken-down trucks, parking in a field of stubble by the side of the dirt road.

"Let's not hang around," he said to Freddie Mueller.

"What's the matter?" Freddie said, a knowing leer on his blunt face. "Scared?"

Gordon glanced over toward the improvised auctioneer's platform that had been hammered together in front of the yawning barn door. A nervous sheriff's deputy who kept fingering his holstered pistol was talking to a man in city clothes.

"I just have better things to do with my Saturday, that's all," Gordon said. He felt conspicuous in his good tweed knickers and argyle

Victor Sondheim

sweater and belted coat with matching cap. At least Freddie was wearing knockabout clothes. And long pants.

At seventeen, Gordon was a tall, well-put-together boy with almost his full growth—too big for knickers, which he hated. He had extracted a promise from his mother that this would be the last pair, after he wore them out. He had conventional sandy-haired good looks, with the pale blue Sinclair eyes, and an unblemished complexion, unlike Freddie, who was going through the pimple stage. The light blond fuzz on Gordon's cheeks had lately started to grow wiry, and it was his ambition to shave every day, not just twice a week, as at present.

"Oh, yeah?" Freddie challenged him. "Like what?"

"Well . . . we could go to the movies. *King Kong*'s playing at the Strand."

"Betcha don't have a dime."

"Bet I do."

Actually, Gordon had been hoping to borrow the dime from Freddie till he could go home and get paid for doing his chores. Freddie always had money in his pocket. His father owned the Mueller Feed and Grain Company, the most prosperous business in town. Freddie got an allowance of twenty-five cents a week, and he didn't have to do chores for it.

It had been Freddie's idea to come to the farm sale. He always knew where to find excitement. Dutch Hansen's place was only a couple of miles out of town, a flat sprawling spread with three enormous storage barns built in more prosperous times, and a tall narrow-shouldered Gothic house whose windows were blind with dust and faded drawn curtains. Gordon and Freddie had ridden out from Beulah on their bikes, now leaning against an abandoned chicken house farther down the road.

They had a good view of the proceedings from their vantage point across the barnyard in front of one of the facing barns. They were sprawled comfortably on a bed of yellowed cornstalks heaped on an abandoned broken-wheeled wagon. The projecting peak over the hayloft above protected them from the steady drizzle. The wagonload of corn had evidently been abandoned last fall when the wheel broke. Dutch had made no attempt to finish unloading or to fix the wheel. The barn was already half full of rotting corn. With corn at ten cents a bushel, it was cheaper to burn it for fuel than to try to sell it. A smudge of burning corn hung all over the Iowa countryside these days.

"Look," Freddie said, pointing.

A tall spare man with a pompadour of white hair was moving

among the farmers, talking to little groups here and there. The sheriff's deputy was giving him the eye.

"So what?" Gordon said.

"That's the guy," Freddie whispered. "The Holiday man. I saw him in town that time they blockaded the highway and turned over the milk trucks."

"We'd better get out of here," Gordon said uneasily.

Like everybody else in this part of Iowa, Gordon was acutely aware of the farm holiday movement. The dissident farmers had been gaining in strength and boldness since last summer. They barricaded the roads with barbed wire and railroad ties and chopped-down telephone poles to keep produce from getting through to the cities. They blew up bridges. They'd held Sioux City and Council Bluffs under siege, and armed with pitchforks, they'd faced down the machine guns of the National Guard. They mobbed courtrooms to prevent farm foreclosures, and they'd been known to tar and feather mortgage agents. They had a song: *"We'll call a farmer's holiday, a holiday we'll hold . . . we'll eat our wheat and ham and eggs, and let them eat their gold."* The movement was spreading to other states, and Gordon's elders talked darkly of revolution.

"My pa says they're bol-bolsheviks," Freddie said authoritatively.

"Huh, they're just dumb old farmers," Gordon snorted.

One of the deputies was wading through the mud toward them. He planted himself in front of the wagon, hands on hips, and stared up at them. He was a narrow-shouldered man with a seamed face, and the gunbelt looked too heavy for him. "You boys better get on out of here," he said.

"We ain't doin' nothing," Freddie said.

"Is something going to happen?" Gordon said.

The deputy looked him over. "Ain't nothing going to happen," he said. "Goddamn outside agitators come in here stirring up trouble, that's all. Go on now, you don't belong here."

"Mr. Hansen said we could stay," Gordon said, improvising wildly. "He's our cook's cousin."

The deputy looked at him closely. "Your name Sinclair?" he said.

"Yes."

The deputy spat into the mud. "I guess you can stay. Just keep out of trouble."

"Yes, sir," Gordon said. "What's it all about?"

"You ought to know. Your father turned him down for a loan. He's got a chattel mortgage for four hundred dollars that he can't pay. They'll take his stock and machinery for that. After that's settled, he's got a foreclosure ahead of him. The papers are being filed at the courthouse this morning."

"My pa says this farm's worth thirty thousand dollars," Freddie put in.

The deputy eyed him sourly. "I guess he'd know. You're the Mueller boy, aren't you?"

Freddie nodded.

"Thought so. Well, it'll be knocked down for a lot less than thirty thousand, you can count on that." He glanced contemptuously over toward where the man in city clothes stood talking to the auctioneer. "That's the man from the insurance company over there. Came all the way from New York. After they take the farm away, old Dutch'll still owe a deficiency judgment."

"But that's not fair!" Gordon burst out.

The deputy spat again. "No, it ain't," he said, and walked away.

There was an eddying movement at the front of the crowd. The auctioneer was mounting the platform. He was a large, florid man with a new straw hat and a red bandanna neatly tied around his neck. He wore a flannel shirt and heavy twill trousers held up by bright red galluses. He climbed ponderously into a rickety kitchen chair that had a big black umbrella tied to a piece of two-by-four nailed to the chairback. He fished a big gold watch out of his watch pocket, looked at it, and put it back.

"I thought you wanted to leave," Freddie said to Gordon. He rolled his eyes back. "'Mr. Hansen said we could stay.' 'What's it all about, sir.' Oh, boy!" There was grudging admiration in his tone.

"Shut up," Gordon said.

The auctioneer hammered for attention. The farmers stood silently in the cold drizzle, waiting. A dozen husky boys wearing black shirts pushed their way through the crowd, taking up strategic positions. The farmers made way for them, then closed up again.

Gordon glanced over toward the house. Mrs. Hansen, a plump woman in a starched high-necked apron, was bustling over a long table that had been set out on the porch. Even in this extremity, Iowa hospitality demanded that she put out refreshments for the crowd that had come to see her possessions taken away. No one had made a move toward the table, and no one in this crowd would. Dutch Hansen came out, a worn, leathery man in his sixties, wearing a collarless dress shirt and faded overalls with an ancient black coat over them. He trudged through the mud toward the barn, his head down, meeting no one's eyes.

Freddie poked Gordon in the ribs with his elbow. He took a crumpled leaflet out of his pocket and smoothed it out. There was a

long list of livestock and machinery, ending with: "Other articles too
numerous to mention." The auctioneer's name was at the bottom:
COL. BOB R. QUICK.

"He's got that prize Holstein bull that won the ribbon at the fair
here," Freddie whispered. "That's worth more than any old four hundred dollars all by itself. My pa says—"

"*Shhh!*" Gordon said.

Hansen led out the first animal, a great dun gelding with hairy
fetlocks and a still-shaggy winter coat. He urged it to a place in front
of the auction platform and brought it to a halt. Instinctively, he
reached up to pat its broad muzzle, then, shamefaced, withdrew his
hand.

"What am I bid for this fine workhorse?" Colonel Bob chanted.
"Five years old, broke to the plow, fine deep chest, firm quarters and
gaskin." He looked around at the crowd.

There was an unnerving silence from the crowd. Muddy boots
shuffled. People avoided one another's eyes. Gordon noticed a young
farmer, off to one side, whispering to his wife. They were a thin, worn
couple, wearing shabby clothes, and the girl was holding a bedraggled
baby whose face was shielded from the rain by a corner of grimy blanket. He had a guilty look on his face as he whispered, but he must
have needed a plough horse pretty badly.

Colonel Bob tried again. "Who'll start the bidding off with fifty dollars? Fifty dollars for a sound animal with good wind. Hell, make it
forty, and I'll throw in the harness!"

The young farmer turned from his wife and started to open his
mouth. Somebody jostled him, hard, before he could make the bid. He
stumbled and regained his balance. He tried again, and suddenly
found himself hemmed in by men in black shirts.

"A nickel!" somebody shouted.

Gordon followed the voice and saw a burly man who needed a
shave. He thought he recognized him as one of the Hansen neighbors.
The tall thin man with the white pompadour was standing at his
shoulder.

Colonel Bob looked unhappy. "I hear a nickel," he said.

The young tenant farmer was standing tight-lipped, looking embarrassed. A space had been cleared around him. The black-shirted men
had moved away.

"I'll raise that," a rough voice yelled. "Ten cents!"

Gordon turned his head. The bidder was another Hansen neighbor,
a dour middle-aged man named Schott.

"Ten cents," the auctioneer repeated. He took off his straw hat and
mopped a bald head with a handkerchief. "Listen here, Gus . . ."

"Are you gonna get on with it?" Schott said.

There was a low throaty growl from the farmers. Gordon's eye was caught by a movement at the front of the crowd. One of the farmers there was dangling a noose in his hands, twirling it around to show it off.

"I hear ten cents," Colonel Bob said unhappily. "Who'll make it fifteen?"

There was laughter, some of it ugly, some of it nervous. But the tension was broken. "Hell, I'll make it fifteen!" somebody shouted.

"Do I hear twenty?" Colonel Bob said, playing it out.

"Sell 'im!" a voice called out.

"Sold for fifteen cents!" Colonel Bob said and slammed his gavel. The man who had bought the horse went over to talk to Dutch Hansen. They exchanged a few words, nodding, and the man took the halter and led the horse back into Hansen's barn.

After that it went faster. A mare went for a dime, the cows for a nickel apiece, fifty hogs for a quarter. The famous Holstein bull, out of respect, was sold for a dollar. Dutch Hansen bid on him himself, ashamed to offer less than twenty dollars, but the men gathered around him, somebody clapped him on the shoulder, and Colonel Bob, pretending he hadn't heard the bid, knocked it down for a dollar. Then he untied the black umbrella and climbed down from the platform, taking the crowd with him through the sheds. Gordon and Freddie followed, on the fringes of the crowd. Nobody paid any attention to them. A McCormick-Deering Farmall tractor with a four-row cultivator, a mower, and an eight-foot binder went for the grand sum of seventy-five cents. A disc harrow went for a dime. A Ford truck went for twenty cents. The insurance agent from New York trailed along indignantly as they stopped at each new piece of machinery and bid on it on the spot. Gordon was close enough to hear him protest to a deputy, the nervous one who'd been fingering his gun. The deputy snapped: "It's all legal, there's nothing we can do. You can go back to town and complain to Judge Boehm if you want."

When the "auction" was over, all of Dutch Hansen's livestock, machinery, household goods, and sundries had been sold for a total of eleven dollars and forty-three cents. A committee of farmers solemnly counted out the money in small change and crumpled bills, and turned over the bill of sale to Hansen, who stood there with tears running down his leather cheeks.

Gordon and Freddie watched from the shadows of a tack room while the farmers filed out, laughing and talking. Outside, in the field near the road, engines sputtered and coughed and came crankily to life. The Holiday man was standing over by the big barn door, talking to a couple of the farmers.

The insurance agent should have left it alone, but he marched self-importantly over to the Holiday man and started to harangue him. "You haven't done Mr. Hansen a bit of good, don't you understand that? He's worse off than before. If there's been a proper auction, he might have reduced the deficiency on the chattel mortage. Now we'll just have to go through the whole thing all over again, and when we foreclose on the property—"

"Ain't goin' to be no more auctions," one of the farmers said. "And ain't goin' to be no foreclosure."

The insurance company lawyer ignored him—his second mistake—and continued to scold the white-haired man from the Farmers Holiday Association. "Reds, that's what you are! You and that Milo Reno of yours and your whole damn bunch of bolshies! Well, you found out in Council Bluffs that you can't go against the authorities, and if it takes more tear gas bombs and machine guns to teach you people to be good Americans, we'll teach you another lesson, by God!" He stood there, panting and faintly ridiculous, a little potbellied pink-faced man with mud on his glasses. Gordon had to admire his spunk.

"We ain't reds, mister," the white-haired man said quietly. "We're just farmers."

There was a lot of nodding and grumbling from the men clustered around the entrance. The lawyer had angered them with his reminder of Council Bluffs, where a thousand irate farmers had stormed the county jail and released fifty-five fellow pickets. They'd been dispersed with machine guns, and tear gas had been used against crowds that included women and children. Gordon's father had shaken his head at the story in the paper and said, "They're pushing those fellows too far."

The Holiday man said: "We've got the corn and the hogs and the beef you got to eat, and the milk you got to drink. Seems to me you got nothing but the mortgages."

"You're talking revolution!" the lawyer said, his face growing purple.

"They talked revolution at Bunker Hill and the Boston Tea Party, too!" said the farmer who'd first spoken up.

A murmur of agreement went up around him.

"We'll just see what you have to say when Judge Boehm signs the foreclosure papers on the Hansen place!" the lawyer flared. He picked up his briefcase and started to march out the barn door. Nobody made way for him.

"You ain't foreclosing on old Dutch!"

Somebody gave him a shove, knocking him against the doorframe. "You and that Judge Boehm been foreclosing too many farms in this county!"

The lawyer was slammed against the doorframe again. His glasses fell off, dangling from one ear, the frame bent. He reached up to put them right, and somebody hit him in the face.

The Holiday man tried to shove his way through. "There's no need for that, boys. Let's not make any trouble for Dutch. We sent a committee to talk to Judge Boehm this morning. We're going to try to talk him into postponing all foreclosures, like the other judges."

The lawyer stooped to retrieve his glasses. One lens was cracked. He stood there, his face gone white, blood running from his nose.

"Committee, hell!" a farmer growled.

"You men will regret this," the lawyer said in a trembling voice.

Freddie moved out of the shadows of the tack room for a better look, and Gordon pulled him back. He didn't care for the way things were developing.

Rough hands pushed and slapped the lawyer out into the rain. The barn emptied out fast. When Gordon thought they wouldn't attract attention, he nudged Freddie out into the barnyard. They took shelter under the dilapidated eaves of an attached outbuilding.

There were still about a hundred farmers hanging around outside. They turned to see what was happening. Some of them drifted over to join the pack of men who were shoving and kicking the lawyer across the barnyard. The Holiday man was following the group, trying to get them to stop, but they weren't paying any attention to him.

When the sheriff's deputies saw what was happening, they came running over to stop it. It might have ended there, with the farmers glad to have an excuse to let the lawyer go after an exchange of insults, but one of the deputies overreacted.

It was the nervous one again. He wanted the comfort of a gun in his hand. He fumbled with it as he ran through the mud. Before he knew what was happening, a dozen farmers had grabbed him and wrested the gun away from him. It went sailing high in the air to sink into the muck of the hog pen. The farmers surrounded the deputy, pinning his arms by his sides. Gordon heard someone say, "Now you just quieten down, Lester, and don't go gettin' trigger-happy."

The other two deputies had been prepared to overlook a lot, but the delicate truce was shattered when they saw one of their own number being manhandled. They quickened their steps and came wading over. They weren't fools enough to try to draw their guns, and they didn't get the chance. A solid wall of overalled men crowded them. Their gunbelts were pulled off and thrown away. Nobody hit them, and they didn't give anyone cause to. They were just penned in by bodies.

"I know you, Fritz Ackley," Gordon heard one of the deputies say.

"I know you, too, Frank Lyman, and I know your sister Margaret's husband, and your cousin Luther who bought Oscar Heimer's place over near Linn Grove after Oscar was evicted, and no one around there will talk to him or his wife, and his neighbors won't help him with the threshing, and he can't have a telephone, and the postman won't deliver his mail, and his children can't ride the school bus, and none of the children'll talk to *them,* and you just better think about your cousin Luther, Frank Lyman."

The deputy had nothing to say after that. A nervous excitement had overtaken the farmers. For the moment nobody was hitting the insurance company lawyer. They stood pinning his arms, the great mass of them surging aimlessly this way and that while they tried to figure out what to do next.

"Let's go get the judge, too!" someone yelled.

There was a rush toward the field of parked cars. Engines raced. About twenty of the cars rattled off on the road to town, filled with unshaven men who waved jack handles and pieces of knotted rope out the windows.

"C'mon," Gordon said. "Let's get out of here."

"Are you crazy?" Freddie said. "I'm gonna watch."

Against his better judgment, Gordon stuck by Freddie's side. They had their backs pressed against the red tile wall of the silo, while rain dripped down past their faces from the overhang high above. From their protected place in the ell formed by the connecting structure, they could see most of the farmyard.

The farmers were getting noisy now. They frog-marched the unfortunate lawyer in the direction of the hog pens. Gordon caught a glimpse of a faraway face that must have been Mrs. Hansen's looking out of a window in the house; then another hand yanked the curtain shut. The few women present were being hustled out of sight by their husbands.

"Tar and feather the son of a bitch!" came a cry.

"Ain't got time to heat tar," somebody else brayed, "but we got something damn near as good!"

The lawyer had disappeared under flailing arms. They had him on the ground, packed so tightly around him that they were getting in one another's way. As Gordon watched, a blue serge jacket, its sleeve ripped off, was flung high into the air. If fluttered down to fall into the mud. It was followed by a pair of trousers.

"Lookit that!" Freddie said with appropriate awe. "They stripped him mother naked!"

Gordon caught flashes of the lawyer's pale soft body being jerked this way and that, and finally flung sprawling into the manure pile. Busy hands plastered him all over with gobs of pig manure. The rain had made it as sticky as cement. The man's glasses were gone and he had a dazed look. For a moment Gordon saw the white face, its mouth working like a gasping fish, then someone slapped a handful of black slime all over it.

"Careful, boys, he got to breathe!" a voice said.

There was laughter. "Yeah, we sure want him to breathe!"

When they were finished, they rolled him in straw. They stood back and let him get to his feet. He staggered in front of them, a shaggy haystack of black excrement and yellow straw in the approximate shape of a man.

"Somebody git a ladder!" a voice yelled.

Gordon felt obscurely ashamed of what he was witnessing. He was reminded of the dancing bear he'd seen once at the county fair in Spencer, a bedraggled mangy creature that had tottered aimlessly on its hind legs, a cruel ring through its nose, until somebody from the exhibitors' committee expelled the trainer from the grounds.

"Lookit 'im standing there with his thingamajig hanging out!" Freddie said gleefully.

"You stink," Gordon said.

"Aw, Gordon," Freddie said, and fell silent.

Some of the farmers had found a wooden ladder in a tool shed. They thrust it between the lawyer's legs and lifted it to their shoulders, making him ride the narrow edge like a hobby horse. His bare toes scrabbled for support on the lower edge and he clung desperately with both hands, trying to keep from falling off.

"Splinters!" somebody chortled. "Now you be sure to find all the splinters!"

The mob was in high spirits. They carried the ladder round and round the barnyard with rowdy shouts and scraps of off-key song while the grotesque straw man swayed and tried to keep his balance. In the midst of the hilarity, there was the sound of automobile engines. The expedition to Beulah had returned.

The lead car came clattering and popping into the barnyard, its klaxon crowing triumphantly. It was a big, square rattletrap Ford with narrow tires and foggy windows, and it promptly sank up to its axles in the mire. Eager hands wrenched a door open, and they hauled out Judge Boehm.

The judge was a stringy, dried-out old man with a turkey neck and a meager face squeezed between two vertical pleats. His heavy severe coat hung open, buttons ripped off, showing loose trousers hitched high on suspenders, with a small round belly peeping out of the top like a stolen melon.

He stood rooted in the mud, looking with disgust at the spectacle in the barnyard. "Turn that man loose!" he demanded in a thin querulous voice. "You, deputies, why aren't you stopping this?"

Gordon moved back farther into the shadow of the silo.

"You ain't giving orders no more, Judge!" one of his captors said. Somebody struck the judge from behind, and he sank to his hands and knees in the mud.

They gathered around him, the encrusted lawyer forgotten.

"Swear!" a black-shirted man bellowed. "You swear not to sign no more foreclosures!"

The judge looked up at his tormentors. He'd lost his false teeth in the mud and his face looked like a lizard's. "I won't swear to any such thing," he said, his voice trembling. They lifted him to his feet and dragged him over to the base of the windmill. It made a creaking sound as the vane struggled to keep the circular fan of blades facing into the wind; the oil in the gear case must have leaked or dried up long ago.

"Swear it!" the shouts came.

"No!" the judge said in a hoarse voice.

One of the younger men shinnied up the tall steel framework of the windmill tower, carrying a rope, while his friends cheered him on. He threw the rope over a crossbar. Down below, eager hands retrieved the rope ends. One end had been fashioned into a noose.

They stood the judge on the concrete square of the pump platform and waved the noose in front of his face. "Swear, god damn you!"

The judge swayed and almost fainted. They held him propped up, his knees sagging.

"No," he whispered, "I'm not going to swear."

They draped the noose around his neck. There was a commotion as one of the deputies tried to break free. Gordon saw that it was Frank Lyman. "You'll all go on trial, every one of you!" he was shouting.

Freddie grabbed Gordon's arm, his stubby fingers digging painfully into muscle. "They can't hang a judge, can they?" he said.

It all seemed strange and far away to Gordon. He was surprised at how calm he felt. "I don't know," he heard himself saying. "Maybe they just want to throw a scare into him." He was thinking of the machine guns that had been issued by the sheriff in Council Bluffs and the call for federal troops when the farmers got out of hand, and wondering what would happen in Beulah if nobody stopped what was happening in Dutch Hansen's barnyard.

The Holiday man must have been thinking about that, too, because he was trying to shove his way through the packed crowd to the base of the windmill. Before he could get there, a couple of husky farm boys hauled on the end of the rope and lifted the judge nearly off his feet. He stood there on tiptoe, his face growing purple, and they let him down again.

"Will you swear?"

Gordon saw the judge shake his head. This time they hoisted him clear off the ground. He dangled there frighteningly for a moment, clawing at the noose. They dropped him and he crumpled to his knees.

"Are you goin' to swear?" they said, pleading with him now.

Gordon could see that the farmers had become frightened at what they were doing, but didn't know how to stop. The judge was an old man; the next time would probably kill him.

It was the Holiday man who gave them an out. Gordon saw the pompadour of white hair bob as he stooped deliberately to pick up a clod of mud. "He wants Dutch Hansen's farm so much, let him have it!" he shouted, and threw the clod. It struck Judge Boehm on the cheek, leaving a smear.

Somebody else threw a clod, and then the air was full of flying dirt, pelting the judge. "Hey!" one of them yelled. The men converged on the platform. Gordon could see what was happening, because the platform was raised a foot or two. They had the judge's trousers pulled down and they were filling them with dirt.

Freddie was staring, transfixed. Gordon had to shake his arm. "Let's get going!" he hissed. All the farmers' attention was concentrated for the moment on the scene at the base of the windmill.

Gordon gave Freddie a push, and then the two of them were making their way around the yard, keeping as much as possible to the shelter of the outbuildings. They got all the way past the third barn before anyone noticed them, and even then it might have been all right, except that the wrong man saw them.

"There's the goddamn banker's son!" somebody shouted, and Freddie started to run. That attracted more attention, and the next moment a couple of dozen men had detached themselves from the outside edges of the crowd and were coming after them.

Gordon broke into a trot, but the sticky mud kept pulling at his feet in their thin shoes, and one of the shoes came off. Ahead of him he could hear Freddie sobbing for breath. He hobbled on with the nightmare drag at his feet, and then one of the pursuers managed to clutch a handful of his jacket. He smelled a whiskey breath. Hardly aware of what he was doing in his terror, Gordon lashed out and for the first time in his life hit an adult. His fist crunched into a stubbled face. The man cursed, and Gordon, breaking loose, found firm ground and ran like a hare across the field.

He didn't look back until he reached the chicken house down the road. Freddie was there, wheeling out his bicycle. "Criminey, you should see yourself!" Freddie said. Gordon was covered with mud, had a long scratch down his cheek, and blood on his knuckles. His bare knee stuck out of a long rent in the hated knickers. At least, he found himself thinking, I won't have to wear knickers anymore.

The farmers were a couple of hundred yards back, tiring faster than the boys had, but still coming on. One of them had a pitchfork. Gordon could see the man whose face he had bloodied, stumbling across the soggy furrows. Freddie thumbed his nose at all of them and rode off, wobbling a little till he got started. Gordon threw a long leg over his bike and pedaled off after him.

They separated at the corner of Elm Street. Freddie looked again at Gordon's torn and muddy clothes, gave a parting whistle, and said, "Your pa is goin' to whip you for sure!"

"He doesn't whip us," Gordon said. "But there'll be extra chores and no money till the clothes're paid for." Secretly, he hoped that the knickers were beyond mending.

He wheeled his bicycle around back, hoping to sneak in through the kitchen without being seen. His uncle Elroy's old Plymouth, a tall black coupe with a rumble seat, was pulled up in the long driveway behind his father's gleaming maroon Pierce-Arrow Twelve. Guiltily, Gordon remembered that he had been supposed to wax and polish the Pierce-Arrow today.

He left the bicycle next to the garage and went around to the kitchen door. When he was only halfway up the stairs, the door flew open, and his uncle Elroy was framed there, bleak and angular in his rigid black suit, his pinched face thin-lipped and disapproving.

"Where you been, boy?" he said. "Your father's killed himself."

3

Harry's Place opened at ten, and by noon it was already full of regulars who were taking the hair of Friday night's dog or getting an early start on Saturday night. There were a lot of Yalies in the crowd as usual, some townies and their girls from the Hill, and a table of family people dressed in their Sunday best. Among the solitary drinkers at the bar were a rumpled reporter from the *Register,* and a New Haven trainman taking a chance by being in uniform, and the off-duty police lieutenant whom Harry paid, a saturnine man named Hanrahan. The big corner booth was occupied by a party of noisy theatrical people who'd come up from New York the night before to see the opening at the Shubert. The bank holiday had left them stranded, but Harry was giving them credit.

Over at the scarred oak table under the Spy prints that tradition reserved for law students, Bradford Sinclair, Jr., stretched his long legs and peered into the gloom. Brad was a lean, rangy fellow with the long Sinclair jaw and a touch of ginger in his hair. His expensive tweed sports jacket was impeccably pressed and his flannels were a calculated disgrace. He affected the negligent slouch expected of a graduate student. He was very good at it.

"The Law," he said sententiously, raising his glass in the general direction of Hanrahan, who fortunately did not notice. "Long may it waive. Excuse me. Be waived."

He downed the raw bootleg rye in a gulp, then washed it down with Harry's more reliable beer. He signaled Angelo, the waiter, for another ball-and-a-half.

"Sinclair, old man," Binky said with a belch. "You're drunk."

"I sincerely hope so," Brad said.

Binky swallowed some more of his own drink, making a face. He was a large, soft young man with patent leather hair and remarkably pink eyes. His real name was Charles Foxcroft Holworthy III.

They both looked sorrowfully at the third man at the table, a fellow third-year law student named Dudley, who was sleeping blissfully with his cheek in a puddle of beer. Dudley had survived three all-night speakeasies and a riotous party on Whalley Avenue at an off-campus residence maintained by students of the Divinity School, but he had begun to waver about dawn.

"Disgraceful," Binky said blearily.

"Shocking," Brad agreed.

"He has failed to uphold the honor of Delta Kappa Epsilon."

"The Drunken Dekes, of undergraduate memory."

"Ah, yes."

"And he is *not* doing his part to flout the Volstead Act."

"And time is running out," Binky said, his nose twitching. "If that Roosevelt chap keeps his word, places like Harry's will soon be *legal*."

"A sobering thought indeed."

Binky shuddered. "Don't *say* things like that, Sinclair."

Brad lit a cigarette to cover his boredom with the conversation. He was not as drunk as he seemed, but he had a reputation to uphold. He was acutely aware of the fact that he was a member of his present crowd only by sufferance. People like Binky and Dudley and their friends had known since the age of five who their classmates at Yale would be, and what clubs they would belong to when they got out. Their names had been on the waiting lists since birth. Brad was only the son of an obscure midwestern banker, and had attended public school in a place no one had ever heard of called Iowa. It was only the fact that he was too amusing a fellow to ignore, and that he never tried to push, and that he was academically brilliant without being a greasy grind that had got him into the Dekes in his junior year and Skull and Bones in his senior.

Brad worked hard at being amusing, and he worked harder at his studies than he would have been willing to let his classmates know. He had been careful never to get involved with a frat brother's sister or any girl in their immediate circle. That would have been overreaching.

Instead, he was engaged to a New York girl whose father had Harvard connections. From that safe distance, Brad's Yale credentials looked good. Her name was Gilda Stanhope, she was beautiful, and it was already tacitly understood that on graduation, Brad would be offered a position in the prestigious New York law firm of her father. Stanhope would see to it that his daughter's husband got into the Links and the Union Club and the Knickerbocker and perhaps, when Brad had made his way in the world, even the Century. His Yale connections would stand him in good stead for the rest of his life.

A shadow fell across the table. "One ball-and-a-half," Angelo said. He was a small wiry man with a large head and dark liquid eyes, wearing a butcher's apron over his shirt and vest. Brad knew for a fact that he carried a sap in his rear pants pocket.

"Thank you, Angelo," Brad said. "Is this the wood alcohol with burnt cork or the furniture polish with caramel coloring?"

"It's good stuff, Mr. Sinclair," Angelo said reproachfully. "It just came off the boat."

"What boat is that? Charon's ferry?"

Angelo gave him a hurt look. His eyes moved sadly toward Dudley. "You shun't let him sleep it off like that here, Mr. Sinclair. It gives the joint a bad name." He glided off with his tray into the noisy murk.

Some madman had put a nickel in the piano. It began tinkling out a manic arrangement of "Has Anybody Seen My Gal" that sounded as if it were being played by a hopped-up pianist with three hands. The noise level in the room rose to compensate. Over at the corner table a pale ingenue with hair like milled brass was shrieking at a squat chinless man in evening clothes who had his hand down the back of her dress: ". . . and Mannie said I could of had the part, but they wanted the Hope Williams type. . . ." Three businessmen having Harry's forty-cent lunch were arguing about politics. "Mussolini," one of them was saying loudly. "That's what we need in this country to get us out of this. A Mussolini."

The reporter from the *Register* slid off his barstool and made his way through the smoke to the men's room. On the way he stopped at Brad's table.

"Congratulations on winning your case at Moot Court, Sinclair. I saw the story in the *Yale Daily News*."

Brad lounged disinterestedly in his chair. "Yeah, thanks."

"I hear you're an odds-on favorite for this year's Stone Prize, too," the reporter persisted. He was a small rumpled man with a gray hat pushed way back on his head.

"That's up to the justices," Brad mumbled, looking away.

The mock proceedings at Moot Court were taken very seriously at

Yale, and were reported in the *Yale Daily News* as if they were real trials. Brad had been a minor celebrity all week because of the clever though unorthodox tack he had taken in what had been generally conceded to be a hopeless case. There was even talk that his tactics might be written up in the *Yale Law Review* as a classic. Brad was uncomfortably aware that Binky was tired of hearing about it.

The reporter wouldn't go away. "Reason I recognized you is my son's a second-year student at the law school. You probably know him. Name of Kevin Tully. He thinks you're the cat's pajamas. Talks about you all the time."

Brad remembered Tully, an earnest horse-faced individual who had tried several times to strike up awkward conversations with him, and who had a reputation as a grind and a meatball. The sort of person it would be fatal to be seen being friendly with.

"No, I don't know him," Brad said, feeling Binky's bright malicious eyes on him.

"Sure you do. *Kevin.* He really looks up to you. Says you're going to go far. Make a name for yourself in jurisprudence if you want . . . maybe all the way to the Supreme Court. Says you're too good to be another gold-plated Wall Street lawyer. How about it, Sinclair? Is that your ambition?"

Brad slouched elaborately. "My ambition," he drawled, "is to collect a courtesy card from every speakeasy on the Eastern Seaboard between New Haven and New York. A life's work, sir, and I'm barely begun."

He fished in a bulging wallet and spilled his collection of dog-eared speakeasy tickets across the table. He had everything from the Dizzy Club to Jack and Charley's "21," most of them autographed by the owner. It was always good for a conversation-stopper.

Across the table, Binky stirred into life. "It is Mr. Sinclair's theory, sir," he said in his best preppie's accent, "that we can put this country on its feet again by substituting boozelines for breadlines."

Tully's face closed like a book. "You Yale swells," he said. "Spoiled. Got it made. Fifteen million unemployed out there, people living in Hoovervilles and fighting over garbage that your fine restaurants are kind enough to save for them, and you don't give a damn. Girls and country clubs and a place in your fathers' firms, that's all you care about." He shook his head in disgust and lurched off to the men's room.

"Tedious little rooster," Binky said.

"What can you expect of a man who wears a bow tie?" Brad said.

Angelo was back. "Your friend's name Dudley?" he said. "There's a couple of broads outside saying they know him."

Brad and Binky exchanged glances. "Brother Dudley came through," Brad said. "He *told* me he'd talked those girls at the reverend's party into meeting us here after they had a nap and freshened up. Rotten of me to doubt him."

"Wait a minute," Binky said. "They might not be the same ones."

"I better see," Brad said. He heaved himself from his chair. "Take me to the ladies," he said to Angelo.

"They ain't no ladies, Mr. Sinclair," Angelo said.

He followed Angelo across the crowded floor. The nickel piano was playing a breakneck version of "Stardust" now, all octave doublings and broken-note runs. The brassy ingenue was squeezing the chinless man's knee while shrilling: "Bosoms! That's all they want now, Milton Berle and bosoms! Does Nazimova have a bosom? I ask you!"

Angelo slid open the eye-level slot in the steel door and let Brad peep through. Outside in the alley were three young women, townies, a little overdressed for the middle of the day in silk stockings and calf-length dresses with complicated lapels, rounded in front by the new uplift brassieres that had replaced the flat look of a few years back. They all wore fussy little hats with identical curled bobs peeking from beneath the tiny brims. They looked like an act.

"Is it okay to let them in?" Angelo said.

Brad frowned at him. "I'm surprised at you, Angelo," he said sternly. "Can't you tell Prohibition agents when you see them? The blonde is Eliot Ness in disguise."

"Aw, Mr. Sinclair!" Angelo said. He rattled chains and slid back bolts and opened the door.

"Hi," the blonde said. "You were the one from Kansas. Brad?"

He looked her over. She had a coarse, pretty face. Too much lipstick and rouge. Eyebrows plucked almost to pencil lines.

"Iowa," he said.

"It's all Kansas to me," she said.

"It sure ain't New Haven," one of the other girls said.

The girls handed Angelo their dripping raincoats. The blonde said, "I'm Marge Doyle, I don't know if you remember, and this here's Teresa Cipriano."

"Terry," the other girl said. She was dark-haired with a sallow complexion and a hint of fuzz on her upper lip, and she had painfully thin arms sticking out of floppy sleeves that ended just below the elbow.

"I remember," Brad lied.

"And this is Helen Gilmore, she wasn't there last night, she came because Mildred couldn't make it, Mildred, the girl with the fox collar."

"Last *night?* More like this morning, I hear," Helen giggled. She was a chunky redhead with a lot of face powder that didn't succeed in hiding her freckles. She looked placid and good-natured.

Brad led them to the table and pulled up extra chairs for them. "What's the matter with *him?*" Marge said, looking doubtfully at Dudley.

"Just taking a nap," Brad said. "He'll be good as new in no time. Life of the party."

"Hey, what are *these?*" Helen said, pouncing on the courtesy cards that were still scattered across the table. "Oh, boy, lookit this! Jack and Charlie's! You been *there?* Is it like they say it is?"

"Mr. Sinclair has been everywhere," Binky said, "everywhere that vice smiles and virtue frowns. He's the man who put the sin in Sinclair."

"Oh, yeah?" Marge said. She turned to Brad. "I thought you were the minister's son."

"That's right," Brad said. "It runs in the family. My father's a divine and my mother's a nun."

"Hey, I don't like that kind of talk," Teresa said.

"An Episcopal nun," Brad said.

She looked at him suspiciously. "Oh, I guess that's all right, then."

"He's kidding you," Marge said. She turned to Brad again. "But you go to the Divinity School, though, you and your friends?"

Binky had just caught on. "Actually, we're all—"

Brad kicked him under the table. "It's all right, brother Charles. Dudley *told* them."

"I don't mind," the redhead, Helen, said.

"You boys from the Divinity School are sure a wild bunch," Marge said.

"We're making hay while we still can," Brad shrugged. "Once we're ordained—"

"Enough, enough," Binky said jovially. "Let's get the ladies a drink."

Brad signaled Angelo. The girls, with no hesitation, ordered gin with a ginger-ale chaser. Helen asked for a cherry. Angelo tilted his big head toward Dudley. "What about him?" he said.

Brad reached across the table and lifted Dudley by the hair. Dudley's eyelids twitched and he made a small sound. Brad lowered his head gently.

"I think I detect signs of life. Let me see if I can get his head under a faucet." He got up and walked around the table. Binky helped him get Dudley's legs under him.

"Think he'll walk?" Binky said.

"I'll give it a try," Brad said. "You entertain the girls."

He managed to walk Dudley across the floor to the men's room, one arm across the back to support him. Dudley's eyes were squeezed tight. He draped Dudley across the cracked sink and splashed cold water in his face.

"Okay, okay!" Dudley muttered. He swayed, and Brad caught his elbow. "I'm all right," he said, his hair dripping. "I could hear everything. I just couldn't *move!*"

"What made you tell those girls we were from the Divinity School?" Brad said.

"They're hot for the cloth. One of the guys at the party told me they sneaked that Terry into Bushnell house one night. *Bushnell,* for Chrissake! She took on the whole dorm."

"Can you make it back to the table?"

"Sure." As Brad turned to go, he grabbed him by the arm. "Listen, buddy, can you do me a favor?"

"What?"

Dudley lowered his voice. "You got any frenchies on you?"

"Don't you ever carry your own?"

"Come on, Brad, you don't need them *all.*"

Brad got out his wallet and silently handed a couple of the tightly rolled packets to Dudley. Dudley put them in his pocket, looking relieved.

Brad opened the door to a blast of noise. The piano was rattling out a chorus of "I Can't Give You Anything But Love," and somewhere in the gloom a whole table was singing or humming along with it.

As Brad reached the table, the din suddenly stopped. Brad looked up and saw that Harry had pulled the plug on the nickel piano.

"Hey, everybody quiet a minute!" Harry yelled through the residual noise. Talk started to fade in the room as customers turned their heads to see what was happening.

Harry was a great big battered-looking man with a face like a granite cliff and a dent in his head that looked as if it had been put there with a fire axe. The story, which Harry encouraged, was that he had had a difference of opinion with some out-of-town muscle about where he would get his beer. Harry was proud of his beer, which he got locally. Brad privately believed what a friend in premed once had told him: that the dent looked like a birth trauma caused by forceps; though he never would have said so aloud and taken the risk of it getting back to Harry. Whether you believed the story or not, Harry was an impressive figure with his banana fingers and broken nose and foghorn voice.

"What's he doing?" one of the girls said.

"Shhh," Brad said, patting her hand.

Harry was fiddling with the dials of the big table-model Majestic he kept behind the bar for sporting events, to accommodate his betting patrons.

"It's after one o'clock," Harry announced. "Time for the Roosevelt speech."

There were good-natured catcalls from various parts of the room. The businessmen's table booed loudly. "Hoover or hell!" some diehard shouted, mouthing one of the campaign slogans. "I'll take hell!" somebody else retorted. At the table adjoining Brad's, a weather-beaten old man in a shiny blue suit, who looked as if he might be a retired railroad brakeman, looked up from his boilermaker and said to no one in particular: "It's Roosevelt or revolution, that's all there is to it."

"Shud up!" Harry rumbled.

"What's come over friend Harry?" Binky said. "This unwonted interest in public affairs?"

"Wants to see if Roosevelt has anything to say about Repeal," Dudley said.

"The beer drinkers put him up to it," Brad said.

Binky cocked an eye owlishly. "Oh, he'll have something to say for the beer drinkers. And those striking farmers of yours in Iowa. And the Bonus Marchers. And the apple sellers. The man's a traitor to his class."

"Say anything to get elected," Brad agreed. He remembered that Binky's uncle, like a number of other rich men, had barricaded himself in his country estate and hired armed guards in expectation of Armageddon.

"He *is* elected," Binky said. "And now God help us all."

"God can't help us," Brad said. "It'll take another Mussolini."

"Hey, you better cut that out. . . ." Terry began angrily.

"*Shhh!*"

The radio had warmed up, and was crackling into life. The speakeasy fell suddenly, eerily silent. Something extraordinary was happening in the room. Brad looked around at the theater people, all at once grown thoughtful, at the toughs and their girls, the old drunks at the bar, the family men in their preserved threadbare suits. He could see on the beaten faces, on the hardened and cynical faces, a common yearning for hope.

"So help me God!" Roosevelt's high penetrating voice cut through a sizzle of static. Evidently Harry had tuned in just at the end of the oath. Brad shifted in his chair and listened with the rest.

There was no pause. Roosevelt went directly into his speech. "President Hoover, Mr. Chief Justice, my friends. This is a day of national consecration, and I am certain that my fellow Americans expect that on my induction into the presidency I will address them with a candor and a decision which the present situation of our nation impels. This is preeminently a time to speak the truth, the whole truth, frankly and boldly."

Brad was struck by the chill, wintry tone of the voice. This was not the jovial, outgoing Roosevelt that the country had become accustomed to during the election campaign and the four months of limbo that had followed. It was a little scary. The drinkers in Harry's felt it, too. There was an uneasy rustling of feet and clothing.

"So first of all," the President was saying, "let me assert my firm belief that the only thing we have to fear is fear itself—nameless, unreasoning, unjustified terror which paralyzes needed efforts . . ."

Brad shivered without knowing why. "Somebody walking on your grave," was the way his uncle Elroy had put it once, when as a small boy Brad had tried to describe the sensation.

". . . our distress comes from no failure of substance," Roosevelt went on grimly. "We are stricken by no plague of locusts. Nature still offers her bounty and human efforts have multiplied it. Plenty is at our doorstep. . . ."

Brad slumped deeper into his chair. He had a strange sense of communion, as if the radio with its glowing orange dial connected him in some mystical fashion with the millions of other radios that were alight at this identical moment—radios in shabby furnished rooms, in farm kitchens where the men had come in from the ploughed raw fields to hear this, in the sagging wooden tenements smelling of cabbage and hall toilets, in the shantytowns that festered in public parks, in the suburban neighborhoods where jobless men dressed in business suits each morning and pretended to go to work, in the expensive clubs where the frightened rich drew together for the comfort of their own.

". . . The money changers have fled from their high seats in the temple of our civilization," the grim accusing voice went on. "We may now restore that temple to the ancient truths. . . ."

For the first time the audience applauded. Brad could hear the sound, like the breaking of distant surf, through the loudspeaker. Somebody in the bar began to applaud, too. Brad looked around and saw that it was one of the family tables, middle-aged people in decent worn clothes.

". . . These dark days will be worth all they cost us if they teach us that our true destiny is not to be ministered unto but to minister to ourselves and to our fellow man. . . ."

The ringing phrases followed one after another, echoing through Brad's head: "Our Constitution is so simple and practical that it is possible always to meet extraordinary needs by changes in emphasis and arrangement without loss of essential form. . . . I shall ask the Congress for the one remaining instrument to meet the crisis—broad executive power to wage a war against the emergency, as great as the power that would be given to me if we were in fact invaded by a foreign foe. . . ."

Binky leaned across the table. "What's the man saying?" he whispered savagely. "He's asking us to make him a dictator!"

Nobody paid any attention to him. Dudley was sitting erect, his jaw hanging open. The three girls were staring transfixed at the radio. A corner of Brad's mind had stirred uneasily at Roosevelt's extraordinary choice of phrases, but the force and bleak majesty of the speech carried him inexorably along.

Roosevelt was winding up now. "We do not distrust the future of essential democracy. The people of the United States have not failed. In their need they have registered a mandate that they want direct, vigorous action. They have asked for discipline and direction under leadership. They have made me the present instrument of their wishes. In the spirit of the gift I take it."

A roar of applause and wild cheers came through the loudspeaker when Roosevelt finished. The customers in Harry's sat stunned and exhausted for several seconds. Harry switched off the radio. Little by little, the speakeasy came back to life. Somebody called for another beer. A hum of conversation grew, punctuated by the tinkle of glasses. Brad could hear the arguments starting. "Discipline," one of the lunching businessmen said. "That's what the Eyetalians have under Mussolini, and that's what we need here." He was overheard by one of the boys from the Hill, who eyed him dangerously. "You said it," one of the other businessmen agreed, his head bobbing vigorously. "They had a run on the banks there, too. You know how Mussolini stopped it? He said one little word, and they were standing in line all day to redeposit."

Binky had recovered his poise. "How about it, Sinclair?" he said wickedly. "Are we going to drive the money changers from the temple?"

"The bankers, you mean?" Brad said.

"Yes indeed, the bankers."

An image of his father popped into Brad's mind, the long scholarly face with the silver-rimmed glasses, and the neat white hair with its few remaining flecks of rust. He crossed his fingers as he had when he was a child and said, coolly: "That's right, brother Charles. It's up to us ministers' sons to overturn the tables of the money changers. And let's not forget the seats of those who sell doves."

He felt unaccountably depressed. The whiskey seemed to have

burned itself off, leaving a bad taste in his mouth. He looked around for Angelo so he could order himself another one.

Marge leaned forward, resting her breasts on the table. "Hey, let's quit all this talk about politics and religion, huh? I thought we were here to have a good time!"

"Right you are," Brad said with forced gaiety. He reached under the table and patted her knee. The mechanical piano was plugged in again, finishing out its last roll. He managed to catch Angelo's eye, and returned his attention to Marge. "How about another goddamned drink?" he said.

It took them until almost five to get the girls back to their rooming house, and then only with a firm promise of dinner afterwards. Binky phoned ahead and got one of their classmates to decoy Mrs. Quinn out of the way while they smuggled the girls upstairs. Mrs. Quinn was not one to make a fuss about noises emanating from the upper reaches of the rambling old Victorian structure, but it wasn't a good idea to affront her standards of propriety too blatantly. The quiet one, Helen, had shown a surprising capacity for Harry's gin, and she was the one who supported a floppy-limbed Dudley up the staircase rather than the other way around. Terry was draped like an anaconda around Binky's neck and calling him brother Charles. They separated at the top of the stairs, and Brad steered a giggling Marge into his room and got the door closed without any sign that Mrs. Quinn had been alerted.

"You're not, are you?" Marge said, sprawling across the day bed.

"Not what?"

"What you said. You don't even go to the Divinity School, do you?"

"There's Methodist in my madness. . . ." he began.

"Cut it out, Brad. Your name's at least Brad, isn't it?"

"Yes. It's at least Brad."

"Okay, then. No more jokes, all right?"

"No more jokes." He dropped down on the day bed beside her. The mattress gave a little bounce.

"That's better," she said. "I know this house. Law students and loaded. You loaded?"

He laughed. "You don't believe in pussyfooting, do you?"

"*Are* you?"

"Not in that sense. Not like brother Charles and friend Dudley. I'm just a small-town banker's son."

"Banker. That's loaded in my circles. Terry's father, he's a stone-mason, he'd kill her if he knew where she was. My dad, he works for New Haven Tire and Rubber. He'll never go any higher. Me, maybe I'll marry a rich man some day." She looked at his face searchingly. "You'll go a lot higher though, won't you? You made up your mind."

"Sure," he said lightly. "I've got the world by the oysters."

"You use people, don't you?" she said. "You're a cold son of a bitch. You'd do anything to get ahead."

"No, not anything."

"I'll bet!"

"Look," he said, growing angry, "if you want to call the whole thing off—"

She gave a little triumphal laugh. "What do you know, I got him mad. He has some feelings after all. See, other people can do it too."

It was his turn to laugh. "Okay. Point proven."

"And all the time you thought I was just some stupid little townie, didn't you?"

"No, I never thought that."

"Actually I like you better than your friends. They're a pair of, I better not use the word. I'm glad I got you."

"I had my eye on you, too."

She was twined all around him, her skirt riding up past the tops of her stockings, and he had the buttons on the complicated lapels undone and his hands under her dress trying to pull apart all the hooks and eyes in back with fingers that had gone stiff and numb from alcohol. Her tongue, hot and slick, darted into his mouth like an avid little animal. He got the last hook undone and felt her breasts fall free. She gave a little sigh. He started working on her girdle. She twisted her head away and said, "Have you got any you-know-whats?"

"Yes," he said, peeling the girdle down.

Somebody rapped on the door. "Sinclair, are you in there?" The voice belonged to a fellow named Stoddard who had a room at the end of the hall.

Marge broke free. "Tell him to go away," she said.

"Stoddard, get the hell out of here," Brad said. He grabbed at Marge and pulled her to him again. Her body had gone rigid.

"Sinclair . . ." Stoddard's voice was hesitant. "You've got a phone call."

"Get the hell away from that door!"

There was a brief pause. "I think you better answer it, Sinclair. It's long distance." He hesitated. "Something about your father."

Marge struggled to a sitting position. The mood was broken. Smudged lipstick blurred the outlines of her mouth. She smoothed down her skirt. "You better take it," she said.

"I'll be right back," Brad whispered. He got up and fixed his clothes.

The phone was at the end of the hall, the receiver dangling and making noises. Brad put it to his ear.

"Hello?"

"I've been trying to get you all afternoon." The voice buzzed distantly, like flies behind a windowpane. It sounded aggrieved. It took Brad a moment to recognize it as his uncle Elroy's. The hallway tilted and swooped: all the drinks and the sudden standing up doing it to him. He reached out for the wall to steady himself, hearing the insect buzz in his ear.

"What's the matter?" he managed to say, his tongue gone thick.

"Are you drunk? I said you better get on a train here right away. You're the oldest. You'll have to settle the affairs."

"Affairs?" he repeated.

Elroy showed his exasperation. "Didn't you hear me? Your father. He's gone and shot himself."

4

On that gray Saturday morning of March 4, 1933, while her oldest brother, Bradford junior, was drinking bootleg whiskey with his eastern friends in a New Haven speakeasy, and her youngest brother, Gordon, was watching a mob of farmers come close to hanging a district court judge, June Alice Sinclair, known as Junie, the baby of the family at fifteen, was in the hayloft of a falling-down barn just outside of Beulah, finding out for the first time what it felt like to be kissed on the mouth by a boy.

Junie took after her mother's side of the family, the Everetts with their New England roots that her mother kept bringing up to her father, and she had her mother's thick dark hair and eyebrows, deep brown eyes, elfin chin, and small perfect white teeth. Her hair was tied up in a red ribbon this morning, in that hateful childish fashion that her mother insisted upon, and she was wearing a brown corduroy jumper and sensible blouse with a snug lisle vest under it. She envied the spun-blond hair of her grown-up sister, Pamela, and wished that she was allowed to have a real wave permanent and wear rouge and lipstick, too.

Her mother never would have approved of the boy she was kissing. Floyd Kinney's father wasn't even a farmer with a place of his own—only a tenant farmer. More than half the farms in Iowa were run by people like the Kinneys these days. It was the depression that had done it. Every February the country roads were alive with gypsy caravans of battered trucks and wagons heaped with household goods, the herds of gaunt livestock trailing behind. February was moving time for tenants, time to pull up stakes and settle in someplace new, so you could get a crop in the ground by March. It was long past time for the Kinney clan to join that weary tide, but there was some problem that Junie didn't understand, though Floyd had tried to explain it to her.

No one except Gordon knew about Floyd. He had appeared one day in her English class three weeks after school started, a shy, gangling, homely boy in patched clean overalls, his raw wrists and big red hands sticking out of an outgrown shirt. He wore no socks and—some of the boys snickered—no underwear. He was two or three years older than the other kids in the class—almost a man. He paid no attention when they made fun of him. He kept to himself, patient as a horse, tensed over his textbook with his lips moving slightly as he tried to follow the lesson. Junie's heart poured out to him.

He could barely read. She realized that with a shock one day when Miss Ritterhouse called on him in class. He stood by his desk, his face growing redder and his voice fainter as he tried to stumble his way through a short recitation from *The Merchant of Venice*. Miss Ritterhouse let him sit down after the first line, and she never called on him in class again.

Junie was intrigued by him—this almost-grown person who towered a head above most of the boys in class, and yet was as ignorant as a baby about things that she and her friends took for granted. When she got to know him, she found that he had never been to a movie, never owned a sled or a pair of roller skates, never eaten an ice cream sundae. It was a dreadful ordeal for him to accumulate a nickel for a new Masterpiece tablet or find a penny for a pencil, and sometimes he disappeared from school for days at a time for the shame of not having them.

He never walked her home. Neither of them was courageous enough for that. And he never would meet her at the library, because he was ashamed to be seen there in his overalls. Junie felt grown up when she helped him with his homework: *she*, helping a boy who was older than her brother Gordon and almost as old as her brother Jeremy away at the University of Chicago.

"We had our own farm oncet," he had been saying just a few minutes before the kiss. He was leaning back against a clump of hay, a straw in his mouth, his school tablet with his shaky downhill writing put aside. "I remember it real well. I must of been ten or maybe twelve. Big white house, fresh-painted red barn with tin ventilators, red tile silo. Brand-new Aermotor windmill, shiny as a pin. Crick running right through, corn fields on one side, pasture on the other. My brother Purley and me use to sneak off from chores and go fishing, and Pa never minded much in those days."

"What happened?" Junie said.

From where she was sitting beside Floyd in the loft, she could look out through the open bay and see the Kinneys' place. The buildings looked mean and shabby. The animal shed leaned crazily, a door hanging off its hinges, and she could see daylight through the walls. The paint on the house had flaked off years before, leaving silvery diseased-looking board exposed. A couple of bedraggled chickens pecked at garbage in the kitchen yard.

"Pa lost it," he said without rancor. "They sold it for taxes. He couldn't pay no more after times got hard."

"I wish this old depression was over," Junie said.

"Pa says it ain't never goin' to be over. He says we're goin' to have hard times forever."

"Things will get better, you'll see!"

He shook his head. "Can't. Can't get better. Don't do no good to work hard, 'cause the harder you work the less you have. Two and a half cents a pound for hogs! Costs more than that to feed 'em. You know the Mueller Feed Company in Beulah, they list corn at *minus* a penny a bushel? You want to get old man Mueller to take a bushel of corn off your hands, you got to pay *him* a penny. We kept warm this winter by burning ours."

"But *if* things get better some day, what would you do?" she persisted.

He took the straw out of his mouth. A dreamy look came into his eyes. "I'd git me a farm of my own."

"Tell me about it." She tucked her shoes under her skirts and waited. They had played this game before.

"It's goin' to have a red barn and a house with a sittin' porch, and the tallest Aermotor you ever saw, and I'm goin' to have a corn picker and a tractor. No more ploughin' with horses, no sir! And I'll have hogs—feed 'em my own corn. No more old man Mueller. Hogs, that's where the money is."

Junie was impressed. Here was a real ambition—not like the silly boys at school who talked about being aviators or African explorers. Floyd's prosaic vision was like the things grownups talked about. It could really and truly come true some day. It could! And here she was, teaching him about things she knew about that he didn't. She hugged her knees to herself, feeling old and wise.

"You know what I wish?" she said. "I wish I could live in Europe

and be a ballet dancer like Greta Garbo in *Grand Hotel*. My father's
going to take me to Europe some day, but just for a trip. My mother
says that a trip to Europe should be part of every girl's education. My
sister Pamela was supposed to go when she was eighteen, after she got
out of Mount St. Claire Academy, but Daddy said business was bad
that year, that was when the depression started. That's why I'm going
to Beulah High instead of Mount St. Claire. Mummy says that when
business improves, she'll get Daddy to send us together, Pamela and
me, and she'll chaperone us. Can you imagine being in a real Paris
hotel and hearing people speak French?"

She chattered on happily. They sat companionably while she talked,
side by side, their bodies almost touching. She didn't feel mean, telling
Floyd about things he'd never see in his whole life. She always told
him the stories of the movies she saw. He enjoyed hearing about them
—like looking into a shop window at all the candy you couldn't buy
and imagining what it would taste like.

She was so overwhelmed by a feeling of tenderness for him that she
laid her head on his shoulder and snuggled up a little. It was all right;
he was almost like one of her brothers.

Neither of them intended it. But he turned his head to say something just as she moved, and their faces brushed. She felt a jolt, as if
she'd had an electric shock, and she realized that Floyd had given a little jump at the same instant, too. That little twitch of mutual surprise
had brought their lips together, and without premeditation they corrected for position and began to kiss.

She never had been kissed on the mouth before. At spin-the-bottle,
she always had turned her cheek so that the big wet disgusting smack
landed off center. Floyd's lips were unexpectedly dry. This close there
was a sort of cheesy smell, and she found herself remembering those
poor missing teeth of his in the back that gave a sunken look to one
cheek. All the while they kissed, Floyd strained to keep his big red
cracked hands motionless by his sides. Out of the corner of her eye
she could see the fingers working.

"Floyd!"

They gave a guilty start and moved away from one another. It was
Floyd's mother's voice, calling from the kitchen door.

"I got to go to dinner," Floyd said, standing up.

"I better go home," Junie said, gathering up her books. Country
people always ate earlier, but even so it was a half-hour walk into
town, and she'd have to start soon if she didn't want Mrs. Hansen to
be mad at her.

"You . . ." Floyd's voice sounded strangled. "You kin eat with us."

"I better not." She didn't relish the thought of sitting down to table with Mr. and Mrs. Kinney and Floyd's brothers and Floyd's sister-in-law Sue Ellen and her children.

"Nobody ever got turned away from the Kinneys' hungry," Floyd said. "That's what Pa says." His voice was rough and he looked a little frightened.

"But your mother doesn't even know I'm here. . . ." she began.

"You're eatin' with us," he said with finality.

When she followed Floyd into the kitchen, Mrs. Kinney was at the stove, stirring around a big pot of potatoes and turnips. "Set down," she said, then looked around and saw Junie.

Junie wondered if kissing a boy made you look different, but Mrs. Kinney didn't seem to notice anything. Floyd said at once, "Ma, Junie's staying to dinner."

"Of course she is," Mrs. Kinney said. "You just set right down, Junie. Floyd, you go fetch an extra chair."

"I don't want to be any trouble," Junie said.

"You ain't no trouble, child. Now just set down." But Junie had seen the terrible look that had crossed her face before she turned again to busy herself at the stove. For the first time it occurred to Junie that there might not be enough food to go around.

She looked around at the kitchen. The floor slanted, and you could see the bare laths in the wall in places where the plaster had crumbled away. There was no hand pump on the sink; the Kinneys had to haul all their water from outside. The woodbox beside the old black iron stove was filled with cornstalks and dry cobs. There was no tablecloth on the table, and that seemed strange to Junie. The table itself was a fine old yellow oak dining table that had seen better days. It had massive carved legs and a top that was two inches thick. It must have weighed a ton, and Junie could imagine the struggle it must have been for the Kinneys to load it on a wagon every February when it was time to move.

She took her place at the table. Only Mr. Kinney and Floyd's older brother Wesley were seated so far. Sue Ellen's two-year-old was sitting on the floor playing with a headless thing that had once been a doll.

Mr. Kinney nodded gravely at her. He was a lanky, used-up looking man with sparse brown hair and a nondescript face covered with a three-day growth of whiskers. Like Floyd and Wesley, he wore a patched shirt and faded overalls. "You make yourself at home, Junie," he said. "We're just waiting on Purley and Sue Ellen. They went to an auction sale down the road. They'll be back directly. Does your ma know you're here?"

She was saved from having to answer by the arrival of Purley and his wife. Purley seemed to have lost even more flesh since the last time she'd seen him. His eyes burned darkly under a ridge of brow that seemed like parchment stretched over bone. Sue Ellen followed him in, holding her baby wrapped in an old blanket. Her dark hair hung limp from the rain. It was hard for Junie to remember that Sue Ellen was actually younger than her own sister, Pamela.

Purley gave Junie a tired nod, then sat down at the table opposite her. Sue Ellen sat down beside him, holding the baby. The little girl got up from the floor and started to whine until Mrs. Kinney picked her up and set her down in the chair next to Sue Ellen.

"You git it?" Mr. Kinney said to Purley.

Purley shook his head. "It was one of them penny sales. Every farmer in the county must have been there. They take care of their own."

"You're better off without it," Mrs. Kinney said from her place at the stove. "No good comes from taking advantage of a man's misery, Purley Kinney. You'd have got no sleep nights."

"Oh, I'd 'a slept, all right," he said with a short, bitter laugh. "I need a plough horse a sight worse than that insurance company does."

Wesley spoke up from his seat next to Floyd. He was the bachelor. He had a soft face for a Kinney, and he wore a pair of bent wire spectacles with a piece of adhesive tape all the way across one cracked lens, giving him a half-blind look. "Ain't nobody worried about takin' advantage of Pa's misery when they took *his* place away from *him*," he said.

"That's the truth," Purley went on. "I'd 'a had Dutch Hansen's good plough horse, I could 'a farmed me a piece of land of my own! Sue Ellen and me, we could 'a rented that Calvin place on the other side of Beulah. Man can't get a *start!* Damn insurance companies and bloodsucking bankers own *everything*. . . ."

"Purley!" his mother said sharply.

Everybody was looking at Junie. Or trying not to look at her, which was the same thing. She shrank in her chair, as embarrassed as they were. Junie didn't know much about business, but she knew that her father's bank held the Kinneys' seed loan, whatever that meant. Floyd had once mentioned it, in his first astonishment at being friends with a banker's daughter.

As soon as Purley realized what he'd said, he started talking quickly to cover it up. "Anyway, there was a riot. . . . Got Sue Ellen and the baby out by the road, but a feller who was there told me. I won't say what those boys did to the insurance feller, but they near lynched Judge Boehm."

Mr. Kinney was incredulous. "They put their hands on a judge?"

"They sure did. They drug him right out of his courtroom."

Mr. Kinney shook his head. "I don't know what the country's coming to."

"Revolution, that's what it's coming to," Purley said. "Farm holidays, bank holidays—it can't go on this way. And that Hoover sitting in Washington, saying the depression'll go way if folks just quit talking about it. Quit talking about how their kids are hungry!"

Everybody relaxed. The blame was now safely far away in Washington.

"He says if someone could get off a good joke every ten days, our troubles would be over," Wesley said.

That exhausted the subject. They all fell silent while Mrs. Kinney served them their dinners. Junie watched her as she clomped to the table in the unlaced man's shoes she wore and ladled food out of the pot. There were no serving dishes and no greens on the table. Boiled potatoes and turnips, biscuits and boiled pork, that's all there was to it. There were more turnips than potatoes.

"Well, there's the last of old Cleo." Mr. Kinney sighed as his wife speared a piece of meat onto his plate. "Dressed out at six hundred pounds, she did!"

Junie couldn't help noticing that her own portion of meat was bigger than anyone else's. "Please . . ." she said. "That's enough."

"Nonsense, child," Mrs. Kinney said, and dumped what looked like the last piece on her plate.

The Kinneys didn't say grace; they just started eating. They all ate very fast. If anyone had eaten that fast at the Sinclair table, Junie's mother would have said something. Junie did her best to keep up. The potatoes were small and withered, the last of the winter hoard. The turnips looked as if they'd been frozen over in the ground all winter. At home, Jeremy always refused to eat turnips, saying they were feed for horses. It was a fact that they would always grow when nothing else would, but there wasn't much nourishment in them. The pork was gristly and tasteless. When the Kinneys had all finished, Junie had barely started. She had to sit there and eat, while they all tried not to look at the food on her plate. It was a nightmare. The amount of food in front of her seemed impossible to manage, but she didn't dare leave a single scrap.

"Have another biscuit," Wesley said.

The noon whistle went off in Beulah, a mile away, and Mr. Kinney and his eldest son looked at one another. "One o'clock in Washington," Mr. Kinney said. "The nauguration 'll be starting 'bout now. They said they'd carry it on the Red Network."

"I'll git it, Pa," Floyd said. He slid out of his chair and went over to the radio sitting on a kitchen shelf. There was no cabinet, just dusty naked tubes. It was connected to an automobile battery; the Kinneys had no electricity.

"You think things'll be better under Roosevelt?" Purley challenged while they waited for the set to warm up.

"Can't get any worse," Mr. Kinney said.

"He's a rich man," Purley said.

"He says he's for fair farm prices, and that's good enough for me." Wesley cleared his throat. "That Hoover, he says the farmer's not *supposed* to make much money."

Junie welcomed the little exchange. It took attention away from her eating. She got another mouthful of boiled turnips down. It seemed as if there was just as much food on her plate as before.

The radio began to crackle. A piercing whistle went up and down, like a teakettle. Through it all could be heard the faint sound of band music.

"Battery's almost dead," Purley said.

"Floyd, you're good with radios," Mrs. Kinney said. "Can't you do anything?"

"I'll try, Ma," Floyd said.

He tinkered with the terminals of the battery and blew dust from the radio tubes. The signal came in a little stronger. Junie could hear a scratchy voice: "I, Franklin Delano Roosevelt, do solemnly swear . . ." All the Kinneys had their eyes fastened on the radio. Her knife slipped on a piece of gristle and squeaked against the plate, but nobody noticed.

Stolidly she chewed while the voice went on. ". . . Values have shrunken to fantastic levels . . . the means of exchange are frozen . . . farmers find no markets for their produce. . . ."

Mr. Kinney rocked back and forth, his head nodding in agreement. The little girl started to whine; Sue Ellen slapped her absentmindedly, and she stopped.

Junie tried not to make any noises as she ate. Something important was going on here in the Kinneys' kitchen. It was like listening to a sermon in church. It sounded sort of like a sermon, too.

". . . The money changers have fled from their high seats in the temple of our civilization. . . . These dark days will be worth all they cost us if they teach us that our true destiny is not to be ministered unto, but to minister to ourselves and to our fellow men . . ."

With despair, Junie realized that she'd been so caught up in the radio broadcast that she'd forgotten to chew. The stringy meat and those horrid turnips were dry in her mouth, impossible to swallow. She wished she had a glass of water.

". . . The task can be helped by definite efforts to raise the value of agricultural products, and with this the power to purchase the output of our cities. . . ."

"He said it, by God!" Purley crowed. "Hot damn!"

Mr. Kinney didn't reprimand Purley, as he had Wesley. He was sitting there with tears rolling down his stubbled cheeks. Junie thought maybe she better look away from him.

". . . It can be helped by preventing realistically the tragedy of the growing loss through foreclosure of our small homes and our farms. . . ." the radio voice went on.

"Same as he said durin' the election," Purley said. " 'Cost of production,' don't you see? But he didn't *have* to say it now. He don't need the votes now!"

It was impossible. She *couldn't* finish what was on her plate. She couldn't even swallow what was in her mouth. And soon the radio speech would be over, and their eyes would be on her again, and all the food she'd wasted. And then there would be more food, biscuits and molasses, or something, and Mrs. Kinney wouldn't let her help with the dishes, and she didn't know how to do dishes anyway in a kitchen like this, with no sink and that big pot of water heating on the stove.

There was a sound from outside: the rattle of an old car pulling up, and the noise of chickens squawking and scattering. An auto horn went *ooga ooga*.

"What damn fool is that?" Mr. Kinney muttered, and started to get up. A moment later somebody gave a perfunctory rap on the kitchen door and walked in. It was an old farmer in overalls and frayed sweater and a cap with earlaps.

"Well, if it ain't Frank Salter!" Mr. Kinney said. "Come on in, Frank. Set down and listen to the nauguration. You hungry?"

"Can't set," Salter said, rocking on his heels, his eyes roving. All of a sudden his eyes gave a pounce and landed on Junie. "This the Sinclair girl?"

Mr. Kinney looked longingly at the radio. ". . . there must be provision for an adequate and sound currency. . . ." Roosevelt was saying through a howling storm of static. Mrs. Kinney answered for him quickly: "Yes, she is. Just here to help Floyd with his school work. Junie, this here's our neighbor down the road, Mr. Salter."

Salter nodded to himself. "Her brother thought she might be here. Her uncle knowed I had a phone and called me."

Junie knew that something awful was going to happen. She could tell from Mr. Salter's eyes. They were fixed on her, narrowed, full of pity. She got up from the table, her mouth full, and waited.

"You best come along with me, girl," Mr. Salter said gruffly. "I'll ride you into town. Somethin' bad's happened to your father."

Little Orphan Annie was off, replaced by Ernie Holst and his Hotel Lexington Orchestra, and the couple in cabin D were at it again. They liked to do it to music. All afternoon the sound of heavy breathing and creaking bedsprings had come through the thin walls, in rhythm first to Concert Miniatures, then to Jack Denny and his Waldorf-Astoria Orchestra, then to Henry King and his Hotel Pierre Orchestra, then Eddy Duchin's Orchestra, the Radio City Organ, Walter Logan and his Viennese Ensemble, and the Lady Esther Serenade. They had paused for fifteen minutes to listen to Vic and Sade, had twirled dials frantically during the early afternoon when all the networks seemed to be carrying the Roosevelt inaugural speech until they found a local station featuring the Sioux City Melody Twins at the Keyboards, then paused in their labors once more to listen to Orphan Annie get Daddy Warbucks out of a jam. Now there was a steady, industrious sound of bedsprings again.

Pamela Sinclair twisted her head around on the rough, unstarched pillowcase and tried not to hear the sounds, but it was no use. The tourist cabins—two rows of cheap plywood boxes on stilts—were spaced no more than a dozen feet apart, and some freak effect of resonance from cabin D's walls made the sounds carry.

She looked around at the room. Flimsy paneling painted a pale pink that showed the dirt. Raw studs exposed at one end where a panel had been removed and never replaced. Dresser with peeling oak veneer and a cloudy mirror. Kerosene heater, resembling a dented milk can on three galvanized legs. Naked lightbulb in the ceiling, and a bedside lamp with a painted shade. Tin wastebasket with an empty whiskey bottle that had been left there by the last couple.

She sat up in bed and reached for one of Carl's cigarettes, trying to ignore the rhythmic little cries that the woman in D was now starting to make. Smoking: that was another thing that Carl had taught her to do. She had put her slip back on, but she still felt naked. She heard the toilet flush, and she shivered.

Pamela was a tall slender girl with a fine-drawn blond beauty. She had a smooth, translucent skin, delicately blue-veined at temple and throat and breast. She had the ice-blue Sinclair eyes, and the long precise upper lip and chiseled nose of her paternal grandmother, her father was fond of telling her. She wondered what her father would say if he knew where his little girl was now.

Carl came padding out of the bathroom in his shorts. "Where's that boy?" he said.

"Maybe he forgot."

He gave a short laugh. "He didn't forget. Not at those prices."

She looked at him, then away. It still didn't seem right to be looking at Carl Fuller—or any man—without his clothes on. Three months ago she couldn't have imagined such a thing. Though he was still under thirty, he had seemed to her to be a member of her father's generation, one of those serious important people in business suits whom you saw in offices and banks and places like the county courthouse, and whom you were made to say hello to by your parents. Now he was standing there in his undershorts, a square blocky man with thick shapeless legs, his body covered with black curly hair from the hollow of his neck to where it fringed over his waistband. He was already getting a little bald on top.

He sat down heavily on the bed and put his hand under the sheet.

"Please, Carl, not now," she said.

"What's the matter? That's what we came here for, isn't it?"

"I should be getting home. It's after six."

"Listen, I already paid two dollars for this cabin. It's ours for the night. I mean as much of the night as we want. Look, I can send the kid out for something to eat in a little while, and I promise to get you back home before midnight. Okay?"

"I don't like it here."

"You've been here before. You liked it all right then."

"Shhh! Don't talk so loud."

He looked puzzled for a moment, then tilted his head. From the cabin next door came a series of long-drawn-out cries in a woman's voice, followed by a single masculine groan. The timing was perfect. Ernie Holst's Hotel Lexington Orchestra finished a rendition of "Stardust" with a wail of saxophones and a flourish of cymbals.

"So that's it," he laughed. "That's why you've been so stiff. Good God, Pam, they can't hear us! They don't *want* to hear us! Why do you think they brought a radio with them?"

"I feel as if they're right here in this room with us. I can't help it!"

"I *tried* to get the end cabin, didn't I?" he said impatiently. "But you know this place. It starts filling up Saturday noon right after the gypsum mills over to Fort Dodge let out."

"That's another thing. This sneaking around in places like this, outside of the county. Eating in those dreadful roadhouses where no one will recognize us. Not being able to tell anybody. How long is it going to go on like this?"

He looked uncomfortable. If he had been wearing a shirt, she would have said his collar was too tight. "Now, Pamela . . ."

"How long?"

He sighed. "We'll just have to be patient, darling. You know how I feel about you. But there are problems. Legal problems. And until they're settled, she mustn't know about us. *No one* must know. And besides, it would be cruel to tell her prematurely. God knows, we haven't lived as man and wife for the last two years, but she deserves something better than a kick in the face."

"I know, Carl," Pamela said miserably. "I'm sorry."

"That's my girl." He chucked her under the chin. "And anyway, you wouldn't want your family to find out, would you?"

Her heart began to beat faster. It always scared her when he talked like this. "Carl . . ."

"Think of what it would do to your mother. And your father. The daughter of the town's banker having an affair with a married man! How do you think the board of directors would feel about that in a place like Beulah?"

"Carl, please don't . . ."

"Lord knows, it's bad enough when a girl your age is seen going around with a *divorced* man. But at least that's legal. Did you know there are still criminal adultery laws in the state of Iowa?"

"Carl, please don't talk like that," she said, really frightened now.

"I'm only trying to point things out to you," he said. "And anyway, you're not twenty-one yet, are you?"

"My birthday's in September. But . . ."

"There, you see." He took one of her hands and patted it. "You see why we have to be careful, don't you? For a while?"

"Yes, Carl," she said, subdued. He was right, she thought. He always was. It wasn't going to be easy, marrying a divorced man. There would be talk. Her parents would be unhappy, but they'd stand by her. She knew her father would give her all his support; he'd do anything to see her happy. And if things got too bad, they could move—to another state, if need be. They could make a good life for themselves. Carl was only eight years older than she. That wasn't so much. Until now she'd only been a silly girl, going to dances with silly boys. Now she felt like a woman.

She had first seen Carl at the Christmas dance at the country club, hobnobbing with the other stags and disappearing from time to time into the cloakroom. Her brother Brad had pointed him out to her as one of the county's rising young lawyers, a man destined to go far in this corner of Iowa. "The biggest frog in the puddle," Brad had said with that newly acquired almost-sneer of his that she didn't like. Carl Fuller, he explained, was a fair-haired boy at the courthouse, and a lot of business got thrown his way: wills, foreclosures, settlement of county claims. Those five-dollar fees added up, and Carl was in line for bigger things.

Brad hadn't mentioned that Carl Fuller was married. By the time she found out, it was too late.

It had seemed all right to let him drive her home from the dance. After all, she had been introduced to him by her brother. And Brad, who had brought her, had disappeared—most likely in pursuit of that Dottie Helm whom everybody told stories about. And there were other young people in the car. Carl dropped her off last, didn't try to kiss her, for which she was grateful, and asked for a date. On that date, and the next one, and the one after that, he contrived not to come to her home. He would pick her up after her piano lesson or after a shopping trip in the next town or, pleading lack of time, have her meet him at the courthouse. There would be a good movie forty miles away, or dinner at a new roadhouse that no one in Beulah had ever heard of. On the fourth date, full of champagne and compliments, she lost her virginity in the back seat of his brand-new silver-gray La Salle Eight.

He told her the following night. "Honest to God, I wanted to tell you, but I kept putting it off. Estelle and I are married in name only. We don't sleep together. She can't have children anyway. We only stay together because of appearances. . . ." After a while Pamela got used to the idea. She gave herself to Carl again that same night. It seemed too much trouble to break off the relationship.

She knew it couldn't go on this way forever. After all, she told herself, it wasn't as if she were breaking up a marriage. Carl had been very clear about that.

The radio in D announced something called O'Leary's Irish Minstrels. Accordians and hilarious tenor voices. There was some rapid switching of the dial until they found another hotel orchestra. A man's voice said, clearly, "No, the other way."

Carl was pressing himself against her, scratchy as wool. She tensed up, but he went right ahead anyway, inserting a hand between their bodies to squeeze her right breast. He always started that way. There was a knock at the door, and she pulled away from him.

"There he is," Carl said.

He went to the door in his shorts, not bothering to put anything on. Pamela pulled the sheet all the way up to her chin and turned her face to the wall.

"You the party with the rye?" the kid's voice said.

"Scotch. I said scotch."

"He's outa the scotch. Not till next shipment. You gotta take the rye. Or he got gin."

"Oh, all right, give me the rye. Where's the ice I asked you for?"

"The ice ran out."

"The ice ran out," Carl said with heavy sarcasm. "All right, how much?"

"Four fifty."

Carl set the bottle on the dresser and got his trousers off the chair. He rummaged in the pocket for his wallet. "Here. And this is for you."

"Oh, thank you kindly, sir."

"Don't get fresh."

Pamela heard the door close, and turned around. Carl was pouring an inch of whiskey into the two glasses that stood on the dresser. He went into the bathroom with one of the glasses and added water. He handed that one to her.

"Drink up."

"I don't want any."

"Go on, it'll loosen you up."

"I can't go home with liquor on my breath."

"For Chrissake, we're supposed to be having fun!"

"Well, drinking isn't fun for me."

"Drinking isn't the only thing that isn't any fun for you!" he said petulantly. He reminded her at that moment of a big, blocky baby, and she felt sorry for him.

"Oh, all right," she said, and drank the rye down like medicine.

He downed his own and poured them both another one. "That's more like it," he said. He sipped his drink and listened to the jouncing of bedsprings from D. Pamela could see that it excited him. "I don't see why it bothers you," he said. "I think it . . . sort of adds something. . . ."

By the time she had another drink, the sounds next door didn't bother her anymore. They were far away. Her own body was far away, too. She felt a kind of numb warmth all over. The whiskey was a friend. Maybe, she thought, maybe it wouldn't hurt this time, the way it always did those times when she didn't want to and Carl plunged ahead anyway.

And then, as he continued his methodical massage, she did feel a faint stirring in that faraway body of hers, and she wished that it were not so utterly impossible to find the words to tell Carl not to hurry her, to give her time. Did husbands and wives, she wondered, ever discuss this thing they did with one another?

The couple in D were taking a rest. On the Red Network, the national news was on. ". . . and at this hour, only hours after taking the oath of office as this country's thirty-second chief executive, President Franklin D. Roosevelt is already swearing in his Cabinet in the Oval

Room at the White House. The Senate has already given hasty confirmation in an unprecedented . . ."

The radio hummed and whistled as the man in D searched for a station with music on it. Instead, he got the Des Moines station with the statewide news. ". . . and this bulletin just in. The chairman of the board of the Beulah Trust Company in Calhoun County, Thayer W. Chadwick, has issued a statement urging depositors to stay calm after the bank's president, Bradford D. Sinclair, was found dead in . . ."

The voice disappeared in a burst of static as the occupants of cabin D managed to find a station with ballroom music on it.

Pamela had the feeling of being suspended in a frozen moment. She seemed to be looking down from a great height at her own body, tiny and sharp, lying across a doll's bed in a slip while a little hairy man in undershorts crouched over her. Then the illusion passed, and she was back in her body, feeling Carl's paralyzed hand on her breast, her head still reverberating with the echo of a voice that said her father was dead.

She pushed Carl aside and sat up. "Take me home," she said.

"Now Pam . . ." he said, looking frightened.

"Take me *home!*"

"You'll attract attention like this. Now first you've got to get hold of yourself. . . ."

She put on her clothes in the bathroom, a narrow crypt of painted plywood containing a yellowed sink and toilet and a shower like a tin coffin. When she came out, Carl was knotting his tie, and putting what was left of the whiskey into the pocket of his overcoat.

It was forty miles home, over dark country roads until they hit U.S. 20 past the Twin Lakes. Pamela sat huddled in the corner, while Carl reached over and patted her hand from time to time, telling her how important it was to keep calm. He gave her a stick of gum to chew, to take the liquor off her breath. She insisted that he keep the radio on. There was one more news bulletin at nine, and this time she heard it all. No cause of death was given, but Thayer Chadwick was still assuring depositors that the Beulah Trust would be open again when the bank holiday was over, and that the death of Bradford Sinclair had nothing to do with the bank's closing.

Carl entered Beulah through a side road and let Pamela off in a dark street, two blocks from her home. He didn't get out of the car. He reached across to open the door for her, and as soon as she was out of the car he pulled the door shut and drove off.

The front door wasn't locked. She let herself in without having to use her key. She heard subdued voices from the parlor. The door to

her father's study was sealed with three strips of paper tape, and there
was some kind of official paper nailed above the knob.

Her brother Gordon came out of the parlor and looked at her without saying a word. He looked older than his seventeen years. His face
was very pale, and there was a long scratch running down one cheek.
It was puffy and bruised under the eye. He was wearing a pair of
flannel pants that were too long for him; they must have belonged to
Brad, because Gordon was already taller than Jeremy.

"I heard it on the radio," she said.

"He shot himself," Gordon said. "It's awful in there. Aunt Ottilie is
lording it over Mrs. Hansen, having her run around with coffee and
food every five minutes. Dr. Davis was here. He gave a sedative to
Mother. She's upstairs in bed. You better talk to Junie. She's taking it
pretty hard."

She wanted to put her arms around him, but he turned and walked
back into the parlor. She followed him.

Aunt Ottilie was sitting on the plum-colored velvet couch, a butler's
tray in front of her heaped with cups and saucers, plates of half-eaten
sandwiches, and a mound of Mrs. Hansen's little Swedish cakes. She
was dressed in a stiff black dress, a cameo brooch that had once
belonged to Pamela's mother pinned at the collar. Her gray hair was
pulled back in a tight bun. Junie, looking small and trapped, sat beside
her on the couch. Uncle Elroy was sitting facing her in a straight-
backed chair that had been pulled up to the couch.

Aunt Ottilie stopped talking and lifted a face as withered as a baked
apple. When Pamela bent over to kiss her on the cheek, she sniffed.
"Whiskey on your breath."

Elroy looked up bleakly from the Bible he'd been reading. "It's
about time. Your mother's in shock." He said it as if it were her fault.

"I came home as soon as I heard," she faltered. "The radio . . ."

"They didn't tell the full story, no sir," Elroy said, his long bony
skull bobbing with satisfaction. "That Mr. Chadwick, he took charge
of the police and the coroner and that sassy newspaper fellow. Fine
gentleman."

"I know what happened," Pamela said. "Gordon told me." Her legs
felt weak; she looked around for a chair to sit down in.

"I called that brother Bradford of yours," Elroy went on, looking
like wrath. "He'll take a train out of New York tonight. I'm still trying
to get Jeremy. Called his dormitory three times, and he still isn't
there."

"The masses," the man in the lumberjack shirt was saying importantly. "A man like Roosevelt will never understand the masses."

"But he declared war on the bankers," Sylvia Harris said, her big dark-fringed eyes staring up at him. "You have to admit that he declared war on the bankers."

Jeremy Sinclair sat miserably on the sagging couch, a glass of sticky wine punch in his hand. Sylvia had ignored him ever since the man in the lumberjack shirt had wandered over. His name was Norton, and he had black fingernails though his hands were otherwise scrubbed pink, and he was supposed to be a real live member of the Communist Party or something.

"Rhetoric," Norton said smugly. "Phony rhetoric meant to deceive the proletariat. All that talk in the inaugural speech about money changers in the temple! Roosevelt's *real* purpose is to buy time for capitalism. If he *did* succeed in improving conditions in this country, it would just delay the revolution."

"I see." Sylvia nodded. "Then you're saying that Roosevelt is the *real* enemy of the working class?" She was a thin intense girl with narrow hips and a billowing peasant blouse. Until Norton's arrival, she had been lecturing Jeremy severely about the class struggle and the new social realism in the novels of Farrell and Dos Passos. She hadn't been much impressed by the fact that Jeremy had had a poem published in the Iowa literary magazine, the *Midland Monthly,* before it folded.

Jeremy stared moodily at his shoes, and wished he hadn't polished them that morning. Everybody at the party seemed to be talking brightly and knowledgeably about art and expressionist drama and the latest five-year plan in the Soviet Union except him. He'd surreptitiously taken off his necktie and put it in his jacket pocket soon after he arrived, but he'd never qualify as a member of the masses with polished shoes.

Jeremy had inherited his thick black hair and fine-boned good looks from his mother. He looked satisfactorily poetic, if only he had realized it. Like his sister Junie's, his eyes were deep-set, dark, and expressive. He was agonizedly ashamed of being nineteen, from Iowa, and a virgin.

He got up with his drink and moved away. Published poem or not, he couldn't compete with Norton, who was at least thirty, had proletarian fingernails, and had visited the Soviet Union.

". . . and I'll tell you another thing," Norton was saying. "There is absolutely no discrimination against Negroes in the Soviet Union. . . ."

Jeremy pushed his way through the crowd toward the kitchen, where an ice-filled bathtub held a punch bowl and a quarter-keg of beer. He had paid a quarter to get into the party, and drinks were another ten cents apiece. The money was going to the defense committee for the second trial of the Scottsboro Boys in Alabama. Jeremy didn't know much about the Scottsboro Boys, but he couldn't say no to Sylvia Harris when she approached him after English class and told him the party would give him a chance to meet a lot of writers and artists and intellectuals, and "find out what's going on in the world." It was being held in a cold-water flat in Chicago's South Side. The walls were covered with bright abstract paintings by the hostess, and the furniture seemed to consist of things like orange crates covered with batik and mattresses on bricks.

"Oops! Sorry!" A small muscular girl in a leotard top bumped into him, spilling his drink. She looked him over. "Are you the Dada sculptor?" she said.

"No, I'm . . ."

But she had already turned back to her companion, a short round man with a beret and goatee, who was saying: "Diaghilev, hell! When Diaghilev died, ballet died with him, and good riddance! Martha Graham, that's who to keep your eye on!"

Jeremy edged past a group who were gathered around a man in an open-necked work shirt who was sitting on a kitchen chair, playing a guitar and singing a song about somebody named Joe Hill. On the fringes of the group, a short gray-haired woman festooned with beads was haranguing a very tall young man with acne: "Open struggle, that's the answer. Have you read William Z. Foster's new book, *Toward Soviet America?*" As Jeremy passed, she gripped his arm with surprising strength and hissed: "Jay Lovestone is a traitor, don't you agree?"

Jeremy murmured something politely unintelligible and broke free. He waited in line at the punch bowl and held out his jelly glass.

"That'll be ten cents, comrade," the man serving the punch said cheerfully. He was a bald-headed little cricket of a man, wearing an apron.

"Oh, I'm not a . . . that is, I don't belong . . ." Jeremy began, flustered.

The little man peered at him suspiciously. "You're not a socialist, are you?"

"No," Jeremy said truthfully.

"Good. Then there's hope for you. Socialists are fascists, you know that?"

"No, I didn't know."

The little man laughed. "That's the new line. Well, don't bother your head about it. Have a good time. Pick up a girl. We're glad to have you. We've raised almost seventy bucks for the committee so far."

He ladled some punch into Jeremy's glass and took a dime. That left Jeremy a quarter: enough for two more drinks and a trolley ride back to the campus. He turned to go and collided with the next person in line, spilling half of his drink.

"Hey, watch where you're going!" It was a tough-looking bearded man in a black turtleneck sweater and a knitted seaman's cap. He was either the Dada sculptor or the proletarian novelist. Jeremy forgot which.

"Sorry."

The bearded man elbowed past him and said to the little crickety man at the punch bowl: "None of that crap. Where's the bottle of Irish you're supposed to have stashed at four bits a knock?"

It was the proletarian novelist. His name was Berry, Jeremy remembered now, and he had written a highly regarded book called *Blood on the Loom*, about a textile factory strike. Sylvia had held it up to him as the sort of thing he ought to be trying to write, if he wanted to be a real writer some day.

Jeremy pushed his way through the batik curtain into the next room. The man with the beret and goatee was still monopolizing the girl in the leotard top. "Stravinsky's finished," he was saying vehemently. "Finished! Without Diaghilev, he had nothing to say. Copland, that's the composer to watch!"

Jeremy sidled past them regretfully. If he wasn't going to get anywhere with Sylvia, the girl in the leotard top had been his second choice. She looked very bohemian, he thought, and probably had a liberated attitude about sex.

The party's other display celebrity, besides Berry, was a massive Negro man in a neat middle-class blue suit and necktie. He was standing off by himself near a window that opened onto a fire escape. Nobody seemed to be talking to him. He was the only Negro at the party. He was smoking a cigarette, a faint, sardonic smile on his face. His shoes, Jeremy noticed, were polished, too.

"Beautiful, isn't he?" a voice said at Jeremy's elbow. "So primitive!"

Jeremy turned and saw the gray-haired woman with the beads who had seized him by the arm before.

"Ma'am?" he said.

"Our brothers in arms!" she said, her fingers digging into his biceps. "This is going to be the biggest thing for the cause since Sacco and Vanzetti. Imagine! Railroading a fourteen-year-old boy on a charge of rape!" At the word *rape*, her eyes glittered.

Jeremy was embarrassed. Rape was not one of the subjects he had been brought up to discuss with a gray-haired woman old enough to be his grandmother.

"I guess it's pretty awful," he said.

"He can stay here tonight," she said, looking across at the Negro man. "I know it's hard to make arrangements in a strange city for a colored person."

"I suppose so," he mumbled. He tried to edge away, but she had him in a grip of iron.

"You'll talk to him about it?" she insisted.

Jeremy gave her a bewildered look. "Well, I haven't exactly met him yet, but I'll be glad to—"

"Aren't you with the committee?"

"Committee?" he repeated stupidly.

"International Labor Defense. Didn't you come out from New York with Bernard? I saw you sitting with him."

"Bernard?"

"The man in the black-and-white checked shirt."

"Oh, you mean Norton."

"That's his Party name. Don't you know anyone here?" Her manner softened. "Where are you from?"

"I'm going to school here in Chicago. I—"

"Where do you *come* from?"

Jeremy stared down at his polished shoes. "Iowa. A little place in the western part of the state called Beulah, that you probably never heard of."

"But that's marvelous." She squeezed his arm. "It's so *genuine!* So *American!* Is your father a farmer?"

"No, actually he's—"

"What's your name?" she rushed on, without giving him a chance to answer.

"Jeremy. Jeremy Sinclair."

"You people are doing marvelous things out there, Jeremy," she said. "The farm strike. The fight against the oppression of the banks and the insurance companies. You're in the front lines. You're showing the rest of us what this struggle is all about."

"Well . . ."

"Have you met Mother Bloor?"

He knew who Mother Bloor was. There were editorials about her in the papers back home. She traveled around the state, dressed in rags, with a well-dressed young man who was supposed to be her son-in-law, getting up on a box and trying to speak to the farmers whenever they held a meeting. They always booed her down. The Farm Holiday

Association had warned them against outside agitators coming in and giving the movement a bad name.

"No, I never actually met her. You see . . ."

Grasping his arm, she propelled him across the room toward the couch. "A farmer's son from Iowa! Just think, and Bernard never mentioned it! I'm going to give him a piece of my mind!"

Norton, or Bernard, or whatever his name was, was still talking about Roosevelt's radio speech to Sylvia. ". . . first he lulls us with all this talk about preserving democracy in America. The crackdown comes later—"

He broke off in annoyance as the gray-haired lady appeared with Jeremy in tow.

"Oh, hello, Marianne," he said without enthusiasm.

"Listen, Bernard, you've got to see that that perfectly beautiful black man stays here tonight."

"Negro, Marianne. They don't like to be called blacks. It's a derogatory term from the colonial past."

"Oh, Negro, then! What do you say?"

"We found a place for him with a colored family for the night. Then we've got a rally in Toledo."

"Be a dear, and talk to him."

Norton looked her straight in the eye. "They'd really rather stay with their own kind."

"Nonsense. He'll jump at the invitation. Do what you can, dear."

Norton sighed. "All right."

"You didn't tell me Jeremy was from Iowa," Marianne said.

Jeremy looked hopefully at Sylvia, but she showed no awareness that he'd been brought into the conversation.

"Iowa," Norton said condescendingly. "Ah, yes, the heartland of America."

Jeremy's smoldering temper rose. "That's right. We're not very sophisticated there. We just grow corn."

"Don't get mad, kid." Norton looked amused. "A lot of good things are going on in Iowa right now. Good old Mother Bloor racing round the countryside, stirring up the farmers. That's where the revolution will start in this country. Iowa."

He's kidding me, Jeremy thought with wonder. He doesn't take any of this seriously. He's just playing a part, with his lumberjack shirt and dirty fingernails. That's the way he gets girls.

"The farmers don't need Mother Bloor or anyone else to stir them up," Jeremy said with some heat. "They've suffered enough. They don't want to be exploited by anyone—even you people. Sure, there's a lot of talk of revolution in Iowa. But nobody wants it to come to that!"

"Bravo," Norton said dryly, and Jeremy immediately felt like a fool. "I applaud your sentiments, my young friend, but you're politically immature. The point is that you Iowa farmers *do* need outside direction. Your leader, Milo Reno, has been trying to *avoid* bloodshed. But we *need* an incident to arouse the masses. A big, juicy incident."

"Yes," Marianne said, looking sweet and grandmotherly. "The revolution must be born out of blood."

"A spontaneous uprising of the masses," Norton said in a dry, lecture-hall tone. "Then a disciplined, organized minority can take over. That's the way it happened in Russia. First the February Revolution. Then the October Revolution. Look at it this way—your Iowa bumpkins will have the honor of sacrificing themselves to a, hmmm, greater cause than support of farm prices."

"Martyrs," Marianne said eagerly. "Every revolution needs martyrs."

Jeremy flushed. He knew he ought to take offense at "bumpkins," but he didn't know how to do it without looking foolish in front of Sylvia. He was no match for someone like Norton.

"B-b-but you're talking about people *d-d-dying.* . . ." he stammered.

Norton got to his feet. He clapped Jeremy condescendingly on the shoulder. "You're young. These ideas are new to you." He turned to Marianne. "Let's go talk to that beautiful Negro of yours."

Jeremy sat down beside Sylvia quickly, before anyone else could take Norton's seat.

"I think he lacquers his nails. Right over the dirt."

"Don't be childish!" she snapped.

Another fumble. He felt his face grow warm. "Well, it's easy for *him* to talk about people in Iowa shedding their blood."

"You're in no position to criticize him. You should be in the fight with your people, instead of hiding at the university writing decadent poetry."

When she said "your people," she sounded as though she were referring to some distant, primitive tribe, instead of the Germans and Scandinavians and Scotch-Irish who were Jeremy's neighbors back home. But Jeremy took heart from the fact that Sylvia's manner had become noticeably friendly beneath the severity. Marianne's endorsement of his Iowa origins had impressed her. Maybe it wasn't so bad to be a bumpkin after all.

"It isn't decadent." Jeremy had been trying to imitate T.S. Eliot, whom he had just discovered.

"*All* poetry is decadent unless it's placed in the service of the masses," she said sternly. "It's been part of a bourgeois preoccupation with art for art's sake up till now. What we need is more working-class poetry."

"Well, I'm just trying to learn," he said lamely. "I don't suppose I'm very good at it."

"Jeremy," she said. She actually took his hand. "You should be *proud* of your origins. I can understand your trying to better yourself. But you should never forget your class."

She gave his hand a friendly squeeze. Jeremy hardly dared to believe the change in his luck. Sylvia was pressed against him on the crowded couch, the side of what felt like a very large, loose breast under the peasant blouse plastered against his arm. He felt himself blushing.

"We never thought much about things like that back when I was growing up," he mumbled. "Most folks just sort of figured that everybody was as good as everybody else."

"Your family was politically naive," she said with a tolerant smile.

"I guess so."

"I suppose your father voted for Roosevelt."

"Good God, no!" Jeremy said. The idea came as a genuine shock. Jeremy couldn't have imagined his father voting for anyone but a Republican, ever. He had supported Hoover vehemently, even though the depression had made it almost respectable to vote for the New Deal. The country, he had said, had to be protected from Roosevelt's radical ideas. Jeremy wondered what his father would say if he could see what kind of company his second oldest son was keeping now.

"Well, I suppose a lot of people in your state voted for Norman Thomas," she said grudgingly. "They don't understand that the Socialist party is intellectually bankrupt."

Jeremy hardly knew how to answer. Sylvia's view of the state of affairs in Iowa was so wildly far from reality that it defied response. She had been born and brought up in New York, and she thought of Chicago—*Chicago!*—as a "hick town," she'd told him earlier. She described the area north of Yonkers as "the country."

"Uh . . . I don't s'pose the folks back home really understand the difference between the various . . . umm . . . revolutionary factions," Jeremy said. His innate midwestern courtesy kept him from contradicting her directly. In point of fact, Jeremy himself was still trying to figure out the exotic distinctions between Trotskyites and Mensheviks, Communists and Marxian Socialists, Syndicalists and Anarchosyndicalists, and all the rest of the radical groups who figured in campus arguments. It was throughly bewildering, after coming from Beulah High, where no teacher had ever mentioned the words "Soviet Union," and the map in his geography textbook showed a blank space for the place Russia was supposed to be.

Unexpectedly, Sylvia laughed. "No, I don't suppose they do under-stand. But they're learning. Is your father in the Farm Holiday move-ment?"

"Well, not exactly . . ."

"You should make him understand the importance of solidarity. Does he own his own farm, or is he a tenant?"

"Well . . . uh . . . he isn't a farmer."

"Isn't a farmer? What is he?"

"He's the president of the bank," Jeremy burst out. "But . . ."

Sylvia snatched her hand away. "A *banker?*" Her lip curled. "You're a *banker's* son?"

She'd raised her voice. Some people in the immediate vicinity turned their heads to look. The man sitting to Jeremy's right on the couch, a fat bearded man in a work shirt, paused in his conversation with a girl in a shapeless green sweater and peered at him as if he were some sort of biological specimen.

"No wonder you were so snotty about Mother Bloor!" Sylvia went on, her voice dripping with scorn.

"Well, I can't help who my father is," Jeremy said, and immediately felt guilty and disloyal.

"No, you can't," she said. "You were born into a corrupt, privileged class, and when the revolution comes, it will sweep people like you away."

"Now just a minute, Sylvia . . ."

"And to think I listened to all your talk about how you were going to write the great proletarian novel someday!"

She got up, taking her breast from Jeremy's arm, and walked away. Jeremy sat there, his ears burning. Nobody sat down in the seat Sylvia had vacated. The conversation went on around him as if he weren't there. After a while he became aware that Sylvia had joined the folk-song group. They were singing a song, something about "there'll be pie in the sky by and by," a little off-key, and Jeremy thought that Sylvia looked magnificent with her dark hair flying and her blouse disarrayed as she threw herself into the verse.

Depressed, he finished the punch that was left in his glass and stood up. He put the glass down on one of the batik-covered orange crates and went to the door. Nobody seemed to notice him. As the door closed behind him, he could hear the sound of singing.

It was two in the morning when he got back to his dormitory. There were still lights under some of the doors. He let himself into his room quietly, so as not to disturb his roommate, a rabbity-looking kid from Indiana named Butterfield, who wore enormous goggles and had a perpetually dripping nose. He wasn't in the mood for one of Butterfield's all-night discussions about sex and cosmic meaning.

But the desk lamp was on, and Butterfield sat up in bed as soon as the door opened. He was wearing his glasses. He always went to bed with them on. "You better call home right away," he said. "They've been trying to get you since this afternoon."

Jeremy hung his raincoat on a peg. He took his necktie out of his jacket pocket and draped it over a chair. He still felt depressed.

"I'll call in the morning. Who was it? My mother?"

"No." Butterfield gave him an odd look. "I think you better call now. They're waiting for your call."

"At two in the morning? What's wrong?"

Butterfield blinked. "Your . . . your father. I'm sorry, Sinclair. Some man says he's dead."

Jeremy called collect from the pay phone in the commons room. He got a sleepy-sounding Gordon. "Yeah, that was Uncle Elroy who called. He and Aunt Ottilie left about midnight. They're coming back in the morning. Daddy's body is at the undertaker's. Jere—" Gordon's voice broke. "They say he stole some money."

Jeremy lost his nickel in the phone. That left him fifteen cents in his pockets. When he tried to borrow train fare from his roommate, Butterfield looked distressed. "I haven't got it, Sinclair, honest. I went to the bank Friday to cash my check from home, and I couldn't even get near the front door. People were going crazy. There were mobs of them, trying to get their money out before it was too late. When the banks closed at three, there were still thousands of people waiting, getting pushed back by the cops. And this morning there was the notice about the bank holiday. Nobody knows when it's going to end. I don't think you could raise a nickel in this whole dorm. People are trading things. Some of the grocery stores'll take IOU's if they know you."

Jeremy and Butterfield went round the dormitory, knocking on doors, waking people up. Most of the fellows were sympathetic. In the end, Jeremy raised enough for a day-coach ticket as far as Cedar Rapids. It would be another two hundred miles to Beulah in the western part of the state.

"What are you gonna do after you get to Cedar Rapids?" Butterfield asked.

"I don't know," Jeremy said. "Hitch a ride. Hop a freight. I'll get there somehow."

"How are you gonna eat?"

"I won't."

Butterfield looked furtively around the room, then went to the closet and came out with a burlap bag. "Take it," he said. "It's a ham. I got it from home. I was gonna use it to trade with. And why don't you take your typewriter? Maybe you can swap it in Cedar Rapids for a ride."

Jeremy had been planning to take the typewriter anyway. It was the only thing of value he owned. He didn't tell Butterfield that he had no intention of trading it in Cedar Rapids. He'd trade the ham instead, and go hungry. He was going to need the typewriter. He picked up his twin burdens and took a last look around the room he'd lived in during his first year at college. He had a feeling he wouldn't be coming back.

He stared moodily out the window of the elevated train all the way to North Western Station, the ham and the typewriter on the seat beside him. There were no lights in the sky. A wall of cloud hung between heaven and earth, blotting out the stars. The great office buildings were dark. The lights that he saw were below, in the dirty concrete canyons of the city, where flickering red flames marked the alleys where homeless men warmed themselves over fires made of scrap wood.

The shame wouldn't go away. He kept hearing the echo of his own glib voice saying, *I can't help who my father is.* He knew with utter certainty that he'd never forget the words, or forgive himself for them.

Grand Central Station was a madhouse. It was impossible to get near the ticket windows. Under the lofty vault of the ceiling, hordes of frantic people roiled like ants in the dusty light that filtered down from above. The train announcements hovered, blurred and remote, above a pandemonium of noise.

Brad glanced at his watch, worried now. The Chicago express was due to leave in half an hour. He looked around the immense waiting room, with its ranks of dark wooden benches. There was still no sign of Gilda. She'd said over the phone that she would meet him on the woman's side.

On the bench opposite, a bum was stretched out asleep, his tattered clothes stuffed with newspapers. A belligerent-looking businessman with a face like roast beef and a neck like a bull's was sitting bravely beside him, bulwark between the bum and the ladies on the bench. Next to Brad, a weedy little man in a moth-eaten overcoat was reading a scavenged copy of the Sunday *Mirror*. The front page showed a picture of the presidential inauguration with a huge headline: ROOSE-VELT ASKS DICTATOR'S ROLE.

The man folded the paper carefully and said to Brad: "Want to read the paper?"

"No, thanks." Brad looked the other way.

But the weedy man wanted to talk. "Some mess, huh?"

Brad grunted.

"They won't take anything but cash at the ticket windows."

"I know."

Brad had tried to write a check for a compartment on the Twentieth Century to Chicago. He'd had enough money in his wallet to get from New Haven to New York, but he hadn't thought any farther ahead than that. He hadn't taken the bank holiday very seriously. When the ticket agent turned him down, he tried to cash a check at the Biltmore, where they knew him. They'd refused him regretfully. He could put a drink, a meal, or a room for the night on the tab, but cash was in short supply. Then he'd crossed the street and tried the Yale Club. It was the same story there. Next he'd walked three blocks with his suitcase and tried the Harvard Club, where he'd been a guest of J. DeWitt Stanhope. Finally, in desperation, he'd called Gilda and asked if she could put her hands on some cash.

The weedy man leaned over confidentially. "They're cracking down here. At Penn Station, too. A lot of characters have been waltzing up to the ticket windows and asking for change for hundred-dollar bills. Even thousand-dollar bills. Some of 'em tried to cover up by buying Newark tickets. But no soap. You walk up there with a hundred-dollar bill now, and you're outa luck."

"Mmmm," Brad said, and looked away again. He fixed his gaze assiduously on a *New York Times* that the beefy businessman had unfolded. It featured the same front-page picture as the *Mirror*. The part of the headline he could read said: WILL ASK WAR-TIME POWERS IF NEEDED.

"You waiting for a train?" the weedy man said. He had bad breath, and could have used a bath and an application of Odorono.

"You could say that," Brad said.

"Me, I gotta get to Bridgeport by tomorrow, but . . . . oh, oh!"

He suddenly stood up, so quickly that he dropped his newspaper. "See ya, buddy," he said, and walked away.

All around Brad, people were rising from their seats as if on signal, and hurrying off. In only a moment, the long benches were half empty. Brad looked around and saw a man in a blue railroad uniform, followed by a cop, advancing slowly down the aisle.

"Tickets," he was saying mechanically. "Show your tickets."

The beefy man across the way had his ticket virtuously displayed. He had edged away from the sleeping bum, with all the room that had been left on the bench by departees.

The uniformed man stopped in front of Brad. "Where's your ticket?" he said.

"I'm waiting for . . ."

"You've got to show your ticket."

"Look, I'm trying to tell you. I'll buy my ticket as soon as . . ."

The man wasn't listening, wasn't even interested. His eyes flicked over Brad's expensive clothes as if pricing them. The cop stepped forward, gripping his club. "On your feet, bum."

Brad stood up, trembling with rage. He had never been treated like this in his life, and he knew that, despite himself, he was about to act stupidly.

"Now, see here . . ." he began.

The cop, a gleeful look on his face, tightened his grip on the club. At that moment there was a crash of glass from the opposite row of benches, and the cop and the trainman both swung their heads around. The bum had dropped a bottle he had secreted somewhere about himself, and smashed it on the floor. He stirred slightly in his sleep and whimpered.

In three swift strides, the cop was standing in front of him. The beefy businessman got up and edged away. The cop raised his club in the air and whipped it with tremendous force against the soles of the bum's shoes. There was a sharp crack, and the bum screamed. He jerked to a sitting position like a jack-in-the-box.

"Stand up, you son of a bitch! You can't sleep here!"

When the bum tried to put his feet on the floor, he moaned with pain. His legs wouldn't support him. There was a spreading dark stain on his trousers, and Brad saw with disgust that he had left a puddle of urine on the bench.

"Get him out of here, Delaney," the trainman said.

"Hell, I ain't gonna *touch* him," the cop said.

While they were arguing, Brad picked up his suitcase and walked away. He was still shaking with anger. Halfway to the newsstand that divided the twin waiting rooms, he saw Gilda Stanhope.

"Brad!" she cried, running toward him on precarious high heels. She was stunningly beautiful in a sheer silk frock and an exorbitantly luxurious mink coat draped carelessly across her shoulders. Her face glowed, framed by a close helmet of glossy black hair, and her perfect bow lips were parted in a dazzling smile. Her invulnerable freshness was out of place amidst the dank stale odors of the Grand Central waiting room. She made Brad feel seedy with his hangover and the grittiness from his trip.

"Gilly, love!" he said. He put down his suitcase and swept her into his arms.

She kissed him. "Oh, Brad, I was so sorry to hear about your father! Daddy said to tell you that he's sorry, too. How did it happen?"

He looked her straight in the eyes. "Some sort of accident, I gather. He was cleaning his old army pistol."

"How awful!"

"I don't know how long I'll be gone. I have to straighten out the family affairs."

If J. DeWitt Stanhope and his lovely daughter, he thought with wry amusement, only knew that the Sinclair family affairs included the embezzling of bank funds. With any luck, they'd never know. Certainly the directors of the Beulah Trust would agree that it was not in the bank's interests to let a story like that get out. Brad was damned if he'd go through life being known as an embezzler's son.

"Daddy said he was sorry to miss you. He wanted to have a talk with you."

That would be about the junior partnership, Brad was exultantly sure. Oh, there would be a decent period of apprenticeship first, starting with law clerk, then assistant to the Old Man to see how he handled himself, but Brad would have bet his soul that his name would be on the door within five years.

"With any luck, I'll be in New York next weekend as usual," he said. "I would have seen you Friday, but I had to hit the books."

A vast distorted voice came from overhead. "Now boarding for the Twentieth Century Limited for Chicago."

"Oh," Gilda said. "Here's the money. Daddy said not to worry. He had plenty to spare in his cashbox. Will this be enough?"

She dug into her purse and held out five one-hundred-dollar bills.

Brad sighed. It could have been worse. She could have brought him one five-hundred-dollar bill.

"Listen, Gilly-silly, this is very important," he said. He put his hand under her chin and tilted her head back so that he could look into her eyes. "I'm taking two hundred. Got that? Give the other three back to your father right away. Don't spend any of it. I'll write you a check for the two hundred. Make sure you give it to him. It'll be good as soon as the banks open again."

"Daddy says not to worry."

"I do worry. Now don't forget and go spending one of those bills, all right?"

"All right, Brad, if you say so."

"That's my Gilly-silly."

He took out his checkbook and scribbled a check for two hundred dollars to J. DeWitt Stanhope. He didn't dare make it for more, because he knew that there was exactly two hundred and twenty-two dollars in his account. If there was anything in life that Brad was not about to do, it was to write a rubber check to J. DeWitt Stanhope.

"All aboard," the loudspeaker said.

Brad took one look at the howling mob around the ticket windows and decided that it would be no use trying to get near them—even if he had something smaller than hundreds. He took Gilda by the elbow and propelled her toward the departure gate.

"Aren't you going to pick up your ticket?" Gilda said.

"No time."

"Why not take a later train?"

She squeezed his arm, and Brad was almost tempted.

"I've got a pash for the lobster Newburg on corn bread they serve aboard the Century," he said lightly. "I wouldn't think of traveling any other way."

They had arrived at the gate. Passengers were being let through one at a time after their names were checked against a list. A reporter and cameraman stood by, ready for any celebrities who might be embarking today. Brad peered through the gate and saw the long red carpet unfurled the length of the platform, a row of potted palms lining its edge.

"But you can't get aboard the Twentieth Century Limited without a ticket," Gilda said.

"Wrong. You can't get aboard without a *reservation*. It's easier to get into heaven without absolution than to get aboard the Twentieth Century without a reservation."

"But . . ."

"I phoned it in from New Haven. With any luck, my name's still on the list."

"How . . ."

"All I have to do is talk my way through that gate. And you're going to help me. Once I'm on board, I'm going to charm myself into a drawing room. Half the drawing rooms on the Century are empty these days. And today'll be especially confused. The conductor will be glad to take care of me once the train is moving."

She giggled, then tried to look contrite. "I'm sorry, Brad. I know it's awful about your father and everything, but honestly, you take the cake."

He enlisted a redcap with an exorbitant tip that represented the last of his original bankroll. The man stood by with the single suitcase, his eyes fixed uneasily on the station clock. "Cap'n, that train gonna leave without you," he said.

"Don't worry about it. Just stick to me like glue when I go through that gate."

He turned to Gilda. Her eyes were big. She had an alert, eager look.

"Now kiss me, and make it last. Everything depends on the timing.

I'm going to hit that gate just as he's folding up. I'm going to be in a panic about missing my train. I'm not going to give him time to think. I'm going to paw through his lists till I find my name. Then I'm going to run for the cars as the train starts moving, with a redcap huffing and puffing after me. There'll be eager little sweaty hands to pull me aboard, and nobody is going to ask to see my ticket until it's too late."

She giggled again.

Ten minutes later, Brad was sitting in his drawing room, watching the jumbled scenery slip by and drinking an illegal martini he had tipped the porter five dollars for. The martini was excellent. He still had over a hundred dollars left.

He hadn't for a moment considered anything less than a drawing room. Not with two hundred dollars in his pocket. He would go first class until the money ran out.

5

It was a very private service. Young Allan Whiting, the assistant rector at St. Andrew's, had been sent, rather grudgingly, by the Reverend Dr. Bertram to officiate at graveside. Dr. Bertram himself had not been much in evidence this morning, considering the fact that it had been the funeral of one of his most prominent parishioners. The Sinclair family was not too popular in Beulah at the moment.

"Your fathers did eat manna in the wilderness, and are dead," Allan read, his sheep's face pink and solemn over the clerical collar. He coughed delicately. He looked embarrassed.

Brad listened impatiently, the rain trickling down his face. He was sure that the passage from John had been chosen by Dr. Bertram, the old bastard. He put out an arm to steady his mother. Gordon was standing at her other side, holding an umbrella over her. The runoff was dripping down Brad's collar.

"I am the living bread which came down from heaven," Allan droned on. "If any man eat of this bread, he shall live forever." A discreet distance away, the two gravediggers leaned on their shovels and waited.

Brad glanced over at Junie to see how she was taking it. She was standing between Pamela and Jeremy, her eyes downcast. Jeremy had an arm around her shoulders. She looked small and neat and vulnerable in her dark navy coat and knee socks, her white-gloved hands decorously crossed, her feet in the shiny black patent leather pumps pressed tightly together. She and Jeremy looked alike, with their dark hair and deep-set eyes, the pale skin around the sockets discolored from lack of sleep. Jeremy looked angry. He always looked angry these days. It was a stage he was going through. He'd arrived late last night, dusty and exhausted after hitching a ride from Cedar Rapids in a cattle truck, carrying only his typewriter, an undergraduate scowl on his face. Standing next to them, Pamela was a creature from another race. She had the same coloring as Gordon, that unblemished peach-skin complexion and the pale blond hair. Brad was the one who had inherited all the Sinclair freckles.

The Sinclairs with their mixed genes, he thought. The fine, favored, insulated Elm Street Sinclairs, or what was left of them, standing by the grave of their progenitor. Perhaps poor uncomfortable Allan had been right to remind them. The days of manna were gone.

". . . and I will raise him up at the last day," Allan finished, and Brad felt a violent tremor go through his mother's body. Mary Sinclair had been too bright and crisp and controlled all morning. The Everett pride had stretched her taut.

Judge Tanner came toward them, hurrying ahead of Elroy and Ottilie. He was a frail, tidy, erect old man with iron-gray hair and mustache. He had been the Sinclair's legal advisor and a close family friend for as long as Brad could remember. He had got Brad out of that scrape with the girl from Railroad Street when Brad was seventeen, and he had been Junie's godfather. Other than Uncle Elroy and Aunt Ottilie, he was the only person who had come to the cemetery.

"Shall we get back to the house, Mary?" he said. "I'll ride with you, if that's all right with Brad. No need to go to my office. Let's get this thing over with."

"Oh, yes, how kind of you," Mary Sinclair said brightly. Her eyes seemed focused on a place somewhere beyond the judge.

Brad relinquished her arm, and the judge turned her around, gently but firmly, and headed her toward the gate. The gravediggers were already moving toward the coffin, and Brad saw why the judge had been so abrupt. Gordon seemed not to know what to do for a moment, and then he followed his mother and the judge. Brad was surprised at how much Gordon had shot up in the last six months. He was wearing a new blue suit with long pants. The last time Brad had seen him, he had been wearing knickers. He needed just a little filling out.

"Can I give you a lift back to the rectory?" Brad said to Allan.

"That would be nice of you," Allan said. He shook his head. "A terrible, terrible thing."

"Yes. Well." Brad turned to Elroy, who was just coming over. "Would you and Aunt Ottilie like to come back to the house?" he said.

Elroy sniffed. "It's a long drive back to Fort Dodge. And seeing as how we're not invited to the reading of the will . . ."

"His own sister!" Aunt Ottilie said. She was wearing stiff black, and her stays cut into her torso with a fluted effect, giving it the shape of a sectioned tangerine.

"You have to understand that it's not up to my mother," Brad said, making an effort. "Judge Tanner set up the ground rules. I gather there's some family business to discuss. I'll give you a call tomorrow."

"You can save your nickel," Elroy said. "If we ain't invited, we ain't in the will."

"And after all the things your uncle's done for that father of yours over the years," Ottilie said tartly.

Brad refrained from comment. It had been very much the other way around. His mother's older brother Elroy had been a failure all his life. His sister's marriage to Bradford Sinclair, Sr., had kept his head above water. There had been a series of small sums tactfully described as "loans" all through the years. It had been Brad's father who had kept Elroy from losing his home in 1921 when he fell behind in his mortgage payments. When Elroy had lost his job in 1923, it was Brad's father's influence that got him his present job as bookkeeper at the gypsum mill in Fort Dodge.

"We'd better catch up," Allan Whiting said.

He was looking worriedly toward the cemetery gate. There were about a dozen people standing beyond the iron bars. As Mary Sinclair approached with Judge Tanner and Gordon, a low murmur went up from them.

Brad got to his mother's side in a few long strides. Jeremy was keeping close to Junie and Pamela.

"That's them," one of the crowd said. He was a slat-thin, angular man with a face as gray as newspaper, his hat drooping and soggy from standing in the rain. "Where's our money?"

"Who are they?" Brad said.

The judge spoke without turning his head. "Depositors."

A stout woman with broken veins in her face said: "There's no food in the house, and I can't get what little I have out of the bank. How am I supposed to feed my kids, mister? Tell me that!"

Allan fiddled nervously with the chain around the gate. He avoided looking at the people outside.

"They got our money, that's what!" the gray-faced man said. "Stole it and shot himself, and now they've got it salted away somewhere!"

The angry murmuring grew louder.

Judge Tanner faced them. "Bradford Sinclair's death has nothing to do with the bank closing," he said in a flat, careful voice. "The banks are closed all over the country. President Roosevelt's made the bank holiday nationwide. When the banks reopen, you'll all get your money. Now, go home. This is disgraceful! These people have come to bury their dead!"

The crowd made no move to leave. Allan, red-faced, got the chain undone.

"Jeremy, you drive Mother and the judge and Gordon in the Pierce-Arrow," Brad said tightly. "Just get away as quickly as you can." He looked over at the mob. "What's wrong with those people?"

There was a look of harsh satisfaction on Elroy's narrow face. "But Peter said unto him, Thy money perish with thee, because thou hast thought that the gift of God may be purchased with money," he recited.

Judge Tanner shot Elroy a look of fury. Brad glanced worriedly at his mother, but she hadn't reacted at all.

Allan swung the gate open and they all filed out, with Brad, Gordon, and the judge forming a protective circle around Mary Sinclair. Jeremy hurried the girls after them, and Elroy and Ottilie followed, with Allan bringing up the rear.

"There they go," a voice hooted after them. "The high and mighty Sinclairs, with their fancy clothes and their expensive cars!"

Mary Sinclair seemed not to have heard. She walked on in her widow's black, a waxen beauty with a fixed, gracious, inappropriate smile on her face. She got into the back seat of the Pierce-Arrow with Gordon. Jeremy closed the door after her and went around front and climbed in with the judge. Brad saw his aunt and uncle disappear into the tall, boxy Plymouth with its narrow tires, and herded Junie and Pamela into the cream-colored Stutz he'd bought the previous summer. He'd got it for practically nothing, though it was only three years old and in mint condition, after hitting his father up for the money. The understanding was that he'd use it in Beulah and the family would use it as a second car while he was gone. Gordon had his eye on it, but didn't have a license yet, thank God!

The Stutz's eight cylinders came to life with a smooth purr of power, and Brad followed the Pierce-Arrow and the Plymouth coupe down the drive. As the three-car cortege moved slowly off, the crowd moved indecisively from the gate. A clod of mud hit the rear window, and Junie started to cry.

"One of those men is in the congregation at St. Andrews," Allan said in a shocked tone. "I recognized him. I'll have Dr. Bertram speak to him." Evidently you didn't throw mud if you were a member of Dr. Bertram's flock.

In the back seat, Pamela had her arms around Junie. Junie was still crying.

"There's nothing," the judge said.

He faced them over Bradford Sinclair's broad green-topped desk, the parched elderly skin of his face varnished by the dull yellow light that slanted down from the tall windows of the study. Mary Sinclair, looking vague and serene, sat between Gordon and Junie on the deep leather couch against the wall. Brad, Jeremy, and Pamela were in straight chairs that had been drawn up in an arc across from the desk.

Brad glanced at his mother, then said: "What about the household account for the monthly bills?"

"That's frozen, too," Judge Tanner said. "Thayer Chadwick has a lien on everything, in the name of the bank. The checking and savings accounts, the house, the car, Mary's jewelry. There was about four hundred dollars in cash in a desk drawer, and they impounded that, too, when the police searched the study."

"You mean we can't even pay our light bill? Or the phone?"

The judge sighed. "No."

"The servants!"

"You'll have to let them go, of course. The sooner the better. This afternoon. Do you want me to tell them?"

A muscle twitched in Brad's jaw. "No, that's up to me. Dad would have expected it. But letting them go, just like that, without any notice! That's rotten. It's worse than rotten. We owe them a week's pay for this month already."

The judge looked shrewdly at Brad. "Don't you have any cash at all?"

Brad thought of the hundred dollars and change he had left over from J. DeWitt Stanhope's money, and the twenty-two dollars he still had in his New Haven checking account. It would take more than half of that to pay the four servants a week's wages. Then he thought about money for food. It had never occurred to him to worry about such a thing before, but somehow the Sinclair family was going to have to eat while this thing was being straightened out.

"No," he said, looking the judge in the eye. "Not enough, anyway."

The judge shuffled some papers on the desk, then said: "There's the Stutz. The title to that's in your name, and you're not a minor child. They can't touch that. Not for the moment, at any rate. You ought to be able to get a few hundred dollars for it."

"No," Brad said. "I'm not selling the Stutz. Not yet."

"You can't dispose of the furniture. That goes with the house. Or the silver or anything valuable. That includes Mary's fur coat. You can take personal possessions."

Brad's lips tightened. "The clothes on our backs, eh?"

"That's about it."

Jeremy spoke. He looked angry, as if he were blaming Judge Tanner. "But they can't take our house! Can they?"

"I'm afraid so," the judge said gently. "But the proceedings will take a while. You ought to have at least sixty days before you have to move."

"They'll turn off the lights before that," Gordon said unexpectedly, then clamped his mouth shut.

"But where will Mother go?" Jeremy said.

Judge Tanner cleared his throat. He looked over at Mary Sinclair. "Won't her brother take her in? And June Alice is a dependent child. She'll have to go with your mother."

Mary Sinclair stirred on the couch. Her long throat and her face were as pale and as beautiful as a cameo above the dead black of the crepe. "We'll have to cut down," she said in a reasonable voice. "I understand that. Bradford was always saying that, after the stock market crash. That's when we let the chauffeur go, don't you remember, children? We'll have to shop more carefully. And we'll have to let Helga go, poor thing. We can give her a month's wages. We can get along without a parlor maid."

Brad started to get out of his chair. "Mother . . ."

Judge Tanner stopped him with a gesture. "Wouldn't you like to go upstairs and rest awhile, Mary? It's been a tiring day. Perhaps June Alice could go with you and help."

"Yes, yes, you're very thoughtful, Edmund. It would be nice to lie down for just a little while. Junie, you can come along and help Mother to take out the pins in her hair."

"Yes, Mother," Junie said in the voice of a little girl. She stood up with her mother. Mary Sinclair left the room with a rustle of crepe and taffeta, standing very straight.

"Judge . . ." Brad said.

Judge Tanner waved a hand. "Your mother will be fine, Brad. Just give her a little time to adjust. This has all been a shock. But she's got a lot of stuff in her, your mother has. Don't forget, she raised the five of you."

"Judge, we've got to save the house. Can't you see about getting the lien removed? You said that the insurance policy the bank held on his life was for fifty thousand dollars. That ought to be more than enough to cover his shortages."

The judge picked up a piece of paper from the desk. "That's what your father thought. He made a full confession. Very detailed. He'd been fiddling with the bond account for almost three years. It was such a mess, thanks to Thayer Chadwick and his friends, that he was able to get away with it. Your father was a *good* banker, believe it or not. He fought hard to keep the bank from taking on so much bad paper—those foreign securities that Chadwick's cousin Edgar wanted to take a flyer in, and some of the more stupid of the mortgage foreclosures around Beulah that left the bank holding nothing, when they might have brought in a little income if the farmer had been allowed to hang on. If your father had been allowed to have his way, the bank could have kept its head above water, and Chadwick wouldn't have had to press so hard for the payments on your father's bank stock. The stock itself would have been worth more. Ironic, isn't it?"

"It's the whole rotten system!" Jeremy growled from his chair. His thick black hair had finally come loose from that morning's slicking-down, and was hanging down over his forehead.

The judge looked at him curiously. "Yes, it is. The way the damned banking system works, any bunch of Main Street grocers can get together with a few thousand dollars and start a bank. When they get into trouble, their depositors are out of luck. Maybe this Roosevelt can reform the banking system, I don't know. But that's what's been happening here in Iowa and all over the country since 1929."

"But the Beulah Trust isn't just one of those rinky-dink banks!" Brad protested.

"Might as well be. Chadwick's grandfather and a few of his friends started the bank under the old state banking system. They couldn't issue paper currency, but that was about all they couldn't do. When the law was changed in 1863, they had no trouble in getting their new charter. They've been running it as a private fiefdom ever since. Made such a mess of things that they had to hire your father after the war to straighten things out. Too bad they didn't let him run it the way he wanted to."

"What do you mean?"

"Son, if that bank holiday hadn't been declared last Saturday and given them a breather, the Beulah Trust Company would have gone under. Your father said so in his suicide note. I don't blame Chadwick for getting the note suppressed. He don't want it getting around what bad shape the bank's in."

"Well, then, let's get the suicide note back," Brad said eagerly. "It'll give us something to fight with."

The judge gave him a sad look. "That note's in the police chief's pocket. And the chief of police is in Thayer Chadwick's pocket. And there they'll both stay."

"All right," Brad said impatiently. "Forget the note. I'm getting to be a pretty fair lawyer, thank God and Yale, and we ought to be able to do something with that insurance policy the bank took out on my father's life. There's language in there to the effect that the proceeds are intended to 'recompense the bank for losses incurred by the death of the insured'! Chadwick probably thought he was being smart with that clause, but he outsmarted himself! That language changes the intent of the policy from just a simple life policy with the proceeds going to the bank in the event of my father's death. If we can get it into court, in front of the right judge, we can make a case to the effect that the policy fully covers the amount of my father's embezzlement. . . ."

"Defalcation," the judge said dryly.

"Defalcation, then," Brad said with a bitter grin. "You see what I'm driving at, Judge. Legally, the bank can't dip into the grave twice—collect on the policy, and then recover their losses from my father's estate. In fact"—the grin changed into a look of surmise—"I'll bet we can get the leftover few thousand—after the losses are covered—for my mother—"

"Just stop that right there," the judge cut in. "Stop telling yourself fairy tales. The liens cover shortages of over a quarter-million dollars."

Brad's lips went white. "My father wasn't a liar, whatever else he was. He confessed to taking forty-seven thousand dollars, and that's what he took. He killed himself over it. He had no reason to lie."

A tired look came over the judge's small, withered face. "Son, don't you understand what's happening?" he said pityingly. "A suicide makes the perfect patsy."

"What's he talking about, Brad?" Jeremy demanded angrily.

"That money your father took wasn't the only shortage," the judge said. "I can't prove it, but Chadwick and his cronies have been dipping into the till, too. Now they're in the clear. It all gets blamed on your father."

"They can't get away with it!"

"Oh, they can get away with it, all right. They'll collect the fifty thousand on that bank policy. And they'll claim the proceeds of your father's personal policy—that's another fifty thousand. Your mother'll never see a cent of that. It's part of the estate, don't you see? And they'll recover your father's bank stock—that'll be worth something some day. And they'll sell off the house and the car and the personal property. Ought to get another fifty thousand for that if they hold it till conditions improve. That'll give them a hundred and fifty thousand dollars, more or less, to keep the bank afloat and save their own necks. And your father's estate will *still* owe them another hundred thousand dollars—not that they ever could collect it." He paused and cocked his gray head. "And there's not a thing you can do about it."

"The hell I can't!" Brad said, and stood up.

First he went upstairs to see his mother. She was dozing, her black hair spilled across the starched white pillow, the beauty of her profile like a knife edge. She lay still as a drowned person in the dim watery light that filtered through the curtain. My mermaid mother, he thought as he bent over to kiss her. He noticed for the first time that there were strands of gray in her hair.

Her eyes suddenly flew open, and she gripped his wrists with desperate strength. "They can't, they can't!" she said.

"Can't what, Mother?"

She looked confused. "I forget." She let go of his wrists and fell back, instantly asleep again.

Brad went over to the window, where Junie sat in a high padded chair, a book in her lap.

"How is she?" he said. "She seem all right?"

"She was talking a lot while she was getting ready for her nap, just about a mile a minute, all about when she was a young girl, and how she met Daddy, and how beautiful the wedding was."

He squatted down in front of the chair and squeezed her hands. "You'll stay with her till she wakes up, won't you?"

"Sure, Brad."

"Good girl." He gave her hands another squeeze and stood up.

As he turned away, she said, "Brad?"

"What is it, pun'kin?"

"Are Mother and I really going to have to go live with Uncle Elroy?"

"We'll see about that, honey. Nothing's settled yet."

"Because he's so grouchy, and he's always quoting from the Bible, and he always makes you feel like you're doing something *bad!*"

"Give him a chance, honey. Uncle Elroy takes God a little more personally than the rest of us. He means well."

"And he keeps looking at my chest."

Brad laughed. "You'll have to get used to that, pun'kin. You'll be grown up soon."

"Brad?"

"Yes."

"If I have to go live with Uncle Elroy, couldn't Gordon come live there, too?"

"I just don't know, baby."

"Because I can talk about things with Gordon. Pamela's so far away these days."

"She's grown up, honey. And you will be, too, pretty soon."

"I don't see why we just all can't stay together!"

When he left the bedroom, he was shaking with anger. By the time he got downstairs, he was back in control of himself, the shallow charm slipped on like a glove. No one could have guessed that he ever had felt an unseemly emotion.

Jeremy was waiting for him in the foyer when he went to get his coat. "I'm going with you," he said.

"The hell you are. You're spoiling for trouble. This has got to be handled right."

"Oh, you cold bastard!" Jeremy said. He turned away, the tears springing to his eyes.

The crowd outside the bank wasn't as big as Brad had expected. After four days of a world without money, people had had time to get used to the idea.

These were the diehards. They stood around on the sidewalk and curb in loose, formless clusters of twos and threes, kept well away from the granite face of the building by the single policeman on duty. They were predominantly men, the collars of shabby overcoats turned up and hats pulled down, wearing that furtive, guilty look that lack of money imparts. There was one sprightly old man marching back and forth with a homemade sign that said: LIFE SAVINGS GONE— NOTHING LEFT BUT CHARITY. A grim, determined fat lady in a coat with a bedraggled fur collar sat in a kitchen chair in the middle of the sidewalk, a carpetbag and a picnic basket beside her, looking as if she were prepared to wait out doomsday.

Brad parked the Stutz a good distance down the street and walked toward the bank, his own overcoat collar turned up and his hands in his pockets. Eyes turned dully to follow him as he approached the steps. Once or twice an hour, somebody tried, not very hard, to get past the cop. It wasn't very interesting, but at least it was something to watch.

"You can't get in, mister, move on," the cop said warily. He was a bulky young man with a tight uniform collar and a stiff new white cover on his cap.

Brad looked over his shoulder, then leaned confidentially toward the cop and said: "Mr. Chadwick wants to see me."

The cop's eyes were taking in the tailored coat from J. Press and the sharply creased dark blue trousers Brad had worn to the funeral. "Yeah? You with the bank?"

"My name's Sinclair."

"Oh . . . one of the . . ."

"Yes, one of those."

"I don't know, Mr. Sinclair. Mr. Chadwick said nobody but the state examiners and the federal people."

"It's bank business," Brad said, letting just enough impatience show.

"Well . . ." The cop looked around. "You better come around the side with me."

Brad followed him around to the alley, feeling the eyes of all the people out front follow him. The old man with the sign stopped in his tracks, standing feet apart, shouldering the broom handle with its tacked board as if it were a weapon. There were a few dispirited hoots and jeers.

The cop unlocked the metal gate to the alley, and locked it again behind them. He pressed the buzzer next to the narrow iron door set in the wall, and a slot opened.

"Open up," the cop said. The door creaked open, and he said, "You know this guy? He says Mr. Chadwick sent for him."

"Hello, Nils," Brad said. "Don't you recognize me?"

The man in the bank guard's uniform peered uncertainly at Brad. He was a skinny, knob-jointed man of about sixty, with a Sam Browne belt across his narrow chest dragged down by an enormous holstered revolver.

"Mr. Bradford," he said.

"It's been quite a few years. You used to have a piece of candy for me when I dropped by to see my father."

"You've filled out some since I saw you." The guard was uneasy. "Mr. Bradford, I'm sorry about your—"

"Thank you, Nils." Brad cut him short. "Will you let Mr. Chadwick know that I'm here?"

"His . . . his office door is closed. Mr. French and Mr. Edgar Chadwick are supposed to be here at four, and he left word that he wasn't supposed to be disturbed."

Brad breathed more easily. Until this moment, he hadn't been sure that Chadwick would be at the bank today.

"Yes," he said lazily. "That was the idea. There's just enough time for him to fit me in first."

"I gotta get back," the cop said, looking from Brad to the guard.

"Go right ahead," Brad said. "Thanks."

He walked through the door as if he expected the guard to step back for him, and the guard did. Brad had noticed long ago that when you acted as though you knew what you were doing, people behaved as they thought you expected them to.

Brad strode across the marble floor, the guard hurrying to catch up. The big green shades were drawn over the plate glass windows, and the bank had the lighting of an undersea grotto. There were half a dozen people working in the place: a man behind the gilt bars of one of the teller's cages wrapping packets of currency, a man in a vest sitting at one of the desks behind the oak rail going through piles of maroon ledgers while a girl with a pad and pencil sat beside him, a few clerks fetching and carrying huge untidy stacks of records from filing cabinets. They all stopped what they were doing to look at Brad.

He walked through the low wooden gate without hesitating and hung his hat on a rack as though it belonged there. He didn't try to barge into Chadwick's office; with his exquisite sense of just how far he could go, Brad knew that would get him stopped, and lose him control of the situation. He lounged against a handy desk and waited while the guard tapped diffidently on Chadwick's door. The guard went in, leaving the door open a crack. Brad heard Chadwick's voice, heavy and impatient, and then the guard came out, giving Brad a curious look. "Go on in," he said. Brad slid off the desk. He'd known that with the bank employees watching, Chadwick could not have sent him away without seeing him.

"Sit down, Brad. I can only spare you a moment. You've grown up since I last saw you. Let's see, you were just going into your second year at Yale."

Chadwick leaned back in his chair, a large soft man with shiny pink cheeks. He had a high, smooth forehead, bulging outward like a baby's, with brown hair plastered wetly across the top of his head and curling forward at the temples, like a Roman bust. He smelled of cigars and expensive cologne.

Brad drew up a chair, close enough to make Chadwick uncomfortable.

"You've changed, too. You're fatter."

"*What!*" Chadwick surged up in his chair, then decided that Brad was joking and sank back, a frown on his big forehead.

Brad crossed his legs negligently, in no hurry to talk. He tapped a cigarette out of his pack of Luckies and made a big production out of lighting it. He took a puff and looked at the ceiling.

"You didn't send flowers," Brad said finally.

"No," Chadwick said. "Under the circumstances."

"Ah, yes, the circumstances."

Chadwick frowned again, but Brad had gauged his tone nicely, so that there was nothing Chadwick could take offense to without seeming a fool.

"All very regrettable," Chadwick said. "It must be tough on your mother."

"And you're making it tougher."

"What? Oh, the lien. There's nothing personal about that, Brad. It's purely a matter of bank business. You see, in cases like these, it's the responsibility of the board to recover as much as possible for the stockholders . . ."

"Who comprise the board."

Chadwick's color deepened. "I said, there's nothing personal."

"Yes there is. My brothers and sisters and I take it very personally."

Chadwick sat up straight in his chair and began to push things around on his desk. "I'm very busy, Brad. Now if you'll just . . ."

"I'll bet you're busy. Getting things ready for the examiners?"

"Yes, I am." Chadwick's patience was gone. "We've got a shortage of a quarter of a million dollars to account for. We'll recover a hundred fifty thousand at best from your father's estate. To get credited for it, we'll have to convince the examiners that the legal work is well along. And that will still leave us with a loss of a hundred thousand."

"My father confessed to taking something a bit under fifty thousand dollars. Your insurance policy on him covers that."

"What he confessed to and what he took are two different things. In cases like this, the presumption is—"

"The presumption is my father's the fall guy."

"What are you insinuating?"

"You and your cousins thought you got away with it, didn't you?"

Chadwick drew in his breath sharply. "Go on," he whispered.

"My father was a very methodical man. He kept records. What makes you think that suicide note was the only piece of paper he left behind?"

Chadwick gripped the edge of the desk with both hands. His cheeks were as livid as raw meat. "Get out!" he choked. "You cheap blackmailing punk! Your father was a thief, and you're nothing but a dirty rotten extortionist!"

Brad stood up and ground out his cigarette on the corner of the desk. "Thanks," he said. "You've told me what I wanted to know."

"Get out!"

Brad paused at the door. "You'll get your hundred thousand, Chadwick. Some day, somehow, you'll get every cent of it. There are five of us. That's our way of spitting at you."

He walked out of the office, angry with himself for having lost his temper. The bank employees were in frozen postures, their faces turned toward him, and he realized that they had heard the shouting. The guard, Nils, scurried ahead of him to open the door. Halfway across the marble floor, he realized that he had left his hat behind. The hell with it, he thought. Let him have that, too. The guard passed him through the gate and he walked away without looking back.

6

"Quadratic equations," Judge Tanner said, "whatever they are. How are you at them?"

"I won the math medal two years in a row," Gordon said. "It's my best subject. That and history."

He was clear-eyed and freshly scrubbed, his close-cropped blond hair standing up in a stiff brush. He wore the new blue suit, with a handkerchief sticking up out of the pocket.

"Mathematics and history," the judge nodded. "Good. That's what the congressman told me they emphasize. Gordon, the regular West Point exam starts the first Tuesday in March. You've already missed a day. Do you think you can catch up?"

"I'll have to, sir," Gordon said. "Won't I?"

"That's a good answer. A fine answer. You've got spirit, boy."

Brad gave Gordon's jacket a final brushing. "How did you wangle it, Judge?" he said.

"I still have a few remaining shreds of political influence," the judge said wryly. "But you can thank your father. He and the congressman served together in the First under Pershing. They both were wounded at Chateau-Thierry."

"Come on, Judge," Brad grinned. "Politicians never do anything for sentiment. A congressman can make exactly two West Point appointments. He has to get mileage out of both of them."

"The name Sinclair still means something in these parts. Your great-grandfather, Brigadier General Zephaniah Sinclair, Beulah's own Civil War hero and the delight of the county courthouse pigeons. Gordon will be carrying on a great military tradition, et cetera, et cetera." He turned away and looked out the window. "The congressman doesn't know yet how your father died. It's just local gossip so far, and he doesn't get back to the district much. Chadwick will keep the scandal under wraps until the examiners are finished. By then, Gordon will be on his way. I didn't expect many more favors from the congressman anyway."

"Thanks, Judge."

"Don't thank me yet," the judge said gruffly. "A West Point 'appointment' is nothing but a chance to take the tests. There are three nominees for each vacancy. Gordon's only the first alternate. He wouldn't have had a chance at all if the original alternate hadn't turned out to be married and disqualified himself. You'd be surprised how many candidates try to conceal a marriage, or lop a year off their age." His mustache twitched with a little smile. "Another thing that disqualifies you is something the regulations call 'extreme ugliness.' I don't think Gordon has any worries on that score."

"All I want is a chance," Gordon said. "Whatever happens, I'll never forget this, Judge."

"Tell you a secret, boy. The principal nominee is a horse's ass. Boy named Braithwaite, son of the district chairman. Can't stay out of trouble. I looked into him. He's going to be one of those that either fails or resigns before September. You just pass this test and show up at the Point in September, and that's all I'm going to say."

Gordon broke into a big smile. "Imagine, going to school and getting paid a salary for doing it."

The judge shook his head. "Wish I could do something for Jeremy, too. I don't know what's going to come of the boy, having to quit after a year of college. He's got a good mind, but no discipline. And you, Brad, only another year to go on your law degree."

"Don't worry about me, Judge," Brad said cheerfully. "I'll land on my feet. Come on, Gordon, it's an eighty-mile drive to Camp Dodge. Colonel Pemberton is waiting for you with a pile of exam booklets and a stopwatch."

Gordon started for the door. "I'll just say good-bye to Mama first."

"Don't bother her," Brad said quickly. "She's resting. We can call her from Des Moines tonight."

"If they haven't turned the phone off," Gordon said bitterly.

Brad got Gordon to Camp Dodge in under two hours. He drove the Stutz lovingly, watching it eat up highway, savoring the feel of his hands on the wheel, feeling a part of the machinery through his foot on the clutch. The Pierce-Arrow was smoother and more powerful with its twelve cylinders, but the Stutz belonged to him. He was determined to enjoy it while he could. He stopped on the outskirts of Des Moines to see that Gordon had a hearty breakfast, spending thirty-five cents of his dwindling funds for a thick slab of ham, two eggs, toast, milk, and a wedge of apple pie. He himself had a cup of black coffee for a nickel. The sight of the food so early in the morning turned his stomach. He delivered Gordon to the gate on time, and had a few words with Colonel Pemberton. The colonel looked at Gordon's erect posture with approval. Brad gathered that Braithwaite was a sloucher. He was unable to get a glimpse of Braithwaite or the second alternate. He told Gordon he'd pick him up at the end of the day, and set out to find a place to stay for the next few nights. The hotels in Des Moines ranged from three and a half dollars to a dollar a night. Brad didn't like the look of the dollar hotels he saw; they would have been all right for him, but not Gordon. He found a cabin camp outside of the city for seventy-five cents a night. It was plain but decent, with two beds, a little kerosene stove, and a table where Gordon could study. The couple who owned it would serve breakfast for fifteen cents.

He spent the rest of the day wandering around Des Moines. The city was full of movie houses, and he squandered a dime on a balcony seat to a movie called *Grand Slam,* which seemed to be about a lot of bridge games between Loretta Young, Paul Lukas, Glenda Farrell, and Frank McHugh. Bored, he walked out in the middle and found a cheap speakeasy near the railroad tracks where he drank beer until it was time to pick Gordon up.

"How'd you do?" he said as Gordon climbed into the Stutz.

"Okay, I guess. There wasn't much math. They didn't even get into solid." He was frowning.

"What's wrong?"

"Nothing. Forget it."

"Come on."

Gordon hesitated. "It's that Braithwaite. He cheated. He had a crib sheet up his pants leg. Colonel Pemberton never noticed."

Brad's hand paused halfway to the ignition. "That simplifies things, Gordie. If he gets caught, you're in."

"He isn't going to get caught, Brad. The guy's good at it."

"Then you'll have to clue Colonel Pemberton."

"But that would be squealing."

Brad half turned in his seat and faced Gordon. "You've got to grow up sometime, Gordie, and this is the time. If you don't get that appointment, there's nothing for you. No education. No life. No roof over your head, even, and no food. I can't support you. Jeremy and I are going to have to take off on our own after we get Mother and Junie settled. Elroy won't take you in. It's going to be tough even to get him to take Pamela in till she gets fixed somehow. You're on your own. It's too bad, but you're going to have to do all your growing up between now and ten o'clock tomorrow morning."

"No!" The word burst out of Gordon. "I'm not going to snitch on Braithwaite, and that's all there is to it."

"You stubborn Scotch lunkhead! Don't you know he'd do it to you? This isn't some kid's game you're playing! Don't you know what goes on at the big West Point cramming schools that guys like Braithwaite go to—the dirty tricks they learn to knock competitors out of the ring? And if you ever *get* to the Point, you'll be *expected* to squeal on cheaters. They call it the Honor Code!"

"Dad taught us that gentlemen don't snitch," Gordon said.

"Dad also taught us that gentlemen don't steal," Brad said brutally.

"You'll say anything, won't you, Brad?" Gordon was close to tears. "Anything to get people to do what you want."

"Look, Gordie," Brad said in a placating tone. "I want to see you get some sort of a start in life."

"I know you, Brad." Gordon's face looked too old for the peach fuzz on his jaw. "You make believe you give up, then you get your way some other way! Right now you're planning to go to Colonel Pemberton yourself, behind my back, aren't you? *Aren't* you?"

Brad said nothing.

"If you do, I promise you I'll walk out. I mean it. I want to go to the Point, but I won't get there that way."

Brad turned on the motor. "All right, if that's the way you want it."

"It isn't the way I want it. I'd rather be like you. But that's the way it's got to be."

Brad put the car into gear and headed southeast toward Des Moines. This isn't my week, he thought. My virtuous brothers.

Gordon sat stiffly, his face turned toward the window, watching the rolling prairie flow by. Ahead the granular skyline of Des Moines was coming into view above the greening fields. Gordon twisted round and said: "I'm sorry, Brad."

"Forget it. Let's have some supper. I noticed a pretty good restaurant on Grand Avenue. I'll buy you the fifty-cent special."

At the end of the week they drove home. Braithwaite had not been caught. Gordon was certain that he'd done well on the examination, but he was in a depressed state about his chances. Brad had tried to cheer him up, the last day, by promising a small celebration in Des Moines and a movie afterward; *King of the Jungle* was at the Paramount, with Buster Crabbe as the new Tarzan. Gordon had never before turned down a Tarzan movie, but this time he surprised Brad.

"Let's go right home," he said. "We haven't got much time left there."

As soon as they entered the house and dropped their suitcases in the front hallway, Gordon sniffed the air and said, "Darn that Jeremy! He was supposed to take care of the furnace while I was gone. Just smell that. I better go fix the damper. I bet the darn fire's out."

"Why don't you let it go till morning?" Brad said. "It's not going to get too cold tonight."

Gordon gave him a baleful look. "We might as well keep warm," he said. "What's the point of saving coal? We can't take it with us." He turned around and headed toward the cellar.

Brad wandered toward the rear of the house. It was oddly empty and silent. There was a noticeable film of dust on the grand piano in the living room. All the furniture had accumulated dust since Helga had gone. There was only one lamp on. No one had been in the living room since dinner. That was the biggest change of all. Until now, the living room had always been warm with human presence in the evening. His father would take a second cup of coffee with him and sit in the green velvet armchair, reading the evening paper and chatting with his mother. Gordon and Junie would be sprawled on the rug in front of the radio, reading the comics and listening with half an ear to *Buck Rogers* or *Bobby Benson* until they were overruled in favor of something like the *Chase and Sanborn Hour*. Sometimes, in a spasm of family spirit, they'd all work on a picture puzzle together, and the card table displaying the triumphant result would sit in the middle of the floor for days afterward, getting in everyone's way, until Mrs. Hansen put her foot down. In summer, one of the children would be sent out for ice cream, and though it would have been unthinkable for the Sinclairs to sit on their front porch like ordinary people, to be seen by the evening strollers and greeted by them, sometimes friends would drop by for ice cream and gentle conversation and lemonade from the pitcher always left in the electric icebox by Mrs. Hansen.

He heard the sound of running water from the kitchen and went in. Pamela was at the sink, her sleeves rolled up and an exasperated expression on her face, scraping and scraping at a big iron frying pan. A smell of grease and burnt meat hung in the air. Dirty dishes were everywhere.

"I can't even *cook*, Brad, do you know that?" she said, almost in

tears. "I'm not good for *anything!* Mother never taught me. I don't
think she knew how herself, and Mrs. Hansen never wanted me in the
kitchen when I was a little girl." She stamped her foot. "I'm *useless!*
And I ruined a good roast and wasted the money you gave me! And it
was eighteen cents a *pound!* And I think I ruined the pan, too!"

"Why isn't Junie helping you with the dishes?"

"It's my turn tonight. She's a good kid. The two of us have worn
ourselves to a frazzle trying to run this house. I don't see how the servants did it! Mother just doesn't know what's going on. She just stays
in her room and expects to be waited on. And Jeremy's no help. He
just spends all his time sitting around and sulking."

"I'll have a talk with him."

"I wish you would."

Brad climbed the back staircase to the third floor. Jeremy's room
was up there, a cramped slope-ceilinged room amidst the Victorian
cupolas. It had originally been intended as a maid's room. Jeremy had
moved all his possessions up there when he was thirteen, even though
there was an empty bedroom on the second floor opposite Gordon's.
Even then he'd been a loner.

The door was ajar and there was a light burning. He knocked once
and let himself in. Jeremy was packing. A suitcase lay open on the
bed, crammed to overflowing with socks, shirts, underwear, and books.
Jeremy's battered portable typewriter was beside it.

"What's up?" Brad said.

"I'm taking off, that's what's up," Jeremy said, continuing his packing without looking around.

"You going back to school?"

"Are you kidding?"

"Your tuition and room are paid up till the end of the term. I could
let you have a few bucks, and maybe you could get some kind of a job
to take care of incidentals till June."

Jeremy turned around and straightened up. "What's the point? You
don't get any prizes for finishing one year of college. If I'm getting
kicked out of the nest, I might as well start now."

"Where are you going?"

"I'm heading east. I'm hoping that eventually I can make it aboard
a ship to Germany."

"Germany?" Brad raised his eyebrows.

"What's so funny about that? Living is cheap there if you're an
American. Four trillion marks to the dollar."

"Your information's a little out of date. This fellow Hitler is getting
their inflation under control. And the dollar's going down. Roosevelt is
talking about going off the gold standard."

"Living's still cheap there. I talked with a fellow who was in Berlin just a few months ago. A Dadaist sculptor I met at a party. He says there's a place called the Bonner Platz that's full of artists and writers. Sort of like what Montmartre in Paris used to be during the twenties."

"I've heard about the Bonner Platz," Brad said dryly. "They call it the Red Block."

Jeremy flushed. "You can make fun of me if you like, Brad. But Berlin is where things are happening today. Brecht and Weill, Gropius, Kurt Schwitters, the Berlin Deutsches Theater, and Max Reinhardt. You probably never heard of any of them."

"I've heard about Berlin. My corrupt capitalist buddies get there too, you know. Lady wrestlers and midgets and nude cabarets and freak nightclubs." He shook his head. "Hitler's shutting all of that down."

Jeremy was really blushing now. "I'm not going to Berlin for that stuff."

Brad sighed. "What are you going to do once you get there? Besides mingle with your friends on the Bonner Platz, that is?"

"You're really crummy, you know that, Brad? I'll tell you what I'm going to do. I'm going to find a cheap place to live and I'm going to write a novel."

"A novel? You've never even written a short story."

"How would you know? Anyway, that's what I want to do. Be a writer. I'm through with the whole rotten system here in this country!"

Brad looked around the cramped warren that Jeremy had lived in the last six years. The objects in the room bore witness, in a sort of archaeological reconstruction, to the former Jeremys. There were the laboriously constructed model airplanes, hanging by wires from the ceiling and growing dusty. The stack of *Boy's Worlds* with the stories and serials that Jeremy had followed through the years. The roller skates hanging by their straps. The Daisy air rifle. The clipped newspaper pictures of cowboy actors pasted to the wall. The untidy stacks of books. They seemed to bear no relation to the fierce young man that Brad saw before him now.

Maybe Jeremy was right, he thought. The orderly world that had made promises of a comfortable, measured life to Jeremy and the rest of them had betrayed them all. Perhaps it was better for Jeremy to drop out of a system that had nothing left for him.

"Do you have any money?" he said.

Jeremy resumed his packing. "I sold my old bike and most of my books and some of my good clothes. My watch, too, that Dad gave me when I graduated high school. Took them down to the pawn shop over by the tracks. I got three and a half dollars for everything."

"You're not going to get very far on three and a half dollars."

"I'll go as far as it'll take me. I can hitchhike, hop freights. I can eat on forty cents a day. I've got it worked out. It ought to last me till I can get to New York."

"When are you leaving?"

"In the morning."

"It's going to be tough."

"I'll make out."

Brad hesitated, then took out his wallet and looked inside. The hundred was going fast. He took out a ten and two fives and handed them to Jeremy. "Take it."

Jeremy's face twisted with indecision.

"Go ahead. You're going to have to get along till you can find some sort of job in New York."

"Thanks, Brad. I'll send it back when I can."

"Forget it." He stood up and went to the door. He turned at the door and looked back. Jeremy was standing there with the twenty dollars in his hand. He looked very young.

"Jere?" he said.

"Yeah, Brad?"

Brad had been about to say "good luck," but he thought that he'd been serious enough already.

"Say hello to Hitler for me," he said, and left the room.

Brad slept late the next morning. He didn't want to see Jeremy off. When he came downstairs in his bathrobe, Pamela was at the piano, playing something by Chopin. He thought she looked pretty, sitting there. She had given up permanents, and her hair hung, fine and straight, halfway to her shoulders.

"Hi," she said, turning her head and going on playing. "I hope I didn't wake you up."

"I didn't hear a thing."

"I'm trying to get in all the practice I can. It's going to be strange, not being able to play the piano anymore. I wish it didn't have to be sold."

"It goes with the house."

"I know. I can't seem to make Mother understand that she can't take her furniture with her to Uncle Elroy's. She keeps walking around the house, looking at the different pieces and trying to make up her mind which things will fit."

"Did Jeremy say good-bye to her?"

"Yes. She's got it into her head that he's going back to the University of Chicago. She didn't listen to a word he said. And he didn't try very hard. Is he really going to Germany?"

"He thinks he is."

Pamela sighed. The music came to a dead stop in the middle of a passage. "Well, at least he has something to do with his life. And Gordon. I'm sure he'll get to West Point. That makes two of us. Brad, what am I going to do?"

"You'll have time to figure it out, Sis. Elroy will take you in till you get a job or get married or something. Christian charity, he calls it. He's big on Christian charity. You'll have to share a room with Junie, but you'll manage. Maybe it won't be long."

She looked at her hands. The fingernails were chipped, the fingers discolored from dishwater. "A job. There aren't even jobs for people with skills this marvelous year of 1933. Men. What am I fit for? I can play the 'Minute Waltz' and 'Für Elise' on the piano, and I can do needlepoint. The good sisters at St. Claire taught me to be a lady. They taught me a lot about deportment. I'm very good at deportment. I can walk across a room with a book on my head, and I never cross my knees, and I can sit down in a chair without moving my pelvis an inch."

"Look, I'll try to find something for you. Just hang on. I'll send Mother money whenever I can to keep Elroy from getting too upset about the room and board."

"What are you going to do, Brad?"

"I'm working on it," he said.

The call from Judge Tanner came a week later. "Brad, is Gordon there?"

"No, he's out looking for a job. He looks for a job every day. He has this crazy idea that there are jobs around Beulah."

"I just got a letter from the Point. Gordon passed his exams. Got the highest score in the state."

"What's the use? He's only the alternate."

"Not anymore he isn't."

"What do you mean?"

"That Braithwaite fellow. I told you he could be depended upon to be a horse's ass. He's gone and gotten some girl pregnant. Daughter of a very important family. Don't ask me how I know. They're going to keep it a secret so Braithwaite won't get disqualified for the Point. Idea is that she'll take a little flat somewhere near West Point so she can be close to her rapscallion, and so that folks back home won't see her belly grow. After his first year, when it's legal for him to be married, he'll acknowledge her."

"Judge, we can't tell the authorities."

"Why not?"

Brad explained Gordon's ultimatum. "He's a stubborn mule, Judge, but that's the way Gordon is."

"He's quite a boy. Your father would have been proud of him."

"Yes," Brad said curtly.

"All right," the judge said. "There's no need to upset Gordon. We'll just let nature take its course. Mobilization day at the Point—'M day,' they call it—is July first. Braithwaite has two months to make an ass of himself. I'm willing to bet that they catch him sneaking off to see his bride in the first two weeks. If Gordon shows up in September, they'll take him in."

"We'll get him there, Judge. Somehow."

The judge hesitated. "There's just one thing."

"Yes?" There was a sinking feeling in the pit of Brad's stomach. He was afraid he knew what was coming next.

"Cadet's pay is $1,072 a year. That'll cover his expenses, and let him save something toward his lieutenant's uniform at graduation. But he's got to turn in three hundred dollars to the treasurer as an advance on uniforms and equipment before they'll let him in."

"Three hundred dollars?"

"That's right. He can't get in without it."

Brad stared at the wall. The wallpaper pattern was busy, confusing to the eye. He tried to focus on it, and his vision blurred.

"Brad, are you there?"

"Yes. I'll get the three hundred, Judge. I'll have it for you by the end of the week."

"Where are you going to lay your hands on three hundred dollars?"

"I'll have it for you, I said!" Brad hung up the phone. He was pleased at the fact that his hand was remarkably steady.

Three hundred dollars. He could get at least that for the Stutz.

She helped him on with his topcoat. His bags were packed and at his feet. He'd taken the expensive pigskin bag that had belonged to his father, even though that was one of the "articles of value" specified on the lien. He knew he'd be able to sell it for something in New Haven.

"Good-bye, Sis."

"Good-bye, Brad. Take care of yourself."

"Don't worry about me. Keep an eye on Junie, will you? And Mother."

"I will. Are you going to see Gilda when you pass through New York?"

"No."

"I'm sorry, Brad, I was just asking."

"That's all right. No, I'll see her again after I get connected. The Stanhopes don't know anything about all this yet."

He had made his plans like a thief plotting a crime. He had enough money to get to New Haven. He'd clear out his things there. He could sell his law books and most of his expensive wardrobe. There would be plenty of takers, at bargain prices, among his fellow students. That fellow Kevin Tully, the reporter's son, had admired the English sports jacket. And there was always a market for secondhand law books. It would give him some kind of a stake until he got started in Washington.

"Brad . . ." She looked at him with her clear blue eyes. "Are you sure you're doing the right thing?"

He gave her a twisted half-smile. "What can a brilliant law student within a year of his degree, and without a snowball's chance in hell of getting it, do with his life? Easy. All the action is in Washington now. Roosevelt's Brain Trust is in the saddle. He's surrounded himself with Iowans, did you know that? Henry Wallace, his new secretary of agriculture. Until a couple of months ago, good old Henry was just our homespun editor of *Wallace's Farmer and Iowa Homestead.* And then there's Harry Hopkins—another neighbor from the Hawkeye State. We Iowa hicks are a helpful lot. I won't have any trouble getting introductions."

"But . . ."

"I don't have a law degree, Pam, but neither do most of the people who'll be descending on Washington now for some of the pickings. But I'm a genuine Old Blue from Yale, and I've got legal training, and I'm presentable, God knows! There's going to be a need for thousands of bright young men with some law training to do the donkey work of drafting legislation for the New Deal."

He tilted her head back and gave her a light kiss on the cheek. There were tears in her eyes. "It's rotten, Brad. We had it all. Everything. And now it's gone. Blown away. With just one little bullet."

"The Sinclair inheritance."

"What?"

"The Sinclair inheritance. Disgrace. Debt. Broken-off lives. That's the patrimony our dear father left us. Well maybe it isn't a bad start in a world that's gone smash."

"Brad, I know you're bitter, but—"

"Bitter? I'm not bitter. We're going to take this Sinclair name we've got hanging around our necks, the five of us, and we're going to walk out into that storm that's going on out there, and we're going to stuff it down their throats!"

He picked up his bags and walked down the steps. It was a lovely spring day. The archway of elms over the street was turning green with little tender budding leaves. The Pierce-Arrow was waiting at the curb, sleek and maroon, shining from the final polishing Gordon had given it.

He had the day-coach ticket in his wallet. He'd be sitting up all night in a crowded smelly car, full of unwashed human bodies. Coach was all he'd had money for after selling the Stutz and paying Gordon's three-hundred-dollar deposit at West Point, and paying Mrs. Hansen and the other servants what his father owed them.

He threw his bags into the back seat of the Pierce-Arrow and climbed behind the wheel. The hell with Chadwick's collection agents. They could pick up the car at the station. This was going to be the last chance he'd have to ride in style.

Book II

A New Wind Rising

June 1933–June 1934

7

"What did you say your name was?" the girl at the desk said, her hand over the mouthpiece of the phone.

She looked harried. Her curls had gone limp in the stifling heat, and two dark stains showed under the arms of her frilly blouse. Like the other two girls in the outer office, she was trying to type, answer the jangling phones, and greet people all at once.

"Sinclair," Brad said. "Bradford Sinclair. I'm a neighbor of Mr. Wallace's from Iowa."

The girl looked at him doubtfully, then down at a clipboard on her desk. "I don't see your name on the list, Mr. . . ."

"I phoned earlier," Brad lied. "I'm supposed to be down for Friday morning."

"I don't know," she said. "He's awfully busy right now. They're closing the government offices at two o'clock on account of the heat."

"I'd hate to disappoint him," Brad said with a modest smile.

The voice on the phone was distracting her. She rolled her eyes helplessly at Brad. "A neighbor, did you say?"

"From Iowa," he assured her.

She sighed. "Why don't you have a seat and I'll see what I can do."

"Thanks," Brad said, but she was already talking into the phone again.

He took his place on one of the crowded benches and looked around, comparing himself with the others. The anteroom was filled with sweaty, sour-smelling men, their white suits wilting in the ninety-degree heat. "A subtropical climate" was the way the British Foreign Office officially classified Washington. White suits and straw hats were what you wore when the weather turned hot. Brad's own white linen suit was better tailored than any of those he saw around him, but he knew that this was the last day it would look respectable. There was no more money to get it cleaned. The shirt still looked all right, but it was beginning to feel grubby.

He balanced the stiff new Panama hat on his knee. The hat made the difference. It bore the label of one of Washington's best haber-dashers. It had cost him four dollars—a week's lodging at the bachelor boarding house he'd found on G Street—but it was an investment. The girls at the desks always looked at your hat first. They couldn't see your shoes till you walked away.

He'd stayed too long in New Haven and New York. That had been a mistake. The good jobs were gone in Washington by the time he got there. Roosevelt's New Deal had moved with breakneck speed. Hordes of bright young men had descended on the Capitol in those first cru-cial weeks to staff the agencies that were administering the emergency programs. Brad had tried for three weeks to get an appointment at the Department of Agriculture. He'd heard that the new general counsel, Jerome Frank, was hiring fledgling lawyers as if they were going out of style. But without a law degree, Brad knew he'd have to go over Frank's head.

"You looking for a job, brother?" the man next to Brad said.

"What?" Brad swung his head around and saw a small, sallow man with yellowing eyes and bad teeth. He had a grimy collar and wore a dilapidated straw hat with a little cresent broken off at the rim, as though a horse had stepped on it.

"I was in Commerce, myself," the man said. He coughed and spat on the travertine floor. "One of Roy Chapin's boys. Got the boot when that Roosevelt crowd came in, but I still got connections."

Brad began to edge away. Failure was a contagious disease. You didn't let yourself be seen talking to people like this, even in waiting rooms.

"This new crowd," the man went on. He spat again. "Smarty-pants college boys. Think they know it all." The yellow eyes were on Brad, knowing and malicious, taking in the Palm Beach suit, the silk tie left over from Brad's Yale wardrobe, the expensive hat.

Brad let his eyes wander toward the ceiling. He studied a rosette in the molding intently.

"Who do you know in there?" the man demanded.

The receptionist rescued Brad from having to reply. "Mr. Sinclair," she called. "Mr. Wallace will see you now."

Brad got to his feet. Envious eyes turned in his direction. There had been a noticeable drop in the noise level in the room at the sound of the secretary's name.

"Hey, I was here first," the sallow man said indignantly.

"I told you before, you need an appointment, Mr. Garvey," the girl said. She looked past him toward another of the waiting men. "You can go in now, Mr. Oakes. Mr. Fortas is free."

Brad left the new Panama hat on the rack by the bench. It had done its work. "Hat in hand" wasn't the impression he wanted to make when he walked into Henry Wallace's office.

Wallace already had a visitor with him when Brad poked his head through the door: a balding young man not much older than Brad himself, with a pleasantly homely face and a nose that was slightly askew. He turned and looked at Brad with alert, humorous eyes.

"Come on in, Mr. Sinclair," the secretary said from behind his desk. "Mr. Stevenson was just leaving."

Stevenson paused on the way out to shake hands with Brad—a thoughtful gesture in what Brad had discovered to be a city with generally rude manners—and Wallace said: "Mr. Stevenson is one of the new attorneys on Mr. Frank's staff."

"But not one of his favorites," Stevenson laughed. "I had a couple of years at Harvard, but I went home to Illinois. Got my law degree from Northwestern. Jerry Frank likes to surround himself with Harvard men. Alger Hiss, Lee Pressman, John Abt . . ." He was sizing Brad up with shrewd eyes all the while, evidently coming to the conclusion that Brad was a job seeker. "You're not a Harvard lawyer, too, are you?"

"Yale," Brad said. He didn't add that he had failed to collect his law degree.

"That's all right," Stevenson said graciously. "Abe Fortas and Thurman Arnold are Yale men, too. Sometimes I think this department needs fewer lawyers and more farm specialists anyway." He turned to Wallace with a mischievous smile. "Do you know what Lee Pressman said at the macaroni code meeting the other day? He wanted to know what the code would do for the macaroni growers."

Wallace laughed—somewhat uncomfortably, it seemed to Brad. "You'd better get back there then, Adlai, before he has the macaroni crop ploughed under."

After Stevenson left, the secretary turned apologetically to Brad and said: "Adlai has a fine legal mind, but not everybody appreciates his sense of humor. I'm afraid it'll get him in trouble some day."

Brad stood there, not knowing what to say.

"Sit down, Sinclair," Wallace said, waving at a chair. "They tell me at the desk that you're a neighbor of mine from Iowa, and that I've *got* to see you." He chuckled. "First thing I learned in Washington was to do what the girls at the desks tell me I've *got* to do."

Brad eased himself into the chair, taking the opportunity to study the man everybody in Washington said was one of Roosevelt's most trusted advisors, and whom Huey Long called "Lord Corn Wallace." Henry Wallace was a rumpled, awkward man in his middle forties, with faraway blue-gray eyes and a mop of brown hair turning gray. His vest was unbuttoned, his tie pulled carelessly loose. He was tilted back in his chair with one foot resting on an open bottom drawer of his desk, in what should have been a casual pose but wasn't. He seemed strangely ill at ease, and Brad suddenly realized that the secretary of agriculture was wondering where he might have met his brash young visitor—and was actually worried about offending him.

Brad searched his brain for what he knew about Wallace. His eyes strayed to a cracked and varnished portrait hanging on the oak-paneled wall opposite the desk. That would be Wallace's father. He could see the family resemblance. The elder Henry Wallace also had served as secretary of agriculture, under Harding and Coolidge. Probably in this very office. The Wallaces were practically a hereditary dynasty. They had been enormously influential in agricultural affairs for three generations, through the family publication, *Wallace's Farmer*. Young Henry had broken with the Republican faith of his forebears only recently. He hadn't liked the way farmers were faring under Hoover. He had come out in support of Roosevelt's New Deal during the election. Roosevelt's own knowledge of farming was sketchy. He had been glad to add an expert like Wallace to his team. Wallace not only was a notable thinker on the social and economic problems of farming, but was a distinguished plant geneticist. His experiments had contributed a greatly improved hybrid seed corn to the world.

He was also a bit of a mystic. While practical and down-to-earth about farm matters, he was reputed to dabble in Eastern religions and the occult. "A spiritual window-shopper," one newspaper columnist had called him. Brad found himself reminded of the phrase as he tried vainly to make contact with the secretary's absentminded gaze.

"The girl must have misunderstood me," Brad said with a laugh. "I did say I was from Iowa, but I'm not exactly a neighbor. I come from Beulah."

"Ah, yes . . . Beulah . . ." Brad could almost see the statistics clicking into place in Wallace's brain. "Bad situation there. Very bad. Tenancy rate way up in your county. Almost sixty percent. All those foreclosures. That's where they almost lynched that district judge, wasn't it? Boehm was his name?"

"Yes, sir," Brad said.

Wallace seemed to relax a little. He had a handle on the situation now. "Well, I'm always glad to see a fellow Iowan. Farm delegations come through all the time. What can I do for you, Sinclair?"

"I want a job, sir."

There was no point beating around the bush. The neighbor story had gotten him in here. He had Wallace's somewhat wandering attention. He had to make the most of it without wasting Wallace's time.

"A job?" Wallace pronounced the word as if he were having trouble with its definition. His gaze went up to the ceiling, out the window to the glassed courtyard, then back to Brad's face again. "Have you tried Senator Dickinson? He's always glad to help a constituent from Iowa."

Dickinson had been the first person in Washington Brad had seen. He had put on his best Republican face and commiserated with the senator for the allotted five minutes about how that maniac Roosevelt was trying to usurp the power of the Congress and overthrow the Constitution. The senator had told him he was a fine young man. And he had gotten a handshake. That was all.

Brad shook his head. "I'm not a Republican. Not anymore. I'm not interested in what Senator Dickinson can do for me. My father would turn over in his grave, but Roosevelt's the only hope of putting this country on its feet again."

He stared sincerely into the secretary's evasive blue-gray eyes, one ex-Republican to another.

Wallace laughed nervously. "It sounds to me as if you ought to try for a job in the Emergency Relief Administration. Harry Hopkins is an Iowan, too. He threw together a staff pretty fast, just as soon as the Congress made his agency legal last month, but he might have an opening available."

Harry Hopkins had been the second person Brad had tried to see, after Senator Dickinson. Wallace was right about a staff being thrown together quickly. All the jobs had been taken.

"I don't want to work for Emergency Relief," Brad said. "They're treating symptoms, not causes. Agriculture is where the action is." He leaned forward. "That's why I came to the Department of Agriculture first."

There was a brief silence. Wallace played with a pencil on his desk. "You're a very outspoken young man," he said finally.

"I've heard the farmers around Beulah talking revolution," Brad said.

The secretary's wandering eyes lit briefly on Brad's silk tie. "You don't look as if you grew up on a farm, Mr. Sinclair."

"I have legal training," Brad said. "That's the important thing."

"Well, of course that's Mr. Frank's department. . . ." Wallace said.

Brad's heart sank. He was back to square one. What he needed was for Wallace to pick up the phone—if only to get rid of his visitor—and call Jerome Frank's damned office and say something like: "I'm sending a young man named Sinclair down to see you for a minute. . . ." He could take it from there. A call like that could be parlayed into a job.

But the secretary made no move toward the phone. Instead he began to ramble on about the problems of the farmer, about the new cotton acreage reductions and wheat price supports he was planning to put into effect.

". . . ploughing a standing crop under is a terrible thing to do when people are going hungry, but it's got to be done. This is a terrible moment of history. . . . We've got to make it possible for the farmer to earn a living or we'll all go under . . ." There was a visionary look in those distant eyes. ". . . but when we get back to some sort of sane society, we can take off the brakes and step on the gas. . . ."

Brad listened with waning hope to the flood of words. At last it came to him that this strange, awkward man didn't know how to get rid of a visitor. He got to his feet.

"Thanks for your time, Mr. Secretary."

A look of relief came into Wallace's eyes. He walked Brad to the door. "Come back again," he said. "Maybe something will open up in a couple of months."

As Brad walked down the long corridor, he heard Wallace say to his secretary: "Will you get me Mr. Frank on the phone. And have Mr. Pressman come in when he has a chance." He suddenly realized something else. Wallace was too shy to buzz for his own secretary. He got up and went to the door every time he wanted her. He grinned bitterly. It was too late to go back and press his case now.

When he got back to the waiting room, his hat was gone. Hanging in its place on the rack was a battered old straw hat that had a little crescent-shaped gap broken off the frayed rim. He looked around the waiting room for the sallow little man who had worked for the Commerce Department, but he was gone.

"Son of a bitch," Brad said.

The heat struck Brad in the face as soon as he stepped outside. The sun was blinding. The temperature had climbed to what felt like a hundred. He took out his handkerchief and mopped his brow.

He stood on the busy corner, getting his bearings. He was facing the Washington Monument across the bustling traffic of Fourteenth Street. Down the block to his left was the corner of C Street. Here was where the ragged and hungry veterans of the Bonus Army march had erected one of their shantytown camps last summer. President Hoover had sent the army under General MacArthur to drive them out with tanks and machine guns. There wasn't a trace of the camp now. Everything had been burned, bulldozed, cleared away.

To his right, a quarter mile away, was the enormous limestone mass of the Department of Commerce building. It was the largest government office building in Washington, completed only last year: Hoover's valedictory monument. A good many of Roosevelt's emergency agencies were setting up shop there, for want of office space elsewhere. This was where the fixers went when they descended on Washington, drawn like ants to honey. Brad shrugged. There was still an hour left of the morning, and he had nowhere else to go.

A streetcar clanged by, shedding sparks. It stopped just past him and began disgorging passengers. Brad had been here long enough to recognize the types. Sweating government clerks, clutching precious transfers, the seats of their trousers marked by the straw benches. Washington matrons in flowered summer dresses. A careful Negro or two. Families of heat-stunned tourists, their faces registering dutiful awe as they stared across the manicured parkland at the stark slender spire of the monument, the shirt-sleeved men fingering cheap cameras, the tired wives trying to keep the children from dashing across the tracks toward the monument grounds.

Brad looked at the streetcar regretfully. The dime fare was more than he could afford. He watched the trolley close its doors and lurch forward. With a sigh, he joined the flow of foot traffic heading north up Fourteenth Street.

By the time he got to the Commerce Building, he was perspiring heavily. He could feel the sun beating down on his bare head. Ruefully he looked down at his Palm Beach suit with its disappearing creases. A man carrying a portfolio bumped into him, then hurried on with a mumbled apology. Brad circled round a pushcart selling fruit, crossed Constitution Avenue, and walked around to the main entrance of the building.

He paused to look up at the façade while a stream of people hurried past him. The Department of Commerce was impressive in its vastness: eight acres of ponderous masonry squatting opposite the cool greenery of the Ellipse. It was also tasteless. Its architects had tried to disguise its massiveness with a fake adaptation of the Italian Renaissance palazzo style. The colonnades and sculptural pediments were pathetically out of scale for a structure so immense, and six floors above, there was an attic story roofed with red mission tile. As if to mock its pretensions, a peanut vendor was peddling his wares among the parked cars at the curb.

Inside, it was a cross between a pharaoh's tomb and a Roman bath. The milling crowd, fighting to get at the reception desks, was dwarfed by the height of the ceiling.

Brad squirmed his way through the throng toward the far end of the lobby, where a map of the world was punctuated by flashing buttons. Before he was halfway across, he was stuck like a fly in resin. He gave up any idea of asking directions. Who should he try to see, anyway? Some official in the Bureau of Standards? Fisheries? The Patent Office with its legions of specialized lawyers? The Census Bureau? It hardly mattered now.

He let himself be borne along in a flood of people to the elevators. He barely managed to squeeze himself inside. There was a lady in the crush. All the men took off their hats. Brad was ahead of the game. A half dozen conversations buzzed around him.

"Where's Johnson? He's not listed on the board."

"In that suite of offices opposite Coast and Geodetic Survey that used to be empty. He's still collecting a staff."

Brad pricked up his ears at that.

"It's a madhouse in there," the voice went on.

"I hear the person to see is Robbie," somebody else said confidentially.

The elevator door opened before Brad could get a further clue as to the identity of the "Johnson" who was collecting staff. He got his shoes stepped on as everybody moved aside to let the lady out first. The men filed out after her, clapping their hats back on their heads. Brad followed.

An officious little man with a toothbrush mustache marched up to him and demanded: "Which way to Conference Room B?"

"I'm sorry, I don't know," Brad said.

"He doesn't know," the man said in an aggrieved tone. "None of them know anything." He scurried off down the nearest corridor.

Brad shrugged and set off in the direction of what seemed to be the most promising traffic. He had hardly taken a step when a hand grabbed him by the arm.

"Can you help me?"

"I beg your pardon?"

A gentle soul in his sixties, whose face was as smooth and unlined as a child's despite his gray hairs, was looking up at him with a shy, anxious smile. He had on a shabby dark suit and a high old-fashioned collar, and he carried a polished cigar box lovingly under his arm.

"The examiners turned me down, but I know if I could get in to see the assistant commissioner, he'd take a look at it."

"What?" Brad couldn't follow him.

"My invention." The man tapped his cigar box. "It's a machine that runs on sunlight. The examiners classified it as perpetual motion." He beamed up at Brad hopefully.

"I'm sorry, but I don't—"

"I understand," the man said with a sad smile. "You can't show favoritism."

He turned to walk away. Then he turned back and said: "Can you at least tell me where the assistant commissioner's office is?"

"I'm sorry, no," Brad said.

"That's all right," the inventor said. "I know you have your job." He plodded off with his cigar box.

Brad scratched his head. Then suddenly he understood. It was because he wasn't wearing a hat. These men thought he worked here. The same scene was probably being duplicated all through the miles and miles of corridors of the Commerce Building, as the favor seekers approached other hatless men to ask them directions or advice. Brad grinned.

Twice more, as he prowled the busy corridors, people stopped him to ask him questions he couldn't answer. He was beginning to get tired of it.

"Pardon me, young man."

This time his questioner was a tall, harsh-faced man in his fifties with two deep lines drawn from the sides of a knife-edge nose to the corners of a thin-lipped mouth. Brad looked with interest at his clothes. The man was wearing a silk custom-tailored suit that must have cost more than a hundred dollars. He didn't have to carry his own briefcase, either. He had an entourage of flunkies to do that for him: three sweating young men with identical shiny leather portfolios and a heavyset goon who looked like a bodyguard.

"I can't find General Johnson. He's supposed to be on this floor. We've been all around it twice."

So the mysterious Johnson was a general! If, Brad thought, he was the same one.

"He's in that suite of offices opposite Coast and Geodetic Survey," Brad said confidently. "He's just setting up. They haven't put the signs up yet."

The man in the silk suit looked impatiently toward his flunkies. One of them said quickly: "I know where that is, Mr. Tewkes. We passed it a few minutes ago."

"Thanks," Tewkes said. He looked Brad up and down. Brad noticed that the bodyguard was scrutinizing him, too, chewing a toothpick, his straw hat pushed back. There was the dull metallic glint of a gun butt showing between the beer belly and the unbuttoned suit jacket.

"Glad to help," Brad said.

"What kind of mood is Old Ironpants in?" Tewkes said.

"You can imagine," Brad said. "The place is a madhouse."

"I'll bet," Tewkes said sourly. "Everybody trying to get to him first. If I don't get in to see him before that son of a bitch Green does, I'm cooked."

"The person to see is Robbie," Brad said in an appropriately lowered tone of voice.

Tewkes turned to the trio of flunkies. "Got that?"

"Yes, sir."

He swung back toward Brad. "I appreciate the tip. I won't forget this." Abruptly he thrust out a hand. "I'm Harrison Tewkes. Mid-Central Steel."

Brad returned the grip. Tewkes's hand was hard and strong. "Sinclair," he said. "Bradford Sinclair."

"I hear he's a crusty old bastard. That true?"

Brad shrugged.

Tewkes chuckled harshly. "The son of a bitch must still think he's leading cavalry charges." The provocation was deliberate. He watched Brad's face for a reaction. "No offense?"

"I don't mind," Brad said truthfully.

Tewkes laughed and clapped Brad on the shoulder. "You're a rare one, Sinclair." He turned on his heel and marched off with his little army.

Brad waited until they were almost out of sight before following them. It was one way of finding out where the suite of offices opposite Coast and Geodetic Survey was. He trailed them at a distance, through corridors thronged with hurrying people, almost losing them a couple of times. The traffic seemed to be getting denser and denser in the direction they were traveling. Once Tewkes encountered someone he knew: a chubby dark-suited man chomping a cigar. Brad hung back while they talked. Then a delegation of men with Kiwanis buttons in their lapels, laughing and horsing around, blocked Brad's way, and by the time he got past them, Tewkes and his party had disappeared. Brad spent the next twenty minutes circling the corridors in the area, trying to pick them up again.

Then he saw it: a wall sign that said Coast and Geodetic Survey, and opposite it the entrance to a jumbled working area in which a lot of temporary partitions had been set up. On the way inside he collided with a party of disgruntled-looking men with jowly faces and fraternal paunches.

"John L. Lewis," one of them was saying. "It's just an invitation for that goddamned John L. Lewis to come in and try to organize the miners."

"Let him try," another answered. "I'll have two hundred Pinkertons with machine guns waiting for him."

"Section Seven-A," a third man said earnestly. "The collective bargaining provision. That's where the trouble is."

They swept past Brad without apology, leaving him to brush cigar ash off his sleeve. He stepped out of the path of the traffic and looked around.

The place was the madhouse he'd promised Tewkes. He was in a broad corridor that was alive with people. The sound of ringing phones came from the open office doors lining the corridor. Impatient hopefuls were continually sticking their heads inside the doors and getting rebuffed by the people inside. There was a slow authorized trickle in and out. Desks and filing cabinets were pushed haphazardly against the corridor walls, still waiting for moving men to carry them inside. Some of the government workers couldn't wait. They were sitting at the corridor desks, trying to work in the midst of the hubbub.

Tewkes's entourage was about fifty feet away, loitering outside a door that seemed to have a swarm of people hovering like midges around it. One of the whey-faced young men was sitting on a crowded bench, his straw hat on his lap. The other two were leaning against a wall. The heavyset bodyguard was sitting on the corner of an unoccupied desk. Tewkes himself paced impatiently, glancing at his watch.

Brad strolled toward them, hands in pockets. Tewkes stopped pacing and looked up with an expression that might have been construed as an attempt at a friendly smile.

"Your tip worked, Sinclair," he said. "We had a little talk with Robbie first. Old Ironpants is going to see us as soon as he's through with those textile people he has in there now."

From the open door came the roar of an enraged bull elephant. "That's a lot of bunk, guff, and hooey!"

Brad could hear a faint murmuring demurrer.

"I don't want to hear any more of that blah-blah!" the enraged voice cut in. "Are you trying to tell me that child labor will *eliminate itself* within ninety days of approval of the code because if we apply the minimum wage to children, *there won't be any financial advantage to it?* Is that it?"

There was more agitated murmuring.

The crash of a fist on a desk put a stop to it. "Well that's *not good enough!*" The rage gave way to heavy sarcasm. "If child labor in the cotton mills is going to 'eliminate itself,' as you put it, then you gentlemen ought not to have any objection to specifically outlawing it in your industry's code. . . ."

Tewkes turned a perspiring face to Brad. "Your boss plays rough, doesn't he?"

Brad made a noncommittal noise and sank down gratefully in the vacant chair at the desk. He was too hot and tired to try to explain to Tewkes that he didn't work for Old Ironpants Johnson, whoever he was. There were papers scattered across the desktop. Shamelessly he picked up the top sheet to try to get a clue as to what he had blundered into.

Tewkes glared at his bodyguard. The man shrugged, and with an insolent look at Brad, picked himself up off the corner of the desk and went over to wait with the flunkies.

Brad looked at the paper in his hand. It was some kind of memo from the Department of Labor. It seemed to be about a tour that Labor Secretary Perkins had made of some steel plants in McKeesport and Homestead, Pennsylvania. At Homestead, town officials and the police had tried to prevent Madame Perkins from speaking to dissident workers at the town hall and in a park. She had finally defied the police by taking the men to the post office—U.S. government property. The picture she got was grim: half the mill workers unemployed, the rest working part time at an average wage of seven dollars a week. She had reluctantly concluded that the Labor Department would have to break precedent and act as advocate for the workers in the formation of the "codes," and she was recommending that William Green of the AFL be designated "labor advisor."

Brad glanced over at Tewkes. The industrialist had resumed his pacing, oblivious to everything but his wristwatch. The three flunkies with their briefcases were watching their boss. It was hard to believe, but none of them had noticed this incredible document that was lying in plain sight.

An outraged bellow from inside diverted Brad's attention before he could pick up the next paper.

"Judas Iscariot! Even the good Lord only mentioned turning *one* cheek! We're not getting anywhere here! Now I want the bunch of you to go back to your hotel and apply the seats of your pants to some hard chairs, and not come back here till you've worked it out yourselves. And if there are any carpers, critics, or crabs, you can give 'em a punch in the snoot from me!"

Chairs scraped. The meeting evidently was over. A quintet of solid, important-looking men filed out like abashed schoolboys. One of them lit a cigar defiantly.

They were hardly out of earshot when Brad heard the voice inside rumble: "By God, I wore more skin off on my saddle riding with Georgie Patton against Pancho Villa than would make a dozen men like them!"

There was a female giggle, quickly stifled. A moment later, a pert attractive girl in her late twenties came to the door and singled Tewkes out. "You and your party can come in now, Mr. Tewkes."

Tewkes motioned to his people to follow. The fellow on the bench sprang to his feet, briefcase in hand. The bodyguard started to shamble along after them, chewing his toothpick. The girl looked at him in distaste.

"Not you," she said. "You wait outside." She turned to Brad and said impatiently: "Please don't sit there. Go on in with the others."

Brad shrugged and got up. On his way through the door, he looked back and saw the girl sitting down at the desk he had just vacated. She looked annoyed.

Inside he found an almost bare office that had been formed by putting up a temporary partition in a long bay that couldn't have been more than fifteen feet wide. The clatter of dozens of typewriters came from the other side of the partition.

None of it seemed to bother the man who sat at the cramped desk in the middle of the room. He was a burly, red-faced man wearing a blue shirt with its collar open and sleeves rolled up. His jacket hung over the back of the chair. His clothes looked as if they had been slept in. His eyes were red-rimmed from lack of sleep, and his hair was mussed. The desk he sat at was a rat's nest of papers, cigarette butts, and crumpled Old Gold packages.

"Herbert Hoover spent seventeen million dollars on it," he was fuming to Tewkes, "and it's the worst-planned and least efficient modern office building in the world." He swept a beefy arm around the cubicle. "Look at it! It reminds me of the pay toilets in Union Station!"

Tewkes laughed uncomfortably. He and two of his assistants were sitting on straight-backed chairs drawn up in front of the general's desk. The third assistant was perched on the end of a couch that was piled with stacks of papers.

The general broke off his harangue to look up at Brad. "Well, sit down if you're going to be a part of this meeting," he said genially.

The only other chair in the room was at a small desk angled at one side of the general's desk. Brad pushed a typing table aside, sat down, swiveled the chair around to face the others, and tried to look intelligent.

"Well, I'm glad to have Sinclair here," Tewkes said. He was forcing himself to be agreeable. "He's been very helpful."

The general looked puzzled for a moment. "It's fine that Mr. Tewkes has so much confidence in you, Sinclair," he said absently. He turned to Tewkes again. "Robbie says it's urgent that you see me. Go ahead, I'm listening."

Tewkes grunted, "I don't like Seven-A."

"Nobody likes Seven-A. Your buddies at the Iron and Steel Institute are screaming to high heaven about it, but it's written into Title One of the Industrial Recovery Act, and you're stuck with it."

The general fished the last Old Gold from a pack on his desk, lit it, and crumpled the empty pack. He tossed it at an overflowing ashtray and missed.

"The act isn't even law yet," Tewkes said poisonously. "Your department doesn't exist, legally."

"The President's signing the act into law this afternoon," the general said. "You can read about it in the papers tomorrow. I'm due at the Cabinet meeting in a couple of hours so he can tell me personally that he's naming me administrator." He glared triumphantly at Tewkes.

Brad was impressed. General Johnson, whoever he was, had access to the President.

"We're willing to allow unions," Tewkes said.

"Company unions," the general spat.

"Goddamn it, Seven-A will kill us!" Tewkes shouted.

The general shouted back, only louder: "Men have died and worms have eaten them! But not from paying human labor thirty cents an hour!"

Tewkes looked startled at the outburst of sudden oratory. The general looked as if he were enjoying himself. Brad had to admire the performance.

Tewkes collected himself. "Grover," he snapped. "Do you have those figures on wages?"

The straw-hatted flunky on the couch sat up spine-straight. He fished a paper out of the briefcase balanced on his knees. "Mid-Central Steel is prepared to offer forty cents an hour in return for pricing concessions," he recited. "For a forty-eight-hour week, that comes to a nineteen-dollar-and-twenty-cent wage."

The general took a long drag on his cigarette. He shot a hooded glance at the other two flunkies. "You boys ready to back that up?"

They started pawing desperately through their briefcases while Tewkes glowered.

"Never mind," the general said sarcastically. "Baloney doesn't have to be written on a piece of paper to be baloney." He turned his red-eyed gaze on Brad. "What's the matter, Sinclair, no briefcase?"

"No sir, no briefcase," Brad said.

"What do you have to say about it?"

Brad thought furiously. He was a small boy again, listening to the mysterious conversation of grown-ups. Or caught daydreaming in law class, without a glimmering as to what the topic was. He'd always got by, throwing a few of their own words back at them till he could get his bearings. This "Seven-A" everyone was so excited about had something to do with collective bargaining. And what was it that Labor Department memo had said?

"Nobody's working forty-eight hours," he said. "Half the men are laid off. The rest are averaging seven dollars a week."

General Johnson's eyebrows shot up in surprise. "Well, Tewkes," he laughed, "*I* didn't say that. Sinclair did."

It was Tewkes's turn to look puzzled. His eyes darted from Johnson to Brad and back to Johnson again. "Our mills are working at a fraction of capacity," he said defensively. "The demand for steel's been dried up since 1929. We've got to keep our prices low to compete."

Johnson's voice rang out theatrically: "No one—*no one!*—is entitled to low prices achieved by the degradation of human labor! And no industry which depends for existence on less than living wages has a right to continue to exist! This dog-eat-dog business of price cutting is economic slaughter!" His hand slapped the desk with such force that all the litter on it jumped up.

Brad figured he had nothing to lose by jumping into this Alice-in-Wonderland conversation one more time. "Excuse me, General. Why don't you ask Mr. Tewkes about those pricing concessions that Grover mentioned?"

The general smiled grimly. "We were bound to get to that, weren't we?" He turned to Tewkes with cold distaste. "All right, Tewkes, you know what we're talking about as well as I do. We've got a quid pro quo here. You fellows go along with a little collective bargaining and we'll go along with a little price fixing. The important thing is to get the country on its feet again. You boys have been screaming about the antitrust laws since Teddy Roosevelt. Now's your chance to get around them." He glared. "Within limits!"

"I spent twenty years breaking the back of the steel union in my plant," Tewkes growled. "I'll be damned if I'll let that son of a bitch William Green get a foot in the door now!"

"Don't be a horse's ass," the general growled back at him. "I just talked to Myron Taylor over at U.S. Steel. He's pressing for adoption of a code now, even if it means outside unions. Why do you think that is? He's got his eye on that bundle of concessions on price policy, that's why. And Charley Schwab at Bethlehem is leaning."

"I'm not Charley Schwab and I'm not Myron Taylor."

The general sighed. "Sinclair," he said wearily, "Mr. Tewkes told me he has confidence in you. What's your advice to him?"

"Go along with the code," Brad said promptly, remembering the memo on the desk outside, "or the Department of Labor's lawyers and Bill Green will get it done without you."

Johnson's eyebrows rose again. "That's confidential," he said, "but sure, that's what's going to happen. Big Steel has armies of high-priced lawyers. The steelworkers have no one. Frances Perkins has agreed to present their case, with Bill Green as her labor advisor."

"That bitch can't use a federal agency to—"

"Watch your mouth!" the general said dangerously. "Nobody uses language like that about Miss Perkins in my presence."

"The codes aren't legally binding," Tewkes said tightly. "You can't pressure me. I don't intend to go along."

A vein was pulsing in General Johnson's thick neck. "You'll go along," he thundered, "or you'll be left out in the cold when everybody else in your industry does. Oh, I know well that there's the possibility of an Iscariot in every twelve! But even Judas hanged himself for shame!" He thumped the desk. "Anybody who trifles with this great chance to lift the country out of economic hell is guilty of a practice as cheap as stealing pennies out of the cup of a blind beggar! And do you know what's going to happen to the chiseling fringe who prong pennies while their neighbors are fighting in the war against depression? They'll get the Danny Deever treatment! We'll rip off their buttons and cut off their stripes and break the bright sword of their commercial honor in full view of this suffering nation! It's a sentence of economic death! And that transcends any puny penal penalties in the law!"

He leaned back in his swivel chair, breathing hard and drumming his fingers on the desk. He and Tewkes glared at each other while the clatter of typewriters came through the partition.

Brad tried to keep a straight face. It had been an extraordinary performance. The general enjoyed invective, all right, but Tewkes didn't. "You crazy old windbag!" he choked. "You can talk to my lawyers!" He got up and stalked out. The three straw-hatted flunkies followed him, like puppets jerked along by strings.

Johnson chuckled, the flush of combat fading from his face. He swiveled his chair around and saw Brad.

"You still here, son? You better hurry on out after your boss. You have some fence mending to do. In fact, after the advice you gave him, I'd be surprised if you still have a job."

"I don't work for Harrison Tewkes, General," Brad said. "He thinks I work for you."

"He thinks you . . . *what?*"

"I don't know how he got that impression. I met him outside. I came here to see about getting a job."

Johnson's color rose alarmingly. Then the scowls turned into roars of laughter. "Oh, that's too rich! I thought you were one of Tewkes's milksop assistants! And all the time he was sitting there thinking you were *my* aide! Wait till I tell the President this one! He can't stand Tewkes and that whole crowd! Did you see the look on Tewkes's face when you called him a liar about his workers' wages? By God, we had him on the run, didn't we?"

He slapped his thigh with a meaty hand and roared again. On the other side of the flimsy wall the typewriters had stopped.

"I told him to talk to Robbie before he tried to see you," Brad ventured.

The tears rolled down Johnson's rough cheeks. "Stop it, Sinclair, you're killing me!" He threw back his head and bellowed: *"Robbie!"*

Someone came to the door. It was the pretty girl whose desk Brad had appropriated. She gave Brad a narrow look.

"Robbie, fill out the payroll forms for Sinclair here," the general said. He leveled his blue eyes at Brad. "Sinclair, what d'you do?"

"I studied law at Yale, but—"

"Put him on the legal staff with Richberg. Assistant deputy's salary, at two thousand six hundred a year. That all right with you, Sinclair?"

Brad could hardly believe his ears. Was this all there was to it? He had gotten a job because he had wandered into a government building without a hat.

The general heaved himself to his feet. "I better shower and change before I go to the Cabinet meeting. Spent the night on that couch there. The President will probably have the press there for the announcement. Then I have to fly to Chicago to kick this thing off. The army has a plane waiting for me! With a desk in it!"

He turned to Brad, his face flushed with excitement, and clapped him powerfully on the shoulder. Brad smelled a rich haze of tobacco and bourbon.

"Congratulations, Sinclair! You'll be telling your grandchildren about this! You're in on the first day of the Blue Eagle!"

The general charged out of the office, struggling impatiently into his rumpled jacket as he went. The typewriters on the other side of the partition started up again. Brad turned to the girl. She was surreptitiously sliding shut the bottom drawer of the general's desk with her foot, but not in time to keep Brad from getting a glimpse of a whiskey bottle.

"Robbie . . ."

"Miss Robinson," she said coldly.

He smiled ingratiatingly. "I'm sorry. Can you tell me what—"

"I'll get the employment forms for you to fill out. You understand, of course, that there'll be a fifteen percent deduction from the salary that General Johnson mentioned, as part of the federal economy drive."

"Miss Robinson . . ." He caught her eye as she was starting to turn away from him. "What the hell is the Blue Eagle? And who is General Johnson?"

She looked genuinely shocked. "Everybody in Washington knows who General Hugh Johnson is! He practically wrote the National Industrial Recovery Act single-handed. And President Roosevelt knows he's the only man who can administer it."

"You mean he's been setting up these offices and hiring people before he's been *appointed?*"

"We've been working for weeks," she said proudly. "We're hiring a hundred people a day. Maybe we're not official yet, but all the important people in the country know who they're going to have to deal with. They've been flocking here by the thousands, the manufacturers and the labor leaders, trying to get in on the ground floor. And it's 'See Robbie, get on the good side of Robbie.' They think I'm just a secretary, but they soon learn differently." She gave a harsh triumphant laugh. "General Johnson's going to name me assistant to the administrator, at a deputy's salary, as soon as the appointments list is approved by the White House."

"Hugh Johnson must be quite a guy."

"He's a *wonderful* man! He's part of President Roosevelt's Brain Trust. You don't see his name in the paper all the time, like Mr. Moley or Mr. Tugwell or Mr. Baruch, but all that's going to change now!"

Her eyes were shining. Brad reminded himself never to say a critical word about General Johnson in Miss Robinson's presence.

"But what's all this about a Blue Eagle? What agency am I going to be working for?"

Robbie suddenly realized she had been talking too freely. Brad saw her pretty face close up like a flower at dusk. "The NRA," she said in a brisk, businesslike tone.

"The NRA?" he repeated stupidly.

"The National Recovery Administration." She gathered up a bundle of papers from the general's desk and headed for the door. "Come along with me, and I'll give you those forms to fill out. Be here tomorrow morning at eight o'clock sharp."

Someone was pounding on the bathroom door. "Come on, Sinclair, you've been in there ten minutes! The rest of us have to get to work on time, too!"

It was Monckton's voice: Monckton of the loud socks and dirty jokes and odious table manners, who always managed to scoop up half the butter for his mashed potatoes before anyone else could get to it, and who always grabbed the comfortable armchair in the parlor for the Sunday-night radio programs. He had some kind of job in the Department of the Interior, and visited an aunt in Arlington on Sunday afternoons.

"Just a minute," Brad murmured.

He took his time wetting down his hair and dabbing at the spot on his sleeve with a wad of damp toilet paper. The white suit would do for today—but just barely.

"Sinclair!"

Mrs. Rafferty had left a can of furniture wax under the sink with the cleanser and disinfectant. It was a fair substitute for shoe polish, Brad had learned. He rubbed it into the cracked leather with another wad of toilet paper, then flushed the paper down the toilet so that Mrs. Rafferty wouldn't figure out why the furniture wax had been going so fast. Then he unhooked the door and walked out.

"What's the matter, Sinclair, fall in?" Monckton said. He strode past Brad, a newspaper under his arm. Brad stared regretfully at the paper. It was Willison's newspaper, all three cents' worth of it, left on the hall table when Willison was through with it, and Brad had hoped to get his hands on it first this morning of all mornings.

He went downstairs to the shabby front parlor that Mrs. Rafferty had converted into a dining room for her lodgers. Dulcie, the maid, was already serving breakfast. A half-dozen loners had staked claims to the small tables, and the usual chummy crowd sat at the big table in the middle, clattering utensils and filling the room with muted conversation.

Brad surveyed the small tables. There was Campbell, secure behind the barrier of his dandruff and halitosis. Old Mr. Hamilton, who would start reminiscing about the Taft administration at the drop of a hat. Poor rabbity Horton, who thought no one knew he had lost his job at the Bureau of Fisheries, and pretended to go to work each morning.

Brad sat down opposite Horton, who looked up, blushed guiltily, and busied himself with a jellied roll. Dulcie came over with a tray, a stolid, walnut-colored woman in a gray uniform and soiled apron. Brad shuddered at the lumpy oatmeal. Saturday was oatmeal day.

"Just black coffee," he said. "And a slice of toast."

He sipped his coffee, trying not to look at the scabrous pink wallpaper. It was worse in the morning, made horrible by the dirty sunlight that was strained through the net curtains. The alternative was to stare at the tablecloth. Tablecloths at Mrs. Rafferty's were changed on Sunday and turned over on Wednesday. He would have known it was Saturday even without the oatmeal.

Monckton came down, looking pleased with himself. He had the newspaper with him. He sat down with his cronies at the big table, his back to Brad, and put the paper down on the empty chair beside him.

". . . and I say Sharkey will knock out this Primo Carnera bozo in the first . . ." someone was saying.

"Hey, fellows," Monckton said, looking around to make sure Mrs. Rafferty was nowhere within earshot, "you hear the one about Sally Rand and the electric fan?"

"We're talking about the match, Monckton. . . . Schmeling coulda taken Sharkey easy, like he did three years ago, if Baer hadn'ta knocked him outa contention last week. . . ."

"It'll just take a minute. . . . See, she got caught in . . ."

Brad reached out and deftly pinched the newspaper. Monckton, deep in his story, didn't notice.

The headlines were splashed over the front page:

PRESIDENT STARTS RECOVERY PROGRAM;
JOHNSON CHOSEN 'DICTATOR' OF INDUSTRY:
ICKES NAMED TO HEAD PUBLIC WORKS

Brad skipped quickly to the part that would tell him about his new boss. Hugh S. Johnson was a salty character who had grown up in a sod prairie house on the edge of Indian territory; had been a classmate of Douglas MacArthur's at West Point; was an ex-cavalry officer who had ridden with the Pershing expedition into Mexico in 1916; had drawn up the Selective Service plan and served as head of the draft during the World War. He had worked with Bernard Baruch on the War Industries Board, mobilizing American production. After the war, he had become a plough manufacturer for seven years, heading the Moline Plough Company, and then had become a troubleshooter for Baruch, riding herd on the companies that Baruch invested in. It was Baruch, advisor to presidents, who had loaned him to Roosevelt during the campaign.

The lead story called the Recovery Act the most sweeping law in America's history. The President, it said, had "assumed unprecedented control over the nation's economic life." It was the culminating achievement of Roosevelt's first hundred days in office. An exhausted Seventy-third Congress had finally adjourned after putting through the President's programs, and FDR himself, after signing the final bill, had taken a special train as far as Boston on his way to Cape Cod, where he would board the schooner *Amberjack II* for a vacation cruise up the coast of Maine.

There was something in the story that made Brad frown. Hugh Johnson had been appointed administrator only of Title I of the act. Unexpectedly, Title II, the Public Works program, had been given to a Cabinet board headed by Harold Ickes, the secretary of the interior. A budget of $3,300,000,000 went with Public Works. It seemed to Brad that President Roosevelt had taken a lot of clout away from General Johnson.

You couldn't tell from Johnson's speech. There was a second story about Johnson's plane—the army plane with the desk in it—being forced down by fog in Pittsburgh. He had rushed to the nearest radio station to broadcast his speech over a hastily arranged NBC hookup that would take his words to the waiting coal operators in Chicago. He had delivered an impassioned, extemporaneous tirade. "The idea," he said, "is simply for employers to hire more men to do the existing work by reducing the work hours of each man's week and at the same time paying a living wage for the shorter week." Each industry would have to abide by a "simple, basic code." Those who cooperated would be entitled to display the NRA symbol—a blue eagle with the motto: WE DO OUR PART. Those who didn't cooperate would get "a punch in the nose."

Brad read on, fascinated by the general's pugnacious prose. What had he got himself into?

"Hey, Sinclair, how about giving me back my paper?" Monckton's voice grated behind him. "We wanna look up something on the sports page."

Wordlessly, Brad refolded the paper and handed it over. "Stay away from electric fans, Monckton," he said, getting up.

Outside, he recklessly hailed a cab. It would have cost him a dime to take the bus, with a free transfer to the trolley that stopped in front of the Commerce Building. A taxi would cost him twenty cents, plus a nickel tip.

He could afford it now. And on his first payday, he promised himself, he would leave Mrs. Rafferty's dreadful boardinghouse forever.

He leaned back luxuriously in the seat to enjoy the sight of all the government girls in their flimsy summer dresses, hurrying to bus stops along the tree-shaded sidewalks, their high heels announcing them on the cobblestones. They far outnumbered the men in a lot of government departments, and the early morning rush hour showed it. Washington was the ideal city for a young bachelor to live in. Brad warmed at the thought of the good times he would begin to have here in this strange, synthetic city now that he had some money again.

Then the driver cut across a side street, and the long shadowy defile of the alley that was hiding behind the brick row houses flashed past. He saw the leaning shanties made of scrap wood and tin, the narrow outdoor privies, the half-dressed Negro children playing in the rubbish. Clearly visible past the squalor, the Capitol dome gleamed whitely in the distance.

"Takin' a short cut through the Nigra section ef you don't mind," the driver said in a soft, gentle southern accent.

Brad turned from the window. "All right," he said.

There were a lot of Negroes in Washington, too, more than Brad had ever seen, even in New York. They weren't allowed in the restaurants or movies or department stores, but you could see the men working with pick and shovel where the new government buildings were going up along Constitution Avenue, the women working as maids in boardinghouses and private homes. There were even a few of them working in the federal departments, though they couldn't eat lunch in the government cafeterias. Brad felt a mild twinge of curiosity. Were alleys like that where the maids and laborers came from?

"Let me off on the Fourteenth Street side," Brad said. "I'll tell you which entrance."

"Yes, suh."

The curb outside the Department of Commerce was already crowded with the parked automobiles of early birds. Roosevelt's government hummed from early morning till far into the night. Brad felt around in his pocket for change and came up with a quarter. "Thank *you*, suh!" the driver said, touching his cap, when he saw the tip.

The typewriters were busily clacking at the NRA when Brad strode down the long corridor. He glanced at his watch. Seven-thirty. General Johnson inspired a lot of staff enthusiasm.

Robbie was nowhere in sight. The desk outside the general's door was vacant. The door was ajar. He rapped once and pushed his way inside. Robbie was on her knees beside the general's desk, fishing an empty bourbon bottle out of the wastebasket.

"Get *out!*" she said. "You wait outside!"

He made no move to leave. "It's all right," he said gently. "I won't tell."

She got to her feet and shoved the bottle into a large manila envelope that already had paper stuffed into it to hide the contours. She looked around distractedly.

Brad held out his hand. "I'll get rid of it for you," he said. "Don't worry. *I* work for him, too."

She hesitated a moment, then handed it over to him.

"He got back from Pittsburgh about five this morning," she said. "He came right to the office. I found him here, very upset, when I opened up at six-thirty, but I managed to talk him into leaving. He promised to check into a hotel. I don't think anybody saw him leave. He'll be all right by Monday morning."

"He did all right in Pittsburgh," Brad said. "I read his speech in the paper."

"He *drove* himself to do it," she said. "You don't know what it took out of him. He said he was a soldier, doing his duty. After what they did to him."

"Title Two? Giving the Public Works to Ickes?"

"They didn't give him any warning. They had it all arranged. He walked in at the end of the Cabinet meeting after being kept waiting outside while they fixed it up. The President had a big smile on his face. He praised Hugh . . . General Johnson . . . to the skies, and told him he was about to sign the bill and appoint him administrator. They all sat there and let General Johnson thank them and make a speech about how he was going to devote his life to the great project. Then the President said, as smooth as silk, that it would be an inhuman burden on any one man to administer both Title One and Title Two—that's what he called it, an 'inhuman burden'—and that he was going to divorce Public Works from the program and have Ickes administer it. Ickes made a big thing of acting surprised. He said, 'This is rather sudden, Mr. President,' and everybody at the table laughed. The general couldn't talk. All he could say was, 'I don't see why, I don't see why.' He told me he was ruined."

"There was too much pork barrel in Public Works," Brad said. "Three billion dollars' worth. The President wasn't about to hand over all that power to one man."

"He was going to quit. He said he couldn't do the job now, that it was impossible, that he had to get out. That Perkins woman kept him away from the reporters."

"Frances Perkins? The secretary of labor?"

"She got him in her car and drove him around Washington for hours, till he cooled down. They visited every park in Washington. She told him the President needed him. She told him he couldn't quit now and spoil the President's vacation. He promised to wait. Then she drove him to the army airfield to get on the plane for Chicago. They had the engines running, waiting for him."

"Is he going to stay?" Brad asked as casually as he could manage. She started to open her mouth, but the phone rang.

"Hello . . . Oh, Mr. Taylor . . . Just a minute, I'll see . . . I'm sorry, General Johnson's in conference. I don't know when he'll be out, but I know he wants to talk to you. If you can hold the line a minute, I'll see if I can pass him a note. . . ."

She cupped her hand over the telephone mouthpiece and kept it there for a long time, her eyes fiercely commanding Brad to silence. After two or three minutes, she spoke into the phone again.

"Hello, Mr. Taylor? General Johnson couldn't come out, but he told me to tell you that he got your proposal, and it looks fine to him. He says that he'll modify the language on hourly demands the way you want, and put it through in time for the hearing. . . . Yes, he'll take personal responsibility for it. . . ."

Robbie hung up. Brad was a bit stunned. Whatever commitments this trim slip of a girl had made in the general's name, they sounded like substantial ones. He stood there, the manila envelope with the whiskey bottle in it grown awkward and heavy in his hands.

She seemed to have recovered her self-possession. She turned to Brad briskly and said: "Does that answer your question? Yes, he'll stay. Don't worry, you still have a job."

8

Gordon Sinclair stood poised in the weeds at the side of the track, all his muscles tensed, the lumpy canvas bag in his hand, listening to the long rising wail of the approaching freight. All around him, casting spindly shadows in the early morning light, were the waiting bums, at least a hundred of them.

Bums. Gordon rubbed the golden stubble on his jaw, looked down at his scuffed shoes and shapeless trousers, and wondered if he looked like a bum yet, too. It had been four days now, four days without a shave or a bath; he knew he smelled, and he was only as far as Cedar Rapids.

Footsteps shuffled behind him. "You gonna flip th' freight to Chicago, sonny?" a husky voice said.

Gordon turned around and saw a bleary-eyed man in a heavy twill jacket that had dried vomit down one lapel. The man's shirt was in ribbons, its collar ripped away.

"Well, uh, yeah," he said warily.

"Boy like you, you need someone to show you the ropes." The bum's eyes roved over Gordon's still relatively intact clothes, the canvas bag. "You travel with me, sonny, I'll treat you right."

"No thanks," Gordon said politely. "I'm traveling alone."

The man reached with a filthy hand for Gordon's arm. Gordon took a step backward.

"Ahh, ya dumb gonzel," the man said, and walked away. Gordon watched him approach another boy, a frightened-looking kid of about thirteen, wearing discarded army breeches and a ragged cardigan. The man fumbled in his side pocket and handed the kid something that looked like a lump of bread, and they walked off a little way together. Gordon had been on the road long enough to know what they called men like that. Jockers, or wolves. The boys who went with them were called punks, or preshuns.

Gordon cast his eyes over the ragged assembly that crowded the edge of the cinder track. An awful lot of them were boys, many younger than himself. Girls, too, dressed in boys' clothes. Their families, if they had any, were no longer able to feed them. The boys tended to band together for protection. Gordon had been invited to join one such group and had declined.

There were men here and there in the crowd who didn't look like bums. They wore threadbare suits, grimy with soot or scorched by cinders, but if they were lucky they still had a decent change of clothing rolled up in their bundles. They were new to the road, like Gordon himself. They rode the rods or hopped boxcars in a desperate search for work, hoping to send money to their wives and children.

There was even an elderly couple traveling with a dog, a small white-and-black mongrel named Spotty, wearing a length of frayed and knotted clothesline. Their name was Clegg. They had lost their home three years earlier for some incomprehensible reason. Gordon had spoken with them during the ride from Waterloo. Mr. Clegg was small, gnarled, and bald, in overalls that were too large for him. Mrs. Clegg was large and shapeless, in a long shiny black dress, and her legs, when she hitched up her skirts, were a mass of welts and purple blotches. Gordon spotted the Cleggs now, resting in the shadow of the water tower, looking down the track like everybody else.

The train was in view across the flat prairie, belching great clouds of dirty black smoke. There was an instinctive surge toward the track.

"Back, get back, you sons of bitches!" one of the railroad bulls shouted, and the surge halted, breaking like a wave against the invisible line that separated the weeds from railroad property.

There were two of them, bulky red-faced men in shabby clothes, looking not much better than some of the bums. But they swung long hickory clubs, and Gordon had seen the pistols sticking out of their pants pockets.

He edged as close to the cinder roadbed as he dared, and waited. It wasn't fair, he thought. It was just plain mean. They couldn't keep people off the freights anymore. They were too many to chase. But they made it as hard as possible. The unwritten rule was that no one could board a freight until it started to move.

He kept a tight grip on the canvas bag, his knuckles whitening. It was the one his father had brought home from France in 1918. In it were Gordon's good blue suit and patent leather shoes and a clean shirt, so he could present himself at West Point. Hidden in the cracked pair of shoes he wore was the twenty dollars he'd managed to save by working at odd jobs all spring. Brad had tried to give him some travel money before he had left for Washington, and Judge Tanner had tried to force a few dollars on him, but he'd refused them both. The three-hundred-dollar advance on his uniforms and equipment had been sent to the treasurer at West Point by postal money order. That was enough for him to take. And he'd told Brad that he'd pay back every penny of it. The twenty in his shoe would have to keep him alive until September, when he showed up at the Point.

Absently he picked a piece of straw from his trousers. His clothes were still full of hay from the weeks of sleeping in the hayloft of Uncle Elroy's barn. There was no room in the house for him. Pamela slept on a cot in the little attic room they'd cleared out for Junie, until she could move out. Brad hadn't found a job for her yet. He hadn't sent any money home yet, either. His postcards contained vague references to some big job he expected to get soon.

Gordon had been allowed to eat at Uncle Elroy's table. Aunt Ottilie grudgingly set a place for him whenever he showed up at suppertime, but it hadn't been very pleasant. He had found food outside as often as possible, working all day for some farmer for his supper, or eating at the Jewel Café in town whenever he could scrape up the thirty cents they charged for the three-pork-chop dinner. Some days he'd just plain gone hungry rather than face Aunt Ottilie's beady eyes, or hear Uncle Elroy complain again about the lack of word from Brad.

It was an untenable situation. He'd known he couldn't go on sleeping in the barn all summer, so he might as well be on the road a couple of months early. He still had to get to Chicago and cross all of Indiana and Ohio, and half of Pennsylvania and New York State.

The locomotive gave a couple of shrill hoots. There was a hiss of air hoses, a shriek of iron on iron, and the train was grinding to a halt beside the water tower. The two railroad bulls prowled the cinder border, their glances challenging the long line of bums. A hobo in a chopped-off overcoat tied with rope around the waist took a tentative step toward a boxcar when he thought no one was looking, but one of the bulls wheeled around suddenly, and with a bellow of rage, rushed the man. The hobo stepped back into the protection of the crowd. He was lucky. Gordon had seen a man shot dead in the railroad yards outside of Webster City.

The sun climbed higher. Somebody down the line collapsed and was dragged back out of the way. At the tower the spout folded up, and the fireman rang the bell. A ripple of anticipation ran through the crowd. A brakie crawled from under a car and hopped smartly aboard. The locomotive gave a great huff, and all the couplings groaned, but the ragged mob still held their ground. The two bulls stood, hands on hips, looking disappointed that no one had made a break for it.

Then there was a violent jolt as the couplings jerked tight, and the long parade of cars began imperceptibly to move.

At once the line of people surged forward, swarming across the cinder path with their bundles and water jugs. The railroad dicks stood and watched.

Gordon ran with the others. He spotted an empty boxcar a hundred feet farther on and made for it. The first wave had already reached the train and were climbing over flatcars and gondolas. Beside him a man stumbled and cursed. He saw a one-legged man stump along on a homemade peg leg whittled out of a two-by-four, a burlap sack slung from his shoulder, catch a handhold, and swing himself expertly up. Old Mrs. Clegg was already aboard, her lumpy purple legs dangling from a flatbed, while her husband ran alongside, handing the little dog to her.

Gordon sprinted past to the boxcar with the open door, and tossed his bag inside. He got his hands on an iron brace and was almost jerked off his feet. The train was picking up speed. His legs pumped desperately, trying to match the pace, and then he heaved himself up. Willing hands inside caught him and pulled him through. "Thanks," he said, panting.

He looked back toward the water tower. A dozen or more people, too slow or too hesitant, hadn't made it. They stood in the cinder path, shoulders sagging, and watched the cars rattle by. The railroad bulls were already moving toward them, clubs in hand.

One of the bums made a last desperate snatch at a boxcar ladder as it swayed by. The train was going too fast now. The bum, legs flailing, swung like a pendulum, then lost his grip. Gordon, sick, saw him fall between the cars.

"Jesus!" said the man who had pulled him into the car.

"You gotta be quick," another bum said. He was a sandy-haired man with cheeks caved in from lack of teeth.

"Lotta arms and legs lost under them wheels," an old-timer said sagely.

They were all looking at Gordon's canvas bag. Gordon retrieved it without making a big thing of it.

"You look pale, young feller," the old-timer said. "You wanna take a little drink of this white line?" He pulled a bottle of colorless liquid out of the front of a grimy shirt.

"No, thank you," Gordon said, edging away.

"It's good stuff, none of your smoke."

"It's dehorn and you know it," the toothless man said.

The old-timer cackled. "Squeezed it out myself and strained it through a whole loaf of bread. It's safe as mother's milk." He took a long pull at the bottle, the alcohol running down the stubbled chin. Gordon could see newspapers stuffed in the tattered sleeve as he raised his arm.

Gordon had made it a rule never to travel in a car with more than one or two men in it, unless it was a large, generalized, sociable crowd. The next time the train stopped, at a junction point past a small town, he dropped to the ground and walked down the length of it, looking for a better place. There were no railroad dicks here, and the train's small crew went about their own business. A lot of the transients were taking the opportunity to stretch their legs or relieve themselves by the side of the train.

It was a long train, more than a hundred cars till Gordon lost count, but there weren't all that many choices. Bums never tampered with a sealed boxcar, only the empties, for fear of terrible retribution at the next railroad yard. A lot of the gondolas and flatcars were uncomfortable or dangerous—those with shifting loads of pipes or machinery, or the grain hoppers that you were liable to roll off if you fell asleep.

The next boxcar he passed was too crowded. Somebody had a fire going in the middle of the steel floor, boiling water in a tin can, and there was no backrest space left along the walls. He saw an open door a few cars down and headed for that one.

As he drew close, a young boy in frayed khaki fatigues stepped into his path. He couldn't have been more than fifteen, but his thin sallow face had middle-aged lines in it.

"You gotta have a dime," he said, shaking his head.

"What?"

"You gotta have a dime to get in. You got a dime?"

"No," Gordon said. He tried to step past the boy, and instantly there were two more of them, dropping down from the open door.

Gordon studied them cautiously. They were smaller than he was, starveling children with that strangely loose skin on their matchstick arms that he had noticed in others like them, but something made him afraid of them.

"Or a nickel," one of them said. "A nickel's all right too."

"Let him look," the other boy said. "Go 'head, take a look."

Gordon peered into the dark interior of the car. There were about a dozen bums in there. They seemed to be lined up, waiting. There was an overpowering smell of cheap wine and dehorned alcohol emanating from inside. Six or seven more young boys, in torn sweaters or olive drab castoffs, were ranged along the walls, arms folded. As Gordon's eyes adjusted, a pile of rags in the corner suddenly came to life. It was a bum in a flopping coat and drooping hat, getting to his feet and pulling his trousers up from around his ankles. As he stood, he revealed a maggoty white form that resolved itself into a skinny little girl, naked as sin, lying on a pile of blankets.

Gordon stepped back quickly. The three boys were watching him.

"Go ahead, we'll watch your bindle for you."

"You gotta lose your cherry sometime."

Gordon walked away, his ears burning. Behind him he could hear the high, forced, whooping laughter.

He got aboard again just in time. The train jerked into motion with no warning but a sudden crash of metal, and he caught hold of the nearest iron ladder. He climbed to the top deck, the bag awkward in his hand. He was near the tail of the train. It stretched out ahead of him, an articulated serpent at least a mile long, eating the shiny, endless rails. The bums didn't seem to have spread this far back. He could see a few top-riders here and there, the closest a hundred yards away.

He scrambled along the center boardwalk on all fours, his back humped high, while the train rattled and lurched, and jumped across to the next car. A peek over the side showed him an empty with its door ajar. Hanging over the side, he tossed his bag inside. Then, waiting for a smooth stretch, he dangled from the edge of the roof, swung his legs inside, and collapsed in a heap on the floor.

When he had caught his breath, he looked around. He was in an old car with a rotten wooden floor littered with moldy straw. There was a man snoring loudly at one end. Gordon looked him over. He was a big-shouldered man with a craggy, ruined face half-hidden by a greasy felt hat tilted over his eyes. There was iron-gray stubble on a shelf of jaw. One big, twisted hand with knuckles like walnuts was wrapped around the neck of an empty bottle. He didn't look particularly dangerous. Gordon sat down in the corner farthest from him, and pulled his canvas bag close.

He opened the bag and took out the last of the sandwiches he had brought with him. The bologna smelled a little funny when he unwrapped the waxed paper, and the bread was stale, but he wolfed it down. He wished he had thought to bring a water jug with him, like all the others. At least he had a peach left, going soft but still juicy. He finished it, still hungry.

Despite the bouncing of the car, he felt groggy. He hadn't slept at all the previous night, waiting with the others in the predawn dark for the freight that was supposed to stop at the water tower. He tried to slide the door shut, but it wouldn't close all the way. Someone—the unconscious bum in the opposite corner—had spiked it to keep from being locked in. The sunlight streaming through the door made no difference. After another mile or two of clicking rails, Gordon was fast asleep.

When he woke, it was dark. He could see starlight through the half-open door. All his joints ached, and he had to go to the bathroom.

There were presences in the boxcar. Three men, hunkered down, talking low. When he stirred, the silhouetted heads turned in his direction. A match flared, and he saw jack-o'-lantern faces: gap-toothed grins and shadow-pooled nostrils in the orange flame.

"Hey, our sweetheart's awake," one of them laughed.

He drew back against the wall of the car, hugging his canvas bag close to him. It was out of the question to get up and pee out the door. He didn't know why, but he couldn't have done it in front of these men.

"Look at them cheeks. Peach fuzz. How old are you, kid?"

Gordon kept silent.

"Hey, I ast you a question." The man's voice was growly with adult authority.

Gordon swallowed. "Seventeen," he said.

"Seventeen! Why ain't he just a little lamb?"

The others laughed. With shock, Gordon saw that one of the men squatting there had his pants open and was fiddling with himself. He didn't think grown-up men did that. "Hey, Billy," one of them said in a voice that had a strange, shaky excitement in it, "I think you got a place to put that thing."

The three of them got up and stood around him in a semicircle. They loomed above him, breathing hard, smelling of sweat and urine and cheap whiskey. Gordon started to get up, but a heavy hand on his shoulder pushed him down.

"Let me up," he said.

"What you got in the bag, kiddo?"

"Leave me alone."

"Hey, that ain't nice, kid, talking like that."

"What do you want?"

They laughed. A bar of moonlight traveled across the car floor as the train rounded a curve. Gordon saw a scabby face, a shiny mouth.

"We ain't gonna hurt you, kid. We're just gonna break you in, see?"

Suddenly there were rough hands on his arms. Gordon lashed out, trying to get to his feet.

"Ow! The little son of a bitch got me on the nose!"

A fist drove into Gordon's midsection, knocking the wind out of him. Something hard, like a piece of wood, bounced off the side of his head, and for a moment he was blind, dazed, and rubber-limbed, everything peppered with little lights. He found himself pinned face down on the dusty straw. Somebody was kneeling with all his weight on the small of his back, and forcing his wrists up between his shoulder blades. He felt as though his arms were about to break. Somebody else was sitting on his legs. He struggled, and got a clout on the head.

"Hold still, you!"

Hands fumbled at his belt, and then he felt his trousers and undershorts being peeled down to his knees. "Ain't that cute?" a voice snickered. "Smooth as a baby's cheeks."

"Go ahead, Billy, you first."

He could smell rotten breath close to his face, and then something blunt and fleshy was pressing against his buttock. Gordon thrashed wildly, and for a moment the weight was off his legs. The men cursed. A thick gob of something went splat on the floor beside his face. It looked black in the moonlight.

"God damn him! He started my nose bleedin' again!"

"Hold him, I said!"

The weight was back on him. The hand he'd managed to free was pinned again. A calloused hand explored his flesh. Gordon sobbed with rage and humiliation.

"Leave the boy alone." The voice was a thick rumble from across the car.

The hand withdrew, and Gordon felt the weight on top of him shift as the three bums turned their heads to look around. Gordon managed to crane his neck in the same direction.

It was the bum who'd been sleeping off his drunk in the corner of the boxcar. He heaved to his feet, a great big man in the ruins of a dark pinstriped suit and collarless shirt. He was still clutching his empty bottle by the neck.

The one called Billy spoke first. "Back off, pops. This ain't none of your business."

"I'm making it my business. Let the boy up."

Billy laughed. "Look at the old rum-dum. He can't even stand up."

The man with the bottle swayed on his feet. He blinked, as though in pain. "You ain't cornholing the boy," he said.

Billy stood up, not bothering to button his pants. He picked a wooden slat off the floor. Gordon was sure it was what he'd been hit with.

"Hold on to the little lamb a minute, boys," Billy said lazily, taking a step forward.

There was a crash of broken glass, and the big old bum was standing there with his bottle all wicked-looking shards. He'd smashed its bottom against the side of the car. Billy cursed and stepped forward, swinging his club.

Somehow the old bum caught Billy's wrist and stepped inside the swing. The jagged glass flashed in the moonlight. Billy screamed and dropped the club. Gordon could see that his whole cheek was ripped open, showing the white of teeth. Blood dripped down to the floor.

In the moment that Gordon felt the hands holding him relax, he twisted with all his might and squirmed free. He scrambled to his feet, holding his pants up with one hand, and backed quickly away. He saw the wooden slat lying there and snatched it up with his free hand. He continued to back up, crouching, waving the club in front of him.

"Aw, come on, Knobby," one of the bums whined. "We was just having a little fun."

"You know who I am?" the man with the bottle said. "Good. Then you know I mean what I say. You got your warning. I carved your chum careful-like. I left him his eyeballs."

They looked at Billy. He was on his knees, dripping blood, afraid to touch his face with his hands.

The man Gordon had given a bloody nose managed a sick smile. "We don't want no trouble. Look, we'll find another car. Soon as the train stops—"

"You're not staying on this train, grease tail. You and the other dingbats are jumping off at the next soft grade."

"Have a heart, Knobby."

Gordon's rescuer feinted with the broken bottle. The other tramps shrank from it.

"I'm all heart, jungle buzzard. Otherwise I'd 'a shoved this glasgie slasher up between your legs where it belongs. Now get over by the door. A curve's coming up."

The three of them lined up at the open door, including the moaning Billy. Gordon watched, aghast. When the train slowed for the curve, two of them jumped at once into space. The third hesitated, and Knobby helped him along with a boot in his rear. The train was going about fifteen miles an hour. Gordon saw the three men tumble down the slope into a gully.

"God, I hate them jockers!" Knobby said in a voice filled with loathing. "You all right, kid?"

Gordon was too stricken to answer. His bag was gone—with the good suit and shoes and shirt he would have to be wearing when he reported to the adjutant at West Point in September. The first bum to jump had grabbed it and taken it with him before Gordon could move to stop him.

The old bum's name was Knobby Kerrigan. He was unsympathetic about Gordon's loss. "You asked for it, carrying a good bindle around with you like that. The trick is to travel light, see? You scatter your stuff around your body, in different pockets and all. You got two shirts, you wear 'em both. Or you can cop a new one off a wash line. Too many bindlestiffs on the road nowadays. Amateurs. Not like the old days."

They sat side by side in the jouncing boxcar, waiting for dawn. At one point, Gordon had dangled his legs outside the door, enjoying the breeze, and Knobby had snapped: "You crazy? That door slides shut, it'll slice your legs off at the knees! I got it spiked good, but you can't never be sure. There're a lot of stumpies and halfies hopping around because they didn't have no respect for what a train can do." He snorted. "Amateurs! Depression babies!"

Knobby himself had been on the bum since 1908—long before the depression had sent a mob of millions of homeless men and children out to ride the rails. He hadn't always been a bum, he said—and then suddenly clammed up. Gordon took it with a grain of salt; during his four days on the road, he'd heard a boast of better days many times.

"Yeah, it was different in them days," Knobby mused. "Nowadays you can't get on a red ball without there are a hundred 'bos on it already, takin' the best places. And you don't hardly dare ride the passenger jobs anymore—the bulls are all trigger-happy about anyone they catch riding the rods or the blinds now that they can't keep us off the freights. In the old days, sometimes a brakie would let you warm up in the caboose in cold weather, even give you a cup of coffee if you looked clean and were sober. Now they'd as soon throw hot ash down at you, or lower a spike on a wire so it'll bounce up when it hits the ties and knock you under the wheels."

He stared morosely at his broken bottle, mourning the few drops of sneaky pete it had still contained when he'd smashed it.

Knobby had spent a quarter century perfecting his craft. He carried the routes and timetables of hundreds of trains in his head. He knew the schedules of the Big Four mails by heart, and all the best red ball expresses, coast to coast. He knew where the best junction points were, which yards had the toughest bulls, who the most dangerous cinder dicks were, and what territories they covered. He knew every hobo jungle between Maine and California, every soft town, all the best missions where you could get a handout without having to get down on your knees and pray for it. He'd crossed the United States a hundred times, following the seasons, moving on when a town dried up.

"But my traveling days are about over, kid. Gonna find a nice soft jungle and turn into a jungle buzzard—me, Knobby Kerrigan!" He laughed and a fit of coughing overtook him. He took out a dirty handkerchief, and Gordon was horrified to see him spit blood into it.

"There's this place I heard of, see." Knobby's rasping voice turned almost gentle. "The town's soft. The Sallys put beef in the beef stew, the cinder cops never roust you, and there's a handout at every kitchen yard. There are never no night riders come down to the jungle to shoot it up for fun, and when cold weather comes, you can get yourself arrested and the sheriff's wife, see, she cooks pretty near the same food for the cagebirds that she puts on her own table, and nobody never sells you no bad alky that'll make you blind."

He sighed and stared out the door at the bleak moonlit landscape rushing past.

Gordon swallowed. "Gee, Knobby, how do you get there?"

Knobby gave a short harsh laugh. "Haven't you heard, kid? You ride the Wabash Cannon Ball. To the end of the line."

"Well, I hope you get there someday. It sounds okay."

"Oh, I'll get there, never fear. But not for a little while yet."

Knobby broke into a fit of coughing again. He didn't seem to want to talk anymore. He slouched back and pulled his cap down over his eyes. Gordon couldn't tell if he was asleep or not.

Gordon sat propped against the wall in the dark, hugging his knees, listening to the miles click by. The constant bouncing of the empty car was making him sore all over. He felt crawly and dirty. He would have traded his soul for a bath with soap and hot water. In his mind he could still see those filth-encrusted hands that had touched him. He wondered if you could catch a disease that way. Jeremy would know. Jeremy knew about things like that. He remembered the story Jeremy once had told him about the man who couldn't ever get married because he had been spoiled by sitting on a toilet seat with germs on it. But of course, Gordon thought, he could never talk to Jeremy about it, or any other living person.

He shuddered.

Stop it, he told himself. He clenched his fists and straightened his spine. Then he took a deep breath and imagined that there was a blackboard in his mind that was being wiped clean by a wet eraser. It worked, the way it always did, whenever he wanted to stop thinking about forbidden subjects and concentrate on something constructive.

Gordon began to make a plan of action, and immediately felt better. He still had the twenty dollars hidden in his shoe, after all. He just wasn't going to be able to use it to live on, that was all.

He'd get through the summer somehow. Odd jobs. Breadlines. Panhandling, if he had to. Twenty dollars was more than enough to outfit himself. Ten dollars for a new suit, fifty cents for a white shirt, shoes for four dollars, forty cents for a tie. Do without a topcoat—he could get away with it in September. And he could buy a secondhand suitcase and stuff it with newspapers. Stop at a barbershop before reporting to the adjutant and splurge twenty cents on a haircut, a dime for a shave with hot towels.

Once he was admitted to the Point, all he'd need would be his uniform, anyway.

But he'd learned his lesson. Knobby was right. Travel light. He'd wait until he got to New York State, wait till September to buy that one good suit of clothes.

He was going to have to be a bum until then. It was possible to live that way. Knobby had done it for twenty-five years. All those hundreds of boys and girls he'd seen riding the rails were doing it. And they had nothing to look forward to, the way he had.

It was daylight. Flat, low sunlight streamed into the car, picking out dust motes from the straw. Knobby yawned and stretched, then got to his feet with a cracking of joints and took a long leak out the door.

"Chicago coming up, kid. Another couple hours."

Gordon joined him at the door. "I was there once before."

Knobby yawned again. "Yeah?"

"When I was thirteen, my father took me and my brothers there for a weekend. That was before he started to worry about money all the time. He took us to a show and the fights, and a couple of swell restaurants, and we stayed at a big hotel. It was swell."

"Different now, huh, kid?"

Gordon managed a tired smile. "I guess so. We took a parlor car then."

Knobby began scratching vigorously. "Damn! I think I got cooties again!"

"Knobby?"

"Yeah?"

"Can I get a train on through Indiana and Ohio in Chicago?"

Knobby laughed. "You can get to anywhere from Chicago. It's the hobo capital of the world. More track going in and out of Chicago than any other city in the good old U.S. of A."

"Would . . . would you show me where I can hop a freight east?"

"What's your hurry, kid? It's a hobo paradise. More flops, more missions, better handouts, even now, with all the amateurs. I always lay over in Chicago a couple of weeks. East of Chicago it starts to get rough for a bum."

"I got to get east, that's all."

Knobby looked at him shrewdly. "When's the last time you ate, kid?"

"Yesterday morning, I guess."

"And it wasn't no grand feed, neither, I bet."

Gordon remembered the stale bologna sandwich. "I guess not."

Knobby rubbed his white-whiskered chin. "I'll tell you what. I gotta check in at a mission. I usually stay away from them places. I'll do a lot of things for a meal, but I hate getting prayed at." He snorted in derision. "Knobby Kerrigan never was no mission stiff, to get down on his knees for a pork chop. But I gotta get rid of these cooties. A man gotta keep himself clean, don't he?"

He glared at Gordon belligerently.

"Sure, Knobby," Gordon said.

Knobby nodded, mollified. "That's right. The Sallys run a place on the main stem where you can get your clothes deloused. I'll take you there with me, see that you get fed. Then in the morning I'll put you on a red ball heading east."

"Sallys?"

Knobby looked at him in disgust. "Salvation Army. Don't you know nothing?"

Gordon hesitated. "I don't know, Knobby. . . ." He remembered all the remarks his father had made about accepting charity.

"What's the matter with you, kid? Chicago's a tough town. You stick with me, those jockers won't bother you. They'll think you're my punk. You go into one of them shower rooms alone and—"

"Shower room?"

"Whataya think I've been talking about?" Knobby said impatiently. "You get yourself fumigated, take a hot shower . . ."

That decided Gordon. He felt that he couldn't live with himself until he got clean again.

It was dark again by the time the train finally jolted to a stop in the city yards. Gordon peered out the door and saw the dim boxy shapes of hundreds and hundreds of railroad cars stretching parallel to infinity, lit here and there by the harsh flaring points of carbon lamps. There was a dank river smell in the air.

"Tough luck, kid," Knobby said. "It's prob'ly too late for Sally, but we'll try anyhow."

Knobby dropped to the gravel and motioned Gordon to follow. All up and down the track, vague shadowy figures were spilling to the ground and dispersing through the yard.

"Let's get outa here fast," Knobby whispered.

Gordon hurried after Knobby down the long dark alley between the lines of freight cars. Abruptly Knobby stopped. Gordon halted beside him.

Far ahead a lantern was swinging in slow circles like a disembodied spark. It disappeared, then winked into existence again. Knobby threw his head back, listening. Gordon could hear the chuffing sound of a steam engine somewhere in the darkness behind them. The sound speeded up, going faster and faster, then suddenly stopped. Knobby's wide shoulders relaxed.

"It's okay, kid. They're humping."

A horde of skinny shadows poured past them. It was the gang of boy tramps from the boxcar with the girl in it. Gordon couldn't tell which one of them was the girl. The last one to pass looked back over his shoulder and hissed, in an evident panic: "Deeks on the way!"

The band of children dived under the boxcar and rolled across the tracks to the next alley. Gordon started to follow, but Knobby's big hand shot out and grabbed him by the collar, yanking him back.

At that moment there was a tremendous ring of clashing steel, and the whole line of cars suddenly jumped forward five feet and rolled to a stop.

"What's the matter with you?" Knobby said angrily. "Didn't you hear me say they were humping?"

Gordon stood there in a cold sweat. If Knobby hadn't jerked him back, he would have been under the wheels when the cars rolled forward.

"Damn fool kids," Knobby muttered. "No wonder you see so many of them without a foot or a hand."

He resumed his listening posture, as intent as a person at a symphony concert. Gordon could hear the slow faraway huffing of the switching engine again. He couldn't tell what it meant to Knobby, but Knobby nodded, apparently satisfied.

"Okay, kid, crawl under. Hurry it up, now."

Gordon swallowed his fear and scrambled beneath the freight car. He emerged on the other side in a scrubby patch of milkweed growing through the cinders. They picked their way from track to track. Once a brakie, inspecting bearings with a lantern, looked up at them and Knobby stiffened, but the man decided to mind his own business and bent back to his work. They were near the edge of the yard, beginning to hear traffic noises from the city beyond, when their luck ran out.

"Hold it right there, Willie!"

Yellow light splashed on Gordon's face. Beside him he could sense Knobby deciding not to run, and he stood where he was. "That's right, kid," Knobby whispered. "You could get plugged in the back by some of these bozos."

The man came sauntering up, a bulky shape behind his lantern. The glowing red end of a cigar indicated where his face was.

"You bums stay outta this yard!" he yelled, his voice rising in fury. "By Christ, I'm gonna break your lousy heads open!"

Gordon could see the weighted sap swinging from the bull's hand. A very large revolver was stuck through the front of his belt.

"Please, boss," Knobby whined. "We wasn't doing nothing. We just got off, see. We thought it was all right."

Gordon was amazed at the sudden change in Knobby's appearance. He was half crouched over, the big shoulders hunched, making himself look smaller. Gordon could hardly believe that it was the same man who had outfaced three younger tramps with a broken bottle.

"Oh, you thought it was all right?" the bull said with heavy sarcasm. "And who told you that?"

"Guy down the line," Knobby mumbled.

"What?"

"Down the line. In Rockford."

Without warning the bull swung the sap. It caught Knobby on the shin. Gordon could hear the sharp crack. Knobby howled and hopped up and down, clutching his leg. Gordon was surprised. He hadn't figured Knobby for a person who made much fuss about anything.

"Try again," the bull said.

"Honest, boss," Knobby whimpered. "It was a brakie there. He said they didn't bother you much in the yards here."

"He told you wrong, didn't he, crumb?"

"We didn't mean nothing, boss. Let us go. We'll be on our way. We won't come back here, no sir!"

The bull turned to Gordon. Gordon squinted against the glare of the lantern.

"You with him?"

Gordon cleared his throat. "Yes, sir."

"You a fruiter?"

Knobby said quickly: "He's just a dumb kid. He don't know anything. He just ran away from home. Wasn't nothing to eat in his house."

The bull laughed, an unpleasant sound. "There's been a lotta robberies in this yard, see? We gotta be careful."

"Sure, boss," Knobby said in an abject tone of voice.

"Mind if I search you?"

"Go right ahead, boss," Knobby said, almost eagerly.

Gordon was puzzled. He couldn't understand why the yard detective would ask permission to search them, after the way he had been acting. It was as if he and Knobby were playing some kind of a game, and the rules had changed.

The man was leaning close to Knobby, patting him down. The lantern was resting on the ground. His face was close to Knobby's, and Gordon thought he heard him whisper something. Knobby muttered something unintelligible.

"Your turn, kid."

The detective loomed over Gordon, his legs wide apart. Gordon could smell the man's tobacco breath, the sweat from his clothes. "Will you give me everything I find?" he said.

Startled, Gordon said, "Yes." He didn't know what else to answer.

The detective started feeling Gordon's clothing. His hand darted into Gordon's pants pocket.

"What's this?"

"It's a Ventrilo," Gordon said. He had sent away to Street & Smith's *Wild West Weekly* for it. It had cost him a dime. He had never been able to make it work the way the ad said it was supposed to.

"A what?"

"A Ventrilo. You can throw your voice with it. Or do bird calls."

"Ahhh!" the detective said in disgust. He flipped the little semicircular object out into the darkness. Gordon heard it fall somewhere on the gravel.

The fat hand was in his other pocket. It closed around the coins it found there: the seventy-five cents change left over from the dollar he'd broken to buy the loaf of bread and pound of bologna.

"That's more like it. Got anything else?"

Gordon, terrified, remembered the twenty dollars hidden in his shoe. What if the detective made him take off his shoes? He knew with utter certainty that if he lied to the detective, and the detective then found the money, he would be beaten with the blackjack, maybe until he was dead.

"No," he said.

The detective pocketed the coins. "Okay. Now beat it, the both of you. I'm giving you a break. Don't let me catch either of you around here again."

Gordon thought of looking for the Ventrilo, but when Knobby

started walking quickly away, he followed him. A sudden blow between his shoulder blades made him stumble. Instinctively he looked back and saw the detective raising his blackjack for another blow. He skipped out of the way before it could land.

"Damned yardie," Knobby growled when they were out of earshot. He spat into a patch of weeds. His voice had taken on its normal gravelly tone. He looked suddenly bigger again. His blocky shoulders were held at their usual height once more.

Gordon sneaked a hand between his shoulder blades to probe the bruise there. It felt awfully sore for being hit just once.

Knobby was rubbing his shin. "How much he get, kid?"

"Seventy-five cents."

Knobby looked up in surprise. "I didn't know you had that much. You should of told me. I could of worked something. Me, he got the fifteen cents I always keep tied in a handkerchief and hang down inside my pants. They always feel smart when they find it. Takes their mind off the rest of the frisk." He gave a dry chuckle. "And all the time I had a one rolled up tight in my cuff."

"Gee, Knobby, weren't you scared?"

Knobby spat again. "Of him? Naw. Listen, kid, yard bulls like that are the lowest of the low. The ones you got to watch out for are the train deeks."

They had reached a rotting board fence at the edge of the yard. Knobby glanced in both directions, then swiftly pulled a couple of boards loose. He squeezed through the opening and Gordon climbed through after him. They were on a dingy side street with sagging wooden porches and weed-filled yards. All the streetlamps were broken. Ahead was a glow of light in the sky. Knobby headed toward it.

"You ever go through Nebraska, see, you stay away from the C, N and W line between Grand Island and North Platte," Knobby rambled on. "There's this deek name of Walsh rides that stretch. Mean son of a bitch. He just shoots, see. He don't give you a chance to jump off. What he likes to do, he walks along the top deck and shoots down at anyone riding between cars. Little kids riding the baggage blind, anything. And don't try riding inside no battery box, neither. He knows that trick. He checks every one."

Gordon was impressed. "Gee, Knobby, do you know them all?"

Knobby laughed. "Not all, kid. Just some of the bad ones. And they know me. The worst is a guy named Featherstone, works the track east of here along Erie. Jake Featherstone. Got away from him four times. He knows my face. Knows I ride through his territory every year. It drives him crazy. I have a new dodge every time. He swore to get me."

Knobby fell silent. Gordon tried a couple of times to coax more of the story out of him, but Knobby wouldn't answer him. They were in a more built-up neighborhood now: wooden tenements of three and five stories, each with its own rickety porch. A starved cat ran across their path toward a row of garbage cans. It didn't look anything like the Chicago that Gordon remembered.

"Knobby?"

"Hah?"

"Is this really Chicago?"

"Whataya mean?"

"It doesn't look big enough."

Knobby gave a wheezing laugh that started him coughing again. "Oh, it's big enough, kid," he said.

9

The Salvation Army was housed in a narrow stone building between a barber college and a pawnshop. Gordon could hear them singing inside as he approached.

"Well here goes," Knobby said, and pushed the door open. The music swelled, a hundred faltering voices and a wheezing harmonium:

"Stand up, stand up for Jesus. Ye soldiers of the cross . . ."

Gordon looked around the entryway. It was festooned with tired banners and painted slogans about love and salvation. A pink-faced old man in a high-collared blue uniform sat at a yellow oak desk. Under the leather visor of his cap he resembled a baby that had been instantly aged and preserved with a coating of paraffin.

"No more beds tonight, boys," he said, looking up.

Knobby advanced to the desk, his hat in his hands. "We just thought maybe—"

The Sally didn't wait for him to finish. "The kitchen's closed for the night, brother. We're just having evening services. Would you care to join us?"

Knobby twisted his hat in his big hands. "Well, uh, thanks, but—"

"Come back tomorrow, brother. Early." The old man's eyes glittered behind gold-rimmed glasses. "Haven't I seen you before?"

"Me? No. I never was here before. . . . Uh, thanks . . ."

Knobby edged toward the door, still holding his hat. Gordon, with a last backward look at the banners and slogans, followed him into the street. The door closed on the singing:

". . . *put on the gospel armor, each piece put on with prayer*. . . ."

"Too bad, kid," Knobby said. "Well, it was worth a try. Come on."

Gordon followed Knobby down the street. A drunk reeled out of a doorway, and Gordon had to step into the gutter to avoid him. He hurried to catch up to Knobby again, passing a Gypsy fortune-telling parlor with beaded curtains hung across the dusty glass. A swarthy woman in a peasant blouse called out to him, "What's your hurry, handsome?" and he blushed without knowing why. Knobby was waiting for him in front of another converted store window that was draped with blue cloth and painted with a gilt Calvary cross. A faded streamer proclaimed: DIVINE HOPE MISSION. Each of the three steps forming the base of the cross bore a word:

SOLDIERS

OF

HOPE

"Take a deep breath, kid," Knobby said.

Gordon thought Knobby was just being rhetorical, but when they pushed through the door, he was assailed by a miasma of old cabbage, urine, and boiled socks. An unpainted plywood partition made a sort of waiting room with backless wooden benches pushed against the walls. The slogan IT'S NEVER TOO LATE FOR JESUS was lettered foot-high across the plywood in an amazing shade of puce. The floor was white octagonal tile. A wizened gnome with a bald head shaped like a bean was pushing a mop across the floor. The mop seemed to be doing nothing more than moving a tidal wave of dingy water ahead of itself, redistributing the sludge.

"Say, friend, they serve supper yet?" Knobby said.

The gnome jerked his head around and showed toothless gums. "Too late, too late," he cackled.

"Come on, friend, they ain't dished it out yet, have they?"

The gnome looked around as if he were checking for eavesdroppers. "They already passed out all the work tickets. I'm just finishing up here, another minute. You got to go to the sermon."

"You can show us where, can't you?" Knobby said in a wheedling tone. "That's all I'm asking."

The shrunken little man gave a final swirl with the mop. He picked up the bucket, with the mop in it. "Follow me," he said.

He disappeared through a flimsy door in the plywood, leaving muddy tracks in the tile. Knobby pushed Gordon through ahead of him.

They followed the gnome down a narrow hallway. A man with a puffy white face that looked as if it had been dipped in cornstarch sat behind an oak balustrade. He was wearing a uniform that seemed to Gordon to be an exact replica of a Salvation Army uniform, except that instead of the "S" insignia on the collar there was a replica of the stepped cross he'd seen in the window.

"He isn't a Sally, is he?" he whispered to Knobby.

"Naw," Knobby whispered back. "That's just their dodge."

They approached the railing. Another of the ever-present signs was painted on the wall behind the uniformed man. This one said: WHEN DID YOU LAST WRITE TO MOTHER?

The gnome said with a malicious gummy grin, "Two more fallen brethren, Colonel."

The colonel raised his eyes. "It's late, brothers," he said.

Knobby had his cap in his hands. "This ain't one 'a them hungry missions, is it, Reverend?" he said humbly.

The colonel recoiled as if he'd been slapped in the face. "No one is ever turned away at the Divine Hope Mission," he said. "Here, you men sign the register." He pushed a greasy ledger across at them.

Knobby scrawled something painfully, then handed the pencil stub to Gordon. Gordon was about to sign his name when he saw that Knobby had written, in a big, careful hand: "Ulysses S. Grant." With a nervous glance toward the colonel, Gordon scribbled: "John Quincy Adams." The colonel took the book back and closed it without bothering to look at the signatures.

He handed each of them a dog-eared square of cardboard. "Here are your work tickets. In the sweat of thy face shalt thou eat bread. Now get your tails up to the evening service."

Gordon glanced at his ticket. It said: "Kitchen Cleanup." Knobby stuck his ticket in his hat without looking at it.

As they mounted the stone steps, Knobby said in a voice that Gordon was sure was loud enough to be heard by the colonel: "They can't even give you a lousy plate of beans without you get down on your knees for it."

The gnome looked around in alarm. "Can it, brother! I went out on a limb for you!"

"Ahh, what do you know," Knobby said. "You're just an old mission bum."

"I am not," the old man said, close to tears.

"No? How long you been here with the Hopers?"

"Since December," the gnome said miserably.

"Yeah, see?"

"It was a cold winter," the gnome quavered, but Knobby had lapsed into silence. The gnome looked hopefully toward Gordon. Gordon, embarrassed, stared at his feet.

The services were being held in a big, bare room that looked as if it once had been a storeroom. A little wooden platform had been raised at one end, railed off by sawhorses. A homely colorless girl in a poke bonnet and blue cape sat stiffly at a rickety old upright piano. Three ladies with tambourines stood nearby, waiting. There was a drooping American flag and a placard that read: WHERE WILL YOU SPEND ETERNITY? At the front of the little stage, a sweating fat young man in a too-tight uniform stood, hands clasped behind his back, aggressively surveying the sea of bums before him.

There must have been more than two hundred of them filling the rows of folding chairs, hats in laps. They sat hunched in their clothes, patient as beasts.

"You stink!" the preacher screamed at them. He pinched his nose between thumb and forefinger and turned his face dramatically toward the ceiling. "You stink in the nostrils of the Lord. But I say to you that if you let Jesus into your hearts, you'll smell like lilies!"

He paused to glare at the latecomers. He waited impatiently while Knobby and Gordon eased into seats in the rear. Knobby took off his cap.

The preacher paced, hands behind his back again, head cast sorrowfully down. "Oh, the Devil's a crafty one, friends. He's hiding in that can of Sterno, hiding in that jug of sneaky pete. . . ."

Knobby leaned over to the man next to him. "What's the word, brother?" he whispered hoarsely.

"Bad news, friend," the man whispered back. "They watered the stew tonight. And cut all the pieces of corn bread in half. I saw it. I was on kitchen detail when they told the cook they was running short."

Knobby gestured with his chin to the fat young man on the platform. "He don't look like he's goin' hungry, does he?"

The man laughed. "Do any of 'em?"

Gordon recognized the man. It was the one-legged tramp he'd seen running for a train with such surprising agility the day before, near Cedar Rapids. The crude peg leg was stretched out in the aisle now.

Gordon studied the homemade contraption with interest. It was simply a couple of lengths of two-by-four nailed together at the bottom and separated near the top by a short piece of wood that formed a crossbar. A cushion of rags in the fork made a soft place for the man to rest his stump. An old army belt was wrapped around the whole business to keep it in place.

"Pretty good, huh, kid? At least I don't have to worry about finding a shoe for that one."

Gordon blushed. He hadn't realized he'd been staring. An involuntary glance at the man's other foot showed him a shoe that was in ruins. It had no heel at all. The sole flapped loose, revealing dirty toes.

"The blink over there's my chum," the one-legged man went on.

Gordon looked past him and saw a pale, thin boy of fifteen or sixteen, wearing a ragged army shirt that was too big for him. His face was streaked with coal dust, evidently from the gondola he'd been riding in. He turned briefly toward Gordon, and Gordon saw that he had only one eye. The empty socket was weeping, making a wet track through the grime on one cheek. The man with the peg leg patted his knee.

"Strike out the Devil!" the preacher was saying.

Gordon jerked guiltily to attention. Up on the platform, the chubby young man, his collar open and his face turning red, was going through the motions of winding up an imaginary baseball and pitching it.

"Get on God's team!" the preacher shouted. He bent with effort to dust off an imaginary plate. "Hit a home run for Jesus!" He swung an imaginary bat and then shaded his eyes to follow the flight of the ball into the infinite.

"Who'll stand?" the Hoper's voice throbbed. "Who'll stand up for Jesus?"

"Oh, Christ," Knobby muttered beside Gordon. "It's testimonial night."

There was a vast uneasy stirring in the sea of rags. Knobby, his big shoulders hunched, stared resolutely at the floor. Nobody got up.

The preacher whirled on a rheumy old bum sitting in the first row. His finger stabbed out. "You! You'll stand up for Jesus, won't you, brother?"

The old bum rose unwillingly to his feet. He mumbled something unintelligible.

"That's right, brother," the man on the platform said. "You were a sinner, but now you're saved!"

The next to rise was a dish-faced young man who boasted of his past successes with women, ignoring the catcalls from the audience. A gaunt, sober-faced man, twisting his cap in his hands, confessed to deserting his wife and children after not being able to find work. "That's all right, brother," the Hoper said. "The Lord forgives you."

Again and again, the plump forefinger shot out, jerking people to their feet.

Gordon watched the proceedings with interest. It wasn't anything at all like the services at St. Andrew's, with Dr. Bertram's dry, restrained sermons and the seemly procession of communicants to the rail. Gordon was particularly impressed by the dish-faced man's confessions, which were extremely graphic.

He was caught unprepared when the fat finger thrust in his direction, and the preacher roared: *"You!* Get up, get up! Jesus wants you for His team! Don't say no to the Lord! On your feet and spit it out!"

Gordon stood up slowly, his mouth dry.

"Spit it *out!"*

Gordon opened his mouth, but nothing came out except a squeak. He could feel everybody's eyes on him. He tried again.

"That's all right, sonny," the preacher said quickly. "The Lord knows what's in your heart. There, now, don't you feel good all over?"

Gordon sat down in confusion. Knobby hissed at him: "You dumb donkey! What'd you get up for?"

Gordon's ears were burning. Was this what it was like to be saved? He didn't feel any different. Uncle Elroy said you could tell when you were.

The horse-faced girl had begun to play the piano. It was tinny and out of tune. She didn't play as well as Pamela. It was all block chords. The three ladies with the tambourines had moved to the front of the stage, their faces eager. Their voices rang out, thin and clear as flutes:

There is a fountain filled with blood . . .

The fat preacher was prancing back and forth, waving his hands at the audience. "Chime in, boys, chime in, whenever you get the tune. Give it to 'em again, sister, nice and loud!"

Gordon glanced at Knobby. He was sitting defiantly, his lips pressed tight. The one-legged man had hoisted himself upright and was singing lustily off-key. Beside him, the one-eyed boy was moving his lips silently. The hall filled with a vast dissonant droning over which you could hear the high distinct voices of the tambourine ladies. Gordon got his throat unstuck in time to finish out the first verse, loud and true:

. . . And sinners, plunged beneath that flood,
Lose all their guilty stains . . .

There were more hymns and then they were released. The bums got gratefully to their feet and shuffled off to the dining hall.

Gordon found himself standing in line behind Knobby in a long, dim hall arranged with crude trestle tables and backless benches. A man tried to edge past Knobby. Gordon didn't see what happened, but all of a sudden the man was bent over, gasping, clutching his side below the ribs.

"You didn't have to do that, brother," the man said reproachfully when he got his breath back, but Knobby didn't bother to look at him.

Up ahead, there was a commotion at the window. A gangling man in a wool seaman's cap had reached in with both hands and grabbed a whole tray of corn bread before they could stop him. He was trying to get away with his prize when the men around him knocked him to the floor. They scrambled like animals for the fallen corn bread. It was gone, down a dozen scraggly throats, before the sailor could get to his feet again. A couple of tough-looking Hopers in uniform appeared and hustled the sailor out of the room.

"Bastard," Knobby rumbled without looking around. "The 'bos at the end of the line were gonna go hungry anyways. Now . . ." His big shoulders shrugged eloquently.

The line started moving again. The man ahead of Knobby, when it was his turn, said with a sad, tired smile: "How about beef stew with some beef in it?" It was evidently an old joke.

"No beef in the stew today," the man behind the window said. He was large and sweaty, with blue jowls. "I'll give it to you without the stew, okay?" He handed the man an empty bowl.

The man stared, stricken, at the empty bowl. "I was just—"

"End of the line, bud. Start over."

The man's shoulders slumped. He headed toward the end of the line, carrying his bowl.

Knobby kept his mouth shut when it was his turn. He took his food and, balancing it carefully, walked over to the nearest empty table.

Gordon stepped up to the window. Through it he could see a dank steamy cave where men in limp white aprons toiled over cauldrons. He followed Knobby's example and took the food without comment.

He sat down on the bench next to Knobby. The other men at the table hunched over their food, surrounding it with their arms as if they were afraid it might be taken away from them. The man across from Gordon, pock-faced with a yellowish crust on his lips, caught his eyes and held them.

"Don't you want that, kiddo?" he said, and before Gordon could react, a grimy paw shot out and pounced on the corn bread.

There was a blur of motion, and the pockmarked man's wrist was pinned to the table by Knobby's gnarled hand. The square of corn bread tumbled out of his grasp.

"You like to broke my arm, mister," the man said, nursing his wrist.

"Keep your hooks to yourself, see?" Knobby said, staring the man down. He turned to Gordon. "Take your cake, kid."

Gordon looked at the corn bread. It was not possible for him to eat it after it had been handled by the pock-faced man. "I guess I'm not too hungry," he said.

Knobby stared at him in contempt. The corn bread lay in the middle of the table for the next few moments. Finally one of the other men said apologetically, "I guess I'll take that if you don't mind, mister," and reached out quickly for the corn bread.

Gordon finished his stew in a few hurried spoonfuls. The other men were already wiping up the remains of the skimpy meal with their corn bread. He was still hungry. He could have eaten four or five bowls that size.

After the meal, there was an inspection of their work tickets. "Annie Oakleys," Knobby called them. Most of the early arrivals already had theirs punched. "Splittin' stovewood, wouldn't you know it," Knobby sighed. "Well, at least I don't get to clean the toilets. Let's see your Annie, kid." He inspected Gordon's ticket. "Kitchen duty, huh? It must be that choirboy face of yours."

Gordon's partner in the dishwashing job was the one-eyed boy. "Just call me Blinky," he said when Gordon asked his name. A "blinky," it seemed, was hobo slang for any train rider who lost an eye.

"Yeah," he said, "I was riding the rods down Galveston when it happened. Live cinder blew into my eye. Burned it right out. I usually tie a handkerchief over the hole when I'm riding. Cold hurts inside my head if I don't."

Blinky was from New Jersey. His father had been out of work for two years. "We took turns eating, us kids. There wasn't enough food to go around. I was the oldest. The old man kept looking at me. He didn't say anything, but I knew what he was thinking. So one day I just left."

"Couldn't . . . couldn't your family go on relief?"

Blinky laughed out loud. "We *was* on relief. We got two and a half dollars a week to feed seven of us. It wasn't too bad for a while. The teachers used to chip in so that kids who came to school without any lunch bag got a sandwich or an apple or something, but then things got too tough for them, too, with all the payless paydays. Miss Foster, I know she used to come to school hungry herself."

When Blinky asked Gordon why he had gone on the bum, Gordon was embarrassed to answer. "My father died," he said, and that seemed to satisfy Blinky.

Gordon kept trying not to look at Blinky's empty eye socket. "But don't . . . don't you wish you could have stayed home?"

"Naah! Things are swell, now. With this eye, I can get a handout anytime. People feel sorry for me. Especially the women. If I knock on a door and ask for a glass of water, the woman usually gives me a swell feed if her husband's not home. And it's good for panhandling, too. I can make a nickel or a dime anytime I want. Peggy showed me how."

"Peggy?"

"My partner. He showed me how to snitch clothes, too. Off of clotheslines is easiest. But you can hook clothes through a bedroom window with a stick, too. A kid can carry a stick through an alley, and a cop doesn't think anything of it. I got Peggy that swell pair of pants right off a chair while the guy was sleeping. There was change in the pocket, too. But I got to get him a shoe pretty soon. He says we're gonna stay in Chicago awhile. It's a swell town."

Blinky did a lot of talking, but Gordon noticed that he didn't do much work. He stood there with the towel in his hand while the dishes Gordon washed stacked up higher and higher. Finally Gordon had to take a towel and reduce the pile.

When it came time to wash the greasy pots and pans, the scummy yellow soap the bull cook had given him wasn't much good. It just spread the grease around. And there wasn't much hot water, either. The bum who was supposed to feed firewood to the stove and keep kettles of water boiling wasn't paying attention to his job. None of the supervising Hopers seemed to care. They seemed to think the work was punishment or something, but they didn't care if anything actually got done.

"Excuse me," he said to the blue-jowled cook. "Do you have a Mystic Marvel?"

"A *what?*"

"You know, that sort of copper sponge. Or just plain Brillo. And a can of Sunbrite?"

A Mystic Marvel and Sunbrite were what Mrs. Hansen always used to clean greasy pots. Gordon had often helped her before he got too old.

"Look, kid, you've still got twenty minutes to go on your work ticket. So get back to the sink."

"Oh, it'll take me an hour to finish up. But I need some kind of cleanser for the pots."

The cook gave him a shove toward the sink. "You work till your time is up, see. And don't try to goldbrick again."

When Gordon and the other vagrants were shooed out of the kitchen, there was still a pile of unwashed utensils. Gordon wondered if they would be used to prepare the next day's meal without being cleaned.

They were herded back into the dining hall. The benches and tables had been shoved back against the walls and piled high. Whoever had swabbed down the floor hadn't done a very good job. There were little pools of scummy water everywhere.

"There's Peggy," the one-eyed boy said.

The crippled man hopped across the damp floor toward them on his pine contraption. His powerful shoulders lifted alternately with each step. He'd managed to wash the grime off someplace, and his shovel face looked spruce despite a day's growth of stubble.

"Bastards," he said. "I asked them for a shoe, and they said no clothes for guys passing through. Just the local relief cases."

He glanced ruefully at the ruined shoe. It had deteriorated visibly in just the last two hours. The sole was now almost completely detached. It was wound round with spliced pieces of twine to hold it on. Gordon felt sorry for the man. He was embarrassed that his own shoes were still in such good condition.

At the far end of the hall, the colonel appeared in the doorway, the thick ledger under his arm. His floury white face surveyed the milling tramps with distaste. He held up his palm like a traffic cop.

"No beds," he said in a satisfied tone. "No beds for transients. Just for locals."

Sheets of newspaper and the brown waterproof packing paper used by the railroads appeared from under coats and sweaters. Men flopped to the floor, one after another, as if struck by a mysterious plague. The floor began to fill up from the walls, which were evidently the most desirable locations.

"We better try the chapel," the one-legged man said to his companion. He turned to Gordon. "You want to come with us, kid?"

"Well . . . uh . . ." Gordon looked up and saw Knobby picking his way across the strewn bodies. He was moving stiffly, as if all his joints had rusted.

"That's okay," the crippled man said. He took Blinky by the elbow. "Let's go."

Knobby reached Gordon with difficulty. He stood panting, his clothing sprinkled with wood chips and sawdust.

"What was the peggy saying to you?" he demanded.

"Nothing," Gordon said.

"Stay away from him, kid. I don't like his looks. That punk he has with him, neither."

"He isn't so bad," Gordon said. "He just—"

"Didn't you get us a spot?" Knobby said.

"I—"

"For Chrissake!" Knobby exploded. "I thought you'd have brains enough to get us a spot."

"Gee, Knobby, I'm sorry. I—"

"Never mind, kid," Knobby said wearily. "Let's have a look at the chapel."

Outside, in the murky corridor, Knobby paused to take off his cap and wipe his forehead. His breath was making a strange wheezing sound, like an old reed organ. A coughing fit doubled him over. It stopped when he spit something into his handkerchief.

"They sell the wood, did you know that?" he said. "They get it free from the railroads for charity. Old redwood ties. Then they get bums like me to chop it up for a nickel's worth of food and they peddle it for firewood. That's for charity, too."

He started wheezing again.

The chapel was just as packed with bodies as the dining hall. All the folding chairs had been stacked against the walls, and the floor was a tangle of old rags with people in them. There was even someone sleeping on top of the piano.

"Cripes," Knobby said.

There was a half-moon patch of empty floor at the far wall. Knobby made his way toward it, lifting his feet over the sprawled forms. Gordon tried to be careful, but curses followed in his wake. The vacant spot turned out to be in front of a lavatory door. The door itself had been taken off its hinges. The toilet was overflowing and unapproachable.

"No thanks," Knobby said. He steered Gordon out into the center of the room again. By some miracle, there was a vacant space big enough for one person. Or it would have been big enough if there hadn't been an outstretched hand across the middle of it, fingers clawed, palm upward. Knobby picked the arm up by the ragged cuff and folded it back across its owner's chest. The man stirred and moaned in his sleep, but didn't wake up.

"You take this place, kid," Knobby said.

"What about you?"

"I'll find a spot. Or make one."

"All right, Knobby. Thanks."

Knobby sighed. "I don't suppose you got any paper on you?"

"No."

"Take some of mine." Knobby reached inside his coat and pulled out crumpled sheets of newspaper that had been lining it. He didn't look quite so bulky now. He peeled off about half the sheets and spread them over the damp floor. "Always travel with paper, see?"

"Thanks, Knobby," Gordon said, but Knobby already had turned away and was threading a path through the carpet of sleeping men.

Gordon stretched out on the newspapers. He pulled off his old sweater and rolled it up under his head for a pillow. It was stifling in the room. He thought of taking off his shoes, but he had learned his lesson. The shoes would stay on his feet, where they were safe.

He flexed his toes and felt the crumpled, comforting texture of the twenty-dollar bill under his sole. It was his passport to West Point.

It felt funny, going to sleep without brushing his teeth or washing his face. But his toothbrush was gone with the canvas bag. And there was nothing in the world that could have induced him to go near that lavatory, anyway. He said his prayers mentally, sure that God would forgive him for not kneeling.

He looked around at the huddled forms spread out around him in the semidarkness. There was just a pale illumination filtering in from the hallway doors along one side of the meeting room, but his eyes were getting used to the gloom.

He had the odd sensation that he was not looking at individual bodies, but a bodyscape: a single coagulated mass. It reeked of sour breath and fetid armpits and mildewed feet, like the exhalation of a vast dying beast. With an effort, Gordon dispelled the illusion and separated the flattened monster into people again.

The old geezer lying next to him, whose arm Knobby had pushed aside, was all nose and jutting chin, like a Punch-and-Judy puppet. Beyond him was a snoring man in a baseball cap, his round oafish face glistening with unhealthy sweat. And a slight form whose patched pea jacket had fallen open to reveal the unmistakable curve of a girl's breast under a sweater. Her hair was tucked up under a wool cap to make her look like a boy. The girl moaned in her sleep and drowsily pulled the coat closed again.

Gordon turned his head and saw a pair of eyes staring into the darkness. The eyes snapped shut so quickly that he couldn't be sure if they had met his. It was Peggy, lying on his back, breathing deeply and evenly. Gordon recognized the inverted A of the wooden leg on the floor beside him, its straps undone. He tried to locate Blinky nearby, but couldn't find him.

A disturbance erupted across the room. A drunk was trying to get to the toilet, stepping on half a dozen people. He didn't make it in time. Someone yelled, "You dirty son of a bitch!"

Gordon squeezed his eyes shut and tried not to listen. He couldn't sleep. It was impossible. He was just going to have to lie here awake all night and wait it out. And while he was telling himself that, he fell asleep.

He woke with a terrible taste in his mouth. It was light. Around him, men were moving, coughing, spitting on the floor. There was a drift toward the exits. The big room was half empty already. He saw a bum urinating against the wall, looking furtively over his shoulder to make sure a Hoper wouldn't catch him at it.

He lay there a moment, trying to collect his thoughts. As soon as he moved his leg to sit up, he knew something was wrong.

He looked down at his feet. Only one foot had a shoe on it. The other was wearing only a sock. The shoe that was missing was the one with the twenty dollars in it. He hadn't felt a thing.

He looked at the thing that had been left in its place. He'd seen it before. It was the sorry wreck of a shoe, its sole flapping loose and held on by pieces of twine tied around it.

Knobby found someone who remembered seeing the man with the peg leg leave. "The peggy? Yeah, he left before light, him and his punk. Stepped on me and woke me up. Guess they din't want breakfast. The Hopers, they keep the front door locked at night, but you can get out through the alley if you know how."

Knobby was furious at Gordon. "You got a good pair of shoes like that, almost new, you tie the laces around your wrist and you sleep with them under your head!"

Gordon was too mortified to tell Knobby that there had been money in the shoe, too. Losing the shoe itself had been bad enough. And it made it somehow more humiliating that only one shoe had been stolen. He tried to imagine the surprise of the one-legged man and the one-eyed boy when they had found what was inside.

"I'm sorry," Gordon said miserably.

They stood in the sour city sunlight, on the sidewalk in front of the mission. The cement was hot against the sole of Gordon's stockinged foot.

"Well, we got to get you a pair of shoes, that's for sure." Knobby sighed. "You can't go hopping around in one shoe. You ain't flipping no fast freight for Indiana this morning."

Gordon limped down the hot sidewalk after Knobby. A desiccated old storekeeper sweeping out the doorway of his secondhand clothing shop leaned on his broom and regarded them with disapproval.

When they were far enough from skid row, Knobby stationed Gordon in a doorway. "Now watch me, kid. I'll do it for you this time. Keep an eye out for cops."

For the next two hours, Knobby panhandled. His favorite technique was to startle some absentminded pedestrian by suddenly appearing in front of him, hand out. Some of them actually jumped. He avoided prosperous-looking men, and concentrated on those who looked a little shabby. He hit young couples, but never approached a woman alone, except for colored women.

"Fifty cents. Not bad for a morning," Knobby said. "Before the depression, I could make four, five dollars easy in Chicago. Too early for the hookers to be out. They're usually good for a nickel or a dime. And priests. If you give them a good story, you can get fifty cents or a buck out of them. Bucks, that's what we used to call a priest in the old days. Forget about ministers. They're tight with a nickel. Come on, kid, let's get you your shoes."

They went back to West Madison and the secondhand clothing store they had passed. The dried-up proprietor looked at Gordon with distaste when he limped in. The damp sock picked up sawdust from the floor, leaving a track.

"We need a pair of shoes for the kid, uncle," Knobby said.

The old man sniffed. "So?"

"A pair of thirty-five-cent shoes."

"Thirty-five-cent shoes I ain't got. Sixty-five-cent shoes I got."

Knobby stood in the middle of the jumbled tables heaped with goods, silent and stubborn.

The old man shrugged and shuffled off. He came back with a pair of black-and-brown saddle shoes. The soles were broken and the heels worn down. "Fifty cents," he said.

"What's he gonna do with those? Go dancing? Come on, how about a pair of clodhoppers. Forty cents."

The old man looked down at Gordon's feet, gauging the size. He went off again and came back with a pair of well-worn brogans. They were stiff with sweat and smelled. But the soles were thick, and the heels were only half worn down.

"I don't think—" Gordon began.

"Okay, we'll take them," Knobby said. "Forty cents."

The old man made no move to hand them over. "Forty-five."

He waited until Knobby produced the money. But Knobby kept the money in his fist. "The kid got to try them on," he said.

"Sixty-five-cent shoes you try on," the old man said. "Forty-five-cent shoes you don't try on."

Knobby handed the money over with a show of reluctance, and the old man relinquished the shoes. "Come on, kid," he said, and started toward the door.

When they were almost outside, the proprietor's dusty voice said, "Wait a minute. The boy can put the shoes on here. He don't have to go outside."

"And leave the old shoe here, huh?"

The old man said nothing.

"Give us a dime for the old shoe, whataya say?" Knobby said.

"What would I do with one shoe?"

"How would I know? Sell it to a peggy. Match it up to make a pair."

In the end, the old man handed Knobby a nickel. Knobby laughed in triumph as they left. "I got a dime, kid. Let's see if I can mooch another dime, and we'll get something to eat."

"He was kind of mean, wasn't he?"

"The uncle? Naw, he was okay. They fit, don't they?"

Fit wasn't exactly the word. Knobby had had to stuff a little newspaper in the toes. "Better than too tight," he'd said. "You want a little leeway."

"Will you take me to the train yard and show me how to find a freight east now?" Gordon said.

"Tomorrow, kid, okay?" Knobby said vaguely.

"But . . ."

"Hey, look at that," Knobby said with sudden animation. His eyes were across the street, and he made a move in that direction. "A priest."

"No tobacco, drink, or playing cards," the Sally said. "Or dice. No dice, either. Anybody attempting to smuggle any of those items inside will have them confiscated. He will be expelled, and he will not be admitted. Is that understood?"

The Sally was a plump, thirtyish man whose uniform collar was too tight for him. His face looked very young until you got close to him and saw the network of fine wrinkles that covered it, like cracks in a marble egg that had been dropped. He had trouble with his *l*'s—not exactly as lisp, but "expelled" had come out something like "expewled." He stood behind the counter under framed, faded pictures of General Booth and his daughter Evangeline, both in full uniform.

Idly, Gordon wondered how you could be expelled before not being admitted. He took another shuffling step as the line of naked men inched forward. It was a sorry display of fishbelly flesh, sagging bellies, and protruding ribs, of sores and rashes and wasted muscles in arms and legs. Knobby was ahead of him, his big frame marked with old scars. The line moved another step, and Gordon went with it, his clothes bundled under his arm.

"You can keep your shoes," the Sally said. "But check your vaw-luabwles here."

The Sallies ran a delousing station, as Knobby had promised. They had checked in at four-thirty, after Gordon had spent the afternoon watching Knobby drink up the last of the money that the priest had given him. Twenty-five cents of it had gone for an enormous plate of sausages and mashed potatoes and baked beans and a glass of milk for Gordon. Knobby had professed disinterest in having anything to eat, himself. Instead he had downed the nickel beers and ten-cent shots of whiskey until the last penny was gone.

"Might as well spend it all," he'd said. "You show up at Sally's with more than twenty cents in your poke, and they send you to the New Century with a bed ticket." The New Century was a twenty-cent hotel, like the Workingman's Palace, run at a loss by the Salvation Army.

When Knobby reached the counter, the plump Sally sniffed suspiciously. "You been drinking, brother?"

"Me?" Knobby said cheerfully. "Drinking?"

He dumped his pile of clothes on the counter and stood like a gladiator with his knotted muscles and old scars, staring the Sally down. The Sally blushed and handed him his ticket.

Gordon followed Knobby into a steaming shower room where sallow, emaciated men stood about under rows of showerheads sticking out of the walls. At the far end, a few men were washing out their socks—the only item of clothing they had been allowed to retain—at laundry sinks. An attendant handed Gordon a towel the size of a washcloth, and a bar of strong-smelling green soap, and made a highly personal suggestion as to how thoroughly he should wash himself. Shoes and the clothing tickets went on a wooden bench running the length of the side wall, where the showering men could keep an eye on them.

Gordon turned the spray on as hot as he could stand, and scrubbed himself raw. The scalding water felt wonderful. It was the first time he'd felt clean since the horror of the boxcar.

The tiny towel wasn't much help. He dried his face and hair with it and rubbed himself down. Before he could retrieve his shoes, the attendant was in front of him with some kind of canister and hose.

"Close your eyes." The attendant sprayed him with something that stung, in his groin, armpits, and hair. "Rub it in good, okay?"

Knobby already had his shoes on. He was scratching himself vigorously. "They're going crazy, the little bastards," he said with satisfaction. "I can feel it. They always itch you worse while they're dying."

The attendant handed everybody a flannel nightgown, recently boiled. They filed to the dining hall, looking like a band of scruffy apostles.

The meal at the Salvation Army wasn't much more filling than the one at the Divine Hope mission. There was a bowl of thin vegetable soup and a plate of boiled beans, with two slices of stale bread, probably bakery returns. The bread was thinly spread with margarine.

Afterward they were led to the chapel for a sermon, delivered with weary resignation by a spare, birdlike old man with an English accent. "Just try, fellows," he said. "That's all the Lord asks." Then they sang hymns while a stout woman in a poke bonnet played an asthmatic old harmonium. The hymns were mostly familiar and simple, and Gordon sang with a will. He was yawning from the food and hot bath by the time they finished, and the scene began to take on an odd, otherworldly quality: the rows and rows of scrawny necks sticking up from the flannel gowns, while the bums with their lumpy, abused faces struggled to follow the harmonium, like a choir of raffish angels.

The dormitory was a surprise. It had beds in it. They were narrow cots, packed so close together that they seemed another floor, eighteen inches above the real one. Each one had a stiff gray sheet, smelling of lye, and a thin blanket. The nightgowned men waded into the room, like people walking through a field of knee-high wheat, and Gordon saw that there was a narrow aisle between every row of three beds. The man in the middle bed had better not have to get up during the night.

"The Sallies're all right," Knobby said grudgingly. "Clean, at least."

Gordon yawned and rubbed his eye with a knuckle. He sank down gratefully on the nearest vacant cot. He remembered to tie the laces of his new shoes around one wrist and tuck them under his pillow before he fell into a stunned sleep.

He woke once in the middle of the night. A flashing red advertising sign somewhere outside gave a pulsing illumination to the field of swathed forms surrounding him. He wondered what had awakened him, and a moment later realized that it was Knobby, thrashing around in the next cot.

"Can't sleep," Knobby whispered. "Ain't used to a damn bed no more."

Knobby rolled himself up in his blanket and dropped to the floor through the narrow crack between cots. Gordon looked around the dormitory and saw at least a dozen more empty cots. Apparently there were others who, like Knobby, had been on the road too long.

In the morning, Gordon turned in the ticket for his fumigated clothing and got an unpleasant surprise. His right trouser leg was missing. It seemed to have been burned off in a perfectly straight line at mid-thigh. There was a scorched line on the other leg at the same spot.

"Hanger must've got too hot," the delousing attendant said laconically. "Next."

Knobby appeared at his side, big and menacing. "Aintcha gonna give the kid another pair of pants?"

"No clothes for transients," the attendant said.

"You can't send the kid out in the street like that."

"Sorry, friend."

"Them was a good pair of pants."

In the end, Gordon was handed a pair of greasy overalls that someone had left behind. They were too big on him, and had a triangular rent at one knee. He looked down past the rolled-up cuffs to his floppy secondhand shoes stuffed with paper. His transformation to bum had been completed.

"Come on, kid," Knobby said. "Let's go."

"Collect your work ticket across the hall," the attendant told them. "Two hours. Then breakfast."

"Oh, we never take no breakfast," Knobby said. "Just a little champagne with a crumpet. Come on, kid. Let's find you your red ball outa this burg."

"It's a glory," Knobby said. "A train made up of empty freight cars. It'll take you as far as Fort Wayne. From there you can pick up a Wabash to Toledo. Look for the mark on the boxcar door, like I showed you."

He stood blinking in the sunlight of the freight yard, looking up at Gordon sitting in the door of the car he had pried open. He had taken off his cap, and the bald head and wrinkles across his brow made him look old and tired.

"I'll remember, Knobby."

"You're dumb not to stay in Chicago, at least till you make a road stake. You could have it in a week. Kid looks like you, there's a poke-out at every kitchen door."

"I've got to get moving, Knobby. I told you, I have someplace I have to go to."

"Yeah, yeah. Look, here's a jug of water and a cheese sandwich I got you. Never travel without a jug of water. You get locked in a car, you could be dead by the time they open it at some yard."

He passed up a gallon wine jug and a sandwich wrapped in wax paper. Knobby had made Gordon wait in Grant Park for an hour while he went off on an expedition.

"Thanks, Knobby."

Knobby looked uncomfortable. He fumbled in his jacket pocket. "You better take this, too. Don't worry, it ain't stolen. I got it in a hock shop."

He handed Gordon a wicked-looking folding knife. Its blade was at least five inches long.

"Go on, take it," he said harshly. "You hit a jungle, you just flash it, see, like you're testing the blade with your thumb. The jockers won't bother you then."

Silently, Gordon pocketed the knife.

Somewhere ahead, a bell clanged three times. Knobby glanced nervously down the track.

"Remember what I said about keeping your legs inside. And if you hafta get off a moving train, you hang down by your arms and you let your feet touch first. You take great big steps. You lean back, then you let go. You don't want to end up a crip."

"I understand, Knobby."

Air hoses hissed. Freight cars grated and crunched all down the line. The train jerked into motion.

"So long, Knobby. Thanks for everything."

Knobby stood watching, his gnarled fists clenched, as the open doorway began to move past him. "Aaah!" he said, and with a sudden motion he swung himself aboard.

"What the hell," he said, not looking at Gordon, "I might as well go as far as Fort Wayne."

10

Rain spattered against the taxicab window. Pamela Sinclair looked out and saw a dreary street with some kind of factory chimney at the end of it. It was a street of sagging frame houses and wooden storefronts, some of them boarded up. There was a smell of brick dust in the air.

The cab pulled up in front of a dilapidated Victorian house with an untended front yard. The driver turned around, one arm draped over the seat. He was a stocky redhead with freckles spattered across a rustic face.

"This is it, miss," he said. "Number two-forty. You sure you got the right place?"

She wiped a little clear patch on the fogged glass and peered out. A tarnished plate on the gatepost said HAROLD McKAY, M.D.

"Yes," she said.

"That's fifty cents," he said apologetically. "Being across the river and this part of town."

She opened her purse and dug for change among the crisp twenty-dollar bills that Carl had given her. The driver's eyes widened when he saw the quarter tip.

"Thank *you*, miss. Do you want me to wait?"

"What . . . ? Oh, no, I don't think so."

He came around the side and opened the door for her. "I'm sorry I don't have an umbrella. Here, take my paper."

"Thank you." She spread the crumpled newspaper over her head and ran for the porch, hampered by her tight skirt. The house was set well back, and by the time she reached shelter her powder-blue suit was soaked, and despite the newspaper, her fine blond hair was limp around the edges of the little cloche.

She thought she saw a flutter of grayish curtains out of the corner of her eye. Before she could use the knocker, the door opened and she was facing a blowsy raw-cheeked woman in a faded kimono.

"Excuse me," Pamela said. "I'm Mrs. . . . Mrs. Brown. I called Dr. McKay from—"

"Get in quick, honey," the woman said.

She stood dripping in the foyer. "He said . . . he said . . ."

"I know," the woman said. "Wait here." She left Pamela standing there while she disappeared through a door at the end of the hall.

From where she stood, Pamela could see into a parlor with threadbare tasseled furniture and a worn Oriental rug. There was an odor of dust and chloroform. Her knees felt weak. She twisted the dimestore wedding ring that hadn't fooled anybody. It certainly hadn't fooled the cabdriver. He had called her "miss" without thinking about it. She was certain the hotel clerk had looked closely at her, too, when she registered as "Mrs. Brown."

She had paid for two nights in advance out of one of Carl's twenties. Two and a half dollars a night for a green-papered room with its own sink, twin beds with modernistic headboards, and a window that looked out on the main street of downtown Des Moines. It was a fairly good hotel, but not as good as the one she and Mother had stayed at during shopping trips to Des Moines in better days.

Carl had been utterly shaken when she had told him she thought she was pregnant. All the confidence had drained out of his square, blue-jowled face. He looked more vulnerable than she had ever seen him, and she felt sorry for him.

"This couldn't come at a more awkward time for me," he said. "They've got it all set up for me to run for the state senate next year. Old Schleswig's retiring. If they like the way I handle myself, it could mean a judgeship in two years. But they'll drop me like a hot potato if there's the slightest whisper."

"I'm sorry," she'd said miserably.

"Are you sure? You can't be sure, can you?"

She blushed. "I've missed my . . . my period twice," she said, dropping her voice.

"You mean you haven't been to a doctor?"

She was horrified at the thought. "How could I go to Dr. Davis? He *knows* me! Since I was a little girl. And anyway, where would I get the two dollars?"

Carl had agreed with her promptly. She mustn't visit a doctor anywhere in the county. He had pulled ten dollars out of his wallet, and armed with a cheap ring, she had found an old country practitioner some fifty miles distant. His name was Struble.

"You're two months gone, all right, Miz Brown," he'd said with satisfaction. "I don't need one of these newfangled mouse tests to tell me that. Let the young fellows carve up mice if they want to. As far as I'm concerned, all the signs are there. The fatigue you've noticed. The morning sickness. The urge to urinate more frequently. The full feeling you've noticed in the breasts."

Pamela had sat there numbly.

"Doesn't show yet," he'd gone on. "But you'll begin to notice some changes in your body in the next few weeks."

She clutched her purse in her lap. The thought of Aunt Ottilie being able to tell was terrifying.

"What kind of changes?"

Dr. Struble looked at her shrewdly. "Little pot belly at first. Breast enlargement. Nipples getting darker."

No! It couldn't be happening! Pamela felt her hands and feet suddenly grow cold.

"Are you all right, Miz Brown? Maybe you'd like to lie down on the couch for a few minutes."

She stumbled to her feet. "No . . . no . . . I've got to be going. . . ."

He escorted her to the door, showing concern. "You just go on home, and tell Mr. . . . Brown. Now, the two of you ought to be *happy*. Having a baby's a mighty fine thing—even in a depression year like this one."

Carl was coldly reasonable this time. He'd had time to think it over. "A divorce is out of the question at this stage in my career," he'd said. And then, with forced jollity: "Anyway, you wouldn't want to beat the baby to the altar by a month or two—and with a newly divorced man at that! People would be talking about it for the rest of your life."

"I don't care, Carl."

He patted her hand. "You don't know what you're saying. You've got your whole life ahead of you. Now listen to me. I've made inquiries. Don't worry, your name was never mentioned. Fellow I know down at the courthouse had a little trouble with his girl friend last year, and *her* girl friend knew somebody. A doctor in Des Moines. A *real* doctor, not one of these country women with a knitting needle.

It's safe as a hospital. Name of McKay. He had some trouble with the county medical association, but he's still got his license. He's a convenience to some of the holier-than-thou members of the association with rich patients that they're too yellow to soil their hands on themselves. He's safe as a hospital, believe me."

When she comprehended what he was saying, she went cold.

"No, I can't—"

"You can and you will. Now you're going down there, goddamnit! It's all arranged."

He gave her a hundred dollars in new twenties. "This is all I could lay my hands on at short notice without attracting attention," he said. "Estelle goes over the monthly expenditures like a hawk, but she doesn't know about everything I get in cash. It ought to be enough. Doc McKay charges fifty. There'll be plenty left over for a train to Des Moines, a hotel, meals. Hell, take in a couple of shows while you're there. That new Spencer Tracy movie that hasn't come to Beulah yet, *The Power and the Glory*. Think of it as a vacation. Listen, you can keep any money that's left over."

He thrust the money into her unwilling hands.

"Pam . . ."

"Yes, Carl?"

There were beads of sweat on his forehead. "You'll think up a good story to tell your mother and your uncle, won't you?"

"Yes, I'll think up a good story."

And she *had* thought up a good story, she thought bitterly. But her mother, lost in her own pink clouds, had paid no attention. "Have a perfectly *lovely* time, Pamela dear, and I think it's so nice of your friend's mother to invite you." Uncle Elroy had treated her explanation with sour skepticism, comprehending only that she was going to spend all night out, for two or three nights in a row. That night, before supper, he had read from Kings, Nine, taking special satisfaction in the part about dogs eating the flesh of Jezebel.

So here she was, standing in Doc McKay's shabby hallway, dressed in the nice powder-blue suit that was so impractical in the rain, and wondering how she was going to get back to her hotel room afterward.

The blowsy woman came back and squinted with puffy eyes at her. The woman's kimono was agape, disclosing a valley between heavy breasts the texture of corned beef. A thin gold chain glinted in the hollow. Pamela wondered who she was. Surely not Mrs. KcKay. And not a housekeeper, either, dressed like that.

"This way, honey," the woman said. "Try not to drip water."

She followed the woman to a small cluttered office in the rear. A glass-fronted cabinet filled with moldly books covered most of one wall. She saw a flyspecked diploma with Dr. McKay's name in Gothic script on it. A plain metal table was bolted to the floor in the center of the room. Over in one corner, a dented zinc kitchen boiler containing instruments of some sort sat on a gas ring.

A heavyset white-haired man in vest and shirt-sleeves got up from behind a scratched rolltop desk and shuffled toward her. He had a hound's face, all dewlaps and wattles, crisscrossed with little broken veins. He smelled powerfully of whiskey.

"She drove up to the door in a cab, Doc," the woman said.

McKay blinked watery blue eyes at her. "I told you to get off at the corner."

"It was raining," Pamela said.

"It was raining. Oh, that's good. That's rich."

Pamela stood rooted, not sure what to say.

He sighed. "Let's have it."

"Have it?"

"The money. You brought the money, didn't you?"

"Oh, yes." She found the wadded bills, the two twenties, and the ten from the change the hotel clerk had given her, and handed them to McKay. He started to put them in his pocket, then saw the woman looking at him. He sighed again, and peeled off the ten and gave it to her. She stuffed it somewhere down inside her bosom.

"All right," he said. "Remove your lower garments and get on the table. Delia will prepare you. Don't worry, she's a trained nurse."

Pamela fumbled with the fastenings of her skirt. She felt oddly lightheaded. It hadn't occurred to her that she would have to take off her things one by one in front of these two people. She had assumed there would be a screen or something. Her fingers were clumsy. She would have to wriggle out of the skirt, step out of it. And then there would be all the awkwardness of the garters and the stockings. And what would she do about the slip? Hike it up? She wished she'd given more thought to a practical costume. But what sort of an outfit did you wear to an abortion anyway?

Doc McKay had turned away. He was washing his hands at a sink against the wall.

"Don't be shy, honey," the woman named Delia said. "Doc's seen a million of them. Here, you might as well give me the jacket too. I'll hang it up so it won't get wrinkled."

The table was cold against her spine. It wasn't even a proper examination table. It was too short to stretch out on, but of course she was going to have to elevate her knees anyway. Delia was swabbing her with something cool and astringent.

"I can't shave you," the woman said cheerfully. "There can't be any

signs of medical attention. Just in case. But don't worry, honey. Everything'll be all sterile. A girl doesn't walk away from Doc McKay's with
septicemia. That's the last thing we want."

Pamela was rigid with tension. She was listening with only half an
ear to the woman's babble. Her head was swimming from her tipped-
back position and the closeness of the room. So she wasn't paying attention when the woman suddenly leaned over and whispered in her
ear:

"You'll burn in *hell.*"

Pamela's head jerked up. She thought she had imagined the words.
They rang in her head like a voice left over from a dream. The
woman's rouged and swollen face was close to hers, the eyes shiny
with malevolence.

"What?"

She tried to sit up, but the woman pushed her down again.

"It's a sin," the woman hissed. "Don't you know it's a *sin?* You're
murdering your *baby* and you'll burn in *hell* for it."

Pamela gasped. She felt as if she were suffocating. "Please," she
whispered, "please . . ." She felt the sudden tears welling up in her
eyes, blurring the mottled cheeks that crowded her vision.

"Delia!" Doc McKay's quavering voice came from across the room.

The face was withdrawn. The woman was suddenly bustling with
brisk efficiency around her again. "It's all right, Doc. The poor thing's
just a little upset. It's only natural."

"Delia, will you come over here and help me with this?"

The woman gave Pamela a quick bright smile and went over to
McKay. He was trying to do something with the instruments in the
boiler, and he was making them rattle. Pamela blinked her vision clear
and saw his old hands trembling.

"Oh, Doc," Delia said reproachfully.

She went to the scarred desk and got a whiskey bottle and a jelly
glass. She poured the glass half full, measuring it professionally, and
handed it to him. He took it with both hands. He drank it down in one
long, grateful gulp, and handed the glass back. He wiped his mouth
with the back of a hand he had just washed. After a moment, his
hands stopped trembling.

McKay shambled over, something bright in his hand. Pamela
stretched her neck to see. He was holding a long stiff wire bent into a
loop at the end. All at once she was terrified. It was going to be now.
Right now. The woman switched on a green-shaded gooseneck lamp
and bent it to shine between Pamela's legs.

She smelled the whiskey on his breath. Whiskey for the doctor, nothing for her. It wasn't fair. Pamela felt an absurd childish resentment. Even the dentist gave you gas.

"Can't . . . can't I have ether? Anything?"

"Are you crazy? I want you up and on your feet right after this, sister."

"Don't worry, honey," the woman said. "It'll be over before you know it."

At the foot of the table, the doctor abruptly sank to his knees. The woman braced herself behind him and leaned over to grasp Pamela's ankles. Pamela, raising her head, could see only the doctor's pink scalp. The woman's bosom hung over it like a canopy. The thin chain she wore dangled free. A tiny gold cross glinted over the doctor's head like a miniature portent.

The wire loop was painful and scratchy sliding in, but it wasn't too bad until he forced it past some obstruction, and then there was a sudden wave of nausea. Pamela gripped the edges of the table, afraid she'd throw up. He was scraping now, scraping and twisting, all the while cursing under his breath. The burning rawness of it seemed to go on forever, then there was a bright stab of pain and it was over. The woman let go of her ankles. The doctor handed the woman a blood-soaked wad of cotton. She took it fastidiously through a door, and Pamela heard a toilet flush.

The doctor went over to the sink in the corner and scrubbed his hands. Then he had another drink to steady himself. The woman came back with towels, old soft towels that had been laundered many times. She wadded one up and put it between Pamela's thighs. As she leaned over, she whispered: "Your baby wasn't baptized. Now he'll burn in hell, too." Pamela looked up to see the expression of flushed malicious triumph and turned her face toward the wall.

They let her lie there another half hour, the metal cold and hard beneath her. She used up two more towels. Then the doctor came over and said, "You can't stay here, sister. Up, up."

"I'm still bleeding," she said.

"That'll stop." He turned away.

The strawberry-haired woman helped her get dressed. She expertly tore a towel in half and stuffed it into Pamela's panties. "There, that ought to last till you get back," she fussed. "What a nice skirt. You should have worn something a little fuller. Oh, well, I don't think it will show too much." Every move was agony. Pamela had to keep her thighs clamped together and move in mincing steps. She could feel the blood seeping, and prayed that it wouldn't soak through until she could get behind the locked door of her hotel room again.

"Here, dear, if you have any pain you can take these."

Pamela looked down at the little tin the woman had thrust into her hand. It was aspirin.

"Can I call a cab?" She was surprised at how steady her voice was.

"From here?" The doctor was outraged. "Nothing doing. There's a drugstore at the corner."

The wait at the drugstore until the taxicab came was a nightmare. She loitered by the phone booths in the rear, feeling the sticky dampness grow, wishing she dared to sit down at the marble slab of the fountain, while the soda jerk shot curious glances at her between customers. Then there was the agony of the ride back to downtown Des Moines, feeling every bump. And the long, long walk through the hotel lobby to ask for her key, feeling the secret warm trickle halfway down her thigh, almost to her knee. In her room, she wrapped the soaked panties and the horrid wad of toweling in newspaper and hid them in her suitcase for disposal later.

She was unable to leave her room for dinner. The thought of food nauseated her anyway. She woke by the gray light of dawn to find that she had soaked through the hotel towel, that there were spots on the sheet, but that the bleeding had stopped during the night.

She packed the towel with her things. People were always stealing hotel towels. It was the final mortifying touch, to know that the chambermaid would think she was a thief.

On the long slow train ride back, in a day coach like a traveling oven, she thought of Carl. There could be other babies, when she was a married woman, when the time was right. She stared out the dusty window and clung to the thought that she had done it for him.

Carl didn't like her calling him at the office, but when her train pulled in she thought she had better use one of the pay phones at the station to let him know she was all right, and to find out when she would be seeing him again. She felt she couldn't face returning to Uncle Elroy's tall narrow house with its spiteful atmosphere and constant bickering until she had at least heard Carl's voice again.

She got to Carl's secretary after the third ring. "Hello, may I speak to Mr. Fuller, please?"

There was an imperceptible hesitation at the other end. "Who is calling, please?"

Pamela knew the secretary had recognized her voice: the girl who called from time to time and didn't give her name. She recognized the stiff tone of disapproval that the secretary was never able to disguise.

"Just a friend."

"Will you hold the line for a moment."

Pamela waited. The big station clock said ten forty-five. This was the best time to call him. Carl never left for lunch before eleven-thirty.

She had to wait a long time: almost two minutes by the clock's second hand. She began to worry that her nickel would run out. Then the secretary came back on the line.

"I'm sorry, but . . . Mr. Fuller isn't here."

"Oh. When will he be back?"

"I really don't know."

"Well, will he be there later this afternoon?" She could sneak out of the house after noon dinner, she supposed, and use the pay phone at the Woolworth's to call him.

"Mr. Fuller will not be available this afternoon." The undertone of satisfaction in the secretary's voice was unmistakable.

"Oh, why not?" Pamela fought to keep the sound of panic out of her voice.

"Mr. Fuller will be leaving early to take Mrs. Fuller to a dinner at the country club. It's a special fund-raising dinner given by the county committee. Mr. and Mrs. Fuller are the guests of honor."

"Oh," Pamela said. But the phone was already dead.

11

The mosquitoes were thick along the riverbank. Gordon slapped at his neck and stumbled through the darkness after Knobby. A few scattered campfires burned dull red through the trees.

"The jungle's still there," Knobby said. "Sometimes the town cops clean it out for a while. You got the onion?"

Gordon dug in his overall pocket and handed the onion over. He'd dug it up in a farmer's field a couple of miles back. Knobby had said that a couple of miles was far enough away. The rule was that you didn't steal, beg, or make a nuisance of yourself anywhere within a mile of your jungle.

"Onion's always good in a stew," Knobby said. "Always bring something, see, and you're entitled to an equal share. Tomorrow we'll hafta hustle a gump or something."

A gump, Gordon knew by now, was a chicken. Live and stolen.

He tripped over a tree root, and then he and Knobby broke through into a small clearing. One side of the clearing was a wall of underbrush formed by a steep slope rising to the railroad tracks above. On the other side, a path led down to the river.

"There's the mulligan," Knobby said, pointing his chin at one of the fires. A circle of listless scarecrows sat with their backs against tree trunks, watching another man with a shovel handle stir something in a small oil drum that had its top third sliced off.

Hands in pockets, Knobby sauntered across the clearing, taking a circuitous route toward the drum. A few heads lifted as the two of them passed.

Gordon looked around at the hobo jungle, not knowing what to expect. The trees glittered with bright things—pieces of mirror, cans, tin pie plates, all hung from nails. A jumble of crude lean-tos sagged against the steep bank, pieced together out of scrap lumber, cardboard, tar paper, corrugated tin.

In front of one of the ramshackle lairs, an emaciated man with the beard of a prophet was diligently squeezing the contents of a ragged handkerchief into a cup. A discarded Sterno can lay nearby. Another man sprawled unconscious, clutching a milk bottle that still held a trace of some cloudy liquid. Despite the warm night, the bearded man was shaking uncontrollably. Gordon could hear him mumbling to himself as they passed.

A hand like a bird's claw shot out and caught Gordon's ankle. The prophet shrieked something that sounded like *"Gimmish, gimmish, awwwrrgh!"*

In a panic, Gordon broke loose and caught up with Knobby. He looked back to see the claw grabbing at air, and realized that the bearded man was blind.

"Damn crazy smokies," Knobby growled. "They'll drink anything. Canned heat, ether, anything. They'll dissolve illuminating gas in milk. Or gasoline. Steal the milk offa doorsteps, give an honest bum a bad name. Drink that smoke till it drives them loony. I ain't never gonna be like that, no sir!"

Gordon remembered the sight of Knobby lying senseless in the boxcar with a bottle in his hand the first night he'd met him, but he said nothing.

"Gas hounds and jungle buzzards," Knobby went on angrily. "What a place. Wasn't like that in the old days. Even a bum can have pride. He don't have to be a buzzard and eat some other bum's leavings. This was a good jungle once. The Wobblies usta use it on their way through, you know that? They had pride, I'll give them that. But when there were enough of them, they took over. They wouldn't let anybody in the jungle unless he had a red card. There were some pretty good fights, I'll tell you. But you don't see too many Wobs now. They stopped coming through here about 1919. That was after that Centralia thing. I hear they tarred and feathered those guys and cut off their peckers. The Wobs made up a song about it. Yeah, they had pride in their own way."

Gordon stumbled along, not trying to follow Knobby's ramblings. Knobby got like that sometimes. He'd picked up a pint bottle of what he called "good alky" at the last little town they'd stopped at, and finished it before getting off the freight here.

The ring of men looked up as they approached.

"Hi there, Shorty," Knobby said. "I brung something for your mulligan." He held out the onion he'd taken from Gordon.

Shorty stopped stirring. He was a withered little man with a pink shrunken face. "If it ain't Knobby Kerrigan. You staying a while, Knobby?"

"Just passing through. I ain't like you, Shorty. I ain't no jungle buzzard."

Shorty looked pained. "I ain't no buzzard, Knobby, you know that. But I got a bum leg now. I'm getting old. What's the sense of moving around? This place is as good as any. You ought to settle down yourself."

Knobby looked over at one of the hovering scarecrows. "You still here too, Dacey? I thought you were heading south."

Dacey started trembling even before Knobby stopped talking. It was a sort of impersonal, automatic trembling, like the shakes of an abused dog when someone talks to it, even kindly.

"It's tough down there, Knobby," he said in a hoarse whisper. "You can't get past Atlanta now. It's thirty days on the chain gang. I can't do that."

"Hell, Dacey, you don't have to go through Atlanta. You can ride the L and N through Birmingham."

Dacey shook his head. "It isn't the same. Not with Roy gone. I can't make it on my own."

Knobby turned to Gordon. "Roy was his partner," he said conversationally, as though Dacey weren't there. "They used to do wood carving all winter in Florida. Carve stuff out of cigar boxes. Then peddle it in New York. But Featherstone caught them on their spring trip. Killed Roy. He redlighted him. By the time he got around to beating up Dacey, the train'd slowed down some. But Dacey got broke up pretty bad."

At the mention of Featherstone's name, Dacey had started weeping. The tears washed tracks through the grime on his cheeks.

Gordon was embarrassed, but Knobby and the others paid no attention. They seemed to regard Dacey's weeping and trembling as an entirely natural affliction, like a cough or the sneezes.

Gordon looked more closely at Dacey and saw that he was smashed up indeed, like a man made of broken sticks. One shin bent inward at an impossible angle, so that Dacey had to walk on the outside edge of one shoe. His left forearm had an extra bend in it, too, and two fingers of the hand were mashed flat, as if stepped on. And one side of Dacey's face was caved in, as if the cheekbone had been splintered.

"What's Featherstone up to these days?" Knobby said. "He still working the Erie corridor east of here?"

"He's just as bad as ever, Knobby," Shorty said. "There was a young fellow come through here last week who ran into him. He got away with a few busted ribs, but he saw old Jake bust up a whole car of 'bos with that lead-tipped blackjack of his."

"Same tricks as before?"

"Yeah. He tries to smash a kneecap with the first swing so they can't jump off and run, then he comes back and busts them up one at a time later. Did fourteen men, the fellow said. Took over an hour at it. Some of 'em tried to crawl away, busted knee and all, but Featherstone just laughed and dragged them back till he could get around to them. This young fellow saw it all. He was hiding in the weeds. He was afraid to move, in case old Jake saw him."

"That bastard!" Knobby said. "Some time some bum's gonna get *him* with the first swat, then *he's* gonna have a whole car full of 'bos work on *him* for an hour."

Shorty shook his head. "Don't try it, Knobby. In case you're thinking about it. Old Jake, he has a new trick if he catches you with dusters or anything."

"What's that?"

"The young fellow saw it all. Featherstone found a pair of brass knucks in one 'bo's pocket. Oh, that made him mad. He saved that 'bo till last. When the train started to move again, he dragged him over to the track and held both his wrists down against the rail till a wheel ran over them."

Gordon felt sick. All his life he'd been brought up to respect policemen. He couldn't believe that such things went on in the world, and that nobody knew about them.

Knobby had fallen moodily silent. That surprised Gordon. He would have expected Knobby to fly into a rage at the last Featherstone story.

"What does redlighting mean?" Gordon said.

Shorty appeared to notice him for the first time. "That's when you kill a person by throwing him off a move-fast, sonny," he said. He looked Gordon over, then looked at Knobby quizzically.

Knobby scowled. "There a shack me and the kid can use?"

"You can have old Cal's shack. He died day before yesterday. I cleaned it out good."

"Old Cal, you'd *have* to clean it out good. He was the dirtiest old man I ever seen."

"You know what I found in there?"

"What?"

"Stones."

Knobby looked blank. "Stones?"

"Not that kind. His stones. You know. You remember the trouble he had."

"Oh, yeah, he was always moaning."

"Well he saved them. Every time he passed a stone, he saved it. Kept it in a little pillbox with the date on a piece of paper inside. He must have had fifty of them. I couldn't figure out what they were at first."

"What was he gonna do with them?"

"Beats me."

"What did you do with them?"

"What do you think? I threw them away."

Knobby frowned. "You should of saved them. Old Cal, that's all he ever made in his life. Stones. He prob'ly knew it. You should of put them away someplace."

"What for?" Shorty dipped a tomato can into the stew and tasted it. "Mulligan's ready. You and the kid can have those cans hanging on that tree over there. You tell him he got to wash the stuff he uses and put it back when he's finished? Look, kid, tomorrow you mooch the potatoes. That's your job, see? There's a farmer the other side of town. You hoe a few rows of corn for him, he'll let you pick over last year's potato field. You look like you're strong."

The scarecrows began to shuffle forward, holding out their tin cans. Shorty ladled the stew out to them, using a battered old saucepan that still had a handle. No matter what the size of the man's can was, he got the same measured portion. Gordon thought the stew was delicious, better than the thin stuff he'd been given at the mission. There were pieces of real beef and sausage floating around in it. Afterward there was coffee, boiled in a five-gallon can from a dozen individual contributions by hobos who carried little packets with them. There was even sugar, passed around until it ran out.

Later, while Shorty was busy cleaning up, Knobby took Gordon aside and said: "Don't worry, kid. We ain't gonna stay here long. Just a couple of days till I rest up."

But the couple of days stretched into a week. When Gordon pressed Knobby about it, he was elusive.

"What's the hurry, kid? The apples ain't gonna grow any faster, you get to New York a few days sooner. Don't worry none. I'll take you where you want to go. Sure I will. Didn't I say I would?"

Every morning Knobby spruced up. He washed his face in the river and shaved with a piece of broken glass. "I'd rather shave with glass, if it's broke right with a good edge, than a dull razor any day." His shaving mirror was one of the automobile rearview mirrors that were nailed to trees all over the encampment. Then he'd walk three miles to the small Ohio town nearby, or hit the country lanes, and spend his morning mooching his share of the mulligan.

He took Gordon along on the first few expeditions and pointed out the techniques. "A tough-looking old bum like me, see, I'm lucky to get a poke-out. They don't want me in the house. They gimme a sack of leftovers, maybe, and hand it out through the door. A kid like you, that's different. Keep that peach fuzz shaved, keep your hands clean. Look for a yard with toys in it. Look for a window with the ice card out. If she needs ice, she probably wants to get rid of some of the old food in the icebox. If the woman asks you in the house, wipe off your feet. Take off your hat. Don't talk much. Don't act like you *wanna* tell her your hard-luck story. Make her *ask* you, see. She'll ask you, all right, then you get seconds. You can say you got a little brother down the road who ain't ate. You gotta act bashful. I guess that ain't hard for you, kid."

At first, Knobby used Gordon as part of his pitch. He'd leave him standing conspicuously out in the road while, hat in his hands, he gestured earnestly toward him. Then he saw that Gordon didn't like it.

"Okay, kid," he said resignedly. "I guess you ain't cut out to be no shill, and I sure as hell ain't no punk-grafter." After that, Gordon was on his own.

He asked for work at every house he hit. There was a trick to doing this without actually having to do any work for your handout; the kid tramps who passed through the jungle called it "nickeling up." But Gordon wanted to work.

He weeded kitchen gardens, split stovewood, mowed lawns, dug post holes in the broiling sun. There hadn't been much cash in the town since the depression, but Gordon got fed, and most times got some food to take away with him—a leftover slice of roast, a half loaf of stale bread, a few cookies, a peck of somebody's garden beans for Shorty's stewpot. Sometimes he got a nickel or a dime, too. He washed the barbershop windows in town and got a dime and a free haircut. Once he labored for six hours chopping wood for a lady who promised him a meal when he finished. When the last cord was split, she told him to go away before she called the police. He helped with the haying at the farm Shorty had told him about, the one where the farmer let hobos from the jungle dig for last year's unharvested potatoes. He worked hard and well for two days, not for money but for the hearty country meals that the farmer apologetically said were all he could afford. When the haying was finished, the farmer gave him fifty cents anyway, then offered him a job if he would stay on. There would be no money; just a roof over his head, his clothes, and all he could eat at the family table.

But Gordon needed money.

He had started a special fund for the outfit he would need to present himself at West Point. He kept it tied in a handkerchief, hanging down inside the waist of his overalls the way Knobby had shown him, each coin wrapped separately in a piece of newspaper so it wouldn't clink.

Only money he had worked for went into the special fund. Any money he got as a handout he gave to Shorty for the running of the camp.

He had a revised budget worked out. A suit was out of the question now. He could do it for six dollars, not counting the shoes. A dollar for a white shirt and a tie. Two dollars for a pair of pants. Two dollars for a pullover sweater. A dollar for socks and underwear.

He had over a dollar saved already. Surely he could earn the other five before September. He had almost two months.

When he had exhausted himself working, or worn himself out walking, he would return to the hobo jungle. If Knobby had not returned yet, he would help Shorty with the few simple chores—gathering firewood or cleaning up—or talk to one of the bums.

Nobody bothered him. New arrivals at the jungle were encouraged by Shorty to believe that Gordon was Knobby's preshun. One look at Knobby's craggy face and scarred fists was enough to intimidate even the toughest jockers. "You don't care what they think, kid," Knobby said. "They're just grease tails."

Gordon enjoyed talking to Dacey, the broken-up wood-carver, once he got used to Dacey's fits of weeping and trembling. They didn't mean anything. Dacey would go right on talking through them, like a determined person with a stammer. If you couldn't understand what he was saying, you would wait until he got enough control of himself to try again.

"J-just a g-good sharp jackknife is all you need, G-Gordon," Dacey said, his fingers flying. A shower of wood chips fell to the floor continuously while he worked.

"Gosh, Mr. Dacey, how long does it take you to make one of those?"

"This little dresser? A couple of hours."

Dacey seemed happy while he worked. He lost himself in the job, and sometimes forgot to tremble for an hour or more.

"I never saw anything like that before," Gordon said admiringly.

The object Dacey was whittling was a miniature dresser, complete with three little drawers that worked, painstakingly carved claw feet, and an elaborately framed mirror fitted with an oval glass pried from a wrecked auto in the town dump.

It was made entirely from thin, built-up layers of soft orange-crate wood. The walls of Dacey's thin shanty were stacked with broken packing crates and cigar boxes he had scrounged. They bore labels like "Huston's Digestive Biscuits" and "Florida Fruit Company."

"Oh, lots of tramps carve. Didn't you ever see a bird tree? Those're always popular. Little wooden tree with dozens and dozens of birds covering the branches. Some tramps like to do jewelry boxes. Roy and me used to like to carve toys for the children. Once we made a whole circus with over five hundred pieces. That was before . . . before . . ."

Dacey's teeth had begun to chatter. His hand was shaking so badly that he had to stop carving. Shorty had told Gordon that Dacey had never been like that before the railroad bull, Featherstone, had smashed him up. The beating had turned him to jelly inside. He dreamed about Featherstone every night. Gordon had heard him screaming.

The fit passed. Dacey went on, as if nothing had happened: "See how I do it, Gordon? You notch every edge, all over. Then you notch another layer, a little smaller, and fit it to the first. Then another, a little smaller than that."

The notched edges, built up in pyramidal layers, produced an incredibly elaborate surface effect. Gordon couldn't believe it had all been done with a pocket knife.

"It's beautiful, Mr. Dacey."

Dacey was pleased. "I'll make you something tomorrow, Gordon. A pencil box, maybe. This one I'm making now is for a dollhouse. I'm making a whole set of dollhouse furniture for a little girl in town. Chairs, beds, everything. Her mother's going to give it to her for Christmas. I get a real good feed every day while I'm working on it. When I finish the whole set, she's going to give me a dollar."

"Gee, Mr. Dacey, I think it's worth more than a dollar."

"That's what I've been told. One fellow I made a comb and brush holder for, he had me sign it with my name. He called it . . . what did he say? . . . 'folk art.' Imagine that. He said it would be in a museum some day."

Knobby came back then. He had a bottle with him. That meant he had been able to get money in addition to food. Knobby was taciturn. Gordon knew he would spend the rest of the afternoon and evening drinking himself senseless.

Shorty helped Gordon drag Knobby into old Cal's shanty and take off his shoes. Gordon would guard the shoes tonight.

Shorty sniffed the empty bottle. "Grain alky," he said.

Knobby never touched smoke, no matter how badly he wanted a drink. It was always grain alcohol or cheap wine or reliable bootleg rye. He was terrified of going blind or losing his mind.

"Someday somebody'll slip him some bad dehorn, and that'll be the end of Knobby," Shorty said.

"Why does he do it, Shorty?" Gordon said.

Shorty's face split in a toothless grin. "All bums drink, kid," he said.

"He's getting worse, isn't he?"

"Well . . . he's relaxing his standards while he's stopping here. You don't have to keep your wits that sharp when you're not on the road."

"He's getting worse," Gordon said stubbornly.

Shorty sighed. "He's got shack fever."

"Shack fever? What's that?"

"That's when you're afraid to hop a freight anymore, kid."

"Knobby? Afraid?"

"It's been building up a long time, kid. He stays here a little longer every year. He's been forcing himself, the last few trips. I think his nerve finally broke. He don't want to admit it yet."

"He was all right till he got here," Gordon said accusingly.

Shorty nodded sadly. "It's the track east of here that he's afraid of. That bull that works the Erie shore. Jake Featherstone."

"That's not true! Knobby told me he *enjoys* outwitting Featherstone. It's a kind of game with him."

Shorty glanced over at the comatose bulk of Knobby. "He got it into his head that he's gonna die, and that Featherstone's gonna kill him. I don't know why. There's worse bulls than Featherstone. Knobby got away from Humpy Davis himself once. He's got away from Featherstone without a scratch. He can do it again. And anyway, the chances of running into Featherstone are about a thousand to one. He can't be everywhere. He ain't the devil."

Knobby made a moaning sound in his sleep. He raised both fists in an odd gesture, then let his hands drop.

"You shouldn't have told him that story when we got here, Shorty," Gordon said.

"If I hadn'ta told him, he woulda heard it from some 'bo passing through. It's a jungle story now. Anyway, I'm glad I told him. He's got to make up his mind to settle down 'stead of pushing himself all the time for one more trip, and one more after that."

"It would kill Knobby to settle down. He told me he never wants to be a jungle buzzard."

"Listen, kid, what do you know? Knobby's an old man, don't you know that? He's sick. He can't grab iron no more. It'll kill him if he keeps it up. And it won't be Featherstone what kills him, either. He'll slip off a roof, or freeze to death in a boxcar goin' across the Hump."

"He'd rather go that way than die a little bit at a time."

"It's his time, kid. He held it off a long time, but it's his time to wrap himself up in that Tokay blanket."

The image of the smokies at the far end of the encampment flashed through Gordon's mind. Angrily he rejected it.

"You just want him here, that's all," he said bitterly. "You don't care if it turns him into another rumdum. You're afraid of getting old and dying alone yourself, aren't you? *Aren't* you? And you know that Knobby brings back more food and stuff than anybody else!"

Shorty looked at Gordon sharply. The squashed pink face turned away for a moment. When Shorty finally turned back to Gordon, his tone was different.

"He needs peace, don't you understand that? I don't know what he thinks he owes you, kid. Maybe you remind him of his own kid. If he's still alive, he's old enough to be your father, but the last time Knobby snuck back to look at him through the window, he must of been about your age. Don't you understand that Knobby's driving himself bananas trying to get up enough nerve to grab iron one more time? And it's your fault."

All at once Gordon felt guilty. He looked away.

Shorty pressed his advantage. "You owe *him,* don't you, kid?"

Gordon remembered the shadowy boxcar and the three menacing tramps. "Yes," he said.

"You want to do Knobby a favor?"

"Sure I do."

Shorty leaned forward. "Take off by yourself, kid," he said softly. "Some time when Knobby ain't around. Leave him be. I'll take care of him. He'll keep on hitting the bottle, sure. But I'll see he don't become no woody."

The mouth in the center of the collapsed face closed and disappeared into its crease. Shorty looked at Gordon thoughtfully for a moment, then got up and left the shack. Over on the pile of corrugated cardboard that served him for a bed, Knobby was twitching and moaning, in the throes of a nightmare. Gordon strained to hear what he was saying.

"Don't do it, Jake," Knobby was pleading. "This is my last ride, I promise you."

Gordon hesitated at the gate to the dooryard, looking for a clue. It was a white frame house in need of paint, like so many others in the town. The grass grew tall, full of weeds and dandelions, and some garden tools had been left out to rust. Not a promising sign. But there was a chalked symbol on the gatepost that had been left there by some tramp long ago—half rubbed out but still visible. It was the bisected circle that Knobby said meant "soft touch." Under it was another smudged cipher that Gordon didn't recognize: a sort of a fat *W*. Gordon decided to give the place a try.

There was no sign of a dog around. Gordon pushed the gate open. It gave a squeal of unoiled hinges. The fence itself was fancy—its pickets not running in an even line across the top, but graduated to form scallops—but its paint was neglected and there were a number of missing boards.

He climbed the porch steps and knocked. Inside, somewhere in the back of the house, a radio played dance music. The shades were half drawn. No one came to the door. He knocked again, feeling uncomfortable. He was just turning to leave when the door opened.

"You don't have to break down the door!"

The woman who stood there was perhaps thirty, with hair the color of brass and a sullen pretty face gone a little puffy under the chin. She wore a kimono, though it was already ten in the morning. The straps of a slip showed through the thin crepe. Gordon lowered his eyes so as not to see.

"I'm sorry, ma'am. I just wanted to know if you wanted anything done around the place."

She studied his face till he blushed. "Oh, you're the boy who does yard work."

"Yes, ma'am."

"I saw you yesterday mowing the Shelbys' lawn."

"Yes, ma'am, I've been working on this street for the last three days."

"I'm Mrs. Hoskins."

"Yes, ma'am."

"Well?"

He blinked. "Excuse me, ma'am?"

"What's your name?" she said impatiently. "You have a name, don't you?"

"Oh, I'm sorry, ma'am. Gordon."

"Well, Gordon, if you want to mow the lawn and clean up the yard, I'll pay you a quarter."

He could hardly believe his own good fortune. A dime or fifteen cents in cash was all he had been getting for lawns.

"Yes, *ma'am!*"

"My husband's away a lot. He sells farm supplies. Not that anybody's doing much buying these days. And when he's home, he's not much good for doing the chores. He just sits around reading westerns and expects me to wait on him." Her smudged red lips pouted at Gordon.

Gordon was embarrassed. He didn't think he ought to be listening to Mrs. Hoskins's personal business.

"I'll get right to that lawn, ma'am."

"Are you hungry?" she said suddenly.

"No ma'am," he lied. "I had something to eat this morning."

"I guess I can make you a sandwich or something when you finish. The lawn mower's in the shed."

The lawn mower was rusted into uselessness. Gordon guessed that Mrs. Hoskins was right about her husband not being much use around the house. When Gordon tried to push the mower, it froze up after half a revolution. There was no oil or grease in the shed, but a 1928 Reo Flying Cloud coupe sat up on blocks, also shamefully rusting away. Its wire wheels were laced with cobwebs. Gordon didn't suppose anybody would be trying to start it up in the near future. He drained a pint of thickened oil out of the crankcase and used it to lubricate the lawn mower. It seemed to work pretty well after that, except that it had a tendency to catch and buck every once in a while, driving the handle into Gordon's midriff.

It took him a couple of hours to mow the overgrown lawn with the recalcitrant mower, and when he finished, his hands were blistered and his midriff was black and blue. It was a hot July day, and there wasn't much shade, and Gordon had to take off his shirt while he worked. He didn't have any underwear anymore, and when he looked down past the bib of his oversized overalls, he could see himself, all the way down. But nobody else could tell, from the house or from the street, and it was cooler that way, so he didn't worry about it.

When he was through with the lawn, he picked up all the debris he could find, clipped the hedges with the rusty shears he found in the shed, and weeded the flower bed. Mrs. Hoskins hadn't bothered to plant any annuals that spring, but somebody who had once lived there had established a lot of nice perennials—peonies and daylilies and primroses—that were being choked out by weeds. When Gordon finished, they looked as if they might have a chance. After that, he lo-

cated some spare slats, and with a hammer, nails, and crosscut saw
that were rusting away at the back of the shed, he repaired the gaps in
the fence so that the scalloped effect was unbroken. If the Hoskinses,
he thought, ever broke down and bought a can of white paint, the
fence would look as good as new again.

By the time he climbed the porch and knocked on the door, it was
already past two o'clock. Inside the house, he could hear the radio
playing the two o'clock story, *Just Plain Bill*. Bill was giving Elmer
Eeps a haircut. "Just stand up for what's right, Elmer," he was saying,
"and you'll always win out in the end." An organ swelled, and a Dr.
Lyons's Tooth Powder commercial came on.

Mrs. Hoskins still hadn't gotten dressed, or combed her brassy hair.
"Come on in the kitchen," she said, "and I'll fix you something." She
didn't seem to be much interested in the lawn or the fence.

Gordon fumbled with his shirt. He didn't want to put it on in front
of Mrs. Hoskins. He hadn't been expecting to be asked inside. They
usually fed you on the porch or in the yard.

"Don't bother about that," she said. "It's hot." When he continued
to stand there, she snapped impatiently: "Will you get *inside!*"

He followed her through the darkened house. It was cool inside.
From what he could see in the dimness, he concluded that Mrs.
Hoskins wasn't much of a housekeeper. Laundry was piled on the din-
ing-room table. Ashtrays were overflowing.

The kitchen was brighter, but just as messy. The sink was piled with
dishes. A coffee cup with a smear of lipstick on its rim stood on the
counter, with soggy cigarette butts floating around in the remaining
inch of coffee. The electric refrigerator was expensive, though—a five-
year-old Kelvinator without a coil on top. Mr. Hoskins must once
have been in the chips.

"Sit down," Mrs. Hoskins said.

He sat down at the porcelain-top table. His lunch sat in a little space
that had been cleared from a litter of mayonnaise and mustard jars,
open cereal boxes, soap flakes, ashtrays, dirty dishes, and a pitcher of
cream that had gone sour. The lunch consisted of a bologna sandwich,
a glass of milk, and a big wedge of store pie still in its tin plate. There
was a faint trace of lipstick on the rim of the glass.

"Go on," she said. "I'll bet you're plenty hungry."

Gordon was ravenous, but he was embarrassed to eat in front of
Mrs. Hoskins. She hung around the kitchen, watching him. A lot of
women liked to watch a tramp eat, but it always made Gordon uncomfortable. When he finished his milk, she poured him another glass,
then put the bottle back in the refrigerator. He didn't hear the refrig-

erator door close behind him. "God, it's hot!" she said. "Days like this, I could stand in front of the refrigerator all day, cooling off."

He went on eating stolidly, not turning around to answer. With half an ear he listened to the music on the radio. He wished it were later in the afternoon, so that he could have heard part of *Jack Armstrong* or *Buck Rogers*. One of the things he missed most since he had left home was listening to the kids' serials.

He didn't realize she was standing behind him until she leaned across him to put a piece of fruit on the table. Her hand rested on his bare shoulder. He stiffened, but she didn't remove her hand. He could feel the softness of her breasts against his back through the crinkled texture of the kimono.

"You have nice shoulders for a kid," she said.

Against his will, Gordon had an instantaneous physical reaction of the most embarrassing kind to the warmth of her body. He froze in the sudden realization that she could look right down the front of his billowing overalls and see what was happening to him. Before he could straighten up, he felt her hand snake all the way down inside his overalls and grab hold of him.

An involuntary sob broke from Gordon's throat. To his intense dismay, he felt himself give way, entirely without volition, the way it sometimes happened while he slept, even though he willed it *not* to happen. His ears burned with shame.

"Boy, you must have been hard up," she said. She sounded annoyed. "Say, how long has it been since you had a girl?"

"I . . . I . . ." Gordon couldn't talk.

"Never mind," she said. "At your age, you'll be raring to go again in a couple of minutes. Lemme just wash my hand in the sink here. You can wash out your overalls in the bathroom. We'll have all afternoon while they're drying."

Later, on the towel-draped couch in the darkened living room, surrounded by dirty cups and glasses and ashtrays, she said, "That was more like it. Get me a cigarette, will you?"

Gordon padded in his bare feet to the coffee table and got the pack of Chesterfields and some matches. When he turned back, Mrs. Hoskins was struggling to a sitting position, the pink slip draped around her waist like some crazy, complicated sash. He resisted his impulse to look away, and watched her while she pushed her arms through the straps and settled her breasts into place, and pulled down the bottom part to her knees again. He had discovered that she didn't mind being looked at. And oddly enough, he found that he didn't mind being naked in front of a woman.

She took a deep drag on the cigarette. "How old are you, anyway?"

"Seventeen."

"I never would have guessed it. You look a lot older. You're a good-looking kid, you know that?"

Gordon blushed. But he was pleased. The fact was that he had grown at least an inch during the summer and filled out considerably. He was hard and bronzed from all the outdoor work.

Mrs. Hoskins continued to study him. She blew smoke through her nose, and suddenly her eyes narrowed. "Say, don't tell me that was your first time, for God's sake?"

Gordon, in a state of confusion, mumbled incoherently.

She laughed. "Don't worry, you did just fine." She stubbed out her cigarette and stretched a fleshy arm toward him. "Come on over here, bashful. You look like you're ready again."

At the end of the afternoon, his overalls dry and freshly pressed with the help of the iron she had loaned him, Gordon prepared to go. He felt pleasantly drained. The afternoon's events already were beginning to take on the soft edges of a dream. But he felt changed, as if a burden had been lifted from him.

The nightmare of the boxcar was over. He hadn't thought about it once. The nagging fear of having somehow been spoiled was gone, erased forever. A warm rush of gratitude toward Mrs. Hoskins suddenly made his eyes fill.

"You better leave by the back way," she said. "Wait a minute, I want to make sure my snoopy neighbors aren't around."

She peered through the screen door, clutching the kimono around her. Gordon, intensely aware of the close damp warmth of her, of that strange female mustiness mingled with the smell of face powder and tobacco and toilet water, struggled for the words to express the way he felt.

"I . . . before I go . . . that is . . ."

"Coast's clear," she said briskly. She went to the kitchen table and got her purse. "Wait a minute, here's your quarter."

He stood dumbfounded, his jaws still working around the wad of words.

"Well, take it, dummy," she said impatiently. He felt her press the coin into his palm and close his fingers around it. She pushed him toward the door. "Come back tomorrow, okay?" she said.

Gordon waited until he was around the corner. Then he threw the quarter down the first sewer he came to.

Knobby was already started on his evening bottle by the time Gordon got back to the jungle. Gordon tried to talk to him, but Knobby was in one of his morose moods, staring glumly into space.

"Knobby, I've got to leave."

"Sure you do, kid . . . plenty of time . . ." Knobby took a pull on the bottle. His eyes were vague.

"It's almost August already."

"Mmmm, yeah . . . when the time comes, I'll take ya. . . ."

"I'm leaving tomorrow, Knobby."

"Yeah, yeah, we'll talk about it. Tomorrow."

Gordon gave up. "Aren't you going to eat anything, Knobby? Shorty's building a good stew tonight."

He couldn't get an answer. Knobby was far away, lost inside himself. Gordon got up off his haunches and went over to the cookfire.

"Here," he said, thrusting a sack to Shorty.

Shorty looked inside the sack. "Spuds? Is that all you could get?"

"Yes."

Potatoes were no accomplishment for Gordon. He had what amounted to his own private store of them. The farmer he had done the haying for had told him to help himself to any still-edible potatoes he could find in last year's abandoned trenches. He could go dig himself a peck any time he felt like it. Gordon always brought Shorty a few potatoes in addition to anything else he had managed to scrounge.

"You were gone all day. Didn't you get any yard work?"

"What if I did?"

Shorty looked at him shrewdly. "You bring back any money?"

Gordon suspected that Shorty knew about his stash. He could feel the weight of it now, hanging down his thigh in the knotted handkerchief. He didn't have to count it. He knew to a penny how much was there: three dollars and thirty-five cents—more than half of what he needed, not counting the shoes. The quarter would have made it three dollars and sixty cents.

"No."

"What happened? The lady stiff you?"

Gordon kept stubbornly silent.

"All right, all right," Shorty sighed. "I can roast the potatoes. We're having the minister's face tonight." He gestured toward the pig's head he was cooking. "That new guy brung it, the crip faker with the crutches."

"Shorty," Gordon said.

"Huh?"

"Is there a train out of here tomorrow? Going east?"

Shorty put down the broken-off shovel he had been using for a frying pan and looked Gordon in the eye. "There's a slowboat freight to Buffalo stops at the water tower in the morning. It waits there about twenty minutes."

"Thanks, Shorty."

"It leaves early, just after sunup. You can be on it before Knobby wakes up."

"Don't worry, I'll be on it."

Shorty nodded. "You're a good kid. I'll save you some bread and cooked meat to take with you."

"Don't bother. Can I take a jug?"

"Sure, kid, anything."

"Shorty . . ."

"Don't worry, I'll see he stays away from smoke. Old Knobby, he's pretty smart."

"Thanks."

"You'll make out all right on your own, kid. Knobby showed you the ropes. You learned from the best. I seen you toughen up since you got here."

Gordon said nothing. He fingered the knife in his pocket, the one Knobby had given him. The fact was that he felt a little scared and elated at the same time at the thought of traveling by himself.

Shorty became very busy. He bustled around the fire, clanging his makeshift utensils. "How about a hand, kid? Wanna stick those spuds on those wires and put 'em in the fire?"

Gordon woke up before dawn. Over at the other side of the lean-to, Knobby was snoring heavily. The stink of cheap wine filled the air. Knobby would be out cold until at least mid-morning, and he wasn't going to be feeling very good when he woke up. Gordon thought of writing a note, but there was nothing to write on. Shorty would say the right things.

He gathered up the few things he would be taking with him and went down to the river to wash. He was the only one there at this hour. He stood naked in the shallows and splashed himself clean, using the communal soap that had been left in the crotch of the shaving tree. The water was cold. It was still too dark to shave. He brushed his teeth, making a paste of the soap, then put the toothbrush back in his pocket along with the knife, the cardboard-wrapped razor blade, the matches, the hoarded safety pins, and the other necessities. Then he filled the jug Shorty had let him take with water from the river.

On his way back through the encampment, he was intercepted by Dacey.

"I heard you were leaving, Gordon. H-h-here's the pencil box I promised you."

Gordon inspected the little carved case. Even in the half-light, he could tell that it was exquisite. The sides and sliding top were crowded with tiny hearts, birds, stars, mystic eyes, and other standard motifs. Dacey must have worked for hours on it.

"Thank you, Mr. Dacey. It's beautiful."

Dacey's eyes shone with pleasure through the automatic tears. "I signed it with my name. On the bottom. See?"

"I'll keep it for always." He hesitated at making a further revelation, then decided it didn't matter anymore. "I may be using it soon."

The effort of speech had been too much for Dacey. He began shaking again, like a wet dog. "G-g-good luck, G-G-Gordon," he managed through chattering teeth. "B-b-be c-c-c-careful along the Erie."

Gordon thrust the pencil box deep into his pocket. Later he could put his razor blade and matches and other stuff in it. The knife he would keep separate, where he could get at it quickly.

"I will, Mr. Dacey." He left the trembling man standing by the path on his crooked leg, the tears running down his smashed face.

The freight chugged up to the water tower shortly after dawn, as Shorty had promised. It was a long, ponderous, straining train with an old, soot-blackened engine. It was hauling a lot of gondolas filled with sand and gravel, and flatcars with heavy, lashed-down machinery. A brakeman glanced at him without curiosity and went about his business. Gordon strolled openly to the train with his water jug, and tested boxcar doors until he found an empty. He slid the door open and crawled inside. The car once had held packing crates of machinery, judging by the splintered remains of a couple of big lids. There was sawdust on the floor, and plenty of thousand-mile paper in case the nights got cold. Gordon found a wooden cleat and spiked the door so that it wouldn't lock shut.

He settled in a corner and waited. Two brakies passed by outside, talking. After a while there were three toots from the engine.

Before the train started moving, a face appeared in the crack of the door. The door slid open two feet, and a big wide-shouldered man heaved himself into the car. It was Knobby. His rough-hewn face was blotched with the morning dreadfuls, and his eyes were bloodshot, but he attempted a jagged smile.

"I guess I'll ride with you a little farther, kid," he said. "I ain't ready to retire yet."

12

"Mama won't be coming down to supper," Junie said. "I'll bring her a tray in her room."

"Again?" Aunt Ottilie sniffed. "That is the third time this week."

"She isn't feeling well."

"In *this* house we all sit down at the table when it's time to eat. *We* don't have a house full of servants to do all the extra work. And it's high time your mother understood that she doesn't anymore, either."

She sliced off a tiny sliver of butter and pounded it savagely into the bowl with the potato masher. It disappeared immediately.

"I'll fix the tray," Junie said quickly. "I don't mind. Mama doesn't want very much anyway. I'll just take her some tea and toast, and one of those oranges."

Aunt Ottilie looked past Junie to where Uncle Elroy sat at the kitchen table, thumbing through his Bible. "That high and mighty sister of yours," she said. "Mary Sinclair thinks she's the Queen of Sheba. She never lifts a finger around here. As if that little money that Bradford Junior sends is enough to pay for three extra mouths to feed."

"'Charity suffereth long,'" Elroy said severely. "That's what the Good Book says."

"With butter up to twenty-eight cents a pound," Aunt Ottilie went on, her lips tight. "And oranges—twenty-six cents a dozen. Not that I begrudge them."

Elroy nodded agreement. " 'When thou doest thine alms, do not send a trumpet before thee.' Corinthians."

Aunt Ottilie rattled pots and pans. "And that other one, off to the Good Lord knows where! You'd think she'd be *grateful* to have a roof over her head. You'd think she'd make some effort to find work instead of mooning around being a burden to other people."

Junie prepared the tray, her eyes downcast. That isn't fair, she thought. Pamela *did* look for work. She'd even managed to find a job for two weeks at Woolworth's, playing the piano in the sheet-music department till they told her that her style was too classical and they got somebody else. There just weren't any jobs around here for *anyone*, let alone a girl like Pamela, who never had been trained to do anything useful. She was trying to teach herself to type now: you had to hand it to her. Brad was going to find her a job with him in Washington—but it was just going to take *time,* he'd said in his last letter. It wasn't as if Uncle Elroy was going to have to support them forever. Gordon was already gone. Then there would just be Mama and herself.

She buttered the toast, spreading it as thinly as possible, so as not to make Aunt Ottilie any madder. Mama liked it dry anyway. Her stomach was delicate.

She sectioned the orange, spreading it in petals to make the tray prettier for her mother. No, Aunt Ottilie wasn't fair. Brad was sending ten dollars a week now that he was working in Washington, and Uncle Elroy collected every cent of it. Uncle Elroy only made about thirty-five dollars a week himself at the gypsum company office.

She started toward the stairs with the tray.

"Now don't waste time," Aunt Ottilie said. "You still have to set the table."

"Yes'm," Junie said.

"And you didn't empty the pan under the icebox."

"I'll do it right after supper."

"Don't forget. You better do it before you do the dishes."

"Yes'm."

She mounted the steps, balancing the tray. She could feel Uncle Elroy's eyes on her, peering over the tops of his glasses. It made her self-conscious. She was outgrowing the brown jumper. She wouldn't be able to wear it to school this September. Where was the money for new clothes going to come from? She had asked her mother if she could hold back some of the money Brad sent her just for one week, instead of giving it all to Uncle Elroy, but her mother had smiled vaguely and said, "Now, now, dear, you'll just have to make do. You can do that, can't you, like a good girl? Your uncle Elroy works very hard to take care of us. You remember how Daddy was always telling us we mustn't be extravagant."

And then there was the other thing. Junie blushed, thinking about it. Pamela had brought it up. "You can't go on wearing those vest things. You're almost sixteen. You can't go back to school without a bra. If Mother won't do anything about it, then *I'll* talk to the old skinflint. I don't care if he *does* call me a Jezebel for mentioning it out loud." Pamela had tried giving her one of her old bras, but it didn't fit and it just made her look worse.

She pushed open the door to her mother's bedroom. Mary Sinclair was sitting propped up against the pillows in her silk bed jacket, looking pale and otherworldly with her fine chiseled profile and long black hair spread out on either side like wings. Junie immediately felt small and clumsy next to the fairy-tale vision that was her mother.

"How very thoughtful of you, dear," her mother said with the gracious smile that had made Junie's heart leap for as long as she could remember.

The room was lovely, too. It didn't look like any other room in Uncle Elroy's house. Mary Sinclair had made it into a room from their past life in the big house on Elm Street, with the old flowered curtains and the silk hangings and the fine old chiffonier that they hadn't been supposed to take with them, but that Brad had secretly transported one night lashed to the roof of the vanished Pierce-Arrow.

Magazines were spread out all around her mother on the satin quilt: *Ladies' Home Journals* and *Vanity Fairs* and the issue of *Collier's* with the exquisite Maxfield Parrish painting of dream castles on the cover. All of Mary Sinclair's subscriptions had run out, but she read the old issues over and over again, as if they were new.

"The tea's only made with tea bags, Mama," Junie said. "Aunt Ottilie doesn't keep real tea in the house."

"That's all right, dear," her mother said, pouring tea into one of Aunt Ottilie's thick cracked cups. "But I wish that next time you'd serve it in the good bone china. Things just *taste* better out of fine china and crystal. You'll have to remember that when *you're* grown up and running a home of your own."

"We don't have the bone china anymore, Mama. Don't you remember? We had to leave it behind."

"Did we?" Mary Sinclair frowned for just a moment, then her lovely face was serene again.

"Mama . . ." Junie was about to bring up the subject of her school wardrobe again, then thought better of it. Her mother was in one of her forgetful moods. Mama forgot a lot, lately. "I got a postcard from

Gordon in the afternoon mail. He's in Ohio. He says he's fine, and that he hopes to report to West Point early, if he can."

"That's fine. I wish Gordon had stayed with us until September. But he's always been an ambitious boy. I suppose he was anxious to get a head start on his studies. I sometimes wish Jeremy shared Gordon's ambition. You be sure to show Jeremy the postcard from Gordon at supper, won't you?"

"Mama . . ."Junie was close to tears. "Jeremy's not here. He's in New York. We got a letter from him last week."

A puzzled expression crossed Mary Sinclair's face, then vanished. She smiled brightly. "Of course, dear. He's going abroad. Your foolish mama! I do wish he'd go back to the university in the fall, but I suppose it won't hurt him to take a year off at his age. Travel is broadening."

"Yes, Mama." Junie bent over to kiss her mother's cheek. It felt as cool as marble against her lips.

"Now you go right downstairs and don't keep Aunt Ottilie waiting for supper. Remember that she's working hard to make a home for us. Shoo, now! Give them my apologies and tell them that I'm sure I'll be feeling well enough to join them tomorrow."

"Good night, Mama. I'll be back for the tray later."

As she tiptoed out, her mother was already reaching for the bright splashy cover of a 1929 *Vanity Fair*.

Cousin Winthrop and his doughy blond wife, Doris, were sitting at the unset table when she got downstairs. Winthrop was moist and rabbit-faced, a narrow-shouldered young man of twenty-two. He and Doris were living here until he got on his feet. Uncle Elroy had found him a job with one of the gypsum company's suppliers, but it didn't pay very much. The three bedrooms on the second floor were occupied by Uncle Elroy, Aunt Ottilie, and Mary Sinclair, so Winthrop and Doris slept in the converted sunroom on the first floor. Junie had the attic room, a hot airless space partitioned off under the slanting eaves, where she would have to share the single iron bed with Pamela until Pamela left.

"Where *have* you been?" Aunt Ottilie snapped. "Table not set and everybody waiting!"

"It'll only take me a minute," Junie said, and began hurriedly to set out plates and silverware. It did not occur to her to wonder why Doris couldn't have helped. Doris never did anything. She was Expecting.

Afterward, while she was cleaning up in the kitchen, she could hear them all talking in the parlor. The topic of the conversation was Pamela.

"Conceited," Doris said. "I don't know what she's got to be conceited about."

"Just like her brother Bradford," Winthrop said in his wobbling voice. "Wild. Drinks and smokes and I don't know what."

"What do you expect?" Uncle Elroy said. "Bad blood."

At first she thought it was Pamela, returning a day early from her trip to Des Moines to visit her old classmate from Mount St. Claire.

The door creaked open, and a long shadow leaped across the raw floorboards, thrown by the attic light outside. "Pamela?" she said sleepily, and sat up in bed to see the angular outline of a prophetic gowned figure against the unpainted wood.

"Who are," a harsh voice said. "Who are and the sister of a who are."

It was Uncle Elroy. She rubbed her eyes and struggled to make some sense out of what he was saying. He sounded angry, as if she had done something wrong.

"What's the matter?" she said, frightened.

He was standing by the side of the bed, barefoot, in a thin summer nightshirt. The light behind him streamed through it, and Junie turned her head away, but not before she had seen something that she knew she wasn't supposed to see, like the long shadowy outline of a hambone.

"Don't you turn your shameless eyes from me!" he said in a furious whisper, trapping her thin wrist in fingers of gristle. "Don't turn from righteousness now after looking upon sin! What filth has your who are sister taught you, answer me!"

"Uncle Elroy, you're hurting me," she whispered back, afraid she would wake up Aunt Ottilie or her mother.

He ground her wrist in his fingers until the small bones grated. "Displaying yourself. Displaying yourself in those tight clothes. Is that what she taught you, to tempt a decent man to sin?"

"I don't know what you're talking about. Those are the only clothes I have."

"Running off to give yourself to a dirty farmboy on the very day your thief of a father died. Do you think I don't know about that? Little harlot!"

He was breathing hard. He shook her violently.

Junie began to cry. She remembered the kiss she had shared with Floyd in the loft and felt ashamed.

"Pretending!" he hissed. "Pretending, with the body of a harlot!"

With a swift unexpected gesture, he tore her nightie open. He stared at the swelling buds that had grown to be such an embarrassment to her this year. A rancid, goatish odor came from his stringy body.

"Please, Uncle Elroy," she sobbed, her eyes wide with terror and shame. "Please go away!"

Somehow his nightshirt had become hiked up. She had the impression that he had pulled it up himself.

"Who are," he wheezed. "Take hold of the lust your brazen ways have incited and beg forgiveness for your sin!"

He was guiding her hand. When she understood what he was trying to make her do, she yanked herself away so hard that she broke free. She tried to roll away quickly, off the other side of the bed, but he flung himself on top of her, groaning. The suddenness of the movement made a slat give way. It rattled to the floor and the bed collapsed.

Uncle Elroy sat up straight, looking frightened. Junie took advantage of his inattention to roll off the caved-in mattress and cower against the sloping eaves, as far away as she could get. Uncle Elroy's turkey neck was stretched, his head tilted, listening in fear. Junie listened, too, expecting the sound of a voice downstairs, an opening door, a light.

There was nothing. Not even the creak of a bedspring, the sigh of a sleeper. The falling slat that had sounded so loud up here hadn't awakened anybody.

Uncle Elroy looked so scared and shocked that she would have felt sorry for him if she hadn't been so frightened herself. He lifted his face to the bare laths of the ceiling and whispered, "Praise be. Praise be for deliverance from iniquity."

He turned a seamed, forbidding face toward her. "Come here, girl."

Not knowing what else to do, she went over to him, clutching the nightie around her chest. He got stiffly down on his knees and pulled her over beside him.

"Kneel to the Lord," he said. "Kneel and pray for forgiveness."

Terrified, she knelt and prayed with him. She didn't know what he wanted her to say, so she moved her lips in silence. He seemed to have forgotten all about her. He knelt beside her, whispering harshly to himself for a long time. At last he rose creaking to his feet, the nightshirt hanging shroudlike to his bony shins.

"For the sake of your mother," he said, looking straight at her, "I'll say nothing of your wickedness. But your aunt Ottilie would not be so forgiving. So hold your tongue, girl. No one will believe the lies of a wanton and a slut."

She could see his chin trembling. He stared at her another moment, then turned on his heel. She heard the careful tread of his bare feet on the stairs, and a moment later the attic light went out.

She stayed up all night, afraid he'd come back. In the morning, after Elroy and Winthrop had gone to work, she went to her mother's room. Her mother was lying in bed, leafing through an old *Collier's*.

"Mother, can I talk to you?"

Her mother passed a tragic hand across her forehead. "Is it important, dear? Mother has such a headache. Would you be a good girl and get me an aspirin and a glass of water?"

Junie bent over and kissed her, then went and got the aspirin.

"Thank you, dear. Now you'd better go down and see Aunt Ottilie. She's quite upset with you this morning."

Junie gave a little start. "She is?"

"Yes, dear. She had to bring me up my breakfast tray herself. Wasn't that nice of her? I know you're on school vacation, dear, but you mustn't lie in bed all morning. You must try to be a help to your aunt Ottilie and uncle Elroy."

"Yes, Mama."

Pamela returned a little before noon, looking wan and drained. She dragged her suitcase behind her as if it had suddenly grown too heavy.

"Back in time for dinner, I see," Aunt Ottilie said sarcastically.

"I'm not having anything," Pamela said tiredly. "I'm not very hungry." For a moment her eyes showed a flash of their old fire. "Don't worry, I won't be an expense today."

"You got a letter today from your brother Bradford."

"Thank you." Pamela took the envelope. It seemed thick.

"Aren't you going to open it?" Ottilie's eyes glinted with curiosity.

"I'll read it later. I'm going upstairs to unpack."

Over on the divan, Winthrop sat reading the morning paper. He and Elroy almost always came home for the noon meal. Winthrop, with the freedom his route gave him, usually got there a little earlier.

"Item in the paper about your friend Carl Fuller," he said, a malicious expression on his chinless face.

"Brad's friend," Pamela said.

"Brad's friend, then. The county committee's throwing a fund raiser for him tonight. Looks like he's going in for politics in a big way."

"Politics." Aunt Ottilie sniffed.

"They say he'll go far," Winthrop continued. "Yessir, with a wife like that behind him. They say she goes everywhere with him lately. She's a big help to him." Winthrop turned to the comics page and immersed himself in *Homer Hoopie*.

Junie, busy setting the table, happened to look up then. She was the only one who saw the terrible expression that crossed Pamela's face, as if Winthrop had been telling her of someone's death instead of just talking politics.

"I've got to unpack," Pamela said, as if in a daze of fatigue. She stumbled toward the staircase on feet that seemed to be dragging weights.

"I'll help," Junie said, wiping her hands on her apron and following.

"June Alice!" Aunt Ottilie shrilled.

"The table's set," Junie called over her shoulder. "I'll be back in a minute."

She felt she had to talk to somebody or die. She was thankful that Pamela had returned. At least Uncle Elroy wouldn't be scratching at the attic door tonight with Pamela there with her. She didn't know what she'd do when Pamela left.

Pamela opened the suitcase on the bed. Junie started taking things out and folding them.

"Where's the blue suit?"

"I threw it away."

Junie was shocked. "Threw it away?"

"It was soiled."

"Couldn't it be cleaned? I mean that was a *good* suit."

Pamela sat down on the bed and passed a hand over her eyes. "Junie, *please!*"

"I'm sorry. Aren't you feeling all right?"

"No."

Junie hung back. She didn't know how she was going to open the subject with Pamela in a mood like this. "Aren't you going to open the letter from Brad?"

Pamela looked down at the envelope as if she'd forgotten it. She slit it open with her thumbnail. "More Brad promises, I suppose. Charm and daydreams."

The money spilled out on the bed. Money and train tickets. The two of them stared at it. Pamela snatched up the letter and began to read.

"He's found a job for me! In a senator's office! I can start anytime. He's arranged for me to stay at a women's residence until I can get a place of my own. And look at these train tickets! It's Pullman all the way! Oh, the crazy fool! How did he get his hands on so much money after having a job only six weeks? He even sent me an extra twenty-five dollars for expenses on the way!"

Junie, reading over her shoulder, said, "What's a legislative assistant? And what's a quid pro quo?"

"A quid pro quo, little darling, is a kind of sticky stuff like birdlime that your clever brother Bradford uses to snare legislative assistants and other rare species with."

Junie shuffled her feet. "When are you going?"

"Today. This afternoon. I'm catching the first train to Chicago and changing there. I'm not spending one more night under this roof!"

"Oh."

"Don't look so stricken, Junie-bug. You knew I was going to have to leave sometime. Things will get better here. I'll send a little money home whenever I can. And with Brad and Gordon helping out, things won't be so grim around here. Uncle Elroy and Aunt Ottilie won't be able to treat you and Mother like charity cases anymore. They're greedy for the money, you know. They've never seen so much of it, no matter what they say. That's why Mother's such an honored guest. They're terrified she'll leave. You just stick it out another two years. Then no one can stop you."

"Pamela . . ."

Pamela took her by the shoulders. "For heaven's sake, put a smile on your face. It isn't as if I've been such awfully good company for you lately. I'm sorry about that. I'll tell you all about it someday. Look at the bright side. You're going to have this bed to yourself from now on."

Junie twisted her face into a smile. "All right."

"That's better." Pamela hunted in her purse, then turned to Junie again. "Here, honey, I want you to take this twenty-five dollars."

Junie backed away. "That's for you. Brad wanted you to have it."

"I've got almost thirty dollars of my own left over. I'll tell you about *that* someday, too. I want you to take this money and buy yourself some clothes for school with it. You can't go bursting out of that old jumper anymore. And for heaven's sake, buy yourself a bra!"

Junie took the money and put it in the pocket of her jumper. "All right, Pam."

She helped Pamela choose the things she would take with her, and sat on the bulging suitcase until the latches could be closed. Pamela hugged her. "Good-bye, baby. Take care of yourself."

Sitting through the noon meal was torture for Junie, with Uncle Elroy sneaking furtive little glances at her over the tops of his glasses, and the four of them talking about Pamela and her departure, even while Pamela was still within earshot, on the other side of the screen door, standing on the porch with her suitcase waiting for the taxicab.

As soon as she finished the dishes, Junie climbed the stairs to the attic. She felt as if she were going crazy. She had to be alone to think about what to do.

There were sounds coming from her room, little mouse sounds. She pushed the door open a crack and peeked inside. Aunt Ottilie was in there, her back to her, going through Pamela's things to see what she had left behind. Silently Junie closed the door and tiptoed downstairs.

She was almost all the way to the front door, unnoticed, when Doris's voice sounded at her back. "June Alice, where are you going? You know the ironing has to be done this afternoon. And you've got to be more careful when you do that ruffled blouse of mine this time. The last time you—June Alice, come back here. . . ."

Junie went through the door without answering or looking back. She could hear Doris bleating through the screen all the way down the walk to the gatepost.

The August heat was like a furnace. People were walking in slow motion, like sleepwalkers, the men with their jackets over their arms, mopping their foreheads with wilted handkerchiefs, the women fanning themselves with a hat or a hand. The summer of 1933 had been one of the hottest and driest within memory. Hardly a drop of rain had fallen. The corn crop was a disaster. Junie had heard the farmers talking around the stores. It was even worse to the south and west of Iowa, they said. In Nebraska and Kansas, the dry topsoil was beginning to blow away. The farmers there, they said, only half joking, had to dig out their tractors with shovels before they could use them.

Junie walked downtown and loitered in front of store windows, clutching the twenty-five dollars in her pocket. She saw a beautiful dress in the window of the New Paris Dress Shoppe, a very grown-up crepe with jabot neckline, and realized with awe that she could walk in right now and buy it. But what would happen when she brought it back home? She'd have to tell Aunt Ottilie about the money, and probably she'd have to return the dress.

She turned away from the window and wandered across the street to the Strand theater. A Busby Berkeley musical was playing: *Gold Diggers of 1933*. The picture outside on the easel looked glamorous, with lots of dancing girls in frilly costumes. She hadn't been to a movie since her father died. The last one she'd seen had been that sort of sentimental one with Mary Pickford and Leslie Howard, *Secrets*, that she'd tried to tell Floyd about. She could go in right now for the matinee; it was only a dime out of all the money in her pocket. But it would be hotter in the movie than it was outside, and she suddenly realized that she didn't feel like seeing a movie anyway.

What she really wanted to do was to go back and see the old house on Elm Street one last time.

It was a half hour's walk in the broiling sun. When she reached the cool shade of Elm Street, with all the fine old houses set back on their lawns, she felt as if she didn't belong there. Suddenly she was afraid that she'd see one of their old neighbors. She bent down her head and walked faster. She went by some little kids playing jacks on the sidewalk; she recognized the Blake twins, but they didn't count. Probably they didn't even remember who she was; she was a grown-up to them now. Mr. Eldridge's gleaming midnight-blue Franklin was parked at the curb, but none of the family or servants was about.

She stood in front of the house for a long while. It looked different with its drawn blinds and untended lawn; Gordon had always kept it mowed and raked. There was a For Sale sign on the lawn. The windows looked dusty. She found it hard to believe that she had ever lived here.

All at once she felt that she herself wasn't real. What must she look like to people passing by? An overgrown girl with a thick neglected tangle of raven-black hair, her scraped knees showing in a brown dress that was too small for her. Whoever that girl was, it wasn't Junie Sinclair, not Junie Sinclair with a beautiful mother and dignified, important father, who lived in a fine big house on Elm Street. No, if that girl were to ring the Blakes' bell or the Eldridges' bell, the maid would tell her to go away. Who, in this strange new world, was there left to talk to?

Floyd.

She hadn't seen him since she'd moved to Uncle Elroy's. It was too far to walk, from the other side of town and then out into the country. But she'd already been walking for an hour and a half. From here, the Kinneys' place was only two or three miles.

There was no place else to go.

Floyd's brother Wesley was tying a wooden barrel full of bedclothes to the rear bumper of an ancient black Ford that she hadn't seen before, when she came hobbling into the dooryard.

"Junie!" He looked up and regarded her with grave surprise, pushing the tape-patched eyeglasses back up on his short inconsequential nose. "Floyd's out back, helpin' Purley load the truck."

Junie looked around, bewildered. The Kinneys' place looked strange. As if nobody lived here anymore. There were no chickens running around the yard. The kitchen garden looked devastated: the wire down, the pole beans picked over, all the root vegetables pulled up. The door of the cow shed hung off its hinges, and the stall for old Hester, the milk cow, had been dismantled. Wooden store boxes tied with cord stood piled on the porch of the house, and through the open door she could see only bare floors.

"Another hour, you wouldn't 'a caught us. We're almost ready to leave."

"Leave?" Junie felt an icy fist close over her heart. "Where are you going?"

"Oh, somewheres west," he said vaguely. "Things is better there, they say. We've got kin in South Dakota. Thought we'd stay there for a while, till we can figure something out. Then, maybe, California, Pa says. They say there's work out there for willing hands during the harvest season."

He went back to knotting ropes around the barrel, slinging them over the flat roof of the car and down across the windshield to the front bumper. Junie could see rolled mattresses and burlap sacks tied to the roof.

Wesley paused, proud of his work. "Ain't she a beauty?" he said, patting the car's tall flank. "Purley got her for fifty dollars, what we sold off the horses and plow for. Spare tire and all."

Junie mumbled a few words of admiration, then fled out back. The rickety old wooden stake truck, a one-and-one-half-ton Reo Speed Wagon that had been popular some years back because it was so cheap, was piled high with tools and household goods. The missing chickens were crated in a makeshift coop tied to the top. Purley and Floyd were still loading from the heaped baggage in the barnyard. Both of them were shirtless, the straps of their faded overalls rubbing against their raw sunburned shoulders. Floyd was up on top, straddling a mound of lashed junk, while Purley passed him up things from below.

"Floyd," Junie called.

Purley nodded a greeting at her, setting down a washtub filled with turnips and undersized potatoes, and wiped his hands on his thighs. Floyd climbed down the slatted side of the truck and sauntered over, squinting against the sun.

"Wesley told you?" he said.

"Yes."

Floyd had grown during the summer, too. He wasn't a boy any longer. He was a man, lean and hard, with stubble sprouting out of his cheeks and the same look of hollow deprivation around the eyes that his older brother Purley had.

"We couldn't even get a seed loan at the bank this year," he said, rubbing his cheek with an embarrassed gesture. "I guess you noticed the fields on the way in. We didn't plant. I guess it was a good thing after all. All the corn's dying in the drought anyway. We would have just ended up owing more money to the bank and Mueller's."

The mention of the bank made her feel guilty. "I'm sorry, Floyd," she said, and then she looked at him and realized that he didn't know why she had said it.

"We sold the livestock to some of the neighbors for about a dime on the dollar," he said, still embarrassed. "They don't have much, either. They're keeping it quiet so that the Mueller Feed Company won't find out. We owe them for two seasons. It don't sit right with Pa to leave owing a man money, but we got to have a stake to get west. I hated to see old Hester go, though."

"Floyd . . ." She sensed his agony and squeezed his hand in a gesture that startled them both. After a moment, they let go of each other.

"Sold most everything," he went on. "Beds, chairs, the plow and the harrow, the seed drill, even Ma's second-best cookpot that she'd had since she was married. Didn't get much for it. They knowed we had to sell. Too many other folks selling their things now. We kept the hand tools, though. We'll need them to get day work."

"I . . . I'm sorry to see you go, Floyd." She remembered her manners. "And Purley."

A grin split Purley's tired old-young face. "Heck, Junie, it don't matter none. Us Kinneys are used to moving around. The bank owns the house and the fields, anyway. Owns us, too, if you want to know the truth. Only difference this time is we're moving farther."

"And how are Sue Ellen and the baby?" she said politely.

"Just as right as can be."

She suddenly felt dizzy. "Do you think I could have a drink of water?"

Floyd was at her elbow, supporting her. "Maybe you better sit down for a minute."

He took her into the house. Mrs. Kinney was down on her knees, packing dishes between blankets in a box, her men's shoes unlaced and her gray hair straggling down her cheeks with the humidity. "June came to see us, Ma," Floyd said. "Kin she have a glass of water?"

"Why child, did you come walkin' out all this way in the heat?" she said.

"I didn't mind," Junie said.

"And you're living out your uncle Elroy's now, clear the other side of Beulah, too!"

"It's not so far."

Mrs. Kinney drew her a glass of water, then inquired ritually and unhurriedly about the health of her mother, her sister, and each of her brothers in turn, and her uncle and aunt. Then she looked out the curtainless window at the sun and said, "No way you can get all the way back there on foot by suppertime. They'll be worried. I wish we had a telephone. I'll have Wesley drive you back to town."

"I don't want to go back!" Junie burst out.

"Why, child!" Mrs. Kinney said in surprise.

"I hate it there!"

Over by the door, Floyd looked more embarrassed than ever.

"You mustn't say such a thing," Mrs. Kinney said in an even voice. "Why, you'd just hurt your ma if she ever heard you say a thing like that. Now if you stay out past supper, you're going to worry her."

"She doesn't know whether I'm there or not half the time. She forgets where she is. She thinks my brother Jeremy is still living at home."

Mrs. Kinney shot Floyd a troubled look. "Well, sometimes in this life, troubles cloud a person's mind. My own grandma Pultney for one. But that doesn't mean we should regard them less, remembering what they were. And anyway, your uncle Elroy and his wife will be worried about you."

"No they won't!" she blurted. Then, unexpectedly, she could feel the tears hot on her face. "I'm afraid to go back."

Mrs. Kinney was silent for a long time, watching her cry. Then she turned to a fidgeting Floyd and said in her matter-of-fact tone: "Floyd, you go on back out to the truck and help Purley."

Floyd left, looking relieved. Mrs. Kinney turned to Junie and said, "Now child, you just tell me what's troubling you."

Junie, to her amazement, found the whole story spilling out between sobs. Mrs. Kinney listened, her face grim and set. When Junie finished, she said:

"You can't stay there, child. That's all there is to it. Wait here."

She left the room. Junie heard her tramp in her men's shoes through the hollow house, and then through the thin walls she heard Mr. Kinney's voice, and Mrs. Kinney talking to him.

". . . the child can't go back there . . . mother is plain touched, no help to a young girl, sister gone . . . old billy goat, and him a church-going man, too, from what I've heard . . . only thing to do, and I don't give two pins for what the law says, it was the law that put her in that house with that old reprobate . . . Sue Ellen for company . . . seeing as how she and Floyd favor each other . . . when the time comes we'll find a preacher and make it proper. . . ." And Mr. Kinney's rumbled, indignant assent.

Mrs. Kinney returned, looking stern and definite. "You can come with us, child. We'll make room somehow. Shouldn't be any trouble at all, with a truck and a automobile, too. Wesley can ride with Pa and me in the truck. Purley'll have Sue Ellen and the baby in front with him, and you and Floyd can ride in the back seat with the older girl. You'll be a help to Sue Ellen that way, takin' care of the child. And land, we'll have to get you out of that dress, child. It's indecent now you've grown out of it. Sue Ellen can spare you a cotton dress to wear, she has three. . . ."

Junie found herself with her face buried in Mrs. Kinney's soft anonymous apron, sobbing in great gulps while Mrs. Kinney stroked her head.

"Hush, Junie, everything's all right. You're a Kinney now, as far as all of us are concerned."

Two hours later she was sitting with Floyd in the sprung back seat of the old narrow Ford, the little two-year-old asleep in her lap, crowded round with the Kinneys' possessions. Pureley was humming to himself as he drove, and the baby was making little comfortable gurgling sounds as Sue Ellen nursed him. When she turned her head, she could see the truck with its towering load swaying and leaning close behind them.

Ahead through the square windshield was a declining sun, huge and red in the western sky. None of them knew that in the Dakotas the dust storms were gathering.

13

A fog was rolling in from the lake, obscuring the stars. Knobby leaned out and peered into a white wall of mist. Gordon sat listening to the measured clack-clack of the wheels. He couldn't imagine what Knobby hoped to see out there. All that Gordon could make out was the occasional pole that loomed out of the vapor and marched slowly by. Somewhere ahead was a cluster of lights that never seemed to get any closer, blurred cotton balls making halos in the void.

Knobby drew his head back inside and eased the door shut. "I know this stretch of track," he said. "Feel that loose roadbed? After all these years, they ain't got around to fixing it yet. We'll crawl along like this till we get past the next town, then red-ball it the rest of the way. We'll be in Buffalo in an hour, kid!"

He couldn't quite keep the elation out of his voice. Gordon tactfully refrained from comment. It had been a tense journey. Knobby had made them change trains twice without saying why, even though the original slow freight would have gotten them to Buffalo long before now. Knobby operated on hunches. The reason for his jumpiness remained delicately unspoken between them.

Now Gordon was able to relax, too. He knew what Knobby meant. In an hour, they would be out of Featherstone's territory for good. There were no bulls riding this freight, nor had there been any on the previous two trains. Knobby was already beginning to be ashamed of his jitters.

"It's a piece of cake from here on out, kiddo. Hey, how would you like to see Niagara Falls like the other tourists? Can ya spare a day?" He laughed, and Gordon laughed with him. "Then the good old New York Central'll take us direct to Albany. I'll put you on a rattler going down the Hudson. That's where you want to go, isn't it? Somewhere down there? Me, I think I'll head up to Saratoga Springs for a while, see what's doing there."

He rummaged in the small gunnysack he carried. "Here, let's finish off the gut. I grabbed it offa Shorty. When we get to Buffalo, I'll blow us to a meal on the stem. I got a dollar."

Gordon munched his sausage. Knobby finished off his in three big bites, and was just taking a swig of water from the jug when he suddenly paused and tilted his head.

"What's that?"

"What?"

Knobby frowned. "We're slowing down some more."

Gordon listened and realized that the rhythm of the clicks was slackening. Knobby got up and stared into the swirling haze.

"There's a westbound stopped on the next track. They're making signals."

Gordon felt a series of small jolts and heard the hiss of hoses as the train ground to a halt. Knobby stood by the crack of the door, seemingly frozen. Outside were faint voices, trainmen hailing one another.

"I don't like this," Knobby said. "I'm gonna go out and check. Wait here and don't move."

"What if we start up again?"

"I ain't gonna be that far that I can't grab iron."

Gordon was uneasy. "Knobby, why take a chance on their seeing you? Why not stay put?"

"Wait here, I said," Knobby growled. He lowered himself out the door, and a moment later Gordon was shocked to realize that Knobby had slid the door all the way shut, violating one of his prime rules. He tried the door, but it couldn't be opened from the inside. He settled back to wait in the dark.

After a while, the train on the adjacent track chugged into life again. Gordon could hear the cars rattling by, picking up speed. It was a long train. It seemed to take forever before the last car clattered past and the sounds faded into the distance. And there was still no Knobby.

He heard a scraping sound, and realized somebody was trying the door. Metal clinked. There was the rasp of the drawbar and the door slid open. Momentarily, a bulky pair of shoulders was silhouetted against the white blankness outside, and then Knobby was in the car, breathing hard.

"Sorry I locked you in, kid, but the bulls only check the open boxes. You had a jug of water. The worst that could of happened is you'd go hungry a few days till somebody opened the car in Buffalo."

Before Knobby closed the door to its inch of crack, Gordon saw his face. Even in the ghostly light, Gordon could tell that the color had drained out of the weatherbeaten cheeks. He remembered Knobby's coughing fits.

"Are you all right, Knobby?" he said.

Knobby's breath came in accordian wheezes. "I saw him," he said. "Just for a second in the flare light, but you couldn't miss him. Featherstone and his big jaw."

"Are you sure?"

"It was him, all right."

"Did he see you?"

"He didn't have to see me. He can smell a bum, the way a weasel smells blood."

Knobby crawled over to the corner and hunched down with his back against the wall. Gordon had once taken a baby rabbit away from a neighbor's cat. For some reason, the memory came back to him now, the way the rabbit had just hunkered down, making no effort to run away, even though Gordon had pulled the cat off it.

"Look, Knobby," he said. "Let's get off right now. We can wait for another train. I bet we could even *walk* to Buffalo from here in four or five days!"

Knobby shook his head. "This train is the one place Featherstone *ain't*. I saw him get back on the westbound. I waited out there in the weeds until it was gone."

"Okay, then. But just the same . . ."

Knobby shook himself all over, like a dog drying off. "Aaah, what am I scaring you for? Don't pay no attention, kid. It probably wasn't Featherstone anyway. I get so I see him everywhere."

The train gave a jolt and started to move. Even Gordon could tell that the track had become smoother. The click of the rails came faster and faster as they picked up speed.

"We're on our way," Knobby said. He became determinedly cheerful and animated. "This ain't no Wabash Cannon Ball, but we're on our way. Hey, did you know the Cannon Ball goes so fast it gets there before it leaves? It took off one day, and it's up there somewheres in the sky." He hummed a snatch of tune, off-key. "Yeah, there'll be pie in the sky when you die. Hey, we'll have pie in Buffalo, kid. No missions this time, I promise you. Hey, you ought to come to Saratoga with me. The race crowd'll be easy pickings."

"Knobby . . ."

"Huh? Wazzat?"

"I'm going to West Point."

"I got booted off a train across the river from there, once, hadda stay in town overnight." He laughed with forced gaiety. ". . . tried to pling a dime from one of them sojer boys, like a dummy . . . they don't let them carry no money on them. . . ."

"Knobby, listen to me. I've got an appointment to West Point."

Knobby sighed. "Sure you have, kid."

"It's true."

"I know it's true, kid. You ain't cut out to be no bum. I knew that the minute I saw you."

"I owe you a lot, Knobby."

"You don't owe me *nothing*, kid!" Knobby said savagely. "Nothing! Who you owe, you owe your father. He's the one who made you. That's how come you turned out all right. I got a boy, too, you know." He laughed bitterly. "I wonder how he turned out, with a bum like me for a father. He'd be twice your age by now. That's why I left, so he could grow up without me around to shame him. There was this trouble I got into, see. . . ."

He drifted off into silence. After a while he lifted his head and said, "After you become a sojer boy, kid, think of old Knobby sometimes, won't you?"

"Sure I will, Knobby," Gordon said.

A smile relaxed the creases in Knobby's battered face. They sat quietly, facing one another across the car, listening to the peaceful clunking of the wheels. Gordon fingered the carved pencil box in his pocket, almost dozing.

He didn't know what brought him alert. Across from him in the dimness, Knobby's big frame had gone rigid.

"He's here," Knobby whispered.

"What?"

"Featherstone. He's on the train. I can tell."

"Where?"

"He just walked over the roof of this boxcar."

Gordon looked at Knobby sharply. He'd thought that Knobby was over that. "I didn't hear anything."

"You won't never hear anything, kid. He walks like a cat on those rubber-soled shoes."

Gordon shivered in spite of himself. "He *can't* be on this train,

Knobby. You told me yourself that you saw him get on the west-bound. You stood there and watched it till it was gone."

"I can *feel* it when he's near," Knobby said matter-of-factly. "It was like somebody walking on my grave when he went by overhead."

Gordon decided to humor Knobby. "Why don't we just shut the door all the way and lock ourselves in?" he said reasonably. "You said a bull never bothers about a locked boxcar. Somebody will let us out in the yards in Buffalo, sooner or later. Even if it's a yard bull . . ."

Knobby shook his head vehemently. "I ain't locking myself in a trap where Featherstone can get at me. He's gonna come back. That's his way. He must of seen the door open a crack. He checks everything. Some bulls don't bother, but Featherstone does. But he gotta check everything out first, line it all up, so that if there's any riders on the train, he knows where every one of them are before he starts raising hell. He's gonna take a nice, careful look at everything—the rods, the bumpers, the possum belly. And when he's finished, we're gonna see that big door open wide and old Jake come swinging down from up top like a gorilla, with that blackjack sticking out of his hip pocket."

Despite the words, Knobby didn't seem at all panicky. His tone was calm and reasonable, like that of a man discussing a problem in math-ematics.

"We can't jump off, Knobby. We're going too fast."

Knobby had risen to his feet. He was over at the door, his face at the crack, sniffing the air like a bloodhound.

"I foxed the bastard four times. Old Knobby ain't through yet."

"What are you going to do, Knobby?"

"I'm going to make a jerk out of him again. The 'bos will be telling the story from here to Albuquerque, and it'll get back to old Jake."

"But how, Knobby?" Gordon was getting frightened. Knobby's mat-ter-of-fact behavior had half convinced him that the detective was on the train.

Knobby raised his eyes to the ceiling. "He'll be at the tail of the train soon. Give him another ten minutes. Old Jake, he always works front to back. Then he'll start back the other way. All we got to do is keep ahead of him. Ahead of him and out of sight while he works his way forward."

"But Knobby—"

"That won't be hard. With the fog, he can't see more than a couple of cars ahead. Besides, there's lots of gondolas and flats to keep us out of the line of sight."

Gordon stared at Knobby, appalled. "But what if he catches up with us?"

"Look," Knobby said impatiently. "It's gonna take him at least ten minutes to reach the tail. Then another ten minutes to get back to here. Then he'll waste another five, ten minutes letting himself into this car and trying to figure out why we ain't here, and getting himself up top again. By that time we'll have a half-hour head start. We just keep ahead of him, like I said. Even a cat-foot like Jake, it'll take him an hour to work his way all the way front from here. We'll be in Buffalo long before then. We drop off first time the train slows down enough."

"But Knobby, how can we get up top with the train moving? The ladders are at the ends of the car. We can't reach them from the door."

"The same way Jake does with them gorilla arms of his. Only there's two of us."

He slid the door open. The wind howled past. Gordon estimated they were doing close to fifty miles an hour.

"Boost me up, kid."

The car creaked and yawed, leaning from side to side.

"You'll get killed."

"I'll get killed for sure if I stay here and wait for Featherstone. Like a rabbit in a trap."

Gordon got down on his knees and braced his back against the edge of the doorframe, facing inside. Knobby mounted his shoulders. The thick-soled brogans dug into Gordon's collarbone. Knobby was heavy, too heavy for Gordon to lift by himself, even with all the back muscle he had put on this summer.

They timed the swaying of the car, and as the car began to lean inward, Gordon heaved with all his strength. At the same time, Knobby hauled himself upward, his big gnarled hands clutching the edge of the roof. Gordon got all the way to his feet before pitching forward and falling on his face. He saw Knobby's legs kicking above him and heard the frantic scrabbling sound on the roof. And then, before the car could start to lean outward again, Knobby was safely on top.

His face hung upside down into the car. "I got my legs hooked under the boardwalk. Grab my wrists."

They locked on to each other in an acrobat's grip, and Knobby reeled Gordon in. For a terrifying moment, as the boxcar tilted outward, Gordon found himself dangling wildly, legs flailing. Then the car swayed the other way, giving him momentum, and he scrambled up on the roof beside Knobby, panting.

"For a minute there, I thought you was hamburger," Knobby said, looking down at the gravel. "Come on, let's go."

Gordon looked back toward the rear of the train. The cars were swallowed up in billowing fog. His imagination supplied a dark anthropoid shape crouched just out of sight. He shivered and followed

Knobby along the narrow raised platform that formed the spine of the car.

They crawled forward, driven by a dreadful urgency, scuttling humpbacked on their hands and the balls of their feet. Gordon, sucking wind through his open mouth, could taste the smoke and grit from the invisible engine ahead. At the gap between cars, they rose to their feet like drunken puppets, balancing themselves for the leap across.

The car after that was an open gondola, filled with gravel. The lip of the gondola was a good four or five feet lower than their roof. Knobby leaped feetfirst and sank to his knees in the stuff. Gordon followed his example. He waded after Knobby through the loose gravel, feeling it drag at his legs like a nightmare quagmire, while his nerves screamed at him to run. At the far end, Knobby looked up at the shimmying cliffside of the next boxcar. There was no way to jump up that far from their shifting footing. He motioned Gordon to follow, and straddled the rim of the gondola, his feet searching for the iron rungs of the outside ladder.

They were resting on the bumpers between cars, preparing to swing across and climb the next iron ladder, when Gordon happened to look up. He saw a shape pass overhead, silhouetted against the blind white sky. It was the black outline of a man with a big jaw, a trick of foreshortening making him appear to be taking a gigantic stride across thin air.

Knobby gave a hoarse gasp. "It's Featherstone! Comin' from up front! How did he get past us? He ain't human!"

They flattened themselves against the steel wall. The gondola had a slight overhang at the ends, and they were hidden from that side.

"Maybe he didn't see us," Gordon whispered.

"He saw us, all right."

A moment later there was a shower of gravel from above. A mocking tenor voice said, "Stay right there and wait for me, bum. I'm coming after you." The rich treble surprised Gordon; somehow he hadn't expected Featherstone's voice to be pitched so high.

"Up the ladder, quick!" Knobby's voice jolted him out of paralysis.

Gordon hesitated. "You go first," he said to the older man.

"I'm right behind you! Don't waste time!"

Gordon scrambled up the ladder and threw himself across the boxcar roof. Instantly he pivoted on his belly to give Knobby a hand. He saw the dark unwieldy bulk of Featherstone swarming down the side of the gondola, moving nimbly despite his size. He was incredibly quick. For a frozen instant, Gordon's mind fixed an image of protruding jaw, battered derby, shabby black coat, and baggy pants. It struck Gordon that Featherstone looked like a bum himself. Then the big man was at the bottom of the ladder, stepping easily from bumper to bumper, and reaching with frankfurter fingers for Knobby's ankle.

He plucked Knobby off the ladder, laughing. Knobby's reaching hand was torn from Gordon's grasp. Gordon looked down to see Knobby sprawled across the couplings, one arm raised to protect his head.

"Don't do it, Jake," he said.

The blackjack paused in mid-swing. "I know you, bum," the tenor voice said. "I seen your face."

The blackjack came down, not on Knobby's head, but at a point between neck and shoulder. Even up above, Gordon heard a crunch like splintered boxwood. Knobby screamed. His raised arm fell limp and boneless. The other hand held with a death grip on to the coupling. The blackjack rose and fell again. This time it struck Knobby on the point of the other shoulder. Knobby's hand let go of the coupling, and he started to roll off. Featherstone, with no sign of haste, hooked his thick fingers into the back of Knobby's collar and the crotch of his pants. With his legs braced between cars, he lifted Knobby, almost effortlessly. Knobby's arms hung like empty sleeves. With a grunt, Featherstone swung him back and out and let go. Gordon had a glimpse of Knobby's upturned face, the eyes mad with terror, as Knobby went sailing out into white emptiness. The train was rattling over an iron bridge at that point, and Knobby's body hit the granite abutment. It bounced once and tumbled into the chasm below.

Fear lent agility to Gordon. He got to his feet despite the jouncing of the train and sprinted at a half crouch for the end of the car. Even so, Featherstone was quicker. As Gordon dove for the ladder, the detective was already on the roof, running along the centerboard as lightfooted as a rope dancer. Sobbing, Gordon slid down the rungs, heedless of barked shins. A derby rose above the car's horizon like a black moon, and Gordon found himself staring up at Featherstone's pelican jaw.

The blackjack whistled down. Featherstone's big face wore a blissful expression. Instinctively, Gordon jerked his head aside. The loaded sap struck the point of his shoulder instead, and Gordon realized in a despairing instant that Featherstone had been aiming there all along. His whole arm immediately went numb, and a moment later, like lightning after thunder, came a bright flash of incredible pain. The arm dangled uselessly. He couldn't even move his fingers.

Helplessly, he clung there with his one good hand and watched Featherstone raise the limp tube of shot again. Head or other shoulder, he was finished if it touched him. He kicked out with both legs and went tumbling out into space, just as the blackjack hit the iron ladder with a force that burst its leather skin and scattered little lead pellets all around him.

The train had begun to slow down after the bridge, otherwise the impact would have killed him. He hit a grassy bank with his bad shoulder with a force that drove the breath out of him, and went rolling down into a gully. He lay at the bottom, a mass of bruises, unable to move or catch his breath. Somewhere overhead, an invisible train gave a long fading whistle.

Gordon lay there for an hour, listening to the river sounds. When he finally attempted to get up, he found that he could walk with a limp. His arm was still paralyzed, but there was an unpleasant tingling sensation in his fingertips that gave him hope that it wasn't broken. A leg of his overalls was ripped in an enormous flap from knee to ankle, and the bare leg he could see was bleeding from a dozen scratches.

With his good hand, he felt around in his pocket. Miraculously, the fragile pencil box that Dacey had given him was intact.

He examined his surroundings. The train had been slowing down. Perhaps that meant he was near a junction point, or even the Buffalo yards. If there was a hobo camp nearby, it would be situated along the riverbank.

Down near the water's edge, he found a worn path disappearing into underbrush. There was a stick poked into the ground there, supporting an empty tin can turned bottom up. He had learned Knobby's lessons well. He followed the path, limping, until he smelled smoke. Sniffing, he could detect burnt grease that meant somebody had forgotten to keep an eye on the mulligan.

He shuffled forward into the clearing, wishing that he had brought an onion.

The jungle had one more lesson to teach him.

This one was rougher than the place Shorty had run. It was full of hard, bleak, quarrelsome men with the flat accents of easterners. They had drifted here from the Pennsylvania coal mines and steel mills, refugees from hunger and company goons. They had run away from slow starvation in the mill towns of New England. They had fled the breadlines and vacant-lot Hoovervilles of New York City. They didn't invite conversation.

Gordon kept to himself. He foraged his own food in the surrounding countryside, and slept in one of the shallow burrows in the riverbank that a previous occupant had lined with tar paper and curtained with a scrap of rotting tarpaulin.

He was not molested. His shoes weren't worth stealing, and he had learned how to flash the knife Knobby had given him so as to discourage unwelcome attentions. He contributed enough to the communal pot to be tolerated.

His arm was not broken. A grizzled ex-pug from New Jersey explained it to him the night of his arrival. "It's an old cop's trick. He hit you where the nerves run over the socket. You'll have the use of the arm in a day or two." His injuries from the fall kept him stiff and limping, but he didn't think he had sustained anything worse than a couple of cracked ribs. He gave himself a week before he'd be ready to travel again.

The clique that ran the camp was under the leadership of a sack-bellied bully called Cuz. Once they had intercepted a Negro bindle stiff coming down the path from the river. Colored people were not welcome here. They had dragged him into the bushes, and Gordon had heard the pleading cries and the thuds of fists. Cuz and his cronies came back grinning, with a side of bacon they had gotten out of the Negro's bindle. It was divided that night. Gordon declined a share.

Another time they had caught a hijack stealing a pouch of tobacco from a sleeping man. Gordon had watched from the sidelines as they dragged the thief into the clearing, shouting, "Hang the son of a bitch!" "Let's spread 'im over the fire and toast the bastard's marshmallows for him!" The hijack, a bedraggled little rat of a man, cowered in terror while they voted on his punishment. In the end they lashed him to a tree, stripped to the waist, and took turns whipping him with a leather belt until he fainted. Cuz used the buckle end. When the man came to, he screamed when they helped him put his shirt back on. They emptied all his pockets and confiscated the money and food they found. Then they drove him out of camp with orders not to show his face in any hobo jungle down the line.

The child tramps who passed through the camp usually traveled in small packs for protection, but one night a scrawny little runt of a kid came in alone, dripping from a cloudburst. He couldn't have been more than twelve or thirteen. He had a pale thin face with dark circles under the eyes, and wore patched tweed knickers, tennis shoes out at the toes, and a frayed cardigan and old summer cap, both of which were too big for him. He hung wistfully around the fire, but nobody offered him anything. Finally Gordon went over to him and said, "What's your name, kid?"

"Ollie," the kid said in a childish, reedy voice.

"When's the last time you ate, Ollie?"

The kid thought it over. "Yesterday, I think. A lady gave me a piece of pie."

Gordon took a good look at Ollie in the flickering firelight. Under five feet, probably not more than eighty or eighty-five pounds. Small boned. The knickers looked like the remnants of the clothes he had run away from home in, so he couldn't have been on the road too long. On the other hand, Ollie's skin had the gray, granular texture and looseness around the wrists that suggested long malnutrition.

"Come on with me, kid," Gordon said gruffly. "I'll give you something."

Ollie followed Gordon warily. A couple of tramps by the fire watched incuriously. It was live and let live here. Gordon's little store of food was undisturbed. He took out his knife and cut off a generous portion of the liverwurst the butcher in town had given him in return for the long afternoon spent swamping out the back of the shop, and made a thick sandwich with the stale bakery bread. Ollie wolfed it down, then looked longingly at the remainder of the liverwurst. Gordon made him another sandwich, and gave him an apple from the bag of windfalls he had gathered. That seemed to be enough. Ollie rubbed his eyes with a grimy knuckle and gave a yawn.

Gordon showed Ollie where the unoccupied riverbank caves were; a lot of the old-time tramps refused to sleep in them in summer on the theory that it was "unhealthy." He found some dry cardboard for the kid to use as a bed.

As he was returning to his own grotto, he saw one of the men sneaking over to Ollie's cave. It was one of Cuz's buddies, a notorious jocker named Red. Gordon doubled back and got there before Red did. He squatted down in front of the cave opening and opened his knife with a practiced flick of the wrist. As Red came level with the mouth of the cave, Gordon was cleaning his fingernails ostentatiously with the knife. Red shrugged and went back the way he had come. Gordon poked his head inside the cave for a look. Ollie was fast asleep on the cardboard, sucking his thumb. Gordon waited in front of the entrance for another twenty minutes before he was sure that it was safe to leave Ollie alone.

The next morning, Gordon got up early and went down to the river's edge to bathe before the other men were up and about. There was a little inlet around a bend that gave you a chance of privacy. Gordon waded thigh-deep in the cold water, his clothes and shoes rolled up under his arm.

As he ducked under an overhanging branch, he saw Ollie standing in the water with his back to him, splashing water in his face. Ollie was painfully thin, with a protruding spine and narrow hairpin hips. His pale skin was stippled with red mosquito bites, some of them bloody where they had been scratched. Ollie must have sensed Gordon's approach. He half turned, and Gordon saw that Ollie was a very young girl, with small developing breasts the size of demitasse cups.

Neither Gordon nor Ollie said anything about it in the days that followed. But Ollie hung around Gordon a lot, avoiding getting too close to the older, rougher men.

Gordon tried to look after Ollie without being too obvious about it. It was a way of paying back Knobby for looking after him when he needed help. He shared the food he got on his foraging expeditions, begged a pair of old shoes from a Catholic children's shelter in town to replace Ollie's rotting sneakers, and stood guard around the bend when she bathed in the morning.

But despite his efforts, others in the camp had begun to notice Ollie too. The short hair and urchin face, the narrow hips, the boy's clothes that hid the undeveloped breasts, were a good enough disguise for casual contact. But after four or five days, some of the men were beginning to take a closer look at her. Gordon began to be aware of the curious eyes that followed the two of them when they went down to the riverbank together.

"Ollie, you shouldn't stay around this place much longer," he said, feeling uncomfortable.

"Why not?" she challenged.

He took a different tack. "Where's your home?"

"Huh?"

"Where do you come from?"

She wrinkled her gamine nose. "Oh, just some little hick town near Syracuse you probably never heard of."

"Syracuse? That's not so far."

"I been to California and back."

That shook him. "By yourself?"

"Not all the way. I traveled with some kids. Then I traveled for a while with this older girl, Helen."

"Why don't you go home?" He had a vague idea of taking her with him as far as Syracuse when he left, and seeing that she got within striking distance of her hometown.

"What for? To get smacked around some more?"

"It can't be that bad. I'll bet your ma would be real glad to see you."

The elfin chin trembled. "Like fun she would."

"You could be there tomorrow," he persisted.

"No *thanks!*" She brought the chin under control. Gordon thought he never had seen such bitterness in a child's face.

"What made you run away anyhow?"

She faced him defiantly. "Mama got a new fella, and she didn't want me around no more."

And that was all he could get out of her.

It rained all the next day. It cleared up by evening, but the mosquitoes were bad, and most of the men and boys in the camp lingered around the half-dozen cook fires, where the smoke helped to keep them off. There was a bucket of fresh coffee at Gordon's fire, and people kept drifting over for a refill. Every once in a while somebody would wander off into the bushes for a leak. A harmonica wailed somewhere out in the dark. Gordon sat with his back against a stump, sipping coffee out of the tin can he used for a cup, keeping half an eye on Ollie. She was huddled inconspicuously at the edge of the circle of firelight, he was glad to see; perhaps the talk he'd had with her had done some good. But he didn't like the way Cuz kept looking at her. The big man, arms and shoulders bulging in a hole-riddled T-shirt, had his head together with his pal, Red. They were grinning and nudging one another.

Gordon saw Ollie put down her tin mug and get up unobtrusively, heading for the bushes. A moment later, Cuz lurched to his feet, hitching his pants up over his sloppy belly. Gordon saw him wink at Red before following Ollie into the underbrush.

Gordon put his cup down and got up silently. He circled round the edge of the clearing in case any of Cuz's friends were watching, and pushed his way through the vegetation until he intersected the path. Something on the ground caught his eye: a short length of two-by-four that someone had left there. Gordon picked it up.

At first he thought he had lost them. Then he heard sounds up ahead: the snapping of twigs and the rustle of dead leaves, as though something large and heavy was thrashing around on the forest floor. A moment later there was a sharp gasp, and then the unmistakable sound of ripping cloth.

Feet pounding, he broke through to an open space, the length of timber in his hand. The starlight showed him a white blob whose shape made no sense to him until he realized it was a man's T-shirt with the pale protuberance of buttocks beneath. Cuz was on his knees, his pants down around his ankles, kneeling between Ollie's skinny legs. The knickers, ripped, had been flung aside. Cuz was pinning Ollie's shoulder down with one hamlike hand, the other hand forcing her legs apart. Past the big man's shoulders, Gordon could see Ollie's meager childish face staring rigidly at the sky.

Gordon bounded forward, swinging his club. It bounced off the side of Cuz's head with a vibrant woody sound. The force of the blow knocked Cuz sideways. Gordon rolled the body all the way off the girl. Cuz was loose and heavy, breathing with a rattling sound in his throat.

Gordon turned to Ollie. She struggled to a sitting position. She was naked below the waist, all spindly shanks and jutting hipbones and the sparse dark triangle of puberty, and Gordon tried not to look directly at her as he handed her the torn knickers.

She made no move to take the knickers from him. Her face was slack with grief. "What did ya do that for?" she complained. "He was gonna give me a nickel."

Gordon trotted beside the freight car, half twisted around, gripping the iron ladder with both hands. When he had matched pace with the train, he swung himself aboard.

He hung there until he caught his breath, then climbed to the roof and wormed his way forward until he found an inviting flatcar with big vague machinery shapes shrouded in tarpaulins. He settled down out of sight between two swathed masses. Dacey's pencil box was hard against his thigh, and he could feel the dangling pouch of coins down inside his overalls, against his skin. They were all he had been able to take with him; luckily he kept them on his person most of the time. He hadn't dared to go back to the jungle even to take a jug of water.

Ollie had begun screaming at him. Gordon had been astonished at the stream of sewer invective that poured from the childish lips. He hadn't ever been sure what some of the names she called him meant. She had arranged it with Cuz, she told him, and then was going to take on his friends, and Gordon had spoiled it for her. Her voice had attracted the others. Gordon had heard them crashing through the underbrush, and had barely made it to the railroad crossing in time.

He fingered the wrapped coins through the fabric of his clothing. There was almost enough.

A sound in the shadows brought him to alertness. He felt for the knife in his pocket. Something moved and a face came peering round the draped canvas.

It was only an old stew bum, half drunk and harmless. Gordon let go of the knife.

"Saw you running to catch this freight, sonny," the old man cackled. "Hee, hee, you sure look like you was in a hurry. Where you going, you can't wait to get there?"

Gordon looked up at the darkness filled with stars. "The army," he said. "I'm going to join the army."

14

"C'mon, hurry it up, Sinclair," Feely, the day manager, said. "Get those tables over at the far end cleared off. We need more cups and saucers."

Jeremy hurried to obey. "Tables" wasn't the most accurate description. At Macfadden's Penny Restaurants, the customers ate standing up at a sort of chest-high counter. He piled dirty dishes on his tray and took a swipe at the countertop with the dingy wet rag he carried.

"Whattsa matter, college boy, can't you keep up?" Murph, the dishwasher, said as Jeremy staggered into the kitchen with his loaded tray.

Murph was a large, pale, fleshy young man wearing an apron over a disintegrating grayish undershirt. He always had a cigarette dangling from his mackerel lips, somehow getting away with it despite the Macfadden prohibition against smoking. Murph liked to goose unwary busboys who weren't quick enough walking away from his sink, or give them a sly, painful snap of a wet towel across back of the neck. Jeremy had made the mistake of telling him about his six months of college the first day on the job, when he had been misled by Murph's apparent friendliness, and his life had been miserable ever since.

"What are you complaining about?" he said in an attempt at New York-style repartee. "I gave you a rest, didn't I?"

He scraped the food off the dishes and stacked them, inwardly burning with chagrin at having fallen behind again. As he turned to go, a jolt like an electric shock caught him between the thighs, almost lifting him off the floor. He spun round to see Murph, a sly grin on his face, immersed to the elbows in soapy water. He closed his mouth without saying anything. It just made matters worse if Murph got a reaction out of you. At least he hadn't dropped a tray of dishes, like the unfortunate busboy who had been fired the day before.

Feely was still outside, a frail, scrappy bantam surveying the crowded floor with his tiny hands on his hairpin hips.

"Taking a little nap in there, Sinclair?" he said sarcastically. He cinched his tourniquet of a belt still another notch to keep his bunched trousers from sliding down, and disappeared into his cubbyhole.

Cheeks hot, Jeremy waded doggedly out into the sea of eating stands again. His black hair hung tousled down his forehead and his legs were aching, but jobs in New York were hard to come by and easy to lose. There were always plenty of takers. He'd spent more days standing in the crowd behind the rope at the Free Employment Agency than he had working. So far he'd been a messenger, a sandwich man, a dishwasher, a dockworker, a porter, a stockboy.

"Hey, if it isn't the poet! How're ya doing, kiddo?"

A man in a gray fedora, hunched over one of Macfadden's mealy hamburgers, looked up as Jeremy tried to slide away the dirty dishes at his elbow.

Jeremy bristled, then recognized Roger Dixon, the pulp writer he had met at the party in the Village. It was Roger who had told him about Macfadden's Penny Restaurants in the first place. A lot of the pulp writers ate there between checks. When times got really bad, they ate free at the Automat, making tomato soup out of the catsup on the tables, the hot water intended for tea, and the crackers you could snitch at the soup counter. Roger was smiling, but he looked embarrassed.

"I thought you sold a novelette to *Dime Detective*," Jeremy said, looking over his shoulder for Mr. Feely and making a show of polishing the counter with his rag.

"Oh, I did, I did," Roger said. "Ten thousand words at a penny per pearl. But they pay on publication. Payday's Friday. In the meantime . . ." He shrugged and gestured at his plate.

"It's not bad," Jeremy said loyally.

"Oh, no, not at all," Roger said hastily. "And reasonable, reasonable. Where else can you get a hamburger for four cents? And the roll to go with it for a penny? And coffee for two cents? A sumptuous repast for only seven cents. I may even splurge and have the two-cent dessert. A little dish of sweetened mucilage is just what I need to top off the meal. Fuel for the Muse! All praise to Bernarr Macfadden for his charitable works!" He sighed. "I do wish he'd give this particular writer a more direct blessing, though, and buy one of my stories for *Liberty*."

Jeremy looked over his shoulder again and saw Mr. Feely emerging from his grotto, a small livid pixy in a black bow tie.

Jeremy again made a show of polishing the counter, then began backing away with his tray. "Don't worry, Roger," he said nervously. "You'll break into the slicks sooner or later."

Roger sighed again. "They say that seven years of the pulps spoils a man for better things." He fixed Jeremy with his frank blue eyes. "How's the poetry racket going, kiddo?"

"Okay, I guess." He regretted having mentioned the poem he'd had published in the defunct *Midland Monthly* to Roger, but at the party in the Greenwich Village loft, surrounded by real writers and artists, and fortified by several glasses of bathtub gin, he'd been desperate to dredge up some accomplishment of his own.

He tried to break away again, but Roger's voice halted him.

"Why don't you try writing for the pulps? There's no dough in that poetry stuff. Bunch of bearded bums reading their poems in a cellar and getting pennies pitched at them."

Jeremy wouldn't have admitted it to a successful author like Roger, but after the party he had banged out a western short story on his portable typewriter. So far it had collected nothing but printed rejection slips.

"Uh . . . I want to write serious fiction," Jeremy said, edging away. "Look, Roger, I've got to get back to work."

"Sure, kiddo," Roger grinned. "Why don't you try some pseudo-science fiction for a start? I hear F. Orlin Tremaine at *Astounding Stories* is paying two cents a word."

Jeremy tried to avoid Feely on his way back to the kitchen, but it was too late.

"This isn't a social club, Sinclair. Talk to your friends on your own time."

"Sorry, Mr. Feely."

In the kitchen, Murph was waiting for him with an empty drainboard again. "What took you so long, college boy?"

Jeremy managed to get out of the kitchen without being goosed. He worked furiously, and Tony, the other busboy, came back from his relief, so that by the time the place started to empty out a little, the two of them were able to keep ahead of Murph.

Then, just before the evening rush, Naomi Weinbaum walked in.

Jeremy's heart skipped, then almost stopped. The last thing in the world he wanted was for Naomi to see him in this place.

She was standing in the doorway with a tall, good-looking fellow in expensive summer flannels, who was looking around with conde-scending hauteur. Jeremy stared at her with impossible yearning, the tray in his hands forgotten. There were never very many women in Macfadden's, and the ones who did come here didn't look anything like Naomi. Men at the linoleum-topped counters nearest to the en-trance stopped eating and turned their heads to look at her, some sur-reptitiously, some openly.

Naomi was a small, exquisite, composed girl with wavy auburn hair and startling brown eyes. Her complexion was luminous, her features perfectly detailed. To Jeremy, she was as stunning as Garbo. She wore a simple printed silk dress with a deep V neckline framed by flaring la-pels, and she carried a summer evening stole negligently over her arm.

Jeremy had met her at one of the Village loft parties that his new friends were constantly throwing, and had been instantly jealous of her escort. She was a couple of years older than Jeremy, and she made him feel hopelessly cloddish and midwestern. She came from a culti-vated German family, and talked casually of the world of art, music, and literature that Jeremy had so painfully discovered for himself in the Iowan desert.

But perhaps the fierce bohemian pose he had assumed made her no-tice him. She had invited him to an afternoon tea and musicale at her house on upper Fifth Avenue the following Sunday. Her father, Max Weinbaum, somebody important in publishing and banking circles, had played the cello in the string quartet that performed at the musicale, and her brother Eric had played violin in the Mendelssohn trio that followed. Jeremy, who knew nothing about music except what he had absorbed secondhand from Pamela's piano lessons, had been impressed. Mr. Weinbaum, a patrician gray-haired gentleman, had been gracious to him afterward, quizzing him about his writing am-bitions with flattering attention. He was delighted at discovering Jeremy's struggling midwestern German, and had pressed the conver-sation in that language until Jeremy's vocabulary ran out.

Jeremy had been a welcome guest at the Weinbaum home since. But he always saw Naomi in the company of other people. He had never summoned enough courage to ask her out alone. Painfully conscious of his one fraying good suit, he affected a bohemian scorn of middle-class values, and hoped desperately that Naomi would find him just a little interesting.

Now she was seeing him in the soiled apron of a cafeteria busboy. She came toward him with the flanneled fellow in tow.

Jeremy hated him on sight.

"Hello, Jeremy," she said with her dazzling impersonal smile. "Marc and I were driving by on our way downtown, and I saw the sign and thought I'd drop in and see where you work."

Marc acknowledged the semiintroduction with a superior nod of his well-barbered head. "So this is where all those pulp-magazine chaps hang out." He took a cigarette out of a gold case and lit it.

"You were so amusing about it at the cocktail party Saturday, Jeremy," Naomi said. "I couldn't resist telling Marc about it." She giggled mischievously. "A penny a word. Four words for a hamburger, you said. Two words for dessert."

Jeremy felt betrayed. His somewhat exaggerated account of his intimacy with the inbred world of pulp writers had been intended for Naomi's ears, even if he *had*—he blushed to remember it—been holding forth to everyone within earshot. He groaned inwardly. How insufferably supercilious and adolescent he'd been!

Marc favored Jeremy with a patronizing smile. "Yes, very entertaining, Sinclair," he agreed. "Imagine these chaps taking their garbage seriously! As if they were *real* writers!"

All at once Jeremy felt ashamed of himself. "I don't know," he said stubbornly. "Dashiell Hammett wrote his stories for *Black Mask* magazine originally, and now the critics are comparing him with Hemingway. And there's a new writer in *Black Mask*, his name is Raymond Chandler, who's as good a writer of hard-boiled realism as Erskine Caldwell or James Farrell."

"You're comparing that pulp trash to *books?*" Marc said incredulously.

"Why not? Dickens and Dostoevski published *their* novels as serials in magazines," Jeremy retorted hotly. Out of the corner of his eye he could see Naomi looking at him with interest. Encouraged, he went on. "Someday I'll bet *The Maltese Falcon* will be considered a classic. And what about H.G. Wells? The critics consider *him* a serious novelist, but isn't that new book of his, *The Shape of Things to Come*, really pseudoscience fiction? I'll bet—"

"Okay, Sinclair, that's it," said a voice somewhere in the vicinity of his shoulder blades. "You had your warning. Now get your things and beat it."

Jeremy turned around and saw Feely standing there, his tiny face like a boiled skull.

"I was just—"

"Beat it. We don't need you around here no more."

Jeremy could see Marc's face registering lofty amusement at Feely's appearance. Naomi was showing polite puzzlement. He turned back to Feely.

"Okay. Just give me my pay for the six and a half hours, then."

"What pay? You ain't finished your shift."

Feely stalked away like a puppet being jerked along by strings, meager bottom and flat shanks twitching.

"What an extraordinary little chap," Marc murmured. "Did you see his shoes? I think he bought them in the boy's department."

Jeremy felt suddenly drained. He'd had three dollars coming to him for the day's work. And he'd been counting on a free meal from the kitchen.

"Ah, well," he said bravely. "I didn't have much of a future around here anyway." He pulled off his apron and rolled it into a ball.

Naomi turned her long-lashed brown eyes on him, comprehension dawning in her perfect face. "You mean that little man just *fired* you? Oh, Jeremy, it's all my fault. I shouldn't have come here to see you."

"Don't let it bother you, Nome. I was going to quit soon, honest. I've almost got enough saved to go to Europe."

It wasn't true. He had ninety-four dollars and change, saved dime by dime from all his jobs. His goal was two hundred. You could book third-class passage for Germany on the Hamburg-American line for seventy-seven dollars, though with luck you might find a freighter or cargo liner that would take you for less. And, he figured, he needed at least another hundred dollars to live on till he got established.

"Be sure to come to the house before you leave. I know my father will want to talk to you. He still thinks of himself as more of a German than an American. Perhaps he can give you some introductions."

Jeremy nodded. "I will."

Marc broke in. "I say, old chap," he said in his imitation English accent, "can I give you a lift downtown? The least I can do is drop you off, seeing that it's our fault you were fired."

Jeremy was tempted to save the bus fare, but he shook his head. He couldn't have faced riding in the car with Naomi with Marc along, and anyway he didn't want Naomi to see where he lived.

"Thanks anyway, but I have some things to do in midtown before I go home."

"Well, then . . ." Naomi said hesitantly.

Marc took her familiarly by the arm and escorted her out the door. Jeremy stared after them. Through the plate glass window he saw Marc put her in a shiny green Stutz convertible that reminded him of Brad's old car, and drive off. He slouched off toward the kitchen, the balled apron in his hand.

He almost collided with Tony, storming out of the swinging doors with a pile of napkin refills for the rush hour on his tray. Tony shot him a poisonous glance.

"Nice going, Sinclair," he muttered. "Now I gotta work the rest of the shift alone."

Murph gave him a pasty-faced grin. "Hey, college boy, I hear you tried to pick up a broad during working hours. Think you'd know what to do with one?"

Without a word, Jeremy tossed the dirty apron into the soiled linen bin and went to get his jacket, hanging on a hook at the rear. As he walked past Murph on the way out, he felt the hard slap of a wet towel against the back of his neck.

All of a sudden his rage exploded. He whirled and grabbed a startled Murph by the wrist and the nape of the neck. Murph was big but flabby. After a brief floundering resistance, Jeremy's wiry muscles got the better of him. Jeremy forced Murph's hand up behind his shoulder blades and dunked his head in the sink of soapy water.

Murph came up spluttering. "What's the matter with you, Sinclair?" he said plaintively. "You crazy or something?"

But Jeremy was already halfway through the swinging doors.

A downtown bus was just pulling away from the curb when Jeremy reached the corner. He made a successful leap for the bottom step, grabbed hold of the railing, and climbed to the top deck. He had it almost all to himself, except for a couple of lady shoppers laden with packages from Saks, and a handful of sightseers gawking at the tall buildings and crowded streets. The conductor was nowhere in sight. Jeremy settled into a rear seat, behind a pair of tourists.

He was still a bit of a tourist himself, even after five months in New York. He never got tired of riding the double-decker buses down Fifth Avenue, even though he could save a nickel by taking the subway. He craned his neck to have a look at St. Patrick's Cathedral, then turned his head in time to see the astonishing towers of the new Rockefeller Center. The tallest of them, the RCA Building, stretched seventy stories into the sky.

The biggest art scandal of the year had taken place in its lobby a few months earlier. Communist demonstrators had swarmed through the plaza, waving banners, and the art world had made a cause célèbre out of it. Jeremy's Marxist friends in the Village had filled him in on the details. It seemed that the Mexican painter, Diego Rivera, who had been hired by the Rockefellers to paint the huge sixty-three-foot mural that would decorate the lobby, had celebrated May Day by inserting a small head of Lenin among the other faces. John D. Rockefeller's young son, Nelson, who had talked the old man into hiring Rivera in the first place, asked the artist to remove Lenin's portrait. Rivera refused. Twelve uniformed guards had escorted Rivera from the lobby, removed his scaffolding, and covered the unfinished fresco with tar paper. Rivera was handed a check for the fourteen thousand dollars due him. His mural was chipped off the wall, and now another famous Spanish artist, José Sert, was working on a replacement.

Jeremy got off at the arch. Washington Square was alive with people taking advantage of the late afternoon sunlight. He strolled through the little park, enjoying the sights: the women pushing their wicker baby carriages, the old men playing chess, the earnest scraggly young men sitting on the benches reading books with esoteric covers carefully displayed, the Italian family groups sternly promenading in their best clothes. The fine, ancient, red brick mansions that faced the park were beginning to be overshadowed by tall apartment buildings, but Greenwich Village still had a character all its own.

Jeremy loitered, in no hurry to get back to his stifling room on Mulberry Street. That was as close to the Village as he had been able to get. His narrow, airless cell in the midst of the slum tenements cost him only three dollars a week. He'd told Naomi and her uptown friends that he lived in the Village, stretching the truth a little.

Bleecker Street was a bedlam of pushcarts and sidewalk stands, of tantalizing food odors, of washing hung out the tenement windows, of raucous Italian voices and people gesticulating at one another. Jeremy never tired of its motion and color. It was nothing like Beulah, Iowa. It was almost like being in Europe.

The East Side swarmed with foreigners: Italians, Jews, Slavs, all jammed together in their own little colonies. Jeremy, with his dark, passionate features, had often been mistaken for a Jew or Italian himself . . . till he opened his mouth. In the dark little shops or the polyglot street markets, elderly women liked to fuss over him.

Crossing Houston Street, he stopped at a pushcart and bought a thick penny slice of German rye bread for his supper. The vendor was a venerable bearded Talmudist who was a little off his turf.

"*A dank,*" Jeremy said, as the old man sawed away at the dense loaf for him. In German, it would have been simply '*danke.*' Yiddish, he had discovered, was surprisingly similar to German, and he could generally make himself understood.

The old man looked up. "*Binst du Yiddish?*"

"*Nein,*" Jeremy said. His brief triumph vanished as the expectant look on the old man's face faded. Deflated, he said, "*Gott helf,*" and walked away with his bread.

"*Zeit gesunt!*" the old man called after him.

Jeremy's building was a remodeled tenement, shouldered on either side by grimy brick façades festooned with iron fire escapes. A canny landlord had converted it into a rooming house. The entrance was blocked by a bunch of tough Italian youths lounging on the stoop. They stared through him as if he didn't exist as he squeezed past them into the gloomy hallway.

He climbed the rotting stairs with the bread under his arm, worried about the rent. It was due in three days. Then there would be another rent to pay a week later, and another after that. And food—twenty-cent meals on the Bowery or someplace cheap, day after day, while he looked for a new job. And the subway and bus fares to places that were too far to walk. Jeremy could see his savings evaporating, dollar by dollar, dime by dime, before he could find another job.

Germany seemed farther off than ever. He reached the landing, empty with despair. If only he had another thirty or forty dollars in his pocket right now! He'd leave at once, on the first cheap berth he could find. He might as well starve in Germany as here.

The white corner of an envelope peeped from under his door. The janitor had shoved the afternoon mail in through the crack. What could it be? One of Brad's infrequent scrawls, or a letter from Pam?

He let himself into his room and picked up the envelope. It was from Standard Magazines. Probably another rejection slip. With a resigned sigh, he tore the envelope open. And stared.

It was a check. For fifty dollars.

With trembling hands he read the enclosed note. *Thrilling Western* had bought his story: five thousand words at a penny a word.

The name painted on the bow was BUXTEHUDE. Jeremy stood on the long pier, gazing upward at the freighter's ancient steel flanks. The rust had been freshly scraped away, and there was a new coat of paint on the scarred woodwork of the superstructure. It looked cheap and clean, in contrast to some of the other cargo vessels Jeremy had investigated, which merely looked cheap. The Germans were an industrious race.

It was almost twilight. Half a sun squatted on the Jersey shore, swollen and red. Seagulls wheeled screaming over the greasy waters of the Hudson, competing for garbage. Jeremy could look down the river and see the long rows of piers and covered sheds jutting into the water, the freighters and ocean liners nuzzling at them like nursing leviathans. He recognized the four red smokestacks of the *Mauretania*, lying at rest some distance away, and beyond, the giant *Europa*, one of North German Lloyd's finest ships.

Jeremy grimaced. He wouldn't be traveling in as grand a fashion, but he'd get there all the same.

He turned to look at the shore. All he could see from here was the new elevated express highway, rising above the jumbled warehouses. When it was finished, it would run along the Hudson River from Canal Street to Seventy-second, disgorging its traffic into Riverside Drive. It would carry an unbroken stream of motorcars at thirty-five miles an hour above all the congestion. It was a stupendous idea, an emblem of progress. But Jeremy knew that above Seventy-second, between Riverside Drive and the Hudson shore, the miserable shacks of New York's largest Hooverville stretched for two miles.

No, he wasn't sorry to be leaving his native country.

He peered upward again at the looming curve of the *Buxtehude*'s hull. Perhaps the Germans were managing things better. Hadn't this new fellow, Hitler, promised to end unemployment?

A sailor appeared magically at the top of the gangplank as Jeremy started climbing, a stolid clean-shaven man in a blue-striped jersey and white canvas cap. He saluted smartly, making Jeremy feel impossibly young and sloppy.

"*Entschuldigen Sie, bitte,*" Jeremy said in his best schoolboy German. "*Wo ist . . . Können Sie mir den Weg nach dem . . . dem Verwalter zeigen?*"

The sailor looked puzzled for a moment, then nodded and said: "*Hier entlang, bitte.*"

Jeremy followed him along the deck and up a companionway. He noted with approval that all the brightwork had been diligently polished. They stopped at the purser's cabin, and the sailor rapped discreetly on the door.

"*Wer ist's?*" a muffled voice said inside.

"Heinke," the sailor said deferentially. "*Mit einem amerikanischen Herrn.*"

"*Herein!*" the voice inside said.

The sailor pushed the door open for him, gave him a respectful salute, and left. Jeremy advanced into the cabin.

The purser was a balding, open-faced man with humorous blue eyes, smoking a pipe and sitting at a desk covered with little stacks of neatly grouped papers. He took the pipe out of his mouth and laid it carefully across the edge of the desk.

"Well, young sir, what can I do for you?" he said in English.

"*Ich möchte einen Platz in—*" Jeremy began.

"Please, please," the purser smiled. "English is all right. I must practice, isn't that so? Please sit down."

Gratefully, Jeremy took a seat.

"Now," the purser said with cheerful briskness, "you wish to book passage on the *Buxtehude,* you began to say?"

It was all going much too quickly. "Well, uh . . . I wanted to inquire . . . that is, if you have a berth available . . ."

"We have eight passenger cabins," the purser said. He laughed. "Of course, our accommodations are not as luxurious as those aboard the *Britannic* or the *Bremen,* but we are able to make our passengers comfortable. You have the use of the officers' lounge, and dine at the captain's table. The food is plain but good—good German food. And of course you have the freedom of the decks. And that's more than you can say for the poor third-class passengers aboard a luxury liner."

"How much . . . that is . . ."

The purser sized him up with a glance. "Fifty dollars. American money."

It was fate, Jeremy decided. The amount was exactly what he had received for the western story. And it would leave his saved hoard intact: more than ninety dollars to live on until he could find some way to earn money in Germany.

He would compromise his standards and become a pulp writer, he told himself sternly. If he had done it once, he could do it again. He could mail his manuscripts from Germany. Two stories a month would support him very well. That was only two days' work. He'd have the rest of the time to concentrate on his *serious* writing.

The purser mistook his hesitation. "The fifty dollars covers everything, you understand," he said quickly. "Drinks, wine, your laundry . . . we even have a ship's doctor, which is unusual on a vessel this size. . . ."

"Oh, fifty dollars is fine," Jeremy said. It suddenly came to him that he was doing the Germans a favor, not the other way around. Wasn't there something about foreign exchange . . . ? "When do you sail?"

"Tomorrow evening at eight." He peered anxiously at Jeremy. "Is that too soon for you?"

"No, that's all right." He wouldn't have to pay another week's rent for the room on Mulberry Street. "That'll give me time to cash a check. Can I drop by tomorrow and pay you?"

"Perhaps I can accommodate you now." The purser wasn't going to let him get away. "May I see the check?"

Jeremy dug in his wallet and handed the check over. The purser studied it, knitting his brows.

"From Standard Magazines," he said slowly.

"Oh, the check's all right. They're a big publisher. Their offices are on Forty-eighth Street."

"You are employed by them?"

"Actually, no." Jeremy lowered his eyes modestly. "That's payment for a story."

The purser frowned. "You are a journalist?"

"No," Jeremy admitted. "That's for a western story I wrote."

"Ah!" the purser suddenly beamed. His finger stabbed at the handwritten memo on the check. "I see it here. You have written a 'Thrilling Western.' Yes, yes, cowboys and red Indians. Very colorful. I myself have read the books of Zane Grey. He is very popular in Germany."

He stamped the check with a big rubber stamp and put it away in a lockbox. Jeremy watched it disappear with a sense of relief. He was committed.

"Now, do you have a valid passport?" the purser said. "If not, you must apply early tomorrow morning. It can sometimes take all day."

"I've got one." A passport was the first thing Jeremy had acquired when he arrived in New York. He had carried it around as a talisman ever since.

"May I see it, please?"

Jeremy handed it over. The purser inspected it and made a notation in a ledger. He handed it back.

"You will require a visa from our consular representative in New York. I will give you a document. There will be no difficulty. Why should there be? Germany and America are friends, is that not so?"

"Yes . . . of course."

The purser slapped the desk. Jeremy had the impression that if they had been standing together, the purser would have given him a jovial clap on the back instead. "Good, good," the purser said warmly. "Please be here an hour before sailing time. I wish you a prosperous voyage, Herr Sinclair."

"Thank you," Jeremy stammered, then realized he had been dismissed. Before he knew it, he was on deck again, and another sailor, a handsome blond youth who seemed no older than himself, was seeing him down the swaying gangway.

Outside, the sun had set, but there was still a dying light. From over the water came the faint sound of music: a ship's orchestra playing on the deck of some departing liner.

"Germany!" he murmured to himself.

He packed that night. Everything that would fit into the one big suitcase: the good tweed suit, the good jacket and the one with the leather elbow patches, the more presentable of the shirts, the hiking shoes. The Remington portable typewriter had its own carrying strap. There was no room for all the books he had accumulated.

Ruthlessly he discarded them. They would give the next tenant of the room something to read, if he had a taste for avant-garde poetry and experimental novels. He took the Rilke, and the volume of poetry by Heine. The German language dictionary. The Nietzsche to read aboard ship: heavy going, but he thought it might help him to understand the German character. And *Ulysses* and Eliot's *The Waste Land;* he couldn't leave them behind.

There was time to scribble a few hasty letters. One to Mother, Pamela, and Junie at Uncle Elroy's. A quick note to Brad in Washington. He didn't have Gordon's address, but Brad or Pam would tell Gordon. As for his friends, it would be more fun to send them postcards from Germany, when he got there.

Naomi?

He hesitated. Call her, that's what he should do. Say good-bye in an aloof, brittle, sophisticated manner that would make her sorry that she hadn't been nicer to him. But she was out with that Marc tonight.

Too late, he thought, despising himself for never having worked up the courage to try to kiss her.

He smoothed out another piece of paper on the washstand that served for a desk. *Dear Naomi,* he began, bearing down so hard with his fountain pen that it made a blot. If he dropped the letter in the mailbox tonight, she would get it by the afternoon mail, before his ship sailed. He did not stop to think why that was important to him.

"Are you the passenger?" the pier guard said.

"Yes," Jeremy said.

He lowered the heavy suitcase to the concrete floor of the loading platform. His arms ached from lugging it across town by bus and part of the way by foot. He was a little embarrassed at having been caught without a cab driver to carry it out to the dock for him.

"Name Sinclair?"

"Yes."

The guard jerked his head toward the yawning warehouse door. "Lady waiting for you inside. I told her she could wait aboard, with the friends of the other passengers. They're all having drinks in the officers' lounge. But she came ashore again. Asked if I'd keep an eye out for you."

"Thanks," Jeremy said, puzzled.

He dragged the suitcase through the cargo door and looked around the warehouse interior. It was a vast, gloomy place, smelling of spices and tea. At first he thought no one was around. Then he saw her, a small figure standing over at the far side by some stacked bales. He left his suitcase where it was and hurried over.

"Naomi!" he said. "What are you doing here? Why didn't you wait aboard ship?"

Naomi gave him a wan smile. "Hello, Jeremy. I didn't feel very comfortable there. The ship's officers were rather . . . rude."

"Rude?" Jeremy wrinkled his forehead. He couldn't believe it. The sailors had been extremely deferential the day before, and the purser had been the soul of courtesy. "Well, you come right back on board with me. We'll see about this."

"No, no," she said hastily. "Don't make any kind of a fuss on my account. You're going to have to live with those people for ten days. Anyway, nobody actually said or did anything that I could take exception to. They were all quite correct. Just a little . . . perhaps, brusque." She forced another smile. "I'm probably just overtired. I'd rather talk to you here, anyway. They'll be sending the visitors ashore any minute."

Jeremy peered closely at her in the dim light. Naomi did look tired, tired and vulnerable, her shoulders uncharacteristically slumped. Marc had kept her out late, he thought with a stab of jealousy.

"Well . . . gee," he floundered. "It was swell of you to come and see me off, Nome."

"I got your letter. It was a nice letter. You said some nice things in it. I never . . ." She broke off. "I couldn't let you leave without saying good-bye."

The color seemed to be returning to her face. Some of the old gaiety was back in her voice. Looking at her, Jeremy was struck again by the poignant beauty of her small, perfect features, framed by the glossy auburn hair that curled into either cheek. She was smartly turned out in a plum-colored summer frock and a tiny pert hat with a brim that dropped over one eye. Jeremy couldn't imagine anyone not being absolutely captivated by her, let alone being rude.

"I'll write you from Germany," he said warmly.

"No, no, you'll have better things to do with your time. Promise not to write."

"I don't—"

"Promise." There was an odd note of appeal in her voice.

"All right," he said with an uneasy laugh. "I'll see you when I get back someday."

She wrinkled her nose at him. "By that time I'll be a fat Fifth Avenue matron with at least three insufferable, spoiled children with little fat Prussian necks and sailor hats."

He kept his voice casual. "Marc?"

She nodded. "I'm sorry, Jeremy."

"Listen, Nome, I wish you the best. I mean that."

"Thanks, Jeremy dear. I know you do. You're well rid of me. An ancient hag of twenty-two. Do you have a cigarette?"

He dug out his crumpled pack of Spuds and lit one for her.

"My mother's overjoyed," she said, puffing nervously at the cigarette. "She thinks I'm already past the childbearing age. My father's not so overjoyed. I don't think he likes Marc very well."

"Nome . . ."

"Listen, Jeremy, my father wanted me especially to say good-bye to you for him, too."

"Oh . . ." He blinked. The reminder that Naomi was three years older than he was had thrown him off balance. Now, being relegated to the status of family friend had made him feel even younger.

"My father's very fond of you, you know."

"Well, I . . ."

"He says he envies you, going to Berlin. He had to leave as a young man because of business, and then the war came along. But he's still very much a German at heart." She was talking very quickly, between puffs. "He remembers the old days, the *Kaiserzeit*. He says that Germany is the true land of culture, that America is still too young. *Kultur*, he calls it, even now. Beethoven, Schiller, Goethe. He was very impressed by you, Jeremy. He says he hopes you find what you're looking for in Germany."

Touched, Jeremy said: "That's awfully nice of him to say that, Nome. But why doesn't he go back himself? Just for a visit?"

She shrugged. "He was always going to take us on a holiday there. The whole family. Introduce us to our relatives. Take us all for a stroll down Unter den Linden and show us the Tiergarten. Treat us to a performance at the opera house—he played in the string section there when he was a poor student, you know." She dropped the cigarette to the floor and ground it out with her toe. "But there was never enough time. And now it's too late."

"But why not go?"

Her huge dark eyes stared at him with something like amazement. "Conditions," she said.

"Conditions?" he repeated stupidly.

"We're Jewish," she said impatiently. "You know that!"

"Oh, sure . . . yes . . ."

He felt like an idiot. He'd known that the Weinbaums were Jews, but he hadn't thought about it. Jews were those foreign people on the East Side, like the bearded old man with the skullcap he'd bought the slice of bread from. It took an effort of will to remember that Naomi, and the elegant, urbane Mr. Weinbaum, were members of the same race.

"Well," he finished lamely, "maybe it isn't as bad over there as they say. I mean, from what I've read, they say that this mistreatment of Jews is just a phase. That the Nazis know they went too far, and after all the protest, things will get better from now on."

"That's what my father says. He says the German people won't put up with a thug like Hitler for long. But he's worried. He got these letters from his brother that were hard to believe, and now the letters have stopped."

"Brother?"

"His brother Friedrich. In Berlin. He owns the big Weinbaum department store on Leipziger Strasse. You've heard of *that?*"

"Oh, sure. Yes. Of course."

She gave a bitter laugh. "Well, you know Hitler's program. He promised to overthrow the Treaty of Versailles, get rid of the Jews, and do away with department stores. That's two out of three for Uncle Freddie."

"I'm sure he'll be all right, Nome," Jeremy said uncomfortably. "The Nazis won't bother important people."

"Maybe," she said. "Jeremy, would . . . would you do me a favor?"

He cleared his throat. "Anything."

Naomi looked around the empty shed. Then she took an envelope out of her purse and handed it to Jeremy.

"Could you deliver this letter to Uncle Freddie in Berlin? My father doesn't want to send it through the mail."

Jeremy looked at the envelope. It was blank. "Sure, Nome," he said, and put it in his inside jacket pocket.

"If . . . if he has any answer, would you mind putting it in a letter of your own to my father? Just a sentence or two. My father thinks they aren't as likely to intercept mail from Americans."

"If you want me to. But I'm sure it isn't necessary. My gosh, the Nazis aren't going to fool around with the postal service. Hindenburg's still the president of Germany, after all."

She went on as if he hadn't said anything: "Write him care of George Wilson at the publishing house. You know George. The editor. You met him at one of the Sunday teas. He'll be on the lookout for a letter from you. That way there won't be a Jewish name on the envelope."

"All right, Nome. But this is ridiculous. . . ."

She threw her arms around his neck and kissed him on the lips. "Thank you, Jeremy," she said. "You're very, very sweet and dear."

He was embarrassed to see that she had tears in her eyes. He felt awkward and strange. He had often imagined kissing Naomi for the first time, but he had never imagined it would be like this.

"Well," he said clumsily. "I'd better get aboard."

She smiled at him. "Yes, you don't want to miss the party."

He retrieved his suitcase, and the two of them stepped out onto the pier, Naomi clinging to his arm. They stopped at the foot of the gangway. The river slapped against the sides of the ship, and Jeremy could hear the groan of ropes. From somewhere above came the sounds of music played on a gramophone and the babble of celebrating voices.

"Good-bye, Jeremy," Naomi whispered.

She stood on tiptoe to embrace him and turned her face upward. Their lips met for a long tremulous kiss. They broke apart, both of them a little breathless, and Jeremy saw a sailor standing at Naomi's shoulder.

It was Heinke, the square, stolid fellow who had first shown Jeremy aboard the *Buxtehude*. He touched a hand to his cap—rather more casually than he had the first time, Jeremy thought—and picked up Jeremy's suitcase.

"*Folgen Sie mir, mein Herr,*" Heinke said, clambering up the swaying gangway without looking back.

Jeremy followed him to the deck. At the top, he turned to wave good-bye to Naomi, but she wasn't there.

The *Buxtehude* steamed downriver toward the Narrows, the little puffing tugs falling away from her flanks. Jeremy stood at the rail of the promenade deck, a glass in his hand, feeling a breeze ruffle his hair and listening to the gramophone music coming from the open door of the lounge behind him. Most of the other passengers had crowded out on deck to watch the lights of Manhattan twinkle on in the deepening twilight.

Some kind of ceremony was taking place at the stern. A number of officers and sailors were gathered there to watch as a new flag was hoisted into position on the jack staff, above the black, white, and red stripes of the German merchant flag. The new flag was red, with a crooked-armed black cross outlined against a white circle at the center. A swastika, the bent cross was called. Jeremy had seen news pictures of it, flying at Nazi party rallies and, lately, over government buildings.

The gramophone music abruptly stopped. Jeremy turned his head and saw the purser come out of the lounge. At the stern, the sailors had their arms extended in a rigid salute. A couple of passengers on the promenade deck—Germans, he supposed—were doing the same thing.

The purser joined him at the rail. His name was Graebe, Jeremy had learned, and he came from Düsseldorf.

"Our radio operator was fortunate enough to catch a transmission from Germany," the purser said, nodding at the scene below. "The new flag regulations for merchant ships. Actually, they're not supposed to go into effect until December."

"Oh?" Jeremy said politely.

"A splendid sight, Herr Sinclair," the purser said. "The emblems of the old Germany and the new Germany flying side by side. The Führer himself has ordered it, as a symbol of the vigor and rebirth of the German race."

As Jeremy struggled for some sort of reply, the purser suddenly thrust out his arm in the same stiff salute, looking a little reproachfully, it seemed, at the cocktail glass in Jeremy's hand. Jeremy stood there, feeling silly and useless.

In the salon, somebody turned the gramophone back on. Down on the afterdeck, the sailors were filing away, returning to their duties. The purser gave Jeremy a hearty thump on the back.

"Look, there's the Statue of Liberty coming up, Herr Sinclair," he laughed indulgently. "As soon as we leave it behind us, that drink you're holding will be legal."

15

"Another helping of *Leberknödel,* Herr Sinclair?" the steward said, leaning over his plate with the serving dish.

Jeremy, his mouth full, chewed and swallowed frantically. "No thank you," he finally managed. The steward straightened up, and Jeremy added hastily, "They're very good."

The steward clicked his heels and proceeded to the next place at the table, occupied by the second officer, a sallow, narrow-skulled man with mournful brown eyes. The second officer nodded his head, and the steward spooned some more of the liver dumplings into his soup.

"Herr Sinclair is wise," Graebe said jovially from across the table. "He is saving room for the *Schweinebraten mit Sauerkraut.* Is that not correct, Herr Sinclair?"

"There's always room for more *Leberknödel,*" the red-faced chief engineer, Brakel, grunted, stuffing his mouth again.

"But Herr Sinclair is an artist," the purser said. "And artists have a more delicate constitution than pigs like you, Brakel."

"Oh, I'm enjoying it very much," Jeremy said. "It's just that the portions are so big."

"What did I tell you?" the purser winked. "Did I not promise you that we would treat our passengers well? On board the *Buxtehude,* we are very fortunate. The captain is a stickler—stickler, is that the correct American slang?—for good German food."

Jeremy looked across at Captain Bruning, presiding at the other table. Bruning was a stocky, square man with a broad, weathered face, chewing stolidly and nodding at the conversation of one of the passengers. Jeremy wished fervently that he had been seated at the captain's table. The purser was all right, but he didn't care for the company of the morose second officer or the loudmouthed Brakel. He had been placed here at the second table, he supposed, because he spoke German, and could converse with the German couple, Herr and Frau Schreiber, who were returning home to Hamburg.

The other married couple, the elderly Mr. and Mrs. Willoughby of Ohio, had been teamed at the captain's table with the blond English girl, Millicent Wickes. She worked for a British news agency in Berlin, and had a lively, chatty manner that made her attractive despite a bird-boned frailty and unfortunately protruding front teeth. Jeremy had hardly had a chance to speak to her during the first two days of the voyage. The unattached male passenger favored with her company was a lean, saturnine man named Kleist, who had something to do with the Siemens Electrical Works.

"That pork looks greasy," came the thin, querulous voice of Mr. Willoughby from across the way. "Pork, liberty cabbage, sausage, herring, goose liver . . . is that what we're going to be eating for the next eight days? Can't that fellow in the galley whip me up a good American-style steak and some mashed potatoes?"

There was a soft, apologetic murmur from the steward. Jeremy felt embarrassed at his fellow countryman's behavior. Mr. Willoughby was a retired tool-and-die manufacturer from Toledo, used to ordering people about. He was always delivering diatribes about the superiority of things American, from food to industrial production. He didn't seem to realize that, in setting foot on the *Buxtehude,* he was a guest in another country, with a guest's obligation to be courteous.

"The doctor says that Mr. Willoughby has to stay away from greasy food," Mrs. Willoughby apologized for her husband. "He has a gall-bladder condition."

She lapsed into silence, a watery gray woman who sat stiffly encased in a dowdy high-collared dress.

"Herr Willoughby does not like pork, perhaps he is a Jew," Brakel said with a broad wink.

The Hamburg couple laughed politely. Herr Schreiber leaned forward and said seriously, "Impossible. I myself have seen Herr Willoughby eat the Westphalian ham for his appetizer."

Jeremy was pleased to see the purser and the second officer scowl in reprimand at Brakel. The Germans weren't half as bad as they were made out. All at once he felt impelled to make up for Willoughby's rudeness.

"Herr Willoughby didn't mean anything by 'liberty cabbage,'" he said earnestly to the Schreibers. "It's just that during the war that's what they called sauerkraut, and a lot of older people kept the habit. There was . . . sort of a ban on German things. Even Beethoven couldn't be played in public. I know it sounds ridiculous now. But actually there's a lot of admiration for Germany in my country. I'm a great admirer of German culture."

He glanced nervously toward Willoughby. He'd had to say "liberty cabbage" in English. But Willoughby hadn't caught the phrase. He was fiddling impatiently with his napkin, unaware that he was being talked about.

The English girl, sitting between the captain and Kleist, locked gazes with Jeremy for a split second, a secret, amused smile on her face. Evidently she had overheard. Jeremy flushed and broke the eye contact.

"Ah . . . yes . . . Beethoven . . ." Frau Schreiber said, looking vague. Evidently she didn't know enough English to have caught Willoughby's reference in the first place.

"Culture . . . cabbages, it's all the same to me," Herr Schreiber said comfortably. "I'm just a businessman."

He looked away as his main course arrived and at once began mashing some of his roast potato into the pork gravy.

Unexpectedly it was Kleist who came to Jeremy's rescue. He leaned across the space between the two circular tables and said, "You speak German very well, Herr Sinclair."

"Thank you," Jeremy said gratefully. "I studied it in school. And of course I had a lot of German neighbors in Iowa, where I come from."

"So. You admire German culture," Kleist said, carefully buttering a slice of bread. His sleek, oily head and darting brown eyes made Jeremy think of an otter.

"Yes. Very much."

"So. Have you read Nietzsche?"

Jeremy thought guiltily of the thick, neglected volume in his luggage. He had tried again last night to read a few pages before going to sleep, but as usual had gotten bogged down in the impenetrable prose.

"Well . . ." he temporized, "I'm reading *Thus Spake Zarathustra* now. . . ."

Kleist nodded. "Good, good. You should also read *The Will to Power*. Are you familiar with his theory of the *Übermensch?*"

The word translated as "superman." "N-not very . . . I haven't gotten too far into it yet. . . ."

" 'The magnificent blond brute,' " Kleist quoted. " 'A ruler race is building itself up. This man and the elite around him will become the lords of the earth.' Nietzsche wrote that fifty years ago, but he was a good prophet. That is what is going on in Germany today. The world will see."

The light banter at the two tables had become frozen. The German officers were regarding Kleist with polite deference. It was like, Jeremy thought, what happened when a clergyman came to dinner. Only the Willoughbys seemed oblivious to the change in mood. Mr. Willoughby was glancing impatiently toward the galley door.

The English girl tried to break the ice. "Your precious Nietzsche wants to relegate women to the kitchen and the nursery," she said lightly. *"Küche, Kirche, und Kinder.* Doesn't he say that our only role in life is to breed warriors for the state? And that we should be ruled by the whip?"

Kleist patted her hand indulgently. "No whips for you, Miss Wickes," he said with a perfunctory smile that showed small, crooked teeth. "Why should there be whips for our friends and companions? The English are a Germanic race. And anyway, in the perfect world state, everybody will know their place and perform their duties joyfully."

"Where's my steak?" Mr. Willoughby said peevishly, fussing with his napkin. Mrs. Willoughby tried to soothe him.

"So that's your utopia?" the girl said with a laugh. "Sounds like *Brave New World."*

"Oh, the new Aldous Huxley novel," Jeremy said, grateful for a chance to change the subject. "How did you like it? Babies grown in bottles! Do you think that's what the future will be like?"

But, like a ferret, Kleist would not let go of his subject. "Huxley!" he said scornfully. "A decadent! If you want to know what the future will be like, read Nietzsche. And Hegel. Are you familiar with Hegel?"

"I'm not much on philosophy, I guess," Jeremy said cautiously.

Now it was the purser who tried to bail Jeremy out. "Herr Sinclair is a writer of Wild West stories," he said with heavy jollity. "He does not understand ideology." The word he used was *Weltanschauung.*

"So. Wild West stories." The expression on Kleist's face showed clearly what he thought of westerns.

"He has worked for the American publisher Bernarr Macfadden," the purser said.

"Actually, I'm interested in writing poetry," Jeremy said quickly, before *that* could go too far. "And someday, maybe, a serious novel."

"And how do you find our German poets?" the taciturn second officer put in unexpectedly.

"Well . . . there's Goethe, of course," Jeremy said, remembering Mr. Weinbaum's enthusiasms. "I guess *Faust* is one of the greatest poetic dramas ever written. . . ."

They all nodded their approval, even Kleist. Encouraged, Jeremy went on.

"And Heine. I'm just now reading him. In German."

He saw the scowl on Kleist's narrow face. He'd put his foot in it again.

"*Jude!*" he heard Brakel mutter under his breath.

He was determined not to let that get by him. "A Jew? Well, maybe. What of it? He's one of your finest writers."

"He's not one of *our* writers, Herr Sinclair," Kleist said, a trace of contempt showing on his face. "He's one of *their* writers."

"What do you mean by *their* writers?" Jeremy said, feeling his anger begin to rise.

The English girl was trying to tell Jeremy something with her eyes, and the captain, looking distressed, was industriously carving away at his roast pork.

Kleist was breathing hard. "The German soul will not be free to express itself until our culture is cleansed of Jewish intellectualism and degraded art!" he said.

Jeremy was about to reply, when the captain stopped the discussion by putting down his knife and fork with a loud clatter. The captain looked up at the steward, emerging from the galley with a covered tray, and said blandly: "Ah, here is Mr. Willoughby's steak."

Mr. Willoughby raised a reptilian neck. "About time, too."

The steward hovered anxiously until he saw that Mr. Willoughby was eating, then bowed and busied himself in the serving pantry. At the captain's nod, he poured everybody a glass of sparkling Rhine wine, evidently from a private stock.

Before the captain could propose a toast, Kleist raised his glass and said, "To a new Germany and our glorious leader. *Heil Hitler!*"

The English girl shot a worried glance at Jeremy, then relaxed when she saw that he was picking up his glass with the rest. Jeremy was flattered by her worry, and a little amused by it. Despite his irritation at Kleist, he certainly wasn't going to be rude enough to refuse a toast in a roomful of Germans.

And besides, he saw nothing wrong with drinking to a new Germany. The old one had been no great shakes, with its inflation and unemployment.

"Heil Hitler," the second officer murmured at his elbow.

Everybody joined in the toast except the Willoughbys, who didn't drink.

From up here next to the bridge house he could see the vast flecked circle of the ocean, flatter than the plains of Iowa, stretching out equally in all directions. A stiff following breeze flung salt spray even this high, but the ship rode easily in the wallowing swells, and the sky was a sparkling blue that made his heart ache.

Jeremy liked to come up here mornings. It was the third day out, but he still had not tired of the spectacle of this immense, heaving emptiness. The world had gone, vanished. Here in this greenish void, the *Buxtehude* had become the only reality. The sea was everything he had dreamed of, growing up in the landlocked interior of the country.

He shifted his gaze to the afterdeck. A pair of brawny sailors were setting up the swimming pool. This was a canvas pen, about fifteen feet square, slung from poles. A third sailor was dragging out the hose that would fill it with seawater.

The German couple, the Schreibers, were lounging in deck chairs, watching with good-humored impatience. They were already in their swimsuits. Herr Schreiber was pale and hairy, wearing a striped top whose side cutouts showed rolls of flesh, and a rubber bathing cap whose flaps were rolled up above his ears. Frau Schreiber was bulging out of an orange one-piece suit that made bubbles where it stretched across the tops of her thighs. Jeremy wished fervently that he had a bathing suit so that he could join in the fun in the pool. He'd be making excuses all the way across the Atlantic. He'd contrived a sort of shipboard costume out of his flannels and an open-necked white shirt with the sleeves rolled up.

"Hullo," said a voice behind him. "I didn't see you at breakfast."

Jeremy gave a start. He hadn't heard Millicent Wickes approaching. She was wearing a white sundress that left her bony shoulders bare, and her yellow hair was tied back with a bright turquoise bandanna.

"I was up early," he said. "Cook gave me something in the galley."

She squinted at him. "Earlier than breakfast call aboard *this* tub? God, you Yanks are worse than the Germans! Up at the crack of dawn, I suppose, one hundred pushups and fifty laps around the deck, the perfect start to a terribly efficient day."

"I'm not like that."

"No, I don't suppose you are. D'you have a fag?"

Wordlessly he got out his crumpled pack of Spuds. He had two more in his cabin. If he couldn't make them last for the rest of the voyage, he'd have to buy more from the purser. He'd have to buy a whole carton, because it would look cheap to buy less. He lit the cigarette for Millicent, cupping his hands to shield it from the breeze.

"Bugger-all, one of those menthol things!" she exclaimed. "I don't see why you bother to smoke." She stared carefully out to sea. "You made rather a chump of yourself last night, didn't you?"

His ears burning, Jeremy said, "I don't know what you mean."

"Getting in a tiff with Kleist in front of everybody is what I mean, you bloody fool."

"We were just having a literary discussion, that's all."

"It's not literature, it's politics to them. What they call *Weltanschauung*. The correct world view. Heine and that lot aren't terribly popular in Germany these days. They made a bonfire of their books this spring, remember? On Unter den Linden, right in front of the State Library. I was there with my boss. He was covering the story. They burned Freud. And Einstein. 'Jewish physics,' they called it. Little Doctor Goebbels, the propaganda minister, pranced around the flames. 'Jewish intellectualism is dead,' he told us. They're mad on the subject of Jews. And not just Jews. They burned Gide, Zola, Proust, even your own Jack London." She tossed her cigarette into the sea.

"Maybe there are a few Germans around like Kleist," Jeremy said defensively. "But they're not all like that."

"Don't you understand *anything?*" she said impatiently. "Kleist is no businessman. He may be on the Siemens payroll, but if so, he's been put there to keep the Nazis quiet. All the big industrialists are sucking up to the Nazis. Kleist's real boss is the Gestapo."

"Gestapo?"

"Geheime Staatspolizei—the Secret State Police. It's a terror outfit that Goering set up. There's a power struggle going on. They say the SS will soon take it over under Himmler."

Jeremy was bewildered. "You mean Kleist is some kind of spy?"

"They're all afraid of Kleist. Germans are learning to keep their mouths shut these days."

"Well, I'm not a German," Jeremy said angrily. "And I don't have to be afraid of mugs like Kleist."

She searched his face wonderingly. "You great flapping infant!" she finally said. "You're absolutely fixed on getting yourself into trouble, aren't you? Well, don't expect any help from me. I can't afford to get mixed up in it."

With the sunlight harsh on her face, Millicent Wickes no longer looked like the young girl Jeremy had at first taken her for. He saw all the little lines around her eyes, and put her age at about thirty. It infuriated him that she had called him an infant.

"I can take care of myself, thank you," he said stiffly.

"You're already off to a bad start, you know."

"What do you mean?"

"They've been laughing about your little Jewish girl friend, the one who came to see you off. *Jüdische Fruchttorte,* your friend, the purser, calls her."

The blood rushed to Jeremy's head, blinding him. "They have no right!" he said.

The sudden rage drained away, and he saw Millicent looking at him pityingly.

"You *are* the chump, aren't you? Well I don't think I can afford to be seen spending a lot of time with you. Sorry, love."

She turned away with a toss of her yellow hair and headed toward the companionway to the afterdeck. Herr Schreiber, splashing happily in the canvas pool, saw her and waved. She waved back.

The three sailors who had set up the pool were loitering in the shadow of a ventilator. Jeremy recognized one of them as Heinke, the man who had first shown him aboard. He was bullying the other two, giving them little shoves for no reason that was clear to Jeremy from his vantage point. Heinke, suddenly aware that he was being watched, lifted his face toward the bridge house in a deliberate, insolent stare.

"Radio is the key," Kleist was saying, over the excellent sauerbraten and potato dumplings. "In a modern state, one must use modern methods to influence the great mass of people. That is something your own leaders do not yet understand, Miss Wickes. Your BBC gives its valuable broadcast time to bird watchers and other eccentrics instead of utilizing it for political purposes."

He scraped the gravy off his sauerbraten. Kleist ate like an ascetic. There had been cold lobster first, and he had ignored it.

"Whereas your Doctor Goebbels *does* understand all about propaganda, is that it?" Millicent said brightly.

At the adjoining table, Jeremy kept his mouth resolutely shut, except for eating his dinner. She's egging him on, he thought resentfully. If she can get away with it, why can't I? But he was determined to keep his vow to behave tonight. He found abstract political discussions like this boring anyhow.

"Most certainly," Kleist said, pushing the food around on his plate. "News must be a government monopoly. And to make sure that all the people get the message, Herr Goebbels is instituting production of an inexpensive radio receiver, the *Volksempfänger*—the People's Receiver."

"Lovely," Millicent said. "But I should think they'd be more grateful for a *Volkswagen*—a People's Automobile."

"Someday that too may come," Kleist said seriously. "But first Germany must recover economically. We are still staggering under the burden of reparations imposed by the Western democracies. At Versailles we were stabbed in the back by the rapacious French and by the Jew bankers of America."

It was too much for Jeremy. He glowered at Kleist, but before he could open his mouth, Millicent shot him a warning look.

"Are you referring to the Dawes Plan, Herr Kleist?" she said. "The one that provided a two-hundred-million-dollar loan to get German industry back on its feet?"

"Yes," Kleist growled. "And the infamous Young Plan that replaced it."

"I wasn't aware that Dawes and Young were Jewish names," Millicent said innocently.

He dismissed her remark with a wave of a hand. "It does not matter," he said. "In America, the Jews control everything."

"That's nonsense!" Jeremy exploded.

Heads turned in his direction. Millicent tried to deflect the situation. "But the Young Plan *reduced* Germany's reparations from thirty-three billion to nine billion," she said gamely. "And for the first time it set a specific date for the end of the payments."

Kleist's attention returned to Millicent. "Yes," he sneered. "And what is that date? Nineteen eighty-eight! Practically the end of the century!"

Graebe, the purser, was watching Jeremy closely. "Are you ready for another glass of beer, Herr Sinclair?" he said smoothly. "I can call the steward over."

Jeremy pushed his glass aside. "My father was a banker!" he blurted to Kleist. "And he wasn't a Jew! And he wasn't controlled by Jews, either!" He was so angry that his voice cracked like an adolescent's, spoiling the effect.

Kleist turned a superior smile on him. "Are you sure, Herr Sinclair?" he said.

At Jeremy's table, Brakel gave a little laugh.

"You people like to blame everything on the Jews," Jeremy said, his face burning. "But they've given Germany some of its finest literature and music! That *Kultur* you're so proud of!" In his mind he could see the face of Mr. Weintraub, his expression turned gentle and dreamy, as he played the Mendelssohn trio. "And science, too, even if you *have* kicked Einstein out of your country!" He sputtered inarticulately. "They're . . . they're just as good Germans as you are!"

Around him, the faces had closed like fists. The purser and the Schreibers had become very busy eating. At the other table, Millicent sat with an airy smile frozen on her face.

Brakel leaned over to the second officer and whispered, loud enough for Jeremy to hear, *"Judenfreund."*

Jew-lover, it meant.

The captain, his weatherbeaten face neutral, got the conversation going again. "And how is your steak tonight, Mr. Willoughby?" he said.

Mr. Willoughby had been peevish during all the talk in German that he didn't understand. "The steak's all right," he said grudgingly. "But that turtle soup of yours is going to give me heartburn. Gassy."

"Perhaps Dr. Schumann can oblige you." The captain raised his eyebrows. "Doctor?"

The ship's doctor raised his eyes obediently. He was a tall, angular man with faded blond hair and an old dueling scar down his cheek. His uniform was better tailored than those of the other officers. He had let it be known that he had been assigned to the *Buxtehude* for this trip only because the steamship company wanted him back in Germany in time to sail with one of the large passenger liners.

"Certainly, Herr Willoughby," he said with forced warmth. "Drop by my surgery after dinner, and I'll give you a powder to take."

"Yes, gas is not good," Kleist said, spearing himself another sliver of sauerbraten.

No one spoke to Jeremy during the remainder of the meal. It was fine with him.

He didn't feel like sleeping. He put his shirt and trousers back on and slipped into his shoes without bothering about socks, and let himself out of his cabin to look out at the dark sea and smoke a cigarette.

After a few minutes, the door to Millicent Wickes's cabin opened and closed, spilling a wedge of yellow light across the passenger deck. Millicent came out in robe and slippers to join him at the rail.

"Well, you made a proper mess of it tonight, didn't you?" she said.

"I don't care," Jeremy said. "I'm glad I told them what I thought."

"Yes, you certainly did that."

"You were baiting Kleist yourself," he accused.

"I'm not you, love. I'm an addlepated female, to be humored. I'm just too benighted to understand their divine destiny, and they can condescend to me. The Germans have been on their uppers since they lost the war, and they've got to find someone to blame. The Jews are handy. And you threw it back in their teeth."

"God, they're so *smug!*"

She gave him a curious look. "I had a drink in the saloon just now with the Schreibers and a couple of the officers. Everybody seemed relieved that you didn't drop by. They're calling you the *Judenfreund.*"

"The Jew-lover. Yes, I know."

"Brakel's a swine. Even Kleist doesn't care for him much. He's too low and vulgar. *Gemein.* Too thick with the ordinary seamen. I don't doubt that he's been gossiping with the oilers about the latest indiscretions of the *Amerikaner* with the *jüdische* girl friend."

"She's not . . . not my girl friend."

"I'm sure it's none of *my* business, love," she said tartly. "But do try to watch your step in the future. The officers will behave correctly, but the men are another story. Things can get out of hand. Lord knows, I've seen it often enough in Germany since Hitler bullied his way into the Hindenburg government."

"Don't worry," he said sullenly. "Nobody's going to see much of me during the rest of the trip, except for mealtimes. I'm going to keep to myself till we dock. I've lost my taste for the company of the people on this ship."

"Ow!" she said.

"The hell with the gracious shipboard life! It was just a cheap way to get to Germany anyway. Once I'm in Berlin, I'll forget all about the Brakels and the Kleists."

"I wouldn't count on finding things too different in Berlin if I were you."

"There are tinhorn fascists everywhere. We've got our Huey Long and you've got your Oswald Mosley. You just have to ignore them. Berlin's the place to be these days. For intellectual and artistic ferment . . ."

"So that's it," she said in disgust. "I should have known. Another imitation expatriate! The Left Bank is dead and Paris has lost its bloom. Hemingway's gone fishing in Cuba, Fitzgerald's gone Hollywood, and now all the bright young men are flocking to the Friedrichstrasse to write this decade's *Ulysses!*"

"It's not like that," he said, stung. "Artists and poets just naturally go where it's cheap to live."

"You're too late, Jeremy love. It's all over for the artists and poets in Berlin. Brecht left the day after the Reichstag fire. Kurt Weill and Lotte Lenya followed him. Max Reinhardt was forced to close the Deutsches Theater. Mann ran for his life to Switzerland. The Nazis run the show now, and they don't like your chums."

"That's what my brother told me."

"You should have listened to him. Well, try to stay out of trouble."

"Don't worry," he said angrily. "You better go back to your cabin. Somebody might see you talking to me!"

"Listen, you bloody little fool . . ." She looked at the expression on his face and broke off. "I'll do just that. Good night."

She flounced away, her robe swirling around bare legs. A fan of light from her cabin door widened and snapped shut. Her porthole went dark. Jeremy flipped his cigarette into the black ocean and set off for a walk around deck.

A trio of sailors came toward him out of the murk. Jeremy frowned. Seamen were supposed to stay away from passenger country. He supposed they were taking a shortcut from the engine room or wherever they had been working because they thought it wouldn't matter this late at night. They passed a lighted porthole, and in the pale wash of light he recognized Heinke.

The passageway was narrow here, and he waited for them to step aside as he passed. But they didn't. They came straight on without slowing down, and as they brushed past him, Heinke jostled him. Hard.

There was no apology. They continued on without looking back. He heard them laughing about something, but he couldn't catch the words.

Jeremy rubbed his bruised shoulder, fuming. But he decided not to report Heinke in the morning. He didn't want to get the man in trouble.

They ran into rough weather the next day, a nasty squall that sent big, hard raindrops spattering like bullets onto the decks. Jeremy spent the day in his cabin, trying to read *Ulysses*. He skipped lunch. He didn't feel like facing anybody. He had helped himself to some fruit from the cold-locker when he visited the galley for his early-morning breakfast, and that was enough to get him through the afternoon.

By dinnertime, he was hungry. He was tempted to butter himself a roll and eat it while waiting for the appetizer to be served, as Brakel was doing, but decided to be patient. There was always too much to eat.

The atmosphere at his table seemed to be constrained. The Schreibers and the officers made a few desultory attempts at conversation with one another, but nobody addressed Jeremy directly.

At the adjoining table, Kleist was being obnoxious. "So perhaps a few Jews have had their heads knocked in by some of our overenthusiastic young fellows, Miss Wickes. And we no longer allow them to practice law and the other professions. What of it? What we do with our Jews is our business. What right has the American ambassador, Dodd, to protest? What of the way the Americans treat their Negroes?

Do you see a Negro Supreme Court justice? And what of the Ku Klux Klan and all the lynchings in the South? Does the world protest that?"

Though he was addressing Millicent Wickes, he was speaking in a loud, clear voice that was obviously meant to reach Jeremy's ears. He was speaking in German, so that if Mr. and Mrs. Willoughby caught the references to "Amerika," they had no inkling of what was going on. Every once in a while Kleist would smile fatuously at them, and make some innocuous remark in English.

Jeremy was determined not to let Kleist get his goat. He was relieved when the appetizer was finally served and everybody stopped talking, then groaned inwardly when he saw what it was. Jellied eels! He'd learned to eat a lot of things since he'd left Iowa, but he couldn't face jellied eels. He'd left them on his plate when they'd been served, the first night out, and the steward, surprised that he didn't like the delicacy, had solicitously brought him sardines instead. Jeremy was surprised that the steward hadn't remembered.

"Uh . . . could I have something else instead?" Jeremy said. "Some goose liver and crackers, sardines, anything?"

The steward swept his plate away without replying and disappeared into the pantry. Jeremy waited for him to reappear, but he didn't. The minutes ticked by, with everybody else finishing their appetizers, Brakel smacking his lips loudly. Jeremy looked enviously at Mr. Willoughby, toying with his deviled eggs. It would have been unthinkable to give Mr. Willoughby the jellied eel. Deviled eggs or the paper-thin Westphalian ham, that's all he would tolerate for his first course. Jeremy took another sip of his water. He wasn't going to make a fuss. If the steward had forgotten him, he'd wait for the soup course.

"Who is President Roosevelt's advisor?" Kleist was saying to Millicent Wickes. "Bernard Baruch. A Jew." He smiled at the Willoughbys and switched to English. "I see in the news that your President Roosevelt has made the British and the French very angry by refusing to stabilize their currencies with respect to the dollar."

Willoughby went on munching, a smear of egg on his chin. "The man's an out-and-out communist," he said. "I voted for Hoover."

The steward came out of the pantry and cleared away the appetizer plates. He passed by Jeremy's place without comment. Jeremy looked up to see Brakel grinning broadly. When Brakel saw him looking, he changed his expression to one of bland innocence.

". . . and Henry Morgenthau meets with Roosevelt in his bedroom every morning to set the price of gold for the day," Kleist's abrasive voice went on. "And who is Morgenthau? Another Jew."

The steward emerged from the galley with the soup course, balancing the heavy tray expertly against the ponderous heaving of the ship.

The little wooden barriers had been set out around the edges of the tables tonight, even though the sea wasn't quite rough enough to make them necessary.

". . . but it's not surprising," Kleist continued with a sneer. "Roosevelt himself is a Jew. His real name is Rosenfeld."

It was too much for Jeremy. "Listen . . ." he began loudly.

The steward, standing behind him, suddenly lurched, and a bowl of hot beet soup landed bottom up in Jeremy's lap. Jeremy leaped to his feet. Everybody's eyes were on him.

"Verzeihung," the steward murmured. *"Die Wellen sind hoch . . ."*

He made a few perfunctory swipes with a towel at Jeremy's trousers, seeming not at all concerned, and retreated to the galley.

"What a pity," the purser said unctuously. "Your trousers are soaked. Perhaps you would like to go back to your cabin and change them. I'm sure you can get back in time for the main course."

Jeremy mumbled an apology and left in embarrassed confusion, feeling everybody's eyes on the bloodlike red stain at his crotch and thighs. As he fled out into the driving rain, he heard Brakel laugh.

The door to his cabin was ajar. He frowned. He was sure he had left it closed.

He turned on the light and gasped. The locker door was open wide and all the drawers of the little dresser were pulled out. His clothing, toilet articles, and other possessions were scattered all over the floor, covered with oily handprints. He knelt. Nothing seemed to have been taken.

But his books—all of them: *Ulysses,* the Rilke poems, the precious copy of *The Waste Land*—had been torn apart and defaced. They were ripped down the spines, great handfuls of pages had been torn out, and the covers and every page that was exposed to view had crudely drawn swastikas scrawled all over them in red crayon.

Whoever had done it hadn't known the difference between Heine and Nietzsche. They should have checked with Kleist. The thick volume containing *Thus Spake Zarathustra, The Will to Power,* and *The Antichrist* had been treated just as badly as the rest of them, the theory of the *Übermensch* notwithstanding.

Sorrowfully he picked up some shredded pages of Heine. The words leaped to his eye:

"Those who begin by burning books," the poet had written, "end by burning people."

"You are not accusing any of my crew of thievery?" Captain Bruning said, his face like stone.

"N-no," Jeremy said. "Nothing was taken, but—"

"German sailors are not thieves."

"But my clothes, thrown all over the place, and the oil stains . . ."

The captain stared with controlled distaste at the shabby flannels that Jeremy was wearing. He hadn't been able to get the beet stains out of the good trousers, despite the soaking he'd given them in his little lavatory sink. The front of them still had an embarrassing pinkish hue that made them impossible to wear.

"So," the captain said heavily, "perhaps some young men are not as neat as they might be, yes? And they do not notice that their clothes have not been kept clean. To bring a formal complaint is a serious matter. And whom would you accuse?"

Jeremy flushed. "I didn't leave my clothes like that. And my books . . ."

"They were not new books?"

"No, I got them secondhand."

The captain spread his square hands. "Who can say who had those books before? And nothing was taken."

Speechless, Jeremy stared at the closed face. He turned and left the captain's office without a word.

A couple of sailors were outside, one polishing brightwork, the other mopping the deck. They looked up as he emerged. As he passed, the one who was swabbing the deck was careless with the mop and spattered his cuffs with dirty water. Jeremy didn't feel up to a confrontation. He quickened his step and headed toward the promenade deck. When he rounded the corner, he almost collided with Millicent Wickes.

"Hullo," she said. "You didn't come back to dinner last night."

"No, I lost my appetite."

She looked at him shrewdly. "Something happened."

"Yes." He told her.

"Crikey!"

"The captain isn't going to do anything about it. He told me that those swastikas must have been all over my books all the time, and that I probably just didn't notice them."

"Ah, yes, the Germans invented fairy tales. First the Brothers Grimm. Now Herr Doctor Goebbels. Well, you can't say I didn't warn you."

"No."

"They've kept you from having three meals, haven't they? They ought to discount ten percent of your passage."

"I thought I was getting a bargain. I only paid fifty dollars."

She looked startled. "*I* paid forty. And they still have a cabin they weren't able to fill."

She had reminded him of how hungry he was. "I'll see you at lunch. If I don't die of starvation first."

"You won't mind if I don't go in on your arm, love? I'm sure you understand."

"Oh, I understand, all right."

"Don't be a beast. I'm still cultivating Kleist. My boss wants to do a story on Siemens."

"Then I'd better leave before I contaminate you."

"You're a surly brute, aren't you? I don't wonder you get on the Germans' nerves."

"I'll be in my cabin till lunch," he said, and walked away.

He was so lost in thought that he didn't hear the footsteps behind him. The next thing he knew, someone was treading deliberately on his heels, left foot, right foot, left foot. He stopped and was almost bowled over by the forward momentum of the man behind him. He flailed for balance and his hand brushed a hairy forearm, as hard as maple. He turned and saw Heinke with a smirk on his face.

"What the hell do you think you're doing?" he flared.

The man stared at him insolently. "The ship is too small," he said.

Jeremy's fists were clenched. Heinke waited. No one was around. Despising himself, Jeremy turned and walked away.

The captain's chair was empty. He rarely appeared for lunch with the passengers. As chief engineer, Brakel was supposed to preside in his place. Kleist was absent, Jeremy was glad to see. At least he wouldn't have to worry about the man goading him into losing his temper.

Millicent was being monopolized by Mrs. Willoughby. Mr. Willoughby, she explained in a fretful voice, was indisposed. He was lying in his cabin, suffering from the effects of the rich cream that the cook had so thoughtlessly given him with his breakfast cereal. The doctor expressed regret, and said that he would drop by after lunch and see Mr. Willoughby.

Lunch began with asparagus soup. Jeremy thought that Brakel and the other officers were watching him closely, as if in anticipation of another disaster. He got his soup without incident, however.

He put a spoonful into his mouth, and almost spit it out.

It was so salty that it burned his mouth; almost a saline solution disguised by the pale green of the asparagus. Somehow he managed to swallow the spoonful, and immediately took a long gulp of water.

"The soup," he sputtered to the steward. "It's all salt."

"I'm sorry it's not to your taste, *mein Herr*," the steward said.

Brakel blew on a spoonful of soup and swallowed it. "It tastes all right to me," he said slyly. He winked at the second officer. "How does it taste to you, Pieper?"

"Fine," the second officer said, and hastily devoted himself to his meal.

Brakel! He must have put the cook and the steward up to it. And if a lout like Heinke thought he could get away with being insolent to a passenger, then his attitude must have filtered down to the crew. The *Judenfreund* was fair game.

Jeremy knew it would be no use asking for another bowl of soup. He pushed it aside and helped himself to two buttered rolls.

The main course arrived, a cutlet covered with some kind of thick sauce, with potato salad. It was all right. Brakel seemed to have lost interest in him. Perhaps the practical joke was over. The cutlet was tender enough to cut with his fork. He took a bite, and almost threw up.

The meat was rotten. The thick sauce had disguised it. He spat the putrid mouthful into his napkin, gagging helplessly, and leaped violently to his feet, knocking over his chair.

"Well I never!" he heard Mrs. Willoughby exclaim as he raced for the exit. He barely made it to the rail in time. Wretchedly he heaved up the buttered rolls and potato salad. When his nausea subsided, there were tears in his eyes, and the bitter taste of bile in his throat.

Trembling with anger, he marched back to the dining salon. Conversation stopped as he walked in.

"Not feeling well, Herr Sinclair?" the purser asked solicitously. Millicent watched him appraisingly.

Wordlessly, Jeremy leaned across the table and helped himself to every roll in the basket, stuffing them into his jacket pockets. For good measure he took a hard-boiled egg off the plate of an astonished Brakel and tucked somebody's bottle of beer under his arm.

"I've never seen such manners," Mrs. Willoughby huffed as Jeremy walked out.

Back in his cabin, he arranged his booty carefully on the dresser top. He'd eat it when his stomach quieted down. He'd be damned if he'd let the Germans starve him after he'd paid them for his passage. There were five days to go till Hamburg. At dinner tonight he'd fill up on bread and butter if he had to, and help himself to the community pâté, the cheese, the fruit from the centerbowl.

He turned around then, and saw what they'd done to his good suit.

It was hanging on the inside of the open locker door, where he'd left it after sponging off the machine oil. Somebody had cut a large, obscene hole out of the crotch. The hole was outlined in white paint, and written above it in thick, hasty strokes was the word JUDE.

* * *

"This was all I could swipe for you without attracting attention," Millicent said. "For God's sake, *will* you close that door!"

Jeremy pushed the cabin door shut. Millicent pulled things out from among the balls of wool and knitting needles in her reticule and set them out on the bedspread. There was a roll, an apple, a banana, a fragment of cheese, a couple of sugar pretzels.

"Thanks," Jeremy said. "I mean it."

"Wait a minute. Here's the pièce de résistance." She dug into her reticule again and pulled out an enormous sticky slice of torte, wrapped in waxed paper. "I've suddenly taken to having late-night snacks in my cabin, you see," she laughed.

"This is really swell of you," he said, eyeing the torte hungrily. He'd polished off his luncheon swag early in the afternoon, saving one small roll for bedtime. He'd just been about to eat it when Millicent arrived.

"I thought you'd be wanting something when you didn't show up for dinner. What was all that about at lunch, by the way?"

He told her about the salted soup, the rotten cutlet.

"Crikey!" she said. "They're out to get you, aren't they? Why didn't you come to dinner? Things can't get *too* out of hand with the captain there. Just brazen it out and keep sending food back to the galley. They won't have time to doctor *everything* on your plate."

"I was going to, but I couldn't afford to leave my cabin."

Silently, he showed her the trousers of his suit.

"That's their style of humor, all right," she said. "They think anything to do with circumcision is very funny. Brakel had a joke from one of his oilers that he was passing on over dessert. He kept looking over to my table to make sure I'd overheard. Frau Schreiber made a big show of being scandalized, but she laughed till her husband had to pound her on the back."

"They've ruined my suit and my best flannels so far," he said. "I can't land in Germany with just the clothes on my back."

"No," she said. "Listen, chum, you'll have to work something out yourself. I'm willing to keep up my new passion for knitting, but I can't promise to keep smuggling food to you indefinitely. In any case, a couple of apples and the odd piece of cheese is rather a limited diet."

"I can look after myself," he said with a scowl.

"Can you? You haven't been doing too terribly well at it so far."

She poked a cautious head outside, and left. Jeremy picked up the apple and took a bite.

There was no moon tonight. The stars hid behind scudding clouds.

Once in a while one of them would break free of the overcast, a brilliant point of light that would wink out almost immediately. The sea was a black eternity, unknowable. There were only the disembodied squares of light that were the bridge house, high overhead.

Jeremy felt his way along the deck to the rail. The air was fresh and cool after the storm. He needed a breath on deck after the stifling hours in his cabin. He didn't intend to stray far from his cabin door. If anyone tried to open it, the sudden flood of light from the lamp he'd left on would alert him.

He almost hoped someone would try.

He stood at the rail awhile, breathing the alien salt tang of the ocean, listening to the dull pounding of the ship's engines far below. His stomach was comfortably full for the first time in two days. He gazed at the black void beyond the rail and let his thoughts roam. He could almost imagine himself alone in space, traveling to a distant star. But he remembered a Sunday supplement story he had read, where an eminent scientist had proved beyond the possibility of doubt that there was no known explosive powerful enough to fling itself free of earth's gravity, let alone lift a space rocket too. No, mankind would never walk on the moon. It was fun to think about, but it was strictly Buck Rogers stuff.

The shuffling of feet on the deckboards roused him from his thoughts.

Jeremy turned and saw a cluster of dark, furtive figures moving swiftly toward him. They were keeping close to the cabin wall, out of sight of the bridge house up above and the lookout forward.

Jeremy tensed. These were no sailors taking a shortcut.

Before he could decide what to do, they were crowding all around him. There were four or five of them, dark shapes with indistinct faces, smelling of dried sweat and diesel oil.

"The Jew-lover's out for a stroll," a jolly voice said.

"You should have stayed in your cabin."

"Hey, Jew-licker, want to lick me?"

Another voice, more nervous, said, "Come on, let's get it over with."

No one had touched him yet. Jeremy said, "Get out of my way. Immediately." He was surprised at how firm his voice was.

It almost worked. The two in front of him actually took a backward step. Then somebody grabbed his arms from behind.

"Get his legs, quick!"

Jeremy tried to kick, but he was too late. A burly sailor was hugging his knees, and powerful hands were clamped around his wrists and elbows. He struggled, and they laughed at him.

"Be nice, little Jew-lover," somebody sniggered, and pinched his cheek.

Jeremy seethed with the humiliation of it. They weren't even beating him up properly. They were nothing but a bunch of smirking playground bullies tormenting a younger child.

"Release me at once," he said. "The captain will hear of this!"

"The captain!" the sniggerer said. "This ship has no captain!"

Jeremy turned his head. The face was a vague, paler patch against the prevailing gloom, but he thought the man's bulk and the way he moved were familiar. "I recognize you, Heinke," he said.

"What of it?" Heinke said, turning surly.

"And you too," he said to a man he thought was the sailor who had spattered him with the mop.

"Let's go," the nervous one said.

The others were not to be deflected from their hilarious mood. "Tell us, lover, how is it with your little *jüdische Fruchttorte?* Does she like it the regular way?"

"Shut your mouth!" Jeremy said.

"I think he's a Jew himself," one of them remarked with a laugh.

"Let's have a look and find out," Heinke growled.

Despite Jeremy's violent thrashing, it took the sailors only a moment to haul down his trousers. Somebody produced a flashlight. Jeremy, in an agony of shame and anger, heard them laughing.

"What do you know! He isn't a Jew after all!"

"Look, look, his little *Spargelspitze* is trying to crawl away!"

They collapsed with merriment. They've had their fun, Jeremy thought; now maybe they'll let me go.

Heinke tilted his head. In the stray illumination from the flashlight, Jeremy could see the potato nose, the wide lips parted to show the rotten stumps of teeth. Heinke pulled a large clasp knife out of his pocket and unfolded the blade with a click.

"As he has so much sympathy for Jews," Heinke chuckled, "we should turn him into one."

Jeremy struggled in panic. The sailors held on more tightly.

The laughter had taken on a sort of sick excitement. "Don't cut off too much, Heinke," somebody said.

Heinke tested the edge of the blade on his thumb. "The Jewish bitch will like it better after it's been trimmed," he said.

This can't be happening, Jeremy thought. They're just trying to scare me.

Then there was the shock of someone touching his intimate flesh, pinching the loose skin between thumb and forefinger. "Hold the flashlight steady, Karl," Heinke said.

Oh, my God, Jeremy thought, I've never even had a girl in my entire life, and now I'll never be able to have one. It did not occur to him to scream.

"Hold still," Heinke hissed at him. "If you move around like that, you might make my hand slip."

"Hurry it up," the nervous one said.

There was a burning stab of pain, worse than he could have imagined, and a hoarse scream clawed its way out of his throat. Yellow light spilled across the deck, bringing it back into the universe, and a skinny shadow was framed in an open slice of door.

"What's going on out there?" Mr. Willoughby's elderly voice complained.

The sailors dropped Jeremy to the deck. *"Vorsicht!"* one of them said urgently, and they scattered, still laughing. They voices faded down the companionway.

"What is it, Horace, what's going on?" came Mrs. Willoughby's voice from inside the cabin.

"Stay where you are, Cora," Mr. Willoughby said sharply. "I'll handle this." To Jeremy he said in a harsh, carrying whisper, "I don't know what you're doing, and I don't care. You just get your pants on and get back in your cabin before the ladies see you."

Jeremy tried to raise himself on one elbow and almost screamed again at the bright flash of pain this caused in his groin. He opened his mouth to ask for help, but Mr. Willoughby had already slammed his cabin door shut and shot the bolt.

He crawled the twenty feet to his own cabin door like an inchworm, sliding on one bare hip and pulling himself along with one elbow, while with the other hand he held the trousers that were bunched around his ankles. He was able to butt his door open with his shoulder and roll himself inside. He pushed the door shut behind him and lay on the floor panting, afraid to look at his wound. Warm thick blood ran down his thigh, welling up as if it was not going to stop.

He couldn't touch it. It burned like hot coals when he tried. But after a minute or two he was able to get to his feet in front of the lavatory sink and inspect the damage under a running faucet. It wasn't as bad as he had feared. The knife had sliced right through the foreskin and taken a little nick out of the edge, but the glans was only scratched. He wasn't going to be able to wear trousers until the parted edges of skin knit together again, but he was still a man.

His writer's brain wouldn't keep quiet. I'm an honorary Jew now, he thought with bitter mirth. Very well, then, when he arrived in Hitler's new Germany, he would wear the scar proudly.

* * *

"Herr Sinclair!"

The knock on the door was discreet. A bright shaft of early-morning sunlight streamed through the porthole, bathing the cabin in a golden warmth that washed away the last traces of nightmare.

Jeremy hobbled to the door dressed in a shirt and the sarong he had contrived for himself out of his bath towel. The touch of the towel against his wound if he tried to straighten up was pure agony, and he had to remember to stay bent over.

It was Dr. Schumann, stiffly erect in his blue uniform and gold braid, looking spruce and trim. He put his little medical bag on the dresser and began laying out cotton swabs and alcohol.

"So, you have done yourself a little injury," he said with heavy geniality. "I am afraid you have been doing something that is not nice." He shook his head in mock despair. "Ach, you young men! The things a doctor sees! Well, do not worry, Herr Sinclair, I am sure it is not serious."

"Who told you?" Jeremy said.

"That does not matter," the doctor said. "You will please remove the towel now, yes?"

"Was it Herr Willoughby? Or are they making jokes in the forecastle this morning?"

"Please, I am very busy."

"You can get out of my cabin. Right now."

The doctor regarded him coldly. The dueling scar on his cheek flared an angry crimson. "Your behavior is incorrect," he said stiffly. "I am here to help you and you have shown ingratitude. But what can one expect from a country of half-breeds?"

He closed his bag and left with enormous dignity, leaving the swabs and ointment behind. Jeremy glared at the door.

Millicent Wickes slipped into his cabin in mid-morning. "I can only stay a mo', love. The Schreibers are getting up a shuffleboard game. I brought you an orange and a lovely slice of *Zuckerkirschtorte*." She raised an eyebrow at his shirt-and-towel getup. "Well, aren't you the wee kiltie? Is the Sinclair tartan pink terry? What's up, love? The story is that you can't leave your cabin. For reasons unspecified."

"Some of Brakel's oilers tried to circumcise me."

She stared at him a moment, then broke into laughter. "Excuse me, but that's really very funny."

He flushed. "The hell it is."

She put her hand on his arm. "I'm sorry, Jeremy, but if you only knew. Well, there go my plans for the rest of the voyage. I don't suppose . . ."

"No," he said shortly.

"Hurts even to think about it, does it? Well, worse luck, damn it and all. Be good, love, though I don't suppose there's much else you *can* be for a while."

She left, after a last regretful look at him. Jeremy stared unhappily at the closed door, hardly able to believe what he had just heard. He cursed himself for having been so dense.

Chalk up another atrocity for the Nazis, he thought. They kept Jeremy Sinclair a virgin for another week of his life.

The *Buxtehude* chugged its way up the crowded, smoking Elbe, past the miles and miles of slips and moored vessels, following the buoys that marked the channel. The air was filled with the screams of steam sirens from ships and shore. A great liner passed, on its way out to sea. A brass band on its deck played Spanish music, while passengers crowded the rail and waved.

Jeremy waved back, with feeling. He leaned over the rail, his jacket collar turned up, the wind whipping his straight black hair. He stared with a midwesterner's awe at the cluttered shore with its forest of steel chimneys and giant cranes. Beyond, the complicated skyline of Hamburg rose from the steaming harbor, a vision of strange futuristic buildings mixed in with medieval spires. Jeremy gawked at the cubist bulk of a *Wolkenkratzer*—"cloud-scratcher"—glittering in the morning sunlight. The colossal office buildings rivaled anything he had seen in New York. He had heard that open elevators ran in an endless loop, like buckets on a chain, never stopping, while people hopped nimbly on or off at their floors.

Sailors scurried back and forth on the *Buxtehude*'s deck, strained at capstans, wrestled with the gangplank chains. Jeremy could see Heinke among them, sweating at a thick rope. He looked like any middle-aged workman, the kind you passed at their jobs without noticing.

The other passengers waited in isolated pairs at the rail with their luggage. The officers had no time for them now that they were about to dock. No one looked in Jeremy's direction. The Schreibers stood self-consciously apart, surrounded by worn suitcases, Herr Schreiber already in a gray business suit with elephant-leg trousers. Millicent, in a gay candy-stripe frock and straw hat, was talking animatedly to Kleist, who looked dapper in blue blazer and white flannels. As Jeremy watched, Kleist's hand moved familiarly to Millicent's buttock and patted it like a dog's head. He looked past them to the Willoughbys, who were edging forward to be first at the gangplank, while Mr. Willoughby looked impatiently at his watch.

Surprisingly, it had been Mr. Willoughby who had made a fuss about Jeremy not getting trays in his cabin, after Millicent told him what was going on. He had appeared at Jeremy's door and said, "I don't like you or your fancy communist ideas, young man, and I don't care for your sort of morals, but I'm not going to stand by and see these Krauts cheat a fellow American out of what he paid for." Jeremy never found out what Mr. Willoughby had said, but the meals he was served in his cabin after that were perfectly all right. There were even the little treats that any other passenger confined to his cabin might have expected: a bowl of *Schlagsahne* to put in his chocolate, or a thimbleful of brandy to top off his coffee.

By the last night of the voyage, Jeremy's wound had pretty well closed up, leaving an irregular scar where the edges of skin had rejoined. A reminder, he thought. A useful memento of the state of brotherly love on this planet in this year of our Lord, 1933.

I'm not going to let the bastards keep me away from the captain's farewell dinner, he'd resolved. Captains on passenger freighters traditionally outdid themselves on the last night of the voyage, paying for a special menu out of their own pockets. It was a matter of maritime pride. The Brakel faction expected Jeremy to stay decently out of sight and save everybody from embarrassment, and maybe as a reward his tray would include a paper hat and some party favors.

The hell with that! He could put his pants on by now, though he still tended to walk carefully.

There had been a stunned silence when Jeremy strode into the dining salon. Brakel gaped as he brought a chair over and made room for himself at his old place, as if nothing had happened. Then the captain had said brusquely to the steward, *"Schnell, schnell,* set a place for Herr Sinclair without delay!"* Jeremy sat down with a smile and a nod for everybody, put on his paper hat like the others, and blew an experimental toot on his noisemaker. He pretended to be enjoying himself hugely, despite the damper his presence had put on the conversation. He ignored Kleist's provocative remarks from the next table. There was only one incident: his first glass of champagne had been spoiled by having vinegar added to it. Jeremy immediately poured it into Brakel's half-empty glass, saying with an idiot grin, "Please, Herr Brakel, your glass is empty. Have some of mine." Brakel had sent the champagne back without tasting it, saying to the steward, "Bad vintage," and had been rewarded by a scowl from the captain for wasting good champagne. After that there were no problems.

Now, still pleasantly stuffed with the captain's caviar and pheasant and truffles and roast beef and ice cream cake, he looked out benevolently at the brave new futuristic Germany rising out of the dingy shoreline. The Germans were an energetic people. They could build something fine and clean out of the rubble of war and world depression, once they put the present nastiness behind them. Everybody said Hitler couldn't last long.

He patted Mr. Weinbaum's letter in his breast pocket. He'd deliver it and settle down to write his novel. Let the Germans work things out for themselves. In the meantime, he'd ignore politics and politics would ignore him.

There was a rattle of chains as the gangplank was lowered into place. The *Buxtehude* had tied up at a "dolphin," a clump of pilings in the channel, to avoid wharf charges. A couple of hired motor launches bobbed nearby, waiting for the luggage to be carried down and the passengers to descend. Jeremy hung back. He didn't want to be in the same launch as Millicent and Kleist. He had his day planned: a visit to the famous Hamburg Zoo this morning, a cheap waterfront lunch, then to the Union Depot, and a ride on the much-talked-about Diesel electric train, a streamlined, airship-shaped vehicle that ran the 178 miles to Berlin in only 141 minutes—over seventy-five miles an hour!

A sailor picked up his suitcase and saluted respectfully. *"Hier entlang, bitte,"* he said.

Jeremy followed him to the gangplank without looking back.

16

"Three *weeks* ago?" Pamela said, hearing her voice turn shrill. "Do you mean to tell me that Junie's been missing for three *weeks,* and you haven't let Brad or me *know* about it?"

On the other end of the line, Uncle Elroy did a lot of throat clearing. "Wasn't no point in worrying you till . . . till we knew what was what."

"But I called just last week to speak to Mama. You didn't say anything about it then, and you didn't put Mama on the line, either."

"She was asleep."

"What do the police say?"

He cleared his throat again. "It's . . . it's nothing you want to go bothering the police about."

"You mean you haven't notified the *police?*" This time her voice went stridently out of control. It earned a stare from the two girls who were just coming down the shabby staircase on their way to work, still dabbing at makeup and tugging at silk stockings.

Pamela flushed. There was no privacy in the women's rooming house that Brad had installed her in. It was full of government girls, made independent and a little wild by the salaries they earned—the same as men for equal work. They visited one another's rooms constantly, bemoaned the shortage of single men in Washington, borrowed hair curlers, combs, clothing without asking. Once Pamela had even had to throw away a toothbrush. Boy friends were allowed in the parlor, and though the house rules were supposed to be strict, you hardly dared walk in there on a weekend night unless you were immune to embarrassment.

She had decided to call Junie on the pay phone in the hall before going to work this morning, just to see how she was doing at school, and to make sure that she had used the twenty-five dollars she had given her to buy a new wardrobe. Uncle Elroy had hemmed and hawed, and finally admitted that Junie wasn't there.

Now Elroy was working up to his usual biblical righteousness. "She made her choice, and I ain't a-going to shame this family by having the police in on it."

"What are you *talking* about?" she said, almost stamping her foot with impatience. She glanced at the hall clock. She was going to be late, and there was a big mailing to get out for the senator today.

"She ran off with a no-account tenant farmer's boy, that's what. She was seen leaving town with the family."

"What boy? What's his name?"

"Some trash. Doesn't matter."

"Doesn't *matter*? June Alice hasn't turned sixteen yet. Now, if she was seen leaving town, she can be traced . . ."

"Good riddance!" Elroy snapped. "That's what I say. Now she won't be around to worry your mother with her doings. I won't have the little slut back in this house anyway."

Forcing herself to speak calmly, Pamela said, "Put my mother on. I want to talk to her this minute."

"Bad seed," Elroy raved. "A thief and a suicide for a father, a libertine for eldest son, and a pair of whores for daughters!"

"Hello, hello . . ." Pamela said, but she was speaking into a dead phone. She looked at the handful of coins she had left. There wasn't enough to place a call to Iowa again. She put a nickel in the slot and got the operator to call collect.

"I'm sorry," the operator said. "The party refuses to accept charges."

Pamela lit a cigarette to calm herself. Brad, she thought. Brad will know what to do.

She dug her nickel out of the slot, then dialed Brad's Georgetown flat. She tried twice, but there was no answer. He must have been out tomcatting all night. The Lord only knew whose bed in what part of Washington he was getting out of this morning. She'd have to wait and call him from the office.

Senator Marcus Hale's suite in the Senate Office Building still smelled of fresh paint. It was located in the new wing, just completed that year, which had turned the three-sided structure into a quadrangle. The senator's seniority and connections had enabled him to wangle one of the coveted new offices.

When Pamela walked in, she heard the sound of typing. Two of the girls, Doris and Janine, were already at their desks. Harvey Lucas, the senator's ulcer-ridden administrative assistant, unwound a lanky leg from the arm of the chair he'd been lounging in and turned his homely, acne-scarred face in her direction.

"Well, I've lived to see the day," he said, breaking into a grin. "The day the Iowa whirlwind wasn't the first one in the office. What happened, princess?"

"The senator isn't in?" she said in alarm.

"Marcus? Here before ten-thirty? Never fear. His first appointment's at eleven. That chicken farmers' delegation. But he left some longhand notes on that mailing late last night. The whole thing's got to be changed around. And it still has to get out today."

"It'll get out, don't worry," she said grimly. She took off her hat and patted her hair into place, put down her pocketbook, and sat down at her desk. Her heart sank when she saw the senator's changes. Her typing was still a little slow and uncertain, though she went to night classes twice a week. She got through her work by sheer persistence, staying at her desk when the other girls went out to lunch or went home at the close of office hours.

Harvey kept hanging around her desk. "You must be making an impression," he said. "Marcus actually noticed you yesterday. He said, 'Who's that pretty blond girl over by the mimeograph machine?' "

She laughed in spite of herself. "Give him another year and he might even remember my name."

"Don't be bitter, sweetheart. *I* appreciate you. I don't know how I ever got anything done around here before that rascally brother of yours blackmailed me into giving you a job."

"That's nice, Harvey," she said, "but I'm not going to get this mailing done if I keep talking."

He shook his head. "Looks of flame, heart of ice," he said with mock regret. He unfolded himself from the chair and slouched off to his own office.

Poor, dear Harvey! Shrewd, brilliant, intense—and working himself to death to nursemaid another man's career. His loyalty to Marcus Hale was total. Harvey would die of a heart attack or bleeding ulcers by the age of forty. He had made the expected pass at Pamela the first week she was there. She had fended Harvey off as tactfully as possible, then spent the next week worrying about her job. But Harvey needed reliable help more than he needed sex. He had grown to have a keen appreciation of Pamela's devotion to her duties. And Pamela, for her part, had been surprised, then delighted, to find that she *wasn't* useless after all. That she could do a demanding job, and do it well. For the first time since Carl Fuller had dealt what she had thought was a fatal blow to her self-esteem, she had come alive again.

She worked steadily through the first hour of the morning, giving Brad time to get to his desk in the Commerce Building. How he got away with being late all the time, she didn't know. The Brad charm, she supposed. He had inherited all the dazzle and sleight-of-hand allotted to this generation of the Sinclair family, while poor Jeremy had inherited the reverse side of the coin: all the mulish obstinacy and anger and awkwardness. Gordon was the only steady one.

She tried Brad's number four times, but the switchboard operator at the NRA kept saying, "Sorry, his line's still busy." Brad's line was always busy. He spent half his life on the phone, buttering people up for the gruff, salty General Hugh Johnson.

Finally, on the fifth try, she got through to Brad's secretary, an earnest, intimated girl named Priscilla.

"I'm sorry, Miss Sinclair," Priscilla said. "But Mr. Sinclair's just been called to the White House."

From the outer office, his secretary said reproachfully, "There's a call for you. He wouldn't say who he was." Brad sighed. From the expression on her face, he knew very well that she had recognized the voice, and that it was somebody she didn't approve of his talking to.

"Thanks, Priss. Close my door, will you?"

She gave him a sorrowful look and closed the door. He picked up the phone. He glanced at the newspapers spread out on his desk. He was afraid he knew what he was in for.

"Hello, Brad. This is Drew Pearson."

He sighed again. "Good morning, Drew. To what do I owe the honor of this call?"

"Come off it, Brad. You've seen the morning papers?"

"Indeed I have."

"What's the matter with that boss of yours, anyway? Can't you teach him to keep his foot out of his mouth?"

Brad cast a bloodshot eye over the headline. It screamed: 'MORE THAN A SECRETARY,' GENERAL JOHNSON SAYS. There was a picture of Robbie with it, looking very pretty. Brad had been present when Johnson had committed the unfortunate gaffe. A bunch of reporters had been ragging him about Robbie's high salary. The general had begged them to lay off, saying that she was "no mere stenographer or secretary," but did the work of an administrative assistant. Brad, knowing what was coming, had taken the newsmen aside afterward, and asked them privately not to use it, but the temptation had been too much for a couple of them.

"Well I guess I should thank you for not using it in 'Merry-Go-Round.' I owe you one."

"Bobby talked me out of it."

"Bobby" was Robert S. Allen, Pearson's collaborator on the "Washington Merry-Go-Round" column. Brad had warned the general a number of times to be careful what he said in his presence, but Johnson had replied airily, "Bobby Allen is a friend of mine. He's one newshawk who would never consciously do me an injury." Brad knew that if Allen hadn't used the item, it was because too many other reporters had it, and he was resigned to the fact that Johnson would view this as evidence of "friendship."

"Thanks anyway. I still owe you one."

"Wait a minute. You haven't heard the worst. How early were you up this morning?"

"Not very," Brad said cautiously. "Why?"

"Old Ironpants called the fellows in to complain." Pearson was having a hard time keeping the amusement out of his voice. "What do you suppose he said?"

Brad steeled himself. "What?"

"He looked them in the eye, man to man, and said, 'Boys, you're hitting below the belt.' "

"Oh, no!" Brad groaned.

"I'm afraid it's so."

Brad said carefully: "Are you going to use it?"

Pearson laughed. "It'll be stale by tonight. Every tabloid in the country will have it."

"Thanks again. I owe you two."

"How about right now."

"When I have something really juicy, you'll be the first to know," Brad said lightly.

Pearson said casually: "Mrs. Johnson doesn't get to see much of the general these days, does she? She stays in Virginia while he bunks in the office, or goes rushing around the country with Miss Robinson."

"Sorry, Drew. I have nothing to add. There just aren't any juicy tidbits. Why don't you just go with the below-the-belt crack, like everybody else."

"Your loyalty to Old Ironpants is commendable. But sooner or later you'll have to choose sides, you know."

Brad listened grimly. Pearson was talking about Donald Richberg, the former Chicago law partner of Harold Ickes, who had become general counsel of the NRA, and who now considered himself virtually coadministrator along with Hugh Johnson.

Brad didn't care much for Richberg, a large, balding, cigar-smoking man with an abrasive manner. Richberg had a gigantic ego, had pretensions of being a poet, composer, and novelist. He had already written a somewhat premature autobiography. Despite Roosevelt's economy drive, he had wangled for himself the highest salary in Washington below Cabinet level—fourteen thousand dollars minus the fifteen percent deduction that everybody, including Congress, was subjected to. Richberg, clever and self-serving, had begun to split the NRA into two factions. His staff had cautiously sounded Brad out on a number of occasions. Johnson was slow to see what was going on, though Robbie was doing her best to protect the general.

Brad had walked in on an amazing scene the other day. Richberg had tried to put something over on Johnson without "that woman's" interference, and had locked the general's office door from inside. Robbie had made a scene, pounding with her fists on the door and shrieking, "Let me in!" until Richberg, thwarted, had stalked out.

Brad grinned at the memory. He liked Robbie, and approved of her fierce protectiveness, though he knew she was no match for a powerhouse like Richberg.

What Drew Pearson was doing was inviting him to get on the Richberg bandwagon before it was too late.

But it wasn't time to switch sides yet.

"Well, it's been a fascinating conversation, Drew," he said, "but I've got to get back to work. The general's staging that tremendous Blue Eagle parade in New York today, and I'm holding down the fort in Washington. It's a madhouse here."

"Think it over, Brad."

"Sure, Drew. I think I'll let Don Richberg do his own leaking for a while, though."

The White House call came next. It was from Steve Early, FDR's press secretary.

"Brad, I think you better come over here right away."

"Now? Jesus, Steve, I'm up to my eyeballs this morning. Can't it wait till after lunch?"

"Now," Early said with emphasis, and hung up.

Brad got his hat off the rack and left. As he went out, the phone on his desk was ringing. Priscilla looked up at him with desperate eyes and said, "You *can't* leave! There's a delegation of druggists from Illinois waiting to see you. It's about the new master retail code. They say they want to lynch somebody. I can't locate Mr. Whiteside. And that's your sister on the phone again."

"Tell them Mr. Whiteside is hiding in the men's room. They can set up a gallows there. It has a high ceiling. And be a good egg and take the call from my sister. Tell her I'm on my way to the White House."

"The White House," Priscilla said, mollified. Her eyes shone. "How long will you be gone?"

"I'm not leaving till they appoint me to the Cabinet. If you absolutely have to reach me, I'll be with Steve Early."

"Oh," she said, disappointed. "Another press release."

Steve Early looked up from his desk when Brad walked into his cramped office and said, "Jesus, what a mess!"

Early was a rugged, handsome man in his forties, impeccably dressed in a pinstriped suit with a vest. He had been a crack AP reporter when, during Roosevelt's 1920 vice-presidential campaign, he had been hired as advance man. He had come to Roosevelt's attention again during the 1932 preconvention maneuvering at the governors' conference when—now a newsreel man—he had managed to jockey FDR into a rival governor's footage.

"You mean this morning's headline?" Brad said warily.

"Jesus Christ on a mountaintop!" It was a favorite Earlyism—one of the milder ones. "That's the least of our problems."

"What do you mean, *our* problems? I'm just supposed to be a lowly legal assistant."

Early passed a hand through his graying hair. "You're the only one over in that pile of limestone who speaks my language. Listen, Brad, do you love your boss?"

"Like a father."

"Marvin McIntyre got a call from the leader of a women's group in New York. They're up in arms about the story this morning. They warned Mac that no one wanted Robbie at the NRA rally in New York today. They called her 'That Robinson woman.' "

Brad's expression grew sober. "Bad," he said.

"Do you know Marv?"

"No," Brad admitted.

"He hasn't told the chief yet. He asked me what I thought, and I told him I'd get you in on it."

"I can't tell her not to go," Brad said. "If the general found out, he'd have my hide. 'Impertinent pup' is the least of what he'd have to say."

"How about Johnson's son? The lieutenant. Didn't the general pry him loose from the army and put him on the NRA payroll?"

"Pat? No, you won't get him to strong-arm Robbie for you. He's in a very delicate position over there. He's right in the middle, between his parents. Anyway, he likes Robbie. He depends on her to keep his father away from the bottle."

Early rubbed his eyes wearily. "Christ, what a mixed-up kettle of fish. Well, Brad, you're the only one with any kind of a handle on the situation. What do you suggest?"

Brad thought it over. "Robbie's a sensible girl. She has the general's best interests at heart. But you can't take a chance on her blowing up. It better come from somebody with enough authority to impress her. Not me. And I think she'll take it better from a woman."

Early nodded. "Let's go see Mac."

He led Brad down the hall to a room adjoining the President's office, and pushed the door open without knocking. A frail, skeletal man with hollow cheeks and eyes as bright and inquisitive as a sparrow's looked up as they entered.

"Mac, this is Brad Sinclair," Early said. "The guy I told you about."

McIntyre took Brad's hand in a grip that was warm and feverish. "Steve says you're unscrupulous and discreet," he said mischievously.

"My unscrupulousness has never been called into question," Brad laughed.

Brad took the opportunity to study the man who was closer to the President than any male staffer except the ailing and withdrawn Louis Howe. Marvin McIntyre looked as though a strong wind would blow him away. He couldn't have weighed more than one hundred and twenty pounds. There was a gentle, pixyish quality about him. A fair barbershop tenor and better drinking companion, he had somehow persuaded the White House press corps that FDR's favorite tune was "Home on the Range."

Like Steve Early, McIntyre was a former newsman who had worked for Roosevelt during the 1920 campaign. After the disastrous Cox-Roosevelt defeat, McIntyre, too, had gone to work as a newsreel representative, until Louis Howe had rehired him in 1931.

Early repeated what Brad had said. McIntyre listened, nodding, then stood up. "Wait here," he said to Brad, and left the room.

"Okay, it's in Mac's hands now," Early said. "You'll have to stick around in case there are any questions. You don't mind if I leave you alone, do you, Brad?"

"Not at all," Brad said, pretending to study the view outside the window. McIntyre's office faced the State, War, and Navy Building across a street crowded with parked cars. The immense baroque structure was an architectural monstrosity dating from the Grant administration, a grotesque fantasy of carved stone and proliferating columns. From one of its porches, an antique brass cannon pointed at the White House.

After Early was gone, Brad tiptoed across the carpet to the door leading to the Oval Office. There were no sounds from the other side. He eased the door open a crack and peered inside.

The President's office was unoccupied at this hour of the morning. Brad glimpsed a clutter of ship models, nautical prints, souvenirs; even a stuffed tarpon hanging above the mantel. The desk itself was so crowded with junk that there was scarcely a clear space to work on; Brad saw toy donkeys, ceramic pigs, a white stuffed elephant, a ship's clock, a ship wheel, barometer, ashtrays, two calendars, piles of memorandums. Roosevelt seemed to be a very human President.

He pushed the door an inch wider for a better look at the rest of the office. Just at that moment a door on the opposite side opened, and a tall, slim girl in a shirtwaist dress came through with a pile of folders. She looked to be in her thirties, pretty, with prematurely gray hair.

Her eyes darted immediately to the opened door and to Brad's eye peering through the crack. Before he could step back, she said: "You could get yourself shot by the Secret Service that way."

He jerked away as if he'd been burned, and heard tinkling laughter from the other side. Then there were footsteps and an instant later the door was firmly shut.

Brad didn't care. Now he could say he'd seen the Oval Office. The tall girl had to be Missy Le Hand, the President's private secretary. She, too, was a veteran of the unsuccessful 1920 campaign. She had been asked by Mrs. Roosevelt to come live at Hyde Park after FDR had been stricken with polio, and she had been with the family ever since. The younger Roosevelt children, John and Franklin Junior, had given her the nickname Missy because they could not pronounce Marguerite, and it had stuck. Now she lived, Brad had heard, on the third floor of the White House.

Marvin McIntyre poked his head through the corridor door and said, "Come with me." Brad followed him to a small elevator and found himself standing in a second floor corridor in the living quarters of the White House.

Brad expected to be left standing in the hall, but the next thing he knew, McIntyre was propelling him through a doorway into a large oval room that had been transformed into a study. He had time for a sketchy impression of an overflowing clutter that was even more disordered than that of the Oval Office downstairs: a tiger-skin rug, a canary in a cage, and ship models everywhere—in bottles, on stands, or simply propped against the tall windows.

Through an open door, a voice that he had heard only on the radio or in the newsreels called out heartily: "Is that you, Mac? Come right on in."

Before Brad had time to recover, McIntyre was pushing him unceremoniously into a bedroom, and he was suddenly in the presence of the President of the United States.

Roosevelt was flat on his back in bed while a Negro valet helped him into his trousers. He was a big man, bigger than he looked in the newsreels, with powerful shoulders and a barrel chest, but his legs were wasted and useless. That was another shock for Brad. Though he had known intellectually of the President's disability, the managed news photos hadn't prepared him emotionally for the sight of the valet picking the legs up like lifeless sticks. A pair of heavy steel braces leaned against a corner, looking like torture instruments. Evidently the President wasn't going to bother with them this morning.

Roosevelt flashed the familiar jaunty smile at him and said, as if it were the most natural thing in the world for Brad to be standing in his bedroom: "Marv the Mac tells me you've been a great help, young fellow. I'm going to follow your suggestion."

"Thank you, sir," was all Brad could manage.

The President turned to McIntyre. "I've called Frances. She's on her way over."

McIntyre glanced at his watch. "There isn't much time. I checked the airport. The general takes off in half an hour."

"Let's wait for her in the study. A gentleman's bedroom is no place for a lady," Roosevelt said, laughing at his own joke.

With the help of the valet, Roosevelt levered himself into a small, armless wheelchair and arranged his legs on the footrest by picking up the creases of his trousers. He was so totally unselfconscious and matter-of-fact about his paralysis that there was no question of being ill at ease in his presence.

Brad took the opportunity to surreptitiously study the man and his surroundings. Newspapers were scattered in disarray all over the bedspread; FDR's morning reading included the *New York Times* and the *Trib*, the *Washington Post* and the *Herald*, and the *Baltimore Sun*. A breakfast tray bore the remains of scrambled eggs, toast, and coffee. The President himself looked tired and baggy-eyed despite a night's sleep, though he was forcing a cheerful buoyancy with McIntyre. Brad recognized a kindred spirit; Roosevelt belonged to that vast company of souls to whom the first hour or two of the morning is a shuddering horror.

As the valet was leaving with the tray, the President interrupted his conversation with McIntyre to call out: "McDuffy, will you tell Mrs.

Nesbitt to *please* give me something else for lunch besides hash for a change?"

"I surely will," McDuffy said, "but that lady, she don't listen."

Roosevelt shook his head and said to McIntyre, "Eleanor won't let me fire the woman. Last week it was sweetbreads four days in a row." He added, a little wistfully, "I wish I could have Brunswick stew, just once, but she won't make it."

Brad thought it astonishing and pathetic that, with all his power, the President of the United States couldn't have what he wanted for lunch. But before he had time to reflect further, the President startled him by saying, "Brad the Bad."

"Mr. President?"

"Brad the Bad," the President repeated with a chuckle, and Brad realized that it was just a memory device FDR used. "But not as bad as your boss. Hugh's been a naughty boy, hasn't he?"

"The press likes to inflate things," Brad said cautiously.

The President gave a little nod—almost of approval—and wheeled himself rapidly toward the study. McIntyre and Brad followed. Brad realized that the President had been testing his discretion—inviting him to gossip or criticize—and that he had passed the test.

McIntyre realized it, too. "Nice going, Brad," he whispered as they entered the Oval Room.

The President heaved himself into the chair behind the desk with one powerful motion, and Brad understood why the wheelchair had no arms. There had been movement in the hall outside when the President emerged, probably a Secret Service man reporting on the President's progress, and a few moments later, without any sign of FDR having pushed a button, Missy Le Hand came in with a file folder and a dictation book.

"What have you got there, child?" the President said with mock resignation.

"Some letters that you simply *must* answer, F.D."

"Is there anything *really* important?"

"Mr. Ickes is quitting again," she said wickedly.

The President threw back his head and laughed. Evidently this was familiar banter. "Run along, child. Write him a soothing letter in my best style, and invite him to lunch with me tomorrow."

As Missy turned to go, her eyes lit on Brad and stayed there.

The President caught the look. "Yes, this young fellow will be staying for the meeting. This is Brad"—he repeated his mnemonic device with obvious relish—"the Bad."

"Yes, I know," Missy said, secret amusement in her eyes.

"We've met," Brad said, returning Missy's gaze without flinching.

"If Madam Secretary is waiting downstairs, send her right up," the President said.

Missy nodded, and swung out with a tiny smile.

Brad waited with anticipation. "Madam Secretary" would be Frances Perkins, Roosevelt's secretary of labor. She was an almost frighteningly able woman who had been industrial commissioner of New York State under Roosevelt's governorship. When he became President, he had made her the first woman ever to serve in a Cabinet post, despite catcalls and sniping from labor and the press. She had a teen-age daughter, and a shadowy husband hidden in a sanitarium, but she called herself "Miss Perkins."

Hugh Johnson raved about her: he admired her ability and counted her a trusted friend. Brad recalled that she had been the person who cooled General Johnson off the day Roosevelt had handed Harold Ickes the public works end of the recovery program.

A few minutes later, Frances Perkins sailed in, holding herself stiffly erect and wearing the brown tricorn hat that was her trademark. Her lips were set in a prim line, and she had gone out of her way to make herself look dull in a plain dark dress, but nothing could hide the lively intelligence in her darting eyes. Brad remembered that this formidable woman once had disarmed a gunman in a courtroom, wrestling with him until a guard could come to her aid.

Without preamble, Roosevelt said: "Frances, Hugh's in hot water again. What am I going to do? They're up in arms in New York."

Miss Perkins gave Brad a curious glance, but she didn't say anything and she didn't question his presence. McIntyre said hastily: "Brad's here to help. He works for General Johnson. You can trust his discretion."

"Nobody in New York wants the Robinson girl there," the President said. "Robbie, you call her, don't you?"

The President had modulated to a rich vibrato, his voice all helpless appeal. Overdoing it, Brad thought.

"Yes . . . Robbie," Miss Perkins said.

"They don't want her there with Hugh."

"She shouldn't go with him," Miss Perkins said tartly. She spoke with the kind of Boston accent that Brad had found intimidating in the parents of some of his Yale classmates. "I've been saying that for weeks."

"You saw today's papers," McIntyre interjected. "Brad's been working with Steve Early to try to keep that kind of stuff out."

Miss Perkins, with consummate manners, allowed herself to look at Brad. "Brad Sinclair," he said.

She acknowledged his self-introduction with a nod, then turned to the President.

"I've told her that she ought not to go on these expeditions with the general. And certainly not to allow herself to be photographed with him. It was bound to lead to gossip."

"Well, the gossips are having a field day," the President said. "What do you think we ought to do about New York?"

He's already decided, Brad thought, admiring Roosevelt's acting ability.

Miss Perkins wrinkled her forehead. "If he needs her, let her go by train. No photos of her stepping out of the airplane with him. She ought to stay away from the reviewing stand. She can wait for him in the NRA office if he needs her. The only thing she does is to keep him from drinking. You knew that, didn't you?"

"Does he drink too much?" Roosevelt said, looking surprised.

"You *must* have heard about it by now!"

"Yes . . . yes . . . but he doesn't drink too much, does he?"

"No, not too much. But sometimes it's in public. Anyway, he doesn't need her on the reviewing stand with him."

The President leveled a sincere gaze at her. "Frances, tell her not to go. They don't want her in New York, and it's up to you to tell her."

"Mr. President, what a job to give me!"

"They're still at the airport. Take a White House car. They don't have to observe the speed limits. Go to the airport and get her off that plane."

She looked trapped. "Why don't you send McIntyre?"

An alarmed expression passed over McIntyre's face. "I wouldn't go under any circumstances."

"It's a job for a woman," the President said persuasively. "You'll know how to say it to her."

"She'll take it better from a man."

"No, no, Frances, you go."

She sighed. "Mr. Sinclair, will you come with me? I suppose you can think up some plausible story about an emergency at the NRA office on the way."

Brad thought quickly. "Let me take a folder with me . . . anything."

With an effrontery that surprised even himself, he crossed to the President's desk and picked up the folder of letters that Missy had left there. He dumped them out on the desktop and inserted a few blank sheets torn from the President's memo pad.

Roosevelt laughed. "You're a very cheeky young man. Listen to

him, Frances. He has enough brass to come up with something that
will work."

McIntyre was already on the phone to the White House garage.
"There'll be a limousine downstairs by the time you get there."

Miss Perkins swept out, Brad in her wake. "Do it in a nice way,"
the President called after them.

They crossed the highway bridge with sirens screaming and other
cars pulling out of the way. Miss Perkins leaned forward and said
firmly to the White House chauffeur: "Perhaps you had better turn off
the sirens now. It wouldn't do to attract attention at the airport." She
turned to Brad, sitting beside her. "Oh, dear, I do hope the plane has
already left. I don't relish this at all."

"I'll keep the general busy a few minutes while you talk to her,"
Brad said.

He took his fountain pen from his pocket and printed, on the top
sheet of stolen White House stationery in the folder: PLEASE TALK
TO THE PERSON IN THE BLACK LIMOUSINE NEXT TO THE
TERMINAL.

"What story will you tell General Johnson?" Miss Perkins asked.

"Robbie will make up the story," Brad said. "She's very quick. But
you'd better suggest that she wait until the last minute before saying
anything to the general."

A faint smile struggled momentarily with Madam Secretary's
worried expression. "The President was quite right about you, Mr.
Sinclair."

As the limousine drove into the dusty airport grounds, Brad could
see the general's plane parked on the airstrip, a converted Curtiss Condor bomber with army markings. It had attracted a crowd of the curious, who had deserted the big Ford trimotor that was discharging passengers, and were pressed up against the low wire-mesh gate for a
closer look at the novelty of an army plane.

Beyond the barrier a smaller mob was clustered around the plane.
Brad could make out a tiny figure standing in front of the Condor's
oval door, one foot on a strut. The figure waved a hand expansively.
Brad cringed inwardly. The general was holding forth, as usual. He
caught the glint of sunlight on cameras.

"Let me off here," he said to the chauffeur.

He watched the limousine till he saw it pull under a striped awning
at the side of the terminal building, then pushed his way through to
the front of the crowd at the gate. He reached around for the latch
and let himself through with serene authority, while the spectators
looked on enviously.

He strolled over to the plane. A UP reporter recognized him and called out, "Hey Brad, when is Henry Ford going to sign the automobile code?"

"When hell freezes over," Brad said absently. "We're working on that."

He located Robbie, standing a little to one side, looking pert in a fur-collared coat and a cloche that hugged her skull. She looked at him curiously. The general still hadn't noticed him.

"What is it, Brad?" Robbie said with a frown.

He handed her the folder just as the general turned his head and saw him. "Take a look inside," he said.

Her eyebrows lifted as she saw the White House stationery. She read the message, lips pursed, and with a questioning glance at Brad started toward the terminal.

"Where's Robbie going?" the general said. "We're taking off in about five minutes."

"Something came up at the office," Brad said. "She's making a phone call. She'll be back in a minute."

"Why didn't you—"

"It's nothing important," Brad said smoothly. "But I couldn't resist the excuse to come and have a look at your bomber. I took a cab over."

The general rose to the bait. "Come and have a look inside. There's still a few minutes."

"General Johnson," a reporter called out from the audience he had deserted. "Just a minute, sir. What'll happen to objectors—the ones who won't go along with the code?"

"They'll get a sock right in the nose," the general snapped.

A flash went off, capturing the general in all his glory: red face, hulking shoulders, unpressed suit, shirt collar unbuttoned around his thick neck, his tie askew. Brad shuddered.

The general grasped both sides of the doorframe, put a foot on the little stepping stool that had been placed in front of the door, and heaved himself inside. Brad, with an apologetic backward glance at the reporters, followed.

The desk was there, just as all the stories said it was: a flat-topped oak desk bolted to the floor of the cabin. A small lamp with a shade protruded over it from a bracket in the wall. The four passenger seats had been arranged in a novel fashion: facing one another as if in a Pullman compartment. The Condor was a big plane; there was still room for a narrow aisle forward. An army officer with lieutenant's bars jumped to his feet and saluted. "At ease, son," the general said. "Did you stow my luggage?"

"Yes, sir," the lieutenant said.

"Come on, my boy," General Johnson boomed at Brad. "I'll show you the cockpit."

The pilot was another army officer. He didn't attempt to get up. He was jammed into one of two seats in the narrow cabin, surrounded by a complicated array of dials, knobs, and levers. The windshield was many-paned, giving a view in all directions.

"This young fellow has never seen the inside of an airplane," the general said.

The pilot craned his head around and gave Brad a friendly smile. "This is one of the latest models," he said. "We've still got a few open-cockpit bombers like the Boeing B-9, but this is the wave of the future. No more flying helmet and goggles. All these new instruments to take the place of the seat of the pants—horizon indicator, directional gyro, bank-and-turn—"

"She cruises at a hundred forty-five miles an hour," the general broke in. "We'll be in New York in an hour and a half."

"We should get started," the pilot said. "Is the lady aboard?"

The general looked at his watch worriedly. "What happened to Robbie? You said she had to make a phone call. . . ."

"Here she comes now," Brad said. He could see the small trim figure hurrying toward the plane. The general pushed past him to get to the door.

Robbie poked a head inside. She was standing on tiptoe on the footstool. "I have to go back to the office," she said. "I'll take the train to New York later."

Storm clouds gathered on General Johnson's massive face. "Confound it, Robbie, I need you!"

"I'll take the next train," she said. "I'll be waiting for you in the New York office by the time you leave the reviewing platform."

She gave Brad a dirty look and disappeared from view. Brad leaned around the general's broad shoulder and saw her stumbling on high heels toward the gate. He felt like a bastard.

"*Damn* it!" the general exploded. "I've got a pile of work to get through before we arrive in New York. I haven't even written my speech yet. What am I going to do now?"

Brad discreetly said nothing.

The general's eyes lit on Brad. "I don't suppose you know how to take dictation?"

"No, sir. But I'll split that pile with you."

The general laughed. He thumped Brad on the back and said, "Sit down and belt yourself in, my boy. You're going to take an airplane ride."

* * *

A jammed river of humanity flowed up Fifth Avenue, filling the broad canyon. They waggled their placards and homemade banners, and tried to keep in step with the competing fifes and drums. The sidewalks were clogged with cheering people, and the side streets were bursting with more crowds who kept surging against the police lines and sometimes broke through them. The great NRA parade was supposed to have ended by nightfall, but all along Fifth Avenue the streetlamps were winking on, and there was still no end in sight.

Brad stood unobtrusively toward the rear of the flag-draped reviewing platform that had been set up in front of the stone lions of the Public Library. Down below were massed batteries of cameras that kept letting off flashes. Grover Whalen, in frock coat and top hat, was at the front of the platform under a huge banner that showed the Blue Eagle, clutching lightning and a cogwheel in its claws and bearing the slogan WE DO OUR PART. So were Mayor O'Brien and Governor Lehman, and every other official who had been able to wangle a place on the platform. There were votes this year in being photographed under the Blue Eagle, shoulder to shoulder with Hugh Johnson.

General Johnson was enjoying himself. Still in his rumpled suit, he was returning the waves of the marchers as they passed in front of the stand.

Next to Brad, the man from *Time* said: "The Mussolini salute."

"Come on!" Brad said. "He's just waving."

Brad had cautioned the general not to raise his arm higher than his shoulders. The press was quick to cry "fascist" these days. Johnson was especially vulnerable, because before the election, still violently anti-Roosevelt, he had written an amusing satire about an American dictator he called "Muscle-Inny," which he had circulated among his Wall Street friends.

"The Mussolini salute," the *Time* man repeated with satisfaction, writing in his notebook.

Brad shrugged. He had done his best.

On Brad's other side, the *New York Times* man was haggling with the AP man. "I say two million. What do you say?"

"Okay, two million spectators," the AP man said. "And a quarter-million marchers. One out of three New Yorkers."

They both scribbled in their pads.

A bugle corps marched by, playing "Keep the Home Fires Burning." The Blue Eagle girls marching with them wore abbreviated skirts and star-spangled bunting over their bosoms.

"Look at that," the *Times* reporter said.

"That's nothing," AP leered. "Have you seen Miss NRA?"

"It's Miss Nira," Brad said.

"Huh?"

"Miss Nira. National Industrial Recovery Act." Brad had worked with the mayor's publicity man to find a showgirl and get a seamstress to piece together a costume at the last minute. One of the eagle's strategically placed wings had come unglued, and the press corps had a lot of pictures for their private collections.

"Miss NRA," the *Times* man said decisively, and wrote in his notebook.

It was amazing, all the hoopla that had been organized on short notice by Grover Whalen and the mayor's office. Walter Damrosch was marching with the whole radio symphony orchestra. Al Jolson was leading five thousand movie people. And even the Radio City chorus had shown up in their costumes. The general himself had arranged with the Army Signal Corps to pause in front of the reviewing stand and release a flock of pigeons with greetings to the President in Washington.

But the great mass of the parade was ordinary working people, linked briefly in fellowship with their employers. There were contingents from all the craft unions, the needle trades, barbers, waiters—even a contingent of ten thousand brokers and bankers and their clerks. The mayor, fighting for his political life against a reform candidate named LaGuardia, had let thirty-five thousand city employees off from work to march in the parade.

"Who are those guys with the torches?" the AP man asked Brad.

"The brewers' unit," he said.

"They were planning to march after dark, huh?" the reporter said cannily.

"No," Brad lied. "Nobody thought it would last this long. They must have swiped the torches from a construction site downtown." Actually, Brad had arranged with the city maintenance department for the red flares to be supplied.

"When is it going to end?"

"Beats me," Brad said.

A wire service photographer hoisted himself up from the platform's lower level. "Hey, Charlie," he called through the railing, "I'm going up to Fifty-eighth Street. The crowd's supposed to have pressed itself through the plate glass windows. They're trying to get an ambulance through."

"Check out the cop's horse story first," Charlie said.

There was a report that an enthusiastic throng had picked up a mounted policeman and his horse and turned them over. There had been repeated instances of crowds storming the police lines all along the parade route.

"Okay," the photographer said, and dropped from sight.

The general came stomping back toward Brad. His face was flushed, his eyes inflamed.

"A spontaneous outpouring," he said. "We've given these people hope again."

"Yes, sir," Brad said. The general's old employer, Bernard Baruch, had warned his protégé that he would acquire a taste for publicity, and he had. "By the way, I've arranged with the press to change Miss Nira to Miss NRA. It'll give us better identification."

"Good, good," the general beamed. "Will you hold the fort for me for a couple of hours, Brad? I have to go with the governor to give my speech at that dinner."

"You'll be back?"

"Of course. The governor and I have to be here for the end of the parade." He peered anxiously at the human torrent below. A detachment of men in welders' masks was marching by, looking like a medieval army. "Do you think it'll still be going on?"

"General, I think it's going to last all night."

The general laughed like a small boy. At moments he could be totally ingenuous. It was easy to see why he inspired so much affection. "This is the high spot of my life," he said. "I'm going to tell them so at the banquet."

"They'll eat it up." Brad had helped draft the speech during the plane ride. It was full of hortatory rhetoric about the numbers of people put back to work as a result of the Blue Eagle, of lists of industries signed up under the codes. It needed a touch of the quintessential Johnson.

"I'm going to put the bankers on the hot seat, too. Tell 'em that if they don't supply investment funds to industry, the government will act to loosen up credit."

"Will it?" Brad said uneasily. This was a new one.

"Damn right we will!" the general said. The use of the imperial "we" was getting more frequent with the general lately. It worried Brad.

"General . . ." How was he going to caution the general not to drink at the banquet? For the first time today, he wished that Robbie were here.

"Oh—the governor's waving to me. He's ready to go. You'll watch over things while I'm gone, Brad?"

"You can bet your life on it."

As soon as the general and the governor were out of sight, Brad slipped away. The lobby of the Public Library had been converted into temporary press headquarters so that reporters could use the pay phones there to call in their stories. The cop stationed in the lobby tried to stop him, but Brad flashed the press pass he had talked the mayor's publicity office into issuing to him.

All the booths were occupied. Brad approached a large, rumpled reporter who was filling the open doorway of one booth, chewing on a pencil and squinting at his notes.

"Come on, Fogarty. You càn't take out a lifetime lease on that booth."

"Hey, Brad! How goes it?"

"How about letting me use the phone?"

"I gotta file in half an hour."

"I'll be out in five minutes. Come on, Fogarty, I can keep it warm just as well as you can."

"Okay . . . remember, five minutes."

"Thanks, buddy."

With Fogarty guarding the front of the booth, Brad dialed Gilda Stanhope's number. This was the fifth time he'd tried. The other four times, he'd gotten no farther than a frosty reply from the butler, who told him that Miss Stanhope was not at home, and no, he did not know when she might be expected.

This time the butler told him to hold the line, please. Progress.

But it was old man J. DeWitt Stanhope himself who came on the line. "Sinclair, Gilda doesn't want to talk to you. I don't want you to bother her."

Bad. J. DeWitt wasn't calling him by his first name anymore.

"Is that her idea? Or yours?"

"Why you impudent—"

"I don't believe she doesn't want to talk to me. We're engaged."

"She's breaking the engagement. I'll see that your ring is returned."

Brad fought to control his temper. "Mr. Stanhope. I know that you don't approve of my working for the Roosevelt administration, but—"

"Communists and Jews," Stanhope said in his Harvard accent. "That's who you chose to throw your lot in with."

I take it you're withdrawing your offer of a junior partnership in your law firm, Brad thought wryly. But he resisted the temptation to say it. Instead he tried a placating tone.

"I know what they're saying in all the best clubs," he said. "But believe me, they're wrong. Roosevelt's no radical. My God, he *saved* the banking system. Don't you remember that when he took office—"

"That man is a traitor to his class," Stanhope said coldly. "He's turning this country into another Russia."

"All right, so you don't like the New Deal, and you don't like me. This has nothing to do with politics. It's between Gilda and me."

"Gilda doesn't want to see you anymore. She's been seeing young Grayson Tyler, with my approval, and her engagement to him will be announced after a decent interval. She has no intention of linking the Stanhope name to the son of an embezzler and suicide." The phone slammed down.

Brad found himself shaking with anger. Steady, steady, he told himself, and forced himself to take a couple of deep breaths. In a moment he was outwardly calm.

He couldn't blame Gilda. She didn't have the willpower of a flea. And he hadn't made it any easier for her to resist her father's influence. He had avoided her for two months out of misplaced pride —or vanity—until he had made his Washington connection and had some money in his pockets again. Gilda wasn't the kind of girl to sit around moping. She liked her fun. Grayson Tyler, with his chipmunk teeth and greased-down hair, had at least been handy, and he had Daddy's approval.

Brad hadn't seen Gilda since his last trip to New York, in August, and he had known it was over then. She had driven him all over Westchester in her shiny Marmon, searching for roadhouses and putting off the end of the night. She hadn't returned his kisses with any enthusiasm, and she hadn't let him put his hands on her.

He wondered if a pompous bastard like Tyler had ever figured out how to make love in the front seat of a Marmon without opening the door. If he hadn't, Gilda would soon instruct him.

At least, Brad thought with wry self-appraisal, I'm getting the diamond ring back.

"Hey Brad!" Fogarty was trying to force the door. "Are you through? Freddie Lee from the *Trib* has his eye on this booth."

"Just a minute," Brad said.

He took another nickel from his pocket. He remembered that he was supposed to call Pamela about something, but he was short of change, and it would be too complicated to make a call to a pay phone in a Washington boardinghouse. Tomorrow would be time enough.

He leafed through the Manhattan phone book. What was the name of that Blue Eagle girl, the cute one with the red hair and the Helen Kane voice? He was sure she'd given him the high sign at the photo session this morning. The girls had passed the reviewing stand almost a half hour ago. With luck, she'd be back home by now.

No matter what he'd told the general, the parade couldn't last *all* night.

"Brad . . ." Fogarty was trying to squeeze his hippopotamus bulk into the phone booth with him.

"Control yourself, Fogarty," Brad said. "I've just got one more call to make."

Brad's hand closed on something round and soft under the sheet. "What the hell is this?" he said.

The Blue Eagle girl giggled. "You've got one of my pompons."

He drew it out and looked at it. It was one of the white ones. There were also red ones and blue ones, scattered on the floor and draped across the chair with her star-spangled bunting and majorette's skirt, and the shabby cloth coat that had covered them. Her name was Billie. His phone call had caught her just as she had come through her door, and she had left without even stopping to change her white boots.

"How the hell did it get there?"

She squeaked in her Helen Kane voice. "You don't give a girl a *chance*, Brad! I mean, I was hardly through the door, and wham!"

"Say boop-boop-a-doop," he said.

"You're making fun of me," she pouted.

"No, really, go ahead. I just think it's cute, honest."

"Boop-boop-a-doop," she said suspiciously.

"Again."

"Boop-boop-a-doop."

There was a knock on the door. "Come in," Brad said. Billie dived under the sheets.

A bellboy came in, staggering under the weight of a pile of newspapers.

"These here are the papers you ordered last night, sir," he said. "I got as many out-of-town ones as I could."

"Put them over on that chair, will you."

The bellboy stacked the papers on the chair. "There's a dollar-eighty's worth," he said.

"There's a five-dollar bill over on the dresser. Keep the change."

"Gee . . . thanks, sir!" The bellhop pocketed the bill, eyes goggling.

Billie surfaced a crown of red hair and two enormous eyes over the top of the sheet to see what was going on. When she saw the bellboy looking at her, she pulled the sheets over her head again.

"Put the Do Not Disturb sign outside when you leave," Brad said.

"Yes, sir."

As soon as the lock clicked, Billie sat up, clutching the sheet to her chest. "Why dint you warn me?" she said. "I mean it's so early, and we might still of been you know."

"It's all right," Brad said. "The bellboys at the Plaza take a vow of chastity. Didn't you know that?"

"Yeah? So do priests, and they still got eyes."

"Relax." He got out of bed and went to get the pile of newspapers. He plunked them on the bed and sat down beside them.

Billie yawned. "You're not going to read the *newspapers,* are you? Now?"

Brad didn't answer. He had the *New York Times* spread out in his lap. FERVOR SWEEPS THRONGS, one headline said. *Great Outpouring to Show Faith in NRA Recalls Armistice.* Rapidly he scanned the story. Governor Lehman was quoted as saying, "The demonstration was the greatest New York has ever seen."

Practically the whole front page was given over to the NRA. General Johnson's speech at the NRA dinner was extensively quoted. And R.P. Lamont had quit as "Steel Dictator" because of his clashes with the general. Another story was about the new NRA code for retailers. And President Roosevelt had announced that the government would consider direct loans to aid NRA industries if bank credit continued to lag. The general had known what he was talking about after all; either that, or the President had heard about the general's speech and thought it was a good idea.

"Brad," Billie wheedled, "what's so interesting?" She was draped around his neck, pressing her body against his bare back.

He patted her haunch absently. "In a minute," he said.

He dipped into the pile of newspapers again. The NRA parade was big news on the front pages of papers as far away as Chicago. Almost all the publicity was good, though a few reporters had pursued the idea of the "Mussolini salute." One of them even had printed a photo with a faked arm grafted onto the general; he supposed *Time* magazine would use it too. Several photos showed Brad on the platform, identifying him as "General Johnson's aide." And the *Daily News* had a dandy picture of the Blue Eagle girls, Billie among them, waving their pompons.

He looked up to show it to her, but she was standing by the door, her coat on.

"Sorry, Brad," she said, "but I guess you'd rather read the papers than you know what."

"Don't you want to stay and have some breakfast? I can call room service."

"I'm a working girl. I just ran out of morning."

"Well . . . uh . . . I'll call you the next time I'm in New York."

"You do that."

He went back to the newspapers. He hardly noticed when she was gone.

Brad and the general had to take the train back to Washington. The general's pilot, Lieutenant "Hez" McClelland, had pronounced the weather unfit for flying. Robbie was on the train, sitting by herself in another car. Brad saw her when he passed through on his way to the diner, staring straight ahead, her hands in her lap, dark rings under her eyes. She didn't look up when he passed. He wondered if the general knew she was aboard. He didn't see her get off.

Reporters were waiting for them at the station. The general made an impromptu speech. He promised great things ahead for the NRA, and praised Brad generously as an "invaluable aide." The NRA office, when they got there, was in a fever of excitement over the New York triumph. Robbie was already at her desk, uncharacteristically subdued.

A pile of congratulatory messages and call-backs was waiting on his desk. His secretary said: "Your sister's still trying to reach you. She wants you to call her back as soon as you get in. She says it's important."

"Later," Brad said. He sifted through the call-backs.

He called Drew Pearson first. "I hear Robbie's walking around with the hilt of a knife sticking out of her back," the newsman said.

"I don't know what you're talking about, Drew."

"I underestimated you, Brad. The general's star is still rising after all. Don't hang on to it too long, though."

"I appreciate your concern, Drew."

He bumped into Don Richberg in the corridor on the way to the men's room. Richberg gave him a peculiar look and walked by without speaking.

By five o'clock he still hadn't called Pamela. She had tried him twice during the afternoon, but both times he had been in the general's office for conferences on the bloody coal strike in Uniontown, Pennsylvania. Seventeen men had been shot—fifteen strikers and two company goons —and scores of men had been beaten. The NRA coal code was supposed to have been signed weeks ago, but the mineowners were still dragging their feet.

"The President's losing his patience, Brad," the general said. "Keep it under your hat, but he's calling the coal operators to the White House tomorrow night. John L. Lewis, too. I want you with me. There's going to be a lot of detail work to follow through on."

"I'll be glad to help, sir," Brad said.

The general regarded him with affection. "Well, young fellow, you're going to get to see the inside of the White House, anyway. With any luck, you'll get to see the President, too."

Brad dropped his gaze. "I'll look forward to it, sir."

By the time the general let him go, it was too late to call Pamela at her office. Then he had a drink with a lobbyist who wanted his help in getting the general's ear, and he ended up having dinner with the man and a senate aide who joined them in the bar. Brad explained obliquely that the general didn't accept bribes, and excused himself from the offer of a girl to finish off the night with on the grounds of exhaustion. The senate aide accepted the girl enthusiastically, and Brad broke away after a final drink. When he finally arrived at his flat in Georgetown, ready to collapse into bed, his phone was ringing. He could hear it ringing without pause all the way up the stairs.

"Brad, where have you *been?*" It was Pamela, and she sounded close to hysteria. "I've been trying to get you since yesterday morning."

"I was in New York. It's a long story."

"Junie's gone."

"Calm down. What do you mean, gone?"

Pamela told him about her conversation with Elroy. "Will you call him, Brad? He won't talk to me. It's very strange."

"I'll call the sheriff and make it an official complaint. Then I'll have the *sheriff* call Elroy and throw a scare into him." He thought a moment. "And tomorrow I'll give John Edgar Hoover a call."

"Edgar Hoover?"

"The director of the new Division of Investigation the Justice Department set up last month."

"Oh . . . yes . . . there was an article about him in the *American Magazine*. Do you know him?"

"No, but I can get to him by throwing the general's name around. Homer Cummings, the attorney general, is his boss, and the general swings a lot of weight with Cummings."

"But what can *he* do?"

"The Lindbergh Law that was passed last year makes kidnapping a federal offense. Hoover's an ambitious young fellow. He wants to expand the activities of his division. He's anxious to do favors for the right people in government."

"Oh, Brad, get your feet on the ground!" There was exasperation in Pamela's voice. "The Department of Justice isn't going to send federal agents to Iowa to look into a runaway little girl."

"No," he agreed, "but a couple of phone calls from Hoover to the police in Iowa and Nebraska will make the case look important—get them cracking on it. Junie's probably crossed the state line by now."

"Well . . ." she said dubiously, "maybe you're right."

"Of course I am. Now get some sleep. I'll do what I can."

He decided not to wait until morning to call the county sheriff's office in Beulah. A nighttime call would seem more urgent. He could visualize the place—a rundown cement building, a few blocks away from the courthouse, with the sheriff's frame house attached to it by a sagging clapboard wing. After a dozen rings, he got a yawning deputy.

"It's awful late, mister. Who did you say you were?"

"My name's Sinclair. I work with J. Edgar Hoover here in Washington."

The deputy's voice brightened. "Oh, yeah. That was a real nice piece in the *American*."

"Thanks. Can you put me through to the sheriff?"

"Well . . . if he ain't gone to bed yet . . ."

"Would you have a look? We'll appreciate it."

When the sheriff came on the line, he was not hopeful. "Trail's pretty cold by now, Mr. Sinclair. But we'll do what we can to trace your little sister. I'll send a man around in the morning to talk to your uncle. Knowing the name of the boy won't do much good, though. These tenants, they're just like locusts. They spread out across the land, and they don't set down long enough to leave a trace."

"Will you do me a favor, Sheriff? Give Elroy a call now. It'll shake him up a little. He'll be more cooperative with your deputy in the morning."

The sheriff laughed. "You fellows in Washington sure believe in action in a hurry. All right, Mr. Sinclair. I'll make the call."

"Thanks, Sheriff."

Brad waited long enough for the sheriff to follow through, then placed a long distance call to Elroy's house. Elroy sounded jumpy and defensive.

"Now, don't you get high and mighty with me, Bradford Sinclair. It's not my fault that girl ran away. I treated her in this home like she was my own daughter."

"I don't want to discuss it with you, Elroy. Put my mother on the line."

"She's probably asleep at this hour. Decent folks—"

"God damn you, put her on!"

Brad heard the sucked-in breath. He was afraid Elroy might hang up on him, but after a minute of static, he heard his mother's voice.

"Bradford, dear, it's so nice to hear from you. I couldn't sleep. I was sitting up in bed, reading my magazines. You naughty children never call."

"Mother, I'm calling about Junie."

"Yes, dear." She sounded vague. "I'm afraid she's been very head-strong."

"Mother—did anything happen that might have made Junie run away? It's just not like her. I'm having the sheriff's department look into it. There'll be a deputy out to question Elroy in the morning."

"Yes, dear," his mother said brightly. "All you children have left Mother one by one. You and Jeremy and Gordon and Pamela. I sup-pose I've got to realize that you're grown up. Now June Alice has eloped with a young man."

"Mother—"

"Your father and I practically eloped, too, did you know that? Oh, I was such a silly young girl. . . ."

He listened to the familiar recitation until she ran down. Then he said gently, "You get some sleep now, Mother. I'll call again if I find out anything."

"Bradford . . ." A raw edge of pleading suddenly broke through the serene surface of his mother's voice. "Couldn't you come down here, just for a day or two? I know you're very busy, but you could fly in an airplane, they're very safe now, and be here in just a few hours. . . ."

Brad gave a start. It was just what he'd been thinking. There was something funny about Junie's disappearance. He really ought to be on the spot for a few days to make sure that the sheriff did more than go through the motions.

But the coal conference at the White House was tomorrow night. He'd be in heady company as General Johnson's aide. He couldn't afford to pass it up.

"I wish I could," he said soothingly. "But don't worry, everything's being done that can be."

In the morning he went to see J. Edgar Hoover personally. "Cover for me," he told his secretary. "I'll be back in an hour."

"Miss Robinson wants to see you," she wailed. "She needs a draft revision of the coal code on the general's desk by lunchtime. He wants to show it to the attorney general before the White House meeting."

"Is Attorney General Cummings going to be there?" Brad said in surprise.

"Yes. And so is Secretary Woodin and Mr. Richberg."

He chucked her under the chin. "I'll be back in plenty of time. Get the coal files out and have them ready for me."

J. Edgar Hoover had arranged his office with an effective sense of drama. A special agent told Brad he was expected, and led him through a long outer room through a double door into the director's inner office. The visitor's chair was placed at a distance from the desk to make the director remote. There was no ashtray within reach, another device to put the visitor at a disadvantage. Brad recognized the tactic, and revised his estimate of the director upward a notch.

Hoover did not rise. He was a solid, compact man with muscle that looked as if it might run to fat in a few years. He was brown-eyed and dark-skinned, with a blunt jowly face and pompadoured black hair. He was in his late thirties, and utterly impressive.

"What can I do for you, Mr. Sinclair?" he said. "I'm always glad to help a member of General Johnson's staff."

"Thank you."

"The general's a great American."

"Yes, he is."

The director was as awesomely wholesome as Jack Armstrong. According to the stories in the press, he didn't smoke, drink, or go out with girls. His only hobbies were baseball and fishing. He demanded similar standards of his men. When he had become head of the United States Bureau of Investigation at the age of twenty-nine, he had immediately fired all the political hacks—a third of his force—and decreed that all his agents either have a legal education or be an accountant.

He heard Brad out with total courtesy. Then he said firmly, "I'm sorry, Mr. Sinclair. I'd like to help you, but this isn't the division's kind of case. I'm afraid I can't open a file on it."

Brad understood immediately what Hoover was trying to say. There was no publicity in the disappearance of a fifteen-year-old girl who was probably a runaway. To build up his new investigation division, Hoover needed spectacular cases, like the roundup of the "Terrible Toughy" kidnapping gang that had recently made headlines for the Chicago police. Hoover was now racing the Chicago police for the capture of Machine Gun Kelly.

Hoover also needed successes. He wasn't going to take on a case unless he could be pretty sure that it would contribute to a high conviction rate for his new department. Junie wasn't a very hopeful statistic.

"Oh, I'm not suggesting that you open a file," Brad said blandly. "I just thought that perhaps your agents in Iowa and Nebraska might check—off the record, of course—with some of the county sheriffs there to see if they've developed any leads. Just sort of let them know that your division is interested."

Hoover waited.

Brad sighed. "It would take a load off my mind. General Johnson and I are meeting with the President and the attorney general at the White House tonight, and I'm going to be awfully tied up."

Hoover sat, utterly still, for a moment. Then, in the same cordial tone of voice, he said, "I'll drop a note to my agents in the field. Informally, of course. And I'll place a call personally to the sheriff in Beulah."

Brad stood up. "That's very good of you. My boss will be pleased."

It was a long walk to the door. The director had arranged his office that way.

17

"What is the difference between a duck?"

"Sir!" Gordon barked, bracing himself so hard that his chin went numb, "one of its legs is alike."

He was sitting rigidly on the edge of his chair, occupying no more than the prescribed three inches of rim. Three other plebes sat at the foot of the table with him, bodies stiff, eyes downcast. They were there to serve the upperclassmen. For this meal, Gordon had been designated "water corporal."

"How many lights in Cullum Hall?" the table commandant went on. He was a First Classman named Crowley, a beetle-browed individual with large ears.

"Three hundred and forty lights, sir."

"How many gallons in Lusk Reservoir?"

"Ninety-two point two million gallons, sir, when the water is flowing over the spillway."

One of the other upperclassmen took over. "Are you a virgin, Mister Dumbjohn?"

"Yes, sir," Gordon said, "in my left nostril." That was one of the accepted answers.

The upperclassman stared at him reflectively. "How is the cow?"

Gordon sweated under his tight collar. The other plebes in his class

had had eight weeks of Beast Barracks during the summer to memo-
rize the nonsense litany. But as a despised "September Member," he
had a lot of catching up to do.

"Sir, she . . . she walks, she talks, she's full of chalk. The lacteal
fluid extracted from the female of the bovine species is . . . is . . ."

"Well, mister?"

Gordon looked longingly at the food on his plate. The gravy was
congealing on his roast beef and potatoes. His food had been sitting
there for fifteen minutes of the thirty-minute dinner period, and he still
had not been allowed to eat. Crowley and his friends had it in for him,
all right. None of the other plebes at his table were ridden this hard.

". . . is highly prolific to the nth degree," he finished in a rush.

The upperclassman looked disappointed. Gordon wolfed his food
down while he had the chance. Around him the vast dining hall was
filled with the murmur of conversation and the discreet clatter of
knives and forks.

It had been like this for two weeks now. It wasn't bad enough, being
a September Member and the focus of resentment for all those who
had gone through the hell of Beast Barracks themselves; Braithwaite,
the cadet whose place Gordon had taken as first alternate, had been an
extremely popular fellow. But as Judge Tanner had predicted, he had
made a horse's ass of himself. He had been caught sneaking off after
taps to visit his pregnant bride in the cozy little flat in Highland Falls
their parents had rented for them. A cadet couldn't be married. It
wasn't Gordon's fault that Braithwaite had been expelled, but he was
blamed for it anyway.

The hobo jungle had taught Gordon the art of survival. He was
tougher than Crowley and the rest of them could have suspected. All
he had to do was make it to Plebe January without accumulating too
many demerits. That was when the forty cadets of lowest standing
were lopped off. He had to stick it out until then, no matter what they
dished out.

Otherwise, it would mean that Knobby had died for nothing.

"Mister Ducrot!"

Gordon choked down a mouthful of meat and raised his eyes to
meet Crowley's contemptuous stare.

That was another thing. He had lost his identity. Plebes were too
low a form of life to have their own names. He was "Mister Dumbjohn" or "Mister Ducrot" or sometimes "Mister Dooflicket." Ducrot
was the legendary cuckold who had been invented by an earlier generation of West Pointers, when an alert cadet had noticed that in the
translation exercises in the French grammar "Mr. Ducrot has a son

and a daughter" but "Mrs. Ducrot has three children, two sons and a daughter."

"*Mister* Ducrot, have you checked the water pitcher for goldfish?"

"No, sir," Gordon said slowly.

"You are sadly remiss, Mister Ducrot. As water corporal, it is your duty to make sure there are no goldfish in the pitcher." The other upperclassmen snickered. "Of course, no goldfish ever *has* been found in the water pitcher, but that does not mean that no goldfish ever *will* be found in the water pitcher. *Does* it, Mister Ducrot?"

"No, sir."

"Do your duty, Mister Ducrot."

With the eyes of the upperclassmen on him, Gordon plunged his hand into the pitcher to the wrist and felt around.

"There is no goldfish, sir."

"Louder."

"*There is no goldfish, sir!*"

"Have you explored all the way to the bottom, Mister Ducrot?"

"Not exactly, sir."

"You have explored all the way to the bottom or you have not. Answer yes or no."

"No, sir."

"Do so, then."

Still maintaining his extreme brace, Gordon started to push his uniform cuff back with his left hand.

"One hand will suffice, mister."

Gordon dipped his arm in halfway to the elbow.

"What is your report, Mister Ducrot?"

"There is no goldfish, sir."

Gordon withdrew his dripping sleeve. Crowley stared at it with distaste.

"Your uniform is in a state of unmilitary disarray, Mister Ducrot."

Gordon said nothing.

"You have a soggy cuff, Mister Ducrot."

Gordon kept his mouth shut. He knew Crowley was trying to goad him into answering without having been asked a direct question.

"Yes, I think this merits a report to the Tac," Crowley said with satisfaction. "You'll find your name on the next skin sheet. Do you want to dispute it?"

Gordon flushed. "No, sir."

Crowley went on, "I'd say an offense like yours qualifies you for . . . oh, four demerits and five punishment tours."

Gordon burned with a dull, helpless fury. He didn't mind the punishment tours in themselves. Marching in quick time with a rifle around the Area for five hours was no big deal. But it would cut into his precious study time. Crowley knew that. And trying to catch up by cracking a book after lights out was a serious offense.

They left him alone for the rest of the meal, but he had lost his appetite. When he fell in with his section for afternoon classes, one of the plebes who had been at the table with him whispered out of the side of his mouth, "Tough, Sinclair. That wasn't fair."

Gordon didn't answer. He didn't need another demerit for talking in the ranks.

Sally was heavy. Miss Sally Springfield, that was what the Area birds called the rifles they had to carry. It was funny, Gordon thought; this was the second time he'd had to learn what Sally meant. He wondered if Knobby would have been amused.

The barracks square was filled with other solitary marchers at this hour, quick-stepping in grim silence, making their abrupt about-faces at the end of each circuit. Occasionally a pair of cadets would match their steps for a few paces and march side by side, but there wasn't much point to having company. Not with a Tac officer always alert to catch someone talking.

Gordon stomped back and forth along his invisible line, his gray uniform cape thrown back over his shoulders, his gut sucked in. His muscles ached from the growing weight of the rifle. For the thirtieth time that hour, he passed the cadet approaching from the opposite direction, a freckle-faced redhead named Pease from Gordon's company. Pease looked tired. Gordon had been narrowing the interval between them, little by little. Soon they'd be marching in the same direction. As they converged, Pease's lips silently formed the words "ten minutes."

Gordon let his eyes stray toward the Tac, standing by the big clock overhanging the punishment area. The Tac was one of his math instructors, a trim, sandy-haired artillery captain named Wilson, all spit-and-polish in a tight high-necked tunic, flaring breeches, and mirror-shined boots. He had been wounded with the Second Division at Château-Thierry. The French had awarded him the Croix de guerre. The cadets, with grudging admiration, called him "the Ramrod" behind his back.

It was Captain Wilson who had posted Gordon's name on the day's delinquency report. He had done it on Crowley's say-so, without inquiring into the details of the offense, as most of the other Tacs would have done. Captain Wilson did not encourage the filing of the mitigating explanation known as the "b-ache," which the accused cadet was entitled to submit. And Gordon, with stubborn pride, would not have submitted one in any case.

Captain Wilson was not fond of Gordon. He regarded any cadet who had missed the tempering experience of Beast Barracks as forever being unsoldierly material.

Gordon reached the barracks curb and executed a smart about-face. Miss Sally dug into his shoulder. His right collarbone felt like a mass of bruises. He wished he could switch to left shoulder arms, but that would have been unthinkable. He continued his mechanical marching.

Then he saw the girl.

She was standing over by the Grant Hall entrance, looking amused at the courtyard full of crisscrossing marchers. She was a strawberry blonde with vivid red lips and cheeks colored by the crisp September air. She wore a wine-colored suit with ruffled white at the throat and cuffs and a tiny feathered hat that perched on the back of her head. He supposed she was some visitor who had walked from the railroad station and somehow escaped the officer of the guard at the reception desk in Grant Hall. It was unusual to see an unescorted female at this end of the reservation in the middle of the week.

She stood watching the marching cadets for a moment, then walked in among them. One cadet had to break stride to avoid colliding with her. He stopped short, almost dropping his rifle, then recovered and continued his tour. The girl seemed not to notice what she had done. She strolled through the teeming courtyard as if she were sight-seeing at the zoo. Some of the fellows had slowed up, and were watching her out of the corners of their eyes. One unlucky cadet stumbled.

The girl said something to the stumbler, probably an apology, but he had sense enough not to answer. He marched jerkily away, looking frightened, before she could step into his path. Over by the clock, Captain Wilson was glaring.

Gordon's lips tightened. He gripped Miss Sally's butt harder and quickened his step. A lot of girls were thoughtless. Some of the weekend visitors didn't seem to realize that they could get their boy friends into trouble just by trying to talk to them during formation. He had even seen a girl try to introduce a plebe to an upperclassman.

Now the blond girl was heading in his direction. With a sense of dismay, Gordon realized that she had singled him out. He hoped she wasn't going to be dumb enough to ask him for directions or something.

He had to march in place for a few steps to avoid walking into her. As she passed Gordon, she stared full into his face with a little smile curving her lips. He had seen that expression before, on the lips of a girl at Beulah High named Gloria Rawles, who liked to start fights between boys.

She was walking right up to the Tac. Gordon expected to see Captain Wilson set her straight, with chilly courtesy. But to his amazement, the captain exchanged a few words of conversation with her, then left with her, escorting her from the Area with a hand lightly at her elbow.

He overtook Pease from the rear on his next circuit. As he drew abreast of him, Pease quickened his pace, matching steps with him.

"Pssst, Sinclair," Pease whispered out of the side of his mouth.

Gordon kept his eyes front. Just because the Tac was gone was no reason for breaking rules.

"You like that stuff?" Pease hissed at him.

Gordon ignored him.

"You better keep your nose clean, buddy boy. She's not the fem for you," Pease said, huffing to keep up.

When Gordon still didn't respond, Pease gave a snort of disgust.

"You still don't know who she is, do you, you fungus? That's Nellie Wilson. Old Ramrod's daughter."

He fell back and left Gordon marching alone.

"I don't get it," Hibbert said.

Gordon put down his pencil with a sigh. "It's very simple. Look, all sections parallel to the xy plane are ellipses. If a equals b, then the conic section is a circle."

"Yeah, but why?"

"It *has* to be a circle," Gordon said in exasperation. "Look, I'll show you."

Unwillingly, he pushed back his chair and stepped around to his roommate's desk. He'd already lost an hour's study time during his punishment tour, and he begrudged even the few minutes it would take to make Hibbert see the light. He was behind on his own assignment, and he knew Captain Wilson would call on him tomorrow. At West Point, you took mathematics six days a week, and you were called upon to give a blackboard demonstration every day.

"Thanks, Sinclair," Hibbert said when he finished. "God, I hope it sticks till tomorrow."

Hibbert was a bat-eared kid with acne, whose father was a Maryland contractor. He was hopeless in mathematics, and Gordon knew that tutoring him was a waste of time. Hibbert sat with the goats, and he'd be lucky to make it through to Plebe January. But your roommate was your wife, in West Point parlance, and Gordon felt responsible for Hibbert.

On the way back to his desk, he paused to look critically at Hibbert's sleeping alcove. The mattress was rolled back over the bare iron cot the way it was supposed to be, but the blanket on top of it was folded sloppily, its edges out of alignment.

"Hibb, you're going to get skinned for this, sure," he said.

Hibbert yawned. "It looks all right to me."

Silently, Gordon refolded the blanket for him. The rest looked okay: the shoes freshly polished and lined up under the cot, the uniforms hanging in their proper order, the toilet articles positioned to the precise fraction of an inch. A silver-framed picture of Hibbert's girl friend was on the upper shelf, but that was all right. The rules allowed you to keep a personal photo in that one spot.

He settled back to the chapter on conic sections again. There were three more pages to go. It was still an hour to taps. If he concentrated, he could just about finish.

But he couldn't get Nellie Wilson out of his mind. He kept seeing the red-gold curls spilling out of the silly little hat, the mocking lips, the provocative swing of the hips in the tight wine-colored skirt as she walked away from him. All at once, he thought of Mrs. Hoskins. The image of how she looked, naked, with the pink slip twisted like a rope around her waist, came unbidden into his mind. He shook his head angrily. Thinking about sex all the time, the way some fellows did, just interfered with your studies. And anyway, you weren't supposed to think about decent girls that way. You were supposed to respect them.

"Hibb," he heard himself saying, "do you know Captain Wilson's daughter?"

"Huh? Oh, Nice Nellie? I've seen her around."

"Nice Nellie?"

"She's supposed to be a tease. I wouldn't know. A fellow got expelled over her last year, they say."

"What? How?"

Hibbert put down his pencil and picked at a scab on his face. "Forget about her, old son. She's not for you. She just goes out with Firsts. Anyway, there's no way you can get together with a fem. You don't have any social life till Plebe Christmas, and I can't see Old Ramrod's daughter hanging around for the plebe hops."

"Who says she goes out with Firsts?"

"I says. I saw her heading toward Flirtation Walk with that gorilla Crowley after chapel, Sunday."

It was still a half hour to taps when there was a sharp rap at the door. Gordon looked up in surprise. Before he had a chance to give the "All Right," the door burst open and Crowley walked in, followed by three other upperclassmen.

Hibbert sprang to his feet and stood beside his chair, looking frightened. He tried with one hand to button his coat, realized it was too late, and gave up. Gordon's hand had flown by instinct to his collar at that one sharp rap, and now he stood at attention, stiff and correct.

Crowley looked him up and down without speaking. The other three were grinning. Gordon knew something was wrong. While theoretically any upperclassman could enter the room of any plebe at any time, in practice the subdivision inspector waited until taps for the final inspection, and he didn't bring company with him. And Crowley was the officially detailed inspector this week. He was wearing a red sash and sword as an officer of the guard.

"Who is room orderly?" Crowley said.

"I am, sir," Gordon said. Crowley could have told who was room orderly for the week by looking at the card rank, if it had really slipped his mind.

Crowley ran a white-gloved hand around the underside of the lampshade and checked his finger for dust, then inspected the washbowl. Gordon waited warily. He was sure everything was in order. With a roommate like Hibbert, he would have checked everything anyway, even if he hadn't been responsible for the condition of the room.

"What's this?" Crowley said.

Gordon's eyes flicked toward the sink. He had scrubbed it less than an hour ago.

"Eyes front!" Crowley barked.

Gordon returned his gaze forward, but not before he had seen the tiny pink stain on the rim of the washbasin. It was a drop of the ointment that Hibbert used on his acne. Hibbert must have been at the sink while Gordon had been in the head, and he hadn't bothered to rinse the spot away.

"This place is a pigsty," Crowley said. "The filthy condition of that sink is a disgrace."

Crowley's pals were watching Gordon with anticipation. Gordon knew only one of them by name: a moon-faced cadet sergeant named Stanger, who had been one of the more notorious members of the Beast Detail. Stanger had come prepared. He was holding a naked bayonet in his fist.

"What's the punishment for a dirty sink?" Crowley said, turning to his accomplices.

"Two demerits," one of them said promptly.

"We are compassionate men," Crowley said, deadpan. "I have looked at this cadet's record. In less than three weeks he has received more than half the number of demerits which would make it necessary for him to be reported by the superintendent for deficiency in conduct. Is there not some other alternative?"

"The Tac is not a compassionate man," Stanger said.

"Perhaps this cadet could be made to reflect on the enormity of his offense," Crowley said.

"What better position for reflection is there than to sit on infinity?" one of the upperclassmen said.

"What's that in your hand, Mr. Stanger?" Crowley said.

"By George!" Stanger said with an air of surprise. "I believe it's infinity!"

They kept Gordon squatting over the point of the bayonet until taps, while a terrified Hibbert stood braced, not daring to move his eyes to see what was going on. They'd allowed Gordon to strip to his undershorts; they didn't want blood on his uniform any more than he did, in case he fainted and Stanger failed to snatch the bayonet away in time. Stanger kept pricking him with the point of the blade to keep him off balance.

Hazing under the old system was supposed to have ended after the death of two cadets and the subsequent congressional investigation. But everyone knew that the authorities looked the other way. Douglas MacArthur himself had testified that during his own plebe year he had been spread-eagled over broken glass until he went into convulsions, but he had condoned the practice as being good for the character of the cadets. The only rule now was that upperclassmen were not supposed to touch the plebes physically.

A rule, Gordon thought, as Stanger jabbed him, that was observed in the breach.

Another upperclassman finally took over from Stanger after Stanger complained that his hand was getting tired. Gordon's legs had gone stiff and numb, and he was trembling all over from muscular effort. He clenched his teeth and willed himself not to get a cramp, not to pass out, not to fall over. There was a peculiar roaring in his ears, and the room inexplicably seemed to have grown dim.

From far away he heard taps being sounded, and then all the upperclassmen were crowding through the door, in haste to be in their own rooms before the Tac made his rounds. Hibbert was tugging at his arm, pale and scared, saying: "Come on, Sinclair, try to get up. You've got to be in your bed in about one minute."

There was no feeling in his legs at all. When he tried to stand, he fell over. He lay there while Hibbert, with tears in his eyes, pulled at his arm, saying, "Please!" Then little needles of circulation started. The pain was excruciating, but with Hibbert's help he managed to get to his feet. For a moment he went blind, then the blood rushed back and he could see again. Hibbert unrolled his mattress for him while he stood precariously on legs that had turned to blocks of granite. The seat of his shorts was wet with blood, but the only nick he could really feel was the one pinpoint puncture in his scrotum. That one stung like hell. He fell face forward onto his cot, and Hibbert covered him up to the neck with a blanket before hitting the light switch and diving into his own bunk.

He lay awake in the dark for an hour, fighting the cramps in his legs, listening to the little whimpering sounds that Hibbert made in his sleep.

He didn't mind the pain. It was the lost study time that bothered him.

He hadn't finished his assignment on conic sections. That, he knew, was what Crowley and his friends had intended.

The next night they made him swim to Newburgh.

They hung him over the top of an open door and encouraged him with ribald shouts and the flat of a sword, while he did an imitation breaststroke with straining gut and aching arms.

"Come on, mister, you're not even halfway to Cornwall yet!"

"Kick those legs out, mister! You're swimming, not walking!"

"Watch that wave!"

At this, Stanger would fling a bucket of water into his face.

They let him down at five minutes to taps. His gut was sore and churning, and he felt as if his back were broken. He made it to the head in time to puke in the basin.

There wasn't time for anything else except to mop up the puddle of water and put away the textbooks that had lain open and useless on his desk for the last hour.

The night after that, they handed him a rifle and told him to present arms. He did it almost three hundred times before his arms gave out. As punishment for that, he had to swallow a bottle of Tabasco sauce. The next morning he was so sick that he could barely make police call. He skipped breakfast. Sick call was at mess hall, immediately after breakfast, but he couldn't afford to miss math class. He got to his math section, his face white as flour, and went to the blackboard assigned to him. When you finished working out the problem of the day, you were supposed to stand at attention with the pointer in hand and wait until you were called on. Some of the fellows "bugled"— stayed at the board pretending to work until the recitation period was over, and it was too late for the instructor to nail them. But Captain Wilson didn't tolerate bugling in his class. When Gordon found he couldn't do the problem, he wiped the board clean except for his name, and waited for Captain Wilson to get to him.

"Not prepared, Sinclair?" Captain Wilson said.

"No, sir," Gordon said.

Captain Wilson stood, slim and precise, his face with the small mustache as smooth as porcelain, making Gordon feel lumpish. "Are you ill, Sinclair?"

"No, sir."

"Then there's no excuse for you, is there? You've fallen down badly this week. If you can't bring your average up, I'll have to transfer you to a lower section starting Monday."

Gordon made no reply. He hadn't been asked a direct question. Captain Wilson stared through him briefly, as though he were made of some transparent material, then went on to the next cadet.

Today was Thursday. Marks for the week were posted at Saturday noon. On the West Point scale of three, his standing hung on one tenth of a point. If he didn't give a perfect recitation tomorrow, he was cooked.

That night he did pushups. When his arms finally turned to rubber, he did sit-ups until he lay on his back, unable to move. For the remainder of the three hours between call to quarters and taps, they simply braced him. He stood with his chin pulled in, his aching belly sucked in, his shoulders pulled back, with a piece of tissue paper held between his shoulder blades. Every time the tissue paper fluttered to the floor, he got whacked across the rump with the flat of a sword. Crowley and his raiding party took turns supervising him, one at a time, while the rest of them went back to their rooms to study.

They knew about Captain Wilson's ultimatum. Gordon was sure of it. He had seen one of Crowley's bootlicks questioning a plebe from his math section, the high section that Gordon had been so proud to be in. Gordon was mad, a dull red mad like a cast-iron cookstove top, and that was what got him through the hazing.

During the mad scramble to the Sinks in the five minutes before taps, Gordon arranged his laundry bag and overcoat under the blanket and fluffed them up until they looked right. For the head, he propped the stiff campaign hat on the pillow, brim down, and drew the blanket up over it.

"What are you doing, Sinclair?" Hibbert said, looking apprehensive.

Gordon didn't answer. He unscrewed the socket of his study lamp, left the shade propped realistically in place, and drew out wire until the naked bulb in its socket was under his cot. A flashlight would have been simpler, but flashlights were dangerous contraband for a Fourth Classman.

"Don't do it, Sinclair," Hibbert said. "It's my neck too, if you get caught."

"You don't know a thing about it, Hibb," Gordon said. "You were asleep when I did it."

"But I have to *tell*," Hibbert said, wringing his hands. "Under the Honor Code . . ."

"It's not cheating. You don't have to tell."

"Yeah, but . . ."

"You know what Crowley is doing is wrong."

Hibbert wrung his hands. "Listen, Sinclair, I know it's tough on you. But it's tough on me, too. I'm your roommate. *I'm* not the one they had it in for. They know I had nothing to do with it, but—"

"Do with what?"

Hibbert clammed up. He got into bed and turned his face to the wall. Gordon got his math textbook and notebook and crawled under his cot. He draped the bedclothes all the way to the floor and checked to make sure that no stray light was escaping. Then he settled down with the chapter on the trigonometric functions of general angles.

He fell asleep just before dawn. An outflung arm or leg must have betrayed him. The next thing he knew, a flashlight was shining in his face, and a Tac was saying, "On your feet, mister."

The offense was good for a "slug"—six demerits and twenty-two punishment tours. Gordon would know for sure after he appeared before the bat board and heard their verdict.

But he didn't care. He had managed to finish the chapter and do almost all the exercises. He knew it was all there in his head.

"Hibb," he said, lying awake in his bunk after the Tac had left, "what did you mean before?"

There was no answer from the other sleeping alcove.

"Come on, I know you're not asleep."

"Jeez, Sinclair, leave me alone. It's only a half hour till the sunrise gun."

"Why do they have it in for me?"

"*You* know, Sinclair. Like . . . everybody else had to go through the Beast. They're just giving you your share of it now."

"No," Gordon said decisively. "It's more than that. It's personal. Everybody around here liked Braithwaite, didn't they?"

"*Well . . . you* know . . . it's almost like you got Braithwaite to go through Beast Detail *for* you. Then you got him kicked out and walked in in September."

Hibbert turned over and buried his face in the pillow.

"That's crazy, Hibb."

"I'm not passing judgment on you, Sinclair," Hibbert's muffled voice said. "Hell, I'm your roommate. I'm not too popular myself around here, you know. Braithwaite did a lot of people favors. His family is very important. Did you know that he got himself *recognized?* Crowley and Stanger shook hands with him right in front of the clock tower."

Gordon was taken aback. Recognition, sealed by a public handshake, was a rare honor for a plebe. It ended a plebe's beast status, made him immune to hazing, and gave him upper-class status. The man Gordon had replaced had been a pal of the Firsts.

"What else, Hibb?"

"I've said too much already," Hibbert pleaded.

"Come *on,* Hibb!"

"They're . . . they're counting your demerits. I mean they're really keeping track. If they can get you a hundred fifteen before November thirtieth, the Supe will haul you up in front of the academic board for deficiency in conduct. It's just the same as deficiency in studies. You know that."

"God, I never heard of anything so low."

"Well, what do you expect?"

"What are you talking about? I don't know, honest."

"They say . . . they say you informed on Braithwaite," Hibbert said miserably.

"I wasn't even here!"

Hibbert raised his face from the pillow. "Somebody sent an anonymous letter to the Supe saying that Braithwaite had a wife in Highland Falls."

Gordon lay back and closed his eyes. He could think of only one person who might have sent the letter.

He gave a perfect recitation the next day. Captain Wilson looked at him oddly, then passed on to the next cadet without a word of commendation.

Saturday noon, when the marks were posted, Gordon found that he was still in the top tenth of his class in mathematics. He would stay in Captain Wilson's advanced section.

Later in the afternoon, he was summoned before the board of battalion officers. Only the most serious offenses merited a personal appearance before the bat board.

Gordon stood stiffly at attention in front of the long polished table, smelling saddle soap and leather from six pairs of shiny boots. The ranking officer, a Major Littlejohn formerly of the Eighth Cavalry, said mildly: "Well, you've been quite ingenious, according to the tactical officer's report, Mr. Sinclair. They say that if you give a man enough rope, he'll hang himself. In your case it seems to be a matter of giving you enough electrical cord to electrocute yourself."

Gordon said nothing. Major Littlejohn, he had heard, had once awarded a slug that brought the offending cadet's total demerits to exactly five short of maximum. The cadet had collected the five promptly the following Sunday, and had been thrown out of the Point before supper Monday. It had been the week before graduation. The five-demerit offense had been "laughing at divine service."

"Have you no explanation, Mr. Sinclair?"

"No, sir."

Major Littlejohn seemed disappointed at that. "Mediocre students can manage to limp along at other institutions by studying after hours. That is not true here. You are expected to complete your work within the assigned study time. Is that clear?"

"Yes, sir."

Major Littlejohn shuffled papers. "In less than three weeks, you've managed to collect fifty-five demerits. That doesn't leave you much leeway, Mr. Sinclair. Sixty more demerits over the next two months and you're out."

Gordon kept silent. He could feel his guts coiling.

Major Littlejohn sighed. "Wait over there."

Gordon stood at the other end of the room while the members of the bat board conferred. In a moment they summoned him back.

"Six demerits and twenty-two punishment tours and confinement to quarters."

Gordon's knees went weak with relief. It was an ordinary slug, after all. It would take him a month to work off the punishment tours, but it had been worth it.

"You've got a visitor, Sinclair. To Grant Hall, on the double."

Gordon reluctantly dragged his eyes away from his French textbook and rose to his feet.

"Sir," he said to the cadet officer standing in the doorway, "I'm confined to quarters."

"Your visitor got permission for you. He's some bigwig from Washington. Make it snappy. You've got a half hour."

Gordon put his books away in his locker. He still had assignments in surveying and tactics to get through. The relaxed Sunday schedule had let him get in quite a bit of studying since chapel. Crowley and Stanger were away on weekend passes, and the upperclassman who had been left in charge of Gordon's persecution had been halfhearted and apologetic about it. Gordon had gotten away with some perfunctory pushups, then had been left alone with his books.

The enormous walnut-beamed reception hall was seething with hundreds of Sunday visitors. Gordon had almost forgotten there was a female sex, and the sight of so many mothers, sisters, and girl friends was unsettling.

Halfway across the great expanse of polished terrazzo floor, he located his visitor, standing a little apart, studying the oil painting of General Sherman. Gordon walked over, and he turned around.

"Hello, Gordie," Brad said.

"Hello, Brad."

"I had a little errand over at Hyde Park. The President needed some papers over the weekend. I thought I'd stop off and look in on you."

Gordon said nothing.

"Try to restrain your enthusiasm," Brad said dryly. He looked around the hall. "Look, let's go somewhere where we can talk. Can I buy you an ice cream in the refreshment room?"

"I'm not allowed in the Boodler's till my second year."

"All right. Let's try to find a seat somewhere."

He led Gordon over to the huge center alcove. All the divans and chairs were taken. Brad leaned casually against a carved teak table. Gordon, standing straight, watched with disapproval as Brad took out a cigarette.

Brad looked Gordon over. "Well, you've filled out over the summer, little brother," Brad said. "You've grown up. I hardly recognize you in that uniform."

"Yeah, Brad. I've done a lot of growing up."

Brad had changed, too. He had the same slouching posture, the same careless air. But Gordon could see why the cadet officer had called him a bigwig from Washington. It wasn't just the well-cut suit, the expensive tie. There was something in Brad's bearing that you saw in people who had been around power and authority long enough to know the meaning of it. A couple of officers on the commandant's staff had it, men who had shared great events with Pershing.

"There wasn't much news from you this summer," Brad said. "A couple of postcards."

"I made out all right. I didn't have any money for long-distance phone calls."

Brad took a drag of his cigarette. "Well, you're here. That's the important thing."

"Yeah."

Brad looked at him narrowly. "What's eating you, Gordie?"

"Nothing very much. Just a little letter somebody wrote to the superintendent."

Brad became absolutely still. Then he said casually, "What are you talking about?"

"Somebody snitched about Braithwaite being married. You remember Braithwaite. He was the principal nominee for this appointment."

"Yes, I remember. The fellow who cheated on his exam."

"Why did you do it, Brad?"

Brad raised his eyebrows. "Do what?"

"Cut it out, Brad. I *know* you. I'm your brother, remember? You blew the whistle on Braithwaite, and that's how they caught him."

"Me? Come on, Gordie. Nobody has to blow the whistle on monkeys like Braithwaite. They always trip themselves up. Did the simp actually think he could hide a wife away in a gossip mill like Highland Falls? What did he do, try to sneak away from barracks after hours?"

"You couldn't wait, could you? You saw the summer slipping by, and Braithwaite still hadn't been caught, and you thought you'd hurry things along a little."

"What's the difference, one way or the other? You would have gotten his place anyway."

"It's a big difference to me."

Brad was getting angry. Most people couldn't tell when Brad was mad, but Gordon knew the signs, the carefully controlled tone of voice, the studiedly nonchalant posture.

"What are you going to do, you clunkhead? Resign now?"

"Don't worry, Brad," Gordon said bitterly. "You got your way, the way you always do. Now I've *got* to stick it out. You were counting on that, weren't you?"

Brad visibly relaxed, though the signs of it would have been imperceptible to anyone but Gordon. The familiar ironic tilt of the eyebrow returned.

"I'm glad you're being sensible, baby brother. You've got a chance to make something of yourself now. At least you're getting an education, courtesy of Uncle Sam. That's more than Jeremy can say."

"That's right, Brad, I've got my chance." Hot tears were in his eyes. "But it isn't worth anything to me now."

He turned and started to walk away.

"Gordie!"

The sharpness of Brad's tone brought him around.

"I didn't come here to argue with you. What do you know about a family called Kinney?"

"Ask Uncle Elroy," Gordon said with quick resentment. "He was making things hard enough for Junie when I left. I didn't want to tell him about the kid, but when Dad died and we couldn't find Junie, I didn't know what else to do."

"What kid?"

"What do you want to know for, Brad? So you can interfere with her life too?"

"Junie's run off with the Kinney family."

"Run off with the Kinneys?"

"Yeah. They skipped on their debts, sold off their livestock, and were seen heading west in an old truck and car piled with their household stuff."

Gordon frowned. "His name was Floyd. I used to see him around school. Some of the kids used to make fun of him. He was all patches, and holes in his shoes. There wasn't any harm in him. Junie felt sorry for him. Like a stray dog, sort of. She used to try to help him with his studies. I don't think he could read too well."

"What else can you tell? What was the father's first name?"

"I don't know. He was just Mr. Kinney to Junie."

"What kind of people are they?"

"I never met them. Except Floyd. I used to pass their place sometimes, when Freddie Mueller and I rode our bikes down the road out of town. It was pretty run down. I guess they were okay. Floyd was clean, and all. They were like a lot of other tenants. They did their best. But they never had anything, and they never will."

"And now Junie's with them."

Gordon's eyes blazed. "You *hope* Junie's still with them. But you don't know. How many weeks has it been?"

"Gordie . . . I didn't know she was missing until it was too late."

"And you never bothered to check up on her, did you? You were too busy, with your important job in Washington."

"What am I, everybody's father?" Brad snapped. "What the hell do you know about it? You're in the right place, all right, with that stiff neck and thick skull of yours. You had to make it here to the East on your own. You couldn't unbend a little. You couldn't wait until I found a job. I would have sent you the Pullman fare and let you ride to West Point in style if you'd wanted. Where were *you* when Junie ran off?"

Gordon stood stiffly, hurt clouding his face.

"I'm sorry, Gordie. I didn't mean that. Look, why don't you have dinner with me tonight? Get out of the plebe rat race for a couple of hours. I'll take you to that place on the Academy grounds. The Thayer Hotel. The dining room's not off limits to cadets. I hear the food's pretty good. I can take a room there for the night."

"I'm confined to quarters."

"I've already fixed it up with the commandant. Special dispensation. I've got you a dinner pass. What do they call it here, a DP?"

"*You* fixed it up?" Gordon said tightly. "Oh, boy, that's all I need. Thanks a lot, Brad."

"Come on, Gordie, it's not going to corrupt your principles to take a couple of hours off."

"I can't spare the time."

Brad sighed. "All right." His hand went to his pocket. "Need any money?"

"We're not allowed to have any."

He turned and walked away, his spine straight, his shoulders squared in the tight gray uniform. Brad watched him as he steered a course through the mob of Sunday visitors and disappeared through the arched doorway.

The odd thing was, Brad thought, that he hadn't informed on Braithwaite after all. He had thought about it, but had decided that it wouldn't be necessary.

The bugles sounded the adjutant's call, and the Long Gray Line began to form. As the military band played, the entire cadet body of West Point—three battalions divided into twelve companies—marched out onto the parade ground in perfect unison, colors flying. They took their places in a superb exhibition of close-order drill, over twelve hundred young men identically uniformed in cockaded tarbuckets and gray tunics crisscrossed by white webbing.

Under the shade of the trees at the edge of the parade ground, Brad watched the show with the rest of the Sunday visitors. He squinted, trying to pick out Gordon. They all looked alike, identically tall and straight, even though he knew it was an optical illusion. The companies were assigned by height, with the tallest men flanking the line, and diminishing uniformly toward the runts in the middle. He finally located Gordon about halfway from one end, among the six-footers.

Brad ground out his cigarette in the grass. Despite himself, he was stirred by the sight. The corps put on a good show. He could never have submitted to that kind of discipline himself, but as he watched Gordon, the long serious face bisected by the chin strap, the rifle moving in precision with the rest, he felt an absurd sense of pride.

He lingered until the companies passed in review and marched back to the barracks, then as the crowd of spectators broke up, he headed down the path toward the Thayer Hotel.

As he stolled along the cliffside, he arranged his story in his mind. It wasn't true, as he'd told Gordon, that he had been to Hyde Park on an errand to the President on this particular weekend—though he or Robbie had flown there often enough as couriers for the general.

The errand he was on now couldn't be mentioned to anyone.

Rexford Tugwell had saddled him with it. Tugwell had become head of Roosevelt's "Brain Trust" since Ray Moley—"Holey Moley," his enemies derisively called him—had left the government to start a weekly news magazine. Rex Tugwell and General Johnson had known one another since the early, heady days of Roosevelt's presidential campaign, and these days they often met by the President's bedside.

Nominally, Tugwell was only assistant secretary of agriculture. But he was also Hugh Johnson's ally on the Special Industrial Recovery Board, the Cabinet group to which Johnson theoretically was supposed to report.

"Hugh's disappeared again," Tugwell had said. "Nobody's been able to find him for days." He cleared his throat. "They were making cracks about it at the Cabinet meeting this afternoon."

"He had business out of town," Brad said evasively. The general's periodic binges were common knowledge now, but the polite fictions had to be maintained.

"The board meets Monday afternoon. Ickes will be gunning for him."

"I'm sure he'll be back in time."

It was bad, Brad knew. The board had been fighting General Johnson on the minimum wage. Now they were trying to take authority for final code adoption away from him. Through Ickes, they had the President's ear.

Tugwell hesitated. "Robbie didn't want me to tell you this. She's afraid you'll run to the Richberg people with it. But I know where Hugh goes when he wants to dry out."

"I don't blame Robbie," Brad said with a forthright smile. "If the press found out, they'd be after him there. Wherever it is."

"It's that big hotel at West Point, the one right on the grounds, overlooking the Hudson. Hugh likes it there. I think it brings back memories."

"The Thayer."

Tugwell nodded. "Now for God's sake, don't tell him how you were able to find him. We don't want him to blow up. But get him back here Monday afternoon, sober! He's got to be at that meeting, or he's cooked!"

Brad had the perfect excuse for showing up at the Point. Gordie.

In fact, Brad thought, he was sorry he hadn't thought of mentioning Gordie to the general before. The general, for all his bluster, was a sucker for sentiment.

He had registered under an assumed name. The desk clerk looked puzzled when Brad asked for General Johnson; then, when he described him, said: "Oh, you must mean Mr. Scott. I think you can find him on the terrace at this hour."

The general was sitting in a garden chair, brooding at the Hudson River below. Beside him on a little table was a glass of amber liquid. Brad walked over.

The general looked up as Brad went through a little charade of hesitating and coming to a stop. "Sinclair! What are you doing here?"

Brad feigned surprise. "General Johnson! I didn't expect to bump into *you* on the reservation! I'm visiting my kid brother, Gordon, for the weekend. He's a cadet here."

"He's a kaydet in the corps?" Johnson said, the suspicion fading from his face. "You never mentioned that. Here, sit down, boy. I'll see if I can hail a waiter."

Brad pulled up a chair. He searched the general's face. Johnson seemed clear-eyed, serene, drained, like a man who had wrestled with himself and won. Brad's glance went to the glass.

The general followed his gaze. "That's just ginger ale, Sinclair. You can't get booze here. You'll have to settle for coffee, tea, or soda pop."

"Black coffee's fine."

The general signaled, and a waiter scurried over, very deferential. The view was magnificent. Below the tiers of broad stone terraces, the river was a dark oceanic expanse with toy ships steaming in the distance. The sounds of an orchestra playing Cole Porter drifted from the open doors of the hotel ballroom, where a tea dance was in progress.

"I like to come back here every once in a while," the general said. "Just walk around and see the old sights. Of course they aren't as tough on the plebes as when I was here. It was bare fists to a knockout if you even raised your eyes to *look* at an upperclassman. A boy in my class died from the hazing. They made him drink two bottles of Tabasco sauce. But golly, we had some high old times. I belonged to a bunch we called the Salt Creek Club. We were the tough guys. Our motto was 'Never bone today what you can bugle tomorrow.' Douglas MacArthur and Ulysses Grant the Third were what we called the 'nice boys,' but they raised their share of hell. Once MacArthur stole a cannon from Trophy Point. They finally found it on top of the West Academic Building. It took a detachment of men with block and tackle a week to get the thing down. No one could ever figure out how he got it up there in the first place."

"Oh, Gordie has some stories to tell," Brad said. "Nothing like that, of course."

"This his first year?"

"Yes. He just made it. He was an alternate. The original candidate got kicked out during summer camp for being married."

"Your brother's a September Member?" Johnson said with quickening interest. "So was I. That's the only thing around here that rates lower than a plebe. Well, it'll make a man of him."

"Oh, Gordie's tough."

"Tell you what. Let's take him to dinner here. He can get a dinner pass on Sunday night if he asks. Be a nice change from having to brace in the mess hall."

"I asked him. But he's confined to quarters."

The general chuckled. "The young rascal. But I guess all you Sinclairs are rascals. I'll never forget how you bamboozled Tewkes! And swindled me into hiring you in the bargain."

"I was going to stay, but with Gordie locked up, I guess I'll go back tonight. I just checked out of the hotel. Can I give you a ride back to Washington?"

"You have a car?"

"I just bought one of those new Chrysler Airflows. You know, the streamlined one."

"Streamlined autos." The general shook his head. "You young fellows. The streamlined generation. Always in a hurry."

"Streamlining's here to stay. I can make it back to Washington in six hours. Stop for supper on the way." He looked into the general's face. "Anyway, you're pretty much in a hurry yourself, General."

Johnson laughed. "By golly, I am at that."

"Mr. Ickes seems to think you're too much in a hurry," Brad said.

"Ickes!" Johnson snorted. "Sitting on his public works. He's strangling recovery with his damn red tape!"

"Not to bring up business, but he's been telling everybody that the President's about ready to hand over control of final NRA code adoption to the Cabinet board. At least that was the scuttlebutt in Washington on Friday."

The general's face clouded. "He is, is he? Well, I've been telling the President he ought to dismember the board! Damned interfering busybodies!"

"Doesn't the board have a meeting tomorrow?" Brad said innocently.

"Not without me, they don't," the general fumed. "Where's your car parked?"

They were waiting for Gordon in the Sinks when he came back from evening parade. There were just the two of them, Crowley and Stanger, still in the dress whites they'd worn for their weekend passes.

"Brace, mister! Suck air, suck air!" Stanger shouted at him.

"Enjoying a soft Sunday, are you, Mister Dumbguard?" Crowley said. "Drag in your chin! More! More!"

Gordon strained to obey, feeling ludicrous in his shower robe and bare feet. He didn't know what to do with the cake of soap in his hand or the towel draped over his arm, so he held that forearm crooked outward while his right arm was held rigidly at his side.

"Pull those shoulders back!"

Gordon thought he could smell liquor on their breath. He was astonished. The penalty for drinking was dismissal. A cadet wasn't supposed even to pass a glass of wine across the table to a member of his family while he was on leave.

"Take your slimy eyes off me!" Stanger snarled. "Look front, look front!"

Around them, other cadets were hurrying to or from the showers, anxious to change into proper uniform in time for the supper call. The columns would be forming in another twenty minutes. Crowley and Stanger, still technically on leave, were exempt. Gordon's plight attracted a few curious glances, but not from the plebes, who hastened past with their eyes fixed on the tile floor.

"What do plebes rank?" Crowley demanded.

Gordon repeated the tired catechism: "Sir, the superintendent's dog, the commandant's cat, the waiters in the mess hall, the hellcats, and all the admirals in the whole blamed navy."

"Not you, mister, not you. You don't even rank the superintendent's dog."

"No," Stanger put in. He hiccoughed. "You're not even a plebe. Not yet. You're a johnny-come-lately."

"That's right, mister," Crowley said. "While the rest of the plebes were learning the meaning of being a kaydet, you were having a soft summer in the bosom of your family, weren't you? Lying in a hammock, tickling the girls. Sunning yourself on the beach. Communing with the nefarious John Barleycorn. While certain of your less fortunate brethren sweated in the sun with rifle and field pack. Isn't that so?"

Gordon was getting tired of the silly game. Boys, he thought. They're only three years older than me. He thought about the one-eyed kid, Blinky, who had stolen his shoe in the Chicago mission. Blinky was only fifteen, and counted himself fortunate that his empty socket made it easier for him to beg for food at back doors. He remembered the little girl in the hobo jungle, Ollie, selling herself to syphilitic tramps for a nickel. He remembered his own paralyzing fear as he fled over the boxcar roofs from the railroad detective, Feather-stone, who had killed Knobby.

"Sir . . ." he said.

"Isn't that so?"

It would be so easy, he thought, to slug Crowley on the point of that brutish jaw. Then he could knee Stanger in the belly and rabbit-punch him when he folded, the way Knobby had taught him. And walk out of here before supper. He could hop a train to New York City. It was only a few miles away. He could find some sort of a job there.

But then he thought of the lazy, watchful look on Brad's face when he told him that he had made it impossible for him to quit now.

"Sir, I have spent the summer in the lap of luxury," he said.

Crowley and Stanger exchanged glances. A cadet came out of the showers, hair dripping, gave the three of them a sidelong look, and went out the exit. The Sinks were thinning out now. Every man in the corps would be on the street for mess parade within minutes. Crowley and Stanger kept Gordon standing at attention until the last straggler left.

Gordon was getting worried. How long did Crowley and Stanger mean to keep him standing here? If he missed formation, he was in trouble. He could just about make it if they let him go now. He'd have to get dressed without a shower, but he'd had practice enough running up the stairs, changing his uniform, and running down again in two minutes flat when some upperclassman demanded it.

"What's that in your hand, Mister Dumbguard?" Crowley said.

"Sir, it's a cake of soap," Gordon said.

"Soap is very nourishing," Stanger said.

"Eat it," Crowley said.

Gordon took a bite of soap and gagged.

"Chew and swallow, mister, chew and swallow."

Gordon got the mouthful down.

"You're not finished, mister."

Gordon ate half the bar, feeling sicker and sicker. Then, explo-sively, he puked all over the tile floor.

"Disgusting," Stanger said.

"Disgusting," Crowley echoed. "Clean it up, mister."

Gordon swabbed the floor with his towel, then washed his towel out in one of the sinks. Outside, he could hear the sounds of drums and trumpets as the three cadet battalions marched to the mess hall.

"Delicate stomach," Stanger said.

"It's the lack of salubrious exercise that's responsible," Crowley said.

"We owe it to this young lad to correct that," Stanger said.

"I agree, Mr. Stanger."

Gordon was still feeling sick. His stomach heaved, but he managed to swallow hard. The taste of bile was in his mouth. He wanted to sit down, but they were still keeping him braced.

Stanger went over to the door and looked both ways down the corridor. Then he closed the door.

"Wipe that smile off your face."

Gordon wasn't smiling, but he went through the charade anyway.

"Throw it on the ground and step on it."

He could hear Stanger over by the showers. Then there was the sound of shattering glass.

"Eyes front!"

Stanger rejoined Crowley, back in Gordon's line of vision. There was a smirk on his face.

"About . . . *face!*"

Gordon pivoted around.

"Forward . . . march!"

Gordon marched toward the showers. It was a big tiled area with nozzles sticking out of the wall at four-foot intervals. The floor was still puddled from the men who had just used it.

Then over by the drain, he saw the glass: four or five soft-drink bottles that had been swung against the tile and left there. They must have come out of Stanger's duffle bag, still leaning against the wall. The broken bottoms had been carefully arranged with the jagged ends up. The flowering shards of the necks and the miscellaneous crumbs of glass were strewn among them.

Crowley had aimed Gordon in a direct line toward the glass. Gordon's bare feet slapped the tile, almost there, and he began to get worried, but at the last moment, Crowley halted him. He stood at attention, feeling a stray grain of glass under his big toe.

"Spread your wings, Area bird," Stanger said.

Gordon extended his arms. His robe fell open, making him feel idiotic and vulnerable. His whole abdomen was sore from being sick.

"Bend over."

He was being spread-eagled. Gordon set his jaw in a stubborn line. He was sorry he hadn't slugged Crowley. It was too late now. It would look like he couldn't take it.

"Keep those wings spread!"

Gordon was good in calisthenics. A summer of hopping freights, of chopping wood, digging post holes, and doing other yard work had hardened his muscles. At the daily required gym class, he could continue doing pushups, chinning himself, and working the parallel bars long after most of his division had dropped out.

"Keep mucking, Dumbguard. You've only been going fifteen minutes so far."

The sweat streamed down Gordon's body. His arms felt like lead. The muscles of his abdomen knotted up. Each time, the effort of straightening up was agony. He tried to blank his mind, to keep going in mechanical rhythm.

"Those arms are drooping, mister! Straighten them out!"

He tried, but his arms wouldn't lift any higher. They felt like soft clay. His breath came in a raw wheeze. Crowley slapped him lightly on the face, hissing, "Shape up!" They're not supposed to touch you, Gordon thought with vague wonderment, it's against the rules for them to touch you. Crowley slapped him again. "Do it for Braithwaite."

He had the dry heaves. Gagging, he brought up a thin, bitter stuff. His knees wobbled. His face was suddenly clammy.

Stanger's moon face loomed large, a disembodied thing that swelled in his vision. Stanger's voice, sounding worried, said, "I think we better—"

"Shut up," Crowley said.

He was beyond pain now. His feet were doing little steps on the floor, unable to stay planted, but he couldn't feel them. He had no sensation of bending at the waist. Instead, the glass-littered floor kept bobbing up toward him, over and over again. The straight lines of the tile seemed to heave like ocean waves.

"Jesus!" a faraway voice said.

His knees buckled. He pitched forward. Hands tried to catch him, too late. The last thing he heard before he blanked out was a faint hollow trumpet sounding the call to quarters, and he realized through a surge of darkness that he had been eagled for two solid hours.

An animal sound that was his own voice brought him awake. Before he had time to think, his back arched like a bow. The pain was incredible. He felt as if his spine would snap unless he brought it under control. He bore down with all his might, grunting and panting, and the spasm died down.

"How long has he been like this?" a voice said.

"I don't know. I found him in his bunk when I came back from supper. He never showed up at the mess hall."

Their faces swam into focus. It was Hibbert, looking frightened, and one of the other plebes in his section. Beyond them, at the doorway, he could see curious faces looking in.

Gordon opened his mouth. He thought he was talking, but no sound seemed to be coming out. Another convulsion caught him.

"Jeez! I think he's gonna die. You better call for the doc."

This time he succeeded in making himself heard. "No!" he said through clenched jaw. "No doctor."

"Sinclair, are you all right? You were having some kind of fits."

"I'll be all right. Get the hell out of here."

When the other plebe left, Gordon turned to Hibbert and said, "What happened?"

"I don't know, Sinclair. I swear to God I don't know, and I don't want to know. Your legs are all cut up. I had to pick broken glass out of your knees."

Crowley and Stanger must have carried him upstairs and dumped him in his bed before the battalion got back to barracks, Gordon thought. They must be scared as hell right now.

"Ah!" Gordon cried.

"Sinclair, what's the matter?" Hibbert said, looking terrified.

"Sit on my chest, quick!" Gordon managed to get out through his rigid jaw.

With Hibbert's help, he managed to bring the spasms under control within the next hour. After that, it was easier. His feet kept seizing up and turning inward, the toes curled up, and his hands periodically turned into stiff claws, but he didn't feel as if his back were going to break in two. It was like getting caught by cramps when you were swimming. Hibbert bathed his lacerated knees for him with after-shave lotion, and washed away the crusted blood.

Shortly before tattoo, a pair of grim-faced upperclassmen came into the room and stared at Gordon while Hibbert braced.

"Can he get up?" one of them demanded of Hibbert.

"No," Gordon said through clattering teeth. He felt cold all over now. Goose pimples covered his flesh.

"Do you want the doctor?"

"No."

"Will you be able to get up in the morning?"

"I don't know."

The two upperclassmen turned and left without a word. When the Tac made his after-taps inspection, Gordon was lying rigidly under the sheet, eyes closed, trying to keep his limbs still. One of his legs kept trying to jump up. Hibbert was in his bunk, the lights out.

The flashlight played over Gordon's closed lids, then moved on. It was just an ordinary inspection. Whatever rumors were running through the barracks, they hadn't filtered down to the Department of Tactics.

When the Tac was gone, Hibbert said tentatively, "Sinclair . . ."

"Shut up, Hibb. There's nothing in the rules that says you had to call the doctor if I said I was okay. Go to sleep."

He was awake most of the night. He managed to snatch an uneasy hour of sleep before dawn, when his limbs turned to putty and he didn't have to fight them anymore. He awoke feeling ninety years old.

He kept dropping things, but he managed to dress and hobble painfully downstairs to breakfast formation. No upperclassman harassed him, even though a plebe was supposed to run double-time through the corridors and take the steps two at a time. He marched in cadence with his column to Washington Hall, the sweat rolling down his face.

It was his turn to make the Sammy bird, the queer little figurine that plebes were supposed to fashion out of the potbellied syrup pitcher, napkin, knife, and mustard spoon, with salt and pepper shakers for pop eyes. He tried to drape the napkin properly, but his fingers wouldn't behave, and he gave it up. Crowley looked the other way. Nobody spoke to him at breakfast. It was his chance to eat in peace, but all he could manage was a cup of coffee that his spastic fingers made rattle in the saucer.

It was a very subdued meal, compared to the normal hubbub animating the other tables. Crowley and the upperclassmen kept casting nervous glances toward the marble balcony where the officer in charge sat. Whenever Gordon risked raising his eyes, he could see the curious glances coming his way from nearby tables.

Word had gotten around. They were waiting to see if he would report for sick call after breakfast.

He let them wait. At the end of the meal he took his cap from the rack under the chair and stood at attention with the rest, then marched with his battalion through its doorway.

He was in terrible peril from this moment on. The West Point honor system cut both ways. If he failed to report Crowley and Stanger, and it came out anyway, he'd be pitched out of the Point along with them.

He was safe from the two of them. They hadn't turned themselves in as they were supposed to. So much for the Honor Code.

It was the rest of his company that he was in danger from. By now, even the dullest of them knew that something peculiar had gone on in the shower room. His convulsions had been witnessed by everybody who passed his door and peeked inside. All that was needed was one crack in the wall of silence, and he would be out on his ear.

He had to rely on the other code, the code that nobody talked about at the Point. The code that said you were a fool if you noticed more than you had to.

Hibbert was the one he was in the most danger from. Hibbert was working himself into a state of nerves. He was afraid that if he didn't report Gordon for not reporting Crowley and Stanger, somebody would report him for not reporting.

It was ridiculous.

Gordon had agonized like a medieval theologian during the twenty-five lecture hours when they had attempted to instill the honor system into his raw mind. He had thought it all out, stubbornly. In the end he had relied on his own good sense and strong sense of ethics. Immediately he had felt better about it.

You had to live with the terms of the West Point code. That was the bargain you had made. But you did what was right, no matter what some middle-aged philosophy teacher in an army captain's uniform told you.

Gordon sweated it out all week. The upperclassmen sweated it out along with him. The Firsts were a band of survivors.

Gordon was being tested in a contest that was older than West Point. There is a gentleman's code that began when the first hairy Neanderthal aristocrat looked over his fellow brutes to decide which of them was worthy of being admitted to the inner circle of mastodon hunters.

At the end of the week, nobody in Gordon's barracks had cracked. The plebes had enjoyed a vacation from all but the mildest forms of hazing, for which they were grateful. Hibbert had diarrhea and slept badly, but the unspoken peer pressure had kept his mouth shut too.

On Saturday after the last class, an upperclassman whose name he did not know stopped him on the library steps and shook hands with him.

At least fifty cadets saw it. Across the road on the athletic field, the soccer team was getting in some practice, and from the direction of the clock tower, a large group of Saturday sightseers was being escorted toward Trophy Point by their cadet hosts.

The upperclassman prolonged the handshake. "Heard a lot about you, Sinclair. My name's Stilwell. I'm supposed to be pretty good in surveying and tactics. Drop by anytime if you need any help."

Gordon gulped back his surprise. He had been Recognized. Most plebes had to wait until Recognition Day during June Week for the symbolic handclasp that turned them from beast to human being.

Across the way, the soccer team had halted their practice to gape. The group of Saturday visitors had paused while their escorts stopped and stared. In a minute, no doubt, somebody's aunt would ask what it was all about.

"I mean it, Sinclair," the upperclassman said. "Anytime."

Stilwell pumped his hand once more and left, a trim spare figure in dress grays. Gordon fought back the hot tears that started in his eyes.

Before he could go inside, another upperclassman bounded up the steps. Gordon knew him. His name was Beall, and he was one of the six-and-one-half-foot giants of Company A.

"Good man, Sinclair," he said, grasping Gordon's hand. "Say, have you thought of going in for the football team? You've got the shoulders for it. I can put in a word for you with Captain Rayner."

When Beall released his hand, there was another upperclassman waiting to shake it. And another. And another. Gordon lost count. He stood there, dazed, mumbling his thanks, while a small crowd of the curious gathered in Thayer Road to watch the spectacle.

It was as solemn a promise as is made at West Point. He would never be hazed or braced by an upperclassman again.

The last to come were Crowley and Stanger. Gordon was surprised that Crowley could look him in the eye. But Crowley seemed utterly forthright and sincere as he shook Gordon's hand in view of the others and said, "You're tops, Sinclair. I never doubted it."

He had got his name back. Sinclair. No Ducrot or Dumbjohn or Dooflicket anymore.

Crowley turned to go. Gordon saw his shoulders stiffen. Standing over the clock tower, perhaps attracted by the activity, was the whippet-slim figure of Captain Wilson, wearing the clanking saber and jingling spurs of the Tac. His daughter, Nellie, was on his arm, staring across at Gordon with lazy curiosity.

Crowley started over toward her, then changed his mind and headed toward the barracks, Stanger following. Captain Wilson gave Gordon a long hard look, then walked back toward Grant Hall with a firm grip on Nellie's arm. She turned around once to look at the library.

Gordon, swallowing hard with emotion, went inside the library. A couple of plebes sitting at one of the long tables looked up enviously at him as he crossed to the desk.

The librarian, a nice lady with rimless pince-nez and a black rustling dress garnished by beads and bangles, said: "More books on mathematics and military history, Gordon? Wouldn't you like to read some fiction for a change? The other boys do. I could recommend something light—maybe *Kidnapped* or some Jack London stories. You've got to have *some* relaxation. My goodness, you don't have to be that serious *all* the time, do you?"

"No," he said. "I guess I don't. Not anymore."

It was a small item in the *Washington Post*. Brad sipped his coffee and breezed through it, while in the steel cubicles around him typewriters clattered and telephones jangled.

PRESIDENT ROOSEVELT DISSOLVES
SPECIAL INDUSTRIAL RECOVERY BOARD

Transfers Functions to National Emergency Council

It was just another minor instance of bureaucratic organizational reshuffling. Ho-hum stuff. It was unlikely to mean anything to anybody outside of the Washington rat race.

But its significance would be apparent to everyone who really mattered. The National Emergency Council was a remote coordinating body for all recovery programs. The reins it held were very loose. General Johnson would be allowed to run his own show again.

The general must have set off considerable fireworks at the Monday meeting that Brad had delivered him to. He had grappled with Ickes and Richberg and the rest of them, and won.

Brad was still backing the right horse.

18

Junie got up early that morning. Floyd was still snoring beside her in the big feather bed that Cousin Earl had dragged out of the shed for them and set up in the bare little room off the kitchen that had been a buttery once upon a time.

"Young folks that's just been married need their privacy," Cousin Earl had said, and the rest of the Kinneys had agreed. Ma and Pa Kinney were jammed into the furniture-crowded front room along with Wesley and Sue Ellen's two-year-old, Cindy Lou, and Purley and Sue Ellen and the new baby were opposite, in the old keeping room that didn't have a door, and that everyone tramped through on their way to the outhouse. You could hear the baby crying all through the house. Cousin Earl and Cousin Emma had moved in with the old grandmother in the long narrow back room she used as a bedroom. Grammumum, everybody called the old lady.

There was something in the air this morning. Junie couldn't put her finger on it, but it smelled different, like smoke. She wanted to sneeze. She looked out the flyspecked window, and it was still dark, though down next to the horizon, across the flat Dakota fields, there was a band of dirty light.

She edged along the wall toward her clothes, stepping carefully so as not to awaken Floyd. The billowing mattress occupied almost the whole floor space. Her back to him, she slipped her nightgown down to her waist and held it in place while she pulled her dress on over her head, the way Ma Kinney had shown her a married woman was supposed to.

She dressed quickly and went into the kitchen. Ma Kinney was already up, lighting a fire with cornstalks in the iron stove.

"Morning, child," Ma Kinney said. "Listen to them animals. Lord, something's worrying them!"

Junie listened. A calf was bawling, and she could hear the horses in their stalls nickering to one another.

"The chickens, too," Ma Kinney said. "The chickens is running around as like crazy."

She got the fire going and slammed the iron door shut. She stood at the stove stirring a pot of cornmeal mush, her gray hair, uncombed, straying down her face, her big men's shoes still unlaced. Since the first morning after their arrival, it had been a point of pride with her to get up before Cousin Emma and get things going.

The Kinneys' heavy oak dining table stood in the center of the kitchen. It had been the first thing off the truck. With the leaves in, it was big enough for them all to sit down at the same time. Cousin Emma's rickety kitchen table was pushed against the wall, piled with pots and dishes.

The kitchen's sagging walls were papered with old newspapers. Junie read them over and over; they were the only print she'd had to read since leaving Iowa. She paused to look at her favorite: the Sunday society page with the wedding picture of Barbara Hutton and the Russian prince. Sometimes, secretly, she pretended to herself that Floyd was a prince and she was a princess.

"I'll be back in a minute and help," she told Ma Kinney.

On the way to the outhouse, the air almost choked her. There was a gritty taste in her mouth. She had trouble pulling the door open, and when she looked down, she saw that an inch of fine black dust had drifted against the bottom edge.

There was always dust. Cousin Earl said it hadn't rained from here to Kansas all summer. The topsoil was blowing away, he said. But Junie had never seen it so bad. She looked at the horizon. The sun was nothing but a red smear.

When she got back to the house, the men were up. Pa Kinney was standing barefoot in the kitchen in his overalls, buttoning the top of his union suit. "Wesley," he said, "you better put the tarps over the hoods of the car and truck. Don't want to git sand in the engine."

"All right, Pa," Wesley said, and hurried out.

Ma Kinney said, "You better wet some cloths and stuff them in the window cracks. This here dust's gettin' in the cornmeal."

Junie hurried to help. She sent a proud, shy smile in Floyd's direction, but he was busy with Purley and Cousin Earl, the three of them looking worried and serious, talking man-fashion in low, measured voices.

"We better see to the well," Purley was saying. "That there well gets drifted over, we're finished for sure."

"Gumbo," Earl said. "That's what's blowing out there. That's the kind of dirt they have in the western part of the state. Just won't hold water when the grass is gone."

"Well, it sure blew a hell of a long way," Purley said.

By noontime you could not see the barn one hundred feet away. They stood by the windows with the cloth-stuffed sashes and watched the black snow.

"It's a judgment," Grammumum said. "That's what it is, a judgment."

"Hush," Cousin Emma said, looking frightened. She was a drab, sparrowlike woman, worn out by having babies that never lived. She and Earl were in their fifties now, close in their sorrow. He never reproached her for her childlessness, though Grammumum liked to dwell on the large families of Earl's three brothers.

The old lady wouldn't be silenced. "They plowed the crops under and slaughtered the baby pigs, and now God's sent his judgment."

"The government man," Earl explained apologetically. "Young fellow from the AAA. Said as how they decided in Washington that all our pigs had to be killed to keep the prices up. They paid us, though."

"Don't seem right to kill hogs and plow under a standing crop when so many folks are hungry," Ma Kinney said.

"And spilling milk," Sue Ellen said. "They's spilling milk, too."

The baby began to cry in her arms.

"The fellows spilling the milk ain't government," Wesley said earnestly, fingering his cracked eyeglasses. "That's the Farm Holiday Association. Milo Reno's boys. The idea's the same, though. There's too much milk and corn and cotton and pork, driving the prices down. Got to drive the prices up so the farmer can make a living. That's the government's idea. You see—"

"Shut up, Wesley," Purley said, and Wesley subsided.

"It's a judgment," Grammumum said firmly. "First the drought, then the grasshoppers, now the dust. It's the hand of God."

"It's Armistice Day," Pa Kinney said suddenly.

"What?" Cousin Earl said.

"It's Armistice Day. Today's November eleventh. I've been keeping track. If the Lord sent His judgment, He sure enough sent it on a holiday."

"That's enough talk," Ma Kinney said, a ladle in her hand. "You men set down to dinner before the dust gets into everything. Sue Ellen, you wipe off those plates. Junie, you help me serve."

There were no greens, but there was plenty of stewed corn and pork. Even with the drought, there had been enough withered ears from the fields to fill the crib to overflowing, and Cousin Earl had hidden a sow from the government man. Cousin Earl had refused the ham offered by the Kinneys when they showed up in September, saying he had more than enough to feed everybody. They were getting down to the fatback now, but nobody talked about that.

By two, the barn was half buried. Purley came wading in, dropped the kerchief from his face, and said, "That weaned calf just plain ain't gonna make it. Floyd's out there wiping dust out of its nostrils again, but it's just too skeered to try to live."

"What about the truck?" Pa Kinney said.

"We'll have to dig it out when the dust stops blowing."

"Ain't never going to stop," the old lady said, rocking back and forth in her kitchen chair. "It's the day of God's wrath."

"Ma!" Sue Ellen cried. "The baby's coughing up black!"

The women clustered around the baby. Purley shook his head and went back out into the black blizzard.

The wind died down by next morning. Floyd and Purley had to climb out a window and shovel the drifts away from the door before they could open it. They all went outside and stared at a burned-out landscape.

As far as the eye could see, there was nothing but a wasteland of gray dust. A blood-red sun hung low over a barren and unfamiliar world. The road past the house was gone, fences were buried, trees were strange stunted things with submerged trunks.

The tops of the sheds and the corncrib poked through the dunes, but the chicken coop had completely disappeared. Junie saw a low fence enclosing a little square of sand and realized, after a moment of strangeness, that it was the top of the Kinneys' stake truck.

"Thy wrath is come!" the old lady ranted. "Destroy them which destroy the earth! Hide us from the wrath of the Lamb!" Cousin Emma shushed her and led her into the house.

"Farm's finished," Purley said. He spat in the dust. "It'll never grow corn again."

The men stood apart in a little semicircle, their heads bowed. Junie wanted more than anything at this moment to run to Floyd, to feel his hand warm in hers, but Ma Kinney laid a hand on her shoulder and kept it there.

"Leave 'em be, child," she said.

Pa Kinney cleared his throat. "You and Emma been mighty fine to us, Earl. Mighty fine. But we won't be a burden to you now."

"You're welcome to stay."

Pa Kinney shook his head. "Might be there's enough stored corn to get you and some of the livestock through the winter. But what happens in the spring? Can't get a crop in the ground. Those fields will never grow anything again. We can't do you no good here, Earl."

"We'll help you dig out before we go," Purley said.

"You take my advice," Pa Kinney said. "You'll sell those plough horses if you can, slaughter them if you have to. Don't wait. Before they eat more fodder. And slaughter those cows but one or two and salt them."

"There's the chickens," Purley said. "It was right smart of Ma to think of bringing them in the house last night. Chickens won't eat much corn. Not as much as the cows."

Earl said, "Where will you go?"

"I reckon we'll head south. Follow the crops. Husk corn in Kansas, pick cotton in Texas. I hear they pick cotton as late as December there. Then head toward California and pick fruit. We'll make out."

Wesley had wandered off to investigate the well. He came back, dragging his feet through the grit.

"Well's silted over. The dust got through the boards, the canvas, everything."

"What's down there, boy?"

"Mud. Little wet on top."

"We'll dig it out for you afore we go, Earl. But you get another dust storm and . . ." He left the sentence unfinished.

"I thank you, fellers."

Pa Kinney and Purley exchanged glances. Pa turned back to Cousin Earl.

"Come with us."

Earl stared at his feet. "Can't. We got to stay and take care of Grammumum. We can get through winter. We've got the pig money."

Pa Kinney nodded.

"Come on, boys. Let's git to the shoveling."

For four days they shoveled dust, getting the outbuildings and the machinery unburied. Every moving part of the Reo truck and the Ford was gritty with sand. Floyd drained the oil and strained it through cloth, then put it back in. He took the engines apart and bathed the pistons and bearings in kerosene. When he put everything together again, there were some anxious moments, but after they got started, they ran fine.

The calf had died of fright that first night, and all of the chickens they hadn't rounded up had smothered, but the other animals were all right. On the fifth day, they began slaughtering.

"Want you to take a side of beef, and no arg'ment," Cousin Earl said. "By the time we get through, we'll have more beef salted than the three of us can eat afore it starts to turn. And you take some a' them chickens—some are yours anyways. And as much cornmeal as you kin carry."

Pa Kinney and Ma stood in the drifted yard and nodded agreement. Pride was pride, but sometimes there was no point in it.

The next morning they began reloading the truck, while the women picked through the possessions that littered the yard.

"Emma, you take this pitcher and basin. By rights it should 'a gone to Earl's ma anyway. And you take the marble stand. No use in our hauling it along."

When the last barrel and sack and makeshift coop of squawking chickens had been tied in place, the yellow oak dining table still stood in the yard.

"Ma, we just plain don't have room for it," Purley said, surveying the teetering load. "This truck's springs are carrying everything they kin carry. We don't have no use for a table nohow."

Ma Kinney stuck her chin out and said, "We all ate together off that table all the years we been a family, and all you children were born on that table, and we're taking it with us, and that's all there is to it."

Without a word, the men lifted the table onto the truck.

They left early the next morning. The wheels spun on the sand-covered highway, then caught, and they were on their way. Junie, in the back seat of the old Ford with Floyd and the little girl, twisted around to look through the foggy rear window until the sagging gray roof of Cousin Earl's house was out of sight.

Ahead, past Purley's stiff shoulders, the swaying truck filled the windshield. Riding the top of the load was the oak table, its clawed feet in the air.

Junie felt around for Floyd's hand and clasped it. He stared straight ahead, not saying anything, but his hand squeezed hers.

She wouldn't tell him until she was sure. She had talked to Sue Ellen about it, and Sue Ellen had said doubtfully, "That could be that there's a baby growing inside you, or it might be because you're still young and you ain't settled down to being regular yet. You better wait before you say anything. One more month and you can tell for sure."

* * *

The highway west was jammed with jalopies, a procession of bent tin that crawled like injured beetles across the hard plain.

"Where do they all come from?" Sue Ellen marveled.

"Dusted out, same as us," Purley grunted. He leaned on his horn as the vehicle in front of them, a skinny-wheeled Model T with bedrolls lashed to its rear, came to a dead stop.

"That won't do no good," Floyd said. "You'll just wear out the battery."

"Does *me* some good," Purley said, and leaned on the horn again.

Junie squirmed in the broken seat, working herself around to ease the pressure of a loose spring that was jabbing her in the back. The cheap cotton dress was twisted uncomfortably around her waist. She felt dry and dusty from all the traveling, and the flat, ugly Texas landscape depressed her.

"How much farther do we have to go?" she said.

Floyd swallowed guiltily, and his unshaven Adam's apple bobbed up and down twice. "We'll turn south toward Lubbock soon. Pa figures we can make the Rio Grande valley by day after tomorrow, maybe. We kin stay there awhile if we get work."

"What kind of work?" she said bitterly. She looked out the window at an abandoned farmhouse standing in the middle of a whorl of tractor furrows. One of the new mechanized cotton farms. Whatever had been planted there lay brown and blasted. "I don't think anything grows in the whole state of Texas."

The great dust storm on Armistice Day had just been the beginning. The parched and loosened soil had finally given up its grip on the bones of the land. The whole world had begun to blow away, it seemed to the Kinneys. The battered old radio, when Floyd had been able to trickle enough juice into it before it had finally given up the ghost, had told them that dust from the storms had blotted out the sun in Chicago, had darkened the noon sky as far away as Boston. The farms of Oklahoma were raining into the Atlantic Ocean. The roads were filled with fleeing people, some in flivvers, some just walking.

Junie recalled the other places they had driven through, before Texas. In Nebraska there had not been enough of a corn crop this year to merit the hiring of people to husk it. In Kansas they grew wheat, harvested by big machines. Now here they were in this strange barren place called Texas, crawling along in a flivver parade of Oklahoma people looking for cotton to pick. The side of beef and the cornmeal were almost gone, and the Kinneys' funds were running out. Junie still had most of the twenty-five dollars that Pamela had given her, but the Kinneys so far had refused to touch it.

"Texas is a big place," Floyd said, his knuckly hands working. "It ain't *all* like this. They say it's a Eden down south. Plenty of work. They irrigate from the Rio Grande, y'see. Force the crops. Feller at the last camp said they grow things the year round down there."

He looked miserable. Junie was ashamed of her outburst. Floyd was a good man. He was doing his best. Surreptitiously she patted her belly where the baby was growing. She just wanted to be sure he wasn't born in a tent by the roadside.

"I know," she said. She reached for his hand and quieted its spasmodic flexing. "Everything's going to be all right. Really and truly."

She looked back over her shoulder at the truck looming behind them. Above the heart-shaped radiator, the slot of windshield framed three faces in a row. Pa Kinney sat patient and unquestioning behind the wheel, waiting for traffic to start up again. She tried to remember her own father, but the image wouldn't come, only a vagueness of fine-spun white hair and blind discs of eyeglasses.

Purley twisted round in his seat. "Feller's getting out of his car. Looks like they're stopped all down the line. Something's wrong."

Floyd and Junie leaned out to see. The owner of the Model T was conferring with another migrant. The other man went forward and the Model T's owner came back toward them. He was a young, sharp-boned man in patched overalls, bareheaded, with a smear of black stubble across his lower face.

"Howdy," he said, squinting in at the window.

"Howdy," Purley said.

"Deputies up ahead. They's turnin' ever'one back."

"What do you mean?" Purley said with the quick, smoldering anger that Junie had come to know so well.

The man was softly apologetic. "They said we ain't allowed in their county. No work there anyhow."

"Ain't allowed? We're United States citizens, ain't we? And this here's a U.S. highway. We can go where we damn please!"

Alarm showed in the man's eyes. He changed the subject. "You folks come all the way from Ioway?"

Purley nodded.

"I thought so. Seen your license plates. I'm from Oklahoma. Most of the folks up ahead are. We're sort of travelin' together. 'Bout thirty families."

"Makes it hard to find work, don't it? I mean if there ain't enough jobs at a place."

"A man likes to travel with his own kind." Hastily he added: "Of course you folks are welcome to camp with us tonight."

Purley said nothing. Sue Ellen nudged him and said, "We thank you kindly."

"Had me a nice little place back there," the man said, rubbing his face reflectively with his forearm. "Sharecropped about a hundred acres of cotton, and hired out besides. Had me my own two-mule row cultivator. Then we all got tractored out. The owner said he'd keep me on, seeing as me and the little ones were good workers, but then the dust came, and he just took his Washington money and plowed the crop under. Heard there was work for good pickers in Texas. Feller came through with handbills."

"Well, it looks like they don't want you now," Purley said cruelly.

"Shucks, they're just full up in the next county. We got here too late, that's all. There'll be work farther south."

"With the deputies to kindly move you on," Purley said.

The man looked at him uncertainly. "Well, I better get back to my car. Looks like they're starting to move." He hurried back to the old Model T.

"Purley!" Sue Ellen said. "You had no call to speak to him so mean."

"I'm an American citizen, by God, and nobody can tell me where I can go and can't go."

"It wasn't him."

A stream of antique traffic was starting to flow back in the other lane, decrepit Fords and Dodge Victories and Plymouth Fours and Peerless Sixes, piled high with bales and buckets, with children's bleached faces pressed against the glass, inching apologetically back the way they had come.

"I better tell Pa about the deputies," Floyd said, and was out the door in a flash.

A moment later, Pa Kinney appeared at the side window. "Floyd tells me you're getting smart," he said to Purley. "Now you don't talk back to no deputies, and I don't care if you're the king of Araby. Your ma said to tell you that!"

"Yes, sir," Purley said.

The line ahead started moving, and Pa Kinney hurried back to the truck. Floyd got in the back seat just as Purley put the car savagely in gear.

The roadblock was a couple of sawhorses with red rags tied to them. A couple of deputies stood easily in front of them, thumbs in their pockets. They were sleek, well-fed men in western hats, military shirts and boots, holstered revolvers slung on their fat hips.

Behind the barrier were about a dozen parked cars and pickup trucks. Junie could see a score of loitering men. She had an impression of red faces and dusty ranch clothes and rifles leaning against fenders and running boards. As she watched, someone tilted back a bottle, then passed it along.

Purley pulled up. One of the deputies sauntered over and leaned in the window.

"Now you folks just turn around and go back where you come from," he said gently. "We don't need your kind in this county."

Junie could see the knots working at the back of Purley's jaws, but he answered in a humble tone of voice. "We're just passing through, looking for work."

"Well, there ain't no work. Crop's been picked, folks that picked it been moved along. Now git."

Junie could hear Purley swallowing hard. "We don't aim to settle here. We just got to get through."

The other deputy walked over with a clink and rattle of metal accoutrements. "What's the trouble, Emmett?"

"This goddamn Okie's giving me an argument."

"I ain't no Okie!" Purley flared. "I'm from Iowa. You kin see it on my license plates."

The second deputy put his foot on the running board. "Iowa, eh? Let's see your driver's license."

Purley handed the dog-eared license over, his hand trembling with suppressed rage.

The deputy ripped it across twice and threw the pieces to the ground. "Now you're Okies," he said. "Turn around and get going."

Purley gunned the motor. The deputy cursed and jerked his foot off the running board. The car lurched into movement. For a moment Junie thought Purley was going to make a U-turn, but the car swerved as he tried to go around the barrier.

A gun went off with a sharp crack. Sue Ellen screamed. The car jerked and dropped. A bucket that had been too loosely tied to the fender rattled to the concrete of the highway, spilling dried beans.

Purley was slumped, defeated, over the wheel, cursing softly to himself. Junie could hear the hiss of air escaping from a tire. The deputy called Emmett came running over, his fat jiggling, waving a big blue revolver. Junie was so scared that she couldn't breathe. She clung to Floyd, digging her nails into his arms.

"You son of a bitch, I'm gonna kill you!" the deputy shouted. "Get out of that car!"

The long snout of the gun lay across Purley's neck. Purley was gripping the wheel for his life. Junie could see his bloodless knuckles on the spokes. With his free hand the deputy was trying to drag Purley out the door.

"Please!" Sue Ellen blabbered, throwing herself and the baby across Purley. "I swear we'll leave and never come back!"

Emmett released Purley and took a step backward, breathing hard, his face mottled. The other deputy came up beside him. Junie could see a livid red O on Purley's cheek from the mouth of the gun. Purley's eyes were squeezed shut.

The two deputies stared uncertainly at Sue Ellen and the shrieking baby. Sue Ellen was fastened around Purley's neck. The deputies' eyes roved to Floyd and Junie and the little girl in the back seat. Floyd sat very still. Junie shrank against him. The little girl started bawling.

"Ah, come on!" the other deputy said. He pulled Emmett away from the car. Emmett looked over at the long waiting line of traffic and seemed suddenly to wake up.

"All right, all right, get moving!" He strode toward the stopped vehicles, waving his arms.

"Get that heap of junk off the road," the other deputy said, staring hard at Purley.

"Yes, sir," Purley said, and the deputy walked away.

The rusty cavalcade began to flow, skirting the stricken car and heading back in an easterly direction. With a pang, Junie watched the Kinneys' old Reo stake truck disappear. She had caught a glimpse of Ma's face, staring impassively straight ahead.

"Don't you worry," Floyd said in a low voice. "Pa'll wait for us a mile or two down the road."

The car bumped along on its flat tire as Purley eased it over onto the shoulder of the road, well away from the barricade and the loafing men behind it.

They all got out to inspect the shot-out tire, Sue Ellen carrying the baby. The bullet had torn out a big hole surrounded by hanging shreds of rubber. Junie shuddered, imagining what such a bullet might have done to Purley.

"Well, that son of a bitch sure can't be fixed," Purley said. "And the spare ain't gonna take us far. We're gonna need a new tire, sure as hell."

Junie knew by now that a flat tire was a disaster, if it couldn't be patched. They had had to buy a used tire in Kansas for the truck, and that was the week Ma Kinney stopped buying store bread along the way.

Floyd glanced uneasily at the idlers behind the barricade. "Never mind that now," he said. "Let's get this tire changed and get out of here before those deputies leave."

Purley had no jack; the man who had sold him the car had removed it. He and Floyd levered up the front end with the long side piece from the iron bedstead lashed to the roof, and slid a box under the bumper. By the time Purley changed the tire and got the box and the bed frame tied back in place, the rattletrap Okie caravan was gone. One of the deptuies was removing the barricade. The other deputy came ambling over.

Purley slid hastily behind the wheel. "We're just going, mister," he said.

The deputy looked them all over, his face fat and mean beneath the brim of the Stetson. It was the one called Emmett, who had shot out the tire. "You don't aim to sneak back into this county as soon as our backs are turned, do you?" he said.

"No, sir, we wouldn't do that."

"We just aim to join up with our people down the road," Sue Ellen said anxiously, holding the baby close.

The deputy chewed thoughtfully on his wad. He walked over to the tire that Purley had just changed, leather slapping his thigh. Before Junie realized what he intended, the gun was in his hand. He took aim at the tire and the gun went off like the crack of a whip. The car settled, lopsided.

Junie cried out and reached for Floyd. But he batted her hand aside and dove across the front seat to grip Purley by the arms.

The deputy grinned at them. "That's right," he said.

He walked all the way around the car and shot out the tires, one by one. Junie winced at each explosion. The car slumped with a little jolt three more times. Sue Ellen's two-year-old was screaming. Nobody said anything.

The deputy strolled around to the front of the car, still chewing, and fired a final shot through the radiator. A geyser of steam spurted into the air.

The deputy tilted his hat back. "Walk," he said, and went back to his car.

Floyd let go of Purley's arms. Purley was shaking all over. "Oh, the dirty son of a bitch," he said.

"Purley," Floyd said in an urgent voice, "you better see if that engine will start."

Both of them glanced back to where the locals lounged against the parked cars and ranch pickups. An air of carnival expectancy could be sensed in the crowd. There was some good-natured shoving and prodding. As the deputies drove off, a couple of men with shotguns moved in the direction of Purley's car, in no particular hurry, drawing the rest of the crowd raggedly with them.

The self-starter caught with a cough, and steam boiled out of the hood of the car. "That don't matter," Floyd said. "We can get a little ways down the road afore the engine heats up too much. What's that oil gauge say?"

"She's holding oil all right. The son of a bitch prob'ly just punched a hole in the radiator."

"Git goin'!"

The car shuddered and moved with a grating sound. It rolled down the cement highway on its flapping rims, picking up speed.

"Gonna tear what's left of that rubber to ribbons," Purley said.

"Don't matter. Just keep goin'."

Junie looked through the rear window. The men were running half-heartedly after them. After a few steps, the man in the lead stopped and fired his shotgun in their general direction.

"They had no call," Sue Ellen said. "They had no call at all."

"Anybody coming after us in a car?" Floyd said, his eyes on the instrument panel.

"No," Junie said.

"They had their fun," Purley said.

They jolted along for over a mile on the rims, while the radiator sizzled away. "You better pull over, Purley," Floyd said. He sniffed the air. "The oil's startin' to burn."

"There's Pa."

The slatted wooden box of the old Reo truck rose in front of them. Junie had never been so grateful to see anything in her life. Purley pulled up behind it. They all got out. Ma and Pa and Wesley hurried over to them.

"You're lucky to be alive," Pa Kinney said to Purley. "That depity had that gun at full cock. I seen his thumb all the way back on the hammer when he shoved it in your face. You were almost with the angels, boy." His eyes took in the smoking ruin of the car. "What happened?"

"That fat ol' deputy," Purley said angrily. "He was one son of a bitch. *Tol'* us to be on our way. Then he shot out all four tires and the radiator. With us sitting in the car."

He waited for their sympathy. His mother glared at him. Then, with all her strength behind it, she slapped him in the face.

"You are every kind of a fool!" she said with contained fury. "You've got that wild Derry blood from your great-grandfather Huddersfield who got hisself hanged. None of the rest of us have it. All the time brooding and sulking about the rights of things. Did you think you were just going to keep going down that road when the law said you can't? And that your pa was going to follow you? You think deep and you think deep, but you don't think at all! You quarrel with a sheriff's man when you got Sue Ellen and the two children in the car, and Junie with a baby started! You can get your own fool self killed, but don't you risk my grandchildren!"

Purley stood abashed, his head down, the mark of Ma Kinney's hand flowering on his cheek. Junie was embarrassed. Wesley shuffled his feet, and Pa Kinney was nodding his head to himself. Sue Ellen, holding the baby, looked stoically at the ground while the little girl clung to her skirts.

Floyd had the hood of the Ford folded back. "The hole's high up," he announced. "Bullet went right on through the radiator and bounced off the engine head. Fan's okay, nothing else touched. She'll hold a gallon of water now, once she cools off, and I bet I could ease her down the road a few miles at a time. If I could get her to a gas station and borrow a torch, I could solder her tight."

Everybody's eyes went to the bare wheels. Pa Kinney cleared his throat. "There's the tires."

They all pondered this fact. Wesley said finally: "You can get a new Goodrich Cavalier for four ninety-eight. Four-ply, though. I saw it advertised."

"What do you figure secondhand?"

"Should't be more than three dollars, by rights."

Pa Kinney looked mournful. "Fellow in Kansas charged four fifty for that tire for the Speed Wagon."

"That was a truck tire," Purley put in. "Dual wheel for a one-and-a-half-ton truck."

"Then there's the tubes," Pa Kinney said, staring gloomily at the rags of rubber hanging from the wheels.

They turned to look at Ma Kinney. She was the keeper of the funds. She looked grim.

Junie was almost bursting. "I've still got more than twenty dollars left," she said.

All she had bought for herself was the cotton dress and some underwear on the road to Dakota. The Kinneys had outfitted her from a trunk of castoffs in Cousin Emma's storeroom. She had paid a dollar to the preacher herself, and a dollar for the ring, and she had bought some candy for the little girl, but otherwise the Kinneys hadn't let her pay for a thing.

"That's your keeping money, Junie," Ma Kinney said reluctantly. She glowered anew at Purley. "See what you done?"

"Please," Junie said quickly. "We're . . . we're all the same family."

Floyd remembered having seen a gas station a couple of miles back. They nursed the Ford along on its rims, stopping every five minutes to pour a couple of pints from the drinking jug into the boiling radiator.

The gas station was a ramshackle wooden building with a single Texaco Fire-Chief pump standing dustily in front of it. A flyspecked advertising sign showed Ed Wynn in his fireman's hat and invited radio listeners to tune in Tuesday nights. The building itself served as a general store and post office.

The proprietor was rocking on the low porch drinking Coca-Cola as the two vehicles rattled into the yard. He was a stringy man with a turkey neck that stuck up out of the round yoke of a collarless white shirt. His eyes narrowed when he saw the Kinneys, but he softened up when he understood that they were going to buy gasoline for cash, and were willing to pay for four used tires. He agreed to let Floyd use his welding rig for fifty cents, plus the cost of any solder, parts, and consumed gases.

Purley and Floyd picked over the quarter acre of rusting wrecks out back, and found four tires and tubes the Ford could use. They argued hotly with the owner over the price. "This here tire's worn through two layers." "Yeah, but it's a six-ply." "This tube's got a patch on a patch." "Yeah, but it was just the one puncture, a clean one."

In the end they settled on eighteen dollars for everything. "I bought the whole car for less than three times that," Purley grumbled as Floyd counted out Junie's money.

While Floyd fixed the radiator, Junie wandered through the store, just to look. The owner followed her inside to make sure that she didn't steal anything. The sagging shelves were laden with dusty, unsold things: lanterns, stove wicks, blue cans of Edgeworth tobacco, and brown cans of bag balm for milk cows. Junie fingered the coins she still had in the pocket of her dress. She thought she would buy a penny's worth of candy for the little girl. Then she spent a nickel for a pound of sugar for Floyd's coffee. She knew he had minded going without.

The proprietor pocketed the six cents with a shade more cordiality. "Anything else?"

Junie hesitated. It didn't seem right to spend money on herself. Then she made up her mind.

"I'll have a penny postcard. If you'll lend me a pencil."

"Step over here."

He got behind the part of the counter that was the post office. There was a grated window propped up in front of it, and stacks of untidy shelves and pigeonholes behind. He shoved the card and a pen in a glass inkwell at her.

"What's the name of this town?"

"Dead River, Texas."

The pen's bent nib scratched and blotted. Junie drew the letters carefully, bigger than her usual flowing hand.

Dear Mother,
I am writing this from a place called Dead River, Texas, but I don't know how long I'll be here. I will write as soon as I get settled and let you know where I am. I am Mrs. Floyd Kinney now. I am expecting a baby. We are with Floyd's family. They are wonderful people, so please don't worry about me. I am sorry for the trouble I caused you. Please give my love to Gordon and Pamela and Jeremy and Brad, and let them know that I am all right.
                         Love,
                         June Alice

Outside, a horn hooted. "Junie!" Floyd's voice called.

She pushed the postcard across to the store owner. Tears welled up in her eyes. "Will you mail this for me?" she said.

"Sure will."

She left blindly, clutching the bag of sugar and the penny candy. The Ford was pulled up just beyond the Texaco pump, its motor idling. Purley was just closing the hood. Floyd was sitting behind the wheel. The Kinney family had come to some unspoken decision that he would drive for the time being. Purley slid into the front seat beside him. Evidently Junie was expected to ride in back with Sue Ellen and the baby and the little girl. She climbed inside. It was going to be nice to have Sue Ellen to talk to. Floyd didn't talk much. But she wished all the same that she could be sitting beside him.

They caught up with the Okie caravan just before dark.

"Looky there," Sue Ellen said, pulling Junie's arm. A score of rickety vehicles were parked smack in the middle of a flat plowed field that was overgrown with weeds and dry brush, the boxy old cars and trucks and homemade trailers dispersed in a loose circle. A few tents were already up, and people were starting small fires. Another half-dozen vehicles whose owners hadn't wanted to risk threadbare tires on the hardened furrows were lined up beside the highway, just off the concrete edge. One of them was their friend with the Model T.

"Pull over there, Floyd," Purley said.

Floyd eased the Ford over to the shoulder of the road. The Reo truck wobbled to a stop behind it.

The bony young man from the Model T rose to his feet, a mallet in his hand. He had been pounding stakes for a rude lean-to made from a tarpaulin he had stretched from the angular roof of his car. Three small dirty-faced children hovered listlessly. At a distance, a wraithlike young woman fanned a small brushwood fire under a frying pan propped up on rocks.

"Didn't figure to see you," the man said. "When you didn't come down the road after a while, I thought those deputies arrested you."

His eyes roved to the hole in the radiator grill. Purley evaded the unspoken question. "What do you folks aim to do?"

"We'll hafta backtrack a piece. Go around that county. Fella with us thinks we can get south on the state highway that runs through that little town we passed a way back." He shook his head. "Gonna cost another twenty-five, fifty cents' worth of gas for everybody."

Ma and Pa Kinney and Wesley had climbed down from the truck, and Floyd and Purley had taken this as a signal to get out of the car. Sue Ellen and Junie followed them.

"Our name's McClain. Alva, come on over here and meet these folks."

The woman drifted over, trailed by silent children. Pa Kinney introduced everyone in turn. Then he cleared his throat.

"Be all right if we stop here for the night?"

"Why sure," McClain said. "It ain't our field. Ain't anybody's, looks like."

"We don't want to bother folks."

"No bother. It's just natural for folks travelin' this way to stop together."

"Well, we thank you."

"There's a little creek past that dip at the edge of the field. Still some water in her. A mite muddy, though. And plenty of brush for fires."

They drove slowly across the field, jouncing on the tired springs, and parked at a decent interval from the others. Floyd and Purley went down to the creek to get water. Junie and Sue Ellen gathered brush. They set up their shelter—two wings of canvas draped from guy ropes strung from the truck's tall wooden box, with the flanks of the truck itself for back walls—and took down the mattresses and boxes for sitting.

As Ma Kinney stirred coffee into the pan drippings to make gravy, she suddenly pursed her lips and said: "That McClain family—looks like all they're having to eat is fried dough."

"Those children do look peaked," Pa Kinney agreed.

"We still ain't hungry."

"Potatoes about gone," Pa Kinney said, casting his eyes down. "And that side of beef is starting to turn."

"All the more reason to finish it up quick, while it's still fit to eat."
Pa Kinney got to his feet. "I'll go over and ask them."

"Now mind you ask them right, so they don't feel ashamed. Floyd,
you go look at that beef. Cut away the green parts. Bring me back a
good piece. I kin cut it up and fry it and put it in with the pork."

"Yes'm," Floyd said, and disappeared under the canvas.

"Sue Ellen, get another sack of cornmeal and get some hoecakes
started. They're good and filling. Just leave them to cool. We kin have
them with molasses after, for the children."

"We was savin' the molasses."

"Well we ain't no more. Now scat!"

"Yes'm."

"Junie child, you kin make me up another batch of pan biscuits. You
know how?"

"Oh, yes."

Ma Kinney bit her lip. "You kin grease up the pan with this leftover pork fat. Those poor souls won't know the difference."

The McClains arrived, subdued and skitterish. Alva McClain sat
down quickly on the wooden box that Purley offered and drew the
children to her, shushing them.

"Seems peculiar to sit down at a reg'lar table when you been
campin' out so long," McClain said, gamely striving to make conversation.

"Oh, Ma's real fierce about that ol' table," Purley said. "Makes us
unload it every night."

They ate swiftly, avoiding one another's eyes. McClain apologized
for the children. "They ain't seen no meat for a long time. Shot me a
big ol' stringy jackrabbit 'bout a week ago, but that was all."

"A Hoover hog," Pa Kinney chortled, and that broke the tension.

"Met a fella on the road in a broke-down car hauled by two mules,"
McClain said. "He called it a Hoover wagon."

"Know what they call an empty pocket?" Wesley said eagerly. "A
Hoover flag."

"Yeah, we sure been Hooverized," Purley said.

The children's eyes grew big when they saw the hoecakes. Mrs.
McClain whispered at them to keep them from grabbing. Junie shyly
brought out the bag of sugar and everybody gravely took a spoonful
for their coffee.

"This Roosevelt, think he'll do any better?"

"Well, he's tryin'."

There was a comfortable silence, brought about by stretched bellies.
Somewhere in the darkness a man was playing the guitar and singing.
The scattered campfires glowed redly, each defining a small human

universe in the void. On the highway beyond, cars and trucks went by, each a flash of yellow beams and a rush of sound.

The field was suddenly illumined by a glare and dazzle of headlights as one of the cars turned in instead of passing. It bounced across the field and came to a stop near the circle of tents. The lights stayed on.

Purley rose to his feet. "What's that?"

"Trouble, most likely," McClain said. His voice was resigned.

"We're outa that deputy's county," Purley said angrily.

"Sheriff here probably don't want us, either." He sighed. "We bin on the road a long time. Seems there's always someone to turn us out. Sometimes it's a deputy, sometimes it's the local boys, whiskied up. That's just one car—that's good. At least if it's a deputy, he usually lets us stay for the night. Just be gone in the morning, they always say."

"That don't look like no lawman," Pa Kinney said.

The driver of the car had stepped into his own headlights. He was a chubby man in a western hat and checkered shirt with an open cardigan sweater over it. There was no gun at his waist. He was carrying something tucked under one arm and calling out to the people nearest to him.

"He's passing out somethin'," Wesley said. "Papers."

"Law papers?"

"I don't think so."

A small crowd was growing around the chubby man. He was talking earnestly, thrusting his flyers into the hands of anyone who came close.

"Let's go over and see what's going on," Purley said.

Pa Kinney nodded and stood up. The other men got up with him and started across the field toward the splash of light.

Junie and Sue Ellen looked at each other. "Should we?" Junie said. "Let's."

They started trailing after the men. Ma Kinney said sharply, "You two stay here. You'll find out soon enough what it's about."

Junie helped clear away dishes. Alva McClain was hunched over the pans, the little bones at the back of her neck standing out as frail as a baby bird's, scrubbing away at the grease with boiled water. "Leave it be," Ma Kinney said. "We'll take them down to the creek in the morning." But she went on scrubbing.

The two men came back after a little while. Over in the glare of the headlights, the chubby man was still making his speeches to anyone who would listen.

"His name's Magg," Pa Kinney said, scratching his head. "He says he's a labor contractor."

"From Arizona," Wesley said.

"By God, he's come a long way to trick poor people, ain't he?" Purley said.

"Purley, you mind your language," Ma Kinney said with a sidelong look at Alva McClain.

"Oh, those fellows drive out all the way to Oklahoma," McClain said. "Leave their signs at gas stations. Stop at every roadside camp they pass. Over by Texola, one came with a big cattle truck, looking for pickers on a date ranch, charged ten dollars a head for transportation, taken out of their first wages." He glanced apologetically at his wife and children. "Course he didn't want families."

Pa Kinney spread out a yellow handbill on the ground next to the dying fire. "Wesley, you read this out for us."

Junie edged closer to read over Wesley's shoulder. On the road it was her job to read signs and directions, but this was clearly a ceremonial occasion. She saw a headline in big black type:

WE NEED COTTON PICKERS
5,000 FAMILIES WANTED IN THE BIG
COTTON DISTRICTS

"They're right anxious for pickers," Wesley said. "Says there's a quarter-million acres of cotton waiting in Arizona."

"Cotton," McClain said. "Now that's a crop I know."

Wesley pushed his cracked glasses back on his short nose and said, "Says, big crop, heavy picking. Picking last till February. Cabins or tents free. Good camps. Warm dry winters. Just go to any of the cotton districts and apply at any gin."

"What are they paying?" McClain said.

"A dollar seventy-five a hundred for the long staple, eighty-five cents a hundred for short staple. Says here a good picker can pick up to four hundred pounds a day."

McClain frowned. "It would have to be a good heavy crop to get that."

Purley scowled at the handbill. "It's against Texas law to recruit for work outside the state, did you know that?"

Pa Kinney's finger stabbed out at a little flag emblem at the bottom. "It must be all right. They got the American flag down here."

"Says this bill was put out by an outfit called the Agricultural Labor Service, cooperating with the United States Farm Placement Service," Wesley said.

"That there's a grower's association," Purley said. "They can say they're cooperating with anyone they damn please."

"Purley, I told you to mind your tongue," Ma Kinney said. "I ain't goin' to tell you again."

"If the government's in it, it must be all right," McClain said. "They couldn't say so otherwise." He shook his head. "Seems too good to be true."

"Junie, there are seven of us," Ma Kinney said suddenly. "At four hundred pounds a day, what does that figure out to?"

Junie did the sums quickly in her head. She was proud to have a chance to show off her arithmetic.

"Forty-nine dollars a day for long staple, twenty-three eighty for short."

Wesley slapped the ground with his hand. "Whoo-eey!"

Pa Kinney rubbed his chin thoughtfully. "Now hold on a minute. A woman can't pick as fast as a man. An' maybe four hundred pounds is a mite high. An' it won't all be long staple, you can count on that. Still, we could figure maybe twenty, thirty dollars a day."

"Twenty dollars a day for a family your size ain't bad wages," McClain said. "For us, maybe five, six dollars if what they say is true. The kids are too young to haul a sack, but they kin pick into my sack or Alva's."

"We was headed south."

"So was we."

"What do you folks figure on doing now?"

"I guess we'll have a meeting tonight and talk it over. You folks are sure welcome to come."

Purley stayed away from the meeting. He moped around the camp, saying little, and turned in early.

In the morning, when the Oklahoma people packed up their tents and utensils and assembled once more on the highway, the Kinneys were with them, near the tail of the caravan.

Slowly, like a great tin snake with bedsteads and cooking pots sticking up out of its backbone, the long column of vehicles wound its way along the connecting roads until its head found U.S. Highway 66. It changed course then and headed west, questing toward the New Mexico desert and Arizona.

"There's the postman," Ottilie said, looking out the kitchen window.

"Do you want me to go?" Winthrop said.

"No, no," Elroy said hastily. He put down his coffee cup and got up from the breakfast table. Getting the mail had always been his prerogative. He had never been able to stand the thought of anybody else getting his hands on it first. On the days when the postman failed to arrive before he left for work, Ottilie left the mail in the box until he got home.

"I hope there's a letter for that sister of yours from Bradford junior in Washington," Ottilie sniffed. "He's always late with his check."

Elroy's eyes narrowed when he saw the postcard from Texas, with its scrawled and blotted handwriting. He read it furtively, his back to the house, then crumpled it up and put it in his pocket.

"Was there anything for her?" Ottilie demanded when he got back.

"No . . . no . . . nothing."

"Elroy, are you feeling all right? Your face looks pale."

"I'm fine," he snapped.

"Is that my copy of *Liberty* there?" Winthrop said.

Later, in the privacy of the toilet at work, he smoothed the card out and read it again. He pursed his lips.

"Having a baby," he muttered to himself. "Little harlot."

He tore the postcard up in tiny pieces and flushed it away.

19

The door was heavy oak, reinforced with steel. Imitation dungeon, Brad thought. He pushed the button. A steel slot opened at eye level, but before Brad could speak, the monkey-faced little blonde, whose name was Babs something-or-other, thrust herself in front of him and shouted, "Boo!"

There was an unfriendly silence, then a voice said, "We're full up," and the slot slid shut.

"What the hell," said Brophy, the Hearst man.

Fanshaw, the UP reporter, shrugged and said, "It'll be the same all over the city. Everybody wants to celebrate the last day."

"Oh, boy!" the skinny girl from the Treasury Department pouted. "I thought you said you could get in anywhere."

"Anywhere but Ruby Bill's on a night like tonight," Fanshaw said. "It'll be strictly for the black-tie and dinner-gown crowd. C'mon, I got a bottle of scotch back in my flat." He was weaving drunk already, even though it was barely past five o'clock.

"Nothing doing, buster," the skinny girl said.

"Wait a minute," Brad said. He gently propelled the giggling blonde into Brophy's arms and said, "Hang on to her this time." He rang the bell again.

The Judas hole opened. Brad held a card up in front of it.

"Go away. . . . Oh, it's you, Mr. Sinclair. I didn't recognize you before. How many in your party?"

"Six," Brad said. He glanced at Fanshaw. "Make that five and a half."

Bolts scraped, chains rattled, and the door swung open. A crowd roar washed over them.

"They're off to a good start," Brad said.

The bouncer, a large florid man in evening clothes, whose name was Michael, bolted the door behind them. "I never seen anything like it, Mr. Sinclair," he said. "It's like they're trying to drink it all up before it's too late. Only it ain't too late. They can have all they want tomorrow."

"It's the end of an era," Brad said.

"Yeah, I guess so. I can give you a booth all the way back. Follow me."

As they crossed the floor to their booth, Brad could see that the girls were looking surreptitiously around, trying not to appear impressed. Ruby Bill's was not your ordinary Washington speakeasy, with improvised pine bar and secondhand fixtures. It had a massive, magnificent prewar mahogany bar and backboard, mirrors, oil paintings of fat nymphs, chandeliers, leather booths, and an authentic brass footrail. The booze could be trusted, and the place actually had a reputation for food.

The girls crammed themselves into the booth, twittering and adjusting their hats, and the men squeezed in after them. It was a tight fit; the booth was made for four.

"Sorry," Michael said. "We're going crazy here today. We got a truck waiting at the warehouse to make the run as soon as the announcement comes through. I hope we don't run out before then. Even so, we're better off than most places. We got a big shipment of bonded stuff in from Baltimore last night."

"This is fine," Brad said. He handed Michael a ten-dollar bill.

"Thanks," Michael said. He glanced at the corner of the bill before stuffing it casually into his pocket. He leaned forward confidentially. "Maybe I shouldn't say this to a customer, but we got a tip that the cops might pull a raid tonight."

"On the last day of Prohibition? That's not very sporting of them."

Michael gave a prizefighter's one-shoulder shrug. "Like you say, it's the end of an era. The cops want to go out big, too. They raid a place like this, with all the Washington big shots here, they'll make the headlines."

"Thanks. I'll keep my ears peeled for sirens."

Michael lowered his voice. "You know where the trap is?"

Brad nodded.

Michael straightened up. "I'll send the waiter over," he said, and lumbered off.

Babs was tugging at Brad's sleeve. "Hey, what was that card, Brad, huh? Howdja get us in here?"

Brophy winked at Brad across the table. "Oh, Brad can get in any-where," he said. "They know him from here to Timbuctoo. Show her your collection of courtesy cards, Brad."

"Make sure that's all you show me," Babs giggled.

Brad dug into his inside pocket and took out the thick bundle of speakeasy cards. He removed the rubber band and fanned them out on the table.

Fritzie, the spectacular brunette who worked in the Senate Office Building just down the corridor from Pamela, started shuffling through the cards.

"The Dizzy Club in New York," she said. "I was there once, on a weekend. I never got to Jack and Charlie's Twenty-One, though, and now it's too late."

"There'll always be a Twenty-One," Brad said. "Tomorrow they'll be open for business as usual, only this time with a legal liquor license. So will places like Ruby Bill's."

"It won't be the same though," Brophy said, looking around for the waiter.

Fanshaw raised a drooping eyelid, showing an eyeball like a bloody egg. "What are you going to do with that collection of cards after to-night, Sinclair? Donate it to the Smithsonian?"

"Fanshaw, how do you manage to talk so distinctly when you're half in the bag?"

"Long training, that's the secret."

The waiter appeared, a stocky bullet-headed man with grizzled hair. "What's your pleasure, gentlemen?" he said.

"What's this I hear about bonded stuff coming in from Baltimore last night?" Brophy said.

"I don't know where you heard that," the waiter said evasively.

"They're saving it," Brad said. "They want to get rid of the bootleg stock tonight."

"Business as usual, huh?" Brophy said. "Corn, gin, or Maryland rye."

"Oh, the gin's fine for me," Babs said. "Bring me a little White Rock on the side, wouldja?"

"I'll have rye and ginger ale," Fritzie said.

Fanshaw cocked an eye at Babs. "Smart girl. At least you can see what you're getting."

"What she's getting," Brophy said, "is fifty percent recooked alcohol, forty-nine percent water, and a trace of juniper essence, glycerine, and orange-water compound."

"Oh, the gin's reliable here," Fanshaw said. "I drink it myself."

"Not me," Brophy said. "I'm spoiled. This afternoon I tanked up on twelve-year-old scotch at the Siamese legation. They bring it in by ship from London."

"Did you hear that, waiter?" Brad said. "We can't allow Mr. Brophy to blister his palate on the common brew. What can you do for him?"

He felt around in his wallet for a five, locating it by the turned-down corner, and slipped it unobtrusively to the waiter under the table. The waiter pocketed it just as unobtrusively after looking quickly around.

"Seeing as it's you, Mr. Sinclair," he said, "there's a bottle of pre-war John Walker under the bar that I can serve your friend out of."

"Oh, goody," said the skinny girl from Treasury. "I'll have that too, with ginger ale."

"Give her what she wants," Brad said, and gave the waiter the high sign, which meant that she would get the Maryland rye.

The waiter nodded and hurried off.

"Speaking of the Smithsonian," Fanshaw hiccoughed, "have you heard the sad news about the reptile exhibit? It's gone all to decay. It seems someone drained off the alcohol."

"Go back to sleep, Fanshaw," Brad said. "I'll let you know when your drink arrives."

"We may be drinking that very exhibit tonight," Fanshaw said.

Babs looked alarmed. "Hey, he's kidding, isn't he?"

Brad patted her hand. "Don't worry about it."

Brophy said, "They caught some printers at the Bureau of Printing and Engraving selling the alcohol they use for cleaning the type. They recooked it to get the ink out."

"That's more like it," Brad said. "Essence of hundred-dollar bill in your martini."

The drinks arrived. Babs stuck a pink tongue into her gin to test it before adding the White Rock.

"No snakes, huh?" Brophy said.

"That's what *she* thinks," Fanshaw said. He took a sip and closed his eyes.

"So how is Cissy Patterson treating you?" Brad said to Brophy.

"Hey, I'm sorry about that editorial, Brad," Brophy said. "Cissy may run the *Herald*, but her pal William Randolph Hearst still owns it. The word went out on your boss last month. We gotta rough him up from now on."

"Who was it that thought up the line about NRA standing for No Recovery Allowed?"

Brophy spread his hands. "Hey, listen, Brad, I'm just an employee down there. When Cissy sailed through the office in her black sable last week, one of her poodles bit me." He raised his trouser cuff on a hairy leg. "Look, I'll show you."

"Gee!" Babs said, looking at the scar.

"I'm not the only one," Brophy said. "Dog meat, that's all we are."

"I thought you were intrepid journalists."

"Intrepid journalists, my ass. Do you know what the big journalistic issue is over there? Whether we can take over *Andy Gump, Dick Tracy, Gasoline Alley,* and *Winnie Winkle* from the *Washington Post.* Cissy claims that since Eugene Meyer bought the *Post* this summer, the contract with the syndicate has been up for grabs."

Fanshaw stirred in his chair. "All she has to do is wait for the *Post* to fold, and she'll get the comic strips by default. Meyer can't keep that rag going. It was bankrupt when he bought it, and it doesn't have enough circulation to stay alive."

"He got off to a good start," Brad said lightly. "Putting the Blue Eagle in the masthead right at the beginning."

"So why aren't you out drinking with a *Post* editorial writer tonight?" Brophy said.

"They already support the NRA," Brad said.

"Not for long, buddy, not for long. Wait and see."

Fanshaw's head jerked up. "Even Walter Lippmann's started calling General Johnson dictatorial," he said distinctly before he slumped once more.

"How about it, Brad?" Brophy said. "Is there anything to the rumor that Old Ironpants is going to be forced to resign?"

"General Johnson still enjoys the complete confidence of the President," Brad said blandly. "In fact, he's about to appoint ninety more administrators. I'll give you an exclusive on it."

Brophy shook his head. "Too much government bureaucracy—that's what our line on it is going to be. I'll give you fair warning."

"The general's aim is to get the whole country under the Blue Eagle. He knew the applause couldn't last."

"I'll tell you what the last straw was. It was when he organized the strip joints."

Fanshaw came awake again. "Strip joints?"

"Yeah, there's even an NRA code for burlesque houses," Brophy said. "It limits them to four stripteases a day."

Brad laughed. "The general believes in overseeing every detail."

Fanshaw hoisted himself upright. "I'm afraid I stand with the Hearst people, Sinclair. You New Dealers have gone too far this time. When you start interfering with burlesque shows, it's a threat to the whole free enterprise system."

"Hey, are you guys going to talk politics all night?" the girl from Treasury said. "I thought we were here for a good time."

"You're right," Fanshaw said, waving his empty glass to signal for another round.

Brophy looked around. "Quite a crowd tonight."

"The cream of Washington society," Brad said, "getting curdled."

Babs plucked at the front of her dress. "Gee, do you think I'm dressed all right for here? All them evening gowns. I mean I came right from work."

"You look fine," Brad said. "All them gowns is just showing off. There's nobody out there above the rank of an undersecretary's mistress."

Babs giggled. "You're funny, Brad."

The waiter arrived with the refills, looking red-faced and harried.

"Is this still illegal?" Brad said.

"Yeah. The boss has the radio on. As soon as the word comes through, there's gonna be a round of free drinks."

"What's holding it up?"

"Utah. They're still voting."

Fanshaw shook his head. "Leave it to the Mormons."

"They got a special wire to the White House. Roosevelt'll sign Repeal as soon as the legislature notifies him. That'll make it thirty-six states. Pennsylvania and Ohio already ratified. The radio says the crowds are waiting in Times Square in New York, everywhere. They're lined up outside all the speaks in Chicago. We're gonna bar the doors soon. We can't fit any more in here."

He went away, shaking his head.

"I still feel funny in this old navy wool," Babs said. "Look at that mink that just came in. It cost a thousand dollars if it cost a penny."

Brad twisted his neck and saw a stunning blonde in a lavish calf-length mink coat thrown carelessly open over a clinging silk gown. She wore a rope of authentic-looking pearls that hung even lower than the scoop neckline of the gown. Her other accessory was a swarthy, heavy-lidded man in evening clothes, with a clipped mustache and oily hair parted in the middle.

"That's Sally Collier," Brophy said. "Midnight Sally, our picture-page editors call her. Washington's answer to Zelda. She's a relative of your sister's boss, Senator Hale."

"*The* Sally Collier?" Babs squealed. "The one who went swimming in the Reflecting Pool in black pajamas?"

"The very one. Debutante of the year, two—no, three—years ago. Queen of the Arts Club Ball. Squirter of soda water in the face of Alfred Gwynne Vanderbilt. Comes from an old Virginia family, with money so old it's got whiskers. They try not to notice her goings-on. And by the way, the mink's worth at least three thousand."

"Who's the lounge lizard with her?" Brad said.

"Attaché at one of the Balkan legations, I forget his name. Strictly from Transylvania, if you ask me. Claims to have noble blood, the usual thing. The baron's been trying to peddle him for years."

The baron was a fixture of Washington society. He ran a phony travel agency, but his real business was matrimonial agent, matching fortune hunters to social climbers. He had a seemingly inexhaustible supply of dubious middle-European noblemen whom he offered whole-sale to unwary debutantes whose mothers were willing to pay to have a title in the family.

"She doesn't look like the kind of girl who'd be in the market for the baron's merchandise," Brad said.

"Maybe this guy has special talents," Brophy leered.

The pair had been seated at a small table only a few yards away. The swarthy man snapped his fingers for a waiter. Brad turned away and lit a cigarette just in time to keep Sally Collier from catching him staring.

"Do you think those pearls are real?" Babs said.

"Straight from the oyster," Brophy said. "Drink up, sugar."

When next Brad sneaked a look at Sally Collier's table, the waiter was at the swarthy man's elbow, uncorking a bottle of champagne. Brad was willing to bet that it was sweet champagne. Sweet champagne was exactly the sort of drink that the Moldavian attaché, or whatever the hell he was, would order for a girl like Sally. He was sure he could detect a faint trace of amusement on her penciled lips. This time she caught him looking at her. He raised his martini in ironic salute.

"Hey, something's happening over at the bar," Fanshaw said.

The thickset man in the boiled shirt and stickpins, who was the out-front proprietor of Ruby Bill's, was in a huddle with Michael the bouncer and the three bartenders. A radio was turned up, somewhere behind the bar, and Brad could hear crowd noises and tooting horns. It sounded like New Year's Eve.

The proprietor climbed up on the bar. He rattled a cocktail shaker for attention.

"Ladies and gentlemen! Prohibition ended today, December fifth, nineteen thirty-three, at five thirty-two o'clock!"

There were wild cheers.

The proprietor held up his hands. The noise abated a little.

"Drinks are on the house!"

There was a concerted rush toward the bar. Customers pressed against it, three and four deep, holding out their glasses. The bartenders started pouring liquor indiscriminately into the outstretched tumblers and goblets, spilling booze on cuffs and fingers. One bartender stood on top of the bar, leaning out into the crowd, pouring drinks two-handed. Sweating waiters shoved themselves among the tables, not taking orders but pouring into half-full glasses from bottles on their trays.

"Hooray," Fanshaw said. He drained his glass, holding on to the waiter's sleeve, then held it out for a refill.

Over across the room, a woman had climbed on top of a table and was taking off her dress while a circle of men looked on politely. At another table a young man lay with his head tilted back and his mouth open while his friends tried to dribble gin into him from a height.

"Oh, for a lampshade to wear," Fanshaw said with a belch. "To think that the Volstead Act is finally dead."

"Not till the capital police get the word," Brad said.

Babs looked at the speakeasy cards strewn across the table and said, "You sure must of spent a long time collecting all of them."

Fanshaw said, "Your life's work, gone for naught. You'll never need them again."

"That's right." Brad swept them into a large metal ashtray and began to assemble them into a rickety house of cards.

"What are you doing?"

"I'm making a pyre."

"You can't do that," Fanshaw said. "They're of incalculable historic value. Just think, if some thoughtless Egyptian hadn't done that three thousand years ago, we'd know where the pharaohs did their drinking."

"They're obsolete, Fanshaw. Part of the trash of history."

"Don't be hasty, Sinclair. What if Prohibition comes back?"

A few people at neighboring tables had begun to be aware that something was happening. Brad had the cards stacked a foot high now. A couple of people wandered over to watch.

"What's he doing?"

"It's a burnt offering," Brophy said.

"Good-bye, Prohibition," Brad murmured, and touched his lighter to the stack. The little circle of onlookers began to applaud. Brad glanced up and was pleased to see Sally Collier watching from her table. The Balkan attaché looked disgruntled. She had left her glass of champagne untouched. Instead, she was sipping from what looked like a tumbler of raw gin.

The house of cards collapsed in ashes. Brad's little audience drifted away. Across the room, customers were still surging against the bar, holding out their glasses. The lady doing the striptease on the tabletop was down to her slip, and showed signs of losing her nerve.

Through the clamor of voices that filled the speakeasy, Brad thought he heard rising sirens. Ruby Bill's had never been quite well padded enough to shut out all the street noises.

"I'm getting hungry," the girl from Treasury complained.

"In good time, in good time," Fanshaw said magisterially. He raised his glass, trying to get the waiter's attention.

Brad cocked his head. The sirens had stopped abruptly. "I think we better get out of here," he said.

"Nothing doing," the girl from Treasury said.

"Fanshaw, can you stand up?"

"You heard the young lady," Fanshaw said.

Brad came around the table and tried to haul a resisting Fanshaw to his feet. He got him part way up, then Fanshaw plopped stubbornly down, a dead weight. Brophy, looking alarmed, started to rise.

"Hey, what's going on?" Babs said.

A heavy thumping made the oak door shiver. The revelers in the big main room were making too much noise to notice at first. The bouncer started to pile chairs against the door. One of the waiters rushed over to help him.

Then there was the unmistakable sound of fire axes and splintering wood. The silver edge of an axe blade broke through, flashing briefly. A woman screamed, and there was an eddy of motion in the crowd as people tried to get away from the vicinity of the door.

"Oh, my God!" a man near Brad cried. "If my wife reads my name in the papers, she'll cut me off without a cent!" He was with a large creamy woman in a silver evening gown.

Brad managed to shove his way through floundering people to Sally Collier's table. She and the attaché were among the few customers who were still seated. The attaché had her by the wrist. "Do not worry, my dear Sally," he was saying. "I have diplomatic immunity."

"It's still a damned unpleasant ride to the police station for the lady," Brad said.

The attaché raised pouched reptilian eyes to Brad. Up close he smelled of pomade and mothballs. "Who are you? Go away!"

Sally looked up at Brad with amused recognition. "Boris is telling me that the raid's illegal because Prohibition's over," she said.

"Everybody's name is going to be published in the morning papers," Brad said, "illegal or not."

Behind the sweating liquor agents, a squad of uniformed policemen were trying to untangle themselves from the piled chairs and regroup in some sort of order. A red-cheeked man blew a police whistle and tried to make himself heard above the panic.

"Nobody leaves, nobody leaves! Line up in an orderly fashion against the wall!"

There was more screaming and aimless milling around.

"Oh, dear," Sally said. "Just when Daddy's getting sticky about my allowance."

"There might be a way out of here," Brad said. "But we'll have to move fast."

"This is none of your business!" Boris said furiously. He released Sally's wrist and rose threateningly.

Brad thrust the chair against the back of Boris's knees and sat him down again. "Come on," he said to Sally.

She gathered the mink around her like an Indian blanket and sprang to her feet. Boris, spluttering, tried to rise. With a thoughtful look, she tipped the table over on top of him.

"Poor Boris," she said. "He's so flabby under those rental duds!"

Brad cleared a path for them through the crowd.

"We're heading farther *into* the place," Sally said.

"Trust me," Brad told her.

The mink had slipped off her shoulders and was wriggling its way backward through the crowd as though it had a life of its own. Brad made a grab for it and missed.

"Screw it," Sally said. "I was tired of it anyway."

Brad dragged her past the bar. He noted with approval that every last bottle was gone from behind it except for the White Rock and other nonalcoholic stuff. It had been fast work. Some broken glass was lying around. The door to the storeroom was still ajar. Brad pushed through, hard, almost knocking over the aproned bartender who was trying to slide the bolt.

"Hey, what the hell!" the bartender said.

"Don't let us stop you," Brad said.

"Who the hell are you?"

"We're Moe and Izzy, who do you think?"

"Wise guy!"

"You're wasting time."

The bartender hesitated. "Just don't get in the way." He bolted the door and picked up a last case of liquor. Brad and Sally followed him as he staggered with his burden over to an enormous wooden ice chest standing against the wall.

"What in the world . . ."

The floor of the ice chest had been removed. It stood over a trapdoor, leading down into darkness. The bartender descended. Sally went next, then Brad closed the door of the chest behind him and followed her down the wooden steps.

A group of toiling men were putting the contents of ten-gallon carboys down an open cesspool.

"How did you know about this?" Sally said.

"Every self-respecting speakeasy has a cesspool."

He led her through a labyrinth of stone passages until they came to a short flight of granite steps leading to a wooden hatch. He raised the hatch cautiously for a look, then motioned Sally to come out. They were around the corner from the entrance. Brad could see the squad cars and paddy wagons drawn up at the curb. A crowd had already gathered. They were booing and jeering as the cops and Prohibition agents led out men and women in evening clothes and loaded them into the wagons.

"In the shadow of the White House," Brad said. "I can just see the headlines tomorrow. Come on, I've got my car parked on the other side of Lafayette Square."

Sally looked at the growing crowd, then down at her evening gown. One of the shoulder straps had broken, and she was hoisting on it to keep that breast from tumbling loose. "I'm going to attract attention," she said.

Brad sighed and took off his jacket. He draped it around her shoulders. Sally let go of the strap, hitched up her long skirts, and hurried down the side street, arm in arm with Brad.

When she saw the Chrysler Airflow, she squealed in delight. "Oh, it's one of those funny-looking new cars. It reminds me of the electric train to Berlin."

"You've just come back from Berlin?" Brad said, helping her into the front seat.

"This summer." She made a pout. "It's no fun anymore since that Hitler person came to power. They've closed down the Tingel-Tangel Cabaret and the Negro reviews and all those peculiar nightclubs with the telephones on the tables and the boys with rubber breasts."

"I thought nice girls didn't go to places like that," Brad said.

"Who says I'm a nice girl?" she said, snuggling against him.

He turned the self-starter key. "I'll take you home."

* * *

Home for Sally Collier turned out, surprisingly, not to be a Dupont Circle mansion or one of the smart, newly renovated Georgetown houses, but a rather ordinary flat, not much bigger than his own, in a rundown apartment building on Massachusetts Avenue. She searched through the rooms to make sure the maid had gone, swore when she found that a pot of coffee had not been left, then sat him down on an overstuffed divan and told him to amuse himself with some phonograph records while she changed. Brad found a stack of rather dated records, much scratched and abused, and put one on at random; it turned out to be a Helen Morgan torch song, "What Wouldn't I Do for That Man."

When Sally came out, she had changed from the torn gown to some kind of pale silk wrapper with a collar like a feather boa. As far as he could tell, she wore nothing under it. She tossed his jacket toward him. It missed and landed on the floor. He left it lying there and got up. Sally was a tall girl; even without her heels, she came almost to his cheek.

She let him kiss her and put his hand over her breast. He was sure he felt her breathing quicken, but when he started to guide her over to the divan, she drew away.

"Don't," she said.

Baffled, he let his arms drop. "All right," he shrugged.

"Let's just talk for a while. Put another record on, will you?"

He shuffled through the stack till he found some jazz: Duke Ellington and his Cotton Club orchestra doing "The Mooche." Brad was indifferent to most jazz, but everybody said there was something to it. This one was growling saxes, muted trumpet, and a pounding beat. "Jungle music," the label called it. From the look of the record, Sally had played it often.

"There isn't any booze in the place, and the damn girl didn't make any coffee," she said.

Brad had a flask in his car, but he had a feeling that if he went down to get it, he wouldn't get back into the apartment.

"Well, I don't like stale coffee anyhow," he said. "I don't mind waiting for a fresh pot."

She gave him a vexed look and went into the kitchen. He followed her, and found her staring, mystified, at the components of an electric percolator spread out in the drain.

"Don't tell me," he said.

"I don't have to tell you. You already know. I can't even make coffee."

"Here, I'll show you how."

He found a half-full can of coffee on the shelf. Judging from the contents of the cabinets and an almost bare electric refrigerator, Sally Collier lived exclusively on a diet of stuffed olives, salted peanuts, and pitted dates.

"Your maid doesn't take very good care of you," he said.

"She's all right," Sally said with a toss of her head. "She gets here in the morning in time to make me black coffee and toast. That's all I can face when I get up. I always have dinner out."

"With guys like that bush-league Bela Lugosi?"

She giggled, then cut it off. "You're starting to make a good impression, Brad. Don't spoil it."

"Sorry."

They sat side by side on the divan, drinking black coffee and smoking cigarettes.

"What are you, anyway, Brad?"

"At the moment, a ravening beast."

"No, no," she said impatiently. "Do you *do* anything?"

"I'm a civil servant."

"Civil servant, hell! Civil servants are tense little men with square-toed shoes and patent leather briefcases, and they only make love on the first and fifteenth of the month."

He laughed. "I'm a civil servant all the same. I work for one of Mr. Roosevelt's alphabet agencies, and I make eighty dollars a week."

"Is that a lot?"

Brad glanced at her, then saw that she was serious.

"Quite a lot," he answered gravely. "About half what a senator makes. Since the federal pay cut, anyway."

"They must like you at your alphabet agency."

"I've made myself indispensable."

She swung her legs up and leaned back in the cushions. "Uncle Marcus is a senator. Does that make you half as rich as he is?"

He laughed again. "I'm sure that Senator Marcus Aurelius Hale doesn't have to struggle along on his Senate salary."

"I suppose not." She yawned.

"He has his law firm. And he owns things. Like that cotton plantation."

She looked at him suspiciously. "How do you know so much about Uncle Marcus?"

"My sister works for him."

"Oh." She still looked suspicious.

"Your turn."

"What do you mean?"

"What do *you* do? Besides not make coffee."

"Oh, lots of things," she said vaguely.

"So I've heard. Midnight Sally, the society reporters' delight. Looks like an angel, swears like the devil. Bathes in the reflection of the Washington Monument. Squirts seltzer in the face of young Vanderbilt."

"The reporters like to blow everything up. Besides, Alfred was being very dull that night."

"Why do you go out with snakes like Boris?"

"Oh, I was bored today. And he's been pestering me."

"He and his friends?"

Brad had the impression that if she had had her foot on the floor, she would have stamped it. "Honestly, Brad, you're exasperating!"

"How do you know he's flabby under his duds?" he persisted.

At first she looked as if she were going to be angry, then she giggled. "I don't. Not firsthand. I think he was hoping to show me tonight."

"He came well recommended by the baron, I assume."

Sally giggled again. "I'll say!"

"I've heard about the baron's letters to eligible young ladies. What are they like? 'Get a titled European nobleman before the supply runs out. . . . Heir apparent to the Moldavian throne. . . .' If the kingdom of Moldavia ever comes back, that is."

Sally's giggles were out of control.

"What's so funny?"

"I got a picture of Boris in the mail with his . . . you know, with his trousers unbuttoned. To show what I'd be getting if I married him."

Brad roared. "A titled nobleman, and built like a horse, to boot. What American heiress could resist all that?"

Sally grew sober. "I'm not exactly an heiress, you know. Daddy isn't as rich as people think. And I don't have any money of my own."

Brad couldn't help thinking of the mink coat she had so blithely abandoned at Ruby Bill's. It represented his entire salary for the better part of a year.

"Well, these are tough times for everyone," he said. "Until then you'll just have to struggle along with your apartment and maid and wardrobe and trips to Europe. And the racing stable. Isn't there always something about a racing stable in the *Post*'s 'Top Hats and Tiaras' column?"

Instantly he felt like kicking himself. He was frightened to discover the depths of his own resentment. The words had just come tumbling out. It wasn't like him at all.

She turned on him with quick pique. "Daddy pays the rent on this apartment. And the maid's salary. I don't even know how much it is.

All I wanted was a place of my own. I was going to get some little cheap place and pay for it myself out of my allowance, but Daddy was worried about neighborhoods and we compromised. A very old, dear aunt of Mummy's who everybody in Washington seemed to be terrified of, though I can't for the life of me see why, since her husband the justice died over forty years ago, lives near here, and she's supposed to look in on me every once in a while, but Aunt Cornelia and I have an understanding and she leaves me pretty much alone."

She paused for breath and glared at him.

"Look, I'm sorry—"

"I'm not finished! My mother charges my wardrobe for me, and don't think I'm not going to hear about that damned mink coat from now till doomsday, even though it's three years old and all ratty and out of style! And I go to Europe with my dear cousins who I can't stand! And the racing stable belongs to my brother Charles, and he got it when he turned twenty-one to keep him out of mischief! Only nobody gives a damn about the girls between their coming-out party and the time when they're married off to some rich fart!"

"All right, all right, take it easy. I said I was sorry."

She glared at him some more, then her breathing calmed down. She took a sip of coffee and made a face at its temperature.

"Brad, is money important to you?"

"Is that what's bothering you? For Christ's sake, I'm not after your money."

"Is money important to you?"

Brad thought of the wreck of his father's life, of the wreck of the Sinclair family, of the hundred thousand dollars he had rashly promised to repay to Chadwick after his father's funeral.

"It is now," he said.

"Well that's refreshing, at least. Most of the ones who don't have it tippy-toe around the subject, and the ones who do have it are always droning on about how little they have, as if they're afraid I'm after *their* damn money."

"I'm not a Boris, and I'm sure as hell not one of your rich farts. I'm just a guy with a job who happened to get you out of a speakeasy raid. So long, Sally. It's been interesting."

He was about to get up and retrieve his jacket, when something he felt in the air between them arrested him. She wasn't angry with him anymore, and he realized that he was no longer angry with her, either. With a start they looked into each other's eyes, and he could see her pupils suddenly widen.

Neither of them spoke. He reached for her and planted his mouth on hers. She returned his kiss with sudden greed. After a moment, still joined at the lips, they stretched out together on the divan and adjusted themselves for comfort. With Sally clinging to him, Brad slipped his hand inside the wrapper and found a breast. The nipple was hard as a bullet. She gave a little moan, and he inserted his knee between her thighs. She began moving against him, her fingers digging into his back. Oh, no, he thought, I'm not going to waste that, and he disengaged his knee. When he started to pull the wrapper up over her hips, she suddenly fought free of him. Quick as a cat, she sat up and pulled the wrapper into place around her. Her face was very pink, and she was puffing like a marathon runner.

"Hooo!" she said. "That was close!"

"Was it?"

He felt around on the coffee table for his pack of Luckies and put one in his mouth. He lit it and took a deep drag.

"You're mad."

"No, I'm not."

"You're mad," she said. "I can tell. You're one of those people who turn all super calm when they get mad. Give me a cigarette."

He lit one for her with a steady hand, and after a while the color faded from her face.

"Thanks for not calling me that," she said.

"What?"

"What some boys call you when you don't go all the way. That's why I like to go out with older men. Most of the time they're relieved when they find out they don't have to."

"Well, I'm not relieved. The knee is not an organ of generation."

"You don't have to get nasty."

"Sally," he said wearily. "You're a big girl now. You're not in the back seat of some car after the prom."

"I just like to neck," she said defensively.

"Is that what you call it? Necking?"

"Yes, necking!" she flared. "And I'm pretty damn choosy about who I neck with, if you want to know. You probably won't believe me, you son of a bitch, but I'm practically a virgin!"

"Well, I guess I believe half of that."

"Which half? The practically?"

"No, the virgin."

"Oh, you *are* a son of a bitch. Go get us some more coffee."

He got up and poured them another cup. They sat far apart on the divan, drinking coffee and smoking.

"Look, I don't want to fight with you," he said.

"Yes you do. How come you're hanging around? Why don't you go back and look for that girl you were with? The blond one who looks like a monkey. She probably acts like one, too."

"Are you asking me to leave?"

"I didn't say that."

"She's probably going to spend half the night in jail, getting booked. And when she gets out, I doubt if she'll want to talk to me again."

"*Does* she act like a monkey?"

"I wouldn't know. I didn't have a chance to find out. How come you're so interested?"

"Poor, poor Brad. Tries to act like Sir Galahad, and gets screwed out of being screwed. And it's all li'l Sally's fault."

"Now who's trying to pick a fight?"

"Oh, shut up. Put a record on the Vic."

He got up again. "What do you want to hear?"

"Oh, anything."

"Don't you have anything new?"

"Look in the magazine rack. There's a new band started by somebody named Benny Goodman. They play something called swing. It's a new kind of hot jazz."

The words meant nothing to Brad, but he found the record and put it on. To his ear, it sounded much the same as most other jazz: busy instruments, jumpy beat, with a clarinet tootling in and around all the other music.

"What do you think of it?" Sally demanded, when he returned to the divan.

"Well, it's not exactly Paul Whiteman," he said cautiously.

She laughed. "Poor Brad, you don't know *anything!*" And for the next ten minutes, while the Vic warbled and chirped, she explained why Paul Whiteman wasn't Benny Goodman, and why neither of them was Louis Armstrong and his Hot Five or Bix Beiderbecke and the Wolverines, and what the difference was between Chicago style and the New Orleans style, and other incomprehensible matters. "That Bix surely could blow a horn," she chattered happily, "even though he *was* a white boy!" As she grew more excited, her southern inflection grew thicker. Brad began to feel as if he were a visitor from another planet. He listened and nodded until finally she ran down on the subject of jazz. He brewed another pot of coffee and brought out the jar of peanuts.

Finally he looked at his watch. "It's almost ten o'clock, and we haven't had dinner," he said.

"You don't have to take me to dinner."

They melted together again. Brad found her lips with a sense of dismay. One more time, he thought savagely, then I'm walking out of here.

But her body grew more responsive under his hands, and when he tried to pull away, this time it was she who clung and drew him back to her.

"Do it, Brad," she hissed, "go ahead, do it."

He hesitated. Her body, long and warm, was pressed against his.

"You don't have to be such a damned gentleman," she whispered hoarsely. "I *did* say 'practically.'"

Brad stepped out into the December sunshine, his hair damp from Sally's shower. "You don't have to go," Sally had said, rubbing her eyes and looking at the alarm clock beside the bed. "I don't give a damn what the maid thinks." But he managed, with gentle diplomacy, to make her understand that he was expected to be at his desk in the morning, every morning, even if he did have the title of assistant deputy administrator.

He walked over to the newsstand at the corner to get a paper to read in the cab. The newsy was a withered mushroom of a man in a greasy cap, surrounded by the bright flashy covers of pulp westerns and detective magazines. Brad gave him a nickel and told him to keep the change.

The raid at Ruby Bill's was on the front page. There was a flashbulb picture of patrons being herded into paddy wagons. Brad didn't recognize any of the faces, but in the boxed list of names, he found Brophy, Fanshaw, and the girls. He sighed philosophically. Brophy wasn't going to be able to do him much good at Hearst anyway, with the new editorial policy.

The raid had also netted one Boris Gheorghenescu, who styled himself the Count of Bukovina, a minor principality attached to Moldavia, which had merged with Walachia to form Rumania in 1859, and hadn't existed as a political entity for three quarters of a century. Evidently Boris had not enjoyed the diplomatic immunity that he claimed.

The rest of the news on the front page was minor. Mussolini had threatened to take Italy out of the League of Nations if it didn't renounce the Versailles treaty. Colonel and Mrs. Lindbergh were flying from Africa to Brazil, and were sending progress reports by radio every fifteen minutes. And a House subcommittee had recommended that the federal income tax be fixed at a straight four percent instead of the present four percent on the first four thousand dollars and eight percent of income above that.

Brad folded the paper and tucked it under his arm. An empty cab stopped for a light, and he climbed inside. "Commerce Department, east lobby," he told the driver.

As the cab pulled away from the curb, he looked back at Sally's building. He had promised to see her again tonight.

It was a mistake, he told himself. Sally attracted photographers the way honey attracted flies. And it wasn't going to do him a bit of good. He was still a midwestern nobody working at an obscure government job, and he was only going to be criticized for trying to use her to step into the limelight.

He wouldn't be ready for a girl like Sally for another couple of years.

20

"No, no, there is no Herr Weinbaum here," the maid said, and shut the door in his face.

Jeremy raised his fist to knock again, then let the arm drop. It would be no use. He'd tried repeatedly to reach Naomi's uncle Freddie, both at his department store and here at the house in the Grunewald, and they always acted as if he didn't exist. The last time the butler had threatened to call the police.

He turned and went down the walk. He had barely closed the iron gate behind him when an enormous brindle Alsatian came hurtling from across the corner of the house and flung itself against the bars, its fangs bared. It was a hint. Jeremy had a hunch that if he came back again, the dog's release would not be so nicely timed.

The two men in leather overcoats were still loitering across the street. They followed him with their eyes as he emerged, making no pretense about it. Elisabeth had warned him about the pair after he'd described them for her.

"SD agents," she had told him. "From the Jewry unit. Watching the house to see who comes there. Don't go there anymore, Jeremy."

But the undelivered letter from Max Weinbaum was burning a hole in his pocket. Jeremy had been in Berlin more than three months now.

He walked down the street, eyes stiffly ahead, but not before he had seen one of the SD men speak to his companion, pinch out his cigarette and put the stub in his pocket, and start following him at a distance.

There were no trolleys in this exclusive neighborhood, and the nearest underground station was three blocks away, at the corner where Hohenzollerndamm began. Jeremy walked faster. When he turned the corner he could see out of the tail of his eye that the SD man had speeded up, too, and was keeping pace with him on the other side of the street.

Berlin was having a January thaw, and patches of slush lay on the sidewalks where the street cleaners' brooms had missed them. Children in bright scarves and mittens were tobogganing on the great heaps of dirty snow piled along the curbs. By the time Jeremy reached the station, his shoes were soggy. He still had no overcoat. His jacket collar was turned up against the cold, and his raw hands were thrust deep into his pockets. A woman in a seal coat looked after him with disapproval.

He didn't begin to get seriously worried until the SD man followed him into the station. He had assumed that the fellow would quit there and go back to his post. He went over to the news vendor's kiosk and bought a copy of the *Vossische Zeitung*. Pretending to skim the headlines, he sneaked a look at the SD agent.

The plainclothesman was a lump-faced youth, inevitably blond, like most Sicherheitsdienst agents. Heydrich had a penchant for hiring fair-haired, blue-eyed young men with intellectual pretensions. They tended to be odd types—disaffected university graduates who had been unable to find jobs until the Nazis came to power.

Jeremy bought a ticket and ducked through the gate to the platform. He strode rapidly toward the other end. The SD man fought his way through the crowd after him so as to be in the same car when the train came in.

The train rumbled to a halt and the automatic doors hissed open. The crowd poured inside. Jeremy hung back, waiting until last. At the other end of the car, the SD man hung back too. When the stationmaster bawled, *"All aboard, keep back,"* Jeremy pushed his way out again, to the indignant reprimands of the people around him, and ran for the stairs at the end of the platform.

Behind him he heard pounding feet and a shrill voice yelling, *"Halt! Halt! Fassen Sie den Mann!"* He took the steps two at a time and emerged into January sunlight.

He was in the middle of a block. Above the banked snow he could see the top of a double-decker bus, just beginning to pick up speed after its stop at the corner.

Jeremy plunged into the pile, ankle-deep in melting snow, and slid down the other side in time to grab the safety bar at the rear of the bus. A startled tobacco vendor, pushing his portable kiosk along the gutter, paused and stared at him. Some small children, sledding down the snowbank, pointed at Jeremy and jeered.

He climbed the stairs to the top of the bus, ignoring the passengers who scowled to show their disapproval of the tousle-haired young man with the leather elbow patches who had emerged from a snowbank and boarded a bus in the middle of a block—definitely not a correct thing to do. He took a seat and glanced down at the street in time to see the leather-coated SD agent burst out of the station entrance and look frantically both ways down the sidewalk. It didn't occur to the fellow to search anywhere but the corners, where pedestrian paths had been cleared. If the traffic light had been red, no doubt he would have expected to find Jeremy halted at the curb, waiting dutifully to be caught.

Jeremy grinned. Tiny Ernst used a phrase to describe this trait in the German character. They were *"geborene Untertanen,"* he said: "born subjects." They walked straight lines, crossed at the corners, and didn't do anything unexpected.

The ticket seller came by, a limping old man with a Kaiser mustache and threadbare uniform. "Is there anybody here without a ticket?" he said. Jeremy was tempted to ride free. If you didn't reply, the ticket sellers hardly ever approached you directly, even when they knew perfectly well that you had just got on. Germans were law-abiding people. But low on funds though he was, he couldn't bring himself to cheat. He called the man over, handed him a ten-mark note, and when he received the change said *"Danke."*

At Kurfürstendamm he transferred to a trolley. He had a seat to himself, so he unfurled his newspaper. The lead story, of course, was Hitler's New Year speech. Even the Ullstein papers, with their liberal convictions and large circulation, had to submit to the censors. Every morning the editor of the *Vossische Zeitung* had to report to the Propaganda Ministry along with the other editors to receive the daily handout from Dr. Goebbels and get his instructions on what headlines to feature.

Hitler, according to the story, had praised the eighty-six-year-old von Hindenburg for entrusting the future of Germany to him a year ago. The power given him as Chancellor, Hitler said, had enabled him to "cement the Reich firmly together and call a halt in religious, moral, and cultural decay."

There was front-page news from America. The ailing William Woodin had resigned as secretary of the treasury, and Henry Morgenthau, Jr., had taken his place. The story noted that Morgenthau was a Jew. "The mask is off," Dr. Goebbels was quoted as saying.

Impatiently, Jeremy riffled through the paper until he found his own piece. "An American Visits the Zoo." They had printed it after all. True, they had cut it down to only a few inches, and hadn't given him a by-line; instead it had been rewritten in the third person to make it appear that an Ullstein reporter had interviewed an anonymous sightseer. And they had cut out his main point—that the Berlin Zoo was a parable of life in Germany today—to turn it into an innocuous series of impressions about the monkeys and the elephants.

But it meant that there would be another ten marks waiting for him at the Ullstein office.

It wasn't much, but it would help keep him going. His daydream about writing western pulp stories hadn't worked out. The first one had been a fluke; he had never been able to sell another. But he had found that he could pick up an occasional five or ten marks by doing little freelance jobs for Ullstein and for some of the English-language news services that abounded in Berlin.

Millicent Wickes had put him onto it. He had finally summoned enough nerve to look her up after a couple of weeks in Berlin. She had divested him of his virginity that same night, and a few days later, on learning that he was broke, had introduced him to her boss, Tom Sykes of British Overseas Press Service, thus taking a second major load off his mind.

Sykes was often drunk, and depended a lot on outside material to satisfy his home office. He called it "background." Millicent did a lot of covering up for him. What Sykes didn't take, Jeremy found he could often peddle elsewhere. It took much more of his time than he had anticipated; he sold about one piece in ten, and had yet to get a by-line. But he made enough money to scrape by.

He owed Millicent a lot. She was a good sport, despite her astringent manner. For a while, Jeremy had been afraid that things were growing too serious between them, but it was Millicent herself who had planted his feet on the ground. "Don't be a ninny!" she had snapped when he had hinted that he see her less often. "We're not sewn together, are we? What, me a pram robber? No thank you! Go on, my lad, have your fling elsewhere if you have the itch, but please don't tell me all about it." He still saw her regularly at the Propaganda Ministry with the rest of the news crowd, or when he sold a piece to Sykes.

He refolded his *Vossische Zeitung* and stared glumly out the streetcar window at the Kurfürstendamm. The broad shopping avenue was bustling with holiday pedestrians, though motor traffic was thin. The sidewalk cafés had mostly packed their tables and chairs inside till warmer weather, though there were still places, obstinately alfresco, where a few hardy souls in overcoats sat at outdoor tables sipping chocolate. Only a year ago, he had heard, one could see every sort of vice along the avenue: prostitutes dressed as schoolgirls with pigtails and book satchels, rouged young men in women's clothing. But Hitler, within weeks of coming to power, had closed the transvestite joints, rounded up the homosexuals or forced them underground, and driven the prostitutes off the streets.

Two transfers later, he was on Leipziger Strasse. On an impulse he jumped off the trolley and took a walk past the Weinbaum department store.

The smashed plate-glass windows still had not been replaced. They were covered with raw plywood, smeared with swastikas and painted slogans. Even from across the street, Jeremy could make out the words JÜDISCHES GESCHÄFT, warning passersby away from the store. The same uniformed SA bullies were lounging about in front of the entrance, sloppy, soft-bellied men in brown shirts and swastika armbands and jackboots. The Sturmabteilung—Storm Troops—they called themselves. But, for a change, they didn't seem to be harassing would-be shoppers who slowed down near the entrance. A small trickle of people was actually going inside.

Instead, the brownshirts were busy pushing around a thin young man in shabby clothes who looked like a student. "You're a swine of a Sozi!" a beet-faced storm trooper shouted. "I know your type!"

Jeremy hurried by, glad to escape notice. Being an American was no guarantee of immunity in Berlin these days. A number of American tourists had been beaten in the streets for failing to give the Hitler salute during the interminable brownshirt parades. The beatings went on, despite protests by Ambassador Dodd. Even the son of H. V. Kaltenborn, the CBS radio news analyst, had been assaulted.

He didn't feel quite comfortable until he was back in the workers' district where he lived. Even today, uniformed Nazis hesitated to show their faces in the Bonner Platz and other red hangouts, unless they came in force. This was the scene of last year's pitched battles between Nazis and Sozis, and a lone Nazi who ventured here after dark was liable to get his face smashed in.

Elisabeth was not in her room. Her clothes were flung about untidily, as usual. Jeremy spotted a piece of paper on the floor and stooped to pick it up. It was an anti-Nazi leaflet, the usual dreary stuff, this one showing a crude cartoon of Hitler as a mad dog, foaming at the mouth, sinking his teeth into the leg of a noble fellow who represented the German worker. Elisabeth must have gone out to distribute them, and dropped one. It made Jeremy feel ashamed of his own noninvolvement.

He went down to the beer cellar on the corner to see if anyone knew where she was. It was a dark, smoky place, its street-level windows boarded up against the hit-and-run shootings that had been common last year and the year before. The long tables were packed with surly men in workmen's caps, nursing their beers, but at the far end, against the whitewashed wall, someone was playing the accordian, and there was a crescent of jollity around him.

Tiny Ernst spied him across the room and waved. Jeremy went over and sat down. Willi squinted at him with his one good eye and nodded a lugubrious greeting. Klaus, his hand under the table on Margarethe's knee, wiped the suds off his lips with the back of a hairy wrist and gave Jeremy a great jagged grin that showed the gap where his front teeth had been knocked out.

"Zzzo, Jeremy, how flaps the banner?"

"Same as always," Jeremy said irritably. The story of his near-circumcision at the hands of the *Buxtehude*'s crew had been told and retold with glee at the *Bierstube*. "Has anyone seen Elisabeth?"

Margarethe good-naturedly removed Klaus's paw from her knee. She was a heavy-breasted girl with rosy cheeks and corn-colored hair. "Elisabeth? I think maybe she has gone to Bernhardstrasse to see her mother."

"She was supposed to meet me when I got back," Jeremy frowned.

Klaus belched. "She'll turn up. They always do."

Little Ernst cocked his head like a Berlin sparrow. "No luck again, Jeremy? The butler would not let you in?"

"No, it was the maid who would not let me in this time. They set their dog on me. And an SD man followed me to the subway."

"They all exchanged quick glances. "You did not lead him back to Bonner Platz, did you?"

"No, I lost him. What does it matter, anyway? This isn't one of the Nazi's favorite blocks. They don't need me as an excuse to keep an eye on it."

Again the quick exchange of glances. Klaus clapped him on the back. "Yes, yes, you are right. We are all in their little books, you may be sure."

Willi nodded. "Sooner or later . . ."

Ernst lifted his heavy mug in his child's hands and pounded the table with sudden manic energy. *"Noch ein Bier, noch ein Bier!"* he shouted.

The waiter shuffled over for the empties. *"Und Ihnen?"* he said to Jeremy.

"Bitte," Jeremy said.

Everyone else was having steins. The waiter collected their empties and shuffled off.

"Those were the days," Willi said. "We had the Nazis on the run for a while. It was worth an eye."

"Do you remember the time that fat Nazi from out of the neighborhood came in here by mistake?" Klaus said. "He thought it was one of *their* beer cellars. He didn't know this was our *Verkehrslokale.* The boys took him into the back room and worked him over. The next day a car full of brownshirts drove by and shot the place up. *Bang, bang,* just like Al Capone. I dived under a table, you can believe that! They killed poor Karl, and that sailor down here from Bremerhaven got his ear shot off, what a surprise! The day after *that,* some of *our* boys—they say they were professionals from the Communist war veterans bund—stole a car and shot up that Nazi *Bierstube* on Cosimaplatz. I was the lookout."

"Were you a Communist?" Jeremy said, and immediately felt like a naive idiot.

"Me, no," Klaus said hastily. "I was just helping out. I was just a stupid music student, trying to be another Kurt Weill."

"There are no Communists left in Germany," Ernst said dryly. He held his withered arm close to his body, like a broken wing. "They have all gone underground to await the day of resurrection. The leaders have been arrested. The central committee has fled to Russia. The rank and file are being flushed out, one by one. Then they'll get to us."

"Klaus is a wonderful composer," Margarethe said fervently. "You should hear some of his songs. They are *better* than Kurt Weill. He never had a chance!"

"That's the ticket," Ernst said. "Stick to art, eh, Jeremy? That's all that counts in this crazy world."

"Right," Klaus said. "How's the novel going, Jeremy?"

Jeremy flushed. "Oh, stuff the novel!" The fact was that he hadn't added a word to it in a month. There were some fifty pages of it packed in the bottom of his suitcase, and he was beginning to suspect that fifty pages were all there would ever be. He stared morosely into his beer.

"I know how you feel," Willi said. "I still try to write poetry, but it doesn't seem important anymore."

"How can a man just disappear?" Jeremy said.

"Your Herr Weinbaum again?" Ernst said.

"There's somebody else living in his house. A big new brass nameplate on the gatepost that says Bluecher. And his store's been rented out to concessionaires. And everybody acts like he never existed."

Willi shrugged. "People disappear all the time in Germany these days."

Ernst's bright little eyes lit on Jeremy. "How badly do you want to find this man, Jeremy?"

"I'd give my right arm," Jeremy said fervently.

"One ought not to be so generous with right arms," Ernst said with a hint of malice.

Flustered, Jeremy stammered, "I . . . what I mean is I'd do anything to find out where he is."

"Anything?" Ernst mocked. "Be careful of your language, young Jeremy. Someone there may be who will take you at your word." Ernst's sparrow eyes flicked around the room, then came to rest warningly on Jeremy. On the small pinched face the consumptive patches stood out like rouge spots.

"I mean it," Jeremy said.

Ernst slid off the bench. "Well, I've got to be going." He wound his red scarf around his chin and stood as if waiting, a frail gnomish figure with a queer barrel chest and pinned-up trousers.

"I'll go with you," Klaus said, getting up.

"Well, I never!" Margarethe said, but Klaus had already taken his pea jacket from the hook and was following the little man to the door.

"One more and I've got to be going, too," Willi said.

The waiter stood over them with sullen challenge. Jeremy ordered another round and paid the bill. It came to nine marks twenty, wiping out all but eighty pfennigs of the ten marks he had made for the Ullstein story. He left the change for the tip. Margarethe looked hopefully at him as he stood up, but he mumbled an excuse and left.

Elisabeth was still not in her room, so he sat down on the stained mattress—propped up on bricks because Elisabeth was afraid of mice —to wait.

There was nothing to read except the same tired collection of plays on the windowsill: Shakespeare and Shaw in German, the Revolutionary Theater anthology, the dusty Schiller, and a handful of dog-eared study scripts. He leafed through a copy of *Heilige Johanna* till he got bored with it, then got up and began to pace restlessly. He became annoyed by the pan on the electric plate, still containing the encrusted remains of a can of beans, and took it to the lavatory at the end of the hall near the staircase to wash it out. When he returned to the room, Elisabeth was just leaving with another armload of pamphlets.

"*Hallo,* Jeremy. I can't stop to talk now. I've got to deliver these for Hugo."

Her cheeks were ruddy from the cold outside. Elisabeth always managed to look fresh and sparkling, despite the rat's nest of dark hair that swirled round her head. She was one of those people who took care of themselves rather than their surroundings, and Frau Lemmer, who lived in a room down the hall with her three children, was always complaining that Elisabeth used more than her share of hot water.

"I thought you were going to go to the films with me."

"You don't understand," she said impatiently. "Rudi's managed to borrow a *car!* After we deliver the pamphlets, we're going to transport some duplicating equipment. We've got to move the printing shop again."

"You're going to get yourself in trouble. And it's just plain careless to leave those pamphlets lying around the way you do."

She gave a harsh laugh. "*We* know what we're doing. You're the one who's going to get into trouble, going around inquiring about that Jew of yours. One fine day they'll drag you into an SS barracks and beat you into sausage meat."

"It's ridiculous, this agitprop, or whatever you call it! You're deceiving yourselves. People throw away your pamphlets. They're afraid to be seen reading them. They walk by those slogans you paint on the walls as fast as they can, with their eyes turned away. Everybody knows it's over. It's been over ever since Hitler kicked the Social Democrats out of the Reichstag and made every party except the Nazis illegal. The centrists are in exile, and even Ernst admits that the Communist leaders ran away to Russia! What's left of the opposition is just a headless body thrashing around, thinking it's still alive!"

Elisabeth looked at Jeremy with faint contempt. "You're a spoiled American boy. You don't know what it is to be involved. You stay in your safe little dream and watch others risk their lives, and then you criticize them."

Jeremy felt his face grow hot. "I'm sorry . . . look, this is all new to me."

She sighed. "Poor Jeremy! You're very nice, but someday you've got to wake up politically."

He bustled among her possessions. "At least let me wrap this old sweater around those pamphlets. You can't go out in the street with the titles showing."

She pushed a strand of hair back distractedly. "I wonder if that swine of a policeman is still at the corner. Schinkel, his name is. He's the one who turned poor Paul over to the SS. The chap at the post before him at least had the sense to leave well enough alone. This one will get himself shot one day."

Jeremy knew the policeman she meant. He was an officious runt with a little mustache, gold-rimmed glasses, shaved Prussian neck, and a fussy uniform festooned with every button and piece of braid the regulations allowed. He went to the window and looked out.

"You can't see him from here," Elisabeth said. "Your window on the top floor is the only one on this side of the building where you can get a clear view of the corner."

Jeremy turned from the window. Elisabeth, both of her arms loaded, was pushing the door open with one foot.

"Will I see you later?" he said.

"I don't know," she said vaguely. "It depends. Don't wait up for me."

"Life," Philip said, a weary smile upon his lips, "is a second-rate banquet, and I have supped my fill. . . ."

Jeremy squinted critically at the sentence. Then he x-ed out the *supped my fill* and typed *dined to repletion* in its place. It still didn't look right. He yanked the sheet of yellow copy paper savagely out of the typewriter, crumpled it up, and tossed it on the floor with the rest.

Doggedly he put another sheet of paper in the roller and started all over again. He'd sat hunched over the old Remington half the night, chain-smoking the dreadful German cigarettes, trying to revive his novel. He was going to call it *The Disillusioned*. But everything he wrote looked vapid.

In a fit of disgust, he rose from the sagging couch and pushed away the straight-backed chair the typewriter rested on. He walked over to the window and looked out. Elisabeth was right. You could see all the way to the next corner from here. It wasn't much of a view: ugly concrete buildings and a streetlamp. He could make out a tiny stiff figure strutting back and forth. The policeman, Schinkel. He was working a double shift, the way so many of Berlin's public employees were doing these days. Even a policeman had to make ends meet. There was probably a faded, worn-out Frau Schinkel, a cabbage-smelling tenement, and four or five sniveling children with dirty bottoms. Those were the sort of people he ought to be trying to write about, not world-weary dilettantes copied from Aldous Huxley.

Down below, Schinkel sneaked a yawn. Jeremy looked at his watch. It was midnight, the hour when the Gestapo was reputed to drag people from their beds.

With a sigh, Jeremy went back to his typewriter. He was just settling down when he thought he heard someone fiddling with his doorknob.

As he looked up, the door burst open and three large men in heavy overcoats shoved their way into the room.

"What—" Jeremy said, starting to get up.

"Keep your mouth shut," one of them hissed. One of the others closed the door behind them. The third man went over to the window and looked out.

"Who are you?" Jeremy demanded. "What do you want?"

The man in front looked him over coldly, as if he were trying to decide whether or not to buy a fish that might or might not have gone bad.

"You have been making inquiries about a Jew named Friedrich Weinbaum," he stated.

"What of it?" Jeremy said. An icy sensation tickled the base of his spine.

The man blocking the door said roughly, "I say tie him up, put him in the corner, and have done with it."

Jeremy blinked at them. The yellow ceiling bulb cast raw shadows, hollowing cheeks and chiseling deep facial lines. They were harsh anonymous men in their forties, with the slate complexions of slum dwellers or petty criminals. Their hat brims were pulled down, inking out their eyes. The fellow by the door had an ugly scar at the corner of his mouth that drew his upper lip into a permanent snarl.

"We can tell you where he is," the first man said.

They weren't Gestapo or brownshirts. Jeremy studied them more closely. Each wore a scrap of ribbon in his lapel—red, white, and black in the form of a fishtailed cross. Servicemen's honorable discharge badges. All at once, Jeremy realized who they were. It was part of the education he'd received from Elisabeth and her friends. These were members of the Red Battlefront Alliance, a veterans' organization. The Communists used them to do their dirty work. It was Alliance toughs who, in the months of street fighting that had preceded the Nazi takeover, had cruised in stolen cars and sprayed the Nazi *Bierstuben* with bullets, gangland style.

"Where?" Jeremy said.

"Not so fast," the man at the window said. "First you have to do us a little favor." He was carrying some sort of long parcel wrapped in twine.

"What kind of favor?"

"Nothing so much," the leader said. "We want to borrow your room for one night, that's all. For a look out post."

There was the hint of a wheedling tone in his voice. It was hard for the Alliance men to realize that this was no longer *das rote Berlin*—

"Red Berlin," as the city had been called in the 1920s—and that they were now obsolete.

"What's going to happen tonight?" Jeremy persisted.

"What did I tell you?" growled the man covering the door. "We're wasting our time. Knock him on the head, I say. That way we can keep an eye on him."

"We'll know where he is," the leader said. He turned to Jeremy. "None of your business," he said. "Don't worry, you won't get into any trouble."

"He's a fence-sitter," the scar-faced man sneered. "He doesn't want to get involved."

"Shut up. He's just a *Schriftsteller,* an intellectual. You can't blame him." He turned to Jeremy again. "We know your heart's in the right place. We know all about you. You're no provocateur. You let people like us stick our necks out so people like you can go on writing your poems. Don't worry, nobody's going to get hurt. No rough stuff. We're just keeping an eye out for our chums, see?"

Jeremy blushed furiously. "You can use the room."

"Good," the man said. His manner became brusque. "You can go downstairs now and spend the night with your friend the actress. Don't come back here till morning."

Jeremy stiffened. "What do you know about my friend?"

The man at the window said in an amused tone, "We told you we know all about you. Go on, downstairs. She's there now. She'll be waiting for you."

They had already taken possession of the room. The man with the scar moved Jeremy's typewriter none too gently to the floor and carried the chair over to the window. The one who had done most of the talking took a cushion off the couch and placed it on the window-sill.

"Wait a minute," Jeremy said stubbornly. "What about Herr Weinbaum's address?"

"Nothing doing," the man said. "We'll leave it for you on the dresser."

Jeremy hesitated.

"We'll leave it, I said."

They all looked at him impatiently. The man with the long parcel fiddled with the twine. Jeremy picked up his jacket and left. The light went out before the door closed behind him.

"Jeremy, is that you?" Elisabeth called in a sleepy voice. "Come in, come in, close the door. You're letting all the cold air in."

Jeremy groped his way across the room in the dim blue light from the gas heater. It had been turned low for the night. He tripped over a chair and stepped on something soft—some article of Elisabeth's discarded clothing. He felt around till he located the raised mattress.

"Ugh, your hands are like ice!" Elisabeth was naked between the coarse woolen blankets. "Take off your things and get in with me before you freeze us both to death."

"You don't mind if I stay the night?"

Elisabeth allowed him into her bed, on some mysterious schedule of her own, about once or twice a week, and always kicked him out at two or three in the morning, saying that she needed a few hours of real sleep alone if she was to be any good the next day.

"Of course not, you great dummy! Hurry up, my teeth are chattering!"

The next morning, as he was getting into his clothes, someone knocked on the door. Jeremy glanced at Elisabeth. She was at the cracked mirror over the washstand, carefully applying makeup. She had an early morning appointment at the UFA film studios to try out for a bit part in the new Emil Jannings movie. *"Wer ist da?"* she murmured without looking round.

Willi poked his head inside the door, the black eye-patch covering half of one sallow cheek. He seemed flustered at finding Jeremy there, then managed a *"Wie steht's, Yere."*

"What's up?" Elisabeth said.

"Haven't you heard? All kinds of excitement," Willi said. "Somebody shot the policeman at the corner last night."

"Serves him right, the pig," Elisabeth said imperturbably, continuing to apply her lipstick.

"The story is that some big shot from Russia was supposed to slip into the block last night to make contact with the apparat."

"What do you know about it?" Elisabeth said. "You never belonged to anything except one of those glorified literary groups. I'll bet the district committee never bothered to contact your cell after the Party went underground."

"I could tell you a lot," Willi said mysteriously. "But members of a Group of Five don't talk."

"Group of Five!" she snorted. "Don't make me laugh."

Willi grinned guiltily. "Well, what do you know about it yourself?" he said. "They'd never trust you to be an apparatchik either."

"Maybe not," she said. "But I don't go around shooting my mouth off about things I don't understand." She faced Jeremy. "How do I look?"

"Fine. You'll knock them dead."

"If I get the part, it means a long-term contract, whether they use me later or not. That will pay the rent."

She hiked her skirt to her hips to pull her silk stockings taut, not minding Willi, and inspected herself critically one last time. She rarely bothered to dress up for ordinary auditions. "Shut the door when you leave," she said to both of them, and went out.

"Who was the policeman?" Jeremy said to Willi. "The one named Schinkel who was always making a note of people going in and out of here?"

"I don't know. I think so. They say he was killed at long range with a rifle. The street's full of SS men. They've got an armored car at the intersection. Watch your step if you go out, Yere."

When Jeremy returned to his room, the three Alliance men were gone. The air was stale with cigarette smoke, and the floor was littered with butts. They had helped themselves to his coffee; his two cracked mugs and his water glass were leaving rings on his dresser, and a coffeepot full of grounds stood on the electric hot plate. The manuscript of his novel lay carelessly on the floor with a heel mark on the cover page. The cushion had been removed from the windowsill and replaced on the sofa.

Jeremy walked over to the dresser and found a scrap of paper with writing on it. The paper had been torn from the page he'd left in the typewriter. Scrawled across the top was an address in the Wassertorstrasse.

He went over to the window and looked out. At the far corner he could see the armored car Willi had mentioned. Uniformed SS men swarmed over the area, keeping passersby back.

Something shiny on the floor under the windowsill caught his eye. He bent over and picked it up. It was the brass casing of a rifle cartridge.

The building in the Wassertorstrasse was a shabby tenement smelling of cabbage and urine. A dirty-faced child of eight or nine came past him down the steps, carrying a tin bucket, and glanced fearfully at him before running out to the milkman who was waiting at the curb next to a pushcart that resembled a gun carriage with cans dangling from the shafts.

Jeremy climbed the worn stone steps to the top floor. Someone in the building was playing "Für Elise" on an out-of-tune piano; it reminded him of the days when he had listened to Pamela practice it for hours on end. Behind another of the yellowing doors, somebody was having a family quarrel. The door opened, slammed, and a screaming child came running down the stairs, almost colliding with him.

There were three doors at the top, grouped around the stairwell. A sickly light came from a skylight above. Jeremy checked the apartment number against the scrap of paper in his pocket, then knocked.

There was a rustling sound behind the door, then silence. Jeremy knocked again.

Behind him, one of the other apartment doors opened a crack then closed. Jeremy listened, but heard nothing. "Herr Weinbaum?" he called.

The door opened an inch. A frightened woman's voice said, "Please, what do you want?"

Jeremy caught a glimpse of gray hair, a wraithlike figure in a brown velvet dress. Behind her was a long dingy hall.

"I'm from America," he began. "I'm a friend of Naomi—"

"Please, come in. Quickly."

She closed the door behind Jeremy as soon as he was inside. Down the hallway a voice said, "What is it, Klara?"

"It's all right," she called. She ushered Jeremy into a wretched little parlor that was almost bare of furniture. A gaunt, haggard man with thin white hair sat in a threadbare armchair next to a card table with a lamp on it. He put down an oversize, leather-bound book that he had been reading. Jeremy glanced at the open pages and saw music staves; it was an orchestral score, black with notes.

"Herr Weinbaum?" he said.

The man inclined his head in reply. An answer was unnecessary; Uncle Freddie had the same fine skull structure and long, aristocratic features as his brother Max. But Jeremy was shocked at how old and sick he looked. He had understood that Friedrich Weinbaum was only a few years older than Naomi's father.

"My name is Jeremy Sinclair. Naomi asked me to look you up when I arrived in Germany."

The fine patrician features came to rest on Jeremy's face, and the eyes focused with difficulty. Then, from somewhere inside the man, a spark of ironic intelligence came out of hiding and Friedrich Weinbaum's expression came to life.

"You know Max?"

"He's . . . he's been kind enough to have me as a guest in his house."

"And Max, how is he?"

"He seems very well," Jeremy said.

"Max was always the intelligent one in the family. But his cello technique . . ." He shook his head. "Always too heavy an attack where double and triple stopping is involved. Good enough for Bee-thoven, but not the way to play Bach."

"He . . . he sent you a letter."

Jeremy took the battered envelope out of his pocket and handed it over.

"How long have you been carrying this around?"

"About four months."

"He had no right to ask you to take such chances. But perhaps he did not realize how bad things have grown here."

"I can get word back to him for you," Jeremy said. "Don't worry, it's safe."

The old man in the chair jerked himself erect. "Where are my manners? Please, sit down, Herr Sinclair. This is my wife, Frau Weinbaum. Klara, something for our guest, *vielleicht?*"

"No, no, really I couldn't . . ."

"Nonsense, you must."

Frau Weinbaum fluttered around him. "Of course, you must have something, Herr Sinclair. Sit down, I will be back in a moment."

She had once been a very pretty woman, Jeremy realized. She had large gray eyes, and classic features that reminded him of Mary Astor, grown older. In something other than the dowdy brown dress and with a glow restored to her faded complexion, she might have been a reigning queen of society. With a start, Jeremy suddenly realized that less than a year ago, Klara Weinbaum had been exactly that.

"You will excuse me, Herr Sinclair," Herr Weinbaum said. "I will be rude and read my brother's letter now, while we wait." He opened the envelope and read quickly, his lips pursed. He refolded the letter and put it back in the envelope.

Frau Weinbaum returned with a tray bearing two long-stemmed wineglasses. "Ah, at least they left me a bottle or two of the good Rauenthaler," Herr Weinbaum said.

They sipped in silence for a while. Then Herr Weinbaum said, "And how did you finally find me?"

Jeremy fumbled for a reply, his ears growing red.

Herr Weinbaum inclined his head with wry understanding. "Of course—there are things it is better not to know in Germany today. What I do not know, I cannot be made to tell."

"Sir!" Jeremy blurted, "why don't you get out of Germany? I'm sure that your brother could find you a place in America."

Uncle Freddie waved his hand. "No, no, this is my country. The worst is over. They have taken my business, my house, my savings. I have nothing more that they could want. They will leave me alone now."

"Sir, how can they just take everything away from you? Aren't there laws?"

"Ah yes, there are laws. Certainly there are laws. Everything is done with exquisite legality. First the rowdies in the brown shirts beat up Jews in the streets, smash shops, sack homes. Then the ones in the black uniforms take one into 'protective custody.' Then, in the cellars under the house on Prinz-Albrecht-Strasse, one is persuaded to sign away one's goods. All quite legally. After listening to one's neighbors scream, and doing a little screaming one's self, one is not so brave, let me tell you."

The hand holding the wineglass was trembling. For the first time, Jeremy noticed that the tips of two fingers, the ones in the middle, seemed to be mashed flat.

Frau Weinbaum put a hand on her husband's shoulder and took the wineglass from him. "It's all right, Friedrich," she said, "it's over now."

Jeremy made a move to rise. "Maybe I'd better be going," he said.

"Please, stay. Don't mind an old man who gets carried away. You must not leave before you tell me about Max and his family. I have not received his letters for a year. You will not tell Max about these fingers, please. It is not so bad. There are too many amateur fiddlers in the world already."

"Look . . . if your brother knew that you've lost everything, I'm sure he'd find some way to help you. Why don't you just let me—"

"No, no, you must not trouble Max. It is not so good to attract attention anyway." He smiled ironically. "It is not true that I have lost everything. I still have my life, and Klara and I will not starve. I am satisfied with the bargain I made with the blackshirts, believe me. At least Klara and I will not be sent to Dachau."

"Dachau?"

"Ah, forgive me. You have not heard of Dachau? Well, never mind, the world will learn about the *Konzentrationslager* soon enough. Dachau, Oranienburg—a new idea in the scheme of things." He lapsed into silence.

Jeremy struggled to make sense out of what Herr Weinbaum was saying. Something about concentration camps. It sounded like some sort of military term. But Herr Weinbaum was talking again.

"So tell me all about Naomi. She has grown into an attractive young woman, I'll bet. The last picture I have of her, she was thirteen, and at the awkward stage. And Eric, is he really as fine a violinist as Max claims? I would like to hear him play someday."

There were coffee and little cakes, and Frau Weinbaum became almost gay. She was persuaded to have a glass of wine with them, and they finished the bottle. When it was time to go, Herr Weinbaum put a hand on Jeremy's shoulder and showed him down the dingy hallway to the front door.

"Thank you for coming," he said. Then, in a lower voice: "Do not come back here, Herr Sinclair. I appreciate your good intentions, but it will not be so good for me if you are seen here. Or for you, for that matter."

That night, Jeremy wrote his letter to George Wilson at the publishing house, as he had promised. He wrote it as if it were a letter from an aspiring author to an editor:

Dear George,

I have been working on the manuscript, as you suggested. But I am afraid I am running into trouble. While the leading character remains alive and in good health in my imagination, it doesn't seem quite realistic to portray him as a wealthy, successful businessman. I'm afraid this would lead to a lack of reader interest. How about if I made him a poor man, living in a slum neighborhood like the Wassertorstrasse, anxious only to be left alone? Let me know what you think of this approach. Please excuse the ribbon on this typewriter. I meant to buy a new one, but found the store closed.

Berlin is a beautiful city, and I am enjoying my stay. Of course the weather is bad this time of year, but there is every hope that it will improve.

My fond regards to the family.

> *Best wishes,*
> *Jeremy*

In the morning, he took the letter around to the main post office and mailed it with a batch of postcards. He chose the busiest line, and when he arrived at the window he shoved the whole pile across at once.

The harried clerk held the first couple of cards up to the light and looked at the address, then threw the whole batch into the foreign mail basket without further investigation.

It was a clear, cold morning. Jeremy hopped on a trolley to Prinz-Albrecht-Strasse and got off at the corner.

Gestapo headquarters at No. 8 was an ornate pile of brick and marble that once had been an art school. It dominated the block with its bulk, its massive façade busy with pediments and carved detail. The curb in front of it was empty except for a single parked van.

Too late, Jeremy saw how pedestrians were hurrying by on the opposite side of the street. He couldn't cross over now without being conspicuous. He thrust his hands deep into his pockets and walked by with his head down.

At the Taverne, the restaurant where the American and British correspondents gathered every night to eat spaghetti and complain about Dr. Goebbels's handouts, they made jokes about the place. They told stories about how the rival factions within the SS were always trying to arrest one another, that they didn't dare visit the men's room without notifying a colleague. But it was no joke to the poor wretches locked in the cellars.

He got by, and risked a quick backward glance before turning the corner. Involuntarily he shuddered.

What could Dachau be, that Friedrich Weinbaum feared it more than this grim place?

21

The big round table in the corner was permanently reserved for foreign reporters. Jeremy picked his way toward it across the crowded tavern floor. The proprietor, a big, hearty Bavarian, moved to intercept him, but stepped aside when he saw who it was.

"Hello there, Sinclair," said Kemble, the weedy, droopy-mustached London *Times* correspondent, taking the old briar pipe out of his mouth. "Eaten? Sit down and have a plate of spaghetti or a beer or something."

Jeremy hesitated. He really hadn't earned a place at the table, and he didn't want to abuse the privilege too often, even though there were a couple of empty places tonight.

"Well, just for a minute," he said, squeezing in between the Reuters man and Emmet Hamilton of Allied. "Has Sykes been in?"

" 'Fraid you missed him," Kemble said. "He came in about eight, pretty well swozzled, left in worse shape, and showed every intention of going on the town and getting more swozzled still. Best try him at the office in the morning."

"Morning?" one of the two UP desk men laughed. "Shape he was in, I wouldn't count on finding him till noon, if at all. Millicent will keep him out of trouble by filing some boilerplate for him."

"Oh," Jeremy said. His face fell.

The cruising waiter came over without being asked, detached a stein of beer from the incredible cluster he carried in either hand, and set one, slopping foam, in front of Jeremy. Hamilton raised a stubby finger and got one, too.

Jeremy fumbled in his pocket for a coin. "This one's on me," Hamilton said.

Jeremy started to protest, but Hamilton was too fast for him. "Thanks," Jeremy said.

"Peddling something, Jeremy?" Hamilton said. The Allied International reporter was a fleshy, freckled man in his forties who affected hairy tweed jackets and loud socks.

"Well . . . yes."

"Won't it wait? Isn't this one of your Sykes specials? 'A Walk through the Tiergarten,' or 'The Deutsches Jungvolk, Hitler's Boy Scouts'?"

Jeremy wrinkled his nose. "No, this one's hard news."

"Run into something, have you?" Kemble said, raising his eyebrows.

Hamilton leaned back casually. "Why don't you try me on it? Sykes doesn't own you, you know. The BOPS home office doesn't even know you exist."

"Well . . ."

Hamilton looked amused. "Nobody's going to steal it from you. We've all filed for the day. The beast's been fed. All the home offices and bureau chiefs are busily digesting the big story about Goering turning control of the Gestapo over to that chicken farmer, Himmler, and his blond young chap, Heydrich. Goering gave the bad news to his troops today. Called a press conference this afternoon. All very amicable. But I don't doubt that heads will roll as soon as Hitler looks the other way."

"And as if that weren't enough," one of the UPI pair said sardonically, "we've all got the breathtaking story about Dr. Schacht's new economic decrees. Work and bread, and ground-up acorns in the coffee."

Stung, Jeremy took the story out of his inside pocket and handed it over to Hamilton. It was three and a half pages, double-spaced. Hamilton smoothed out the creases and began reading. After a moment he looked up.

"Is this true, Jeremy? The Ullsteins are closing up shop?"

At the nearby tables, German patrons strained to hear what the foreign correspondents were saying.

"It's true, all right," Jeremy said. "I've got a buddy in the city room at the *Vossische Zeitung*. They're all out of work, as of close of business today. No announcement. I don't know about the other papers, but Goebbels wanted the *Vossische* shut down. They forced the Ullsteins to sell the Ullstein *Verlag,* the printing plant, for next to nothing."

"Tough luck, Sinclair," Jules Cray, the INS correspondent said, putting down a forkful of spaghetti. "Just when you were beginning to get a by-line, too."

"Do you think that's what's important to me?" Jeremy said, turning on him. The jaunty, sophisticated Jules, who always had a flower in the buttonhole of his impeccable pinstripe, became the focal point of Jeremy's resentment. "They've been publishing for over two hundred years. They were one of the great newspapers, like the *New York Times.* And now they're out of business because of this crazy Reich Press Law that says that journalism is a public profession, regulated by law, and that it can't be practiced by a Jew or anyone married to a Jew!"

"My word, does he say all that in the story?" Kemble said, sucking on his pipe.

"He sure does," Hamilton said, skimming the text. "And there's a lot of soapboxing about Dr. Goebbels's daily seminars at the Ministry for Popular Enlightenment and Propaganda."

"Well, you're welcome to young Sinclair's story then," the London *Times* man said. "The home office doesn't want me to be too shrill about conditions here. They only print about half of what I write, as it is. They don't want to offend Lord Lothian and the Cliveden set, all those chaps at the top who see Hitler as a useful counterforce to Red Russia."

Hamilton was already scribbling over Jeremy's manuscript and x-ing out great stretches of it. "Okay, Jeremy, I'll phone it in," he said. "It ought to be good for a sawbuck. Drop by the office tomorrow."

"Thanks, Ham."

"I'm toning it down for you. We'll have to cut out all this inflammatory stuff, turn it into a straight news report."

"You gotta be more professional, Sinclair," the INS man cracked. "A professional lets the customer do anything he wants except kiss her."

Jeremy flushed.

"Don't put so much of yourself into it, boy," Kemble said. "They'll only break your heart for you."

"Lay off him, you guys," Hamilton said. He turned a broad freckled face toward Jeremy. "It's a good story, kid, got some nice inside touches. No by-line, you understand, but I'll tell the desk where it came from."

"That's okay," Jeremy mumbled.

Hamilton stroked his chin thoughtfully. "In fact, I'm going to ask the chief to accredit you as a stringer. You won't get a regular retainer, but we'll issue you a press card, make life a little easier for you in this lunatic asylum of a country."

"You can have one of our cards, too, Sinclair," Jules said. "But you'll have to kiss the bureau chief."

"Ah, shut up," Hamilton said good-naturedly. He got up and went to the phones in the rear.

Somebody had smashed all the streetlamps on one side of the square, and the Bonner Platz was a murky gorge, splotched with deeper shadows. The workers' flats walled off the dim luminescence of the night sky, gloomy masonry slabs dotted with rectangles of feeble yellow light.

Jeremy quickened his steps. As he hurried past the traffic signal box on the corner, he looked up involuntarily to locate his own window. It ought to have been in line of sight. This was the corner that had been the post of Schinkel, the dead policeman. Jeremy could remember him marching back and forth between the signal box and the street sign, his thin shoulders held stiffly back. There was another policeman on duty now, an elderly man with a Kaiser Wilhelm mustache and visored helmet.

The light changed and Jeremy halted at the curb. He had acquired the Berlin habit of waiting for traffic lights, even when there was no traffic. The police tended to be strict about it.

As he waited, he heard a scream farther down the block. It was a man, howling in pain. The howls rose and fell with rhythmic precision, as though someone were working a lever. Jeremy peered down the row of stuccoed tenements and saw the shadowy figures of four or five men milling around in the street. They had another man on the ground, and they were working him over.

The policeman was looking the other way. "Hey, something's going on down there!" Jeremy blurted.

The policeman blinked at Jeremy with watery eyes, but said nothing.

"They're beating someone up," Jeremy said.

The policeman spoke reluctantly. "Everything is in order, young sir."

Down the street, one of the men raised a booted foot and kicked the fallen man. He rolled over in the gutter, and then they were on him again.

"Aren't you going to *do* anything?" Jeremy demanded.

"Best not to meddle, young sir," the old policeman said sternly. "Go home now, mind your own business."

Jeremy stared at the policeman with helpless outrage, then stepped off the curb. The traffic light was still red, but the policeman said nothing. He was taking a great interest in his uniform cuff, flicking a speck of lint off the sleeve.

As he drew closer, Jeremy saw that the fracas was taking place across the street from his own building. Light spilling from an open door outlined the toiling figures. Now he could see that they were brownshirts, beer-bellied men in floppy fatigue caps and leather shoulder straps. Their victim was trying to crawl away from them, hunching himself along like a caterpillar, but they were following him along the gutter, laughing, their arms lifting and falling with some instrument Jeremy couldn't identify. A small crowd had gathered to watch, staying a safe distance away—night workers or people on their way home from the movies or a café.

Jeremy skirted the crowd and headed for his doorway. There was nothing to do. The brownshirts, out looking for trouble, had found some poor Jew to have sport with.

Then he got a shock. One of the men standing in the crowd was the scar-faced strong-arm man from the Red Battlefront Alliance squad that had taken over his room the night the policeman was shot. Jeremy could see the bared incisor glinting in the spilled light. The man's eyes slid over him without any sign of recognition, then the man went back to watching the storm troopers.

Things must have changed a lot in the last three months, Jeremy realized, with the Nazi bully boys daring to show their faces in the Red Block, and with the Kommunistische Partei tough guys standing by helplessly.

Jeremy edged around the melee, almost safely to his door now. With the crowd no longer in his way, Jeremy could see the peculiar instrument the SA men were using to beat their victim with. It was a long, flexible spring with a small ball of lead at the tip.

The thing whipped through the air and chunked into flesh. The man writhing in the gutter gave a shriek of pure agony, and as he rolled over, trying to escape the pain, Jeremy saw the black eye-patch covering one cheek. It was Willi.

Without stopping to think, he took a step forward. Willi took advantage of the distraction to crawl away from his tormenters. "Yere," he called brokenly, "is that you?"

The SA men recovered from their surprise. "There's another of them," one shouted, and two of them ran toward Jeremy, waving their lead-tipped springs.

"Run, Yere, run!" Willi cried.

Jeremy stood, rooted in nightmare. A grinning SA man had planted his booted feet in front of the feebly crawling Willi, blocking his further progress. Now the brownshirt stooped stiffly, grabbed a fistful of Willi's hair, and jerked his lolling head back. Still grinning broadly, he reversed his grip of the ball-and-spring instrument and ground out Willi's good eye with the wooden handle.

Jeremy heard Willi shriek, *"Gott, Gott,"* then the running brown figures were upon him, and a lead ball was whistling in his direction. Instinctively he flung up an arm to protect himself, and the thing struck the meat of his forearm. The pain was astonishing. The velocity of the little lead ball as it thudded into his flesh must have approached that of a bullet, instantly pulping a tiny hemispherical pit of tissue into homogenized jelly.

Jeremy went berserk. Once, as a small boy, he had been tormented every day at recess by a bully, an overgrown lout named Mikey, who was two or three years older. Jeremy was his current project. Jeremy had been small for his age, a scrawny, spidery kid. He had endured Mikey's mean, sly tricks for a couple of weeks—the unexpected swat on the ear, the knuckles dug into the nape of his neck when they were in line, the bending-back of his little finger, the clever grinding together of his elbow bones. On this day, Mikey had sneaked up behind him and poked him in the kidneys with a stick. You were expected to grin, snuffle, and say "Gee whiz." But Jeremy had whirled in sudden rage, his arms windmilling, catching the other boy by surprise and bowling him over. It took two monitors and a teacher to pry Jeremy loose. By then, he was pounding Mikey's head against the ground, over and over again. He didn't realize that he had been bloodied himself until later, when it started hurting. Mikey stayed out of school for two days. He never bothered any of the little kids again.

Now the same senseless fury took possession of Jeremy. He lowered his head and charged, knocking the storm trooper off his feet. They tumbled together into the gutter, Jeremy on top. Jeremy pounded blindly with both fists on the storm trooper's face, until he realized that the man had struck his head on the curb and was limp. The second brownshirt was kicking Jeremy in the ribs. He hadn't felt it. With a bellow of rage he grabbed the man around the legs and shoved, his own legs pedaling against the pavement, until the man went over backwards. Then, somehow, he had one hand clawed under the storm trooper's chin and the other clamped around the wrist of the hand holding the ball-and-spring, and he was shoving, shoving with all his weight. The lead-tipped instrument dropped from the brownshirt's fingers, and the fellow's face started to turn black, the eyeballs bulging.

The other four SA men were scrambling to help their comrade. Somebody threw a brick from a window, and it struck a brownshirt on the shoulder. A rain of bottles and bricks came from the upper stories and the roof of Jeremy's building, and the apartment house next to it —a building that housed a lot of left-wing union members.

"Get the bastards!" somebody shouted. A burly navvy who until now had been part of the watching crowd stepped joyfully forward, fists swinging. Another man in workman's clothes joined him.

The crowd melted away. Except for the two workmen, nobody wanted to be a part of this. Jeremy rose to his feet, his knuckles dripping blood. The scar-faced Alliance man had slipped away too. Jeremy at that moment felt a rush of contempt.

But people were pouring out of the doorways of the two buildings and the building across the street. The Red Block was disgorging its motley company of left-wing students, Marxist intellectuals, muddled artists, and a fair representation of genuine proletarians—socialist factory hands and tract-reading truck drivers. This sort of street battle had been common in the old days, when the Nazis were just a bunch of thugs, detested by the police. Now, after a year of lying low, the Sozis were having one last glorious brawl with their former foes.

Jeremy saw two muscular young Sozis holding a yelping SA man, while a third beat him with his own ball-and-spring instrument. He recognized Klaus, hairy and undershirted, laying about him with a lead pipe.

Down at the other end of the street, a pair of headlights came on and a truck motor roared into life. The truck barreled down the street and screeched to a halt. Bulky dark forms jumped from the truck bed, clubs in their hands. As they came around into the headlights, Jeremy could see that they were more brownshirts, reinforcements from the nearby SA barracks. They had dropped off the squad that had beat up Willi and parked, waiting in case anything happened. The Red Block was still enemy territory.

The SA reinforcements waded into the battle, but people kept pouring out of the buildings. There was a crash of glass as someone threw a paving stone through the windshield of the truck. Jeremy saw two contending figures silhouetted against the glare of the headlights, one with upraised club, one with a sculptor's mallet. Somehow that symbolized the whole struggle for him.

He found Willi, writhing and twisting in the gutter, and dragged him into the doorway, out of harm's way. Willi was groaning, but didn't seem to be aware of anything. In the light of the naked hall bulb, Jeremy could see what they'd done to Willi. Where the remaining eye had been was an empty socket, brimming with blood. A pulped bloody thing hung halfway down Willi's cheek.

Jeremy bent over him. "Willi," he said.

Willi moaned.

"Willi, it's me, Yere."

A sound like a sob came from Willi's throat. "Yere, my eye, is it gone?"

"I can't tell," Jeremy lied. "There's a lot of blood. Don't think about it now. We'll get you to a hospital."

"Yere . . . promise to kill me if it's gone."

"Take it easy."

"Promise!" Willi screamed.

At that moment two wrestling figures came crashing through the door, almost falling over Willi. One was an SA man with a revolver in his hand. The other man, a bearded fellow in a polo shirt, was hanging on to the storm trooper's arm with desperate strength. The gun fired once, twice, sending a shower of plaster down from the ceiling. Two more men came barging into the hallway. They bashed the brownshirt over the head with a plumber's wrench and took the gun away from him. Then all three started methodically to beat him up.

Jeremy hooked his arms under Willi's armpits and dragged him upstairs, a step at a time. Willi seemed to have fainted, and he was grateful for that.

From his window he saw the end of the Battle of Bonner Platz. The brownshirts who were still able to move loaded the more seriously injured onto the back of the truck. The truck thunked off on its slashed tires, its broken headlights dark, a ragtag pack of whipped SA men limping after it. A barrage of garbage pelted them as they retreated.

At least one of the limp figures on the truck had been dead. Jeremy remembered seeing one storm trooper, a big cod-faced fellow, lying on the pavement with his skull split open, his brains spilling out in a gray paste. He felt sick.

By the time the police arrived with their hee-hawing sirens, everybody was off the street. Some of the tenants had had to be carried inside. A litter of rotting vegetables and broken glass, caps and pieces of torn fabric, was scattered across the roadway. The police stood around, staying close to their vehicles, hands on their weapons, glancing nervously up at the blind windows. None of them made any move to enter any of the adjacent buildings. After a while they went away.

A jubilant Klaus burst into Jeremy's room at the head of a troop of celebrating tenants. Behind him, a hulking fellow whom Jeremy vaguely recognized as a metal sculptor who made things out of discarded bathtubs and old plumbing, waved a bottle of cheap brandy.

"Well, Jeremy, we did it! We showed the bastards a thing or two. It was a great victory!"

"It wasn't a victory for Willi."

Klaus glanced toward the couch. Willi was lying there, half conscious. Jeremy had propped him up on pillows and put a towel under his head. The pulped thing dangling from his eye socket rested on his cheek. Jeremy was afraid to touch it. He had made an attempt to wash some of the blood away from Willi's other wounds, but stopped when he saw that tissue was coming away with it.

Klaus frowned. "Some of our chaps will be by shortly. They're taking our wounded away to several different hospitals outside the city limits—so they won't be connected with what happened here. Willi will get the best of care. I'll put in a word. He'll be taken to a private nursing home in Brandenburg. A doctor on the staff is one of ours." He cleared his throat. "It's unfortunate about Willi, of course."

The metal sculptor thumped Jeremy on the back. "It's all thanks to you, Yeremy. If it hadn't been for you striking the first blow, we would have stayed watching from our windows. Well, we're through cowering. All honor to you, comrade!"

He took a swig from the bottle.

Jeremy felt ill. The metal sculptor had put into words what he had been trying not to think about.

Klaus tried to cheer him up. "Don't take it to heart . . . what happened out there just now would have happened sooner or later. It's been a long time brewing. Moscow's been telling the Kommunistische Partei Deutschlands to lie low for the time being. But some of the hot-blooded young fellows in the KPD have been spoiling for a fight—before all the Party strength dribbles away!"

Elisabeth came in, her cheeks flushed and her eyes shining. "Jeremy, you were magnificent! *Herrlich!* I didn't see it myself, but they told me! Fighting six of those brown-shirted swine all by yourself! Giving courage to these wet-bottomed babies!" She flung her arms around his neck. "If you were only politically mature! But you'll learn!"

The metal sculptor was thumping him again. "She's right! The old men in Moscow will be annoyed with you! Hell, annoyed with us! But we showed them that the KPD is still alive and kicking! Have a drink!"

Jeremy wrested himself away from both of them. "Leave me alone!"

The metal sculptor looked hurt. Elisabeth shrugged. Klaus took them aside and said, "Let him be for a while. He's just having his eyes opened."

The men came to take Willi away. They were silent, stony types, like the Alliance men who had used Jeremy's room as a sniper's post in January. Willi screamed when they tried to move him. One of the men gave him a very professional injection, and he quieted down.

The men took time out to dress the tiny hemispherical wound on Jeremy's arm, then carried Willi out on a rubberized mattress pad. Klaus hurried after them, and came back a few minutes later.

People drifted in and out of Jeremy's room all night. They thought he was being modest when he didn't respond to their compliments. Through the open door he could hear the noise of the impromptu party down the hall. He could also see the parade of people passing by on their way to the roof with their armloads of bottles, bricks, and paving stones that they were stockpiling up there. Everybody seemed to have acquired a lead pipe or a chair leg or a kitchen knife. There were guns, too, passed furtively from hand to hand.

A dozen people had taken up a vigil at Jeremy's window. His room afforded one of the best views of the street. There was a fellow with binoculars, and another with a sporting pistol stuck in his belt. When Jeremy looked out of the window himself, he could see a man with a rifle on the roof opposite.

"They're not going to come tonight," a girl said.

"I heard that we have a machine gun," a scruffy art student said. "They're assembling it now in Tiny Ernst's flat."

"All we have to do is hold out for twenty-four hours," the girl said. "They're making arrangements for a general strike. "

"Rumors," a stolid man in a workman's cap grunted.

"The Soviets will help when they see how things are going," the art student said confidently. "They can land troops at Rostock and proceed overland. The people will welcome them with flowers."

"In Austria, just two months ago, the workers held out for four days in the Karl-Marx-Hof and the Goethehof. And just think, the Dollfuss regime brought up tanks and shelled the buildings with six-inch cannon!"

"The Socialists might have won, too, if they'd had help from the Czechs, just across the border, as they'd expected."

"They shot the Socialists at half past five," the man in the workman's cap said dryly. "It is not a game, to challenge the men who run things."

"What do you think, Yeremy?"

Jeremy didn't answer. He continued typing. The couch had been commandeered, so he sat on a cushion on the floor, leaning against the wall, the typewriter on a chair in front of him.

"What's that you're writing?"

Jeremy ripped a sheet of yellow copy out of the typewriter and added it to the stack on the floor beside him. "I'm writing about what happened out there tonight. An eyewitness account. I'm getting it down while it's still fresh in my mind."

Klaus had appeared at the head of a brigade with sandwiches and coffee. "Good, good!" he said. "Tell the outside world. Let them know what's going on here."

Against Jeremy's protests, the yellow sheets were passed from hand to hand. "Not bad, but you should say something about working-class solidarity," the man with the pistol said.

"Comrade, this is ideologically incorrect," a bearded man said sternly. "You talk about the shattered remnants of the KPD making a last stand, when we all know that the official line is that the cadres have been broken up into smaller units and the organizational structure of the Party is intact."

"And why do you say *one* truckload of storm troopers?" the girl complained. "You should say *ten* truckloads. That way our victory will have more political significance."

"No, no, none of you understand," Klaus said magnanimously. "Our young American friend is not writing for the Party press. He is already a respected journalist whose work appears in the American and British newspapers. What he writes will seem to have more authenticity if it is free from any suspicion of propaganda."

"*Seem*, nothing!" Jeremy said harshly. "I'm just writing the truth."

"Of course you are," Klaus said. "You'd better get going. It's getting light. I'll go see if Ernst will assign you a couple of boys to get you out of the block safely."

"I'm not leaving till it's over," Jeremy said. "I started this thing, and I'm staying till it's finished."

"Don't worry, you won't miss the fun. Nothing will happen till after nightfall. I know the Nazis. They haven't even cut off the phones or the electricity yet. They're still getting organized."

Elisabeth was by his side, gripping his arm. "Yes, Jeremy, you must go."

"I don't even know if I can get this printed. I'm just a stringer."

"It's worth a try," Klaus said. "Go ahead. If you want to die, you can come back just after dark. The show will probably start about midnight."

Two hard-faced men in leather jackets escorted Jeremy through a maze of alleys, courtyards, and basement passages that apparently interconnected all the buildings, without having to resort to the street. They helped Jeremy climb down into a damp, vaulted tunnel. A startled rat scuttled off. "Was supposed to be a sewer line," one of them explained tersely. "They forgot about it around Bismarck's time."

At first nobody noticed Jeremy when he walked into the Allied International newsroom. The teletype was clattering away, the boy was running copy, MacPherson was shouting into his tie line, and the two regular staffers were banging away hopelessly at typewriters. All the phones were ringing at once. Emmet Hamilton was nowhere in evidence, which at this time of the morning meant he was out doing something important. Walt Hanes, Hamilton's boss, was methodically penciling his way through a sheaf of bulletins.

Jeremy cleared his throat.

At that moment a five-bell flash rang out on the ticker, and everyone stared at it hopefully. A staffer jumped up and hovered over the machine, waiting for the three bells and the bulletin summary. He tore the tape out of the machine, balled it up, and threw it on the floor in disgust, and said: "Whee, we've got another hot flash from the Paris bureau! They're telling *us!* They have it from a reliable diplomatic source that nothing happened at the Bonner Platz last night."

Jeremy cleared his throat again. "Mr. Hanes . . ."

The office boy elbowed past him and slapped a cablegram in front of Hanes. "It's New York again. They want to know when you'll have something more substantial on Bonner Platz."

"Tell 'em we're working on it," Hanes said. He looked up sourly at Jeremy. "We're kinda busy here, Sinclair. The Ullstein piece was only worth a fiver. Sorry. Sit down somewhere, and I'll have the girl make it out for you, but you'll have to wait."

Silently, Jeremy handed him the sheaf of yellow copy pages.

"What the hell is this?" Hanes scanned the top sheet impatiently. "'The Battle of Bonner Platz: An Eyewitness Report.' Are you kidding?"

"No. I was there."

Hanes was already going through Jeremy's copy, slashing away with his red pencil. "MacPherson," he said without looking up, "get ready to transcribe this for cable. Sinclair, you sit down at a typewriter and knock me out a couple of sidebars, about five hundred words apiece."

Jeremy found an unoccupied desk and hung his jacket from the chair. Twenty minutes later he had a piece called "Dreamers and Nightmares: The Tragedy of Bonner Platz." Twenty minutes after that he had another piece, "Eye of a Poet." "Boy," he yelled, feeling jaded and professional. The office boy picked up his final page and ran with it to Hanes, then, without stopping, ran with the edited previous page to MacPherson. "Good stuff, Sinclair," Hanes said. "Now give me a backgrounder, 'Brownshirts versus Redshirts.' "

"They're not all reds."

"Who the hell cares?"

An hour later, he handed in the backgrounder. It had mostly been pieced together from the AIPS files. Hanes gave him a grudging "Good job, Sinclair. Now stick around, while we wait for questions from New York."

A phone rang. One of the staffers picked it up. "It's Ham," he said.

"I don't want to talk to him unless he's got past that police barricade," Hanes said.

"He's phoning in a story. They're bringing up armored cars in the Bonner Platz. He can hear machine-gun fire."

"Give me that phone," Hanes barked. He listened, nodding his head and writing on a yellow pad.

Jeremy picked up his jacket and headed for the door.

Hanes looked up, covering the mouthpiece. "Sinclair, where are you going? I told you to stick around."

"You don't need me here, Mr. Hanes," Jeremy said. "I'm going back to the Bonner Platz."

All the bus traffic had been rerouted, and the trolleys were skipping the stops nearest to Bonner Platz. Jeremy got as close as he could and walked. He could hear the rattle of machine guns and the occasional thump of a grenade. A lot of people were hanging around in the adjoining streets, as if it were a holiday. "It's like the Spartakist uprising in 1919," he heard an old gentleman with a white mustache say. "Well, the Freikorps crushed that one, and Colonel Roehm's SA boys will crush this one."

The police were turning pedestrians away from the approach streets, and there was a slow molasses tide of people that made progress difficult. A flower peddler whose pushcart had broken a wheel and spilled bouquets into the street was arguing with a helmeted policeman who wanted him to move it immediately. Jeremy was able to get through by flashing his AIPS stringer card. The office boy had gravely delivered it to him while he was typing.

"All right," the policeman said. "Go on straight through to the command post at the barricade and ask for Captain Wenck. Keep your head down. If you get it shot off, it's your own lookout."

Captain Wenck turned out to be an SS officer in black uniform. It was a Gestapo operation now. He studied Jeremy's press card with a fishy eye. "You can wait over there with the other correspondents if you like," he said indifferently. "Tell your superiors that foreign dispatches will be subject to censorship."

About two dozen members of the foreign press corps were standing about behind a huge pile of sandbags, looking frustrated. Jeremy caught sight of Emmet Hamilton, in disgruntled conversation with Millicent Wickes and the correspondent for *Paris-Soir*. Kemble of the London *Times* was there, and he recognized Quentin Reynolds of the Hearst Service risking his neck by standing on an upturned sand bucket and trying to peer over the top.

"Hiya, pal," Hamilton said. "Hanes told me you scooped us all. What's the story?"

"I live in there," Jeremy said.

Millicent pounced on him. "Did you tell Hauptsturmführer Wenck that?"

"No."

"Well, at least you're beginning to acquire *some* sense, love. I expected you'd be blabbing your head off, insisting on being allowed through."

Jeremy's face reddened.

"There's the tenants' register," Kemble pointed out.

"No there isn't," Jeremy said. "I heard it was destroyed during the night."

"My word, they *are* efficient, aren't they?" Kemble said. "For an organization that's supposed to be on its uppers."

"Where's Mr. Sykes?" Jeremy asked Millicent.

"Bloody drunken sot Sykes, you mean!" Millicent said with tight fury. "Sleeping it off with some Chausseestrasse whore, I suppose, leaving me to hold down the fort as usual! It serves him right that you didn't go to him first with your Bonner Platz story, love. I tell you, this time I'm through with the silly twit!"

"You can always come to work for us, Milly dear," Kemble said, lighting his pipe.

"What, and have my bottom pinched by gentlemen? No thank you!"

"Listen!" the *Paris-Soir* man said.

The sharp, authoritative bark of a cannon split the air, quite close. The small-arms fire stopped for a moment, and in the sudden silence, Jeremy could hear the clank of steel tank treads on pavement. Then the rifle and machine-gun fire started up again.

"They're bringing up the heavy artillery," Quentin Reynolds called from the top of the parapet. "It's all over now."

For the next three hours the correspondents stood in small, sober groups, listening as the shooting and the explosions rose to a crescendo, then died down. Then there was the sound of running feet, shouts, the clink of metal. There were a few scattered pistol shots.

Once, unaccountably, there was the roar of a tank starting up again, and the single *whump!* of a cannon followed by the sound of falling masonry and a rising cloud of dust above the rooftops.

"They're not supposed to have tanks, you know," Kemble said quietly. "They've already started to ignore the Versailles treaty."

"No wonder they don't want reporters in there," Hamilton said.

A half hour later, steel-helmeted SS soldiers began to remove the barricades. A convoy of open trucks with high slatted wooden sides, which evidently had been parked waiting in nearby streets, rumbled into the Bonner Platz. Captain Wenck, looking coldly satisfied, came striding over. He had some kind of a leather baton that he kept tapping against the side of his stiff breeches.

"Come," he said. "You will see what happens to enemies of the new Reich."

The correspondents followed him in a straggling band past the wall of heaped sandbags. The Bonner Platz was covered in broken glass, plaster dust, and rubble, but the buildings didn't look anywhere near as damaged as Jeremy thought they would be after the hours of gunfire. There was one gaping hole in the façade of his own building, and the cornice had been bitten off, and all the windows were broken, but mostly it was just pits in the stucco. There was no sign of tanks.

Soldiers with rifles were herding dazed people out of the buildings. Farther down the block, Jeremy could see other uniformed men loading the stretcher cases into closed vans. He could recognize some of the prisoners. He saw the metal sculptor, a scrap of torn, bloody shirt wrapped around his head, being helped into one of the open trucks.

"We want you to write about this," Captain Wenck said. "We want to show the world how our prompt, alert action has saved us from the threat of Russian bolshevism. Your own countries should take a lesson from us."

Kemble pulled on his pipe. "That woman over there doesn't look like a dangerous revolutionary to me," he said.

Jeremy turned his head and saw the soldiers leading out Frau Lemmer, the woman who had always complained about Elisabeth's excessive use of hot water. The youngest of her three children, a towheaded boy of four, was clinging to her skirts and crying.

"Yes," Hamilton said. "What's going to happen to the ordinary tenants, the ones who just happened to be caught in the crossfire? Surely you don't contend that everybody who lives in the block is a red?"

The Gestapo officer compressed his lips. "Naturally the innocent will not be punished. We will investigate each case thoroughly. Those who are not guilty will be released after questioning."

"I say, old chap," Kemble said. "I meant to ask you about your questioning methods."

The first truck was loaded. It inched past them, the people inside jammed like sardines. Two SS men with rifles rode the tailgate. As it passed, a big burly fellow raised his arm in a clenched-fist salute. It was Klaus. Jeremy couldn't tell whether Klaus had seen him. A few voices were raised raggedly in the "Internationale."

"The bloody fools," Millicent murmured. "They're just making it worse for themselves. And for others."

"So. You see?" Captain Wenck said, and walked away, tapping his leg with his baton.

"What was all that about censorship?" somebody said.

"A lot of nonsense," Kemble said. "Goebbels may have the German press under his thumb, but he wouldn't dare try to censor our dispatches." He grinned ruefully. "They're doing that well enough at home. London simply doesn't believe me anymore."

"What's going to happen to all those people they're taking away?" Jeremy said.

"They'll have their teeth knocked out in the SS cellars," Kemble said. "Then they'll be turned over to the SA, and queer Colonel Roehm's men will bash them about some more. Then they'll be shipped off to Dachau or Oranienburg for what the Nazis call 'political reeducation.' But don't try to write about concentration camps, boy. Himmler says they don't exist."

"Oh, come off it, Kemble," Hamilton said. "No wonder London doesn't take you seriously anymore. We're newsmen. We can't write about rumors.

"Quite," Kemble said, relighting his pipe. "They don't exist. But even though they don't exist, Himmler says that the inmates are just there for their own good. Protective custody. It's the only way to guarantee the security of health and life of the *asoziale* elements who cause such annoyance among honest Germans. And if the foreign press tries to spread atrocity stories, he'll make the prisoners suffer for it."

Jeremy remembered Herr Weinbaum's reference to concentration camps. *Konzentrationslager*, he had called them. "Mr. Kemble," he said. "Who gets put in these camps?"

Kemble lifted his eyebrows in surprise. "Oh, Jews, gypsies, Communists, Bible students, homosexuals, Social Democrats, Jehovah's Witnesses. Anyone the Nazis take a dislike to. Some are there simply to be squeezed of their property."

"Documentation, Kemble," Hamilton said. "You need documentation."

Kemble looked at Jeremy. "How about it, lad. You somehow managed an eyewitness report of the battle of Bonner Platz. Think you can get into Dachau?"

The last truck rolled by with its cargo of prisoners. Somewhere above, through a shattered window, a baby was crying. The news people began to disperse. The SS guards wouldn't let them near any of the building entrances. Politely but firmly the reporters were escorted out of the block.

Jeremy followed along with the rest, stepping gingerly through the rubble. Millicent fell in beside him.

"Did you see your German girl friend in any of those trucks?"

"No," he said shortly.

He hadn't seen Elisabeth, or Tiny Ernst, or any of the recognizable Red Battlefront Alliance tough guys. Perhaps they were among the dead or more seriously wounded, but it didn't seem reasonable that *all* of them would be.

"The inner circle always seem to save themselves, don't they?" Millicent said brightly.

"Elisabeth wasn't part of any inner circle," Jeremy said. "She's just an actress."

"Touchy, aren't we?"

They were out of the block, past the sandbags. Ahead, Berlin looked normal, with hurrying crowds, pushcart peddlers, and even an organ-grinder with a little monkey on a chain. Hamilton said, "I'm taking a taxi back to the office. Want a lift?"

"Uh, no thanks," Jeremy said. He didn't want to face Walt Hanes just now, or write another sidebar on Bonner Platz. Whatever dispatch could be gleaned out of the morning's events, Hamilton could write it. Would write it.

Hamilton gave him a hard, curious look. "All right, pal. If I were you, I'd drop by the office this evening, though. Before the ten o'clock cable goes out."

"All right," Jeremy said. Hamilton spotted a taxi farther up the block and raced a couple of other correspondents for it.

"Do you have a place to stay tonight?" Millicent said.

"Not exactly."

"Not exactly," she mimicked. "Do you have any money?"

"I can get along."

He had the draft for the fiver Hanes had given him. He'd have to take it down to the Deutsche Bank on Mauerstrasse and get it changed into marks. And he had a few marks in his wallet. And Hanes would owe him a pretty good sum for the morning's work.

Millicent sighed. "You'd better come home with me."

He stood hesitating. Millicent had a bed-sitting room with a tiny kitchen alcove.

"Don't be an ox!" she said in exasperation. "You have enough for a toothbrush and a spare shirt, I suppose. You can stay till you sort yourself out."

"All right. Thanks."

"Don't exert yourself," she said tartly. "Come along then, you'll have to come back to the office with me first. You can help me patch together something for the London desk under Sykes's name. We can take a trolley. I'll put in a chit for a taxicab. A whopping good chit, believe me! That's the least that Sykes can do to pay me for pulling his blooming chestnuts out of the fire again!"

She glared at Jeremy until he realized with a guilty start that he was expected to take her arm. They walked together to the trolley stop.

Jeremy turned through the arch into the Wassertorstrasse. The new blue wool suit itched. He felt conspicuous, wearing it in this slum neighborhood populated with workmen in shapeless trousers and greasy caps, and screaming children in outgrown shabby clothing. He had bought it with his first regular paycheck from Allied International. He was thinking about moving into a place of his own, but he didn't know how to tell Millicent.

He dodged a pack of small children chasing a ragged little boy who hugged a paper sack of unknown contents, and mounted the eroded steps to the Weinbaums' flat. Somebody was still practicing "Für Elise" on the same out-of-tune piano. In three months they hadn't progressed very much. The same cooking odors filled the stairwell.

Uncle Freddie had told him to stay away, but he had not been able to get the Weinbaums off his mind. He had taken care to see that he had not been followed from the news service office, though this had seemed an excessive precaution. And despite the unsavory system of neighborhood spies and *Blockleiter* the Nazis were haphazardly trying to institute, Jeremy could not believe that a visit from an unknown young man in a blue suit would place the Weinbaums in any danger.

Besides, he had a reason for the visit. In his pocket was a cautiously worded letter from George Wilson at Max Weinbaum's publishing firm hinting that funds would be available if a way could be found for the Weinbaums to smuggle themselves across the border to Austria or Switzerland, and that in the meantime small sums disguised as "royalty payments"—not enough to attract attention—might be funneled through Jeremy to make Uncle Freddie and his wife more comfortable.

He knocked on the Weinbaums' door. Behind the peeling panels, a

Volksradio played military marches. He heard footsteps coming down the hall. The door opened.

A fat doughy woman with hair curlers and missing teeth peered at him suspiciously. *"Wer ist da?"* she said.

"Excuse me," Jeremy said. "I'm looking for the Weinbaums."

"There are no Weinbaums here," she said, and started to close the door.

"Wait!" Jeremy cried. "Herr Friedrich Weinbaum? An elderly gentleman, thin, with white hair. He lives here."

"We live here," the woman said, "and I have never heard of a Herr Weinbaum."

The door closed in his face.

Jeremy stared helplessly at the blank panel, then turned away. The door across the landing was open a crack, and he was aware that someone behind it was watching him.

"Please," Jeremy said. "Can I talk to you?"

The door opened. An old man stood there on one leg and a crutch. He had a discolored nose and white stubble on his face, and he was dressed in a graying long-sleeved undershirt and sagging trousers held by one broken suspender strap, the missing leg pinned up at the knee.

"The Jews are gone," he said.

"Gone? Where?"

"Who cares? Good riddance, I say."

Jeremy started to say something and thought better of it. He made his way down the staircase, feeling the old man's eyes on his back.

At the bottom of the stairs, he almost tripped over a small child scribbling with crayons on pages torn from a book. He stopped and saw that it was music paper, part of an orchestral score.

"Where did you get that?" he said.

"I didn't steal it!" the terrified child said. "I found it in the trash!"

22

The long sloping lawn was splashed here and there with color: the pastel gowns of the bridal party like overturned tea roses, the small brilliant clusters of striped canvas chairs in which no one sat, the vivid canopy of the pavilion from which grave servants in white jackets were dispensing punch and champagne. Under the ancient gnarled oaks, sunburned men mopped their foreheads with handkerchiefs and discussed politics or horses or the market.

Pamela stood decorously in her pale peach bridesmaid's gown and leghorn hat, wondering what to do with the damn bouquet. Sally had thrown it to her as a joke, thus disappointing her cousin Enid, a nasal, annoying girl with buck teeth and shoulder blades. She couldn't throw it away, and she didn't want to be too obvious about forgetting it somewhere.

She could see Brad standing by that strange round-nosed auto of his, shaking hands with his ushers. He had changed to a blue double-breasted blazer and white flannels, and looked very handsome with his coppery hair struck by the sunlight, and his long limbs deployed to express seigneurial ease. He didn't seem at all intimidated by Sally's overpowering family or the crumbling Georgian grandeur of Westbourne and its acres.

Sally was waiting impatiently in the Airflow's front seat, hatless and dazzlingly blond, her wedding gown exchanged for a bright silk print. She had her half of the windshield cranked partway up to provide a breeze when they started. The old shoes and the tin cans were duly tied to the rear bumper. Knowing Brad, Pamela could imagine just how long they would remain there after he and Sally were safely out of sight down Westbourne's mile and a half of driveway.

Brad spotted her and came striding across the lawn. "Got a ride back to Washington, Sis?"

"Herb Willis is taking me."

"Oh, yes, good old dependable Herb. Look, thanks for everything, Pam. Helping me pick out the ring, and holding down the Sinclair family end, and all that."

"It's all right. Have a nice honeymoon. Sally's a lovely girl."

"But a bit above my station, eh?"

"I didn't say that."

"Why not? Everybody else is. Did you see Liz Meredith's 'Washington Tidbits' column this morning? 'Can wild, restless Sally Collier manage to settle down to married life with an impecunious upstart from the Midwest?' "

"She didn't call you an impecunious upstart. She said you were an up-and-coming young official of the Roosevelt administration."

"Comes to the same thing." He glanced over toward Sally, who was puffing on a cigarette and trying to ignore the approach of a large sentimental aunt in a flowered dress. "All that boilerplate about the illustrious Collier family lineage—the two signers of the Declaration of Independence, the Supreme Court justice, the secretaries of the treasury, navy, and God knows what else going back to the Jefferson administration! To say nothing of their having had the grace to fight on the losing side in the Civil War! Liz never used the stuff *I* sent her. Our family's got nobody except Mother's scruffy whaling captains and dull old General Zephaniah Sinclair. And *he* fought on the Union side!"

It was in Brad's usual bantering tone, but Pamela was not deceived. Sometimes, rarely, there was a brief unguarded flicker of the prehistoric creature that lurked beneath the shallow opaque surface that her brother cultivated. She was always startled and a little frightened by it.

"She's here. Liz Meredith, I mean. She crashed the reception. I saw her talking to Sally's mother."

"Is she?" Brad yawned elaborate indifference. "Well she's got moxie, I'll say that for her. At least she didn't blab about how we lost the Sinclair family fortune, such as it was. Everybody assumes Father was ruined in the Crash."

"Is that why you didn't bring Mother east for the wedding?"

His eyes were bland. "Mother isn't up to it. You know that. She stays in her room all the time now."

"And what about Gordon? Why wouldn't he come?"

"Wasn't a question of wouldn't. Couldn't. He's all tied up with his June Week at the Point. Anyway, the plebe class isn't eligible for summer furlough."

Pamela let that pass without comment. There was some kind of trouble between Brad and Gordon. But Brad wouldn't admit it, and you certainly never could get anything out of Gordon when he wanted to be stubborn.

Brad was getting restless. "I'd better go over and rescue Sally from her aunt. If I leave her sitting in the driveway much longer, she'll have to cope with half the Confederacy."

Pamela rose on her tiptoes and gave Brad a peck on the cheek. "When will you be back?"

"I've got two weeks vacation due me. God, I hope things don't fall apart while I'm gone. It's a bad time to be away."

"The Darrow Board's report?"

For weeks now, Washington had been rocked by the verbal fireworks between Hugh Johnson and Clarence Darrow, who at the age of seventy-seven had thrown himself into one last battle—a no-holds-barred investigation of the NRA. The two opponents were well matched in the creative use of invective. The old trial lawyer had taken on William Jennings Bryan himself in the Scopes "monkey trial," but he wasn't prepared for General Johnson. "A more superficial, intemperate, and inaccurate document than the Darrow Report, I have never seen," the general had thundered. "Bloody old Jeffreys at the Assizes never conducted any hearings to equal those." At the height of the ruckus, the two curmudgeons had gone for a peaceful automobile ride together, during which—as Johnson had later allowed to reporters—they had "talked about anthropology, comparative religion, and whether man has a soul."

"The general seems to be holding his own."

Brad shook his head. "He's stretched to the breaking point. I'm afraid he's hitting the bottle again."

"Oh, Brad!"

He laughed. "I'll worry about it after I get back from my honeymoon. So long, Sis."

Pamela watched her brother as he sprinted across the lawn and vaulted into the Airflow's driver's seat. He gunned the motor, and the heavy car rolled smoothly down the driveway, trailing shoes and tin cans from its oddly sloping rear deck. A phalanx of converging relatives dispersed, looking disappointed.

Pamela wandered back toward the striped pavilion. The day was growing hotter. The men were starting to run their fingers around the insides of their collars, and among the lady guests there was a lot of discreet fanning with hats. From the direction of the boathouse, down somewhere at the bottom of the lawn, Pamela could hear the boisterous voices of some of the younger children at play.

"No'm," Custis, the Colliers' elderly Negro butler, said in response to her question, "Mr. Willis go back to the house to make a telephone call."

Herb Willis had promised an early return to Washington. He was a dull, earnest young man who lived a bachelor existence at the Dodge House along with some seventy-five other congressional secretaries. He was a useful prop for keeping other men away from her. Carl Fuller had left a numb, dead spot inside her as far as men were concerned, like a dentist's shot of novocaine. After almost a year, it still hadn't gone away.

Carl had gotten his county judgeship. She had received a newspaper clipping in the mail in an envelope addressed in block letters, with no return address, but with a Beulah, Iowa, postmark. It had shown Carl taking the oath, his needle-nosed wife smiling possessively at his side. Pamela had looked at the picture and hadn't felt anything.

"Oh, Pamela, there you are!"

Sally's mother intercepted her on her way up the curving walk that led to the main house. Mrs. Collier was a lean and sinewy woman with shrewd blue eyes set rather startlingly in a gaunt face that had been burned as dark as dried beef by years of sun. She looked as if she belonged in an open-necked shirt and riding breeches, but she was sheathed—scabbarded was closer to the word Pamela wanted—in the incongruous femininity of a gray silk gown with ruffled sleeves.

"I declare, it's hot enough to fry an egg on a bald man's head! But there's nothing like a June wedding, is there? Didn't the church look just lovely with the pews trimmed that way with field flowers and lily of the valley? I couldn't believe that was my Sally up there! Wasn't she the most *beautiful* bride, standing there in just *clouds* of white? Bradford is a fine young man. Everybody says he's going to go far. What a pity that your mama couldn't be here, but I'll be sure to send her lots of pictures of the wedding and all the clippings for her scrapbook. One day I hope to meet her. . . ."

On and on she rambled in her honeyed southern accent, but her clever blue eyes were on Pamela the whole time.

"We were all so disappointed about your brother Jeremy, but we certainly *do* understand that there wouldn't have been time for him to cross an *entire* ocean, but he *did* send the *nicest* cablegram *all* the way from Germany. He must purely be *brilliant* to be a *for*eign cor-re*spon*dent at barely twenty-*one!* I don't see *why* in the world your brother Gordon couldn't have come to the wedding! Why, it only would have taken one teensy little *word* from George Dern at the War Department to General Connor at West Point, and I'm sure that Gordon could have gotten off from his June Week or whatever it is. But *why* couldn't your little baby sister be here?"

It took a moment for Pamela to realize that Mrs. Collier was actually waiting for a reply. Then she forgot Brad's careful briefing.

"Why . . . uh . . . Junie's traveling out west, you see . . . and, uh, we couldn't get in touch with her in time. . . ."

Mrs. Collier sighed. "These young folk, eloping and such, and giving their poor mamas heartaches."

Pamela searched the leather face warily. The bright blue eyes stared back unwinkingly at her.

"Oh, yes, I had a nice talk with your mama over the telephone. What a pity she isn't well. Your dear daddy was in the banking business, wasn't he?"

"Yes . . . he was."

"Well, Lord knows the Colliers are banking men, and so are the Talbots on my side. My husband, Clay, still keeps an interest in the family brokerage firm in Norfolk, but mostly he's just a farmer. It keeps him busy enough looking after that scalawag overseer of his who runs the tobacco plantation for him. Leaves him no time at all for his horses. Do you ride?"

"No-no, not really."

"What a pity. With your figure you'd look fine sitting a horse. Well never mind, we'll find you a gentle one in the stable tomorrow. We'll have plenty of time to get acquainted when all *this* is over and done with." She gestured around at the lawn full of guests with the white-jacketed Negro servants moving gravely among them. "Clay and I were pleased about Brad, really we were. Sally's so wild and unmanageable. Always has been. I've been terrified that she'd take up seriously with one of those artistic pansies or one of those foreigners with the worthless titles that are always swarming around her." She patted Pamela's arm. "We'll just have to do without your other brothers and your sister, and it will be up to you to represent the Sinclair family tonight."

Pamela said quickly: "Oh, I have to get back to Washington. Tomorrow's a working day."

"Nonsense! I've already asked Marcus, and he says it's all right. So there! It's just a little family supper."

"But . . . but I didn't bring any clothes with me."

"That nice suit you came in will be fine. And tomorrow I can find you some of Sally's old riding clothes. I'm sure they'll fit."

"That's . . . that's very kind of you, but you see, I've made arrangements. . . ."

"Now don't you fret. I've already talked to Herbert and told him you won't be driving back to the city with him. Here he comes now."

Herb Willis, looking distracted, was hurrying down the brick path from the house.

"Oh, Miz Collier, there you are. I just wanted to say my good-byes." He turned to Pamela. "Are you sure you won't ride back with me, Pam? I thought maybe we could have dinner tonight."

"If you'll wait just a few minutes, Herb. I was just explaining to Mrs. Collier—"

"You just run along, Herbert," Mrs. Collier said. "Pamela and I haven't had *any* time to talk, with all the confusion of the rehearsals and all. We'll see that she gets back to the city tomorrow night."

Willis pulled an outmoded turnip of a watch out of his waistcoat pocket and frowned at the time. "I've just *got* to be back in Washington by four. Lyndon's calling a special meeting of the Little Congress. We're having a straw vote on this crazy new social security idea the President proposed. Lyndon's arranged to have Frances Perkins as the speaker."

Herb swore by Lyndon Johnson, the skinny young Texan who worked as legislative secretary to Congressman Richard Kleberg, heir to the gigantic King Ranch. With Kleberg having little interest in anything but gadding about in Washington society, the twenty-six-year-old Johnson had a free hand in running the office. He had wheeled and dealed and taken over control of the venerable discussion group called the Little Congress, composed of legislative staffers. With relish, Herb had told Pamela the story of how Johnson, on the first night of his arrival in Washington, had entered the communal bathroom of the Dodge House four separate times and taken four separate showers, and then the next morning had brushed his teeth five times at ten-minute intervals, so that he could meet as many of the other congressional staffers as possible while they were using the facilities. He hadn't even flinched at introducing himself to the pairs of shoes showing under the booths. "With Lyndon's push," Herb had said admiringly, "he'll be a congressman himself someday."

"Run along now, and don't miss your meeting," Mrs. Collier said. "Don't you worry about Pamela."

"Well, if you're sure . . ."

Helplessly, Pamela watched Herb's awkward figure as he hurried down the path, tails flapping.

"Are you still carrying that fool bouquet, child?" Mrs. Collier said. "Here, give me that."

She hailed a passing waiter, a bent, dignified Negro with graying hair. "Boy, you take these flowers in the house and put them in some water for Miss Sinclair."

"Yes'm," he said with a grin.

"The house is full of strange nigras," she said to Pamela. "I told Custis to hire some extras for the wedding as he saw fit. I think that one's a cousin of his or something. Now look here, I've got to go and make small talk for a while with some of Clay's Richmond relations. You come along with me."

She took Pamela by the wrist and hauled her with an iron grip over to where one of Sally's brothers stood brooding at the gathering.

"Charles, you show Pamela around the place, hear? Now you treat her nice, 'cause she's your sister now." She walked off with long, mannish strides, holding on to her floppy shirred hat with one brown hand to keep it from flying off.

Charles Collier was a gangling, cranelike youth with the face of a plucked hawk. He would be handsome someday. He glared resentfully at Pamela.

To break the awkward silence, she said: "Westbourne is lovely."

"The central house was finished in 1755," he said grudgingly. "Daddy's ancestor, Rufus Collier, brought over a master carver and a joiner from England to do the important work, the paneling and so forth. They were indentured for four years, and then went on to build some of the other big houses in the area. The bricks were fired right here, on what used to be the plantation. See that tobacco leaf finial on the roof? There's nothing else like it in Virginia."

"There must be a lot of history here," she said.

"George Washington really did sleep here," he said. "There's a portrait of him in the dining room by Gilbert Stuart's daughter, Jane." He flashed a sudden grin. "Come on, I'll show you the stables."

She followed him through a quarter mile of green meadow criss-crossed with white rail fences, clutching her straw hat. Past a stately row of oak trees was a complex of horse barns, whitewash gleaming in the sun. An exercise boy in ragged knickers was leading a magnificent blond-maned chestnut filly around a walking ring.

"That's Princess Domino," he said, his face lighting up. "She's a granddaughter of Man o' War. I'll never race her. But she's going to be the foundation of my stable."

"I've never seen a more beautiful horse," Pamela said sincerely.

He nodded seriously. "Jason," he called out. "Bring her over here so the lady can see her."

The boy walked slowly over to the rail, leading the horse. She tossed her blond mane and gave a high-spirited whinny as she approached. "I'll breed her next year, when she's three," Charles said. "I've already made the stud arrangements. The sire is—" He broke off. "This horse hasn't been groomed today."

"No, suh," the boy said. "Luther say he get around to her next."

"What do you mean, get *around* to her? She's supposed to be groomed before she's walked!"

The boy looked frightened. "Miss Sally, she stop by 'bout an hour ago, she say Luther to wash down Brandy, give him a rub and comb out his tail 'fore he do *anything* else."

Charles seemed close to tears. "Luther works for *me*. Daddy said so when he gave me the stable. Darn that Sally anyway!"

Pamela didn't know what to say. "Is Brandy another of your horses?"

"Brandy is Sally's old horse that she had when she was a small girl. He's over twenty now. He's only an old *quarter horse*, and I have to keep him in *my* stable with the thoroughbreds, just because Sally can wrap Daddy around her little finger. He has the stall next to the *heater*."

"Oh."

"Come on. I'll *see* about this."

Pamela stepped around the mounds of manure and straw in her peach satin slippers, hiking up the skirts of her gown. She was trying to figure out how Sally could have visited the stables an hour ago without anyone seeing her. She must have come here, still in her wedding gown, before she went upstairs to change.

"He never even had an English saddle on him, did you know that?" Charles was saying. "Sally always used to ride him western style. Just to annoy Mother, I think. She had the use of one of Mother's jumpers for fox hunting, but once she deliberately showed up on Brandy and scandalized the hunt club."

The horse barn was tall and cool and dim, and smelled of horseflesh and sweet hay. Charles headed purposefully toward a stall that had a worn western saddle hanging on pegs above it. A powerful, bullet-headed Negro in a shirt whose sleeves were cut off to show upper arms as thick as thighs was using a currycomb on an old bay gelding with a white blaze down his face.

"Howdy, Mist' Charles, suh," he said in a profound bass voice. "I just finishing up ol' Brandy here, an' I start on the Princess directly."

"You know you were supposed to attend to Princess Domino first," Charles said, his voice rising to an unfortunate squeak at the end. "That horse didn't need a bath. He hasn't been ridden for years."

"Oh, Mist' Charles," the groom said sorrowfully, "you know Miss Sally."

"Well . . ." Charles said irresolutely, "just hurry it up, will you."

"Yassuh," Luther said. As Charles turned to go, the deep voice boomed out again: "I give the Princess a good sponging yestiday, after Miss Sally ride her."

"She . . . she *rode* Princess Domino?" Charles sputtered. "But *nobody's* supposed to ride her except me!"

"Yassuh," Luther said, lowering his head.

Charles showed Pamela around Westbourne for another hour, but he was withdrawn and sulky. Pamela saw why Sally had a reputation for being headstrong. And where she had got it from.

Sally leaned back in the front seat and stretched like a cat. She had kept her half of the windshield tilted open about an inch, and the sixty-mile-per-hour breeze was blowing her silky blond hair into a tangle, but she didn't seem to mind.

"It's *so* nice to be away from all those *interested* eyes," she yawned.

"It's nice indeed," Brad agreed. He turned east, toward the Defense Highway. "Well, we've crossed the state line now, and this time it's legal."

"Do you think we'll be able to go around in New York without being followed by gossip columnists?"

"The New York gossip columnists persecute their own set of celebrities."

She laid a hand on his arm. "Poor Brad! I've been a trial to you, haven't I?"

"I've enjoyed every minute of it," he said gallantly.

Their six-month affair had been a constant campaign of trying to dodge the gossip reporters. Sally had always provided good copy for them. But Brad couldn't afford too many of the arch and sometimes malicious items. It made him look like a social climber. It didn't hurt to be seen with Sally by a few of the right people, but being plastered all over the papers gave the Richberg faction too great an opportunity to characterize him as a publicity hound. The worst had been the "Top Hats" item that had hinted that Brad was somehow linked with the baron's stable of scruffy eligibles. He had got a retraction on that one, but the damage had been done.

"Well it's over now," she said. "None of those lizards are going to be interested in an old married couple." She giggled. "I bet we could screw in the middle of Rockefeller Plaza in front of Mr. Walter Winchell, and we wouldn't rate an item!"

"The marriage has already been consummated," he said cautiously.

"Not *since!*"

He laughed. "Hold your horses. We're not even to Baltimore."

She cranked the window closed, took out her compact, and inspected her makeup. "Do you have any reservations?"

"None whatsoever. I think you'll do."

"Silly! I mean hotel."

"Well, I called the Ritz-Carlton. Nothing but the best for us."

"You don't have to spend money just to impress me. Any ol' fleabag will do. Mummy isn't running our honeymoon."

"I hope not." His voice was sharper than he intended. Sally grew sober. "It's bothering you, isn't it, Brad? I mean you're letting it bother you."

"I don't know what you're talking about."

"My allowance."

"My bride is entitled to a few creature comforts," he said tightly.

"Well I *am,* damn it! Anyway, it's just to please Daddy. He says five thousand a year isn't enough to live on."

Brad pulled the Airflow over to the side of the road and stopped the engine. "All right," he said, "we can call off the honeymoon."

"That's all right with me!" she flared.

They looked at each other and laughed. A moment later, they were plastered against each other, with all the knobs and handles of the Airflow getting in the way.

"There were some tourist cabins a mile or so back," Brad said. "We don't have to get to New York tonight."

"How can I put it delicately?" Senator Hale said. He put down his wineglass and gave a deep-throated chuckle. "Just before the vote, Huey Long followed the senator into the members' men's room and behaved toward his leg the way a dog behaves toward a fire hydrant. The senator had to go home and change his trousers. Huey's share-the-wealth bill had no chance of passing anyway, of course. But there sure as hell was one less vote against it."

"Marcus!" Mrs. Collier said, hiding a smile. "You mustn't tell such stories. Please remember that there are ladies present."

"Don't you include *me* in that description, Arabella," said Sally's great-aunt Cornelia. "I'm too old and withered to worry about being a lady. Tell all the scandalous stories you want, Marcus."

"What will Pamela *think* of us?" Mrs. Collier protested. "After all, this is her first real introduction to the Collier family."

Pamela tried to maintain her poise as all the alien eyes down the length of the table swung in her direction. Mrs. Collier's "little family supper" had turned out to be a gathering of twenty relations and close family friends in the long formal dining room with its Hepplewhite hunt board and ancestral portraits. The table gleamed with silver and fine crystal, two Negro maids in starched white aprons and caps did the serving, and for the amusement of the guests, Mrs. Collier had even activated the room's eighteenth-century conversation piece: an overhead fan covered with French silk wallpaper that waved gently back and forth, operated from the kitchen by a little boy—one of the maids' children—who hauled on the old pulleys.

"Don't you worry about Pamela," Aunt Cornelia said tartly. "She's no shrinking violet. I know spunk when I see it."

Pamela was grateful for Aunt Cornelia's support. At close to ninety, though she did no more entertaining and though her famous husband had been dead for forty years, Sally's great-aunt was still the doyenne of Washington society. Her dragon's reputation and acid tongue terrorized the newcomers who arrived in town with each new administration, no matter how high their official rank, and her barbed comments were often quoted by a gleeful press. It was she who had quipped of McKinley, when a large crate had been delivered to the White House, that it "contained his pedestal." She was a tiny, frail woman with liver-spotted hands and a wizened monkey-face, but in her fine bones and wide-spaced gray eyes there were hints of her former great beauty.

"Senator Long's gross habits are common knowledge," Sally's older brother Randolph said with an apologetic glance at Pamela. "I saw him in a nightclub once when he grabbed a lamb chop off a woman's plate and ate it on the way to his table. Then he wiped his hand on the cigarette girl's skirt."

"I can't stand the man's boorishness," Aunt Cornelia declared. "When he first arrived in Washington, he decided that nothing would do but that he pay a call on me. So he appeared on my doorstep at nine in the morning with his breakfast still in his teeth, and about fifty reporters behind him, and had the unmitigated *nerve* to address me as 'Cornelia.' 'Cornelia,' he said, throwing his arm around my *fragile* old shoulders, 'we southerners have to stick together.' 'Mr. Long,' I said, 'we wouldn't stick together if you'd wash your hands.'"

Senator Hale threw back his great maned head and roared with laughter. "I wish we had your courage in the Senate, Cornelia," he said. "Nobody dares challenge the Kingfish on the floor. The man's too unpredictable. You never can tell what he might say. But the tourists love him. Whenever he speaks, the galleries are packed."

"He's a law unto himself, all right," one of Sally's uncles said darkly. "Armed bodyguards surrounding him everywhere he goes—even in the Senate, where they're not supposed to be. One of them—

that Louisiana state trooper—even carries a sawed-off shotgun in a paper bag. I'd hate to see him decide to use it in the gallery."

"Marcus," Sally's father said with a frown, "how is that Senate investigation of Huey Long going? Does it have any chance?"

"No chance at all," Senator Hale said. "The judiciary committee dropped the charges like a hot potato. Now they're before the elections committee. *Their* strategy is to stall until the Congress adjourns next week, then request the Senate to discharge it from the duty of investigating Huey—without debate, of course. Roosevelt's sent about fifty Treasury agents down to Louisiana to try to get something on him for tax evasion, but I doubt that they'll get anywhere, either. Huey owns the state. Oh, he might throw them a couple of commissioners or state senators, just to keep them busy."

"Can't the man be stopped?"

"How? Roosevelt took federal patronage away from him, but Huey has more than enough state jobs to take care of his friends. Now he's gone nationwide with his Share Our Wealth clubs. Claims he's signed up three million members since February. He has this ex-minister from Shreveport, Gerald L. K. Smith, traveling around organizing the clubs for him. Smith's quite an orator. I've heard him. Some say he's getting too big for his britches. . . ."

"They're Huey Long's britches, though, aren't they?" Randolph interrupted, smiling. "This Smith fellow wears Huey's cast-off suits, and boasts about it."

"He sleeps on the floor next to Huey's bed like a dog, when it comes to that. Fawns on him. Calls him a superman. We've heard that kind of talk before, in Italy and Germany. There are too many people going around saying that America is ripe for a dictatorship, and that Huey Long fills the bill."

"The man's nothing but a clown!" sputtered a purpling man down the table.

Senator Hale shook his head regretfully. "Roosevelt doesn't think so. Neither does Jim Farley. They take him seriously. Huey says that nothing can stop him from becoming President in 1936."

"You can't mean that, Marcus," Clay Collier said.

"If Roosevelt's New Deal doesn't solve the depression, a lot of impatient people are going to be willing to follow a Man on Horseback. Let's face it, Huey's Every Man a King program has an irresistible appeal. Take the money away from the millionaires and redistribute it. Give every American family a home, an automobile, a washing machine, and a radio. A pension of thirty dollars a month for the aged."

"It's mindless. There isn't enough money to go around."

"Mindless it may be, but when Huey decides to team up with his

natural allies, the way Hitler did, watch out! Father Coughlin, the
radio priest. There's a Goebbels for him! That'll give him the anti-
Semites. Dr. Townsend with his Old Age Revolving Pension plan for
people over sixty. That's ten million votes right there. William Dudley
Pelley and his silver-shirt storm troopers. Oh, there are crackpots
enough to go around."

The senator lifted his wineglass and brooded into it, favoring the
company with what the newspapers liked to call his Imperial Roman
profile.

Randolph broke into the respectful silence that followed. "Have you
heard what Huey Long said about the NRA?" He glanced slyly at
Pamela.

"Randolph," his mother reprimanded him. "Have you forgotten
that your new brother-in-law, Bradford, is an *official* of the National
Recovery Administration?"

"Oh, Pamela won't mind. Huey says the initials stand for Nuts Running America."

Pamela laughed with the rest. NRA jokes were getting to be com-
monplace. Even Brad told them.

"That's enough talk about politics," Mrs. Collier said firmly. The
maids were clearing away the dessert dishes. The overhead fan hung
limp and dead, its pulleys unattended. "Ladies, let's leave these wicked
gentlemen to their brandy and cigars and the scandalous stories they
no doubt wish to tell. We'll join them in the drawing room later."

Instantly, Randolph was behind Pamela's chair. "Thank you," she
said as she rose.

"Well perhaps we'll have *two* Sinclairs in the family," Mrs. Collier
said with leathery kittenishness. "Did you *see* the way Randolph was
making eyes at you all through dinner?"

"Oh, I'm sure he hardly noticed me," Pamela said uncomfortably.

"Randolph's *so* handsome," sighed a random Collier aunt or cousin
whose name, Pamela had confirmed after initial disbelief, seemed actually to be Euphemia. She was a round, wheezy, red-faced woman in
frilly pastels. "He'll be quite a catch for some lucky girl."

"Yes, he's quite good-looking," Pamela said. Privately she thought
that Randolph's face was somewhat puffy, with a self-indulgent mouth.
Charles, she thought, was potentially much handsomer.

"I do wish he'd settle down and apply himself, though," Mrs.
Collier said. "He's almost thirty. He does a little something for Clay in
the brokerage firm, and of course we saw to it that he got himself
elected to the House of Delegates to make himself known, but he can't
diddle about in state politics forever. We'd like to see him run for this

district's congressional seat in thirty-six, but Marcus says he won't lift a *finger* to help him unless he shows that he's serious."

"It must be exciting, working for Marcus in Washington," Euphemia gushed.

"I don't actually work for Senator Hale," Pamela said. "I work for Harvey Lucas, his administrative assistant. I'm just one of the office help, as far as the senator is concerned. Oh, he includes me in his general 'good morning' when he walks through the outer office, but I'll bet I've had more conversation with him here today than I've had in an entire year of being on his payroll."

"Oh, you're just being modest, dear," Euphemia said. "I'm sure you have a very important job with the senator."

"No, really," Pamela protested. "I'm only a grade-four clerk-typist. Until today, Senator Hale didn't even know I existed."

"Nonsense!" Aunt Cornelia said testily. "You're a very pretty girl. Marcus always has an eye for female flesh. He started young. When he was a boy, his parents shipped him out to us at the shore one summer so they could go to Europe. That was when the judge was still alive. Marcus was fourteen. I caught him in the butler's pantry one day with my upstairs maid. He had her *perched* on a serving cart with her skirts up over her head. It had been going on the entire summer! I had to discharge the girl on the spot, of course, or else Marcus's mother would have made a fuss. Dreadful woman, one of the Maryland Webleys. I've never forgiven Marcus; I'd spent four years training the girl properly." She looked sternly at Pamela from the depths of her wing chair, a frail, shrunken creature with fierce eyes. "So you watch out for Marcus Hale, young lady, and don't let him take advantage of you."

"Really, Cornelia!" Euphemia said, fanning herself rapidly with a pastel handkerchief that she drew from the depths of her bosom.

Pamela found herself blushing. "Oh, no . . . I'm sure you're wrong. . . . Senator Hale has always been a perfect gentleman. . . ."

"Don't let that silver hair and Augustan manner fool you," Aunt Cornelia snapped. "Marcus is the same fool billy goat he was forty-five years ago."

Mrs. Collier wagged a finger. "Well, Randolph *isn't* always a perfect gentleman, so you watch out for him, hear?"

Amy Talbot, a faded, pretty woman of thirty who was the mother of two of the small children who had been given their supper earlier in the kitchen, then packed off to bed by the servants, turned from the vanity mirror where she had been drawing a careful mouth with lipstick on a wan face. "Anyway, I think it's so *brave* of you to work in an office and keep busy and all. It must be nice to have something to *do!*"

"Yes, uh, it *does* keep me busy," Pamela said, and bit her lip to keep from saying anything more. The twenty-six dollars a week she made at her job in Senator Marcus Hale's office paid for her rooming house and her meals and wardrobe, and let her send fifteen dollars a month to Iowa toward the maintenance of her mother, supplementing Brad's more substantial check. Mary Sinclair had a full-time nurse-companion now, who at least saw to it that she got her meals on time without complaints from Aunt Ottilie about the extra work. Pamela knew she was lucky. The government pay scale was the same for men and women. The going rate for a girl with her meager office skills in private business was twelve dollars a week.

"But do you think it's fair for a girl to take a job away from a man?" Cousin Enid said. She still hadn't forgiven Pamela for catching the bouquet.

"Oh, hush up," Aunt Cornelia said. "A woman has every bit as much right to work as a man. If I weren't so *ven*erable and crippled with arthritis, I'd get a job myself."

Euphemia hastened to agree. "Yes, yes indeed! Times have changed. A decent girl *can* have a job while she's waiting to be married, and I don't believe what they say about the morals of those government girls . . . I mean, oh dear, I meant to say . . ."

"Euphemia, you don't have any more sense than a mayfly," Aunt Cornelia said. "The first time you opened your mouth, all your brains fell out."

"Ladies," Mrs. Collier said serenely, "shall we join the gentlemen now?"

There was a rush to help Aunt Cornelia out of her chair and fetch her twin canes, but she brushed aid aside impatiently. "Keep your fumbling hands off me, Enid," she rasped. "I don't intend to get wrenched and pulled and dropped on my crumbling old bones. Pamela, you're a good strong quick girl. You come over here and lift me up."

"Do play for us, Pamela."

"Yes, please do."

Pamela looked around the paneled drawing room and saw a circle of polite, attentive faces all turned in her direction. Conversation had stopped. The penetrating voice of Mrs. Collier had seen to that. It was like being a little girl again and made to play for relatives.

"Oh, I haven't played the piano for almost a year," she said, coloring. "I'm sure my fingers have turned to rubber."

"You'll do just fine," Mrs. Collier said firmly. "Now, you sit down and pay us never no mind."

Feeling trapped, Pamela rose as gracefully as she could from the spindly-legged Chippendale settee where she had been squeezed between Amy Talbot and a sullen, silent Charles Collier, and crossed to the old square piano that occupied the place of honor under a darkly varnished Thomas Sully portrait of some Collier ancestor. The keys were yellowed and the fragile instrument looked as if it wouldn't take much pounding. She tried to think of something simple that wouldn't tax her out-of-practice fingers. Something very short. She settled on the little Chopin prelude in A.

The piano had no power, and sounded tinkly, but that suited the piece fine. She played with fingers that felt like sausages, and surprised herself by getting through it all right.

"That was beautiful, I declare!" Mrs. Collier said. "But so *short*. Play us something else."

"No, really I . . ."

"Pamela!" came Aunt Cornelia's commanding tone. "The judge used to say that modesty is a way of showing off. Now play, girl."

Senator Hale rescued her. She was sure he had recognized her predicament.

"First rate, my dear. But that's enough longhair stuff. How about something simple for an old philistine. Do you know 'Allan Water'?"

"I . . . I think so."

"My mother used to play it when I was a boy. We'd all gather round the piano evenings and sing the old songs. 'Allan Water' was always my favorite."

Aunt Cornelia gave a short, caustic bark. "Oh, stop that revolting sentimental mush, Marcus. You're not campaigning for votes now."

The senator laughed. "You can't fool me, Cornelia. I know you're an old softie. Go on, Pamela, play."

Pamela launched into the folk song gratefully. It was a simple, undemanding tune, and she made up a flowing accompaniment to go with it. Senator Hale stood behind her, his hand resting on her shoulder, singing in a vibrant, forthright baritone. On the second verse, Euphemia chimed in with the harmony. She had a high, clear voice, like a little girl's, and she and the senator sounded surprisingly good together. By the time they reached the last verse, half a dozen people had joined in, some raggedly, some lustily, and they all finished more or less together.

"Haven't done that for a long time," Senator Hale said, mopping his brow.

"That was so sad," Euphemia said, sniffing.

"There's nothing sad about some idiotic girl drowning herself just because a man deceived her," Aunt Cornelia snapped. "That song's always exasperated me!"

"We're having ourselves a real old-fashioned songfest," Mrs. Collier said. "Don't stop."

The gathering began to dissolve an hour or so later, when a few of the men, Senator Hale among them, adjourned to a small study for cards and whiskey, and a scattering of the older houseguests, amid yawns, retired to their rooms. Aunt Cornelia tottered off on her canes, helped by a servant. Pamela, seeing her chance, tried to say good night.

"You're not going to bed, like the old fogies?" Mrs. Collier said. "Why the night's still *young!* And we still haven't had our talk."

"It's been a long day," Pamela said.

"Young folks today have no *stamina,*" Mrs. Collier sighed. "Why, when I was a girl, we danced half the night and never went to bed at all. Well, I'll see you bright and early. The maid's laid out some of Sally's old riding clothes in your room. I'm sure they'll fit."

They had given Pamela Sally's bedroom. Once it had been an upstairs parlor; it was too large and public to be cozy. It was no room for a little girl to grow up in. The paneling was superb, with a carved Grecian pediment above the fireplace and two shell cupboards on either side. There was an elaborately scrolled highboy, two brocaded wing chairs facing each other across an expanse of worn Oriental rug, a tall four-poster bed with an embroidered canopy. Sally's old spotted rocking horse was still in a corner, and there was a gilt birdcage that presumably once had held a bird. But these childhood trophies were overwhelmed by the ancestral portrait gallery staring with stern visages from the opposite wall, reminding Sally of who she was.

The riding clothes were laid out as promised: whipcord breeches and a checkered shirt with the label of an expensive shop in them, and boots of old, supple leather. Pamela didn't bother to try them on; she thought that with luck she might make her escape after breakfast. A light cotton nightgown was neatly folded on the pillow, and the maid had provided towels and a new toothbrush.

The windows were thrown wide, but there was no breeze to cut through the stifling heat. Pamela resigned herself to a night of tossing and turning. But the chirping of night insects and the distant whisper of the river were peaceful and reassuring, and sleep tugged at her within minutes.

A bar of light falling across her face awakened her. At first she thought it was morning, then she saw that it was the door swinging open. It was Randolph standing there in shirt-sleeves, his tie hanging undone and his jacket trailing carelessly from one hand. He was unsteady on his feet. He closed the door behind him and switched on the light.

"Hardly had a chance tonight to talk to my new sister-in-law," he mumbled.

Pamela glanced at the shelf clock over the fireplace. "Randolph, it's three o'clock. I was asleep."

"Plenny time for sleep. Ev'body's 'sleep, even Mother. Nobody to talk to anymore, damn them. This is a spesh . . . a special occasion."

He stumbled across the room and sat down heavily on the bed. His face was blotched and his breath reeked of brandy.

Pamela sat up, covering herself with the sheet. "Randolph, please go to bed. It's late. We can talk some other time."

"Hell with that. We're big boys and girls now. We can stay up and talk if we want to without asking Mummy's permission, can't we? D'you have any cigarettes?"

Pamela saw that she'd have to humor him. "All right, I'll have one smoke with you. Just one. Then you'll have to leave."

She reached for the pack of Chesterfields at bedside, holding up the sheet one-handed, and passed it to him. He took one for himself, fumbling the light, and put the pack down without offering her a cigarette or lighting it. He was very drunk. Pamela extracted a cigarette and managed to light it for herself, keeping the sheet pinned up with her elbows. Here in this alien room with the varnished face of the Collier who had been secretary of the navy under Tyler—or was it attorney general under Polk?—glowering at her from the wall, she was very aware of the flimsy nightgown and the explicit shapes of her breasts beneath it.

"Mumsie darling put you in Sally's room," he said with alcoholic harshness. He took a drag on the cigarette and had a coughing spell.

"Yes."

"Dear, cunnin' li'l sister Sally. I'm surprised she didn't marry a horse. Or is there something about brother Brad I don't know?"

He laughed explosively, and started coughing again.

"Randolph . . ."

"I know, I know. Mus'n't talk dirty." He waved his arm in a large uncontrolled gesture, dribbling ashes. "Didn't 'tend—intend anything by it. Jus' funny seeing you in Sally's bed like that, thas' all. You even sorta look like her, with that blond hair and cute nose. I used to come in and talk to her at bedtime before she moved out." He squinted at her, one-eyed. "What do you suppose brother Brad saw in li'l Sally? Think there's anything to Freud and that twaddle about uncosh—un-

*con*scious—incest? Sibling . . . sibling *rib*aldry!" He choked on his laughter.

"Randolph, that's enough. I don't think you're as drunk as you're pretending."

He looked disappointed. "Can't fool li'l Pamela." His speech was less slurred. "I'm pretty drunk, though. Can't blame me for trying. There's courage in brandy, I always say."

He reached out and playfully tried to pull the sheet away from her body. Pamela twisted away.

"Randolph, I think you better leave. Now."

He grinned. "Or what? You'll scream? Not in the Collier household. Think of the embarrassment."

He lunged suddenly, and Pamela found him lying on top of her, his breath overpowering in her face, his hand trying to pull the sheet from between them. She tried to push him off her, but he was a dead weight.

"Stop it," she whispered. "What are you *doing?*"

"Please, Pamela fair," he pleaded. "Just let me for a minute. It won't mean anything to you. It's nothing to a woman. Just lie still for a minute, and you can make me very happy."

She heaved with all her strength and got him off her. His overbred face was flushed and petulant, like a small boy's. He was breathing hard.

"You *spoiled* it!" he said.

"Just get *out* of here," she said, trying to conceal her loathing. "I'm going to forget that anything happened here tonight, and you can do the same. You've had too much to drink. You don't know what you're doing."

A sly look came over his weak, handsome face. "I know what I'm doing all right. Think I don't know about that two-bit courthouse shyster in Iowa? Mumsie made inquiries. But you passed. Mumsie would be pleased. Keep it all in the family. Make a man out of me, she said. If it works, we can be married."

He was staring at the movement of her breasts under the nightgown. The sheet was tangled around her waist. He reached out and grabbed her painfully, as if he were turning a doorknob.

"Get . . . get out of here you . . . you monster," she whispered. The enormity of what he had said left her incapable of action. What had that terrifying woman learned about Carl?

"Come on," he said, squeezing.

Pamela yelped. Someone rapped on the door. "Pamela, are you all right?" a deep male voice said. Randolph jerked his hand away as if it had been burned.

"Come in, oh, please come in," she said.

The door opened and Senator Hale stepped into the room, wearing an old maroon dressing gown over striped pajamas and carrying a tumbler of whiskey. He took in the situation at a glance.

"You'd best toddle off to bed, boy, and don't be bothering ladies in the middle of the night."

"I was just . . . I was just . . ." Randolph's mouth opened and closed, fishlike.

"No doubt," the senator said dryly.

They exchanged a level stare. Randolph stood up. "Just as you say, Uncle Marcus," he said with a smirk on his face. He picked his jacket off the floor. At the door he turned and said, "Good night, dear sister-in-law."

"Are you all right?" Senator Hale said. He set his whiskey glass down on the night table and tilted Pamela's chin back for a look at her face.

Her teeth were chattering, and she had a crawly feeling all over her skin. For a moment she thought she was going to throw up, then she mastered her nausea.

"I'm fine." She remembered the sheet and pulled it up.

"I was just passing by. I couldn't sleep and I went downstairs to fix myself a little nightcap. I thought I heard the sounds of distress. Was Randolph making a nuisance of himself?"

"He . . . he . . ." She couldn't make herself go on. She was flooded with disgust at Randolph's behavior, and still more at the instigation he had received from his awful mother.

Senator Hale looked at her shrewdly. "You weren't in any danger of anything but some unpleasantness from Randolph, you know. He's a pansy, though he hasn't faced up to it yet. Neither has Arabella. She keeps hoping for the best. Randolph likes colored boys. He's going to get himself into serious trouble someday. That's why I won't help him run for a seat in the House, no matter what Arabella thinks."

"I don't think I want to hear any more."

"No—quite right. We're a backbiting family." He threw back his silver head and laughed. "Well don't worry about Bradford. Sally's her own person. She managed to climb out of this snakepit, clawing and scratching all the way. That's what her kicking up her heels for the gossip columns was all about. That marriage will work, though I'm the only person around here who seems to think so. Brad handles himself well, from what I've seen. He won't have any trouble from the Colliers, and neither will you."

His voice was fatherly, comforting. Pamela felt soothed and pro-

tected by his patriarchal bulk looming beside her bed. The worn
bathrobe gave him a reassuringly human touch.

All at once, without meaning to, she began to cry.

A look of quick concern crossed his face. "You're upset. Look at
you, you're shivering."

"No . . . no . . . I'll be all right. I just . . ."

"Here, take a swallow of this. Go on. It'll make you feel better."

Obediently she drank down some of his bourbon, holding the heavy
glass in two hands like a child. It was fiery and powerful, burning all
the way down.

"Better?"

She nodded. The 120-proof bourbon spread a numbing warmth
through her body. She was reminded of the times that Carl Fuller had
forced neat whiskey on her, to calm her down, he said, and she drove
the image from her mind. This was different. She felt at peace. She
yawned.

"Good," he said. "You won't have any trouble getting to sleep now.
I hope you appreciate the bourbon. It's not your run-of-the-mill stuff.
It's the real Kaintuck sippin' whiskey, private from the distillery. Clay
stocks it especially for me." He laughed with simple pleasure. "The
senatorial special. Goes down like syrup, doesn't it?"

Pamela took another swallow. It was too soon for the whiskey to
have taken effect, but perhaps because the taste of it triggered her
body's memory, she began to float.

"That's enough," he said sternly. He took the glass from her hands
and set it down on the night table.

Marcus Hale was almost forty years older than she was, older than
her own father would have been if he had lived. He was a large, powerful man with an air of importance and authority radiating from him
like a tangible aura. It was flattering to be the object of his solicitude,
and Pamela surrendered to the snug, protected feeling that his presence imparted. She listened, drifting lazily, to his low, rich voice as he
droned on about nothing in particular, and it seemed entirely natural
when he took her by the shoulders and kissed her on the mouth.

His kiss was greedy. It demanded a return. His breath smelled of
mouthwash and bourbon and tobacco. It was all very dreamlike and
inevitable. She let him pull the cotton nightgown over her head and
push her with firm insistence down to the pillow. Her hands lay pas-
sively by her sides, fingers curled upward. He loomed in her vision, the
pink straining face with its broad shelf of brow and Roman nose, the
veined eyes, the tufts of gray hair on the slablike muscles of his shoulders. He was wheezing in her ear. His large, coarse hands moved carefully over her body, as if he feared to startle her. He groaned as if in

pain, and she was aware of the faint smell of old flesh under the astringent alcohol. She felt nothing but a pleasant faraway warmth, but that was enough for this time and place.

"Not bad for an old man," he said as he put his pajamas back on. Pamela forgave him the words. She felt fond and indulgent. Men were boastful little boys. He belted his robe. "How did I ever overlook a girl like you, right under my nose?"

He opened the door a little and looked both ways down the corridor. With a last backward glance, he left.

Pamely yawned and stretched. Under the stiff, disapproving gaze of the Collier ancestor who had been a Cabinet secretary under Tyler, or was it Polk, she fell into a deep, dreamless sleep.

In the morning, she didn't see Senator Hale at breakfast. He had left early, Mrs. Collier told her, pleading that he had to get back to Washington.

The Hepplewhite hunt board was laden with an enormous breakfast warming in chafing dishes. Pamela ate her scrambled eggs and kidneys and grilled tomatoes and buttered scones with strawberry jam with a hearty appetite, while Aunt Cornelia looked on and shuddered.

"You're not wearing your riding clothes," Mrs. Collier said.

"No," Pamela said, buttering another scone.

"Well that's all right. We'll wait while you change."

"I've got to get back to the office. I have a lot of work to do."

"But Marcus gave you the day off."

"If I leave now, I can be there for after lunch, anyway."

She stood up.

"Now Pamela dear . . ." Mrs. Collier's voice trailed off as she looked at Pamela's face.

Pamela got one of the male guests to drive her to the station. In the train, as she watched the green Virginia countryside crawl by, she examined her feelings about Carl Fuller. The numbness had worn off, and it didn't hurt at all.

She had come up in the world, she thought wryly. Poor Carl was only a district judge.

23

The pain came again in a great wave that made Junie cry out. The circle of women's faces that hung over her flickered like candle flames.

"Here, bite on this here stick," Miz Garr said disapprovingly. She was their neighbor, a harsh narrow-skulled Colorado woman who lived in the next tent.

Ma Kinney pushed the stick aside. "She kin yell out if she wants. Go on, child. The first one always comes hard."

"Where's Floyd?" Junie said.

"He's hanging around outside the tent, where he hadn't ought to be. I'm going to shoo him away in a little while. It ain't fitting for him to be listening to this. It's past daylight anyway. Time for him to be in the fields with the others, chopping cotton."

"I . . . I'm sorry," Junie whispered, reaching for the gnarled hand. "I should be . . . you should . . ."

"Now you hush," Ma Kinney said. "You worked past your time as it was. So don't you be worrying about doing your share. You'll be swinging a hoe with the rest of us soon enough. As for me"—she glared defiantly at no one in particular—"I aim to take this day off myself."

"All this fuss about having a baby," Miz Garr sniffed.

"Junie's not as strong as some," Ma Kinney said. "She wasn't born to a hard life. But she tries her best."

Junie clutched Ma Kinney's hand. "I want Floyd with me."

"I never heard of such a thing!" Miz Garr said.

"It just ain't proper for him to be in here at this time," Ma Kinney said gently. "Now don't you fret. You're goin' to be jus' fine. Sue Ellen, you come over here and fan the flies off her. I'm goin' out to talk to Floyd."

The pain grabbed and squeezed again. Junie gasped and bit her lip. This time she was able to keep herself from crying.

"Pains comin' closer," Miz Garr said. The two women looked at each other. Ma Kinney hurried out through the tent flap.

Junie clenched her jaw. Her face was clammy. After a while the pain died down. Her arms felt too weak to lift. The interior of the tent swelled into focus again, lit by the lantern hanging from the ridgepole overhead and by the gray light that was beginning to seep through all the threadbare places.

The tent had been provided by the grower. Like the others in the cotton camp, it had been raised over a sort of wooden box without a floor. Some of the camps had wooden platforms for the tents, and some even had shacks made out of pine boards, with proper wooden floors and screens on the windows to keep out the flies. Junie had prayed that her baby would be born in one of those, but they had to keep moving with the swarms of migrant workers who picked the fields bare like locusts and moved on. When her time came, the Kinneys were living in a camp owned by a man named Roscoe T. Perry. Mr. Perry's camp only had tents with dirt floors. There were four privies for every fifty tents, but you couldn't use half of them because new pits hadn't been dug for a long time and they were overflowing. There were a lot of flies in the camp, and no way to keep them out. The camp had once had running water and a cold shower bath, but the county health authorities had turned them off after a typhus scare two years ago, and the workers had to go a mile down the road for water and haul it back in rusty five-gallon cans, backbreaking to carry. Consequently, water for washing and cooking was precious.

When the cotton-picking season had ended in February, the Kinneys had planned to move on with the Oklahoma people they had traveled to Arizona with. A California labor contractor named Mortimer had distributed handbills saying that the pea-picking season would begin in the Imperial Valley about March first. The advertisements had promised a good camp, good water, and a good store. Most of the Okies had packed up and left.

But Mr. Perry had gulled the Kinneys with vague promises of work for those who stayed on. He'd even hinted at tractor work for Purley at two or three dollars a day. Too late, they realized that he was simply trying to get pickers to stay on to clean up the fields. The tractor work went to a small aristocracy of year-round workers who lived with their families on the Perry ranch. For the Kinneys and the other people who had been fooled into staying on, there were only two or three days a week of chopping cotton at fifteen cents an hour.

And now, Junie thought, she had made Ma Kinney miss a whole day's earnings!

The McClains had been tricked by Mr. Perry's promises, too. McClain had ignored the warnings of the more experienced transients. He had been sure that as an experienced cotton man, he could get one of the coveted tractor jobs. But he had used up his small stake, waiting. Finally he had sold off his old Model T just to get a few dollars to feed his children with. Now he was trapped, unable to look for work outside of walking distance, unable to buy food anywhere but Mr. Perry's store, where prices were high.

Ma Kinney was stubbornly determined that the Kinney clan would never become that desperate. Everyone turned over their wages to her, even Purley. She hoarded every penny that wasn't needed for food so that they would have gasoline money and traveling expenses when it came time to pull up stakes for California.

She refused to put up with Purley's impatience. "No, we're not goin' to pick up and go afore knowin' what we're goin' to find. We're not goin' to end up like the McClains, selling the truck for eating money. We missed out on the peas, fools that we were. Missed out on lettuce, too, from what I hear. That's done—no sense crying. Now we're goin' to set here, and not use up our money, till the end of the month. Junie shouldn't travel with the baby so close, anyway. And in July, we can pick figs near Fresno, like that Mexican fella told us."

Junie had learned all there was to know about picking cotton the first day. She bought her own sack for a dollar from the first grower they had worked for in Graham County, just across the Arizona border. A cotton sack was a huge thing, big enough to get inside of it yourself. You slung it over your shoulder by a sort of strap, and dragged it behind you as you worked your way across the field in a half crouch. As the bag filled up, it became heavier, and the strap dug into the raw place on your shoulder, and your back was near breaking from all the stooping. Yet Junie had seen women dragging small babies along on the trailing sack. It was easier pulling the extra weight along than going back for the baby every few yards.

When your sack was full, you brought it to a scale hanging from a tall tripod made of three timbers nailed together. The weigher called out your weight and wrote it down on his tally sheet. You wrote it down, too, if you were smart, so the man couldn't cheat you when it was time to line up and be paid. They always tried to cheat you by at least a few pounds.

It was a good field, that first one, and Junie had picked nearly seventy pounds of the swollen brown bolls. "You done good for a learner," Ma Kinney had told her, and she had swelled with pride until she found out that Purley and Floyd had picked more than three hundred pounds each—almost as much as the circulating handbills said you could get—and that even Sue Ellen had picked twice as much as she had. After that, she drove herself to do better, but it was hard with her belly so huge and the backaches all the time.

She had earned her keep, though. After a couple of weeks she had taken over the record-keeping job from Wesley, by family consensus. She was good at adding up figures, and making sure the Kinneys got what was coming to them at the end of the day. If there was any arguing to be done, Purley did it for her, and the weighing man usually backed down when he saw Purley's scowl and tightening fists.

They made good money, too, with seven of them working, until the Arizona picking season came to an end, and there was nothing to do except work cleaning up the fields at whatever the owner wanted to pay. But Ma Kinney had a milk bottle full of nickels and dimes and quarters and dollar bills, saved from the good months, hidden in the cab of the Reo truck. Ma wouldn't let them spend money on foolishness, like some of the Okies who headed for town as soon as they had two nickels to rub together.

Junie didn't like going to town, anyway. Okies weren't welcome there, and the merchants made them feel it. "Ain't no difference between an Okie and a nigger, as far as I'm concerned," she heard one of the loungers in front of the general store say as she passed by one Saturday afternoon. "Yes there is," another lounger answered. "A nigger knows his place." She was glad Purley had walked ahead; there was no telling what he might have done if he'd overheard.

It was no good telling herself that she wasn't really an Okie. "A blackbird that flocks with starlings is known as a starling," was the way Ma Kinney put it. She forbade them to deny it. "We Kinneys got too much pride to care what trash thinks."

The pain washed over her again and bathed her in sweat. When her vision cleared, Junie saw the dirt-encrusted fingernails of Miz Garr's splayed hand resting on her ballooning belly.

"That was a good strong one," Miz Garr said. She withdrew her hand and Junie saw a grimy print on the spotless white birthing shift that Ma Kinney had sewn for her out of the last hoarded sheet from

Iowa. "Now let's just see how you're openin' up," Miz Garr said, and lifted the hem of the shift.

Junie knew that she didn't want those hands probing her. "Ma!" she cried.

The tent flap opened, and she had a glimpse of Floyd's overalled form walking away in the gray dawn.

"I don't know why this girl takes on so," Miz Garr said.

Ma Kinney tightened her lips at the sight of the handprint. She became very busy around Junie, not looking at Miz Garr. "Sue Ellen," she said, "I told you to keep fannin' the flies off her. Never mind, I'll do it. Wet me a cloth in the can of water over there, so I can wipe off this child's face."

Six hours later the baby still had not shown itself. Junie was woozy with exhaustion. "You got to keep tryin', child," Ma Kinney said gently.

Miz Garr, hovering behind Ma Kinney, said, "Hope it ain't comin' breech first. A gal this size, that's trouble. Baby can strangle in its own cord, be born dead. Lot of things can go wrong. Worst is when you see a foot first. We had an old midwife in Haskell County, a hill woman, who still carried the old child-breaking hooks tied to her apron, in case a baby had to be carved up and dragged out in pieces."

"You hush up now," Ma Kinney said, whirling on her. "Can't you see you're upsetting this child!"

"Well, if a body's help ain't appreciated," Miz Garr grumbled.

"Of course it's appreciated," Ma said quickly. "And we do thank you for looking after Sue Ellen's little ones all those times."

"Glad to be neighborly," Miz Garr said, placated.

Junie screamed. There was a terrible grinding pain, almost continuous. She writhed on the thin mattress.

Ma Kinney felt under the shift. "I think it's coming," she said.

"About time," Miz Garr said.

But it was almost two hours more before the baby's head showed itself. Junie had been in labor for more than a day now. Through a blurred haze, she heard Ma Kinney's voice say, "Push, child, you got to push now." She tried, but her worn-out muscles refused to respond, and that frightened her. Through a cottony film, Miz Garr appeared, holding a knife.

"No," Junie moaned, "don't!"

"It won't hurt," Miz Garr said. "Will it, Miz Kinney?"

"No," Ma Kinney said unwillingly. "I guess it won't."

Miz Garr picked up the edge of the mattress and slid the knife underneath.

"There's some as say a knife under the mattress helps ease the birth," Ma Kinney said apologetically.

There was another heaving spasm. "I can't," Junie sobbed.

"Of course you kin, child," Ma Kinney said. "I'll help you. Now when the next pain comes, bear down hard." She had one hand under the birthing shift, the other on Junie's belly. Junie could feel the calloused fingers exerting a gentle pressure. When the next contraction came, she squeezed her eyes shut and tried.

"You're doing just fine," Ma Kinney said. "I can feel the chin now."

"Head too fast, birth hard at the last," Miz Garr chanted. "Push it back in, Miz Kinney."

Ma Kinney ignored her. There was an enormous heaving thrust, and Junie strained with all her might. Through the pain there was an indescribable feeling of relief.

"Head's through, and it's turned for the shoulder to come," Ma Kinney announced. "Everything's goin' to be all right, child."

And then, in the sunbaked tent, through the buzzing of flies, there was the miraculous sound of a baby crying.

After the cord was cut and tied, Miz Garr, cooing, tried to take the infant. But somehow Ma Kinney's sharp elbow got in the way, and the baby ended up in the arms of Sue Ellen, who bore it away. Ma Kinney stayed with Junie, massaging her belly, until she delivered the afterbirth. Miz Garr had stomped out of the tent, taking her kitchen knife with her. "Go to sleep, child," Ma Kinney said.

When Junie awoke, sun was streaming in through the tent flap. She heard the small sounds that meant people were back from the fields and moving about. Alva McClain, her thin face shadowed by a poke bonnet, was on her knees beside the mattress, scrubbing the boards it rested on with precious water and an even more precious cake of soap.

Mrs. McClain shrank in her faded dress when she saw Junie's eyes on her. "I was just stayin' by you to keep the flies off while your ma rested," she said in the apologetic way she had of talking. "Ain't good to have flies on you after a birth."

"Where's the baby?" Junie said.

"I'll go git your ma," Mrs. McClain said, and hurried out of the tent, her thin shoulders hunched.

They brought the baby to her, wrapped in a piece of a discarded cotton sack that had been scrubbed and boiled until it was as soft as chamois. "It's a boy," Ma Kinney said.

She took the small bundle. It was a horrid little boiled red thing with a distorted head.

"What's wrong with it?" she said, frightened.

Ma Kinney looked at her steadily. Behind her, Alva McClain wrung her birdy hands. "Ain't nothing wrong with it, Junie child."

"Its head!"

Comprehension dawned in Ma Kinney's eyes. "That fool Garr woman skeered you with her stories! A baby's head bones are just naturally soft, child. Sometimes when a woman's too narrow, the head bones git squeezed out of shape so it can get through. It ain't nothing to fret about. In a week or two, the shape of that head will be just as normal as anythin'. My own firstborn, Purley, had a head like that when *he* was born, and you kin see that Purley's all right."

She spoke so matter-of-factly that Junie knew she was telling the truth. "Can I see Floyd now?" she said.

"Why sure, child. Alva, would you go fetch Floyd?"

Mrs. McClain ducked out of the tent. All the women called her Alva now, not Miz McClain. Her status had been readjusted after her husband had sold his car for food money. There was an obscure shame in being that desperate—in not even being able to move on in search of better things—and everybody accepted that, both the McClains and their neighbors.

"Poor soul," Ma Kinney said. "You know that cotton sack the baby's wrapped in came from her. I didn't want to take it, but I couldn't hurt her pride."

The munificence of the gift was staggering. The piece of material might have made shirts for the McClain children, drawers for Mrs. McClain, and undervest for Mr. McClain. Junie didn't want to think about it.

Floyd came in, looking sheepish. He had stopped to put on a clean shirt and overalls after coming in from the fields. His hair was plastered down, and his face and big-knuckled hands were scrubbed raw. He approached the mattress shyly and stood there in mute agony.

"Isn't he cute, Floyd?" she said with preternatural animation. "Isn't he just the cutest baby you ever saw?"

She was all too aware of how she must look. One hand flew to her hair and found, to her amazement, that someone had combed it for her while she slept; probably Sue Ellen.

"He . . . he's sort o' wrinkled, ain't he?" Floyd mumbled.

"Silly! All new babies are wrinkled."

Purley came crowding into the tent with Sue Ellen and Wesley. Sue Ellen had left her children screaming outside. Wesley hung behind, blinking through the twisted frames of his eyeglasses.

"That's a fine baby," Sue Ellen said.

Junie blushed with pride. "Do you want to hold him, Floyd?"

Floyd recoiled, as if someone had offered him a rattlesnake.

"Go on, you coon-footed mule!" Purley said boisterously. "That's your own *son* there. By God, sometimes I thought you didn't know what it was for, but you're sure enough a father now!"

Floyd smiled weakly.

Wesley tried to come to Floyd's rescue. "And . . . and you're an *uncle*," he said, nudging Purley.

Purley looked back over his shoulder at Wesley and said: "And you're a *monkey's* uncle!" Pleased with his sally, he let out a whoop.

"Purley, you quiet down," Ma Kinney said. "That's a beautiful baby."

Realization of what he had said struck Purley. "I didn't mean it that way," he mumbled. "I mean . . ."

"Whatcha gonna call him?" Sue Ellen said.

"I'm going to name him after his grandfather," Junie said.

Bradford Kinney. It had a good solid sound to it. There was nothing left of the Sinclair inheritance but a name, but at least it was a good one. Her father *and* her brother, it would keep on reminding her of them both . . . but she would never call her son Brad. He would be Bradford. Her years of growing up in Beulah were fading like a dream, but a piece of the dream would be alive.

"Pa will be real proud," Purley said humbly, trying to make amends. "And Leander's a fine name."

"We can call him Lee for short," Sue Ellen said.

"Thank you, child," Ma Kinney said. She turned to the others. "Where's Pa?"

"He's gone for firewood," Wesley said. "I'll go tell him." He escaped through the flap.

The shriveled little creature in Junie's arms began to cry. She hugged it against her.

"All you men get out of this tent now," Ma Kinney said.

The AAA man was nervous. "If Mr. Roscoe T. Perry catches us messing around his migrant workers' camp," he said, "he'll have us run off the place with a shotgun."

The photographer from the Federal Rural Relief Administration went right on snapping his pictures. "That's why my boss is coordinating this through the Agriculture Department. He figures that with you along, no grower is going to take a chance on holding up his cotton acreage allotment checks."

"It don't exactly work that way out here," the AAA man said sourly.

He didn't like the photographer that FERA's Rural Rehabilitation

Division had sent out from Washington. The photographer was a city type: young, predatory, and brash. He was sharp-featured and quick-moving, and wore a cheap blue suit and thin city shoes that were covered with dust and cotton lint.

The AAA man couldn't understand why the Federal Rural Relief Administration wanted pictures anyway. His district supervisor had mumbled something about them being needed for the historical record, but among the growers—and even some of the migrants—the picture taking was widely regarded as government spying.

"Jesus, look at that!" the photographer said.

"Look at what?"

"There! That's the picture I want," the photographer said, unslinging his little German camera.

"I don't see anything 'cept a little girl with a dirty face sittin' in the dust playing with a doll without a head."

"That's *it!* That's the picture! With that row of tattered tents behind her, that says it all." He began stalking the little girl carefully, so as not to frighten her.

"Maybe you'd better ask that child's mama if it's all right to take the picture," the AAA man said uncomfortably. "She might want to wash the little girl's face, put a clean dress on her if she got another one, get that broken toy out of sight."

"You don't get it, do you? That dirty face and headless doll are the *point*. That's what makes it art."

He got down on his belly in the dust like a snake, blue suit and all, and inched forward. At the last moment, when the child looked up, the little camera went click.

"Got it," the photographer said, standing up and dusting himself off.

"Crazy man," the AAA agent muttered.

"You don't understand," the photographer laughed. "This is a new art form. Photo journalism. You don't pose the pictures. You show what life is really like. Wait and see, some day there'll be a magazine where the pictures tell it all instead of the words."

The AAA man shook his head in disgust. The way the photographer carried on, a person might think he had a proper professional camera with a tripod instead of that little toy of his. He followed unwillingly as the photographer continued prowling through the camp.

"There's a good shot."

The photographer pointed his camera at a sagging outhouse with daylight showing through its spaced boards and its door hanging half off. An evil cloud of buzzing flies hung over it, glinting green in the sunlight. The stench made it unapproachable. Only a few yards away was a well for drinking water, but, the AAA man was glad to note, the pump handle had been removed and a seal put on it by the health authorities.

"I suppose you call that art, too. A picture of a shithouse."

"It shows conditions in this camp, doesn't it?" the photographer said.

"I suppose it does." The two men fell silent.

The photographer turned toward a row of tents, the AAA man reluctantly in tow. They were old army tents, mildewed and torn, erected on rough wooden boxes. Some of them had stovepipes sticking out of the flaps. Most of them were unoccupied now, after the picking season.

Some men were hanging around outside one of the tents, squatting aimlessly in the dust. A woman came out, spoke to them, and went back inside.

"I wonder what's going on."

They wandered over. "Hi," the photographer said.

The men looked up incuriously. After a while, one of them said, "Howdy."

The AAA man knew it was going to be up to him. "Hot," he said. He took off his Stetson and mopped his forehead to show that he meant it.

The old fellow answered. "It's hot, sure enough," he said, nodding his head.

"Not too many people left in camp."

That was self-evident, so no one answered.

"What's going on in there?" the photographer burst in, jerking his head toward the tent.

They inspected him with mild astonishment. One of the younger men, a lantern-jawed fellow with burning dark eyes under a shelf of bone, took pity on this strange specimen and said, "Woman had a baby."

The photographer darted a feral look at the AAA man, whose heart shrank.

"This fellow over here's the father," volunteered another man, blinking at them through wire-framed eyeglasses that had been taped together.

"Say, that's real fine," the photographer said. The indicated father shuffled his feet uncomfortably and stared at the ground. "Do you think we could take a picture of the mother and child?"

The lantern-jawed fellow rose to his feet. He was shirtless under his bib overalls, and the muscles of his wiry arms were hard knotted cords. "Where did you say you fellows were from?" he said suspiciously.

The AAA man mopped his brow again. "We're from the government. I'm with the AAA, and he's from FERA."

The big Okie scowled. "That's a lot of letters."

"I'm from the Agricultural Adjustment Administration, and he's from the Federal Rural Relief Administration."

The Okie was still scowling, so the photographer added quickly, "Let's just say he works for Henry Wallace and I work for Harry Hopkins."

"We don't want no relief," the man said. "We take care of ourselves."

"No relief. We just want to take pictures."

He was met by four suspicious stares. "How much do you charge?" the old man said.

The tent flap opened and a gray-haired woman wearing men's shoes looked out. "What are you raisin' your voice for, Purley?"

Purley's demeanor turned respectful. "These here fellows'r from the govmint, Ma. They want to take a picture of Junie and the baby."

The woman's raw hands fluttered around her straggling hair. "Oh—will you kindly wait a minute?" She disappeared into the tent. A moment later she came back. "You kin come in now. Junie's decent."

The photographer scrambled to climb through the flap. The AAA man followed and the four men crowded the entrance behind them. The tent was furnished with an overturned bucket and a couple of wooden boxes for seating. The floor was dirt, swept smooth, but somebody had laid down a couple of wooden boards to keep a mattress off the ground. On the mattress lay a pretty little dark-haired girl, holding a wizened infant wrapped in a cotton sack.

The photographer shot the AAA man a look of triumph.

"Great," he said. "Just great. Would somebody open that tent flap all the way? Fine. And would you men stand out of the entrance so you don't block the light?" He was taking charge, the way photographers did, and everybody moved respectfully to obey him.

"Ain't you goin' to use no flash powder?" the old man said.

"No, no, available light's fine," the photographer said distractedly. "Look, would you spread that sack a little so I can see the lettering on it? Fine. Now, honey, you just sit up with the baby in your arms and don't look at the camera."

"Here, I kin fix her hair, maybe tie a ribbon in it," the old woman fussed.

"No, it's fine just the way it is."

The little camera clicked away, while the young photographer danced around in a crouch and crooned to himself. At last he finished, doing something to the camera like the sound of a watch winding. He produced a worn notebook and the stub of a pencil from the pocket of his baggy suit. He gave a sort of false city smile.

"That's a fine-looking baby," he said. "What's his name?"

The girl looked up with shy pride. She couldn't have been much more than fifteen. She was pretty, the AAA man thought, but she wouldn't stay pretty long. Her face was wan and her eyes were ringed and hollow from exhaustion, but she had finely shaped features, like a lot of these people.

"He's named after both his grandfathers," she said, with a trace of something that might have been defiance. "Leander Bradford Kinney."

24

Gordon stood in the shadows outside Cullum Hall and listened to the sound of dance music floating through the upper windows. The orchestra was playing a fox-trot arrangement of "Army Blue." That was traditionally the last dance. In a few minutes, graduation hop would be over.

A cabbie from the long rank waiting in front of the massive marble building spotted Gordon under the tree and came strolling over, a cigarette dangling from his lower lip.

"Hey, sojer boy, how long is this thing going to last?" He was a scrawny man with a cap pulled down low over his eyes, his face waxy in the yellow lamplight.

"Sir," Gordon said, "it won't be much longer now."

The cabbie tilted his head toward the cannon-flanked entrance. "Big shindig inside, huh?"

"Sir, this is the final dance for the First Classmen before they receive their army commissions tomorrow. It's the biggest event of June Week."

From the second-floor ballroom Gordon could hear the sweet sound of the saxophones playing the sentimental tune, and his mind filled in the words:

. . . We'll bid farewell to cadet gray,
And don the army blue. . . .

In his imagination he could see the scene inside. The white and gold walls of the ballroom would be hung with the decorations that Gordon and the other plebes had worked so hard to put up that afternoon. The colored spotlights would be picking out the dancers on the floor; the last dance of the evening was always reserved for your invited drag. And Nellie Wilson would be in Crowley's arms, pressed pliantly against him as he waltzed her around the floor.

Gordon burned when he thought of it. He had no right to, he knew. As Hibbert had told him at the beginning of the year, "Nice Nellie" only went out with Firsts. "You'll just have to wait till you're one too, you poor sap," Hibbert had said. The only reason Gordon had been able to get together with Nellie at all was that she had been stuck at the Point over Plebe Christmas, and the cadet hostess had drafted her and all the other eligible girls at the post to fill in at the plebe hops that week—the only hops that the underprivileged plebes would be permitted to enjoy until they became yearlings. Gordon, in fact, was himself required to attend. Along with the compulsory dancing lessons, it was part of West Point's scheme for turning him into an officer and a gentleman.

Gordon had found Nellie Wilson's name on his hop card for two dances, and afterward she had allowed him to walk her home to officers' quarters, where she lived with her father. Nellie had been sulky about her forced duty, but with the rest of the school away for Christmas, she had no alternative to boredom but the plebe hops, and she had finally condescended to answer Gordon in something more than monosyllables. Gordon had managed to see her again during his week of relative freedom, despite Captain Wilson's glowering intimidation when he called for her.

On the last day, Nellie had coaxed and wheedled Gordon into a stroll along Flirtation Walk, though she knew it was off limits to plebes. It would have meant expulsion if he had been caught. She had led him to Kissing Rock and waited impatiently until he had taken advantage of the iron-clad tradition that a girl had to kiss her escort if she didn't want the teetering boulder to come crashing down on them. But when things had become hot, she had pushed Gordon away and said sharply, "That's enough." When the First Class returned after Christmas, Nellie had suddenly acted as if Gordon no longer existed.

"Yeah," the cabbie said, "I seen the other dances they're holding tonight at the Thayer Hotel and the gym. Every cab in Highland Falls and Newburgh is tied up. How come you ain't inside, sonny?"

"Sir, there is no hop for the plebe class."

"Yeah?" The cabbie wasn't very interested. He ground out his cigarette on the walk. "Jeez, I hate picking up broads here. They don't know how to tip. You'd think their boy friends would ride them to their hotels, or at least slip the driver a little something in advance."

"Sir." Gordon drew himself up. "A cadet isn't allowed to have any money. A woman visitor is expected to pay for herself. And a cadet has to return to barracks after putting her in a cab going off the reservation."

The cabbie pulled back a vulpine lip. "Yeah? I guess you sojer boys don't get much of a chance to get off your rocks. Hey, what's that?"

Above, a harsh roll of drums interrupted "Army Blue," and the hired orchestra swung into "Auld Lang Syne."

"They'll be coming out now," Gordon said stiffly. "Sir."

The crowd came spilling out onto the walk a few moments later. At the curb, drivers who had been sitting on their running boards or lounging against their engines sprang to attention and opened rear doors. The cabbie who had been talking to Gordon turned away to search out his fare and her escort.

Gordon moved closer to the tree trunk, feeling suddenly out of place. He located Crowley and Nellie in the chattering throng. Crowley cut a dashing figure in his white trousers and dress coat, with his big ears and beetling brow shadowed by the white summer cap. Nellie clung to his arm. She looked fresh and beautiful in a lacy sea-green gown that swirled around her legs as she walked. Her strawberry blond hair was done in tight waves that plastered her head like a corrugated bathing cap.

They both caught sight of Gordon. Nellie whispered in Crowley's ear, and the two of them laughed. They crossed the road and set off across the athletic field, bearing right. If they continued in that direction, it would take them not to the Wilson quarters, but to the north end of Flirtation Walk by a roundabout route where they would be unlikely to be seen. Gordon watched them go, feeling miserable.

"Hi, Gordon, what are you doing skulking about here?"

Gordon turned his head. It was Joe Stilwell with his drag. The wiry upperclassman was every inch a soldier in the white-trousered June Week uniform combination, his back ramrod-straight. His date was a pretty, dark-haired girl in a pink gown who hung on his arm with obvious pride.

"Sir, I'm detailed to the decorations committee," Gordon said.

"None of that sir stuff," Stilwell said. "Valerie, this is Gordon Sinclair, the terror of the boxing team and the best shot on the plebe pistol squad. He'll make a heckuva soldier someday."

It was an extraordinary kindness on Stilwell's part to introduce Gordon to his drag. It was thanks to Stilwell's example that Gordon had been treated so well by the Firsts since the hazing incident. Stilwell, as he had promised, had been generous with his time and friendship, helping Gordon with his tactics assignments and including him in the bull sessions where he regaled his barracks mates with anecdotes about his childhood years in China, where Stilwell's father, Joseph senior, had been stationed first as a military attaché, then as a battalion commander with the Fifteenth Infantry in Tientsin.

Stilwell looked at Gordon shrewdly. "You better not hang around here, Gordon," he said. "The Tacs'll be patrolling. June Week or not. I give it a half hour before Captain Wilson comes charging over here with fire in his eye."

Gordon nodded in appreciation. He touched his cap to the girl and turned to go.

"Drop by tomorrow after graduation and say good-bye, why don't you?" Stilwell called after him.

Gordon made it back to camp without incident. The plebes and the Second Classmen were sleeping under canvas this week. They had been turned out of their rooms to accommodate all the old grads who had returned for June Week reunions. The two-man tents were set up in neat company streets, on semipermanent wooden platforms.

Pease, sitting on his cot and industriously polishing a pair of shoes, looked up as Gordon pushed his way through the flap. "Join the army and live in a tent," he said cheerfully. "Where have you been, old son?"

Pease was Gordon's new roommate. Hibbert had flunked out in January and gone to work in his father's construction business until fall, when he would start classes at the University of Maryland. Everybody had been nice to him, and his picture would be printed in the *Howitzer* along with the rest of the dropouts when his class graduated, but he knew and everyone else knew that he would be a failed West Pointer for the rest of his life.

"Over at Cullum," Gordon said shortly.

"Still mooning over our Nellie? She isn't worth it, old son."

"Shut up, Pease," Gordon said.

Pease, undeterred, went on buffing his shoes. "As for myself, I aim to turn into a maniacal hopoid starting next week when we're legal yearlings," he said. "I'll even do my duty and dance with Old Glory."

"Pease, that's a mean thing to say."

Old Glory was what some of the cadets called Gloria Littlejohn, the cadaverous daughter of Major Littlejohn, the cavalry tactics instructor. She was at least twenty-five, and snaggle-toothed, but she never missed a hop. The cadet hostess always saw to it that her dance card was filled.

"I don't know why you're hanging around here anyway," Pease said good-naturedly. "You could have gotten off for your brother's wedding. Compassionate leave, they call it. When a relative dies or gives up his bachelorhood."

"Leave it alone, you parlor snake."

"Why?" Pease said with freckle-faced innocence. "What have you got against brother Brad anyway?"

"I don't have anything against him," Gordon said. He got a can of brass polish out of his footlocker and began polishing his dress uniform buttons savagely. "There are just more important things in the world than going to Brad's wedding."

Joe Stilwell, Jr., was busy packing when Gordon walked into his room. He had a big scuffed leather suitcase open on his bed, and he was laying out toilet articles with geometric precision on top of a compressed stack of shirts and underwear. From down the hall came the unmilitary sound of women's voices and racing children: relatives of the departing graduates. Gordon had passed the open door of his own room and caught a glimpse of the two alumni who were occupying it, a bald, heavy civilian washing his face at the sink, and a middle-aged major, sitting on Gordon's bed and pulling on his boots.

"Come on in, Gord," Stilwell said. "Nice of you to come by. My roommate's long gone. He's been packed all week. I should have done the same. My mother and my sister, Doot, are waiting for me at the Thayer. But we're an army family. They're used to waiting."

"I hoped I'd get a chance to meet your father," Gordon said.

"He's been posted to San Diego. They wouldn't even let him off long enough to attend my graduation. Dad's furious. I can imagine what he's saying about Roosevelt right now. Dad's language can get pretty salty sometimes."

"What happened?"

"It seems there's a shortage of army officers to run the new CCC camps. Civilian Conservation Corps. Put slum boys to work in the forests, planting trees. So all routine leaves between posts are canceled. No exceptions. Goddamn bureaucratic red tape. Dad pulled every wire he could. He even sent a telegram to General MacArthur. But it was no go."

"That's tough."

Stilwell slammed a stack of handkerchiefs into his suitcase. "The War Department's wasting Dad. Four years teaching at the Infantry School at Fort Benning. Now training reserves in San Diego. He's fifty-one, and he hasn't even made full colonel yet. He's talking about retiring."

"Can't he get them to send him back to China?"

"There are no openings. The whole army promotion system is stagnated on account of this damn depression. Dad knows China like the back of his hand. Knows the language. He's a logical choice for military attaché. But he's a year overage. And he doesn't have an independent income."

"From all I've heard you say about him, he'll figure out a way to get back to China someday."

Stilwell suddenly grinned. "They gave him a new nickname at Fort Benning. Vinegar Joe. I think he's proud of it."

"Vinegar Joe Stilwell!" Gordon laughed in appreciation.

"In China they called him Lao Mao Tse. Old Hairy One."

"China must be an interesting place."

"It will be, if they ever stop shooting at one another long enough to turn it into a country. I remember my mother hiding us kids under tables when Feng—he was the one they called the Christian General because he baptized his troops with fire hoses—was having a free-for-all with a couple of other warlords, and the shooting got too close to our house. We had bullets coming through the windows. Dad was away on a mission at the time. My mother complained to the legation that we were under fire, and they advised her that she was taking it too seriously."

"It sounds like *Terry and the Pirates.*"

"China's like that. But it won't be that way forever. Big things are happening there." He stopped and looked seriously at Gordon. "Have you thought about what you're going to do with your career when you leave here?"

"Me? That's still a long ways off."

"It's not too early to start making plans."

Gordon frowned. "I suppose I'll go where the army sends me."

"You're good in math and you've got an aptitude for languages. If you keep on the way you've started, you've got a good chance of graduating in the top ten of your class. That means you get first choice of assignments."

"Well," Gordon admitted, "I suppose I've thought about the Engineers."

"That's not what I mean," Stilwell said impatiently. "Look, Gordon, you have a chance to make something out of your life. But you've got to have a plan. Have you thought about China?"

"China?"

"Everybody's got their eyes on Europe these days. And sure, the next war will probably start there. But the Western powers are sitting on a powder keg in Asia. When four hundred million Chinese finally get themselves organized, they'll be the biggest nation on earth. And don't kid yourself, the United States will have to deal with them. We'll need good men over there to protect our interests." He paused and looked shrewdly at Gordon. "Promotions are slow in the peacetime army, but if you're one of the lucky Johnnies who happens to be in the right spot when the time comes, you'll be able to write your own ticket."

"What do you mean?"

"Japan wants it all. They're not going to stay satisfied with gobbling up Manchuria and installing the puppet emperor. They'll grab for the rest of China next, then southeast Asia. Sure, they got their fingers burned when they went after Shanghai two years ago, but they'll be back. And then it'll be us against them. The Japs know it, even if we don't. In Tokyo, they're putting civilians through air raid drills, where the planes are supposed to be coming from U.S. carriers in the Pacific."

"Us in a war with Japan?" It all seemed farfetched to Gordon, but he was too polite to say so.

"Sure. Logic of empire. A clash is inevitable. Meanwhile, we'd better back the right horse in China. Right now, that's Chiang Kai-shek, like it or not. Chiang's the only one who can pay his soldiers, and the only general with modern equipment. He's got all that Soong money behind him, and he endeared himself to our own conservatives when he kicked the Communists out of the Kuomintang. But he won't fight the Japs. There are those who say he's made a deal with them. He's saving all his strength to knock out Mao Tse-tung."

"Who?" Gordon was getting bewildered.

"Mao Tse-tung, the Communist warlord. Chiang's got him bottled up in Kiangsi province. Cheeky devil. He's actually proclaimed a Chinese Soviet Republic there, and declared war against the Japanese. The Russians are helping him, but then the Germans are helping Chiang. So it's stalemate for now. Chiang's launched four extermination campaigns against his former buddies, but they all bogged down. Now his German military advisors are telling him to starve Mao out."

"But," Gordon said, thoroughly lost, "Chiang Kai-shek rules China. Doesn't he?"

Stilwell looked amused. "He claims to. But it's more like sitting on the lid of a boiling pot, with Mao and Chu Teh and Two Gun Tang and Fire Hose Feng and the rest of them all clawing to get out. Chiang has a lot of things going for him, though. He's Sun Yat-sen's heir apparent. And he was clever enough to marry into the Soong family. And the U.S. is behind Chiang, now that he's a reformed character. When he suddenly became a conservative instead of a revolutionary, it helped. It didn't hurt when his wife converted him to Christianity, either. That got the missionary faction behind him. That's important in China."

"You don't sound as if you like him very much."

Stilwell flashed him a disarming grin. "Dad can't stand the son of a bitch."

A very pretty woman, tall, with a marvelous carriage, appeared in the doorway. "Joe, where have you been?" she said. "Doot and I have been ready since . . . oh!" Her eyes lit on Gordon.

"Mother, this is Gordon Sinclair," Stilwell said. "I've written you and Dad about him."

"I'm very pleased to meet you," Gordon said, discomfited. He hoped Mrs. Stilwell hadn't heard the last thing that Joe had said.

"Joe seems to think a lot of you," she said, melting him with a smile.

"Oh, Gordie'll make a fine officer," Stilwell said. "But right now I need the seat of his pants. Come on over here and sit on this for me while I latch it, will you, Gord?"

Gordon sat on the bulging suitcase. There was still a little pile of personal objects that Stilwell hadn't been able to fit inside.

"Well, drop me a card once in a while, will you?" Stilwell said, fixing his cap. "And think about what I said."

"I will."

"Dad will put in a word for you, if you want. I know he will."

"Thanks, Joe," Gordon said with an effort. He couldn't keep his eyes off Stilwell's brand-new second lieutenant's bars. It didn't seem right not to be calling him sir.

Stilwell hesitated. "Here, Gordie, I want you to have this. I don't need it anymore."

He handed Gordon an object from the pile of left-behind belongings on the bed. Mrs. Stilwell gave Gordon a gracious smile, and the two of them left to join the stream of traffic in the corridor.

Gordon looked down at the thing he was holding. It was a small leather-bound book, supple with years of handling. The gold-leaf letters on the cover were almost worn away. They read: *A Practical Chinese Grammar for Beginners—North China Union Language School.*

Gordon flipped it open. On the inside leaf was a faded inscription: *For my son Joe—his terrible father's first primer. "Ex Oriente lux." From the East light. Pass on the torch.* It was signed with a single Chinese character drawn with a fountain pen.

Gordon slipped the book into his tunic pocket. It was rough enough at the Point to take the two required language courses, French and Spanish, without taking on extra work. But maybe it would be interesting to leaf through the book sometimes.

He lifted his head at the sound of organ music coming from the direction of Mills Road. It was Mendelssohn's "Wedding March." The first of the many postgraduation marriages was taking place in the chapel.

A rush of unbidden sentiment swept over Gordon. The example of the close-knit Stilwell family had affected him more than he'd realized. Maybe, he thought, he ought to relent and send Brad and Sally a telegram of congratulations. There was plenty of time to get down to the telegraph office before he had to report for guard duty.

The impulse passed. It was too late, anyway. Brad and Sally would be on their honeymoon by now.

25

The room waiter said, *"Thank* you, sir!" when he saw the dollar, and bowed backwards out of the suite. Brad lifted the silver cover from Sally's plate and found a caviar omelet, grilled tomato, and a rasher of bacon. He shuddered and put back the cover.

"Your breakfast's here," he called through the half-open door that led to the bedroom and bath.

"I'll be out in a minute, darling," Sally called back. "I'm still steaming in this glorious tub. Go ahead and start without me."

Brad contemplated the starched tabletop with forbearance. There was a silver coffeepot warmed by an alcohol flame, two unequal services, a neatly folded *Times,* and an envelope containing that evening's theater tickets.

"I'll wait," he said.

He strolled to the window in shirt-sleeves and suspenders and looked out at Broadway and Forty-fifth. Across the street he could see the marquees of the Morosco and the Music Box, and, down below, a thriving stream of motor vehicles and pedestrian traffic. He had wanted to stay at the Ritz-Carlton, but once they'd reached Manhattan, Sally had insisted on checking into the Astor, smack in the middle of the theater district. "What's a New York honeymoon *for,* if it's not to store up a few bright lights to get you through another dull season in

Washington?" she'd said. So far they'd seen an S.N. Behrman comedy, the new Cole Porter musical, Sinclair Lewis's *Dodsworth,* and a Noel Coward import with Lunt and Fontanne. Tonight, he had tickets for the new George Kaufman play, *Bring on the Girls,* with Jack Benny, and afterward he was taking Sally to a Harlem nightclub to hear someone named Louis Armstrong.

He opened the window, letting in the street noises and gas fumes that Sally loved, and sat down at the table. He poured himself a half cup of coffee and unfolded the *Times.* The first thing he saw was a story about the general.

STEELWORKERS ASSAIL JOHNSON, BOO PEACE PLAN, the headline screamed.

Brad raised his eyebrows. Two days ago, it had been the Iron and Steel Institute that had rejected the general's plan for averting an industrywide strike. The general had flown in his army bomber to New York with Don Richberg and Robbie, and done some fancy arm-twisting. But evidently it hadn't been fancy enough.

Some of the insurgent steelworkers, it seemed, had suggested that the general "scorch his summer pants at an open blast furnace for twenty-four dollars a week." The general, as usual, had risen joyously to the bait, and had compared his critics to "just so much skin worn off the part of my body that fits into the saddle." Whereupon the labor leaders had sent him an open telegram saying: "We, the undersigned who have just listened to your damnable speech over the radio, denounce you."

Brad sighed. It all made colorful reading, but the fact was that the general had lost his temper and muffed it. He had been under too much strain lately. There was the sniping from the Darrow Board, and the infighting with Richberg, too little sleep, too much booze, and too much gallivanting around the country. The general had barely landed, after heading off a textile strike in Ohio, when the steel thing had come up.

Brad knew what had happened. Some reporter had egged the general on, and there had been no one around to defuse him. Brad sipped his coffee. The general had needed a victory badly in the steel situation. If he went on running himself ragged this way, he was headed for a crack-up.

Sally walked in, glowing from her bath. She was just belting a robe over her slip. "My, don't you look domestic," she said.

He refolded the paper hastily and put it aside. "I was just reading about Hitler," he said. "He's finally going to shake hands with Mussolini."

"The hell with Hitler," she said. "Unless he's playing on Broadway."

She pulled up a chair and uncovered her omelet. Brad watched as she attacked it with a fork.

"I thought you couldn't face anything but toast and black coffee in the morning," he said.

"It's all this screwing," she said, her mouth full. "It does wonders for the appetite. Umm, this is good. Don't you want to try some?"

"Perish the thought."

She sawed at the bacon and popped a piece into her mouth. "I feel so . . . I don't know . . . so *healthy!*"

"And why wouldn't you, safely away from that poisonous sunlight and all that lethal fresh air? Some folks think the way to spend a honeymoon is on an ocean cruise, or lying on a tropical beach somewhere. They just don't know how bracing the smell of gasoline fumes and the sweat of theater audiences in June can be."

Sally giggled. "Mother offered to pay for a stateroom on the *Mauretania* and arrange a letter of credit for us in London at Baring's, so her daughter wouldn't be disgraced. It's *killing* her not to know where we are."

"You didn't tell her?"

"Of course not. We made a bargain, remember? Oh, my poor Brad! Never been anywhere! Don't worry, darling. I know you're going to make scads of money, and then we'll spend all our vacations in London and Paris and Venice. But not Berlin. Definitely not Berlin."

"No, definitely not Berlin." He thought of Jeremy's last letter, full of grim happenings. All the same, he felt a twinge of jealousy at his younger brother's having made it to Europe ahead of him.

"This is much nicer, away from that Washington wasteland. Did the tickets come for the Kaufman play?"

"Right here." He tapped his shirt pocket.

"And are you sure you don't mind going to Harlem afterwards?"

"Anything to make you happy."

She buttered another slice of toast. "I know you think I'm a lowlife, but really, darling, it's very fashionable now. Duke Ellington—I know you can't tell him from Paul Whiteman—just came back from a tour of the Continent. And Louis Armstrong—you know, the trumpet player we're hearing tonight—almost caused *riots* in Paris. Some Frenchman wrote a book about him, *Le Jazz Hot*, it's called. . . ."

Brad listened indulgently as she prattled on, hardly able to believe that he was married to this spoiled delicious creature, who looked like a Pond's ad with her flawless skin and curling blond hair, even if her small perfect mouth *was* crammed with toast and egg.

"What are we doing today?" she said, finally running down.

He pretended to consider. "Oh, I thought that first we'd take a leisurely stroll down Broadway. Gawk at the sights. Inspect the peasants. Then maybe lunch at Sardi's, and back here in time for a shower before the matinee."

"And who's in it?" she said gravely.

"Us. Then drinks here at the hotel, a few laughs with George Kaufman and that other chap, an after-dinner bite at Twenty-One, and your jazz trumpet player."

"What about tomorrow?"

"Tomorrow's program is fresh air. Put the roses back in your cheeks. An excursion on the Hudson on one of those white steamers, surrounded by people in knickers with ukeleles. I'll have the hotel pack us a picnic lunch. And a shaker of martinis packed in ice. Back in time for a nap. Mustn't forget the nap. A shower, a quick drink at the Green Room, then on relentlessly to the theater."

"And Harlem afterward?"

"And Harlem afterward."

"Connie's Inn?" Her southern accent made it "Connie's Iyun."

"Whatever you say."

Connie's Inn, Brad had been given to understand, was the jazz club that had given birth to a review called *Hot Chocolates* by someone with the improbable name of Fats Waller. Now it was a shrine, much visited by Manhattan socialites.

He felt Sally's hand on his arm. "Are you having fun, Brad?"

"Sure I am. I never knew a honeymoon could be so much fun."

"Oh, you!"

"You better put on your dress, or I'll spoil your bath, and we'll never make it to Times Square."

She laughed and got up. "I'll be right back."

He watched her disappear into the bedroom. She had a cute behind, too. He poured himself another cup of coffee from the silver pot. Sally had left some of her omelet. He put the cover back on so he wouldn't have to look at it. The coffee was beginning to do its work. One more cup and he'd feel almost alive.

The phone buzzed. That would be the hotel florist about the flowers he'd ordered for Sally. He wanted them in the suite when they got back from Sardi's.

"Mr. Sinclair?"

"Yes."

"I have a call for you from Washington."

He waited through the buzzes and clicks, and then he heard the crisp New England voice of Frances Perkins.

"Mr. Sinclair, I don't like to disturb you, but I was sure you'd want to know. Please don't blame Miss Robinson. She didn't want to give me the name of your hotel."

He became instantly alert. "That's quite all right, Miss Perkins. Robbie wouldn't have given you the number unless I had told her she could."

It wasn't quite true, he reflected. Robbie would have been no match for the formidable lady who was the secretary of labor.

"General Johnson is in Walter Reed Army Hospital. He's under the care of Colonel Keller. He's . . ." She hesitated. "He's dizzy and irrational."

A sick feeling grew in the pit of Brad's stomach. "I've just been reading about him in this morning's paper."

"Yes . . ." Her voice was embarrassed. "Evidently he wasn't . . . quite himself when he made those remarks about the steelworkers."

There was a silence. Brad remembered the shadowy husband she had in a sanitarium in New York, the husband whose name she had never taken.

She continued, her voice brisk and ladylike once more. "He asked to see me and Senator Wagner. He didn't say why. We went to the hospital with Mr. Richberg late yesterday."

Brad searched his memory. Senator Robert F. Wagner of New York had been trying for some time, with the support of Roosevelt, to introduce a bill calling for the creation of a National Labor Relations Board. But there was a dispute about whether such a board should be located in the NRA or the Department of Labor.

"Yes?" Brad said cautiously.

"General Johnson was extremely vehement, but somewhat confused in expression. He talked about loyalty. He accused us of plotting against him. Mr. Richberg became quite upset. He left the room rather abruptly."

I'll bet he did, Brad thought.

"Hugh takes everything personally," she went on. "He's driven himself into a corner. He doesn't trust me anymore. I'm sorry about that, because I wish him well." She paused. "Mr. Sinclair, he needs a friend."

"You know I'm on my honeymoon."

"I was impressed by your discretion in that . . . previous matter."

Brad turned his head. Sally was framed in the bedroom door, fixing her stockings. She blew a kiss in his direction.

He sighed. "I'll see what I can do. Thank you for calling, Madam Secretary." He hung up.

Sally showed him her legs. "Are my seams straight?" she said. "Who was that on the phone?"

He stood up slowly, and took his jacket from the back of the chair. "Sally, I have to go back to Washington. Something's come up. If I hurry, I can catch an express at Penn Station, be there by about two-thirty."

She stared at him, her small mouth open.

"Look, I'm sorry about the Kaufman play, but I'll get tickets again for later in the week. With any luck, I can wrap things up by evening, get a train back to New York, and be here before midnight. We can still get to the jazz club. They'll just be warming up by then."

Her eyes squeezed tight. He could see tears. "Oh, you son of a bitch!" she said. "You told them where to reach you, didn't you?"

"It's just one day. Not even that."

She followed him into the bathroom and watched with clenched rage as he put his toothbrush in his pocket.

"You can come back at midnight if you want, you smiling bastard! But don't expect to find me here! I've got plenty of friends in New York! I won't have a bit of trouble finding somebody to go to the theater with!"

She had followed him back into the outer room of the suite. He took the theater tickets from his shirt pocket and put them on the serving table.

"Good idea," he said coldly. "Make sure he's a fairy."

She picked up the plate with the remains of her caviar omelet. He got out the door just in time. On the other side, he heard the crash of smashed china.

He called Bob Straus from Union Station. Straus was on the general's side. He had been with Johnson since the election campaign, and had served him as an administrative assistant from the first days, before Congress had made the NRA legal. He was surprised to hear from Brad.

"Brad! What are you doing in Washington? I thought you'd be sunning yourself in a deck chair by now."

"The deck chair sailed without me. What's this I hear about Old Ironpants?"

Straus lowered his voice. "Where did you hear about that?"

"A little bird told me."

"A little bird in a brown tricorn hat?"

"Could be."

"It's a bad business, Brad. He won't even listen to his own son anymore. Pat Johnston and I got Madam Secretary to ask the President to *order* the general to take a vacation. Bernie Baruch is going to Europe for a month, and the President got *him* in on it. The idea was to put together some kind of commission to study economic recovery in Europe and appoint the general to head it. Then, with him out of the way, the NRA could be reorganized—turned into less of a one-man show. But nobody ever said the general was stupid. He found out what was going on, and accused me of conspiring with Don Richberg against him."

"So he's staying put?"

"He's staying put."

"He has a point. If the general lets go of the reins for a month, you can bet that Richberg will cobble together some kind of an NRA reorganization plan that will put Don Richberg on the top."

"It's inevitable, Brad. The general *knows* he's got to resign sooner or later. At least he does when he's thinking clearly. But he's hell-bent on hanging on until he can force Richberg out first."

"What happened at the hospital yesterday?"

"Senator Wagner doesn't want the National Labor Relations Board to be in the NRA. Christ, the NRA is supposed to be a temporary, emergency agency! But the general wouldn't face it. In the meantime, time's slipping by, and the bill's supposed to be introduced next week. So then the senator and Miss Perkins got the general to agree that Richberg would have the authority to write the final draft, and the general would be bound by it."

"So Richberg put the board in the Labor Department?"

"Yeah."

"You can't start doing favors too early."

"It'll make a nice power base for Richberg if the NRA is dissolved. And if it isn't, at least he's yanked another rug out from under the general."

"What happened when the general saw the draft?"

"He started ranting about being sold down the river. Claimed he never had delegated the authority to Richberg. Brad, I think he really forgot."

"That bad?"

"That bad."

Brad took off his hat and wiped his forehead. The phone booth was stifling. "I hope nobody is tapping your telephone," he said.

Straus laughed. "Christ, Brad, this is America, not the Third Reich."

* * *

The nurse said, "You can't go in there."

"It's all right," Brad said. "General Johnson sent for me."

"I don't know," the nurse said doubtfully. "Colonel Keller said no more visitors."

"I'm the general's aide," Brad said, and smiled earnestly.

"I guess I could check with the colonel," the nurse said.

"Thanks," Brad said. "I'd appreciate it."

"You'll have to wait in the solarium," she told him, frowning.

Brad nodded agreeably. As soon as the nurse was out of sight round the bend in the corridor, he pushed his way through the double doors to the private wing. He stopped a tough-looking orderly carrying a bedpan.

"Say, what's General Johnson's room number? They told me at the desk, but I must have got it wrong."

The orderly looked him over. "Twelve, but nobody's supposed to see him, after yesterday."

"Oh, Colonel Keller said it was okay."

The orderly nodded. "That door over there," he said, jerking a thumb. "You ain't carrying no booze on you, are you?"

"Me? In this place? Say, how's Old Ironpants doing?"

The orderly gave a gravelly laugh. "Sobered up. But it'll take him a week to dry out this time."

"Thanks, buddy," Brad said.

He found General Johnson propped up in bed, reading a book of poems. Brad glanced at the cover. Edna St. Vincent Millay. The general never ceased to surprise him. He would have expected Kipling.

"Sinclair!" the general said with genuine pleasure. "How did you get past the watchdogs?"

He laid the book aside, atop a precarious bedside stack of books, magazines, and opera librettos. The general's taste ran to Puccini, Brad saw. An ashtray was overflowing with butts and a crumpled Old Gold pack; they were still letting him smoke.

Brad looked at him closely. He looked terrible. The bulldog face was blotched, the eyes bloodshot, the hair plastered in lank strands against the bulging brow. He had the shakes, too, and was trying to hide it, with one hand anchoring the other against the coverlet.

"How are you feeling, sir?" Brad said.

"Oh, it's nothing serious," the general said. "Just a minor operation. But you know how Washington is. Rumor hungry. Thought I'd try to sneak away for a week or two and have it taken care of, but everybody's tracking me down."

"Well," Brad said carefully, "it's a chance to have a rest."

Johnson attempted a laugh. "My candle burns at both ends."

"But it gives a lovely light."

"Ah, you know my favorite poetess." The general beamed in approval. Then his face sagged. "I'm about to sputter out, son. They're all coming after me."

"You always liked a fight, General."

Johnson's massive head came up with effort. "I'm surrounded by conspirators," he whispered. "They're all against me. Even Straus."

"Straus was only thinking of your best interests," Brad said.

"He sold out to Richberg," the general said flatly.

"That's not true, General."

"Richberg is not my friend. Richberg is not loyal to me."

The general's eyes had gone glazed, and Brad saw that he was losing him. "General!" he said sharply.

Johnson blinked. The big head came up again. "Neither of them could look me in the eye yesterday," he said. "When I asked them if a draft had been written, Richberg turned red. He had to get up and leave the room. Father, I cannot tell a lie. I did it with my little hatchet."

Brad tried to hide his alarm. "Madam Secretary is your friend, sir. You told me so yourself."

"She *was* my friend," Johnson said in a wintry voice. "For a good many months she was my most trusted friend. I used to go to her with my troubles. I think she's *still* my friend personally. But she's trying to build up the Department of Labor. That's only natural. Any zealous official would do the same. We have an honest difference of opinion. My only complaint is that she did not make a clear-cut issue and let it be resolved. But the secretary is a woman, and I don't know anything at all about how to handle that kind of disagreement."

"General—"

"She thinks the NRA isn't equipped to settle strikes. Do you know what she said? I have it on good authority. She said, 'The trouble with Hugh is that he thinks a strike is something to settle.'"

"General, the steelworkers—"

Johnson's hamlike fist hit the bedside table with a force that made the pile of books jump. "A strike against the codes is a strike against the government!"

Brad tried to calm him down. "General, you've done more than anyone would have thought possible a year ago. The Blue Eagle's eliminated child labor, established at least the *principle* of collective bargaining . . ." He tried for the light touch. "When you took this job last June, you said you were a man mounting the guillotine on the hairbreadth chance that the axe wouldn't work."

But Johnson wasn't listening. "They think I don't know," he whispered. "The President had Madam Secretary call Bernie Baruch and ask him if he'd take me back into his organization. They want me to be a number-two man or a number-three man again."

Brad raised his head in sudden interest. This was a new one. It had the ring of truth, despite the general's ranting.

The general clutched Brad's arm in a death grip. A crafty look stole over his face. "Sinclair, when this damned crisis is over and we have the recovery program humming along, there won't be any need for a Department of Labor. Or a Department of Commerce and perhaps some other departments as well. The NRA will carry out all those functions."

Brad could hardly believe his ears. Now he could understand why Miss Perkins had said the general had lost touch with reality.

"Oh," the general waved a hand airily, "the Labor Department can continue to be a research unit within the NRA. I told Madam Secretary that. Sinclair, are you familiar with Mussolini's theory of the corporate state?"

Brad gulped. "No, sir. Look, sir, maybe I better come back tomorrow. I can stay in Washington overnight."

The general surveyed Brad with bleary affection. "You're a good lad, Sinclair. Loyal. Not like some of them. Here, help me up, boy. Ring for the orderly, will you? Tell him I want my clothes."

"Sir, I don't think—"

The general used Brad's arm as a lever to heave himself to a sitting position. He was wearing a hospital nightgown. He swung hairy legs over the side of the bed. In the process of getting to his feet, he knocked the pile of books to the floor.

" '*Con onor muore!*' " the general said in a ringing tone. " '*Chi non può serbar vita con onore!*' "

"I beg your pardon?" Brad said, startled.

"Death with honor is better than life with dishonor," the general said impatiently. "It's what Madame Butterfly sang before she committed hara-kiri with her samurai dagger."

"Sir, why don't you get back into bed." Thoroughly alarmed now, Brad rang for the orderly.

"They want a reorganization plan, do they? I know that Richberg and Madam Secretary have been sneaking round to the President behind my back with all kinds of proposals. I'm going to reorganize myself right out of the NRA. That'll show them! But by God, I'll make sure that no cigar-smoking vulture is going to sit in my place!"

He was in high good humor. He chuckled to himself as he shuffled in his hospital slippers to the washbowl in the corner and began running water.

The orderly came running into the room. "Now, General . . ." he began warily.

"Don't 'Now General' me, you no-stripe hoot owl!" the general roared. "Get me my pants! Mr. Sinclair and I are going back to the office!"

His secretary couldn't meet his eye. "Read Winchell," she mumbled, and dumped the mail on the desk. She turned and fled back to Brad's own office.

He was sitting in Room 3053, the one with General Johnson's name on the door. The general never used it; he worked down the hall in an unmarked office where he wouldn't be bothered. Robbie had let Brad have the unused room for the day, so it wouldn't get around the staff that he was back in Washington.

He had stayed up half the night with the general—keeping him away from booze, and trying to tone down the general's apocalyptic approach to reorganization. He didn't know how well he'd succeeded. With any luck, he'd find out by noon and get on a train to New York in time to take Sally out to dinner.

He unfolded the *New York Mirror* that his secretary had brought, and turned to Walter Winchell's column. Winchell had a pipeline to the White House, and there were often bits of useful gossip.

At first he thought it was the lead item about Missy Le Hand. Missy had surprised Washington by deserting her White House post for a vacation cruise to Europe. The gossip columnists had been reporting breathlessly that she was going to marry Bill Bullitt, the new ambassador to Russia, in a secret ceremony on the Riviera, with Cornelius Vanderbilt as best man.

"Did Missy miss out?" Winchell said. "This reporter has learned that Ambassador Bill, once married to the widow of the head of the Communist Party in the United States, has repacked his bags for Moscow, and that FDR's right Le Hand is on her way back to the U.S., without a wedding ring."

Then Brad saw the other item, halfway down the column.

"What in the world was celebutante Sally Collier, Washington's golden girl, doing last night in a Harlem jazz club with man-about-town Freddy De Vere? She's supposed to be on her honeymoon with her hubby-dovey of less than a week, Bradford Sinclair, Jr., one of General Hugh 'Ironpants' Johnson's bright young men."

Brad's jaw tightened. He wasn't worried about Freddy. Freddy was a harmless, amusing chap who designed theater sets and swallowed his *l*'s. But the gossip item would make Brad a laughingstock at Georgetown cocktail parties for a week.

Thank God for Missy, he thought. She would take some of the heat off.

Robbie came in, looking tired. "Here," she said. "Here's your copy."

He took the mimeographed pages. They were headed *Memorandum to the President. Subject: Reorganization of NRA.*

"Who else saw this?" he said.

"Just you and Ed McGrady. Hugh wants your comments before he writes a final draft."

"Does Don Richberg know about this?"

Robbie's lips tightened. "No."

"Okay," he said. "I'll have some notes for the general in about an hour."

"You can take your time. Hugh's leaving for San Francisco this morning. He'll go over the draft when he gets back."

Brad half-rose from his chair. "He's *what?*"

"He's going to try to settle the West Coast maritime strike."

The San Francisco longshoremen had been out for a month now, in protest against the morning shape-up which gave work only to men whose dues were paid up in the "Blue Book," a company-controlled union. Now, under the protective wings of the Blue Eagle, a new union had sprung up, supposedly a local of the International Longshoreman's Association. The strike leader was an Australian seaman named Harry Bridges. Frances Perkins was attempting to settle the strike, in response to desperate appeals by the West Coast governors. But the strike had spread. Sailors, firemen, cooks had walked out, to be joined by the masters, mates, pilots, and engineers. No ships could move from any Pacific port.

"But General Johnson doesn't have the authority to intervene in the maritime strike!" Brad said. "The President and the secretary of labor want him out of it!"

If General Johnson, in his highly excitable state, went to San Francisco to do battle with Harry Bridges, he could only inflame the situation. Brad knew a disaster was in the making.

Robbie's pretty face closed tight. "That woman!" she said.

"Look, Robbie, can you at least get the general to take Ed McGrady with him?"

McGrady was an experienced labor negotiator. He had already been sent to the West Coast, with Frances Perkins's blessing, as a mediator, though he had been unsuccessful. He would be a moderating influence on the general.

"Hugh doesn't want Eddie there," she said smugly. "He says Eddie's a professional labor man, and is biased. He says he's going to show some steel to those red agitators out there."

Brad tried one final appeal. "Robbie, the general's not up to it. You know that. He should be back in the hospital."

"I don't want to hear it, you devil!" she said, and flung herself out of the office.

Brad turned to the document she had left with him. He skimmed rapidly until he came to the last page. The words jumped out at him:

Application of the foregoing recommendations would shortly make superfluous the present Administrator, who will always be at your disposal in any capacity, important or otherwise, as long as this emergency lasts, but who feels that the task of pioneering this great experiment is about over.

Brad sighed. The Blue Eagle was dead. Oh, it would take a while to bury it. The President was softhearted. He wouldn't let the general quit without arranging some sort of face-saving exit. The President was used to coddling prima donnas; he had to talk Harold Ickes out of resigning about once a week. But the general's ego would make him take the President seriously, and he'd keep looking for excuses to stay on, like Banquo's ghost. There were going to be messy days ahead at the NRA.

He smiled to himself. At least the general had scuttled Richberg. The reorganization plan, he saw, specified that the administrator ("not a one-man job") would be replaced by a board. Richberg would never be anything more than a face in the crowd.

He leaned back in the chair and stretched his long legs out on the desk. It was time to abandon ship. He clasped his hands behind his head and closed his eyes. It was very restful. He could hear the clacking of typewriters in the honeycomb of steel cubicles all around him. Through his flyspecked windows came the clang of a trolley stopping in front of the Commerce Building.

After a while he picked up one of the Washington newspapers that had come in with the mail and scanned the day's headlines. He noted with interest that the House Appropriations Committee had just given Harry Hopkins $2.5 billion to play with.

It was called the "Deficiency Appropriation Bill." What it actually did was allow the President to use unexpended funds from the RFC and the PWA as a slush fund. A lot of that would go to Harry Hopkins's agency, FERA. Hopkins had already put in a bid for a half a billion of the money for drought relief.

Hopkins liked spending money, and he spent it well. His CWA, during its brief life last winter, had put over four million men and women to work in only two months. Some people, who had seen no cash for months or even years, actually got into fistfights over shovels, it was reported.

Hopkins knew how to operate in Washington, as poor Hugh Johnson never had. Almost all of the new emergency fund was going to be squeezed out of Harold Ickes, who no doubt was threatening to resign again today.

And Hopkins came from Iowa, too.

Brad picked up the phone and had the operator get him Aubrey Williams at FERA. Williams was Hopkins's chief assistant, a soft-spoken man in his forties. Brad had gotten to know Williams well several months earlier, when the general had loaned him to FERA on a liaison job.

"Aubrey, can you get me in to see Harry this afternoon?" he said.

"Why?"

"I want a job."

There was silence for a beat. Then Williams said, "The big blue bird is ready for plucking and roasting, then? The stories are true?"

"Let's just say I'm ready for a new challenge. That's the word we always use in the press releases, isn't it? Challenge."

"I don't know, Brad. This afternoon's bad. He has to get dibs on all that lovely new money before someone else gets their hooks on it, and he's getting ready to sail to Europe."

"Europe? What's that got to do with FERA?"

Williams made a rude noise. "He didn't have enough to do, with the work projects and the emergency drought relief, so the President's sending him to talk to Hitler and Mussolini. He's got letters of introduction from the State Department."

"I only need five minutes with him."

Williams gave a resigned sigh. "Okay, I can squeeze you in at three."

"Thanks, Aubrey. I'll be there."

He hung up and dug his train schedule out of his wallet for another look. It was going to be awkward. He wasn't going to be able to take Sally to dinner after all.

26

Hitler's hand was warm, shaking his. Warm, rough, and faintly reptilian, Jeremy thought, like the garden snake he had caught when he was thirteen and kept as a pet in a box in his room until his mother had discovered it and gone into hysterics.

"Sehr angenehm," Hitler mumbled awkwardly, without rising from the table. He withdrew his hand and went back to his cup of chocolate and whipped cream, leaving Jeremy standing there with Hanfstaengl hovering anxiously behind him.

Hitler looked ordinary, sitting at the tearoom table in his blue serge suit—just a puffy, potato-nosed man of forty-five with a little square mustache and a soup-bowl haircut that had left a black forelock straggling across his brow. His eyes were pale blue under a receding forehead, and there were black smudges under them, as if he'd had trouble sleeping lately. There was a fleck of whipped cream on his mustache.

"Herr Reichskanzler," Jeremy said in a rush, while he had the chance, "if I could have a few words for my news service about your meeting in Venice with Premier Mussolini. . . ."

Hitler looked annoyed. "It's all in von Neurath's statement. Hanfstaengl can give you a copy."

Jeremy tried again. "Would you care to comment on Vice-Chancellor von Papen's speech yesterday . . ." he began, but Hitler made a small impatient gesture, and Hanfstaengl dragged Jeremy away from the table.

"Nice try, Jeremy," Hanfstaengl said with a laugh, "but those are the two things he doesn't want to talk about."

He steered Jeremy past the potted palms toward the tearoom's vestibule. The customers at the other tables stared with open curiosity and envy, trying to guess who the shaggy young man was who had been allowed to approach the Führer's table. A space had been cleared around it, and the cold-eyed characters sitting at the tables closest to Hitler were obviously plainclothesmen: sallow toughs who kept their hats on and their hands in their raincoat pockets. Black-uniformed SS men with revolvers dangling conspicuously from their hips stood about near the entrance, and these kept their eyes on Jeremy until he passed through the archway.

It was still easy to get close to Hitler. He hadn't gotten used to being a head of state yet. He liked to give the impression that he was a man of the people, that he was as accessible as when he had been leader of a gang of brown-shirted bullies.

But it wasn't so easy to get an interview these days. Now that Hitler was Chancellor, he didn't need the publicity anymore. Jeremy had thought it a stroke of luck when Hanfstaengl, bubbling over with goodwill, had plucked him by the sleeve and said, "Look, Jeremy, there he goes for his cup of chocolate. Come with me and I'll introduce you."

Hitler still sneaked out to the Kaiserhof Hotel's tearoom, across the street from the Chancellery, once or twice a week. Old habits were hard to break. The Kaiserhof had been his fellow conspirators' meeting place during the lean years, when the Nazis—banned and despised —were maneuvering for power. The kitchen staff made chocolate for Hitler the way he liked it: specially sweetened and with a thick topping of *Schlagsahne*.

It was here at the Kaiserhof tearoom that the impulsive Hanfstaengl had arranged an ill-conceived rendezvous between Hitler and Martha Dodd, the lively, pretty daughter of the American ambassador. Martha herself had told the story to Jeremy and the other American correspondents one night at the Taverne. It seemed that Putzi—as everyone called Hanfstaengl—had decided one day that Hitler ought to have an American girl friend "to moderate his views." Putzi himself had an American mother, had graduated from Harvard, and claimed to be a friend of Roosevelt.

"Martha," he had announced solemnly, "you can be the woman who changes the history of Europe." Intrigued, Martha had kept the date. Hitler, shy as a schoolboy, had kissed her hand, stammered a few words, and that had been the end of it. The theory around the correspondents' table at the Taverne was that Hitler was a virgin.

Outside, Jeremy looked up accusingly at the towering Hanfstaengl. "I thought you said you could get me an interview with Hitler."

"Oh, no, I said I could arrange for you to *meet* Hitler," Hanfstaengl said puckishly. He laughed, spraying Jeremy with saliva. "Cheer up, Jeremy. You can always write one of your local color specials: 'I Shook Hands with Hitler.' "

"Very funny," Jeremy said.

Putzi was a slouching giant of six feet four, with disheveled black hair and a large jaw. High-strung and fidgety, he could babble on about abstractions to the point of incoherence. His official title was foreign press chief, but Hitler kept him on for laughs. He was an accomplished piano pounder, whose main duty was to soothe Hitler to sleep with thundering renditions of Wagner and Beethoven, embellished by Putzi's uncanny vocal imitations of trumpets and other orchestral instruments.

Jeremy had heard him play at parties for the foreign press corps, and had been impressed by his demoniacal virtuosity. It was Hanfstaengl who had transformed a number of Harvard football songs into Nazi marches for the SA bands, most notably turning "Fight, Fight, Fight!" into "Sieg Heil, Sieg Heil!" Putzi was genuinely fond of the American correspondents, and most of them put up with him good-naturedly, despite his tendency to lecture them.

"Don't take it too hard, Jeremy." Hanfstaengl slapped him on the back. "I'll make it up to you."

Jeremy chewed his lip. "Well, I better get over to Dr. Goebbels's press conference. It'll be a mob scene, but I've got to have *something* to file." He looked across the street at the row of government buildings. There seemed to be an unusual number of armed guards. "Say, what's going *on* in Berlin today, anyway?"

The black-uniformed SS detachment in front of the Chancellery had been augmented by a truckload of Goering's special police in steel helmets and green uniforms, parked across Wilhelmstrasse. They had been issued automatic weapons. The two groups eyed one another nervously.

"Going on?" Hanfstaengl said with elaborate innocence. "What could be going on?"

"Come *on*, Putzi, you know what I'm talking about. Why have all the Reichswehr staff officers suddenly started wearing their service revolvers, even the desk types? And I hear that a regiment's been mobilized at Doebritz. And what's this I hear about Roehm's brownshirts being put on forced furlough starting July first? Why is everybody so jumpy?"

"Ah, Jeremy, Jeremy! You are too fanciful!"

"Does it have something to do with von Papen's speech? Goebbels was stupid to try to suppress it. Von Papen smuggled advance copies to all of us foreign correspondents anyway. Is it true that Hindenburg himself was the one who put von Papen up to criticizing the Hitler regime—that he thinks the Nazis have gone too far?"

"The Führer has an appointment with the old gentleman this afternoon," Hanfstaengl said reproachfully. "The two are in thorough accord."

"Is Hitler afraid of a putsch?"

Hanfstaengl affected surprise. "A putsch? By whom?"

It was a good question. All the factions in the Nazi party were at one another's throats: Himmler against Goering, Goering against Roehm, and acting as a brake on all of them, the power of the regular army, with the old-line Reichswehr officers waiting only for a cue from President Hindenburg, who still had the power to declare martial law and once and for all end the mess the Nazis had made of things.

"By the brownshirts. There's talk that Boehm's been drawing up execution lists, with Goering's name at the top."

"The brownshirts?" Hanfstaengl laughed uneasily. "That ragtag bunch of street hoodlums and homosexuals? And Roehm is the biggest pederast of them all!" He clucked disapprovingly. "The stories one hears about what goes on in those SA barracks!"

"Don't change the subject, Putzi. I thought Hitler looked nervous just now. He hasn't been sleeping well lately, has he? You should know."

Hanfstaengl attempted to be jovial. "You mustn't listen to idle talk, Jeremy. Let me ask you, if the Führer were worried, why would he and Goering leave Berlin at such a juncture, to go to a wedding in Essen?"

"A wedding?"

"Yes, yes . . ." Hanfstaengl chattered away in his disjointed style. ". . . a little vacation . . . the *Gauleiter* for the Westphalia-North Rhineland district is getting married. . . . Charming fellow, name of Terboven. . . . A chance for the Führer to sip a little champagne, eat a little cake . . . what's wrong with that, I ask you?"

It sounded fishy to Jeremy. Why would Hitler leave town during a crisis to attend the wedding of a Party nobody in the Rhineland? Jeremy filed Putzi's indiscretion away for future reference.

"And what about Roehm, eh? Eh?" Hanfstaengl babbled on. "He's at the other end of Germany, in Bavaria. For his health." He laughed sardonically. "Yes, yes, it is not good for his health to be in Berlin just now. The Führer made that plain to him. Well, no doubt Herr Roehm will find some apple-cheeked lad to console him in Bad Wiessee."

"Wiessee? That's near Munich, isn't it?"

They had been walking along the Wilhelmstrasse, and they paused in front of the Prince Leopold palace. It was an imposing nineteenth-century building that now housed the Propaganda Ministry.

"Well, I'll leave you here, old man," Hanfstaengl said. "I'm not too popular in the Propaganda Ministry right now."

Jeremy knew what Putzi meant. The quicksilver Hanfstaengl, with his convoluted reasoning, had somehow persuaded Hitler to let him publish a book of anti-Hitler cartoons called *Fact Versus Ink*. The idea was to convince the outside world that a dictator who could make fun of himself wasn't such a bad fellow after all. But Goebbels had been furious. He had responded by trying to undermine Hitler's trust in Hanfstaengl. Goebbels had gone so far as to bring a phonograph record of an English song to a press conference, in an attempt to prove that Hanfstaengl had stolen its tune for one of his own marches.

Jeremy showed his press pass to the guard and was allowed past the colonnaded entrance into the ministry's yawning reception area. Goebbels had hired Hitler's young architect, Albert Speer, to renovate the interior, but Speer had shown too much respect for the nineteenth-century character of the rooms, and Goebbels hadn't like the result. So he had hired another architect to do the interior all over again in what Speer sarcastically called "ocean-liner style."

A Goebbels aide ushered Jeremy into the huge ceremonial hall the correspondents called the "throne room." Usually the daily press conference took place in a small auditorium provided with rows of theater seats equipped with flat armrests for writing. Evidently this was to be a special happening.

Over a hundred reporters were milling around under the high, ornate ceiling, waiting for Dr. Goebbels to appear. A blue pall of tobacco smoke hung over the crowd. A low buzz of conversation filled the chamber. A few lumpish young functionaries of the Propaganda Ministry stood about self-importantly. A thicket of small tables and spindly gilt chairs had been set up along the two longer walls, in deference to teatime later.

He scanned the crowd for familiar faces. Sykes was there, looking hung over but marginally operational. That meant that Millicent was slaving away at the British Overseas Press Office, which was a relief. It had become increasingly awkward bumping into her since that final crockery-throwing row when he had moved out of her flat, but it was hard to avoid encounters in the small, cloistered world that foreign journalists moved around in.

"Hullo, Sinclair," Kemble, the London *Times* man said at his elbow. "Come to see the show after all, have you?"

"What's on for today?" Jeremy said.

Kemble sucked on his pipe, trying to get a spark going. "Dr. Schacht's here to defend the moratorium on German war debts. There's a pile of handouts over by the door if you're interested."

Jeremy frowned. "Is that all? That doesn't seem important enough to rate the throne room."

"Goebbels has something in mind. You can depend on it."

"Think he's going to drop a bombshell? There're an awful lot of rumors flying around Berlin. Did you see all the troops outside? Hess made a speech yesterday accusing 'certain elements in the Party'—he didn't mention any names—of trying to stage a second revolution."

"Oh, they're all in a dither about the Papen speech. He stirred up a hornets' nest. Did you know that someone took a pot shot at Hitler?"

"What? Are you serious? I just saw him."

Kemble took the pipe out of his mouth. "Yes. It was the other day at Goering's estate north of Berlin—that big, vulgar hunting lodge he built in memory of his wife."

"Karin Hall? I filed a piece on it when he showed it off. He showed us around in some kind of a green leather medieval hunter's costume."

Kemble nodded. "Just so. Hermann does love to dress up. Well, Hitler motored up from Berlin with Himmler to attend the reinterment ceremony, and just as some girl in a peasant costume was handing him a bunch of roses, a shot was fired from nearby. Obviously meant for Adolf. Himmler got in the way, though, and took the bullet in the arm. They never caught the chap who did it, but the next day they sacked the SA detachment guarding Karin Hall and replaced them with crack SS men personally selected by Himmler."

"Did you file a story?" Jeremy asked jealously.

"Heavens, no. No one would admit anything. I queried my home office, and—as usual—they said they wouldn't print any unsubstantiated rumors."

"But if there really was an assassination attempt—"

"Shh. Here comes the little doctor now."

The hum of conversation in the big hall died down as Goebbels limped to the rostrum. Hitler's propaganda minister was a frail, miniature figure, barely five feet tall and weighing not much more than ninety pounds, dressed up in a neatly pressed doll's uniform that hardly had room enough for all the pocket flaps and buckled straps.

The limp, everyone knew, was due to a club foot, and the invalid flavor was compounded by Goebbels's delicate hands and fleshless cheeks. But there was something immediately compelling about him all the same. His darting brown eyes, as liquid and expressive as a deer's, seemed to notice everything. The little man's quick, malicious wit terrified Hitler's hangers-on, who knew that one barb from Goebbels could ruin them with the Führer forever.

"I can't imagine what's brought all you gentlemen here in such numbers," he said sarcastically. "Can it be that you've been listening to the stinking lies that have been put about in the last few days by a bunch of back-street sneaks?"

His voice was always a surprise. It was a rich, controlled baritone, full of scorn, giving an actor's performance. The miniature hands moved in practiced gestures, emphasizing points smoothly.

"Before I turn you over to Dr. Schacht, whom I know you're dying to hear from, perhaps you'll be *kind* enough to indulge me while I say a few words about certain impudent scoundels who have had the cheek to question the unity of the German nation under its great and wise leader, Adolf Hitler." He rolled his brown eyes ceilingward in mock disbelief. "These subversive elements would have one believe that criticism of the Führer is *'useful'!*" He almost spat the word. "They weep their false tears and they talk about a 'mysterious darkness' which has fallen upon the soul of the German people. . . ." His voice, by stages, had risen to a fevered pitch, but Jeremy noticed that his gestures were every bit as premeditated as before.

"Oh, no!" Jeremy groaned. "Not another attack on von Papen!"

"Guess again," Kemble said, nudging him. "Look over there."

Von Papen himself had entered the hall unobtrusively, a trim, patrician figure in a dark suit, looking dapper with his clipped gray mustache. Hitler's predecessor as Chancellor was an authentic Junker and former General Staff officer, and the man who had gotten Hitler the job by persuading Hindenburg that the loutish Austrian ex-corporal would be easier to control in the government than out of it.

As the assembled correspondents began to notice him, there was a growing hum of comment and a movement of heads. At the podium, Goebbels smiled ironically.

"I'm surprised he hasn't been shot," Jeremy whispered.

"Oh, no, Hitler wouldn't allow that," Kemble said out of the side of his mouth. "He knows that would be the last straw for Hindenburg and the Reichswehr generals. It would mean martial law and the end of the Hitler gang. And probably the restoration of the monarchy when Hindenburg finally dies, with Prince August Wilhelm as regent. The silly sod belongs to the SA, you know, so that would neutralize

Roehm's three million brownshirts, and the army would mop up the rest."

Goebbels, with an actor's skill, had pitched his voice to cut through the rising hum. ". . . but these elements must give up their hope for a second revolution. Germany is not a banana republic. We have come too far together to spoil things now"—he smiled nastily—"because of an abnormal clique with exotic habits!"

"I don't believe it!" Jeremy said. "He's turning it into an attack on Roehm. He's pretending that von Papen was criticizing the Roehm bunch, not Hitler!"

"Oh, these fellows can turn black into white and white into black without lifting an eyebrow," Kemble said.

Papen, totally unperturbed, was making his way toward the tables at the side, nodding to acquaintances on the way.

"But we National Socialists are generous toward old comrades," Goebbels went on unctuously. "We are always ready to overlook peculiar . . . human *weaknesses,* in the light of past services, and to welcome strayed sheep back to the fold. . . ."

"Now he's holding out an olive branch to the brownshirts," Jeremy said wonderingly.

"That's just a smokescreen," Kemble said. "I shouldn't like to be in Roehm's boots now."

Goebbels concluded his tirade and hobbled over to the tables to join von Papen. The two shook hands and sat down together for a cup of tea.

"That's what this circus was all about," Kemble said, puffing on his pipe. "Hitler's cobbled something together with the Reichswehr and the respectable elements. That little charade over the teacups is to put everybody on notice. We foreign press, like dutiful little servants of Dr. Goebbels, are expected to spread the word."

"But that's crazy. Everyone knows what von Papen said."

"Well it's just been unsaid. *Ungesagt.*"

At the lectern, Dr. Schacht was droning on about the annual interest and amortization of Germany's foreign debt, but he was losing his audience. There was a swirl of movement around the table at which von Papen and Goebbels were sipping tea. Some of the ruder reporters were barking questions, but von Papen smiled and said nothing. A few reporters had already made a dash for the phones in the hall.

"Aren't you going to join the crowd?" Jeremy said in a tone of what he hoped was world-weary cynicism.

"Oh, no, the *Times* doesn't deal in rumors, as they keep reminding me. It will all sort itself out in due course. I've already got my story for today."

"Oh?" Jeremy was itching to ask more, but afraid of showing bad form.

Kemble smiled benevolently. "Yes. It's already written except for a few details. 'Dr. Hjalmar Horace Greeley Schacht, the financial wizard who saved Germany from runaway inflation in 1924, today offered a plan which demanded freer world trade if his country's war debts are to be paid, et cetera, et cetera. Like his plan, the Reichbank's Iron Man was conceived in America and born in Germany. . . .' Think that will get by the desk?"

Jeremy laughed dutifully. "Then you don't think it's any use trying to get a quote from von Papen?"

"Oh, he might be prevailed upon to admit that the tea at the Propaganda Ministry is delightful and that he prefers one lump, not two."

Jeremy looked glumly at von Papen's table. Goebbels and von Papen were both wearing crocodile grins despite their hate for each other, but it was obvious that nothing of consequence was being said.

"Well, I guess I'll go over and take one of Dr. Schacht's press releases," he said.

He left the Propaganda Ministry quickly. Outside, a truck filled with soldiers roared down the Wilhelmstrasse on some unknown errand. Himmler's black-shirted guard in front of the Chancellery fingered their revolvers. Not a brownshirt was to be seen near any of the government buildings, which was unusual.

Hanfstaengl's peculiar words came back to him: *Why would the Führer and Goering leave Berlin at such a juncture, to go to a wedding in Essen?*

Jeremy made up his mind. He hailed a cab that had just deposited some Nazi bureaucrat in front of the Ministry of Agriculture and hurried over to it before someone else could steal it from him.

"What station do I go to, to get a train to Essen?" he said.

"The Potsdamer *Bahnhof* is closest, *mein Herr*," the driver said. "You could walk from here."

Jeremy fingered the coins in his pocket. "No, no, I'll ride."

The driver shrugged and pulled away from the curb.

Jeremy called Walt Hanes from the station. An Essen train, due to leave within a quarter hour, was huffing away on the tracks outside the automatic telephone box.

"Are you out of your *mind?*" Hanes sputtered. "*Essen?* Look, something big's going to break here in the next few days, and I want every available man in Berlin."

"Sorry, Mr. Hanes, I can't hear you. The train's just pulling out, making an awful lot of noise. I've got to run for it. Would you wire some expense money on ahead? To the railway office in Essen. Thanks."

He hung up before Hanes could refuse. He bought a third-class ticket at the window and smiled and nodded his way into the coach filled with seedy office workers and factory hands on their way to the Ruhr to try their luck at the Krupp plants, where, rumor had it, a lot of jobs were opening up because of the new government contracts.

He was going to have to sit up half the night on a hard bench. Even so, he'd get to Essen before Hitler, who, if he ran true to form, would probably fly there in his private trimotor in the morning.

"Isn't it marvelous!" gushed the fat lady in the peasant costume. "With all his responsibilities, the Führer has taken the time to attend a simple wedding breakfast in our town!"

Jeremy, hemmed in on all sides by the crowd, nodded. *"Ungewöhnlich,"* he agreed. "Very unusual."

The Essen market square was jammed with people who were waiting patiently to catch a glimpse of Hitler when he emerged from the ancient town hall, a crazy-quilt medieval structure of dressed stone topped by a half-timbered monstrosity which in turn was topped by a tiled clock tower. It was a fine, sunny morning, despite the smudge of coal fumes that hung over the town from the nearby Krupp works, and those with nothing to do loitered on the steps of the eighth-century cathedral or lounged against the old guild hall and other structures that faced the cobbled square

"Are you *Engländer?"* the woman said, catching his accent.

"Amerikaner," he said.

"Look, maybe that's him now!"

The crowd stirred as the massive oak doors opened a crack, but it was only some minor functionary in a Party uniform with swastika armband who strode importantly to one of the automobiles waiting in front of the town hall, spoke to the driver, and returned.

"You've got it wrong," a jovial, red-faced man in farmer's overalls said to the woman. "The Führer won't be the first to leave. First comes Herr Terboven and his bride." He nudged Jeremy and winked broadly. "When it comes to breaking in the marriage bed, the bridegroom takes precedence over the Reichskanzler, even if he *is* only a *Gauleiter."*

Music from inside indicated that the festivities were still in progress. Jeremy caught the sounds of an accordian swinging into a rustic *Ländler.* The farmer winked again at Jeremy.

Then the double doors burst open and Hitler came storming out, looking grim. A half-dozen aides hurried after him, including Goering, enormous as a hippo in a gray uniform covered with ribbons and medals.

All around Jeremy arms were thrusting stiffly out in the Nazi salute. The farmer and the fat woman eyed him, and he raised his right arm too. Being an American was no protection if you failed to go along with the crowd. Tourists were being beaten up all the time.

Jeremy couldn't help reflecting on how easy it had been to follow Hitler around. All you had to do was join the joyful crowds that sprang up wherever the Führer went. Security was lax outside of Berlin. The four or five plainclothes bodyguards were indulgent toward people who summoned up enough courage to press close, tip their hats, and say a few words of greeting. Hitler's chauffeur would sometimes let admirers trail the supercharged Mercedes for miles before playfully stepping on the gas and losing them in a cloud of dust. Maybe someday, Jeremy thought, leaders like Hitler would surround themselves with bulletproof glass, would travel only routes that had been cleared in advance by security forces. But here in this sunny town square in Essen, no would-be assassin could have looked cross-eyed at Hitler without being torn apart by the crowd.

The crowd moved respectfully aside to let the three cars bearing Hitler's party out of the square. They seemed to be heading toward the Kaiserhof, the hotel where Hitler was staying.

"Excuse me," Jeremy said. "Let me through, please."

The crowd was thick as molasses, eddying uncertainly now that Hitler had left. By the time Jeremy reached the edge of the square, the doors of the town hall had been flung wide, and the bride and groom had come out, followed by costumed maidens scattering flowers after them. The *Gauleiter* was a stocky, bull-necked man, sweating in a heavy black cutaway to which a tailor had sewn a swastika armband. The bride was a robust girl squeezed into a pseudopeasant dirndl and further compressed by a laced green corselet that forced her ample bosom to spill out over the top amid billows of lace. She looked miffed. The Führer had stolen her thunder.

He got to the Kaiserhof perspiring and slightly out of breath. A small knot of people in cheap clothing were loitering near the entrance, being kept at bay by a magnificent doorman. The usual crowd of Hitler watchers. The security men didn't even bother to look them over. They depended on the hotel staff to keep them at bay. The doorman narrowed his eyes as Jeremy came through, then relaxed and touched his hat when he recognized him.

Jeremy had guessed correctly that Hitler would be staying at the Kaiserhof, and had checked in when he arrived. Like its namesake in Berlin, it was a luxury hotel, probably the best in Essen. There had

been some difficulty about his lack of luggage, but youthful arrogance
and a wallet bulging with the telegraphed expense money from Allied
International Press Service had won the day. He had sent a maid out
for a fresh shirt, had his suit sponged and pressed, and his shoes
shined, and now looked presentable.

"Any messages?" he asked at the desk.

The clerk checked his pigeonhole. *"Nein,"* he said. He looked
harassed.

Jeremy nodded toward the entrance, where the crowd of loiterers
could be seen through the open door. "Has the Führer returned? I saw
him leave the town hall a little while ago."

"Yes. Such excitement!" The clerk leaned forward confidentially.
"Now he is having a conference in his suite. Important people are
going in and out. The switchboard has been ringing constantly with
calls from Berlin."

The clerk gestured toward the telephonist's cage behind the desk.
Little red flags were popping up all over the switchboard, and the
young telephonist was frantically plugging in lines.

Jeremy pulled a face to show that he was impressed. He bought a
newspaper and stationed himself strategically in a chair in the lobby
where he could look out through a screen of palm fronds.

He was rewarded three hours later when he recognized a travel-
rumpled official who arrived at the desk with no luggage but a briefcase, and was shown to the lift by a deferential bellhop. It was Goering's assistant, Paul Koerner, a small, mild man whom everyone
called Pilli. Koerner knew Jeremy by sight; it had been his job to fuss
with the press when his fat boss, hunting spear in hand and wearing a
medieval jerkin, had shown off Karin Hall.

Jeremy hid behind his newspaper, but Koerner was in no mood to
notice anything. Jeremy watched the elevator needle and saw that he
had gotten off at Hitler's floor.

Within the hour, a detachment of bellboys staggered through the
lobby with an enormous load of luggage. Goering followed, with
Koerner trotting at his heels. Goering was dazzling in a white Panama
suit, cut from enough silk to have made a parachute. Koerner scurried
to the desk to settle the bill, while Goering sailed grandly out the door.

Jeremy folded his paper and went to the desk. "Say," he said,
"wasn't that Air Minister Goering?"

The clerk was in ecstasy. "Yes, yes," he burbled. "With the
Führer's party. He has been called away to Berlin on important business. Just think, they have ordered up a special plane!"

"Think of it!" Jeremy said respectfully.

He went back to his post, but nothing else happened. At seven o'clock he gave up and went to dinner in the hotel's main dining room.

Hitler's associates came down to dinner in twos and threes, eating quickly and talking in low tones to one another, but Hitler himself did not appear. About eight o'clock, Schaub and Schreck, the Laurel-and-Hardy pair who served respectively as Hitler's bodyguard and driver, pushed their way through into the kitchen and came out with a covered tray. Evidently Hitler was going to have dinner in his room.

Jeremy lingered over coffee, and was rewarded when two members of Hitler's party passed close to his table on their way out. One of them, a gangsterish-looking fellow named Lutze, was saying: "But first he has to fix it up with Krupp."

"When?" the other man said.

"In the morning."

Jeremy finished his coffee and went out to the switchboard. "Can you put me through to Berlin?" he asked.

"In a moment, Herr Sinclair," the telephonist said. "I'm trying to get a connection with Bad Wiessee." He straightened his thin shoulders. "For the Führer."

Jeremy loitered next to the cage. The telephonist was having an argument with the trunk operator in Munich. "No, no, the Pension Hanselbauer in Wiessee! Bad *Wiessee!* You are keeping the Reichskanzler waiting, do you understand me?" Finally he got the pension. "You must call Captain Reichsminister Roehm to the telephone immediately. I don't care if he *is* having dinner with his guests. The Führer wishes to speak with him!"

Jeremy waited. It was obvious that the telephonist was eavesdropping on the call. The man's eyes grew wider and wider. Evidently he was getting an earful. Hitler must have been screaming at the top of his lungs; Jeremy could hear his voice as a furious insect buzz escaping from the telephone.

The telephonist gave a guilty start as he realized that Jeremy was still standing there. "Please take box number three, Herr Sinclair. I can place your call now."

Walt Hanes was still at the office. "Is *that* all you have? Listen, Sinclair, I *know* Goering's back in Berlin. He's put the Prussian police unit on alert, and he was seen paying a call on Himmler. Whatever's going to happen is going to happen right here. Get your ass back to Berlin!"

"Listen, Mr. Hanes. If there were some kind of emergency, why would Hitler stay in Essen? What's here?"

"Nothing except Krupp headquarters." He gave a barking laugh. "Maybe he's going to ask old Gustav for another financial contribution."

"Seriously, Mr. Hanes . . ."

Hanes's voice was heavy with sarcasm. *"Seriously,* kid, Hitler could never've got where he is without the backing of Krupp and his industrialist friends. He still owes them plenty. He doesn't dare make a move without being sure they're behind him."

Jeremy mulled that over. When Hitler had come to power the previous year, one of the first things he had done was to outlaw collective bargaining. Storm troopers had raided every union office in the country, confiscated their funds, and sent the labor officials off to concentration camps. Now, in the big Ruhr factories, it was said, complainers on the assembly lines were sent directly to the local Gestapo headquarters for a friendly little talk.

"Mr. Hanes . . ." Jeremy lowered his voice. "I also found out that Hitler placed a call to Roehm, the head of the SA. He's taking some kind of a cure at a spa near Munich."

"Yeah?" Hanes's voice showed reluctant interest. "What'd he say?"

"I don't know," Jeremy confessed miserably. "But he was mad."

"Great. Just great. That's what I call intrepid journalism. What're you going to file from Essen, kid, a nice little feuilleton on the Ruhr . . . 'Germany's Industrial Heart: Coal, Steel, and Cathedrals'?"

Stung, Jeremy stammered: "Look, Mr. Hanes, maybe if I went on to Munich—"

"Forget it. We've already *got* a stringer in Munich. Good old Pops Schulz."

The "stringer" crack hurt. Jeremy had been on salary for almost three months now, and had scored enough beats to have been given a grudging raise by Allied International.

"I think I'm really onto something, Mr. Hanes. I mean I really think I am."

"If you're working up to asking for more expense money, forget it."

He hung up before Jeremy could protest.

Jeremy woke at dawn, as he had told himself to. He immediately staggered barefoot to the window and looked out. Hitler's car, a dark blue open Mercedes with an enormously long hood, was still parked at the curb. He dressed quickly, then hung around until six-thirty. There was still no sign of activity around Hitler's car. He went downstairs.

At the desk, he found that Walt Hanes had wired money after all— one hundred marks and a message that said: *One more day.* He stuffed the banknotes into his wallet while the desk clerk looked on respectfully, then went to the big, sunny breakfast room facing on the terrace.

He dawdled over sweet rolls and a huge bowl of strawberries with whipped cream. At seven, Schaub and Schreck came in and checked the room out. Their eyes fell briefly on Jeremy, then moved on to the other patrons, one by one. Satisfied, they went back upstairs.

Hitler came in a few minutes later, a convoy of cronies with him. He looked like a man with an advanced state of nerves. Jeremy thought his walk was peculiar; mincing little steps, with an odd nervous twitch that consisted of lifting his right shoulder and jerking his left knee simultaneously every few steps, like a mechanical toy with a missing gear.

The headwaiter fell all over himself, bowing and fussing. Hitler's chief bodyguard, Brückner, spoke brusquely to him, and the party was shown to a large round table in a secluded corner. The help scurried around, moving tables out of the way, scooping up place settings and removing chairs to prevent anyone from taking a seat too close to Hitler.

Jeremy nursed his cup of coffee and tried not to stare too conspicuously at Hitler's table. His efforts were unnecessary. No one would have looked at him if he had been painted purple.

He was surprised by the horseplay at Hitler's table. The second-raters were trying to show off in front of Hitler. Then they would remember that they were supposed to be important functionaries, that people were looking at them, and they would scowl and put on stern faces.

Hitler paid no attention. He seemed morose and withdrawn. Occasionally he would crook his finger and Lutze or one of the others would lean close for a few words. Once Hitler made what was evidently a caustic comment about a huge slice of ham that Schaub had helped himself to, and the bodyguard, turning beet red, pushed it away with a feigned loss of appetite. Hitler, Jeremy remembered, was a confirmed vegetarian.

Hitler himself made a rather odd breakfast of two cups of hot milk, at least nine or ten pieces of Zweiback smeared with marmalade, and several squares of chocolate, gobbling the candy with a furtive greed and wiping the tips of his fingers on his napkin afterward.

When Hitler rose, the entire party scrambled simultaneously to their feet, finished or not. Schaub looked longingly at his slab of ham. The headwaiter was bowing at the table before he could be summoned, and Brückner peeled off bills from a fat wad he took out of his trousers pocket.

Jeremy followed the crowd out into the street after Hitler's party. Hitler, stiffly self-conscious, climbed into the front seat of the supercharged Mercedes beside the driver. Brückner and the bodyguard, Schaub, took the rear bench, and two more members of the entourage occupied the facing jump seats. Five of the remaining men, Lutze among them, squeezed into a second car, also open. The rest, evidently, were going to be left behind.

At first the cars could not move because of the press of people. They surged eagerly around, kept at a small distance by plainclothesmen. But one woman, sobbing with hysterical joy, broke through with a huge bouquet of flowers, which she presented to an embarrassed Führer. He passed it to an attendant in one of the jump seats. Then three or four children climbed the running boards, waving autograph books. Hitler, with a resigned shrug, signed them. A cheer went up from the crowd.

Slowly the cars began to inch their way through the throng. A middle-aged woman, tears streaming down her cheeks, turned to Jeremy and said, "He gives his life for Germany!"

Jeremy joined the hordes trying to run after the disappearing automobiles. A number of juveniles on bicycles were pedaling furiously, trying to keep up as long as they could, and a few of the automobiles parked in the vicinity were starting up their engines. The plainclothesmen and the abandoned members of the party had gone back to the hotel.

As he rounded the corner, he had a piece of luck. A market truck was pulled up at the curb in front of a greengrocer's shop; the driver, a dusty unshaven old man in collarless shirt and shiny vest, had just finished tying down his tarpaulin.

"Ten marks if you follow after the Führer's car," Jeremy blurted, trying not to let his accent show.

The deliveryman stared at him stupidly. "What, what?" he said.

"The Führer's car! I'll pay you to drive after it."

The man's face closed with suspicion, and Jeremy knew he had offered too much. "I'm not a taxi driver," the man said.

Jeremy forced the same kind of ecstatic smile on his face that he had seen on other members of the crowd. "Imagine, what luck coming face to face with the Führer in an out-of-the-way place like this! What a story to tell when I get back home! If only I had a camera!"

"You're not a German," the man said accusingly.

"No, I'm American . . . on vacation . . . but believe me, there are plenty of people in my country who admire Adolf Hitler."

The deliveryman spat in the gutter. "Then you're stupid. All right. Get in. Ten marks. But you'll have to crank the starter."

He moved with exasperating slowness to the driver's seat. Jeremy cranked frantically, and the ancient motor finally caught, with a violent kick that would have broken his arm if he had not snatched his hand away in time. He climbed hastily into the cab. The truck was in motion before he had the door closed.

"We won't be able to keep him in sight long," the driver said.

"That's all right. Just do the best you can."

Jeremy, bouncing in the truck cab's high seat, felt his teeth rattle. But the supercharged Mercedes inevitably gained distance and finally disappeared entirely.

"We've lost them!" Jeremy cried despairingly.

The old man spat on the floor between his feet. "Don't worry, I know where they're headed now. The *Hauptverwaltungsgebäude*."

"Where?"

"Krupp's main headquarters building. Where else would they go?"

"Are you sure?"

"We're on Kortestrasse now. See that? That's Gestapo headquarters. Old Krupp has a direct telephone line to it. He sends troublesome workers there to be disciplined."

"Oh?" Jeremy tried to be noncommittal.

"You can tell your friends in America what it's really like for a workingman under the New Order." He looked sourly at Jeremy's freshly pressed blue suit. "If a *feiner Herr* like yourself knows any working-class people, that is." He spat on the floor again. "Hitler got the workers' vote by talking about National Socialism. In the meantime he made a deal with the bosses."

Jeremy made no response to the bitter outburst. He seemed to have fallen in with an *alter Roter,* an unreconstructed old socialist. Four million German workers had been members of the socialist unions before 1933. Hitler had promptly dissolved their organizations, arrested their leaders, and put them under the "protection" of Dr. Ley, the Nazi labor boss.

On the other hand, the old man could be a Gestapo provocateur, testing him out.

"Here, we're on Kruppstrasse now. We'll be crossing Altendorfer Strasse soon. I'll leave you at the corner. The Krupp police take a good look at anyone coming too close to the main gate."

They had been driving for some time through a strange gray city, growing like a cancer out of Essen's quaint streets and neat squares and spreading out over an area many times larger, a city of smoking industrial sheds and coal piles and grimy cranes, like a suburb of hell. The sky was darkened by a gloomy haze, and you could taste the grit in your mouth. Jeremy felt rather than heard the pervasive thrumming in the air, the collective pulse of giant machines, spread over thousands of acres, thumping away in their sooty caves.

"There, that's the *Hauptverwaltungsgebäude*. What did I tell you?"

The old man braked to a jarring halt. Ahead, down the ashen boulevard, rose a monstrous castellated office building of smoke-stained stone. The two blue open Mercedes were parked in front of the gate, a uniformed guard looking after them.

"You see that bay window on the second floor? That's Krupp's office. That's where he'll take the Führer for a private talk afterward. But first they'll take him to the reception hall and make a fuss with speeches and flowers." He laughed sardonically. "Bertha Krupp won't receive the Führer at the villa. He's not well-bred enough for Big Bertha. She always has a headache when he visits Essen."

"Well . . . thank you very much." Jeremy got out his wallet and gave him a ten-mark note. The old man folded it carefully and put it in his pocket.

"Take my advice, and don't ask for a tour. They don't like visitors."

"Yes . . . well . . ." Jeremy started to get out of the truck, but the old man wasn't finished talking.

"The Easter Saturday massacre of 1923 happened right there, in front of the building. Krupp watched it from his window. It was when the stinking French occupied the Ruhr valley, over the war-debt payments. They sent a machine-gun squad to inventory the vehicles in the central garage across the street there. The whistles blew and the workers laid down their tools. Thirty thousand of them gathered in a crowd. The French got panicky and opened fire. They killed thirteen workers and wounded fifty. My brother-in-law was one of those killed. There was national mourning. The French occupation authorities fined Krupp one hundred million marks for inciting a riot and put him in prison, but in the end they had to withdraw their troops from the Ruhr. The international outcry was too great. Even the British couldn't stomach it. But when the French left, they stole all the new locomotives and trucks and anything else they could lay their hands on."

Jeremy had his hand impatiently on the door handle. The old man looked at him with cold amusement.

"That was when the seeds for Hitler were planted. When we Germans started looking around for someone to give us back our pride. Go on, young American sir, have a look round the Krupp factories if they'll let you in. You won't see any cannon barrels at the forges. No Big Berthas. Typewriters and baby carriages, that's what they'll show you."

The truck backed up with a grinding of gears and turned around. Jeremy walked over to the main gate. The headquarters building squatted amidst a jumble of machine shops that had grown up among the drab houses like blackened mushrooms. Immense chimneys loomed through the haze. Railroad tracks crisscrossed the surrounding pavement. A mountainous heap of coal had been dumped unceremoniously nearby, a dirty reminder to Krupp executives of where their paychecks came from.

The Krupp policemen eyed him suspiciously as he approached. Jeremy put on his best smile and said: "Say, am I in the right place? This *is* the main office, isn't it?"

The older policeman, a grizzled man with a Hohenzollern mustache, frowned at Jeremy's uncombed hair. "Do you have business inside?"

"No, but—"

"No visitors allowed."

"But if I could just ask—"

"Read the sign."

The young policeman smirked as Jeremy read the notice posted beside the gate. It was big—about the size of a Burma Shave sign—and was planted firmly in the ground on two steel posts set in concrete. In forbidding black letters it said: NO APPLICATION TO VISIT THE WORKS MAY BE MADE, SINCE SUCH APPLICATIONS CANNOT BE GRANTED UNDER ANY CIRCUMSTANCES.

It was unanswerable German logic. Jeremy said, "Mind if I wait here? I was hoping I'd get to see the Führer when he comes out."

"You can wait in the street if you like. I can't stop you."

Cheers and applause could be heard from inside the building. Jeremy guessed that Hitler was being introduced. He crossed the street for an overall view. A few other people were standing about, too: a thin housewife with a string shopping bag, a couple of urchins with dirty faces, a young man with a cigarette pasted to his lower lip, a few shabby pensioners. It wasn't as large as Hitler's usual crowd; he had caught this factory street by surprise. The Krupp workmen who crossed the street on errands slowed down and glanced up surreptitiously at *der Krupp*'s bay window, but they didn't stop.

Hitler's autos had been brought across in front of the cavernous central garage to be gassed up. Jeremy strolled over, hands in pockets.

"Some car," he said admiringly.

The young mechanic who was polishing the windshield looked up with a gap-toothed grin. He was a jug-eared kid with a broad, freckled face. "Seven-liter supercharged engine," he said cheerfully. "It'll do over a hundred. Nothing can keep up with it, not even those fancy American models. The Führer sure knows his cars!"

The other mechanics went on working. Jeremy took a step backward to get out of the way of one who was crawling around on his hands and knees, checking the air pressure in the tires.

"Did you get to see him when he went in?"

"No, worse luck. I was working inside. And I'll miss him when he comes out, too. They told us to have the cars ready by two thirty-one and a half, and I'll be off my shift then."

"Two thirty-one and a *half?* It's that exact?"

The boy grinned, and resumed polishing. "Everything runs like clockwork at Krupp's. Even the Führer has to stick to Herr Krupp's schedule when he comes here. Executive luncheons always end at two-fifteen sharp. Fourteen minutes for coffee. One minute for leave-taking. A minute and a half to get downstairs to the cars. And the engines had better be running, I'll tell you that!"

"That's too bad. I can't wait that long. Maybe I'll get to see him when he returns to the Kaiserhof. I'm staying there, too."

"You'll wait a long time, then."

"What do you mean?"

The mechanic smiled happily, pleased to show off his insider's knowledge. "From here, the Führer motors directly southward. To Bad Godesburg."

The Hotel Dreesen in Godesburg was a comfortable, sprawling place with a wide riverfront terrace and a spectacular view of the Rhine. From the balcony of his room, Jeremy could see the ferry landing below and the steep banks opposite with their towering crags and fairy-tale castle.

More important, he could see Hitler, pacing back and forth on the terrace, while the goblin figure of Goebbels limped after him, tiny hands fluttering as he delivered some sort of excited harangue. Schaub and Schreck slumped at a table nearby under an umbrella like a giant mushroom. It had been going on for some time now. Dusk had fallen, and the dimming figures cast long rippling shadows. It was like a scene out of Wagner, complete with dwarfs.

The phone rang in his room, and Jeremy reluctantly turned from the balcony. "I have your party in Berlin now," the hotel operator said. "Please go ahead."

"Having a nice vacation for yourself, Sinclair?" came Walt Hanes's abrasive voice. "You certainly picked a tough assignment this time. A resort hotel on the Rhine, where the tab starts at fifteen marks a night and there's running water and a telephone in every room."

"I had to, Mr. Hanes," Jeremy said in a low voice. He hoped the hotel operator wasn't listening in or, if he was, that he didn't understand English. "Hitler's staying here."

"Of course. He always stays there," Hanes said sweetly. "It's run by one of his old army buddies from the war."

"Please, Mr. Hanes. Something's going on. I'm sure of it. Dr. Goebbels arrived here a couple of hours ago."

"Goebbels? Are you sure?" Hanes was suddenly serious.

"Yes."

"Hmm. Well, don't make too much of it, Sinclair. He's probably just getting the little doctor out of the way."

"Out of the way?"

"Out of Goering's way." Hanes gave a rasping laugh. "After he sent Goering back to Berlin to see Himmler, it suddenly dawned on him that Fatty might take advantage of the general excitement to have our tiny friend killed."

"What do you mean by general excitement?"

"Oh, nothing much," Hanes said, his usual sarcasm revived. "There's a general army alert in effect, that's all. Von Fritsch recalled his top generals to Berlin, and the defense minister seems to have found it necessary to make a public announcement that the army stands firmly behind the Chancellor. In the meantime, Goering's given himself plenary powers. Yes, sir, big things are brewing in Berlin, all right. Nothing, of course, to compare with the excitement of sitting on a hotel terrace overlooking the Rhine and sipping the local wines at fifteen marks a day."

"Please, Mr. Hanes," Jeremy pleaded. "You're covered in Berlin. Let me keep following my lead here."

Hanes sighed elaborately. "Oh, what a sucker I am. It's my one failing. I've wired you some more expense money. You ought to be able to pick it up at the desk in the next hour."

"Thanks, Mr. Hanes."

"Forget it. Stay out of trouble, Sinclair."

Hanes hung up. Jeremy thought he heard a second click on the line. He replaced the phone in its cradle and went back to the balcony. Down below, the terrace was empty.

Jeremy went down to the hotel lounge for a beer. It was no use hanging about the corridor on Hitler's floor, trying to see who went in and out. Brückner or one of the others was always stationed outside Hitler's door, and Jeremy was afraid that someone might realize that he had also stayed at the same hotel in Essen. Besides, there was always the chance that Goebbels might recognize him as a member of Berlin's colony of foreign correspondents.

About eight o'clock, a powerful figure in the showy black uniform and tall peaked cap of an SS officer swaggered into the lounge and called loudly for a stein of *helles Bock*. When it arrived, he took a long draught, wiped the foam off his mouth with the back of his hand, and stared belligerently around.

It was another arrival from Berlin. For some reason, he had not been admitted to the conference upstairs, but had been left cooling his heels until he was sent for. The new arrival was a strong-arm man, not a policy maker. Jeremy covertly studied the coarse, brutal face, and after a moment had him placed. It was Sepp Dietrich, the Bavarian roughneck who commanded the elite SS unit that acted as Hitler's personal guard—the Leibstandarte Adolf Hitler. They were under Hitler's direct control rather than Himmler's, and they were beyond all legal restraints. When Hitler made his public appearances, they rode ahead of him on the parade route, and simply shot into any windows that had not been closed in compliance with police orders. In less palmy days, Dietrich had been a butcher's apprentice, and Jeremy thought that despite the silver braid he still looked as if he belonged in a bloody apron.

Jeremy nursed his beer and kept his head down. At about nine o'clock, Schaub came into the lounge to fetch Dietrich upstairs. Dietrich got up, leaving a half-finished stein of beer.

When nothing else happened after a while, Jeremy paid for his beer and headed back to his room. He stopped at the desk to pick up the expense money that Walt Hanes had wired. The clerk insisted on counting it twice for him before stuffing the thick sheaf of Reichsmarks into a hotel envelope and sealing it in front of him.

As Jeremy put the bulky envelope in his pocket, he looked and saw Dietrich storming through the lobby, looking grim. His interview with Hitler had been brief.

Jeremy followed him outside and saw him get into a waiting limousine. The limousine took off with a shriek of rubber. Just at that moment a taxicab pulled up to the hotel's entrance and deposited an overdressed couple.

Jeremy looked up at Hitler's lighted window. He had taken pains that afternoon to count windows and locate it from the outside. He could see the pacing, hand-waving silhouette and the distorted shadows of the other men thrown on the shade by a low lamp. This conference, or whatever it was, had been going on a long time, and it looked as if it was going to continue for a while longer. Jeremy hesitated, then decided to gamble. He climbed into the waiting cab before anyone else could.

"*Verzeihung*," he stammered, feeling uncomfortably like a gangster in a Jimmy Cagney movie, "can you follow that car, please?"

The taxi didn't move. The driver turned slowly around in the front seat and took a long, hard look at him.

Jeremy suddenly realized the enormity of what he had done—asking a cabbie to trail an SS officer. The driver had certainly seen Dietrich getting in with his silver-braided cap and black uniform. It dawned on Jeremy that he would be lucky if the driver didn't drive him directly to local Gestapo headquarters.

He fumbled in his inside pocket and came up with the thick hotel envelope padded with Walt Hanes's wired money.

"The *Gruppenführer*," he said urgently, "he has forgotten important papers. I must put them in his hands!"

The driver snapped to attention like an old soldier. "At once!" he said. "I can try to overtake him, and attract the driver's attention by blowing my horn."

"Are you mad?" Jeremy said. "One does not make a spectacle in such matters. Follow him unobtrusively and when he stops I will give him the papers without attracting attention."

"Of course, *mein Herr*," the driver said abashedly. He touched his cap, and put the taxi into gear.

Dietrich's car fled north some ten miles to Bonn, which had a small aerodrome. The cab hung well back, at Jeremy's orders. There wasn't much danger of losing Dietrich on the broad, direct autobahn which paralleled the Rhine.

At the edge of the field, they had to stop at an airplane crossing sign while a big trimotor taxied along an access road for a takeoff. When at last they were able to drive through, Jeremy saw the SS limousine parked in front of the terminal's passenger station. Dietrich and his driver were nowhere in sight.

"Shall I wait for you, *mein Herr*?" the taxi driver said.

"No, I'll get a ride back in the *Gruppenführer*'s car," Jeremy said. He paid the driver and got out.

Inside the terminal, he looked at the blackboard. A night flight for Munich was about to take off, with stops at Saarbrucken and Stuttgart. He went through the station building out onto the field.

The Munich plane was waiting on the field under brilliant floodlights. It was a Fokker cabin monoplane with Lufthansa markings and a circled swastika on the tail, an eight- or ten-passenger job. Despite the hour, a small crowd of well-wishers was clustered beyond reach of the propellers to see the passengers off. But something was wrong.

A business-suited man carrying a briefcase climbed backwards out of the oval door, his foot feeling for the step stool. When he was on the ground, someone handed a valise down after him. The next to leave was a fellow in a loud checkered suit, carrying a salesman's sample case.

The oval door closed, and mechanics spun the plane's twin propellers for takeoff. The businessman, shaking his head angrily, was received effusively by a fat lady wearing a fur collar despite the season, and a horsey twelve-year-old in the white blouse and blue skirt of a

Hitler Jungmädel uniform. The salesman, with nobody waiting, trudged wearily toward the passenger station, a dumpy middle-aged man with seal's bristles under his nose. Jeremy stopped him at the door.

"Was that the Munich night flight?" he said.

The salesman put down his heavy case and mopped his forehead. "That it was, sonny," he said in a resigned tone. "A fine state of affairs!"

"What happened?"

"Didn't you see? A pair of Schutzstaffel mugs elbowed their way aboard just before takeoff and commandeered our seats. One of them actually had his hand on his gun, in case we didn't get up fast enough for him, can you imagine that?" He added hastily: "Not that I'm not glad to make sacrifices, like any good German, you understand. Well, I'd better go to the ticket office and see if they'll refund my money. But who's going to pay me for the business I lose if I can't keep my morning appointment, I'd like to know?"

"Isn't there another flight to Munich?"

"Not tonight. From here, anyway. I think there's a later flight from Cologne."

"That's too bad," Jeremy said sympathetically.

The salesman mopped his brow again. "I'm getting too old for this game. See that?" He pointed a pudgy finger at a big Junkers trimotor on the apron in front of the hangar. "That's the Führer's plane. Now *that's* the way to travel. Take off and land whenever you please, no waiting."

"That the Führer's plane over there?"

"Correct. And why *shouldn't* a head of state have his own plane, tell me? That's where we're ahead of America." He picked up his sample case and plodded wearily toward the terminal.

Jeremy strolled over for a better look. The hangar apron was roped off to keep people from wandering too close. Hitler's trimotor was one of the latest models, the same bottle-nosed Ju 52 used by many airlines on their regular passenger flights. It was low-winged, unlike its rival, the Ford trimotor, and it actually had streamlined fenders for its forward wheels. It could carry twenty passengers. It was a lot of plane for one man.

The mechanics had the cowling of the starboard engine off, and were up on stepladders working on it. The propeller lay on the ground. Jeremy edged closer to the rope. Nobody paid any attention to him. A coveralled man came out of the shed, wiping his hands on a piece of cotton waste. "Hurry it up, you fellows," he said. "I've just had a phone call. We've got to have this thing ready to fly by midnight."

"What's the hurry?" one of the grease monkeys grumbled. "I thought we were supposed to have all morning to work on it."

Jeremy turned and headed toward the passenger station. The number painted on the Junkers's fuselage was D-2600. He could call Pops Schulz, the Munich stringer, and have him on the alert to look for the plane, in case Munich was where Hitler would be landing. Pops wouldn't be too happy at being roused from bed after midnight, but maybe the chance of getting a story would mollify him. And he could call Walt Hanes so that a man could be on the lookout at Tempelhof Aerodrome. Berlin was probably where Hitler was heading.

As he sat over coffee in the all-night confectioner's across the road from the aerodrome, he began to get restive. He ground out his cigarette in his saucer and got up. He paid for his coffee and went back across the road to the aerodrome.

A blond young chap from Lufthansa was very helpful. "No, I'm sorry, there are no more flights to Munich from here until seven in the morning. But there is a flight from Cologne in about an hour. There is a restaurant on board, and they will be serving a late supper. If you catch the motor omnibus that stops across the road here five minutes from now, you can just about make it. I'll phone on ahead to Cologne."

"Thank you," Jeremy said.

"Have you ever flown before?" the air steward said.

"No," Jeremy admitted.

"There is nothing to be nervous about. It is quite safe. You will feel no sensation of speed. We will arrive in Munich before you know it."

Jeremy nodded, trying to act as if flying were a natural human endeavor. The air steward gave a little bow, clicked his heels smartly, and went on to the next passenger compartment.

Jeremy settled back in his armchair. It was as large and luxurious as a Pullman seat. The airliner was a giant twenty-passenger ship, with two passenger per compartment on either side of a broad aisle. The chair opposite was empty; Jeremy had the compartment to himself. The windows all had fussy lace curtains, and there were gooseneck lamps above each seat for reading. Except for the mahogany-and-brass handhold screwed into the wall beside each chair, there was nothing to remind Jeremy that the trip was any more unusual than a train ride. He wondered if he could convince Walt Hanes of that when he submitted his expense account.

Once they were airborne, a small table appeared magically in front of Jeremy. It was set with a white tablecloth, silver salt and pepper shakers, a fine crystal cream pitcher, and there was even a vase of flowers. The air steward prepared the meals on a small gas stove in a kitchen compartment at the rear: an appetizer of *Hase im Topf,* delicately cooked Rhine salmon, asparagus and spring potatoes with parsley, and two kinds of wine. By the time the air steward cleared away the dishes, Jeremy was feeling expansive.

"What are those lights?" he said. "Are we approaching Munich already?"

The air steward leaned past him. "No, that's Dachau."

"Dachau?"

"Yes. It's about twelve miles north of Munich. A charming old Bavarian town with a fine castle built by the Wittelsbach rulers in the Middle Ages, well worth visiting. An artistic-looking gentleman like yourself would enjoy the side trip. It's always been a favorite place for landscape painters."

Jeremy suddenly felt queasy. The plane had dipped like an elevator.

"Better hold on to the handgrip now," the air steward said. "We'll be landing in a few minutes."

27

"Well, I'm here," Pops Schulz said. "Where's Hitler?"

He was a round, cozy man with a dab of brown mustache, wearing a fuzzy green Bavarian hat that had a shaving brush stuck in it. He rather resembled the elderly dachshund that he carried under one arm. The dog's name was Wotan, and it kept showing its teeth to Jeremy and growling at him.

Jeremy looked miserably around at the wet grass of the airfield, glistening in the light of the revolving beacon. There had been intermittent gusts of rain during the last hour, and he was drenched through.

"He was supposed to leave Bonn at midnight. He should have been here by now."

"Do you know what time it is, Sinclair? It's three o'clock in the morning, and you got me out of a warm bed to come here."

"He must have been delayed."

"Or you had a pipe dream, and he's not coming."

"What are they doing here, then?"

Schulz looked over at the waiting room, where a handful of men were standing about under an awning. There were a few army officers, some brownshirts whose uniforms showed marks of rank, and a couple of overweight civilians. Schulz took Jeremy by the arm.

"Let's go over and sit in my car."

Jeremy followed him to the car, a red two-seater with a convertible top. Schulz deposited the dog on the rear shelf, where it crouched, growling to itself. Jeremy could feel its breath on the back of his neck.

"All right," Schulz said. "One of those men is Gauleiter Wagner. But that doesn't mean anything. None of those other SA birds are top rank. If they were here to greet Hitler, Roehm himself would have come, or at least Heines or Schmid."

"If you could just wait here with me for a little while. I . . . I need to have a car."

Schulz sighed. "I'm too old and fat for this, Sinclair. Let me tell you about something that happened during one of Hitler's visits to Munich a couple of months ago. He'd just left his regular restaurant, the Osteria Bavaria, on his way to Obersalzberg, when his guards noticed that a car was following the motorcade. They stopped, jumped out, dragged the poor bastard out from behind the wheel, and beat him half to death with rubber truncheons before he was able to explain that he was a waiter from the Osteria, trying to catch up with the Führer to deliver an urgent telephone message that had come in just after he left. The waiter at least could explain himself. You can imagine what they'd do to *me*."

"Something's brewing," Jeremy pleaded. "Everybody feels it. There could be a tremendous story in the works, right here in Munich."

"I'll tell you what the big story is in Munich. Nothing. It fizzled out. I've already phoned in my yard of copy to Walt Hanes, and I deserve a rest."

"Story? What story?"

"Nothing much. A few SA units got overexcited, that's all. They took to the streets—staged a demonstration against Hitler. Half of them were drunk. They were singing their old marching songs and yelling, 'The Reichswehr is against us!' One troop even started to march on Oberwiesenfeld airfield. I met them straggling back. Wilhelm Schmid, the SA *Gruppenführer* here, stopped them on the road and disbanded them."

Jeremy blinked. "There was a brownshirt demonstration here? Against *Hitler?*"

Schulz dug into his pocket and handed Jeremy a crude, hand-lettered leaflet.

"Somebody's been passing these around in all the beer halls tonight, that's all. Got them all stirred up, full of booze and looking for a fight, as usual. Most of them are back in their barracks, sleeping it off by now."

Jeremy examined the leaflet. The Gothic headline said, BE-

TRAYAL! The hastily scribbled text beneath started, *Storm Troopers, take to the streets. The Führer is no longer for us.*

"What . . . what time was this?"

Schulz scratched his nose. "Oh, I suppose it all started some time between nine and ten o'clock."

Jeremy thought back. Hitler's phone conversation with Roehm, the one that had made him so angry, had taken place shortly after eight. It had been some time after that, between ten and eleven, that Hitler had changed his travel plans and told his mechanic to have his plane ready by midnight.

"Listen, I hear a plane."

Schulz cocked his head. Behind Jeremy, Wotan gave a little growl. A few moments later, the airport's searchlight picked out a big three-engine transport. They watched as it bumped to a landing on the grass and taxied toward the waiting room. In the brilliant floodlights, Jeremy could make out the plane's number: D-2600. The small group of Nazi officials and army officers began moving toward it before it rolled to a stop.

"That's it," Jeremy said.

"All right, Sinclair," Schulz said. "So you were right." The dog barked, right in Jeremy's ear.

"Will you follow him?"

"I will *not* follow him. I will drive my colleague, whom I have just picked up at the airport, into the city at a reasonable speed."

"Thanks, Mr. Schulz."

"Why don't you call me Pops, like everybody else?"

"Gee, Mr. Schulz, I—"

"I lived in Chicago for thirty years, did you know that? Came to America when I was about your age. Worked for the *Daily News,* then the AP bureau there. I was full of ideas. Thought I was going to make it big in the magazines. I never managed to lose my accent. The fellows always used to kid me about it." He gave Jeremy a moist, mournful look. "I came back to Bavaria for a dignified retirement, with my pension and my savings, and the loose change I could pick up by doing odd jobs for Allied International and the provincial weeklies. I don't need any excitement, believe me."

"I'm sorry, Mr. Schulz."

"Look," Schulz said, touching his arm.

Hitler stalked from the plane, wearing a long-skirted leather coat and a slouch hat. His face, at this distance, was a doughy blob with a speck of black in the middle. His entourage hurried to keep up with him. Jeremy recognized Lutze, wearing his brownshirt uniform, and tiny Goebbels, dragging his bad foot behind him. Hitler had barely a

word for the reception committee. He nodded curtly, spoke a brief
sentence to the Reichswehr officers with a curious histrionic gesture,
like a woman hiding her breasts with crossed wrists, and headed for the
waiting cars.

"He's riding with Wagner," Schulz said. "That means he'll be going
to the Bavarian Ministry of the Interior first."

Schulz waited until the procession was gone before switching on his
headlights. The little two-seater bumped across the grass and found an
obscure side road that connected with the paved highway. They motored sedately into town through drowsing predawn streets. Jeremy
saw tall gingerbread façades, window boxes, drawn curtains. A milk
cart rumbled, rattling its dangling cans. Munich was a town that slept
late.

As they approached a large, open square, Schulz pulled over to the
curb and turned off his lights. "This is as close as I'm getting," he said.
Looking past two street corners, Jeremy had an oblique view of the
façade of some official building, dripping with Gothic carved stone.
The cars of Hitler's procession were parked in front of it, one of them
so carelessly that its right front tire had climbed the sidewalk. Schulz's
pudgy hands were trembling.

After fifteen minutes, an official car pulled up with screeching tires
and a man in brownshirt uniform jumped out, still buttoning his collar, as if he had just been summoned from his bed. He hurried up the
steps and disappeared inside the building.

"That's Schmid, the *Gruppenführer* who disbanded the column of
marchers," Schulz whispered. "He'll be sitting pretty, after demon-
strating his loyalty to Hitler that way."

Another car pulled up, and another SA official hurried up the steps,
a beer-bellied man who kept patting the holstered revolver at his side.

"Who's that?" Jeremy said.

Schulz was sweating. "I think that was Schneidhuber, the *Obergruppenführer* for the Munich and Upper Bavarian SA."

The dog whimpered. Schulz reached behind Jeremy and picked it
up. He put the little dachshund on his lap and stroked it absentmindedly.

Two police vans were the next to arrive, followed by an open SS
staff car filled with helmeted men. The SS burst out of their vehicle
and rushed into the building, guns drawn. The policemen climbed out
of their vans and followed, reluctantly, it seemed to Jeremy.

"What did you get me into, Sinclair?" Schulz said in a shaking
voice.

"Maybe you'd better get out of here, Mr. Schulz," Jeremy said. "I'll
. . . I'll get out of the car."

Schulz laid a hand on Jeremy's sleeve. "Not on your life. You stay put. I'm not moving this car. We're not doing anything to attract attention."

He slid down in his seat, so that his head wouldn't be visible through the windscreen. Jeremy followed his example. Seconds later, another police van went by, Klaxon hooting. Its headlamps lit up the interior of the automobile and the van rattled past. It did not stop in front of the Ministry, but disappeared down a side street.

"Headed toward the railroad station, it looks like," Schulz said. "On their way to nab the ones arriving by train."

"What ones?"

"There's a conference of SA leaders set for eleven in the morning at Roehm's watering place in Bad Wiessee, the Pension Hanselbauer," Schulz said. He gave Jeremy an odd look. "But you knew that, didn't you, Sinclair?"

"No," Jeremy said.

A few more minutes went by. Then the beer-bellied *Obergruppenführer* appeared, his arms pinioned by two Bavarian policemen. His holster was empty. The policemen propelled him toward one of the waiting vans.

"Holy Mother!" Schulz whispered.

Somewhere above, Jeremy heard a window being opened and hastily shut.

"That makes Schmid the acting commander," Schulz said.

But Schmid was the next to emerge from the building. A pair of policemen frog-marched him down the steps and into the back of a van. The SS men were still inside. The vans drove off.

"Where will they take them, Mr. Schulz?" Jeremy said.

"Stadelheim Prison, I suppose," Schulz said, chewing his lip. "It's the only place that can hold so many."

"So many?"

"Don't play cute with me, Sinclair. How in God's name did you find out?" He slumped farther down in his seat, hugging his dog.

They waited another hour. The little car grew musty with dog smell and the sour odor of human sweat. More police units and SS vehicles raced by, on their way to different points of the city.

The sky was beginning to get light when Hitler stormed out of the building, followed by his small party. They had been joined by two men in plain clothes and a pale young woman in a traveling cape. Hitler had a gun in his hand. The group piled into three of the parked cars and drove off. Hitler was in the lead car, beside the driver.

"Hurry, Mr. Schulz, we'll lose them!" Jeremy blurted.

"For the love of God, Sinclair!" The older man's face was beaded with moisture.

"Please, Mr. Schulz!"

Silently, Schulz put the dog back on the rear shelf. He eased his little car out of the parking space without turning on his lights. He went around the corner, and found his way back to the main artery a few blocks later. Ahead, Jeremy could see the dwindling red sparks of taillights, like a small swarm of fireflies moving in and out and winking on and off as Hitler's three cars intermittently eclipsed one another. There was no other traffic. Once, at a cross street, Schulz jammed on the brakes as a military vehicle crossed his path.

They crossed one of the Isar bridges and headed south. In the gray light of dawn, Schulz was able to get by without headlamps. He was having trouble keeping up with Hitler, now a quarter mile ahead. The little car rattled and shook, and the roar of wind through the canvas top was deafening. Jeremy looked at the dashboard and saw that the engine temperature was rising dangerously.

Hitler's small cavalcade pulled steadily farther ahead. Lorries whizzed by in the opposite lane at quickening intervals; Jeremy was glad of the thickening early morning traffic, which was helping to disguise Schulz's presence on the road.

Then Hitler's squadron of limousines turned off onto a smaller winding road that headed up into the mountains. Schulz licked his lips nervously. Ahead, Jeremy could see the magnificent backdrop of the Bavarian Alps, the crinkled ice-cream peaks glistening in the first rays of the sunrise. The little red car sped past fields of wildflowers, humped pastures dotted with painted cows, whitewashed farmhouses tucked among green billows. In the distance, the three black cars climbed the tilted landscape like running bugs and disappeared over the crest of one of the green folds. The two-seater labored to the top of the same rise and pulled over.

"Mr. Schulz, what are you doing?" Jeremy cried.

Schulz's face was gray. "This is as far as I go," he said.

He looked at Jeremy's face, then judiciously put the keys in his pocket before getting out of the car.

"Come on over here," he said.

Puzzled, Jeremy climbed out and stood by him. Schulz pointed down at a sparkling blue lake set in a hollow of the foothills.

"That's the Tegernsee," he said. "There's no point in my going farther. That's where Hitler's headed. There's no mistake about it now. That town you see on the west shore is Bad Wiessee. It's known for the sulphur springs. Good for neuralgia, they say. The big white building with the chalet roof is the Hanselbauer, the spa where Roehm stays." He gave a nervous laugh. "Sulphur," he said. "That makes it an appropriate watering place for the devil, wouldn't you say?"

"Mr. Schulz—"

Schulz's face was set. "I'm driving back to Munich now. If you have any sense, you'll come with me. You have your scoop. Hitler pays surprise visit to Captain Ernst Roehm, Storm Troop commander. Arrests of brownshirt leaders in Munich rumored. That ought to be enough until the facts come out. It's all yours, Sinclair. I don't want any part of it."

"Mr. Schulz, Hitler had a gun. You saw it."

"What do you want from me?" Schulz burst out. "I'm an old man. All right, come over here."

He opened the rumble seat of the car. A bicycle was crammed into the space, its front wheel and handlebars detached, and along with the tire pump, flashlight, galoshes, and other miscellany, there was a Tyrolean hiking costume tied up into a neat parcel, complete with alpenstock.

"At least change your clothes," Schulz said. "The hiking togs ought to fit you. They belong to my son, Rudi. He's tall and skinny—not like me. Nobody notices hikers around here. You can say you're here for a holiday if you're questioned. Go on, take them."

"Gee, Mr. Schulz, I don't know what to say. . . ."

"You can take the bicycle, too. It's only twenty-five miles back to Munich, and it's downhill most of the way. If you get into any trouble, I'll say you stole the bicycle."

"Thanks, Mr. Schulz."

"I was a young hotshot once, too. In Chicago." He turned away abruptly.

Jeremy took the clothes into a clump of trees, out of sight of passing traffic, and changed. He found lederhosen and a sort of harness to hold them up, a peasant shirt and skimpy leather vest, knee-high socks, and one of the felt hats with the shaving brush. He had to wear his own shoes, but they were sturdy brogans, and didn't look too out of place with the leather shorts.

Schulz looked him over when he emerged from the trees. "You'll do," he said. "Very *gemütlich.*"

He bundled up Jeremy's suit and shirt and stuffed them into the rumble seat. He watched while Jeremy assembled the bicycle with the help of a coin and the small wrench that had been taped to the handgrip. Then, while Jeremy was still lashing the alpenstock to the frame, he turned the car around and left, leaving tire marks in the sward beside the road.

The sound of church bells came from the valley below. Jeremy pushed off and coasted all the way down. The lakeside resort town was still in bed. He met no one except a few parishioners on their way to early Mass, dressed in the obligatory folk costume. The town had a couple of large hotels, and every other chalet along the lake path had a sign, discreet or not so discreet, announcing that it was a *Gasthaus*. It wasn't hard to find the Hanselbauer. It was a large building with a chalet roof, its balconied upper windows facing the lake. It was well set back from the road, with a wide driveway. The three black limousines were parked in front, one of them angled to block the drive.

Jeremy wheeled his bicycle up the drive and left it leaning against a tree. As an afterthought, he untied the knobbed walking stick from the bicycle frame and took it with him. He felt better with it in his hand.

The lounge was deserted. No one had cleaned it up yet from the night before. There were full ashtrays, a few dirty glasses and coffee cups scattered about. A three-handed card game evidently had been played on one of the heavy oak tables; the last hands were still fanned out on the tabletop.

From upstairs came the sound of muffled voices raised in anger. A door slammed, there were scuffling feet, then the sound of someone banging on a door. Jeremy walked over to the open guest book and copied down the names. Someone hasty had been there before him; the top page was carelessly creased and partially torn from the binding. The only names he recognized were those of Edmund Heines, the brownshirt boss of Silesia: a convicted murderer who had figured in a homosexual scandal before Hitler's election; and Count Hans von Spreti, the youthful aristocrat who was almost openly acknolwedged as Roehm's lover. A Dr. Ketterer had signed in late the night before—the last name in the book.

Jeremy put his notebook back in one of the many pockets of the lederhosen and walked through to the dining room, gripping his stick. All the tables were set for what was evidently going to be a large banquet later in the day.

The door to the serving pantry opened, and the landlady came out, looking distracted. She was a billowing, gray-haired woman in a peasant dirndl. Her hands were busy twisting her apron out of shape.

"Excuse me," he said. "I'm looking for a place to stay."

Her eyes automatically took in the leather shorts, the hat with the bristles, the walking stick, but she had no attention to spare for him. There were more of the scuffling noises from upstairs, and her frightened eyes went to the ceiling.

"We have no rooms here," she said. "You must go away."

"Maybe you can tell me—"

The unmistakable sound of a shot rang through the house. Then overturning furniture, a thump of a falling body, cries of pain. A voice made pleading sounds, with rhythmic interruptions as though the owner were being beaten.

"*Ach, du lieber Gott!*" the landlady whispered. She stood twisting her apron, Jeremy forgotten.

A thumping sound was heard on the stairway. Through the connecting arch between the dining room and the lounge, Jeremy saw two men in trench coats dragging a limp, naked form down the steps, bloody head dangling. At first he thought it was a girl, then he saw that it was a man, slender and wide-hipped, with smooth white skin. It might have been Count Spreti, whom he had once seen at a brownshirt function next to Roehm, but it was impossible to tell. The face had been beaten to a pulp. Hitler's chauffeur followed, talking excitedly.

"The swine pointed a gun at the Führer," he was saying. "Thank God Dietrich was quick!"

They dragged the naked man outside. A car door slammed. The two men in trench coats came back without the chauffeur. One of them noticed Jeremy and the landlady standing beyond the archway.

"Get in the pantry," he snapped. "Close the door behind you, and keep your mouths shut."

They climbed back up the stairs. The landlady fled to the pantry, wringing her apron. Jeremy followed. A frightened serving girl was inside, her eyes wide and her mouth open, her hands white with flour to the wrists. Preparations for the midday banquet evidently had been going on; a long marble-topped counter bore pieces of cut-up veal, and a tub of newly peeled potatoes stood nearby.

"What's happening?" Jeremy said. "What's going on here?"

The landlady's mouth worked, fishlike, but for a moment no sound came out. "The Führer!" she wailed. "He demanded to see Herr Roehm. I told him that Herr Roehm was still in bed, that he was sleeping off the injection that Dr. Ketterer gave him last night, but he went right up the stairs. Then the Führer and Herr Roehm began shouting at one another, saying terrible things. . . ."

She trailed off, her lips trembling.

"What happened to Dr. Ketterer?"

"He . . . he's still in his room. They told him to keep quiet, too."

She was in shock. It had not occurred to her to wonder who Jeremy was or why he had the right to ask her questions.

A further commotion broke out upstairs. Jeremy heard the sound of heavy feet coming down the stairway again. He opened the pantry door a crack.

"No, no!" the landlady protested. "We are not supposed to look!"

She clutched at his sleeve, but he brushed her off without turning his head. He had a good view of the foot of the stairwell descending into the lounge. The same two men in trench coats were marching two prisoners along in policemen's grips. Behind them, black-uniformed and jackbooted, came Sepp Dietrich, holding a large revolver. Jeremy was awfully glad to be out of sight.

One of the prisoners was stark naked. He had a muscular, slab-shouldered body incongruously topped by a girlish face with long lashes and full lips. Jeremy recognized him at once. It was the same face that was plastered all over the lurid clippings in the newsroom files: that of the Silesian brownshirt leader, Heines. The other prisoner was a burly young man wearing only an undershirt; he was heavily made up with lipstick, powder, and rouge.

"Do you know what they were doing?" Dietrich said. He seemed to think it was a great joke.

Heines stubbed his bare toe on a table leg and cried out in pain. His trench-coated captor shook him roughly by the neck and growled, "Quiet, you filth!" Heines's face was swollen and discolored, as if he had been thumped about a bit.

Through the crack, Jeremy saw Dietrich and the strong-arm men hustle the unlucky pair toward the exit, then he lost sight of them. A moment later he heard a car door slam. He hurried to the pantry window and looked out through yellow dimity curtains. He could see a portion of the drive, but except for the long locomotive nose of the open Mercedes that Hitler had ridden in, the cars were out of sight. The landlady plucked at his sleeve and whimpered, "Please, you must not."

He was waiting for the sound of a car engine starting up when a revolver shot split the air. It must have been the big Luger that Dietrich had been waving around. Through the open window, Jeremy plainly heard a man's voice blubbering.

"Ask Lutze—he'll tell you I've done nothing! Please, Dietrich, for the love of God!"

"Shut up!" came the harsh answer.

The revolver went *blam*. There was a horrid thrashing sound, and a throaty, gargling noise that could not have been called human. The gun went off once, twice more, and the thrashing sounds ceased. After the first execution, Dietrich must have been too rattled to aim properly. There was a long silence, then a voice said: "Look at that! We can't use this car now." Another voice said: "What about my coat?"

The three executioners came stomping back into the lounge. Jeremy was back at the crack in the door in time to see them go up the stairs again. One of the trench coats was splattered with blood and tissue.

Dietrich's coarse Bavarian face was ashen, and the gun was dragging at his side as if it had suddenly grown heavy.

Jeremy felt sick.

"*Bitte, nehmen Sie* . . ."

The servant girl, with an insane smile, was holding out a glass of water. Jeremy took a sip and felt better.

"It will all be straightened out," the girl said confidently.

An argument was going on upstairs. "Where are the reinforcements?" a hysterical voice screamed. It was Hitler's, almost unrecognizable.

Dietrich's mumbling voice offered excuses. Jeremy caught the words: ". . . bad tires . . . old trucks . . . wet roads . . ."

"*Mein Führer*, you do not need reinforcements now! You have done it yourself! With your own hand!" This voice was that of Goebbels. He sounded jubilant, overexcited. Jeremy could almost picture the little man jumping up and down. They must all have been standing at the top of the landing to have been heard so clearly.

"We must leave immediately!" Hitler gabbled, his voice high-pitched and womanish. "We will all be murdered!"

"But we can't leave Roehm and the others here," a new voice said soothingly. "If they are found . . ." Jeremy thought the speaker might be Brückner.

Someone else growled, "Shoot him now and get it over."

"Just say the word, *mein Führer!*" Goebbels jabbered.

"No, no, why are you all at me?" Hitler shouted. "Let me think!" He must have regained partial command of himself. A moment later he began issuing orders.

"Dietrich, you go back to Munich right away. Hurry. Take one of the cars. Take the bodies with you. Make sure they are covered up. Send two or three truckloads of troops from the Pioneer Barracks here. Tell them to turn back anyone headed for Bad Wiessee."

"*Heil Hitler!*" came a ragged chorus. Everyone sounded relieved.

Hitler seemed to gather strength from the show of confidence. He went on in a firmer voice:

"Find Kempka on the way out. Tell him to commandeer any transportation he can find. We'll keep Roehm and the others locked up in the laundry room until he returns."

Booted heels clicked. "*Jawohl, mein Führer!*" Dietrich came striding down the stairs and out through the lounge.

"My old friend, Ernst . . . how can I bring myself to do it?" Hitler sobbed theatrically. "After all these years . . . fighting side by side in the beer halls . . ."

The others made indulgent, cooing sounds, soothing Hitler as one might soothe a child. Hitler went on, in a voice full of stagy self-pity:

"But I must be strong! I must cut out this cancer, no matter how great my own suffering! Roehm is guilty of treason. He's been plotting against me. Plotting to . . . to hand Germany over to a foreign power. Yes, that's it . . . he's taken bribes from the French ambassador. He and the others. And they tried to kill me! You saw how Spreti reached for a gun. But you saw how I dealt with Spreti, the filthy little pervert! I showed no mercy. I let him know what a gun barrel in the teeth feels like!"

So it was Hitler who had pistol-whipped Spreti, not Dietrich. Jeremy listened with fascination as Hitler worked himself up into a fresh rage against Roehm.

"Of course I knew nothing of Roehm's proclivities until the Reichstag election campaign in 1932. And then that scandal in the newspapers! Boy prostitutes, love letters from Bolivia! You can imagine how many votes that cost me. But I stood by him even then! At least that journalist, Bell, didn't live to write any more such stories. A bullet's cheaper than a libel action, as I told Roehm at the time!"

Jeremy opened the door a crack wider so he could hear better.

"And now this! Plotting with von Schleicher to take over the government. Yes, yes, I know all about his secret meetings with Schleicher. Schleicher will have to go, too. Put him on the list. And the other ringleaders—von Bredow, Papen, Ernst, Strasser, the lot! Yes, we must act quickly in Berlin, too. We'll nip Roehm's putsch in the bud! Somebody call Goering immediately and give him the code word."

Jeremy was amazed at the improvised nature of the impending bloodbath. He had always imagined such things were planned with ruthless competence. But apparently people were going to be done away with almost as an afterthought.

None of it made sense anyway. If Roehm and Heines had been planning a putsch in Berlin, why were they lolling in the backwaters of Bavaria, so unwary that they had been surprised in bed with their boy friends?

They brought Roehm downstairs a few moments later. A half-dozen bedraggled brownshirt prisoners—a chauffeur, a couple of adjutants, and other small fry—were already assembled in the lounge. Jeremy, forgetting caution, opened the pantry door another inch. The landlady wrung her hands and wailed.

The SA leader was a stocky, round-cheeked, bull-necked individual with a bristly mustache and bullet scars on his face. He was naked to the waist, and his hairless fatty breasts glistened with sweat. His captivity hadn't cowed him at all; he was roaring insults at Hitler in a trooper's voice.

"Traitor, *Kot und Harn!* You're the traitor, Adolf, my boy! A traitor to the brown revolution! Sucking up to those rich bastards like Krupp and licking the army's ass! What happened to National Socialism, tell me that? It's in Hindenburg's vest pocket, along with your balls, if you ever had any!"

Hitler bawled insults back. His accent had become more Austrian and rustic, with a lower-class slurring of some words.

"I don't know you anymore, either! What happened to my old comrade-in-arms, the toughest soldier I knew? Wallowing in filth, surrounded by a male harem . . ."

Roehm gave a harsh bark. "I never made any secret of it, Adolf. You should try it, too. That's what you really want, isn't it? Instead of trying to act the man with your niece, and that trained seal, Eva!"

Hitler seemed shaken at the mention of his niece. She had committed suicide, Jeremy remembered. There had been some sort of cover-up. The socialist *Munich Post* had intimated that Hitler had goaded her to it, and given her the gun.

"Listen, Ernst, my old friend," Hitler pleaded. "I'll see to it that you're given a pistol in your cell. At least you can die like an officer and gentleman."

Roehm spat on the floor. "Nothing doing, Adolf. If you want me shot, you'll have to do it yourself."

Hitler flew into a rage. "You have not drawn the correct conclusions!"

"Oh yes I have," Roehm shot back. "That little turd, Lutze, came running to you with stories about me, didn't he? I notice he can't look me in the face. How are you going to reward him, Adolf? Give him my job?"

Lutze started to protest. Jeremy managed to jump back just in time as one of the plainclothesmen came through the pantry door.

"The keys to the laundry room!" he barked at the terrified landlady. He had hardly a glance for Jeremy or the servant girl. He took the keys and went back outside.

Jeremy leaped back to his position at the door. The landlady moaned. "Please, *mein Herr,* this is not our affair. It is better to know nothing. You'll have to go, as soon as they let you. I can't give you a room." She looked in despair at all the banquet preparations. "And what am I going to do with all that veal? Tell me that! It won't keep in this heat!"

The servant girl gave Jeremy a smoky look from under half-lowered lashes. "We could give the young gentleman the spare room downstairs," she said, "until I can clear out one of the upstairs bed-rooms." I don't believe it, Jeremy thought.

"Quiet, you slut!" the landlady said. She looked again at the mounds of floured veal. "Perhaps Herr Roehm will be back in time for the banquet."

No, Jeremy thought. I don't think Herr Roehm will be coming back.

Outside, in the lounge, the prisoners were being marched toward the cellar stairs. "What about Ketterer?" Brückner said.

"Let him go home," Hitler said. "He's only a doctor. Warn him to keep his mouth shut."

Roehm had barely been locked up when there was a sound of truck wheels in the gravel of the driveway. Angry voices could be heard.

Goebbels rushed to a window. *"Mein Führer,* we are lost! It's Roehm's headquarters guard, about forty of them. They're armed!"

"How did they get through?" Brückner growled. "That idiot Die-trich hasn't got his men on the road yet."

"Outside, everyone, before they get out of the truck!" Hitler barked. He was playing another part, that of the decisive, cool-headed hero, but it worked. Jeremy was reminded that Hitler had gotten where he was by climbing on top of tables in beer halls and commanding an un-ruly audience to silence.

"There are only nine of us!" Goebbels wailed. "We'll all be massa-cred!"

"Come with me!" Hitler strode out the door, biting his lip, gun in hand. The others followed. Jeremy noticed that Brückner was skipping ahead to be first.

Jeremy raced to the window. He could see the truck full of brown-shirts halted farther down the driveway. It was a battered old truck with bald tires and gnawed wooden sides. Evidently the SA budget for Munich wasn't overly generous. The men's uniforms looked shabby, too, in contrast to the smart tailoring of SS men.

They were crammed into the open body of the truck, hanging on to the sides. Three men were clinging precariously to the top of the tall cab, and four more were squeezed inside. Even so, Jeremy thought, there couldn't be more than twenty or twenty-five of them, not the forty that Goebbels had mentioned. They didn't look particularly dan-gerous, either, despite the two or three revolvers he could see; just a lot of shabby, ill-shaven men, grown middle-aged in their invented uni-forms, and worried about their jobs.

Roehm had had to cut their pay again recently, Jeremy remem-bered, and even so he had trouble meeting his payroll, which was one reason why he wanted to give his street brawlers official army status.

"Return to Munich at once!" Brückner shouted. "Go back to your barracks and await orders!"

The men stared back sullenly, not moving. There were angry mutters. "Where's Roehm?" someone yelled.

Hitler stepped forward. "Don't you know how to take orders?" he scolded them. "This affair is none of your concern. Roehm is no longer in charge. This is your new chief of staff. Lutze, tell them."

Lutze rose to the occasion. "I am Obergruppenführer Lutze. You will take your orders from me from now on. Return to Munich by the Bad Tolz road. You will meet SS troops on their way here, and they will disarm you."

They hesitated. "Can't you see that it's useless?" Hitler said in a wheedling tone. "Come on, boys, don't make trouble for yourselves."

The brownshirts stirred uncertainly. They might have been prodded into a fight; they understood fights; but instead they had been scolded, then jollied like misbehaving children, and they were disorganized and bewildered. There were more mutterings, and then the truck backed out of the driveway, turned around and left.

"You did it, *mein Führer!*" Goebbels prattled. "Your firm, manly action has saved the day! With a word, you turned them back!"

Hitler preened himself. Brückner and the others fell all over themselves telling him how wonderful he was. Hitler had adopted that peculiar coy stance that Jeremy had noticed at the Kaiserhof: his knees primly together and his hands folded demurely in front of his crotch. The woman in the party, who had hung back until now, came forward and, raising herself on tiptoe and clutching her hat, gave Hitler a peck on the cheek. "Now, now, Fräulein Schroeder," Hitler said, pleased.

A few moments later, gravel spattered in the driveway and a horn beeped. It was Kempka with a commandeered bus, one of the double-decker motor coaches that shuttled tourists to the lakeside resorts.

Hitler stood apart while his men herded the handful of prisoners into the bus. Their hands were tied behind their backs. Roehm, still shirtless, seemed subdued. Goebbels was off to one side of the driveway, deep in thought, dictating something to Fräulein Schroeder, who took it all down in a stenographer's notebook. Jeremy wondered what it was. A death list?

Brückner and the plainclothesmen, guns drawn, boarded the bus to guard the prisoners. One of the plainclothesmen got behind the wheel. Kempka was to drive Hitler, who sat in the car's front passenger seat as usual. Goebbels and Fräulein Schroeder rode in back. Lutze drove the remaining car, with a gray-suited older man for a passenger; this, Jeremy assumed, was Dr. Ketterer.

No one bothered to come back to the pantry to tell them they were free to leave. The landlady, her color back, was issuing a string of orders to the girl, who kept casting sidelong glances at Jeremy. An elderly man in a porter's cap appeared from somewhere, and the landlady began screaming at him. The girl gave Jeremy a lunatic grin as he left.

Jeremy went to the lounge and looked out the window until the bus and the automobiles were out of the driveway, then made a dash for his bicycle, still leaning undisturbed against the tree.

He had to get off the bicycle and push it up the long uphill grade leading out of Bad Wiessee. Long before he got to the crest of the crown of hills, he had lost sight of Hitler's procession. He caught up with them on the downhill side, coasting recklessly with an occasional suicidal assist of the pedals.

He whizzed toward them, unable to stop, the roadside a blur. The road was blocked by the tall yellow bus, the two black cars, and the gray touring car they had stopped in the other lane. The touring car contained three brown-uniformed SA officers who obviously had been on their way to Roehm's banquet. Hitler himself was standing with one foot on their running board, questioning them.

The scene grew in Jeremy's vision. Helplessly he watched the flat yellow end of the bus rush toward him. At the last moment, he squeezed through the narrow space between the bus and the halted touring car, almost brushing Hitler. Someone yelled. He had a distinct split-second closeup of Hitler's puffy face jerking around toward him with an annoyed expression. Then he was through the gap, the front wheel wobbling, trying desperately to stay upright while he half stood on the pedals to slow down.

A mile farther on, they caught up with him. The parade of vehicles swept by, horns hooting angrily. Jeremy picked himself up from the ditch, scratched and bruised, and watched them dwindle. The touring car had been added to the procession, hemmed in between Hitler's car and the bus.

It was noon by the time Jeremy reached Munich, tired, sore, and sweaty. The streets were relatively empty, as if some hive instinct had warned people to stay indoors.

Jeremy saw why when he reached the center of town. The whole area around Königsplatz was cordoned off by army troops. Smart-looking soldiers in steel helmets and the gray uniforms of the Reichswehr stood guard in front of the Brown House, the Nazi party headquarters on Briennerstrasse. An armored car had climbed the bottom steps of the Brown House, its turret turned round to point at the imitation-Greek columns of the Propyläen gate across the way. Hitler's cars and the yellow tourist bus were parked at the curb. They were empty.

Jeremy pedaled over for a closer look. A soldier motioned with his rifle for him to move on. Jeremy rode away, looking back over his shoulder like any gawking tourist.

Twenty minutes later he was at Pops Schulz's flat on the left bank of the Isar. Schulz motioned him in quickly and shut the door behind him. The flat was a comfortable, faded place with overstuffed furniture and untidy piles of books and music scattered around. Wotan yelped at Jeremy, but kept his distance.

"Well, did you get your story, Sinclair?" Schulz said.

"My God, yes! Heines is dead, shot. Another man was shot with him. Roehm was arrested. They've got him locked up in the Brown House, if he isn't dead already. I think they want to make it look like suicide. Where's your phone?"

"The telephone lines to Berlin aren't working. They've been cut off for the last couple of hours."

"They *can't* be! I'm sitting on the biggest story of the year!"

"You can try the phone if you want," Schulz said indifferently.

After a brief, futile argument with the long-distance operator, Jeremy gave up.

"What'll I do?" he said.

Schulz shrugged.

"Maybe I could get a train for Augsburg or Nuremberg and make the call from there."

"Use your head, Sinclair. They'll be watching the railroad station. Especially for people like foreign reporters. And anyway, Berlin will be cut off to outside calls from anywhere."

"I *saw* it, don't you understand? Dietrich was the executioner. And they're going to kill General von Schleicher and Bredow and a lot of other people in Berlin!"

"Have you had any breakfast, Sinclair?"

"Don't you *care?*"

Schulz gave a moist sigh. "Maybe I'm an old has-been, but I haven't been entirely idle. Now, get out of my son's clothes and into your suit while I fix us some lunch. You can take a shower bath in there."

"But—"

"We're going to compare notes and see what we've got, and try to make some sense out of it. Rudi will be back soon. Go and clean up. You can use my razor."

Jeremy gave up and went to shower and change. He felt better when he came out. Pops Schulz had a light lunch waiting on the small balcony overlooking the river: a cold salad of herring, pig's knuckles, and lettuce; meat paste on slices of Dudelhofer peasant bread; head cheese, white sausages, and cold dumplings; and pitchers of light and dark beer. Three places were set.

There was the sound of someone in the foyer. "That'll be Rudi now," Schulz said, looking up.

Rudi came in and sprawled in a chair. He was gangling and red-haired, with a lumpy Adam's apple. "I saw the bicycle downstairs," he said. "You're Sinclair?"

He helped himself to pig's knuckles and pickled herring, and poured himself a beer. Jeremy followed suit. To his surprise, he was ravenously hungry.

"I hung around outside Stadelheim prison, the way you asked me to," Rudi told his father. "They're bringing them in by the truckload. I managed to talk to one of the warders coming off duty—you know, the ratty little guy who takes bribes. I slipped him a few marks. He says they began bringing them in at seven in the morning. The cells are full."

"Seven," Schulz said. "Hitler was busy at the Hanselbauer by then."

Rudi scratched his nose. "He says he saw Hans Hayn in a cell."

"Hayn?" Schulz said. "My God, they're getting rid of everybody!"

"Who's Hayn?" Jeremy said.

"He's the SA *Gruppenführer* for Saxony."

Rudi looked at Jeremy. "My contact also confirmed that Schneidhuber and Schmid were locked up. Those are the two you and Pop saw being dragged out of the Ministry."

"He recognize anybody else?"

"Von Killinger. And Uhl. And von Krausser. They grabbed him getting off the train."

Schulz shook his head. "They've arrested half the SA leadership."

"Koch, the prison governor, isn't too happy about them being in Stadelheim," Rudi said. "My man told me he's worried about what might happen to them while they're in his care. He called Hans Frank —that's the Bavarian minister of justice, Sinclair—and Frank put the prisoners under the protection of a detachment of state police while he tries to figure out the legalities."

"There are no legalities," Jeremy said. "Two men are already dead that I know of for sure. No trial, nothing."

"Frank and Koch won't be able to stall Hitler for long," Schulz said. "He'll steamroller them."

Rudi drew a finger across his Adam's apple. "Then it's good-bye, Roehm. Good-bye, everyone."

Jeremy drew a deep breath. "Hitler's already appointed a new SA head in Roehm's place. A man named Viktor Lutze."

"Lutze?" Rudi said. "Never heard of him."

"He's a nobody," Schulz said. "A retired army lieutenant and an SA *Obergruppen* commander for Hanover."

"Hitler brought him on the plane with him from Essen," Jeremy said. "Roehm accused him of being an informer."

"Informer? Loudmouth is more like it. Probably just shot his mouth off after a few too many beers."

"Well he's commander of the SA now," Jeremy said.

Schulz looked at Jeremy with slow, grudging respect. "You *have* got yourself a story, boy, haven't you? Too bad there's no way to get it to Hanes."

"There's *got* to be a way!"

Schulz helped himself to some more of the sausage and dumplings. He took a swallow of dark beer and wiped his smudge of mustache with the back of his hand. "The Brown House will have to issue an official communiqué sooner or later today. Just to quiet the rumors. I'll file that, along with some man-in-the-street impressions, and that'll earn me my monthly check from Allied International."

"You can wait for the official version if you want to, Mr. Schulz," Jeremy said. "Thanks for the lunch."

He stood up.

"Where are you going?" Schulz said mildly. "They'll be watching the trains and the airport."

"I'm going to ask Goebbels to let me make a telephone call."

The crowds around Königsplatz had grown. The police and the soldiers kept them moving.

"They say it's a revolution," an excited matron told Jeremy. "They say the storm troopers are marching on Berlin to take over the government and hand it over to Russia."

Jeremy wondered how *that* rumor had got started.

He pushed his way through the holiday throngs and got as far as the gigantic pseudo-Greek gate that framed one side of the square. Gray-clad soldiers were spaced between the massive stone pillars, casting beady eyes at any fringes of the crowd that surged too close.

"On your way, on your way, keep moving," a Reichswehr lance corporal said mechanically as Jeremy approached.

"Excuse me, how do I get through?" Jeremy said as firmly as he could manage.

"Move along there, move along. No one's allowed through."

That wasn't strictly true. Jeremy could see a trickle of people, most of them in one kind of uniform or another, moving in and out of the Brown House. At the entrance, they had to stop to identify themselves.

"But I have business inside."

That was true, at least, Jeremy thought.

"It will have to wait. Come back tomorrow." The soldier was getting impatient. He was tired of arguing with civilians.

"Look . . ." Jeremy began. He fumbled in his inside coat pocket for credentials. The soldier's rifle came up with a quick, shocking click of the bolt.

"Hold it!" the soldier said.

Jeremy, sweating in his suit, realized how close he had been to getting shot. That was how nervous they all were today.

". . . I'm an American news correspondent," he said, holding his press card up carefully. It had all sorts of impressive-looking stamps from the Ministry of Propaganda. "Dr. Goebbels, the propaganda minister, is holding a press meeting."

That much was true, too, if you wanted to be literal. Goebbels *would* be holding a press conference eventually. The question was when. And where.

"I don't know anything about any meeting," the lance corporal said. But the rifle lowered a trifle.

"I have to get the official statement from him," Jeremy said. "Look, let me talk with your superior, will you?"

The word *offiziell* did it. "Come with me," the lance corporal said.

Jeremy repeated his story to an unshaven, red-eyed lieutenant who looked as if he had been up all night. The lieutenant listened without particularly paying attention, then passed him along. It wasn't *his* responsibility.

"Corporal Petzl, escort him to Oberleutnant Sieber and see if *he* knows anything about this meeting or whatever it is."

Oberleutnant Sieber picked his nose while Jeremy talked. "Well, if the *Leutnant* let you through, *I* won't stop you." He dismissed Corporal Petzl and called over Sergeant Ganz. "Ganz, take this man to Hauptmann Kunkel and let *him* deal with it."

Hauptmann Kunkel looked Jeremy over and sighed. After all, the young man had been passed through by a *Leutnant* and an *Oberleutnant*.

"They never tell us anything," Kunkel said. "We're just stupid soldiers." He studied the Propaganda Ministry stamps on Jeremy's press card. "All right, go on inside. It's *their* lookout anyway."

The lobby of the Brown House bristled with armed men, hurrying back and forth on incomprehensible errands. There were no Reichswehr soldiers here; just SS men and party uniforms. Jeremy saw Rudolf Hess, Hitler's buck-toothed confidant, in deep conversation with a leather-coated man who was holding a Walther automatic in plain sight. Hess handed the man an envelope, and the man hurried off.

Jeremy climbed the main staircase, unnoticed. Goebbels, he recalled, had an office on the second floor that he used when he was in Munich.

Some kind of terrible row was going on in the second-floor meeting room. Jeremy could hear the shouting voices through the closed double doors as he passed by. A knot of men stood outside, trying to listen. Nobody paid any attention to Jeremy. The doors opened briefly to let a pale, shaken brownshirt come out, and Jeremy caught a burst of almost incoherent words from inside: "Only blood can wipe it out. . . ."

The eavesdroppers clustered around the man who had emerged. "What about Roehm? Has he given the order on Roehm yet?" The brownshirt only shook his head and muttered, "Crazy. *Teppichfresser!* He's foaming at the mouth."

Teppichfresser meant "carpet chewer." Jeremy rounded the bend of the corridor, walking briskly. The SS guard outside Goebbels's door stepped forward to challenge him, but as he did so, the door opened and a plump young man in a double-breasted suit came out, carrying an armful of papers. He was one of Goebbels's flunkies, an undersecretary at the Propaganda Ministry whose main duty seemed to be lighting his chief's cigarettes and fetching coffee. Everyone called him Rosie. Jeremy thought quickly and remembered the man's name. Berndt.

"Berndt! There you are! Where's the doctor?"

Rosie blinked at him. "Sinclair! What are you doing here?"

Jeremy affected surprise. "Isn't there going to be an announcement?"

Rosie blinked again. "Announcement? I don't know. Herr Dr. Goebbels is still in with the Führer. Everything's very confused."

The SS guard had relaxed at the familiar exchange. Jeremy said, "There are all kinds of rumors floating around. Don't you fellows want to issue a definitive statement in time for the evening cable?"

Rosie was flustered. "See here, you can't go wandering around unsupervised like this. Wait here while I go and ask. No, don't wait here, go inside and sit down."

He scurried off with his burden of papers. Jeremy nodded pleasantly to the SS guard, who scowled at him, and went to sit in Goebbels's office.

Goebbels had a classy view. Ceiling-high windows looked out across the Königsplatz at the residence of the papal nuncio. The square was still filled with troops.

The office itself was furnished with a traveling salesman's idea of luxury, in the impersonal high-ceilinged style of a bank or hotel lobby.

A larger-than-life oil portrait of Hitler glowered from one wall. A clutter of papers and salmon-colored folders on the blond-wood desk showed that the little doctor was a demon for work, even when traveling. A sheet of paper had been left in the typewriter. Nobody was passing by the open door at the moment, and the SS guard was out of sight. Jeremy walked over to the typewriter and risked a peek.

The typeface was an unusual oversize Gothic script. The doctor, Jeremy saw, favored wide margins and triple spacing, as befitted a former editor and would-be writer. The document, on stiff, expensive bond, seemed to be the beginning of a rough draft of an official statement, with several false starts:

> *Chief of Staff Roehm, his guilt established beyond question in a mutinous conspiracy of Storm Troop leaders, was executed by firing squad today at Stadelheim prison. . . .*

The last part was penciled through. After some fragmentary lines full of strikeovers, the next version began:

> *Chief of Staff Roehm, in evident remorse at his part in a mutinous plot against the Führer and shame at the revolting circumstances in which he was discovered, committed suicide at 6:00 P.M. Sunday evening. . . .*

That was a good trick. Jeremy instinctively glanced at his watch. It was only three o'clock in the afternoon. The little doctor evidently had the gift of prophecy.

Halfway down the page, still another version began:

> *Despite his complicity in a mutinous plot against the Führer, and despite the Führer's personal disgust at the revolting and immoral circumstances in which Captain Roehm was discovered, the Führer has decided to pardon Roehm in view of his past services. . . .*

So that's what all the shouting was about. Roehm still had a chance after all.

When Rosie returned, Jeremy was sitting innocently in a visitor's banquette a safe thirty feet from the desk.

"He says you can wait," Rosie said. "He's still in a meeting with the Führer, but he may have something to say to the foreign press."

Goebbels limped in about three quarters of an hour later. There were spots of color on his swarthy cheeks. He seemed unnaturally excited.

"You're Sinclair?" he said. "Of Allied International Press Service?"

Jeremy confirmed that he was.

"Why aren't you in Berlin with the rest of your colleagues, Mr. Sinclair?" Goebbels said in his familiar mocking style. "There are big goings-on there today, I'm told."

"I was on holiday here in Bavaria."

"Holiday, is it?" Goebbels hobbled past him to his desk and sat down. He looked at the paper in his typewriter, then glanced sharply at Jeremy. He yanked the paper out of the roller and slipped it into a folder.

"What kind of goings-on?" Jeremy ventured.

Goebbels affected surprise. "Ah, have you not heard? We've put down a revolt. The conspirators have all been arrested. Unfortunately a number of them were shot while resisting arrest. Quite a few of them committed suicide. Yes indeed. General von Schleicher was among the unfortunates. Evidently he had the bad sense to reach for a gun. His wife, too. She tried to shield the general with her body, or so they say." He glanced at his watch. "Goering should be giving a press conference in Berlin just about now to explain how that happened. I've made the Propaganda Ministry available to him."

The little man appeared to be enjoying himself.

Jeremy made himself speak out boldly. "I'm not interested in the reports from Berlin. How about giving me a phone line and letting me report the events in Munich?"

Goebbels lit a cigarette with cupped little hands and sucked on it greedily. Jeremy remembered that no one was allowed to smoke in Hitler's presence, and Goebbels had been closeted with him for hours.

"Why not? Goering will be talking to your press in Berlin this very hour. Why should that fat pig have all the say?"

Jeremy whipped out a pad and pencil. "Thank you, Herr Doktor."

Goebbels negligently pushed a paper across the desk. "What's a few hours? Here, I was going to release this anyway."

Jeremy crossed thirty feet of thick carpet and took the paper. It was a carbon copy of a communiqué. Undoubtedly it was being mimeographed right now.

He skimmed it rapidly:

It has been discovered only recently that a clique of certain exotic leanings has been conspiring to drive a wedge between the Storm Troops and the Party. Chief of Staff Roehm, despite the Führer's long-standing trust in him, tolerated and actually en-

*couraged this subversion. In addition, his well-known queer per-
sonal habits have embarrassed the Party and caused the utmost
difficulties for the Führer, who of course ranks as the highest
leader of the Storm Troops. . . .*

Jeremy glanced at Goebbels. The little man's teeth were bared in a
ferret grin.

He read on. There was very little solid information, just a web of
vague accusations that linked Roehm with General von Schleicher,
with unnamed SA leaders, foreign spies, and "an obscure person, well
known in Berlin, to whom the Führer had always objected."

Goebbels's prose ran on, getting purpler:

*. . . The Führer himself, with incomparable bravery, went
with only a few companions to Bad Wiessee in order to nip the
Roehm putsch in the bud on the dawn of the very day it was to
take place. The execution of the arrests revealed such immorality
that any trace of pity was impossible. Some of these Storm Troop
leaders had taken male prostitutes along with them. One of them
was even disturbed in a most ugly situation and was arrested. The
Führer gave orders for this plague to be done away with
ruthlessly. . . .*

Jeremy scribbled notes rapidly. So it was a "Roehm putsch" now?
This was vintage Goebbels, all right, but it didn't answer the big ques-
tion. Without looking up, Jeremy said: "What about Roehm, Herr
Doktor? You refer to 'arrests,' both here in Munich and by Air
Minister Goering in Berlin, but—"

Goebbels snapped his fingers. Rosie, hovering in the doorway,
stepped forward with an armload of mimeographed sheets.

"Give him the Führer's proclamation, Berndt."

Jeremy took a copy. It was just more boilerplate. This time it was a
diatribe against "banquets," "debauches," and "business trips in expensive limousines or cabriolets" by Storm Troop leaders. You could
glean from it the fact that there was a "new chief of staff of the Storm
Troops," Viktor Lutze, because Hitler had sternly demanded of him
that his brown-shirted followers behave "like men, not apes." But
there was not a solitary word about Roehm's fate.

Jeremy drew a breath sharply. "Is Roehm still alive?"

Goebbels laughed. "You get right to the point, don't you? Well, why
shouldn't you have the scoop? It will be common knowledge by tomorrow, anyway. I was a journalist myself once, and I know how it is. No,
Herr Roehm has taken the honorable way out, and shot himself."

Jeremy hardly dared to look up. "How did he get hold of a gun in a cell at Stadelheim prison?"

The pinched face grew black with synthetic rage. "You ask too many questions! Now get out and write your story!"

"Can I borrow a typewriter?"

Goebbels stared at him incredulously. Then he gave a dry, insectoid chuckle. "Berndt, find him a typewriter and a place to write. Make sure I see it before it goes out."

Jeremy followed Rosie to a small room down the hall. He was rewarded by the sight of Sepp Dietrich pushing his way through the crowd of brownshirts outside the conference room where Hitler was still holding forth. Dietrich, sweating and harassed looking, traded jibes with the brownshirts and disappeared inside, leaving a squad of black-uniformed riflemen in the corridor.

Jeremy thought it was worth a try. "Hasn't Dietrich's firing squad shot Schneidhuber and Hayn and the rest yet? What's the matter, is the prison governor still causing trouble?"

"No, that's been settled. The Führer read him the riot act. Dietrich will get started as soon as—" He broke off. "You think you're smart, don't you?"

"Then Roehm's actually still alive at this moment? But he's as good as dead, is that it?"

Rosie, tight-lipped, escorted Jeremy to a rolling typewriter stand in a corner and waited until he seated himself. "Just stick to the official version," he said.

"Come on, *Röschen,* what's the harm? Your boss is going to censor me anyway, and it'll all be coming out by tomorrow. Who's on the list besides Hayn and Schneidhuber?"

Rosie ostentatiously cleared away folders, memo pads, and the remains of someone's lunch, probably his own.

"But I can definitely put down Hayn and Schneidhuber, right?" Jeremy said. "And of course Heines, Spreti, and Roehm."

Rosie marched out with an armload of file folders. Jeremy grinned and bent to his work.

He thought about all the brownshirts crammed into Stadelheim prison, like cattle waiting to be slaughtered, and about the doomed men who now must be filling the Gestapo cellars in Berlin, waiting until someone could get around to blowing their brains out, and all of a sudden he was almost sick all over Rosie's typewriter.

He swallowed hard and began to type.

Munich, June 30—In an unprecedented night of terror and long knives, Hitler's Germany and the Nazi party have undergone a blood purge that will profoundly affect the balance of power in this nation.

Declared in an official statement to be a suicide is Captain Ernst Roehm, leader of the three-million-man army of Storm Troops, familiarly known as brownshirts, the quasimilitary force that helped propel Hitler to power.

Also confirmed to be dead are Captain Roehm's companion, Count Hans Edwin von Spreti, and SA Obergruppenführer Edmund Heines.

Presumed to be dead, or awaiting execution in Stadelheim prison here, are a long list of brownshirt leaders and political opponents of Chancellor Hitler, including August Schneidhuber, the police president of Munich . . .

He was just putting the finishing touches on it when Rosie came to get him. "He can see you for only a few minutes," Rosie said. "He'll be flying back to Berlin with the Führer as soon as matters are cleared up here." Jeremy gathered up his pages and followed him.

Goebbels was in high spirits. "Back so soon? You Americans get things done, I'll say that. You're almost like Germans. Well, let's see it. I hope you haven't done anything foolish. We're willing to be nice here, if only you'll cooperate."

Jeremy started to hand the pages over, but with a wave of a spidery hand, Goebbels delegated the job to Rosie. Evidently he wanted it to be read to him.

"München, den dreissigsten Juni," Rosie began, and Jeremy realized with a sinking heart that he was going to translate it into German as he went along. *"Während,"* Rosie said, clearing his throat, *"einer beispiellosen Nacht von Schrecken und langen Messern . . ."*

Goebbels frowned. "What is this 'long knives'?"

"It's . . . it's an English idiom," Jeremy stammered. "It m-means something like *Schreckensherrschaft*—a reign of terror."

Goebbels pursed his lips. "Well, why not?" he said unexpectedly. "We'll put a little fear into the hearts of our enemies. Let them know we mean business." He studied Jeremy over tented hands, like a praying mantis. "You have a gift for exaggerated language, Mister Jeremy Sinclair—what I believe you call in English purple prose. You should come to work for us in the Propaganda Ministry. Go on, Berndt."

Jeremy could hardly believe that he had gotten away with it. Walt Hanes edited his copy more than Goebbels was doing.

Rosie stumbled on. Goebbels pricked up his ears at the phrase "confirmed to be dead" and the names of Heines and Spreti.

"Where did you get those names?" he said sharply. "Berndt, do we have a leak at party headquarters? We shall have to put our special unit to work and turn off these dripping taps."

"Do you want me to take out the word 'confirmed'?" Rosie said.

"No, let it stand. I was going to release a few names anyway. Mister Big Ears Sinclair is only anticipating me by a few hours."

When Berndt got to the list of those "presumed dead or awaiting execution," Goebbels held out his hand for the paper. He crossed out two names and handed the paper back to Berndt. A little further on, he objected to some minor detail that Jeremy had thought was innocuous, and still further on he chided Jeremy for his reference to events in Berlin. "Don't concern yourself with things you know secondhand. The rumors will fly in Berlin without your help. They don't have to fly all the way from Munich. Anyway"—he chuckled dryly—"von Papen is not dead yet. We may have a use for the gentleman jockey."

By the time Berndt got to the third page, with its reference to "an authoritative source" and "a high party official," and the paraphrases of Goebbels's own boilerplate material, the little doctor seemed to have lost interest.

"All right, we don't need to go on. You haven't tried anything tricky in that last part, have you?"

Jeremy gulped. "No."

"Good. Don't. Berndt, get him his telephone line to Berlin. Make sure you have an English speaker on the line with him to make sure he doesn't deviate from the text."

"I'll do it myself," Rosie said eagerly.

Goebbels was already back at work, attacking a thick stack of folders with a work addict's relish. Rosie and Jeremy tiptoed out of the office.

"Where the hell have you been, Sinclair?" Walt Hanes's voice buzzed angrily through the telephone. "All hell's breaking out in Berlin!"

"All hell's been breaking out in Munich, too," Jeremy said carefully. "I'm calling from the Brown House. I've got"—he emphasized the next word—"an *approved* statement to read."

"The Brown House, eh?" Hanes abruptly quieted down. "You speaking from Hanfstaengl's office there?"

Putzi Hanfstaengl had a small cubicle on the third floor, next to Heinrich Himmler's office. Foreign correspondents on trips to Munich had learned that they could wander all through the building on the pretext of trying to find Putzi, and sometimes pick up something useful.

"No," Jeremy said, choosing his words. "I'm calling from the Propaganda Ministry's offices here. I guess I'm being favored. No other reporters seem to have gotten through the cordon of troops outside."

"Please, gentlemen," Rosie's voice cut in. "No conversation."

"Who's that on the line?" Hanes said.

"It's Berndt. You know him."

"Yeah, I know Rosie. How's the weather in Munich, Rosie? Things as stormy as they are in Berlin?"

"Please, just take down Sinclair's text."

"Sure thing, Rosie. Wait just a minute, will you? I'll put a stenographer on the line." He was stalling. "But you can't blame us, can you? My God, what a night! Police units screaming through the streets. Machine guns everywhere. Von Schleicher and his wife shot—that's just been confirmed by Goering—and people disappearing all over the place. Even the Vice-Chancellor—I tried to get through to von Papen's office, but he isn't answering his phone, and Goering's police are surrounding the place."

"Oh, von Papen's alive and kicking," Jeremy said.

"Please, gentlemen!" Rosie pleaded. "I'll have to cut you off."

"Hold your horses, Rosie," Hanes said. "Here's my stenographer on the line now. Okay, Sinclair, shoot."

Jeremy began reading. Berndt, in the adjoining room, had his carbon copy with Goebbels's objections marked in crayon. Jeremy tried, by inflection and word emphasis, to communicate the realities of the situation to Hanes. When he finished his own dispatch, he read Goebbels's overwrought communiqué straight, and finished up with Hitler's crazy proclamation forbidding the storm troopers to hold banquets or debauches.

"Wait a minute," Hanes said, "did I get that straight? Did you say he forbids the storm troopers to eat hummingbirds' tongues and seagull eggs?"

"That's what it says here."

"Okay. I just wanted to be sure. Now, who's this Viktor Lutze that you say has taken over as leader of the Storm Troops?"

"He's just *Obergruppen* commander for Hanover. A retired lieutenant."

"Gentlemen, I've warned you," Rosie's voice broke in.

"It's just background, Rosie," Jeremy said. "Mr. Hanes can look it up in his files, anyway."

"Okay, Sinclair," Hanes said. "Good stuff. I'll put someone on rewrite, but you've got yourself a by-line on the main dispatch with the Munich dateline. At least you've given us seven confirmed victims in Munich. That's more than we have here so far. And the announcement of Lutze's name is a scoop. That hasn't been released here yet. And Roehm's suicide is big news. You sure that's confirmed?"

"Yes," Jeremy said. He spoke quickly and clearly. "Roehm is scheduled to commit suicide at six o'clock—"

The line went dead. Rosie came in a moment later, shaking his head.

"Why do you try such tricks? I'll have to tell Dr. Goebbels."

Jeremy sweated it out until Berndt came back. "Am I free to go?" he said.

Berndt was pale. "Yes. He says it will be long past six o'clock by the time you get back to Berlin."

Berlin was relatively calm when Jeremy stepped off the train at the Anhalter Bahnhof the next morning. The vendors were out, and the grounds of the Ethnographic Museum across the plaza from the station were aswarm with the usual family groups. A truck full of armed SS troops sped by, but the Berliners taking advantage of the fine weather to go for a stroll with their children seemed to pay little attention to it.

He stumbled into the office, bleary-eyed and unshaven after sitting up in his compartment half the night laboriously writing out a new story in longhand. There had been a bad moment at Bayreuth when the SS held up the train to search for Munich passengers, but they had lost interest in Jeremy after seeing his American passport. They were after native game that night. They hadn't bothered to examine his notebook.

"Jesus, Sinclair, go home and get some sleep!" Walt Hanes said when he walked in. "You look like hell!"

"I can work, Mr. Hanes. I'll sleep tonight."

"Okay, pitch in, then. God knows we can use another hand. Ham's out getting a statement from Himmler, MacPherson's doing a follow-up on the Goering press conference, and I'll be attending the special tea party Hitler's giving later today in the garden of the Chancellery." He snorted. "Tea parties! And the shootings are still going on at Lichterfeld Barracks and that SS torture cellar of theirs under Columbia House. These people are unbelievable!"

Silently, Jeremy handed over the pages he had written on the train.

"What's this? Christ, your handwriting's terrible! 'Slaughter at the Hanselbauer.' Still the pulp writer, eh, Sinclair? Were you an eyewitness?"

"Well . . . uh . . . not exactly. I was in the pantry. But I heard it all. Mr. Hanes, they dragged Heines and Count Spreti into a car.

Hitler personally pistol-whipped Spreti in the face. Sepp Dietrich did the actual shooting—"

"Kid, this is old hat now. We've already sent through Heines's and Spreti's names. Two more firing-squad victims. We've got newer fish to fry. We're investigating a report that they've gunned down Erich Klausener, the head of Catholic Action, and Probst, the Catholic Youth movement leader. I'm going to put you on the Klausener story."

"Mr. Hanes, I heard Heines begging for his life! The car was so messed up with blood that they couldn't use it to ride back to Munich!"

Hanes handed him back the notebook pages. "All right, kid, type it up. I'll send it through, but I don't think New York will buy it."

Jeremy turned to go. Hanes cleared his throat. "Thanks for the tip on von Papen, kid. You were right. They didn't quite have the nerve to kill him. They were afraid that old Hindenburg wouldn't have swallowed the murder of the Vice-Chancellor on top of everything else. Goering kept Papen and his family safe under house arrest until the butcher boys calmed down a bit. They won't even let him resign. But they shot his press secretary, von Bose. You can still see the pool of dried blood in Papen's office at the Borsig Palace. And they dragged four of his assistants off to the torture cellars. And they killed Papen's ghostwriter on the Marburg speech." He shook his head. "Killing ghostwriters! I gave the story to Ham. I'm afraid he gets the credit, kid."

"That's all right."

"But your Munich dispatch got splashed all over the hometown papers. The New York office is very pleased with it. Here, take a look; even the Paris *Trib* picked it up."

Jeremy scanned the paper that Hanes held out. "But this says that Roehm committed suicide. I heard him refuse! They were going to shoot him in his cell. Didn't you—"

Hanes looked embarrassed. "Yeah, I got what you were trying to tell me over the phone, kid. Smart thinking. I changed the wording of your story the way I figured you wanted me to, but the home office wouldn't buy it. You see, by that time they were getting the doctored version from other sources."

"You mean I stuck my neck out for nothing?"

"Not for nothing, kid. I told you. You gave us the first seven confirmed names and the Lutze announcement. The first authoritative story that anything at all was going on in Munich came out under your by-line. So relax and enjoy it."

Jeremy was so furious he could barely speak. He went to his desk and, trembling, picked up the top flimsy from the pile that had accumulated.

"Yeah, that's right, you can start with that one." Hanes was hovering apologetically behind his chair. "Puff it up. It's an important story. The Nazis must have drafted that telegram for Hindenburg and badgered the old man until he was confused enough to sign it. He's eighty-six and doddering. They say he doesn't recognize the faces of the people around him half the time. He can't last much longer, and then Hitler'll have a clear track."

The flimsy was a copy of a message from Hindenburg congratulating Hitler on his "gallant personal intervention" and "determined action" against treason. "You have saved the German nation," the message gushed.

By day's end, Nazi spokesmen had still admitted only to about two dozen killings, including the seven names that Goebbels had allowed Jeremy to transmit. But reporters were putting together their own lists and pooling them, and it began to look like more than a thousand victims. Himmler's and Heydrich's men were settling private scores, and the butchers couldn't keep their mouths shut.

Some of the stories were horrifying. A man named von Kahr, who had been a political opponent of Hitler ten years earlier, was dragged from his bed by SS men and hacked to death with a pickaxe; his mutilated body was later found in a bog near Dachau. In Breslau, the acting police president was disemboweled by a shotgun held against his belly. A priest who had been in a position to know some of the details of Hitler's unnatural relationship with his dead niece, Geli Raubal, was found in the forest outside of Munich with his neck snapped and three bullets in his heart. Munich's leading music critic, Dr. Willi Schmid, had been playing the cello before supper when four SS men had broken into the apartment and carted him away without explanation. It was believed that he had been mistaken for Wilhelm Schmid, the paunchy *Gruppenführer* whom Jeremy had seen being dragged into a police van during the early hours of the purge.

Coffee and cigarettes kept Jeremy going. He typed steadily through the day, a telephone tucked into his shoulder as he made call after call to verify details. He was just getting up to get his jacket when Hanes came over.

"Sorry, kid. I tried. A cable just came in from the home office. They just don't believe you were in that pantry."

"That's all right, Mr. Hanes."

"Maybe it's all for the best. These Hitler chappies play rough." He shrugged. "You're just as well off not having to look over your shoulder all the time."

"I said it's all right, Mr. Hanes."
He struggled into his jacket and turned to go.

Two weeks later, Jeremy found himself seated next to Kemble in the gallery of the Kroll Opera House, where a special meeting of the Reichstag had been called to hear Hitler's long-awaited speech explaining the Roehm purge. The British correspondent had grown more wintry and seedy-looking since Jeremy last had seen him. Rumor had it that the Nazis intended to kick him out.

"Halloo, Sinclair. Keeping the pecker up? That was a very nice piece you did on the night of the long knives, by the way. I hear you had an even better one, but that your people wouldn't support you. Too bad, old chap."

"Thanks, Mr. Kemble. What's going to happen tonight?"

Kemble pulled at his drooping mustache. "We shall soon find out. The security precautions are extraordinary, aren't they? I suppose our man is afraid some disaffected brownshirt might take a potshot at him."

Jeremy looked round the packed auditorium. Helmeted soldiers— armed with, of all things, swords—guarded all the entrances. Even the guards weren't to be trusted with guns, it seemed. Detectives circulated through the audience, making themselves unpleasant. Jeremy himself had been roughly frisked twice, at the main entrance and in the coat-room, before being allowed to proceed to the balcony space allotted to foreign observers.

"If you're looking for your Ambassador Dodd, he isn't here," Kemble said. "He told Sir Eric Phipps that he'd stay home and listen to the speech on the radio. Said he has a horror of the man, that he wouldn't lend his presence as American representative to dignify a murderer."

"He did?" Jeremy said with some interest. He scribbled a reminder in his notebook.

"Oh, you won't get an interview from him. Your State Department will be trying to smooth that over. The Germans are already boiling over the speech yesterday by your General Johnson, the chap your brother works for in Washington."

"*Used* to work for," Jeremy corrected. "He's with Harry Hopkins now."

Hugh Johnson's vitriolic remarks about the purge had been splashed all over the press on both sides of the Atlantic. The bloodshed, he said, had made him "not figuratively but physically and very actively sick. The idea that adult, responsible men can be taken from their homes, stood up against a wall, and shot to death is beyond expression. That such a thing should happen in a country of some supposed culture passes comprehension."

"I suppose you saw the German protest in this morning's papers. Shows the fine hand of Goebbels, wouldn't you say?"

"Yes."

The Germans had called General Johnson's remarks "so monstrous that a sovereign state never could stand for such vilification of the head of its government." They were equally outraged by Secretary of State Cordell Hull's reply that he had no way of preventing the general from speaking as an individual.

"Your American tendency to moralize," Kemble said. "'Fraid the Johnson incident is going to cause trouble for you Yank reporters here. The Nazis will be looking for some way to retaliate."

"Maybe it'll wake them up back home," Jeremy said fiercely. "Mr. Kemble, they just don't know what's going on here!"

Kemble nodded. "They don't believe me either, y'know. Or pretend not to. By the bye, have you heard the latest on that music-critic affair in Munich, this Willi Schmid fellow that disappeared?"

"No. I'm not supposed to do Munich stories anymore. Pops Schulz complained that I got in his way."

"His widow got a sealed coffin back from Dachau concentration camp. She was forbidden to look inside. One doesn't care to imagine what they did to the poor chap while they had him there. But Rudolf Hess himself visited her to apologize for the mistake in identity. Told her not to grieve, that she should think of her husband as a martyr for a great cause, and that she would get a lifetime pension from the state."

"God!" Jeremy said.

Kemble sucked on an imaginary pipe. Waving a real one around would have been too dangerous at the opera house that night. "Haven't given up on the idea of doing a story on Dachau, have you? You seem to have a talent for getting into places that the rest of us tired old hacks can't get near. Bonner Platz. Roehm's pantry."

"Mr. Kemble," Jeremy said ruefully, "how could I get into a place like Dachau?"

Kemble looked away, then casually back toward Jeremy. "Oh. I don't know. You might try asking Himmler directly, I suppose."

"You're kidding. There's a penalty for circulating even what they call 'true information' about Dachau."

"Mmm. Quite. But Himmler might be getting ready to change his tune, y'know. These fellows are feeling their oats now that they've brought off their bloodbath. Himmler's an odd duck. Not averse to flattery. P'raps he could be persuaded to boast about those camps of his. If he thought it would serve some useful purpose, like terrorizing his opponents. Worth thinking about."

"Mr. Kemble, I don't think I could even get in to see Himmler. Not after my 'long knives' story."

"You don't take my meaning, my boy. He liked the publicity."

It was a dizzying thought. "I'll think about it, Mr. Kemble."

"Shhh. Here comes the Reichskanzler now."

Hitler came striding down the center aisle, flanked by clanking guards, and the house went wild. Down below, on the packed main floor, six hundred brown-shirted deputies leaped like maniacs to their feet and thrust out their right arms in a great chanting salute. Boots stamped on the floor, shaking the building. Jeremy and Kemble rose to their feet, too; it would have been foolhardy not to. Even the massed diplomats in their special section on the first balcony got up; some of them, one could see, somewhat reluctantly.

Hitler, with a masterful sense of theater, paid no attention to the applause and the cheers. He looked neither to the right nor left, and made his aides hurry to keep up with him. Himmler, round-shouldered and potbellied, stumbled on the first step to the dais, and fat Goering had to scramble to get to his place on the stage before Hitler began.

Hitler clutched at the lectern as if he were drunk, and glared wildly at the shouting, stamping mob spread out before him. A hanging lock of hair swayed loose in front of his face. Slowly he lifted his head and raised his hand for silence. He didn't get it immediately. There was a final frenzy of *Heil Hitlers* and arm flinging, growing gradually ragged and unsynchronized; then the deputies sank one by one into their seats, like a great rippling brown carpet being lowered a foot and a half.

Jeremy had to admit it was an impressive moment, superbly staged, as were all of Hitler's appearances. For backdrop, the Führer had an enormous gold eagle with a thirty-foot wingspread, perched on a raised swastika that was circled with gilded oak leaves. The blood-red curtain that extended the whole width of the stage had somehow been gathered so that its folds centered on the circular swastika seal. The total effect was that of a sun with bloody rays shedding their benediction on the man who now stood erect at the lectern, behind a battery of microphones. The bemedaled top brass were deployed at rostrums bracketing the speaker, with Goering, as presiding officer of the Reichstag, enthroned at a raised desk behind him.

The audience was deathly still now. Hitler began to speak, his voice hoarse and throaty with emotion. He spoke with his whole body, swaying toward his audience, tossing his head, shrugging his shoulders, his hands moving in the space around him with a life of their own.

As he gained momentum, he no longer was the unimpressive, pasty-faced man Jeremy had seen at the Kaiserhof tearoom. He seemed to swell, grow bigger. He actually changed color; his face turned a bright pink as the flesh became taut and suffused with blood. Jeremy had no fondness for the Freudian claptrap that passed for clever talk at the American colony's cocktail parties, but he couldn't help remembering somebody's comment that Hitler's reaction to an audience was the counterpart of sexual excitement.

And the audience reacted to Hitler's courtship of them. Gradually Hitler's passionate gestures warmed them up. It was an extraordinary thing to witness. This, Jeremy knew with sudden insight, was the reason for Hitler's power over crowds. He watched the deputies unconsciously leaning forward in their seats. All those little potbellied men with swollen necks had become a single yearning organism that strained toward union with that taut figure posturing before them.

Jeremy was so entranced by Hitler's performance that at first he paid no attention to the words. Then something Hitler said brought the entire audience to its feet, yelling their lungs out. Jeremy gave a guilty start and got out his notebook; he was supposed to be a reporter.

". . . I am ready to undertake responsibility at the bar of history for the twenty-four hours in which the bitterest decisions of my life were made. . . ." Hitler was saying.

Jeremy got it all down as fast as he could. Around him, the hundred or so correspondents in the reporters' gallery scribbled furiously.

Hitler went on, in a tearful orgy of self-pity, to number those who had been shot at sixty-one, those who committed suicide at three, and those who died while "resisting arrest" at thirteen. He himself, he said, spreading his palms outward, had personally ordered only seven of the executions, and had "subsequently recognized" an additional ten killings that had been done without his permission.

Behind Jeremy, Larry Turnbull of the *Chicago News* leaned forward and hissed: "Who's he kidding? That only adds up to seventy-seven deaths. We've got an estimate of more than ten times that, leaving out the ifs and maybes."

A refrain of *shhh*'s from the surroundings seats shut Turnbull up.

For the next two hours, Hitler ranted on, wearing down his audience by sheer exhaustion. By turns he cajoled, threatened, stormed, cooed, sobbed, dripped scorn, grew stern, all the while punctuating his words with those remarkable hand gestures. He played on his listeners with masterly skill, moving them to interrupt him frequently with cheers, applause, and bouts of boot-stamping.

At the end, dripping with perspiration, he shook his fist high above his head and shouted: "If anyone reproaches me, and asks why I did not resort to the lawful courts of justice, then I say this to them: During those twenty-four hours I alone was responsible for the fate of the German people, and therefore the supreme court of the German people consisted of myself alone!"

While the reeling audience struggled to digest this, Hitler leaned forward, supporting himself on the lectern with outspread hands, and said: "Everyone must know for all future time that if he raises his hand to strike the state, then certain death is his lot!"

There was a fantastic explosion of applause and cheers. The deputies rose in one great surge. Hitler walked off without looking at them. Goering, sitting in his high-backed chair, put down the pencil he had been doodling with all through Hitler's speech and pounded his gavel for silence.

Within minutes, a motion was made, seconded, voted on, and the Reichstag had passed a bill which made all the killings retroactively legal.

"They've all dipped their hands in the same pool of blood," Kemble said as he and Jeremy followed the crowd out of the opera house. "No one can point a finger at Hitler now. The German nation just made itself an accomplice to murder."

Three weeks later, the Old Gentleman was dead.

"Sinclair," Hanes said when Jeremy came to work that Thursday morning, "Hindenburg just died. The report came in five minutes ago. I'm sending Ham out to Neudeck to cover the story. I want you to go over to Wilhelmstrasse to see what you can pick up."

Jeremy came back with his story in less than a half hour. Hitler hadn't wasted a minute. He had proclaimed himself both Chancellor and President. His tame Cabinet had passed the law combining both offices while Hindenburg lay dying.

The title "President" wasn't to be used anymore. Hitler was to be known simply as *der Führer.* No elections were to be called. The army went along. That morning, every Reichswehr officer and enlisted man would be required to swear an oath of loyalty, not to the country or the constitution, but to Hitler personally.

Kemble was right, Jeremy thought as he readied his dispatch for cable home. A new wind was rising in Germany, and Hitler was riding it. There was nothing to hold him back now.

Book III

A Sound of Distant Thunder

May 1935–January 1937

28

"Come back early," Sally said. "I may have a surprise for you to-night."

"What kind of surprise?" Brad said.

"If I tell you, it won't be a surprise. Besides, I'm not sure yet."

She got up from the kitchen table and came around behind him. She bent down to put her arms lightly around him and laid her cheek against his.

"All right, I'll try," he said. "I probably don't have a job anymore anyway, after what the Supreme Court did to the New Deal yester-day."

"Do you want another cup of coffee?"

"No thanks. I don't have time." He stood up. "What happened to Alvina?"

"I gave her the day off. Something about her little boy, Henry. Who needs a maid anyway? I only have her to keep Mummy from having a fit. I can make coffee and toast just as well as Alvina can. You have to admit I've come a long way since you married me."

He gave her a peck on the cheek. "That you have. You're domestic as hell. Mother Barbour incarnate." The coffee had tasted like diluted picric acid, and Sally had somehow managed to burn the toast, despite the automatic electric toaster that had been among their wedding presents.

The peck turned into an open-mouthed kiss. Sally clung to him. "You *will* come home early, won't you, darling?" she breathed.

"Sure I will. No briefcase full of work tonight, either. I'll take you to dinner at the club."

"Let's stay home. I can scramble some eggs."

Brad concealed a shudder. "That sounds fine. You're right. Who needs Alvina?"

The morning paper had been delivered too late to read with breakfast for the second time that week, and it was only Tuesday. With a sigh, Brad retrieved it from the tangle of wisteria that cluttered the tiny entrance stoop. He paused for a sour look at the brass knocker and antique fan transom of his house. It was more than he could afford; property values in Georgetown had begun to shoot up since Mrs. Roosevelt had discovered that the area was quaint. But he had managed to fend off help from Sally's mother and swing it on his own. He paid Alvina's salary, too, and her bus fare from the Negro shantytown behind the Capitol where she lived. But he couldn't do anything about Sally's clothes allowance and the other extras the Colliers gave their little girl.

He gave another sour look to the Chrysler Airflow parked at the curb. It was long past time to trade it in for a new La Salle, or at least a Hudson or Studebaker. The beetle-faced Airflow had become somewhat of a joke since its ballyhooed introduction, and Brad got away with driving it only because it was considered an amiable eccentricity that went with his fashionably bohemian address.

Brad climbed in behind the rakishly tilted wheel. Before turning on the ignition, he unfolded the morning paper for a quick look at the headlines.

The first thing he noticed was that the *Post* had removed the NRA eagle from its masthead. They hadn't wasted any time. Brad smiled grimly. All over America today, they'd be peeling the blue emblem off show windows, office doors, factory walls.

SUPREME COURT RULES NRA UNCONSTITUTIONAL, the headline blared at him. And, in a whimsical front-page box: CHICKEN KILLS AN EAGLE.

It was the Schechter Poultry case that had finally done it. "The sick-chicken case," Hugh Johnson had contemptuously called it from his exile in New York; "an absurd case on which to hazard a great and sweeping policy." He had been against Richberg making an issue of it.

The Supreme Court had found it amusing, too. The nine old men had burst into peals of uncontrolled laughter while the Schechter brothers' young lawyer had earnestly tried to explain the fine points of kosher slaughtering. But when the laughing was over, the justices had ruled unanimously that the NRA, in trying to use its incredibly complicated codes as a bludgeon to prevent the sale of diseased poultry, had gone too far down the road of government regulation. Suddenly the legality of the whole of the New Deal was called into question.

Brad had seen the doubt and confusion on the faces of the government clerks and secretaries as they poured onto Constitution Avenue at quitting time the previous afternoon. Five thousand jobs were at stake in the NRA alone. "The Black Monday of the New Deal," the radio commentators were already calling it. Brad didn't relish reporting for work this morning.

He scanned the other news quickly. There was nothing as momentous in the rest of the headlines this May 28, 1935. There had been another minor border incident in Ethiopia, and Mussolini was warning the League of Nations that it was none of their business. Austria had somehow summoned up the nerve to arrest some Nazi agitators, and Hitler was complaining. Huey Long was continuing to maintain martial law in Louisiana on the grounds that he had discovered a plot instigated by Standard Oil to assassinate him. In Ohio, some strikers had been shot.

Brad stifled a yawn. Too little sleep last night. Sally had been inexplicably affectionate and talkative. He refolded the paper and started the car.

A few minutes later he pulled up in front of a dilapidated old office building on New York Avenue, a block and a half from the White House. He was in luck; there was a parking space right in front of the entrance. He bought another newspaper from the blind news dealer beside the front steps, and went inside.

The WPA was on the top floor. That was what Harry Hopkins had decided to call the new agency. Works Progress Administration. Harold Ickes had turned livid and complained to a highly amused Roosevelt that Hopkins had chosen the initials on purpose, so as to confuse the WPA in the public mind with Ickes's own PWA, and get credit for Ickes's relief projects.

He rode a cranky elevator to the top. The Negro elevator man gave him a flashing grin and said cheerfully: "Nice day today, suh."

"You said it," Brad said. He wondered if the man were a federal employee.

He stepped out on his floor. The corridor was stacked with files that had been transferred from the old offices at FERA, still unpacked. A smell of disinfectant hung in the air. The place had been fumigated just before they moved in. Even so, Brad had discovered cockroaches in his desk drawer.

A few of the staff were gathered around the coffeepot in the outer office. The morning paper was spread out on the receptionist's desk. Humphrey Galt, one of the regional administrators, greeted him.

"Hi, Brad. Read the big blue bird's obit this morning? Looks like you got out in the nick of time."

"Oh, Saint Harry's taken quite a few of us NRA refugees in. From the head eagle on down."

Hugh Johnson had just been appointed WPA administrator from New York, after seven months of limbo. He had finally resigned as director of the NRA last October after discovering that his own top deputies had been instructed not to talk to him over the telephone. Even so, Roosevelt had had to take the extraordinary step of asking for his resignation in the presence of two witnesses—Donald Richberg and Frances Perkins—to make sure that he got the message.

The general had departed in a final blaze of histrionics. Hundreds of NRA employees, down to the clerks and messengers, had crowded the auditorium and corridors of the Department of Commerce to hear his farewell speech. NBC and CBS had arranged national hookups. The general had been in rare form. "Very often the crucifixion of a man means more to the thing he is trying to do than all his living efforts," he had declaimed, tears rolling down his cheeks. He had even throbbed out the suicide aria from Madame Butterfly, to the utter astonishment of those present. *"Con onor muore chi non può serbar vita con onore . . .* which to those who know Mussolini only as a shining name means roughly, 'to die with honor when you can no longer live with honor.'" Now he was writing newspaper columns for Scripps-Howard and making radio speeches attacking Hitler, Huey Long, and Father Coughlin.

"Too bad Old Ironpants can't show a little gratitude," Galt said. "Especially when Harry's giving him seventeen million bucks to start him off right in his new job."

"What do you mean, Hump?" Brad said.

The receptionist chimed in. "Oh, didn't you see the new issue of the *American Magazine,* Mr. Sinclair?"

She produced a copy of the magazine from her desk drawer, and Galt handed it over to Brad.

"Page seventy-three."

Brad flipped it open. The article was "Where Do We Go from Here?" by General Hugh S. Johnson. Among other things, the general had characterized the New Deal as "feckless churning."

"Biting the hand that feeds him," Galt said.

"The general just likes to fulminate," Brad said.

"Fulminate, hell."

"Did you hear his crack about Huey Long the other night? He said if an American Hitler ever rides into Washington, Huey knows what part of the horse he can be. Huey's asked the networks for equal time."

Galt scowled. "Huey Long's nobody to trifle with."

Brad handed back the magazine. "Neither is Harry Hopkins. I better get to work."

On his way back, he poked his head into Aubrey Williams's office. "We still in business?" he said.

Williams looked up. "Hell, Harry isn't going to let a little thing like a Supreme Court decision stop him."

"How bad is it?"

"I won't kid you, Brad. Harry talked to Tom Corcoran at the White House last night. Tom says that after the Schechter decision was announced, the justices asked him to come back to the robing room with them. Brandeis let him have it, right between the eyes. Tom couldn't believe his ears. Brandeis said, 'I want you to go back and tell the President that we're not going to let this government centralize everything. It's come to an end. As for your young men, you call them together and tell them to get out of Washington.' "

Brad whistled. "As bad as that? All-out war between the President and the Supreme Court?"

"Don't let it worry you, Brad. We've got our four point eight billion and we're going to spend it."

Brad lifted an eyebrow. "We don't have the whole four point eight. Ickes gets the lion's share for his dams and bridges. We're just supposed to advise and coordinate. That's the way the Work Relief Bill was set up. The President calls us a bookkeeping operation."

"The President would never have been able to get an appropriation that size through Congress otherwise. They don't trust big spenders like Harry Hopkins. It had to look as if Honest Harold Ickes were going to run the show."

"Well, Ickes got what he wanted, didn't he?" Brad said with a straight face. "He resigned twice a week until the President agreed to turn Harry and us into glorified clerks for him."

"Of course the President left a loophole," Williams said softly, "provided Harry was bright enough to find it."

"Ah, yes, the loophole."

"The Works Progress Division," Williams quoted piously, "shall have the authority to recommend and carry on small useful projects designed to assure a maximum of employment in all localities."

"Small being defined as projects costing twenty-five thousand dollars or less," Brad said. "Anything estimated at more than twenty-five thousand to be handled by PWA."

"That's the agreement," Williams said comfortably.

"And?" Brad prompted.

"A half-million-dollar project divided into twenty parts," Williams said, "makes twenty projects costing twenty-five thousand dollars apiece."

They both laughed.

It had taken four months of wily maneuvering by Roosevelt to get the Congress to pass "four point eight," as the press had promptly dubbed the enormously expensive Work Relief Bill that was to supersede the former temporary relief programs like CWA and FERA. A *Washington Post* columnist had waggishly proclaimed the new era in government spending by announcing that the paper had switched to "skinny type" for its headlines so they could squeeze in the extra zeros needed to report billions instead of millions. "If Mr. Roosevelt throws one more digit at us," he wrote, "the *Post* will match the rubber money, dollar for dollar, with rubber type."

Roosevelt purposely made the organization chart for the new relief program so complicated that no one could understand it. It had taken him four news conferences to explain it to the press. But when the smoke had cleared, Harold Ickes had found that his authority had been diluted by an unwieldy monstrosity called the "Advisory Committee on Allotments," whose dozens of members ranged from the secretary of labor to the chief of the army engineers. Hopkins, on the other hand, needed no committee clearances for his "small" projects. To irritate Ickes further, he found that no PWA project could be undertaken unless Hopkins's WPA certified the availability of an adequate labor supply for it. Somehow the money seemed to be flowing to Hopkins's much-derided "leaf rakers" and "shovel leaners" instead of Ickes's dam engineers and construction workers.

"Poor Ickes," Brad said. "He's so tied up with red tape and committees that he can't get anything done."

"And things have to get done, don't they?"

"Oh, Ickes's projects will benefit the country in the long run," Brad said hastily.

Williams became serious. "You know what Harry said. He said people don't eat in the long run. They eat every day."

Brad nodded. "That includes me. Any news on my raise?"

Williams looked uncomfortable. "Harry's working on it."

"I'd like to be able to tell my wife's family that I'm at least a five-thousand-a-year man," Brad said.

Brad made exactly $4,999 a year. Congress, with an eye on future
patronage coming out of Hopkins's incredible money machine, had
tacked on an amendment providing that any administrator making
$5,000 or more had to be appointed by the President "by and with the
advice and consent of the Senate."

"You know how it is, Brad. It'll have to be cleared through Jim
Farley, and he'll have to trade you for some postmasters or something
with a few key senators."

"I know how it is. But my soles are wearing thin."

"Be patient, Brad. Harry only makes ten thousand a year himself,
and half of that goes to his first wife for alimony."

Brad knew that. He also knew that a fund had been raised by former associates to pay Hopkins $5,000 a year to help meet his personal
expenses. Hopkins never had any money in his pocket, except on those
rare occasions when Steve Early tipped him off to something good at
the track.

"Okay, but if Harry tries to borrow any money from me today, I'm
telling him I'm broke, too."

He went on down the corridor, dodging a couple of puffing moving
men who were carrying a filing cabinet.

He had a small office to himself. It was shabby and unpainted.
Hopkins had refused to spend government money to have his new
headquarters redecorated. Water pipes ran across the ceiling and down
the wall, but Brad couldn't complain; Hopkins's own office had visible
plumbing, too.

He sat down at a government-issue wooden desk that was scarred
and gouged by generations of bureaucrats before him, and got to
work. A pile of project proposals was already waiting for him. Hopkins was wasting no time. He had told his staff that he wanted to put a
million people to work within ten days.

Brad worked straight through without stopping until lunchtime. He
was just reaching for his jacket when Corrington Gill, head of the statistical section, leaned around the doorframe.

"Brad, can you see Harry for a minute?"

"Sure. What's up?"

"I think he needs your skills as a propagandist."

Brad got up. "I don't think he needs anybody's help in that department."

Hopkins's office was just down the hall. When Brad walked in, he
was on the phone, his coat off, his shirt collar loosened, and his feet up
on the desk.

"Have a seat, I'll be with you in a minute," he said, covering the
mouthpiece. He went back to barking into the phone. "I don't give a

damn if they *are* Democrats! You can tell the governor we've got the goods on him, and we're not going to allow political kickbacks from relief suppliers. . . . Damn right that comes from the President!"

He sipped from a glass of ice water and chain-smoked as he talked. Harry Hopkins was a lanky stringbean who managed to look boyish and cadaverous at the same time. Despite his sunken cheeks and generally starved look, there was a bright feverish energy about him. Hopkins was appealingly human and untidy in a world of bureaucrats. His hair was like shredded wheat, and, Brad noted, he hadn't managed to shave yet today.

Hopkins slammed down the phone and gave Brad a lopsided grin. "How do you like that? I've just been told that if I ever set foot in Ohio, there's a warrant out for my arrest there."

"Governor Davey?"

"Yep." He shook his head. "Politics has no business in relief."

"But it's here."

Hopkins looked mournfully at Brad. "I took your case directly to the President, Brad. He remembers you. 'Brad the Bad,' he calls you. He's pretty sore at Farley, if that's any consolation. I think we can get around Farley by putting you down as a carry-over from FERA. You were there long enough."

"My FERA salary doesn't qualify me for the raise."

"Don't worry about that. We'll figure something."

"Thanks. As long as you don't get accused of another boon doggle."

Hopkins threw back his head and laughed. The strange phrase had crept into the language a few weeks earlier when one of Hopkins's training specialists had testified to an unfriendly committee that he taught the unemployed the art of "boon doggles"—an old pioneer term for such handicrafts as basket weaving and leatherwork. A delighted press had picked it up, and now the Republicans were accusing all of Hopkins's relief projects of being "boon doggles."

"If they think the basket-weaving project was boon doggling," Hopkins chuckled, "wait till I revive the old FERA federal arts project under WPA. By God, we're going to have projects for writers, artists, actors, musicians! We'll have federal poetry, federal murals, and a federal theater that'll give every small town in America the chance to see plays by Shaw and O'Neill and Ibsen!"

Brad was aghast. "You can't mean it! It would be political suicide! It'd turn WPA into a big fat target for the Republicans at budget time!"

"Why not?" Hopkins snapped. "Artists have to eat, too!"

Brad backed off. "I guess they do. But they can't eat cement and steel. You're going to have to get ahead of Mr. Ickes in that line for four point eight."

"That's why I sent for you, Brad." Hopkins leaned back in his swivel chair. "I need something heartrending."

"Heartrending?"

"I've got a date with Henry Morgenthau over at Treasury. Henry's a sucker for a sob story. I can always squeeze extra money out of Henry by telling him it'll keep children from going hungry."

Brad thought a moment. "Cotton pickers."

Hopkins looked interested. "Go on."

"The research division's working on a study of migratory cotton pickers out west. Nothing more heartrending than that."

"What do you know about cotton picking?"

Brad laughed. "Well, nobody in my family ever picked cotton, if that's what you mean. But I've seen *Tobacco Road.* I'll see if I can work up a little propaganda."

"Pictures. I'll need some pictures to show Henry."

"Careworn mothers? Wistful children? Work-gnarled hands?"

"That's the ticket!"

Brad knitted his eyebrows together. "The research division sent a photographer out in the field last year, when we were still FERA. Lord knows where the pictures are now. They may be over at Agriculture."

"Would you check?"

"I'll call Rex Tugwell right after lunch. He's starting some kind of photo division for the Farm Security Administration. Hired a guy named Roy Stryker, who used to be one of his students at Columbia, to head it. Stryker may have inherited our photo file."

"We ought to have a photo division, too. When it comes to showing hunger, faces mean more than statistics."

"If I come up with anything good, I'll release it to the newspapers."

"Good thinking, Brad. It's what I expect of a fellow Hawkeye Stater."

Brad hesitated. He didn't want to appear to be pushing too hard, but Hopkins had given him an opening.

"As one Hawkeye Stater to another, how about grabbing a bite?"

"I'm skipping lunch today." Hopkins winced and pressed an attenuated hand to his abdomen. "Gotta see the doctor. I think I'm developing an ulcer."

It was easy to get lost in the Department of Agriculture. The place was even bigger than the Commerce Department. The clerk who had been assigned as Brad's guide took him across a third-floor bridge over Independence Avenue to the south annex and led him down vaulted corridors covering a couple of city blocks to an untenanted suite of offices filled with dusty wooden filing cabinets and unpacked crates.

"Mr. Stryker said you can have anything you want," the clerk said. "He doesn't know what he's going to do with most of this stuff. Some of it goes back to the Civil War." He kicked a disintegrating crate. "Like these old glass-plate negatives. We inherited them from the War Department."

Brad laughed. "No, I'm looking for something more recent. There's supposed to be a file of migrant farm worker photos, taken by FERA."

The clerk thumbed through a card file. "Try those cabinets over there." He opened a drawer and took out a folder of prints at random. "This the kind of thing you want?"

The photos were stark and sharply focused. Brad saw shacks made out of cardboard boxes, ragged tents, jalopies staggering under loads of household goods, and the gritty, tired faces of men in overalls and women in cheap cotton dresses.

"Okies," the clerk said. "White trash. I don't know why anybody would bother taking pictures of them, but that's what the boss wants."

"You'd prefer seeing pictures of dams and highway projects?" Brad suggested.

"Mister, these are official *U.S. government photos!*"

"That they are," Brad agreed.

"Now you take these photographers that Mr. Stryker is hiring." The clerk shook his head. "You ever hear of a fella named Ben Shahn?"

"Ben Shahn? But he's a painter. A muralist. Did those Sacco and Vanzetti panels that caused such an uproar."

"He's no photographer, that's for sure. Mr. Stryker, he gave him a Leica and told him to go out and fool around with it. Shahn came back with pictures that were out of *focus!* And Mr. Stryker said they had the right *'feeling'!* How do you like that?"

Brad nodded soberly. "That's nothing. *My* boss is hiring *writers.* Hired a young fellow named John Steinbeck to take a dog census of the Monterey Peninsula."

"A *dog* census?"

"That's right. With government money."

The clerk lowered his voice conspiratorially. "I'll tell you something. I'm a Republican."

Brad made a show of looking over his shoulder. "Me, too. At least I *was* one."

"New Dealers! Well, they won't last long around here."

"That's right. We've just got to bide our time."

"Darn tooting! Well, let me know if you need anything."

"Thanks."

Brad dusted off a chair with his handkerchief and sat down at a desk with the contents of the first file drawer. On second thought he took off his white linen suit jacket so he wouldn't get the sleeves smudged, and hung it carefully from a wall peg.

The photographer, whoever he was, was good. The pictures had a grainy realism that gave them immediacy, and they were all superbly composed. There was one that he was sure Harry would want. It was a photo of a farmer and boy ducking into a half-buried shack to get out of a dust storm. He put it aside.

Within a half hour he had all the photos he needed. He yawned, stretched, and looked at his watch. Four o'clock. A half hour till quitting time. He'd surprise Sally by getting home early.

On impulse, he decided to try one more file drawer. He came out with a thick folder labeled *Arizona*. The first picture showed a rickety outhouse swarming with flies, and a pump for drinking water next to it. Definitely grim. He added it to his collection. The next one was a little girl playing in the dust of a migrant camp with a pathetic headless doll.

He flipped to the next photo, and Junie stared out at him.

He sat still, frozen, forgetting to breathe. It was definitely Junie. She was older. God, she looked ten years older, with a pinched, drawn face and black circles under her eyes. But she was still pretty and elfin, with the huge dark eyes and her lips parted in a tentative proud smile to show perfect small white teeth.

She was lying on a mattress in what looked like a tent. A lantern hung from a ridgepole, and the furniture was wooden boxes. Her shoulders were thin and bare in a coarse cotton shift, and Brad could see that she had filled out to womanhood. She was holding a newborn baby, wrinkled and ugly, that was wrapped in what looked like a gunny sack.

There was no doubt that the baby was Junie's. Brad waited until his heart stopped hammering. He had no idea how much time he had wasted until he looked at his watch again and saw that it was twenty after four. He would have to work fast.

The only clue was the negative number crayoned on the back of the photo. With Pamela's help he had a fighting chance of tracking it down before the government ant heap emptied out for the day. He picked up the telephone on the desk.

The girls were already putting the covers on their typewriters and fixing their makeup when the buzzer rang on Pamela's desk.

"Miss Sinclair," Marcus said over the intercom, "can you come to my office for a minute?"

She got up, patting her hair before she could stop her hand, and crossed with quick steps to the polished walnut door that led to the inner chamber. Harvey Lucas, hunched over his typewriter in his alcove, paused in his machine-gun hammering at the keys to look up at her as she swished past him. She thought she could detect an expression of mournful reproach on Harvey's pocked, gaunt face.

She had her hand on the big brass knob when she heard the phone on her desk start to ring. She hesitated, then pushed through the door, letting it go on ringing.

"Close the door behind you, Pam," Marcus said from behind his desk. He got up and came toward her, large and florid and impeccable, with that imperial head that belonged on a Roman coin, and she felt her knees go weak, the way they always did. He reached around behind her and locked the door.

"Are the girls gone?" he said.

"Harvey's still out there."

"Harvey's *always* still out there. He has no private life. The man is loyalty personified. Don't mind Harvey."

She eluded his grasp and went over to the tall arched window that looked out across the green tiers of Capitol Hill. The walks were flowing with homeward-bound congressional employees sluicing around clumps of tourists.

"Aren't you coming by later tonight?" she said with her back to him. "My roommate's away."

"Pam, you know the Senate may be called into special session on the Guffey coal bill. I promised the majority leader I'd stay available."

"That doesn't come up till next week. I typed the caucus resolution, remember?"

"Joe Robinson may want to meet with some of us informally. With the Supreme Court knocking the NRA out of the box this way, we've got to come up with a new strategy for substituting some of the interstate trade regulations. I don't know how late we'll be."

She turned from the window. The furnishings of Marcus Hale's Senate office were splendid, with a crystal chandelier dangling from the vaulted ceiling, the rich drapes and thick rugs, the American flag and state banner on twin stands in front of the marble fireplace, the massive polished desk. And the leather couch, of course. All of the senators had one.

"You've got another girl, haven't you?" she said.

"*You're* my only girl. You know that." His voice was smooth as butterscotch.

She went on, hating herself. "I'm just a convenience for you, aren't I? Like that brass spittoon in the corner. Silly little girl with a handy apartment on the way to the Arlington Memorial Bridge, so you can stop in for an hour on your way home to your devoted wife. And if you don't happen to have an hour, there's always the couch in your office. Or the desk. My God, once it was even the desk!"

His face adjusted itself into noble lines of concern. "Pam, you know I don't like this arrangement any better than you do. I'd like to spend more time with you, take you places. . . . But I'm a public figure. I take a risk every time I'm seen coming out of your apartment building."

"I have no life of my own, do you know that? Oh, I get to go to a lot of state dinners and diplomatic receptions and official teas with safe young men like Herb Willis, and I've done my duty at cocktail parties on Harvey's arm, and I'm supposed to be the grateful poor relation at the Collier family soirées. Dinner once a month with my brother and his wife included. But most of the time I'm either working outside there next to a girl who chatters all day about Washington bachelors and another one who doesn't know enough to change her underwear and use Odorno, or I'm home opening a can for dinner and washing my stockings and doing my hair and wondering if this is the night you're going to call and say you can manage to stay all night, and can I get rid of my roommate."

"Pam, that's unfair. You know I get away when I can. And we had that weekend at the Maryland shore."

"At that lobbyists' hideaway, you mean?" she shot back. "Where I was stuck all day with two other senators' floozies while the boys went out fishing. Half the Senate and House know about that place. They make jokes about it. Is that what you think of me, Marcus?"

Tears glistened in her eyes, but she would not let him see her cry.

He put a large hand on her shoulder. "Pam, don't. Don't turn us into a joke. It's not that way with us. Sure, there's a lot of fooling around on Capitol Hill that the voters don't know about. Senators and congressmen are only human, and a lot of lonely women work here, and there's a man shortage. But we mean something to one another. At least I thought we did. Life doesn't always work out the way we want it to. We have to take what we can get, and sometimes that's the leftovers. I'm not a young man. Not the young man who should share your life, the young man who *will* share your life someday. Pam, sweetheart, I'll just be a memory for you through most of all those years you have ahead of you; a good memory, I hope."

He was maneuvering her toward the leather couch. He had both hands on her shoulders now, and he was very close. She could feel the warmth of his bulk, and he smelled of mint and alcohol. She knew what he was doing, but she let him do it. It was impossible to resist Marcus Hale. He was overpowering. His presence dazed her. Life had become a dream world, a fever dream where people chattered at her at parties and at work, and she chattered brightly back without hearing what she said, and she went home to eat dinner out of cans whose labels she didn't bother to look at and paint her nails and read best sellers whose titles she couldn't remember and go to an occasional movie with her roommate, a thin morose girl named Willa who came from Ohio and worked at Interior and slept at her boy friend's two or three nights a week. The dream was punctuated by the brief vivid intervals when Marcus wanted her, when she jerked awake to find his solid bulk looming beside her with its barbershop smells and rough textures and that soothing church-organ voice droning on at her. Her body's excitement was remote, separate from her; what mattered was the comforting fact of being wanted. Marcus lately had become brief, brusque, absentminded. But he was the glue that held her life together.

The backs of her knees hit the couch and she sat down. Marcus's hand was pressed against the small of her back. A phone rang distantly in the outer office, then stopped. Harvey must have picked it up; he was still out there. They both poised motionless, but Harvey did not put the call on through. Marcus grunted. He put the rough slab of his cheek against hers and whispered in her ear.

"We've got an hour. I don't have to be at the majority leader's office till then."

"No, she's not here, Brad. Why don't you try her at home in an hour or so," Harvey Lucas said into the phone. He coughed. "You must have just missed her when you called a minute ago."

He dived back into his work. There was a lot to do. The Supreme Court's scuttling of the NRA had piled a tremendous amount of work onto Marcus and the rest of the Senate leadership. The Guffey coal bill was now number one on the President's "must" list, superseding the defunct NRA extension, and there was FDR's controversial Social Security bill to be rammed through committee.

Pamela came out of the senator's office about a half hour later. She did not look at Harvey as she passed, and he did not stop her to tell her about Brad's call. The back of her dress was wrinkled and one of her seams was not straight. But she still looked great, with her chin up and her shoulders thrown back and her blond hair bouncing to that quick, firm step of hers. You had to hand it to Pamela, Harvey thought; she had style.

Marcus appeared at the doorway a few moments later in his shirt-sleeves. His hair was damp; he'd had his head under the tap.

"Call Senator Porteous for me, will you, Harvey? The horny son of a bitch owes me one. Ask him if he can find a place on his staff for a nice, pretty, hardworking gal. I'll return the favor some time."

"I'll call him first thing in the morning, Senator," Harvey said.

"You make sure Pamela gets a *good* job, hear? With a raise."

"I'll do my best, Senator."

Marcus shook his head. "Why do they have to get possessive?"

Brad struck paydirt on his fourteenth call. Paydirt was a harried official at Treasury, working late over the latest redraft sent over by the Senate Finance Committee in the current marathon legislative session. The official's name was Gadsden, and he still had the file with the old FERA vouchers.

"Hold the line, Sinclair, and I'll see what I can do," he said.

He came back on the line a few moments later. "Well, you're in luck. That was one of a series of negative numbers assigned to a photographer named Reisner. Leo Reisner. I've got his receipted vouchers right here."

"Where was that picture taken?" Brad said.

"Well, I can't help you there. It was part of a batch he had developed in a commercial lab in Phoenix. Evidently the contact sheets were sent back to Washington, you see, and a selection was made, and they were printed here. He hadn't submitted any expenses for a couple of weeks at that point, so the picture could have been taken anywhere in a tri-state area."

"Where is this Reisner?" Brad said. "How do I get in touch with him?"

"He doesn't work for the government anymore. He quit . . . let me see . . . in April. A month and a half ago."

"Oh, no!" Brad groaned.

"But I have a forwarding address for him. He had a final check coming to him."

"What's the address?"

"He may not still be there. You know these photographers. Fly-by-night."

"What's the address?" Brad's jaw was tight.

"It's in New York." Gadsden sounded affronted. He read off the address. It was in Greenwich Village.

"Any telephone number?"

"No, no telephone."

"Thanks, Mr. Gadsden. You've been a great help. I appreciate it."

He hung up. When he got the operator back on the line, she was barely courteous with him. "I'm trying to close up the board. It's almost six o'clock. We're only supposed to keep it open an hour after quitting time."

"What about Mr. Wallace and Mr. Tugwell? You give them night lines, don't you?"

"Well . . ." She sounded intimidated by his use of the names.

"I'm Bradford Sinclair." He didn't bother to tell her that he was not with Agriculture. "I don't know how I let Mr. Tugwell talk me into this all-night job. But you don't say no to the undersecretary of agriculture." He gave a confidential, rueful laugh.

"Gee, Mr. Sinclair, that office you're in isn't even on my listing. They just put in the phone lines this morning."

"That's how things go around here."

He waited.

"Well," she said, "I guess I could leave you an open line. But you won't make any long distance calls, will you?"

"No, they'll all be local."

"Okay, then. Hold on a minute while I set you up. Then I'm leaving."

"Bless your heart, Miss . . . ?"

"Gladys."

"I'll be around in the morning to give you a big wet kiss, Gladys."

She giggled. He waited through assorted clicks and buzzes, then when he got a nice steady hum, jiggled the cradle to test it. He had his open line.

He dialed long distance and gave the operator the New York address. She tracked it down for him through information there and reported: "There's no Leo Reisner listed. The building has a pay phone in the hall."

"Try it for me, will you?"

The phone rang a long time at the other end. Somebody finally picked it up. "Yeah?" a girl's voice said. Brad could hear the sounds of a party in progress.

"Is Leo there?" Brad said.

"Leo?"

"Leo Reisner."

There was a pause. Brad heard the girl bellow, "Hey, where's Leo?"

The party noises swelled. Somebody was playing the limerick song on an out-of-tune piano. Drunken voices were raised in chorus. Brad could make out some of the words. It was the one about the plumber from Dee. He hoped the operator wasn't listening. She'd cut off the call.

"Leo went out to get some more wine," the girl said. "You want him to call you back?"

"No, I'll hang on."

"It's your nickel," the girl said. She must have dropped the receiver and left it dangling from the wall. Brad hoped she'd remember to tell Leo when he came back.

He waited about ten minutes. The party sounded lively. Once somebody picked up the phone and a sloshed female voice shouted in his ear: "Hey, come on over, whoever you are!" "Give him a drink, Daisy!" somebody else guffawed, and Brad heard a trickling sound. Leo was going to have a sticky ear. Fortunately, no one hung up.

Reisner turned out to be sober and serious. "They didn't understand what I was trying to do, Mr. Sinclair. They wanted government puff pictures, you know? Maybe I shoulda stayed and connected with FSA. I hear Stryker's trying something different. He's hired Walker Evans and Carl Mydans. Good people. But I'm making out. The editors are starting to get more savvy. There's a rumor that Luce wants to start a picture magazine."

"Do you remember where you took that migrant-mother picture? It was on the same roll as the little girl with the headless doll, and the outhouse next to the water pump."

"Remember? I'll never forget! Jesus, Mr. Sinclair, I never saw people living like that, and I grew up in Hell's Kitchen."

"Take your time, Leo. Be sure."

"It was a cotton camp owned by a big grower named Roscoe T. Perry. The reason I remember is because that cowboy from AAA who was showing me around was so goddamn nervous about what Mr. Roscoe T. Perry would do if he caught us taking pictures of his migrant workers. The place was near the border of Yuma County, just off U.S. 80. That's the royal road to the Imperial Valley for the Okies."

"Thanks, Leo. You've been a big help. I shouldn't have any trouble tracking down Mr. Roscoe T. Perry from here."

There was a burst of party noises. When Reisner could make himself heard, he said: "Excuse me, Mr. Sinclair, but I don't think it's a good idea for you to try to get in touch with Mr. Perry. If he thinks the government is after him, see, he can have those tents down and them poor Okies, whatever ones are still left, kicked off the place in an hour—then, when the government inspectors are gone, install a new batch of pickers. There's no shortage of Okies passing through Yuma County, that's for sure. What you oughta do, excuse me for sticking my nose in, is call the AAA agent out there and have him take you out to the place for a surprise visit, if you get me. I don't remember the guy's name, but you should be able to find it in the department directory."

"Thanks for the advice, Leo."

"Good luck, Mr. Sinclair. I don't know why you're interested in that particular camp, but I hope you nail the bastard. Nobody should be allowed to treat human beings that way."

Brad hung up, sweating. Reisner was right. The chances that Junie was still there were small, but he couldn't afford to risk mishandling it. He glanced at his watch. It was still late afternoon in Arizona. He found a directory of county agents in a bookshelf and placed a long-distance call to Arizona.

"Bud Cooley's the man you want," a western voice said to him, "but maybe I can help you. What do you want?"

"Thanks, but I've got to talk to Bud," Brad said.

"Well, this is his day to go out to Gila, but he'll probably stop in at the office 'fore he goes home. He usually does."

"Will you have him call me? Collect."

When Brad gave his number, the voice at the other end whistled and said, "Long distance? You Washington fellas sure don't mind spending money. It might be late. Will somebody be there to accept a call?"

"I'll be here," Brad said.

He hung up and lit a cigarette. It was getting close to seven. With Pamela's help, he could have placed all the calls in half the time, found Cooley earlier, and waited for his call at home. But he didn't dare leave now. It was getting close to suppertime in Arizona. But he had better call Sally.

When he got her on the line, she gave him no chance to explain. "Where have you been, you bastard? I called your office just before quitting time, and they said you haven't been back all afternoon."

"Sally, honey, I'm sorry. I've been tied up—"

"Tied up! I'll bet! What is she, blonde, brunette, or redhead?"

"I'm in another office. I can't take the time to explain now. I've got to keep this line open. I'm waiting for an important call. I'll be home as soon as I can."

"You swine! You utter swine! Leopards don't change their spots, do they? Why did you have to pick today, of all days? I've got the champagne all chilled."

"What do you mean, today of all days?" Brad said cautiously. Sally hated champagne.

She was crying. "I saw the doctor. We're going to have a baby, you stupid fool! *Were* going to have a baby! I'm not having a baby by a filthy wretch like you! Don't think I'll still be here when you straggle home smelling of cheap perfume! I'll be over in darky town, finding some old mammy who knows how to use a coat hanger! Alvina'll know someone!"

"Sally, listen! I'll be home in ten minutes, and I won't be smelling of any cheap perfume."

"I'll bet!"

"I'm leaving now. Keep the champagne chilled."

He hung up and lit another cigarette. He stared thoughtfully at the phone. He could call Cooley again in the morning. Early. After all this time, one more day didn't matter. Cooley might not even return the call tonight.

He stubbed out his cigarette and put on his jacket. He was careful to turn out the lights when he left. They were always getting little memos about economy.

The Fourteenth Street parking lot had emptied out. The two-thousand-car herd was gone for the day. He found the humpbacked shape of his car with no trouble. Somebody had left a minor dent in the grille. He climbed inside and started the engine. He'd missed the four-thirty traffic jam, anyway. Upstairs in the darkened office, the phone rang awhile and stopped.

"I'm sorry, Mr. Sinclair. Bud ain't here. He was in and left again early this morning. He said he tried to get you last night, but no one answered."

"Is there anywhere I can reach him?"

The voice at the other end laughed. "Lord, no. Ain't no phones where he'll be."

"Would you ask him to call me tonight when he gets back? I'll give you my home number."

"I'm trying to tell you, Mr. Sinclair. Bud won't be back till next week. He's off on his monthly field trip."

He put down the phone softly so as not to awaken Sally. But she stirred and looked at the clock anyway, and said, "Who are you calling at eight o'clock in the morning, darling?"

"Six. It's six o'clock in Arizona. I'm calling a man named Bud Cooley."

"You're all dressed. Why didn't you wake me up?"

He went over and sat on the bed. Sally's body was warm as a furnace. "I thought you needed your sleep. I had a cup of coffee."

She wrapped her arms around him and rubbed against his shirt front. She was bare; last night had not been a night for nightgowns. "Poor darlin', having to get up and work for Mistuh Roosevelt on no sleep." Her southern accent had grown thick. "Ah'll make it up to you tonight. We'll spend a quiet evening at home."

He laughed. "Another quiet evening at home and I'll have terminal exhaustion and a broken back."

"We've got to get in all we can, darlin'. Before you know it, this ole belly of mine'll be out to here." She showed him with her hand.

He put his hand on her belly. It had a fiery heat from the bed. Was it his imagination, or did it feel more rounded; Sally had always been flat as a board. It was awesome to contemplate. Impossible to believe that he had not had another woman for a year, nor did he want another woman than this one.

"I'll take you out to celebrate properly," he said. "Oysters at Harvey's, then we'll go dancing."

Her eyes shone with pleasure. Ordinarily, Brad took her dancing only under protest.

"You don't have to, darlin'," she said. "Alvina can fix us some steaks. I don't mind staying home tonight, really I don't."

He tilted her chin up and kissed her nose. "We'll have a night on the town," he said. "I don't have any reason to stay home tonight."

He reached Cooley a week later. "I don't know, Mr. Sinclair," the AAA agent said. "That was a long time ago. These migrants pick a crop and move on. What makes you think you might still find that partic'lar family on the Perry spread?"

"As I understand it, it was long past picking time when that photographer went out with you and took those pictures. They were among the one family in five that managed to hang on through the chopping season. The way I see it, if that's the case, they'd have been almost certain to hang on another month or two until the next picking season, when the demand for seasonal labor goes up four- or fivefold. I'm hoping that they would have been among those hired to chop cotton again."

Brad had looked up the mysteries of cotton picking in Corrington Gill's statistical study of migratory workers. He had been appalled at what he had learned.

"Well now, you seem to understand how things work out here," Cooley said reluctantly. "Not like most of those fellas that try to run things from Washington and don't know their face in the mirror from the south end of a mule. We almost had a growers' revolution here in February when that fella in the AAA legal division, Alger Hiss, sent out that directive that would have forced the big growers to keep a lot of shiftless workers on the land the year round and let them have their own garden plots and woodlots. I almost got myself tarred and feath-

ered trying to explain it. They didn't calm down till I told them that
Mr. Wallace had fired Hiss and the rest of those pinkos over it."

"What about it, Cooley?" Brad persisted.

"Well . . . when you put it that way . . . sure. There's a pretty
good chance that Okie family stayed put. What's your interest in that
little gal, Mr. Sinclair?"

"I think she may be my sister."

There was a long pause. Then: "No offense intended. I'll see what I
can do. Tell you what, why don't I call Mr. Perry and ask him to have
the sheriff detain her till you can send someone down from Washington
to question her?"

Brad shuddered at the thought of Junie in some filthy Arizona jail.
"No, don't call Perry, whatever you do. I'll fly down. Can you meet
me at the airport in Phoenix tomorrow?"

"Tomorrow?" Cooley was incredulous.

"Transcontinental and Western Air has a new skyliner that makes
the coast-to-coast hop in less than twenty-four hours, with fewer than
a dozen stops. I can catch a plane this afternoon and be in Phoenix by
morning."

"You Washington fellas sure do things in high style. Sure, I can
meet you in Phoenix. It's about a three-hour drive."

"I'll be there."

"Mr. Sinclair." Cooley was hesitant. "You ain't planning to make
any trouble for Mr. Perry over this, are you?"

"No, I'm not interested in Mr. Perry. Just that girl and her baby."

It took him about an hour to set things up. He told his brand-new
secretary that he'd be gone for a couple of days, checking into the agricultural labor situation in Arizona as a part of the ongoing WPA survey of labor resources. When he got back, he'd find some Yuma
County project to tag it onto, and write a report, and that would cover
him. He called TWA and made a reservation to Phoenix through Kansas City and Fort Worth. Then he got the fare from petty cash and
charged it to Corrington Gill's statistical study of migratory cotton
workers. He could cobble together some sort of report for Gill, too.

Sally was understanding. A week of dancing and dining out had softened her up. "Poor Brad," she said over the phone. "You tell Mr.
Harry Hopkins for me that he's a slave driver."

Before leaving, he called Pamela. But when he reached Senator
Hale's office, a strangely evasive Harvey Lucas said, "She, uh, isn't
here at the moment, Brad."

"Where the hell is she, Harv? She never goes to lunch."

"She's uh, working down the hall now. You know what a shark
tank this place is. She went and found herself a better job."

* * *

Bud Cooley was a large, weathered man in cowboy boots and a western hat. He wore a kerchief around his neck, like Buck Jones. He looked at Brad's sleep-rumpled Palm Beach suit and thin shoes, and said, "Kinda rough country where we're goin', Mr. Sinclair."

"I'll get a shine when I get back to civilization," Brad said. "Let's go."

Cooley led Brad past a gauntlet of Indian souvenir peddlers to a dusty pickup truck parked across the road from the passenger terminal. He cast a backward glance at the huge Ford trimotor that Brad had disembarked from. They were still unloading sacks of mail.

"How was the trip?" he said.

"Fine," Brad said. "Pillows, chewing gum, and cotton for the ears. A trained nurse for the flying hostess in case you got airsick. White tablecloths with your meals. Almost as comfortable as a train. Try it sometime. How far to the Perry place?"

"We'll be there by noon." He squinted at the plane. "You'll never get me up in one of those things."

Brad climbed into the cab of the pickup and rested his briefcase on his knees. There was nothing in the briefcase except the toothbrush he'd picked up on his way to the airport yesterday, but it made a nice official-looking prop.

Within five minutes, Cooley, with easy western familiarity, was calling him by his first name. "This your first trip to Arizona, Brad?"

Brad made a noncommittal sound. "Where's the desert?"

On either side of the road, the land stretched in vast green fields cut into squares by ditches. No human figure could be seen.

Cooley laughed. "You're looking at it. Irrigation makes the difference. Only a few years ago, you couldn't see nothin' here 'cept sagebrush and cactus."

"That lettuce?" It seemed a reasonable guess.

"I guess you know your crops, Brad." Cooley shot him a swift glance of approval. "The last fella Washington sent out wanted to know why the cotton fields weren't white. Yep, we grow lettuce here, some spinach, dates, oranges. But the big crop is cotton. It's started to come back after the collapse in the twenties. You'll see it when we get to the newer irrigation districts. It's the large-scale operators who're bringing it back, under the cash lease system."

"Encouraged by the AAA bounties on cotton."

"That's right," Cooley said quickly. "We encourage it. That's why I didn't sound too happy over the phone about your coming out here and bothering Mr. Roscoe T. Perry."

"Is Mr. Roscoe T. Perry one of these large-scale operators?"

"One of the biggest. Him and two other growers control half the acreage in my county."

"So naturally you don't want to offend Mr. Roscoe T. Perry."

"It pays to stay on his good side," Cooley said in a level tone.

"What else does Mr. Perry control, besides all that acreage?"

"He don't control me, if that's what you mean."

"I was talking about migrant pay."

"I guess you could say he pretty much sets the wage scale in these parts."

"He have trouble holding on to his work force between the chopping and picking seasons, does he?"

"It's a big problem for him every year. When the cotton's ripe, you can't leave the open bolls standing in the fields too long. They get discolored and lower the grade. Mr. Perry, he tries everything he can to make sure he has a supply of pickers. The sheriff sends him some. The county welfare board takes everybody off relief, so those who can work have to."

"And those who can't, starve?"

Cooley ignored that. "But you see, these migrants just keep moving on to wherever there's a rumor of higher wages. After chopping season here, a lot of them cross over to California."

"I wonder why. Just shiftless, I guess."

"I told you there was no offense intended," Cooley said in a hurt tone. "I couldn't have figured that little gal was your sister."

Brad suddenly grinned. "Don't worry, Bud," he said. "If we run into Mr. Perry, I won't get him mad at you. Who knows? He might even be glad to see me."

It was high noon when the truck bounced off the highway onto a rutted track that wound its way through an expanse of fields of ugly brown stubble. The sky was the interior of a vast shimmering bake oven, with a blinding smear of sun at its very top. There were no shadows anywhere. Brad's tongue was swollen despite the frequent sips he had taken from Cooley's canteen.

They had crossed a hundred miles of desert before getting to the irrigation district, but this land looked deader. The ditches were dry. In the seared fields, tiny stick-figures flailed with hoes as if they were trying to beat the earth to death.

Brad could see the migrant camp as they approached, a miserable collection of ragged tents and broken-down vehicles. The old army fabric was bleached by the sun. Rusty prehistoric junk lay half buried along the roadside: cans and automobile parts, like the remnants of stone walls in New England. Their progress was blocked by a long, low sedan parked across the road—a custom Cadillac V-16 with whitewall tires and a gleaming finish that had been turned pastel by a light coating of fresh dust. As Cooley pulled to a stop, three men got out, one of them carrying a shotgun.

"You phoned ahead to let Perry know I was coming, didn't you?" Brad said.

"Seemed like a good idea," Cooley said imperturbably.

Brad got out on his side with the briefcase and watched the men approach. The one with the shotgun had a chest like a beer keg and a broad Aztec face. The fellow on the left was just as big, and needed a shave. The man in the middle was short and stringy and bandy-legged, with a rubber-ball belly riding high over his belt and a walk like a bantam rooster. He wore a Stetson and a shoestring tie and twill pants stuffed into his boot tops. As he drew closer, Brad put his age at about seventy.

"This here's private property," Mr. Roscoe T. Perry said.

Bud Cooley had come around from the other side of the pickup. "Now Mr. Perry," he said.

The man with the shotgun stood impassively, looking like a monument. One thick finger rested loosely in the trigger guard, and the other hand was clamped around the barrel, keeping it tilted toward the air above their heads. You could say that technically he was not pointing it at anybody. Cooley did not approach Mr. Perry too closely. He talked across at him, as if there were an invisible fence between them.

"I don't want you govmint people sneaking around here and bothering my workers," Perry said. "I've told you afore, Bud Cooley."

"Now Mr. Perry," Cooley said, smiling and sweating. "This is Mr. Sinclair. He's come all the way from Washington. He ain't here to cause you any problems. He just wants to ask a few questions, and he'll be on his way."

"Damn New Dealers, putting ideas in these people's heads! Can't get them to work as it is, and now there's this WPA luring them away with wages that an honest businessman can't afford to pay! Giving them notions about their rights! Next they'll be wanting electricity and running water and feather beds to sleep in! Wanting to send their filthy offspring to our schools to spread diseases!"

Brad smiled across the sunlit gap at Mr. Perry. He thought about Junie living in one of Mr. Perry's tents, having her baby there within sight of that fly-crusted outhouse. He had a brief, sudden fantasy of springing at Mr. Perry and fastening his hands around that stringy old throat and squeezing it as hard as he could before the man with the shotgun could move. It was very satisfying. He blinked the fantasy away and came back to a world of harsh sunlight.

"You might as well know the worst, Mr. Perry," he said. "I'm from the WPA." The dinosaur smile was still in place, making his jaws ache. The man with the shotgun was motionless in the way a dog is just before you slip its leash.

"By God, you have a hell of a nerve, mister!"

"Bud told you the truth. I'm not here to interfere in your business. Migrant workers' living standards aren't my department. That's between you and your local board of health."

"What do you want here, then?"

"I'd just like to talk to a few of your workers. You see, I know you're losing a lot of your workers to California. What I'm trying to do in these interviews is to establish patterns of migrant movement." He patted his briefcase confidentially. "So I can certify a labor shortage in this area."

Cooley looked confused. Perry scowled. "What's that supposed to mean?"

"Well, you understand that if I'm able to certify a labor shortage in this area, then of course the WPA will cancel any of its September projects in the county that might tend to draw off your work force."

"Can he do that?" Perry said to Cooley.

Cooley pulled at his ear. "I guess."

Brad went on briskly: "September's when your heavy picking season begins, I believe?"

"Damn right!" Perry said.

"On the other hand, we have a situation of labor oversupply shaping up in the Texas cotton districts due to population group migration from the dust bowl areas further east. Leading to a surplus labor pool."

"He means there ain't no jobs for them," Cooley said.

"I know what he means!" Perry snapped. He spat into the dust. "Damn Okies!"

"Now of course I can't make any promises," Brad said. He beamed at Perry. "But if my interviews tend to establish the right pattern of migrant movement, it's entirely possible that we might be able to take some steps, within department guidelines, of course, to provide inducements to move some of that surplus labor pool to where it's likely to be needed."

Perry took off his hat and scratched a bald head. "Are you trying to say that the govmint'll recruit for us in Texas?"

"Oh, no!" Brad said in a shocked tone. "That would be illegal!"

Perry chuckled knowingly. "Sure it is, son." He passed no signal that Brad could see, but the man beside Perry lowered the shotgun to his side.

"How about that," Cooley said.

"Now, you ain't goin' to fill their heads full of those communistic New Deal ideas, are you?" Perry said to Brad.

"I just want to ask a few questions to establish patterns of migration," Brad said. "Where they originated, reasons for deciding to move, size of families, and so forth."

"I'll tell you why they moved," Perry said. "They're just shiftless, that's all."

"I appreciate your cooperation, Mr. Perry," Brad said.

Perry turned on his heel and started back toward his Cadillac. The two oversize ranch hands took a last regretful look at Brad and followed.

"Ain't you going to come with us, Mr. Perry?" Cooley called.

Perry leaned out the window and spat past the running board. "You and your Washington friend kin get your stomachs turned ef you want to," he said. "I can't stand the stink."

The heavy car backed up and swiveled its wheels to straighten out. It edged past the pickup truck and wallowed down the dirt road, heaving on its custom springs.

"Well, I don't know how you did that," Cooley said admiringly.

They climbed back into the truck and inched up the baked dirt track toward the tents. The stench was as promised. Brad recognized the gaping outhouse he had seen in Reisner's photograph. It was leaning farther now. But the cloud of flies hadn't changed. Some enterprising chap had put the pump handle back on, and that was what made Brad gag.

"Seems to me it was that tent over there," Cooley said.

They got out of the truck. People were returning from the fields for their noon meal. Men in bleached overalls. Women in faded sunbonnets. Silent, gaunt children, the smallest of them toddling along wearing just shirts. They stared curiously at Brad's white suit, then hurried past, eyes down.

"Looks like somebody's in there," Cooley said.

Brad could see movement inside the tent, a flash of color through the little rips and worn-out places. His heart hammered within his chest. That could be Junie in there right now, this minute. With a small baby to take care of, she wouldn't be working in the fields with the others.

He put his foot on the crude box platform and Cooley grasped his arm.

"Hold on a minute, Brad. These people might not be much and they might not have much, but this is their home while they're stayin' here, and you can't just walk in without being invited."

Brad looked at his shoe, then put it back on the ground. "Well, then
. . . you want to yell in or something?"

"Is that manners in Washington?"

"Well . . . but . . . how will they know we're out here?"

"They know."

They waited in the dust, and after a minute the tent flap parted. A
small barefoot boy with closely cropped blond hair stared gravely at
them, then went back inside. Cooley put a restraining hand on Brad's
arm, and they waited some more. Brad had time to study the tent. A
rusty elbow of stovepipe poked through the flap at the top. The tent
fabric around it was charred. Brad wondered how many fires there
were in camps like this. The flap parted again and a very old woman,
gnarled with arthritis, came stooping out.

Cooley took off his hat and mopped his forehead. "Morning,
missus," he said.

The woman's eyes took in Brad's white suit and white shoes and
Panama hat without surprise, then went on to Cooley. "We ain't done
nothin'," she said.

"Nobody says you have, ma'am," Cooley said.

"It was that other fam'ly had the typhus, not us. Packed up and left
in the middle of the night, took the body of their little one with them,
gone by the time the deputy got back with the nurse. Prob'ly buried
the baby in the desert."

"We're not from the county health office, ma'am," Cooley said
gently.

"They was the ones that chopped a hole in the floor for a privy
without diggin' a pit underneath," the woman said with rising indignation. " 'Twarn't us. When my man found it, he dug out the underneath
of the tent and nailed a board over the hole." Her eyes lit on Brad
again. "So you can take the doctor away with you."

"He's not a doctor," Cooley said more loudly. "He's from the government. He just wants to ask a few questions."

"What's that?"

"He's from the government!" Cooley shouted.

Brad felt cold in the Arizona sunlight. "This other family," he said.
"Did they have a girl named Junie with them? June Alice?"

Two men with hoes were approaching the tent. They walked more
quickly when they saw Brad and Cooley. One of them was a watchful,
youngish man with blond stubble on his face. The other was an old
codger whose chopped-off sleeves showed sinewy arms that looked
hard as gristle. They gripped the hoe handles with rather too much
emphasis.

"What do you want with my ma?" the younger man said.

Brad faced him. "I'm trying to—"

"He's from the government," Cooley said quickly. "He's just asking about a family that used to live here."

"He had no call to get her upset. She can't tell him nothin'."

"Deef as a post, she is," the old man cackled. "She don't see too good, either, when it comes to that."

"She thought he was the doctor," Cooley said.

"It's that white suit, I reckon," the old man said.

They all had a mild laugh at Brad's expense. He saw their hands relax on the hoe handles. They hadn't been hostile, he realized, just apprehensive. He smiled to show that he thought it was a good joke, too.

"This woman whose baby died of the typhus," he said. "Have you any idea where she might have gone?"

"Huh?"

"You moved in after them," he said, trying to hide his impatience. "They chopped a hole in the floor and you boarded it up. How long ago was that?"

Comprehension dawned in the old man's eyes. "Oh, that weren't here. That was a camp over by Gila Bend nigh three weeks ago."

"She gets mixed up sometimes," the younger man said, embarrassed.

"When did you folks move in here?"

"Just last night. After dark, it was. Mr. Perry's foreman, that Mex fella, tol' us we could have this tent, wasn't nobody in it, and start work in the morning."

"What about the family who had the tent before you? When did they move out?"

The old man shook his head. "Don't know nothin' about no other fam'ly," he said.

Brad exchanged a look of despair with Cooley.

"Tell you who *might* know somethin', though," the old man went on. "The McClains. They've been here longer than anybody, I reckon." He lowered his voice. "Been here since last year."

"Had to sell their car for food," the younger man said with a look of obscure embarrassment.

"Nice folks, though," the old man said quickly. "Real pretty woman, nice young 'uns."

"Where can I find them?" Brad said.

"Well now, I was just about to tell you that," the old man said, hurt. "Two, no, three tents down, that way."

"We thank you kindly," Cooley said.

"You're right welcome, I'm sure. Hope you find that fam'ly."

They went on down the aisle of tents. The sun was getting to Brad. That, and the size of the western sky. For a dizzy second, he had the absurd fantasy that he was walking along an immense fossil jawbone, that the row of bleached, sagging triangles was a stupendous representation of ancient saurian teeth, created in canvas for some unimaginable stage set or paleontology exhibit, and that the people he saw around the bases of the tents were morsels caught between the teeth. He shook off the impression, and caught up with Cooley.

"You all right?" Cooley said.

"I'm fine."

"You should have et breakfast when we stopped. Black coffee ain't enough for a man."

They found the woman at the entrance of her tent, crouched over a small kerosene drum that had been transformed into a primitive stove. A jointed stovepipe of sorts had been improvised out of tomato cans stuck into one another, and a fire door had been punched out of a piece of tin. The noon meal was cooking on top in a blackened skillet. Canned beans, it looked like, with a lardy chunk of fatback melting down the middle. Fuel was a pile of twigs and cotton stalks. A red glare of flame showed through rusted-out patches of the drum.

"Miz McClain?" Cooley said.

She flinched at her name. The fine structure of her face would have made her pretty, as the old man said, if she hadn't been used up by life. She was painfully thin, with skin stretched like parchment over delicate bones. Brad thought she looked tubercular. A small dirty child clung to her apron and stared at them. Two more children, unnaturally silent, hovered nearby.

"Could we talk to you?" Cooley said.

She rose to her feet, hands fluttering at her apron. "I . . . I . . . my husban's in the field. He'll be back mos' any minute now."

Brad took off his hat. "Maybe we could talk to you in the meantime."

"He won't be but a few minutes," she said, alarm showing.

Cooley put a hand on Brad's arm. They waited in the sunlight. Mrs. McClain fussed nervously at the stove, not looking at them. McClain came trudging wearily toward them after a while, a hoe over his shoulder. He was a bony young man with a whipped look about him.

"No, the Kinneys are long gone," McClain said after he had finally absorbed Brad's questions. "They picked up and left just as ever soon as that little gal Junie could travel with her baby. Miz Kinney, she saw to that." His tone was hushed and admiring. "Made them save every nickel and dime they could get their hands on for gasoline and eatin' money so they could get to California and pick the fruit. There's good wages in California, they say. Not like here."

"When would that have been, Mr. McClain?" Brad said.

He already knew the answer. He knew when Reisner had taken the picture. But he couldn't get over the feeling that if only he had waited for Cooley's call that night instead of going home to Sally—if he could just have come to this place a week earlier—he would have found Junie.

McClain scratched a stubbled chin. "Well, let me see now. That would have been way back last July. And there was still cotton to be chopped here."

"Have you any idea—any idea at all—where in California they might have gone?" Brad said.

"Why . . . like I said. Just California."

Cooley gave Brad a look of profound pity. "Tough luck, Brad. Looks like you went to a lot of trouble for nothing."

"The land of milk and honey," Purley said.

He was working in the row next to Junie, but he was drawing ahead of her again. Purley and Floyd were doing three rows to everybody else's two, and had doubled back a dozen times so far this morning.

"California!" Purley said, and spat at the ground. He swung his knife savagely and wrenched another head of lettuce free.

Junie worked as fast as she could, trying to keep up. But the small of her back was pure agony. You couldn't straighten up all the way when you picked lettuce, and you couldn't take the time to kneel. You had to keep moving in a sort of scuttling crouch that left you crippled at the end of the day.

"The promised land," Purley went on bitterly, talking to no one in particular. "Ain't no different than Arizona, 'cept you get to pick more different kinds of crops. Pick the melons in the Imperial Valley, then move on, we don't want you. Pick the apricots in Santa Ana, then get yourself outa our sight, we don't want to look at no Okies. Pick the peas, and thank you kindly. Then move north for the peaches and the cherries. Then the lettuce. They say an Okie is as good as a Mexican or a Jap for lettuce. Then it's back to the Imperial Valley again for the 'sparagus. Now *there*'s a crop! You get to pick the 'sparagus twice in one day, and you can't take time to rest 'cause it keeps growin'." He spat at the ground again.

"Now you stop that frettin' kind of talk, Purley Kinney!" Ma Kinney said from the row on the other side of Junie. "Save your breath for pickin'. You ought to be glad to have food to eat and a place to live while so many folks are goin' hungry."

"Place to live? You call that pigsty they put us in a place to live?"

"I told you to stop that talk. You ain't goin' to improve things by carryin' on that way, and you'll just put everybody in a misery. You don't see Floyd complainin'."

"Floyd ain't got the brains to complain."

"Now you *stop* that! I ain't about to tell you again!"

Junie tried not to hear the quarrel. The lettuce field stretched on forever, an endless striped green carpet with a line of strange crablike creatures moving over it. She was one of them. It was getting harder and harder to remember Beulah, Iowa, or even the last camp. They were all alike, except that some of them had tents and some of them had shacks and some of them just had wooden platforms where you set up your own tent or one borrowed from the camp boss.

She wished she had little Leander with her. No, she corrected herself, little Leander *Bradford!* He was a good baby, even though he cried all the time. It wasn't temper, as some of the women said. It was just colic, and someday when he got over it, he'd be cooing and gurgling just as happily as Sue Ellen's newest child. As soon as they could settle down somewhere, the way Ma Kinney kept promising, she could spend more time with Leander Bradford, and he'd be all right. But right now he was at the awkward age: too old to stay put if you took him to the fields and laid him down on a blanket, and too young to follow, or to help pick, the way the older kids did. He'd be all right with that old woman in the camp taking care of him and Sue Ellen's children.

All of a sudden the lettuce field tilted, and she found herself sitting on the ground with Ma Kinney supporting her, and all the lettuce spilled out of her picking sack.

"Floyd, you give me the water jug," Ma Kinney said. "Here, child, take a sip of this and you'll feel better."

"I'll be all right."

Floyd was there, inarticulate concern showing on his homely face. He hovered over her until Ma Kinney made him go back to picking with the others. The line moved on, drawing the Kinney clan with it. Floyd couldn't afford to stop, Junie told herself. The camp boss, a mean-looking Texan named Rawson, would give the Kinneys' cabin to a more productive family if they fell too far behind. Newcomers were arriving all the time.

"I can work now," Junie said, struggling to get up.

"No, you can't," Ma Kinney said firmly. "That baby's too far along."

"Sue Ellen worked until her eighth month," Junie said.

"You ain't Sue Ellen. You ain't born to this kind of life."

"Neither are any of you," Junie said.

"We've all knowed hard times," Ma Kinney said. "Now you're just a little more delicate, child. You just go back and rest a while. Later on, maybe you can help with the packin' a little. Do you need help gettin' back?"

"No," Junie said, ashamed of herself for feeling so glad. Now she could be with little Leander, play with him and talk to him.

Ma Kinney helped raise her to her feet. They retrieved the spilled lettuce and added it to one of the crates lining the rows.

"Go on, now, and don't you fret," Ma Kinney said.

"All right," Junie said with a tentative smile.

Ma Kinney smiled back at her. She looked at Junie's swollen belly and said, "Maybe this one will be a girl. Be old enough to help with the cooking and the washing and the mending before you know it. Boys are nice, but I allus say a girl is a help and a comfort to her ma."

29

The pounding at the door brought Jeremy blinking out of a swampy sleep and vague dreams of ship's engines and half-glimpsed shadowy figures with something bright in their hands. He had no idea how long it had been going on. He looked at the luminous clock on the kitchen chair beside the bed. It was after three in the morning.

"Open up!" a harsh voice shouted in the passageway.

Jeremy stumbled out of bed and groped for his undershorts. Ilse was rigid under the sheets, not breathing. He couldn't see her face in the darkness, but he could smell her fear.

The pounding grew more violent. It sounded as if heavy boots were kicking at the door in a senseless rage. "You will unlock the door!" the voice screamed. "Immediately!"

Before he could get to the door, the flimsy lock gave way and they came bursting into the room. One of them found the light switch, and the overhead bulb went on, half blinding Jeremy.

There were three of them, in the flamboyant black uniforms of an SS Death's Head unit: shiny boots, silver stitching, all the gaudy metallic frippery of eagles, swastikas, daggers, and double lightning bolts, tall peaked caps tricked out with a silver eagle above and a skull and crossbones on the leather visor.

"You are Jeremy Sinclair," the officer in charge said, not making it a question. He was an angular man with a jaw like a monkey wrench.

"Y-yes, but—"

"You will get dressed immediately and come with us."

"What's this all about?" Jeremy demanded, trying to muster a show of indignation. "I'm an American citizen." But he thought he knew why they had come for him. It was the article he had written about Himmler.

"No questions."

"Where are you taking me?"

"You'll find out," the broad subaltern said with an unpleasant laugh.

"You must put on your clothes at once," the officer said impatiently, tapping his riding breeches with a little whip he carried.

Silently, Jeremy climbed into his trousers, buttoned up his shirt, hopped about awkwardly as he put on shoes and socks. He felt shabby and self-conscious under their contemptuous stares. There was a hole in one sock, a knot where he had tied a broken shoelace together, usually tucked out of sight under the bow. He knew he needed a haircut.

"My passport!" Jeremy said, moving toward the bureau drawer. Whatever happened, he was not going to leave that room without his passport.

But the other subaltern, a cold blond youth with *Untersturmführer* tabs on his tunic, was already rummaging through his possessions. He studied a signed photograph of Ilse in a bathing suit with unnecessary care, then handed Jeremy's passport over to the wrench-jawed officer, who flipped it open for a moment, then put it in his pocket.

"Hey!" Jeremy said.

"Put on your jacket," the officer said.

Jeremy tried to give Ilse a reassuring glance before he was hustled out of the room, but her eyes, huge in a face that had gone chalky, looked right past him as if she did not know him anymore. She was a Dresden girl who worked as a stenographer at the Foreign Office. He had met her three weeks earlier while interviewing her boss.

A black car with curtained rear windows was waiting downstairs at the curb. Jeremy was squeezed into the back seat between the two SS subalterns. The officer in charge got in front with the driver. Nobody spoke. The car started up with a twelve-cylinder purr and moved off through the dark streets.

The car pulled up in front of the building at number eight Prinz-Albrecht-Strasse. Gestapo headquarters was a looming shadow, defined in the darkness by tall phosphorescent rectangles of leaking light. They worked all through the night in this sinister place, but they kept the shades drawn.

Jeremy got out of the car with his three black-clad escorts. As Jeremy climbed the low steps, a piercing scream, suddenly cut off, came from a cellar window.

Inside, a steel-helmeted SS sentry snapped out a Hitler salute. The three returned it negligently and hurried Jeremy through a gloomy catacomb that was illumined by fake electric torches mounted high in wrought-iron cages. A number of bored-looking SS types lounged about on the small sofas placed in wall recesses, smoking and reading newspapers, their showy black uniforms making them look like a lot of extras waiting backstage for their cue.

They took him upstairs to a suite of offices. The rooms were high-ceilinged and spacious, paneled in oak to a man's height and plastered above. A rather plain young woman with her blond hair drawn severely into a bun sat at a desk, typing, as if it were not the middle of the night. She paid no attention to them, and went on typing.

"Sit down over there," the SS officer said.

Somewhat bewildered, Jeremy sat down on the indicated couch. He wished he could go to the bathroom. The two other SS men sat down on either side of him. The officer went through an oversized door of carved oak.

He came back out a few minutes later. "The Reichsführer will see you now," he said.

Jeremy got to his feet slowly. The two subalterns got up with him.

"Go on, go on," the officer said. "Don't keep him waiting."

"What about my passport?" Jeremy said stubbornly.

"Don't worry about your passport," the officer said.

Jeremy got a look at what the secretary was typing as he passed her desk. It was some kind of requisition form with detailed manufacturing specifications and technical sketches. The sketches were of what seemed to be a clamshell press or vise with screws for tightening. The two halves enclosed a vague eggplant form whose shape nagged at him.

Inside, a blond giant in a black uniform closed the door behind him and snapped to attention like a statue. The room was large and plain, paneled with unvarished oak and carpeted with coconut mats. A massive, ugly desk occupied the far corner, under an imitation medieval wall hanging. Jeremy stood facing the most feared man in Germany.

Heinrich Himmler was not a prepossessing figure. Jeremy's first reaction was: Caspar Milquetoast! The former chicken farmer who had become head of Hitler's secret police was narrow-chested and shoulderless, with a weak chin, prissy little mouth, wispy mustache, and watery eyes slitted behind rimless glasses. His round face had an almost Mongolian cast to it. His hands, resting on the desktop, were maggot-pale. Himmler wore the black, gaudily trimmed uniform he had invented for his blond supermen, except that he had added laurel leaf garlands to the other decorations. It seemed a size too large on him.

He blinked nearsightedly at Jeremy and half-rose. "Please, please, sit down," he said in a thin, shrill voice.

Jeremy sat down on a couch as far from Himmler as he could get. Himmler came around his desk and diffidently pulled up a chair opposite him. The Reichsführer seemed nervous about something. He crossed and recrossed his knees awkwardly. He pushed aside a vase of flowers on the round coffee table between them. He cleared his throat and smiled ingratiatingly at Jeremy.

"Yes, yes, I have read your article about me, Herr Sinclair."

Jeremy started to speak, but Himmler held up a puffy hand.

"Please, I understand. It is your job to make me appear tough, strict. Even cruel. Hard. How else is one to write about the head of a nation's security police? I do not mind. I give my life to the state. My family knows me for a decent fellow, and that is enough. Perhaps it is not such a bad thing to make the enemies of the German state know that a stern justice awaits them in my person."

Actually, Jeremy had soft-pedaled the article. Walt Hanes had said, "Christ, that stinking little nut runs a torture factory out there on Prince Albert Street. Know what happens to the Jews who pass through there? I thought you were a red-hot, Sinclair. I'm disappointed in you." But Allied International had accepted the article for syndication. It had appeared in Sunday supplements throughout the U.S. under the title: "Hitler's Top Cop." Jeremy had been paid fifty dollars for it.

Himmler went on: "My office received your request for—what do you journalists call it?—an 'in-depth' interview. You said that Goebbels holds forth daily at the Propaganda Ministry, that Goering makes himself freely available to the foreign press, but—and I quote— 'almost nothing is known of the personal philosophy of the man who runs the powerful organization charged with implementing the Nazi ideals.'"

Jeremy mumbled something suitably noncommittal. He was used to publicity hounds. The rabbity little man's hunger for importance was almost palpable.

Himmler's narrow chest puffed out with pride. "Perhaps it is time. Yes, perhaps it is time."

"I would be grateful, Herr Reichsführer."

"Tomorrow is my thirty-fifth birthday. The Führer himself has sent me his greetings. It is a day which I always celebrate with the most solemn dedication to the holy Germanic spirit."

"My congratulations, Herr Reichsführer."

Himmler was becoming quite excited. His voice rose to a high-pitched squeak. "I live for the day when a revived Germany will resound to the sacred crusade of King Heinrich!"

Jeremy was taken aback. Had Himmler gone completely off his rocker? *"King* Heinrich?" he said cautiously.

"My namesake. Heinrich the First. Known as Henry the Fowler. Next year is the thousandth anniversary of his death. I have built a shrine to him at Wewelsburg." His eyes glittered madly. "When I visit the shrine, I am able to commune with his spirit in my sleep."

"That's very interesting, Herr Reichsführer."

Himmler bounced to his feet, brimming with excitement. Despite the wispy mustache and Prussian neck, he cut an almost girlish figure with his sloping shoulders and wide hips. "I have decided. You will be allowed to view the ceremonies."

"Er . . . when will that be?"

"At midnight, of course. On my birthday." Himmler became brisk. "We will have to hurry. You will travel with my staff. The cars will be waiting downstairs. They will take us to the airfield. My adjutant, Grothmann, will see to your needs. He'll have a spare kit for you. My own batman can shave you."

Jeremy got up off the couch and followed Himmler to the door. "I don't know what to say, Herr Reichsführer. I'm overwhelmed."

A thought struck Himmler. He paused with his hand on the knob. "You don't have any Jewish blood, do you?"

"Not that I know of, Herr Reichsführer."

"One can't be too careful. The Jewish taint is everywhere. We mustn't sully the ceremonies at the crypt."

"Er, no, of course not."

"I have nothing against the Jews personally. I don't believe in needless cruelty. I'm against blood sports, not like that damned Goering, who shoots helpless deer for his pleasure. But the Jew is a subhuman, a racially inferior type. German race scientists have proved this. Eventually we will have a Europe entirely free of Jews. *Judenrein!* But until that glorious day arrives, we Aryans must take whatever steps we can to prevent Jewish blood from contaminating the broad, pure stream of Nordic heredity. No matter how distasteful we find the task."

He marched into the outer office with a runt's swagger. Jeremy followed. The blond secretary was still typing. The technical specifications for the device that the Gestapo was ordering went on for pages, with German thoroughness. Jeremy peeked again. All at once, the eggplant shape became recognizable as an anatomical drawing, and Jeremy suddenly realized the purpose of the little press.

"Blood and soil," Himmler said in a voice that was tremulous with emotion.

"Blood and soil," chanted the twelve SS *Obergruppenführer*s seated at the round table.

"Revenge and right," Himmler quavered.

"Revenge and right," the twelve repeated after him.

Himmler raised his jeweled goblet with a trembling hand. The twelve SS leaders obediently raised their own goblets.

"To the sacred spirit of Henry the Fowler, founder of the First Reich and defender of the holy Germanic peoples against the subhuman Slavic hordes of the east," Himmler said, the tears running down his cheeks.

Jeremy, from his vantage point beside a medieval suit of armor, discreetly snapped a picture with the camera that Himmler's adjutant, Grothmann, had lent him. The flash popped, catching at least one bleary-eyed SS leader in the act of trying to stifle a yawn. Several of them had been roused from their beds the night before, as Jeremy had been, and hadn't had much opportunity for napping since. This crazy King Arthur playacting in Himmler's ersatz Camelot had been going on since lunchtime, and it was almost midnight.

"We are the knights of a new Teutonic order!" Himmler squeaked. Some of his wine went down the wrong way and he had a little choking fit. Recovering, he squared his narrow shoulders and went on: "Our honor is obedience. Our motto is race, obedience, sacrifice."

Jeremy snapped another picture. Everybody blinked at the flash, and tried not to look self-conscious. It was a fantastic scene: the twelve overstuffed men sitting at the oaken round table in high-backed pigskin chairs, with ribbons and sashes and phony coats-of-arms added to their black uniforms, the gigantic blond guards standing around with swords and ceremonial daggers, and in the middle of it all, a little owlish man with a weak chin discoursing on his crackpot theories of a master race.

The dining hall itself was enormous: a one-hundred-fifty-foot-long vault of quarried stone, lit by sputtering torches in wall brackets and hung with huge vulgar tapestries, medieval banners, and shields, swords, and battle-axes looted from museums. Himmler had spared no expense in refurbishing the mountain castle in Westphalia as his private retreat. Wewelsburg, it was called, after the robber knight who had once owned it. It dated from the time of the Huns. Himmler had

spent eleven million marks of state funds rebuilding it according to his
half-baked notions.

Grothmann had shown Jeremy through the private apartments and
allowed him to take pictures. Each SS leader was assigned a room
furnished in a different period and dedicated to one of Himmler's historical heroes. Jeremy had seen the old parchments lying like school
homework on the tables amidst the sample relics that went with the
room. Each *Obergruppenführer* was supposed to study them at bedtime in case Himmler questioned him the next day. But there were
signs that the SS officers were getting bored by all the flummery;
Jeremy had also seen the cheap detective stories and sex novels tucked
away in their unpacked luggage.

". . . and so," Himmler was saying, his bland Mongol features
shiny in the torchlight, "like the holy legions of Henry the Fowler, our
little band of true Nordics must stand as a bulwark to guard the German people against race defilement."

He got up. The blond guard behind his chair towered over him. The
twelve men at the table got up, too, with a creak and a jingle of
leather and tin. Himmler led the way to a trapdoor in the center of the
huge expanse of stone floor. Two of the blond guards sprang smartly
to attention and hauled on an iron ring. The trapdoor opened on a
flight of granite steps. Himmler, almost tripping on his sword, disappeared from view. The twelve SS bigwigs filed after him.

Grothmann glided from somewhere along the wall and appeared at
Jeremy's elbow. The adjutant was a handsome, pale young man with
the requisite blond hair.

"It's all right, Herr Sinclair," he said. "The Reichsführer has said
specifically that you may join them in the shrine."

Jeremy glanced inquiringly at his borrowed Leitz camera.

"But of course, my dear fellow," Grothmann said.

Jeremy descended into the crypt. He found himself in a murky,
round chamber, lit only by flickering candles set in wall niches. It was
like a Halloween party. The twelve costumed SS men were gathered
around a sort of birdbath in the center, trying to look solemn. Twelve
stone plinths were arranged in intervals around the walls. At the base
of each plinth leaned a carved oak armorial shield painted in garish
colors. The heraldic symbols seemed to run to wolves and stags, with a
few death's heads and skeletons thrown in. One of the plinths had a
funeral urn resting on top of it. Himmler approached the plinth and
picked up the oaken shield. It was a particularly spiffy one, with a lion
couchant lifting its head toward a rather unwary stag guardant being
ridden by a skeleton carrying a sword.

Jeremy sidled over to a wall recess and tried to look inconspicuous.

Himmler staggered to the birdbath with the shield, his short arms wrapped awkwardly around it. He set it down in the stone basin, almost smashing his fingers.

One of the *Obergruppenführers* stepped forward with a jerry can of gasoline and doused the shield. Himmler tried to draw his sword out of its scabbard, but it was too long, and his arms were too short. Finally managing to get it out, he held it aloft over the stone birdbath.

"We are gathered here in this realm of the dead," Himmler said in his shaky voice, "to do honor to our fallen comrade-in-arms, Dort, and to speed his spirit to that sacred realm where dwell the spirits of all true Germanic heroes."

He paused, looking impatient about something. Jeremy came to his senses with a start and clicked the release. A flashbulb went off with a pop. Himmler looked pleased. He continued his peroration.

"As was done for the knights of old, we will now burn his arms so that no one may ever sully their honor. *Heil Hitler!*"

"*Heil Hitler!*" the others murmured.

"Our new comrade, Kapp, takes his place at our round table. Kapp, may you prove worthy of your escutcheon."

Kapp knelt on one knee somewhat self-consciously. He was one of Himmler's blond Aryan ideals, gone a bit jowly. Himmler lowered the heavy sword to his shoulder, coming perilously close to slicing off Kapp's ear. Jeremy popped off another flash.

Himmler managed to get the sword back in its scabbard. He snapped his fingers. "A candle!"

One of the men handed him a candle. Himmler touched it to the shield. He didn't step back quickly enough. The gasoline went up with a whoosh, singeing his eyebrows. Everybody stood around gravely watching the wooden shield burn up. Jeremy set off more flashes. The film was gone, but he didn't think he should take the time to change the roll.

Himmler had a surprise for Kapp. "Your own coat-of-arms, especially designed for you by Professor Diebitsch!"

He unwrapped a huge parcel. Kapp's shield was green and purple, with a charging boar, a death's head, and crossed battle-axes. Kapp looked properly grateful. Then there was a lot of mumbo-jumbo involving the Germanic runes, sacred oak trees, and astrological signs.

"Where are the bones of Henry the Fowler?" Himmler declaimed. "We do not know. They have disappeared from their tomb. Can it be that they are now clothed by the flesh of another Heinrich, a new German hero who will lead his own knights to glory?"

Jeremy was asleep on his feet by the time he was shown to his room. The twelve SS leaders were punch-drunk and stumbling. Only

Himmler was still fresh, bubbling over with unseemly energy. Jeremy found an old leather-bound book on his bedside table, its pages flaking away. It had been left pointedly open on a passage about the ancient Teutons and their belief in reincarnation. Jeremy ignored it and fell into a deep sleep filled with nightmares about skulls and dark places.

"Did you get everything you need?" Grothmann asked him at breakfast the next day. "The Reichsführer will be leaving early this afternoon for an inspection of Dachau, so I'm afraid you'll pretty much have to be satisfied with what you already have."

Jeremy stiffened. It had become permissible to mention Dachau guardedly in public ever since the *Munich Illustrated Press* had published an officially approved article with pictures showing the neatly laid out camp streets and vegetable gardens and rows of crop-haired prisoners standing at attention for a "rehabilitation lecture." Walt Hanes had said to him: "There goes your scoop, Sinclair."

Jeremy said carefully, "Well, there are still one or two things I'd like to ask the Reichsführer. Just to fill in the gaps."

Grothmann frowned. "Perhaps I can squeeze you in for a few minutes before he leaves. His schedule is very tight, you understand. Perhaps at lunch?"

"Thanks. It really would make all the difference."

Jeremy spent the rest of the morning wandering around the grounds and taking exterior shots of Wewelsburg. The castle's towers looked out over dense forest. Birds twittered, and once he heard the sound of some large beast crashing through the underbrush. At noon, Himmler's other adjutant, Heinz Macher, came looking for Jeremy. Macher looked exactly like Grothmann: a blond chorus boy with a handsome wax-doll face.

"You are requested to join the Reichsführer in the garden," he said.

Himmler was sitting at a small table with four or five of the *Obergruppenführer*s. They all looked puffy. A servant bowed Jeremy to the place that had been set for him. It was fine china, Venetian glass, and vermeil flatware on a linen cloth. Himmler, looking prim and correct, nodded in friendly fashion at him.

Lunch was roast pork, potatoes, red cabbage, and dark Westphalian beer. "Eat, eat, don't wait for me," Himmler urged, and the *Obergruppenführer*s lowered their heads and fell to. The steward served Himmler a few moments later out of a covered dish. It was a rather peculiar combination of buttered carrots and macaroni.

"My special diet," Himmler explained, following Jeremy's gaze. "You are permitted to say that the Reichsführer has a delicate stomach, brought about by the cares of his office. Hess's cook devised the recipe for me. Hess is a more dedicated vegetarian than even the Führer. He eats nothing but foods of biodynamic origin."

Jeremy got out his pocket notebook and scribbled a few words in it. Himmler lowered his eyes modestly.

"Now, that's the sort of detail I mean, Herr Reichsführer," Jeremy said. "Too bad we've run out of time."

Himmler, his mouth full of carrots, blinked. "It is decided. You will accompany us to Dachau."

The young SS *Sturmbannführer* saluted smartly. "The prisoners are lined up and waiting, Herr Oberführer," he said. "I've had them assembled on the parade ground for four hours now."

"Let them wait," the Dachau commandant said. He was a dumpy, pipe-smoking man whose name was Eicke. "It won't hurt them to stand at attention another hour or two. Help air out some of the stink. First, tea, eh? After the Reichsführer's long journey."

Dachau sparkled with fresh paint in the October sunlight. The pleasant, spacious villas that housed the SS officers were pink and white, surrounded by borders of bright autumn flowers. There were spanking new barracks for the guards, administrative buildings, recreation halls. Beyond, Jeremy could see a barbed wire enclosure, guarded by looming watchtowers, for the prisoners.

Eicke knelt and pinched the cheek of the little blond girl who stood at Himmler's side. "And how is our pretty little Gudrun today? Keeping her daddy company, like a good girl? Some tea would be nice, wouldn't it? With jam tarts."

Himmler beamed. "Say thank you to Papa Eicke," he said.

Gudrun clung, speechless, to her father. She was an exquisite little thing, about seven years old, with pigtails and a peasant dirndl. Himmler had stopped at Tegernsee to pick her up on his way to the camp. Jeremy, waiting outside in the motorcade, had heard angry voices raised in quarrel. The Reichsführer and his wife didn't get along, it seemed. They were separated in fact, if not in name. But he doted on his daughter, and evidently took her along on his expeditions to the camp on his infrequent visits to the area.

Eicke rose with a grunt. "And I must say, it's an honor having Herr Hess come to see us today. You'll bring back a good report to the Führer, won't you?"

Rudolf Hess smiled automatically, then drew his lips quickly closed to hide his buck teeth. Himmler had picked him up, along with other party dignitaries, at the Munich railroad station, where they had arrived by special train. There were a couple of hand-picked journalists with SS credentials. Evidently today's excursion was something special.

Jeremy hung back with the other journalists, where his camera would not look out of place. They were under the eyes of a watchful Grothmann. When one of the others raised his camera to take a picture of Himmler stooping to whisper a sweet nothing in Gudrun's ear, Jeremy snapped a picture too.

"Such humanity!" the photographer said, and Grothmann relaxed a little.

The party straggled across the manicured grounds toward the largest of the villas, with a talkative Himmler in the lead.

"The place was nothing when we took it over," Himmler boasted. "A rotting munitions factory left over from the World War. We put the prisoners to work draining the swamps, as Mussolini did with his prisoners around Rome. We used prisoner labor to plant the gardens, build the houses and barracks, the hospital—even an SS riding school!" He turned toward Hess to emphasize his next point. "Not one pfennig of state or Party money was used to accomplish all this!"

The riding school, Jeremy thought, explained the whips that Eicke and so many of the SS men seemed to be carrying. It made a handy excuse.

They passed an elaborate herb garden, laid out in the shape of a cartwheel, with white-pebbled walks and little white signs marking the various plantings, like a botanical exhibit. A couple of men in striped pajamas were tending it.

"And this is the herb garden," he said. "It is my little *Mädchen*'s favorite spot at Dachau." He patted Gudrun's head. "She already knows the names of most of the plants, and what they are used for."

He beckoned to one of the men in striped pajamas. The man dropped a trowel and shuffled over, looking frightened. He was gaunt, almost a walking skeleton, with a shaved skull and powdery complexion. His upper teeth seemed to have been knocked out.

"You, fellow . . . what was your name? I forget."

"Thielemann, sir," the man whispered.

"Herr Professor Doktor Thielemann, wasn't it?" Himmler said in high good humor. "What was your profession?"

"Professor of botany, sir. At the University of Berlin."

"You see?" Himmler beamed at Hess. "We can draw on high-class talent here. It's not all Jews and Gypsies. Why are you here, Thielemann?"

Thielemann twisted his cap miserably in his skeletal hands. "I . . . I was told that I neglected to give due importance to folk botany in my lectures."

"Yes, yes, you were warned and still you persisted," Himmler said with a frown. "Now I remember. But you are learning here at Dachau. The German peasant has known about the medicinal properties of herbs for centuries. Basil for headaches. Lovage for rheumatism. Tarragon, the dragon's herb, as old peasant women still call it—it heals the bites of mad dogs." He turned toward Rudolf Hess. "Do you know that we are experimenting here at Dachau with cancer-healing herbs?"

Hess raised his bushy eyebrows with interest. "So?"

Jeremy remembered that Hess had a passionate interest in faith-healing. He had founded a hospital in Dresden that specialized in forms of treatment that were not recognized by science.

"Yes, yes," Himmler went on, bubbling over. "And that's only the beginning. I have ideas for medical experiments that we can carry out here. How to bring frozen men back to life, for example. More efficient methods of sterilization. All that will come later. We have a plentiful supply of prisoners we can use as subjects."

Hess wagged a finger playfully. "But will results obtained on Jews be valid for human beings?"

Everybody laughed. Jeremy, feeling sick, managed a weak grin. Grothmann peered at him closely.

Himmler tousled the little girl's hair, and Jeremy had the presence of mind to snap the shutter. "Himmler, the family man," he explained to a wary Grothmann.

"Papa will be very busy today," Himmler said. "I may not have time to show my little *Liebchen* the plants this time. Perhaps Herr Professor Doktor Thielemann can show you through the garden later and teach you the names of some more herbs. Can I trust you to do that, Thielemann?"

Thielemann gave a ghastly grin, all bare gums and rotting stumps of teeth. "Yes, certainly, Herr Reichsführer. I'll be glad to explain about the plants to the little lady."

Gudrun suddenly buried her face in Himmler's uniform and began crying. Himmler immediately snatched her up in his arms.

"There, there, little one, Papa understands. You don't have to see them. They're dirty, ugly. But they can't hurt you. Papa wouldn't let the nasty men hurt you. You can stay in the house and the house-keeper will help you cut out paper dolls while Papa's busy, and then we can go for a ride later. You'll like that, won't you?"

Gudrun sucked her thumb and nodded. Himmler swept on toward the villa, with everybody following.

"Eicke," he said. "I don't like that fellow's attitude. How is he progressing?"

Eicke sucked on his stub of a pipe. "He hasn't come very far in developing a true German pepper plant, as you ordered. He claims hybridization will take at least sixteen plant generations."

Himmler pressed his thin lips together. "He frightened Gudrun. You can do nothing with such scum. Stringent measures will have to be taken."

Eicke snickered. "Fertilizer in the garden, that's all he's good for. At least he can make the plants grow that way."

Jeremy stole a backward glance at the botany professor. Thielemann was the picture of grief, a broomstick man in striped rags, standing with bowed head in the center of the garden. Surreptitiously Jeremy snapped the shutter and hoped the camera was aimed right.

Tea was a cozy affair in front of a roaring fire lit by Eicke's housekeeper against the October chill. Himmler sat on an overstuffed sofa, surrounded by Hess and the other party dignitaries, while Gudrun played on the rug, cutting pictures out of illustrated magazines with the scissors she had been given. Jeremy sat in the second circle with the SS journalists and the younger staff members who had come with their bosses from Berlin.

"Cruelty for the sake of cruelty is not permitted," Himmler was explaining earnestly. "All we have done is to reintroduce old-fashioned Prussian prison discipline. Our purpose is to reeducate these elements. But unfortunately some of them do not appreciate this. So of course we must concede the need for corporal punishment."

Eicke waved his pipe. "Of course we have been hampered in our work by unnecessary regulations. The business of suspending a guard from duty for three days if he is responsible for the death of an inmate, for example." He laughed good-naturedly. "I tell you, we had a positive epidemic of shootings when *that* decree came down from above. The fellows had found a foolproof method of getting a three-day holiday whenever they chose. Fortunately the new regulations remove such restrictions."

Hess laughed politely. He glanced at his watch. "It's getting late," he said.

Himmler jumped to his feet, all apologies. "Of course! You must be getting tired. We can inspect the prisoners now. It won't take long."

Jeremy looked at his own watch. The prisoners had been kept standing at attention for six hours now.

The sign over the gate said: *Arbeit macht frei*—"Work makes you free." Jeremy got a good low-angle shot of it before they went inside, taking care to frame one of the machine-gun towers in the background. Nobody tried to stop him.

"What are those chimneys?" someone in the Hess party said.

He pointed at the factorylike stacks visible across a sea of low roofs. Jeremy marked the location in his mind.

"That's the crematorium," Eicke explained. "Most modern industrial ovens available—very efficient. We solicited bids from the top manufacturers. They fell all over themselves replying."

"Your own crematorium?" another party official said admiringly.

"We have a very large camp population. You can't imagine how many people die here every day. Even that brings money into our accounts. We sell the ashes back to the next of kin for fifty marks."

"A lucrative business," agreed Eicke's young deputy, Lippert. "We even recover the gold fillings from the teeth."

"Amazing," the official said.

The iron gate clanged shut behind them, making Jeremy jump. Himmler started walking briskly past the Bavarian-style administration building that sat astride the gate, drawing the sight-seeing party after him. Jeremy hung back, taking pictures of the party from the rear as it followed the narrow-shouldered, wide-hipped figure, until Grothmann came back for him.

"Come along, Herr Sinclair. You must stay with the rest of the group."

The prisoners were drawn up on an immense asphalt drill field that must have covered acres. The field was enclosed by a double perimeter of electrified barbed wire that was punctuated at intervals by substantial-looking square watchtowers with hip roofs and bands of sliding glass windows at the top. Jeremy saw the snouts of heavy mounted machine guns protruding from the windows. The prisoners could be mowed down in comfort. At the back of the drill field, row after row of long, shedlike barracks stretched endlessly to a railroad marshaling yard in the distance. Jeremy drew in his breath at the size of the place.

As they drew closer, the dense mass of humanity resolved itself into geometrically straight rows of men in zebra stripes. There was no way to count so many, so Jeremy did his best to estimate the distance between rows, the average distance between men in a row, the length of the edges of the living square, doing the rough multiplication in his head. The figure jolted him, and he did his arithmetic again to make sure. There were at least six thousand men waiting out there—the population of a fair-sized city.

Jeremy dropped to one knee to take a couple of quick long shots. The other journalists were doing the same. It seemed like any press junket. He spotted Grothmann turning around to check on them, and hurried to catch up again.

Close up, the faces, the skinny necks, were like an anatomy lesson. Those shaved skulls, the hollowed eye-sockets showing the bone struc-

ture, the cords standing out on the fleshless jaws and throats as though
they were flayed specimens, squeezed Jeremy with a sudden force that
left him breathless. There were varying degrees of emaciation. Here
and there were men who looked almost normal, people from everyday
life whose faces you saw in the streets or crowded buses—men who
might have been doctors, lawyers, shopkeepers, train conductors,
postal clerks—simply gone a bit seedy. Jeremy guessed these were the
more recent arrivals.

Jeremy's face burned. The emotion he felt, inexplicably, was embarrassment, shame. It slowly turned to the dull heat of anger. He fought
to keep himself under control. Deliberately, he forced himself to take
a picture, as the other journalists were doing.

"That's the way, dear chap," Grothmann said approvingly as
Jeremy stood on tiptoe and stretched arms over his head to get an
overall view. "You'll try not to get the ones lying on the ground, won't
you? These are enemies of the state, but we want to make it look like
a proper military formation."

Jeremy nodded, keeping his lips tight. He snapped another picture.

The columns of scarecrows in striped rags swayed and trembled
with the effort of trying to stand motionless. Jeremy could see the
strain in the nearer faces. There were gaps in the line where some of
them had collapsed. The bodies had been left lying. As Jeremy
watched, a man's knees buckled and he fell sprawling to the ground.
One of the roaming SS guards was there instantly, kicking at him and
bawling at him to get up. The man didn't move. He looked dead. The
guard gave him an experimental slash with his whip, but when he got
no response, gave up.

Himmler, hands on hips, was discoursing to his guests on the meaning of the colored triangles sewn on the prisoners' uniforms:

"The green triangles are for common criminals, the red for politi-
cals, the purple for Jehovah's Witnesses. The pink is for homosexuals.
The black is for Gypsies and other antisocial elements. All of them
here are sterilized, by the way. The yellow triangles, of course, are for
Jews. You see how they can be sewn over one of the other triangles to
form a six-pointed star. In the cases where a Jew does not also belong
to one of the other categories, we simply use *two* yellow triangles."

"Ingenious," murmured one of the people in the Hess party.

Himmler paused in front of one of the prisoners. The man stiffened
in terror. He was about sixty, with a craggy brow and prognathous
jaw.

"Now here's an interesting racial type," Himmler said. "Note the
inferior bone structure, the criminal features. The prototype of your re-
pulsive Jewish-Bolshevik subhuman, with its Mongoloid admixture.
What's your name, fellow?"

"Elbers, Herr Reichsführer," he managed through chattering teeth.

"Impossible!" Himmler snapped. "That's an Aryan name." He tapped with his riding crop on the yellow star sewn to Elbers's jacket.

"If I can be of help, Herr Reichsführer." Lippert, the commandant's deputy, stepped forward with a clipboard and some kind of register in purple duplicating ink. He peered at the number stenciled on Elbers's jacket, flipped through pages and announced: "Jewish grandmother. On his mother's side. From Hungary."

"Strange," Himmler mused. "Of course the only way to decide the question scientifically is to compare the skull measurements with the specimens we already have collected for the race science museum. Lippert, you'll see that nothing happens to the head if the body is cremated?"

"Of course!" Lippert snapped his heels together.

"The head should be shipped directly to Dr. Sievers at the Ahnenerbe office in a hermetically sealed tin can filled with a preservative. My aide can give you the details."

"It will be done as you say," Lippert said, making a note on his clipboard.

"You understand that this is to be done only when the Jew dies a natural death."

Eicke broke in with a coarse laugh. "I think the Jew looks sick."

Himmler frowned. "And the head is not to be damaged."

"No . . . certainly not," Lippert said.

"Good," Himmler said. "You'll see that I have a report on the outcome?"

"It will be on your desk no later than a week from now," Eicke promised.

Hess was looking bored. Himmler, with a politician's instinct, noticed it immediately. "Eicke, perhaps you can point out some of our more eminent guests for Herr Hess. The *ehrenhafte* prisoners?"

"This way, this way," Eicke said jovially after a whispered consultation with Lippert and his clipboard. Himmler pranced ahead of them, and the party, with its escort of SS guards, followed.

Jeremy fell farther and farther behind. He knew that he ought to be sticking close to Himmler for the sake of the story he hoped to write, but he couldn't stand being near the man or that dreadful clown, Eicke.

"This one was a big-shot judge." He heard Eicke's voice from two or three rows over. "You recognize him? He's the one who ruled against two of our boys in that murder trial in 1931. He cleans the latrines here now."

Grothmann was coming back for him for the sixth or seventh time, looking annoyed. "Please, Herr Sinclair, you must try to keep up."

"Sorry," Jeremy said. "I just wanted to get a picture down this line of inmates toward that wooden shed." He stared challengingly at Grothmann. "Is that allowed?"

Grothmann hesitated. He assured himself with a flick of the eyes that there were no grotesquely wasted men or men showing the marks of recent beatings within closeup range of Jeremy's lens, then said with a gummy smile: "Of course. We have nothing to hide. Very artistic photo angle. The shed, by the way, is a shower bath, in case you need the information for your caption. Regulations require that each prisoner take a shower once a week for hygienic purposes. See, we're not monsters here."

Jeremy took his time with the picture, while Grothmann tapped his foot. He lagged behind again when Grothmann had to hurry back to answer a question from someone in the Berlin party.

Jeremy walked slowly through the field of scarecrows, feeling like a peeping Tom in hell. With his thumb he surreptitiously worked the shutter release and film advance of the little Leitz camera hanging round his neck. He wanted faces. If he took enough frames, he knew he'd get at least two or three he could use.

He was so intent on what he was doing that he was totally unprepared for what happened next. The frieze of goblin faces suddenly stopped streaming past his eyes, and after a confused moment he realized that it was his legs that had stopped, of their own accord, because one of those waxen masks belonged to someone he knew.

"Herr Weinbaum!" he gasped.

Naomi's uncle Freddie was one of those living wraiths. A part of Jeremy's mind marveled that he had recognized him. Friedrich Weinbaum seemed narrower, distorted, like a film projected at an angle. One cheekbone had been crushed and flattened, the patrician nose was a fleshless beak, the stubble on the shaved skull had turned snow-white, but it was him.

Weinbaum didn't answer. He stared straight ahead with desperate concentration, his clawed hands rigid at his sides.

Jeremy tried again. "Herr Weinbaum, what are you doing in this place, sir?"

"For God's sake, Herr Sinclair, walk on . . . don't speak to me . . ." Uncle Freddie said in a whisper, without moving his lips.

But Jeremy was transfixed. "I'll get you out of here somehow!" he said in a hoarse burst. "I'll make a fuss! They can't do this to a well-known man like you! Your brother! I'll get in touch with your brother! These Nazi swine like money! They'll take ransom . . . they do it all the time—"

"No," Weinbaum said. "It's better not to be noticed. It just makes things worse."

"But—"

"Go, please!"

It was too late. Jeremy became tardily aware of a rustling of ghosts on either side of Weinbaum, and turned his head to see Grothmann striding toward him, black boots shiny, the riding crop tapping impatiently at his side.

"Never mind, it doesn't matter," the apparition said in its ventriloquist's whisper. "I won't make it anyway. The *Blockleiter* has it in for me. He's an ex-clerk of mine . . . a jailbird I gave a job to at the store. All the *kapos* are green triangles. The Nazis think it's funny to let the criminals run things here. I'm going to be assigned to crematorium duty. The crematorium teams only last a month or two . . . they don't want them blabbing. . . ."

Grothmann was only a dozen yards away. The dry whisper came more quickly.

". . . tell Max that Klara's dead. She didn't survive the first month here. It's just as well. I used to see her behind the wire in the women's section sometimes. I was able to throw some of my bread across if there were no guards around. Then she didn't come anymore. One of the women came and told me she was dead. It was good of the woman. She might simply have taken the bread. Klara was too delicate. Tell Max not to be stupid like me. If a Hitler comes to America, he must get his family out immediately. . . ."

The whisper stopped. A shadow fell across the line of prisoners.

"Is this Jew annoying you?" Grothmann said.

"No, n-not at all," Jeremy said. "I asked him what he was here for, but he refused to talk."

A sardonic smile twisted Grothmann's thin lips. "They're not allowed to, except in the presence of camp authorities. They know that." He narrowed his pale eyes at Herr Weinbaum. "All the same—"

A sudden shout from the guards interrupted him. One of the prisoners had gone crazy. He had broken from the ranks and was running toward the electrified fence. It was Elbers, the one Himmler had thought had an interesting skull.

"Don't shoot!" Grothmann shouted, stepping out and waving his arms at the watchtower. A couple of Eicke's subalterns were doing the same. They didn't want a man gunned down in front of the journalists. There was nowhere for Elbers to go anyway. The water-jacketed machine-gun barrel that poked out of the near watchtower stopped traversing. The guards lowered their rifles. Four or five of the guards who were nearest the section of fence that Elbers was heading for raced to tackle him.

The running man flung himself against the wire fence. Perhaps, in his unhinged mind, he had some thought of trying to climb it. There was a shower of sparks, and his hands turned into talons that were fastened to the wire.

The great mass of prisoners seethed and rippled, but kept rank. No one was watching them for the moment. The guards and the people in the visiting party stared in fascination at the fence.

The rag figure hung from the fence, slowly turning black. Jeremy could see wisps of smoke rising. The fence spat and buzzed. One of the guards reached out to pull Elbers down, but his hand was struck down by one of his companions.

"Go to the electrical plant!" someone shouted, trying to make himself heard above the general hubbub. "Tell them to shut off the current!"

Jeremy started walking unhurriedly toward the barracks blocks that fringed the parade ground. The undulating lines of prisoners swallowed him from view. He pushed his way apologetically between the walls of rags, smelling the rich zoo aroma that came from them, a stink of latrine and unwashed flesh. "Excuse me, excuse me . . . *gestatten Sie*," he mumbled over and over again until he broke through the other side of the living square.

He crossed the brief gap with his head down, his hands thrust deep into his pockets, like a man preoccupied with his thoughts, while the flesh between his shoulder blades twitched. Then he was trudging through the mud of a camp street, between long rows of buildings that reminded him of chicken coops and smelled worse. He stayed close to the walls, out of sight of the receding watchtowers.

Here and there he saw people: pale banshee faces behind fogged windows, skeleton figures that shrank into doorways as he passed. They had been left out of the roll call for some reason, perhaps because they were too sick to be put on display. Once a burly man in a beret, with good boots showing under the regular prison stripes, blocked his path, then at the last minute stepped out of his way and stared insolently after him. He wore a green triangle; perhaps he was one of the *kapos* Herr Weinbaum had mentioned.

No one tried to stop him. He was well dressed, walked as though he knew where he was going, and for all anyone knew, could have been plainclothes Gestapo. He took pictures as he went. Once he stepped inside one of the sheds and, holding his breath against the stench, snapped a flashbulb picture of the tiers of shelves that people slept on. A couple of them were occupied by pipestem creatures with lolling skulls who stared at him with incurious eyes.

His mind had gone numb. It busied itself with the technical details of picture taking: correct lens setting, shutter speed, focus. It was a problem in depth of field, composition, nothing more. He stepped back out through the doorway, nodding to himself, a frown of concentration still fixed on his face, and took in great gulps of air.

He managed to keep his bearings, though. The glimpse of tall chimneys as he crossed the camp intersections helped. He came through a row of poplars that screened the end of a square of barracks into a sudden open space.

The crematorium compound was neatly landscaped. There were shade trees, and the lawn had been freshly mowed. Flower beds bordered a low brick building with tall chimneys. There was even a birdhouse on a pole.

Then Jeremy's unwilling eyes made sense out of the great untidy heap on the lawn by the entrance. It was human corpses, thrown in a careless pile, arms, legs, and torsos sticking out helter-skelter. The bodies were naked and terribly emaciated, all arched rib cages and knobby joints and obscenely displayed genitals.

Bile rose in the back of Jeremy's throat, and for a moment the sky darkened and reeled. Then the methodical madman in his brain took over, and he began taking pictures: long shot, then an unwilling twenty paces forward for a medium shot, then the closeups, all with total concentration on the proper f-stop and focus. He finished one roll, changed film and began another, then stepped through the doorway.

It was dim inside. When his eyes adjusted, the first thing he noticed was the stacks and stacks of what looked like clay flowerpots, like displays at a garden shop. The urns, he thought; the urns they sell back to the relatives for fifty marks. Then he saw the oven.

It might have been a commercial bake oven, with the brick arch and the heavy iron door and the metal racks lying nearby. Except that one of the metal racks had not been pushed all the way inside when the crew knocked off work for the day, and a naked foot dangled out of the half-open door.

A notice was tacked on the wall next to the oven, like the placards sometimes seen in restaurant kitchens. It said: *Wash hands after touching corpses. Anyone who does not wash is a pig.*

Jeremy had four flashbulbs left. He took his pictures quickly, but with great care. The smell was getting to him, a sickly burnt smell, like perfumed grease. There were more than twenty frames left on the roll when he finished, but he rewound the film and put it in his jacket pocket. There was a hole in the lining. He enlarged it with his thumb enough to push the roll through, then worked the roll around the rim of the lining to the back of his jacket. He did the same with the previous roll he had taken, the one showing the barracks interior and the pile of corpses on the lawn. He bit his lip, then reloaded the camera. Methodically, he pushed the shutter release over and over again, until it looked as if he had taken most of a roll's worth of pictures. Then he went staggering outside and threw up on the lawn.

Grothmann found him while he was still having the dry heaves. He and the SS guard with him watched contemptuously until he had finished, then Grothmann stepped forward with wrinkled nose.

"My dear fellow, you're not supposed to be in this part of the camp. It's not authorized. May I see your camera, please?" He held out his hand.

Jeremy handed over the camera without a word. Grothmann inspected the film counter and said, "Twenty-nine exposures on the roll. My, you've been busy, haven't you?"

He opened the camera and unwound the film, exposing each frame to the light. "That should take care of it. I'm sorry, but of course you understand that we can't allow pictures of too distressing a nature to go out."

The SS guard had come up behind Jeremy without warning. Grothmann must have made some kind of signal. Jeremy felt his arms seized in an iron grip. Grothmann patted Jeremy's bulging pockets, then helped himself to the rolls of film he found there.

"I'd better take these along, too, just in case. I'll have them developed and returned to you, except, of course, for any that might prove . . . controversial."

"You're censoring correspondents now, are you? I didn't know that was the policy of the Propaganda Ministry."

"Dear me, no. What an ugly word, censorship. We're doing you a favor, Herr Sinclair. Our SS laboratory does excellent work. You'll get free glossy prints of everything."

Jeremy glowered. He knew how he must look to the elegant Grothmann—seedy, sullen, and very young—but he didn't care. "How do you know I won't write about it?"

Grothmann laughed. "You can write what you like, dear chap. A lot of anti-Nazi propaganda gets printed in the foreign press, and nobody takes it very seriously. But pictures are another matter."

"Nobody can dispute them, you mean."

Grothmann looked pained. "There's no need to take that tone, dear chap. The Reichsführer is quite taken with you. He expects a good feature profile out of you, and it needn't be all fawning and flattery, like some of our own journalists are unfortunately prone to do—he understands that, and accepts it. He wants a good press, as you say, and knows it's worth more if it appears to come from an impartial source. That's why he's given you these extraordinary privileges.

Frankly, I was against including you on this little jaunt—but no matter. I do hope the Reichsführer's confidence in you isn't misplaced. I'd be dreadfully disappointed if that were to prove to be the case."

"The Gestapo will be watching to see what I write, is that it?"

"Naturally we take a keen interest in who are our friends and who are our enemies."

Jeremy put on a thoughtful look. "I wouldn't want to get expelled, like Dorothy Thompson was."

"And why should you be?" Grothmann said, looking relieved. "Nobody wants that, least of all us. You have plenty of material for an exclusive, without stirring up controversy."

He clapped Jeremy heartily on the back. Jeremy's flesh crawled at the touch. They started walking back toward the parade ground. Jeremy couldn't stop himself from taking a backward glance at the tangled corpses, heaped like so much garbage on the green lawn.

"We're not ashamed of what we're doing; far from it," Grothmann was saying in his tour-guide voice. "One day the world will thank us. We have plenty of friends in England and America, after all. They'd like to see their own countries purged of their riffraff and mongrel elements, but still shrink from dirtying their hands. We don't want to upset them yet."

Jeremy's stomach churned. Grothmann, with a firm grip on his arm, steered him past a railroad siding where cattle cars were parked.

". . . after all," Grothmann was going on, "there's nothing so terrible about a crematorium, is there? In a place like this, people die. One can't give them all a state funeral, can one?"

The parade grounds stretched ahead of them. The prisoners were still lined up. More of them had fallen. Bodies, unconscious or dead, were being dragged away by trustees. The electrocuted man had been removed from the fence; Jeremy could see a scrap of charred fabric, still caught on a barb, flapping in the raw breeze.

"Ah, here we are," Grothmann said. "I think the Reichsführer is about finished. About time, too. His guests must be freezing in this cold. One doesn't want to discommode influential personages like Hess."

They were passing the column of men where Jeremy had seen Friedrich Weinbaum. Jeremy recognized the big Jehovah's Witness with a purple triangle standing at the end. He slowed down, dragging his feet.

"Looking for your Jew, are you?" Grothmann said with a mocking tone.

There was a gap in the line. Uncle Freddie was gone.

30

Walt Hanes shoved the photos back across the desk. "You've lost your mind, Sinclair," he said. "No newspaper in America is going to print pictures of naked people."

"They're not people anymore, Mr. Hanes," Jeremy said quietly. "They're dead."

Hanes leaned back in his swivel chair. He was red-eyed and rumpled, with his shirt sleeves rolled up and his necktie yanked over to one side. The newsroom was noisier than usual. The teletype hadn't stopped chattering all morning.

"I won't even bother to comment on *that* part of it," Hanes said. "Newspapers don't like to print pictures of dead people. Remember when Art Fellig covered that Brooklyn trunk murder? They airbrushed out the corpse and showed an open trunk. Empty. We're not in business to have our stuff turned down by the clients. In case you've forgotten."

"I haven't forgotten."

Hanes softened a little. "The home office doesn't like us to offend the readers."

"Maybe they ought to be offended."

"Sinclair," Hanes said warningly.

"They're killing people at Dachau, Mr. Hanes!" Jeremy said.

"They're shooting them and starving them and beating them to death. And now Himmler is talking about vivisecting them in medical experiments."

Hanes squirmed uncomfortably in his chair. "Officially the Nazis call it a reeducation camp. They say these people are criminals—that they've committed crimes against the state. Prisons are lousy places the world over, for Christ's sake! Maybe our own penitentiaries aren't so hot, either. Did you see Paul Muni in *I Am a Fugutive from a Chain Gang?*"

Jeremy tried to keep his voice under control. "Mr. Hanes, I counted six thousand people on that parade ground, and those were just the ones who could still stand up. More are arriving by cattle car and closed van every day. They're not there because they committed crimes. They're in that hell because they have the wrong religion or the wrong politics or because they're unemployed. Or because they told the latest joke about Goering to the wrong neighbor. My God, I saw a man condemned to death because his skull was the wrong shape!"

"Still the red-hot, huh, Sinclair?"

"Mr. Hanes, you were the one who told me I went too easy on Himmler in my last piece!"

Hanes pasted another cigarette to his lower lip. "Don't take it to heart, kid," he said without meeting Jeremy's eyes. "You can't reform the world all by yourself. Allied's using your Wewelsburg Castle stuff. Hell of a scoop! 'Inside the Gestapo's Secret Shrine.' Your prose had to be tamed down some, of course. It was real enterprising of you to get those pictures. How the hell did you manage that? The Gestapo delivered the prints this morning, by messenger. But the Dachau stuff is dead as a dodo. You were scooped by the official German News Bureau. We already sent their handout over the wire, with a little light editing. 'A Visit to Dachau.' Too bad you couldn't have got back here with your copy sooner."

"Grothmann saw to that," Jeremy said bitterly. "I was detained till I missed my train, and somehow I could never get to a phone that worked, and when I finally got back to Berlin there were two policemen to meet me at the station about some kind of a misunderstanding about my passport that took all day to clear up."

"Yeah, yeah. Well Dachau's a dead issue now, anyway. All the press services have it. It was of limited interest in the first place— worth a couple of sticks at best. The home office doesn't see any sense in just piling on horrors."

"Sure," Jeremy said. "It's bad taste to talk about killing people for the gold fillings in their teeth, or turning a professor of botany into potash because he couldn't make pepper plants grow fast enough.

While the butchers sit around having tea and jam tarts!" With dismay, he heard his voice rising to an adolescent squeak.

"That's another thing, Sinclair," Hanes said, still avoiding Jeremy's eyes. "You got too personal. That's against Allied's policy. You can't drag the families of public figures through the mud. Himmler might have horns and a tail for all I know, but I'm sure he loves his daughter like any father."

"I didn't . . ." Jeremy couldn't make his tongue work.

"Himmler could make things pretty hot for Allied over a thing like that."

Jeremy found his voice. "Mr. Hanes, I didn't write anything offensive about the little girl. I was just . . . was just contrasting the scene inside the villa, with the housekeeper and the paper dolls and the tea party, with what was going on outside."

Hanes peeled the cigarette off his lip and stubbed it out. "And smuggling out clandestine photos on top of everything."

"You don't care, do you?" Jeremy said, his voice rising. "Nobody cares. They've opened a slaughterhouse for human beings, and it's worth a couple of sticks of type to you."

Hanes swiveled his chair around and began going through a stack of dispatches. Without turning around, he said: "The stuff's been piling up while you were gone. We're short handed around here. The Rome bureau borrowed Ham to cover Mussolini's invasion of Ethiopia or Abyssinia, or whatever the hell they call it. He's been sending dispatches from a flyspeck called Addis Ababa. You can start in by helping MacPherson clean them up. When you finish that, you can do a piece on the German man in the street's reaction to a possible match between Max Schmeling and Joe Louis, now that Louis has polished off Baer and Carnera. I know you don't follow sports, Sinclair, so for your information, Louis is a colored man. Schmeling is Hitler's darling. See what kind of mileage you can get out of that."

He lit another cigarette and began typing away. Jeremy stared at his back a moment, then gathered up his stack of photos and stalked off.

MacPherson was waiting with a sheaf of cablegrams from Addis Ababa when Jeremy sat down. The whole office had heard the exchange.

"You were unfair to him, Sinclair," MacPherson said. "I happen to know he tried to get your story on the wire. He almost got himself fired, arguing with New York. I transcribed the cables. You should have heard what he called them."

Jeremy felt surly. "He should have tried harder."

When he got back to his room that night, Ilse was there, packing up the things she kept in one of his drawers. She looked up, frightened, as he came through the door.

"Frau Wurz let me in," she said. "She had to change the lock."

"What are you doing?" he said. The signed photograph of herself that she had given him, and the nightclub photo showing both of them together, were on top of the little pile of underthings and change of clothing she was stuffing into the shopping bag she had brought with her.

"Please," she said in a small voice, "I do not want you to have these anymore."

He stepped forward into the room and took her by the arm. He could feel her shrink from his touch. "There's nothing to be afraid of, Ilse. See, they let me go. The Gestapo isn't after me, or anything. It was just something to do with my job. And in any case, it has nothing to do with you."

She shook herself free. "I can't see you anymore."

"But why? I told you everything's all right."

"It's better not to take chances nowadays."

"Ilse—"

"Please, you're standing in my way."

He stood watching, with his hands dangling by his sides, while she finished stowing everything in the shopping bag. At the door she paused and said, "Please don't telephone me at my job, either."

"Don't worry, I won't."

She chewed her lip, then said, "You'd better see Frau Wurz. She has a package for you." Then she was gone.

The landlady was a granite-faced lady with a battleship-gray permanent wave. "Such goings-on, Herr Sinclair," she said disapprovingly. "And then gone for three days without a word. I didn't know whether or not to rent out your room."

"Do you have a package for me?"

Her stout, corseted body seemed to shrink in its dressing gown. "I didn't want to take it, but I was afraid not to. The security policeman who delivered it said I was responsible. He was not polite, no, not at all. I had to sign for it. It was fifty marks, plus two marks for delivery."

"Where is it?"

She passed a dry tongue over her lips. "And how am I to explain all the commotion to the other lodgers, tell me that?"

He got out his wallet and gave her sixty marks. "The package," he said.

"And who's to pay for the new lock?"

He sighed and peeled off another fifty. "Will that take care of it?"

The notes disappeared down her bosom. She waddled to the sideboard and got a parcel wrapped in brown paper. There were all sorts of official seals stamped over it. Jeremy started to undo the twine, then when he saw Frau Wurz watching him, he tucked the parcel under his arm and took it back to his room.

He set it down on his bed and tore off the paper. Inside was a clay pot.

It was one of the Nazis' ghastly jokes. He thought he recognized Grothmann's touch. A name, a date, and a place were stamped into the tin lid. They said:

Weinbaum, Friedrich
9.10.1935
Dachau

The beer cellar on Bonner Platz had changed ownership, but it was still the same dim and seedy working-class *Lokal,* filled with tobacco smoke and the stale sweat of men who had spent their day digging excavations or unloading coal barges. The new owner had plastered over the bullet holes without bothering to repaint, and the walls were splotched with irregular white patches that were already turning gray.

Jeremy was too well dressed for the East End. He could feel some of the customers eyeing his brown tweed suit, his good oxfords, his wristwatch, averting their faces when he caught them at it.

"No, I don't know anyone named Ernst," the barman said.

"A little man, almost a dwarf," Jeremy persisted. "He used to work on the canal barges."

"Nobody like that ever comes in here," the barman said. He began to edge away, polishing the glass in his hand.

"He used to come in here all the time. He sat at that table against the rear wall."

Jeremy gestured, and the movement immediately caught the attention of the men who were sitting there. A swarthy man in a seaman's cap muttered something to his friends, then stared rudely at Jeremy until Jeremy dropped his eyes.

"A lot of the old patrons don't come here anymore," the barman said gruffly. "Things are different here, since they cleared that lot out."

"Since the SS troops shot up the Red Block, you mean, and arrested the Communists? I wonder what happened to the ones who got away. I suppose they've all gone underground, those who didn't get away to Russia."

"I wouldn't know anything about things like that," the barman said. He wiped his hands on his apron and went down to the end of the bar to wait on another customer.

A shabby old workman in a torn overcoat and collarless shirt leaned over in Jeremy's direction. "Excuse me, young sir," he mumbled. "I mean no harm, but perhaps it isn't wise to be asking such questions in a place like this. One never knows who might be listening."

Jeremy turned to face him. The old man drew his head in between hunched shoulders, presenting the top of a stained cap with a hint of brown-spotted cheek showing beneath the visor.

"The proprietor is in thick with the *Blockleiter* here, and things get back to the SD office, if you know what I mean," the man went on hastily. "Not that there's any harm in a gentleman like yourself, but it doesn't do to have misunderstandings with the authorities."

"Thanks," Jeremy said. "I appreciate the advice."

The old man lifted his head for a swift appraisal. "If the young gentleman will forgive me, this is no place for someone like you, politics aside. There are still rough customers around here who think nothing of knocking someone over the head for a few marks and throwing him in the canal, even with the new penalty of having one's head chopped off with an axe that Reichsmarschall Goering has instituted."

The barman came back and the old man turned away from Jeremy. Jeremy finished his beer and got up. He was thoroughly discouraged. He'd wasted two whole evenings prowling around the old haunts. Tiny Ernst had vanished from the face of the earth. No one would admit to ever having known him, even though he had been a familiar figure in the neighborhood. Perhaps the little man was in Russia, after all. Jeremy was convinced that Tiny Ernst had been high enough up in the apparat to have merited asylum.

The KPD—the German Communist Party—had broken up into secret groups of five after the Hitler takeover, and gone into deep hibernation. Its terrified survivors shunned contact with each other. Communication with Moscow had been broken.

But somehow propaganda materials from abroad and directives reflecting the Party line continued to filter through. Jeremy had seen some of the pamphlets and Party rags, printed in reduced size so they could be more easily smuggled across borders.

Some kind of Communist propaganda network, with ties abroad, continued to function in Germany. But it seemed impossible to make contact with it.

On the way to the door, Jeremy realized that he'd had too much to drink. He'd stopped at another neighborhood *Bierstube* and a whiskey bar before trying the cellar place. The room was swimming a bit. He noticed vaguely that the rear table, from which he'd attracted stares, had been vacated. He held himself carefully upright and stepped out into the cold night air.

That helped. He walked down the ugly block, past the pockmarked buildings with their boarded-up windows. Had he really lived here once, living on canned beans and lung stew and trying to write a rarified novel about people who didn't exist?

The streetlamp was out. A pool of deep shadow lay across his path. He stepped into it. All at once, someone grabbed his arms from behind. The heel of a hand hit him on the side of the head, stunning him. He flapped like a fish, but he couldn't seem to make his arms or legs do anything. He felt himself being dragged into an alley.

They had him propped against a brick wall. A match flared. In the light he could see the swarthy face and seaman's cap of the man from the rear table. The other figure was too shadowy to make out.

"Get his wallet," the swarthy man grunted. Jeremy could smell alcohol and rotten teeth.

"Get your hands the hell off me," Jeremy said thickly.

A meaty forearm across his throat pressed down, cutting off his breath. A hand felt around in his clothing.

Another match flared. "What do you know, two hundred marks," a voice said. There was a crinkle of paper as the man stuffed the notes into his pocket.

"You've just made a contribution," the man in the seaman's cap said.

Jeremy kicked out and connected with a shin. He heard a howl of pain, then felt himself being spun around and knocked to the ground. His hand found a brick, but before he could do anything with it, they had him pinned down again.

"The little turd almost broke my leg," a harsh voice said near his ear. "Let's finish him off and get out of here."

"Let go of me," Jeremy said, struggling to get up.

"We're not finished with you, sonny boy. You've been going around asking a lot of questions."

"I say he's a lousy provocateur," the other man said. "Come on, let's kick his head in and get out of here before somebody comes by."

"Shut up," the man in the seaman's cap said. He brought his face close to Jeremy. "What's your interest in Tiny Ernst?"

"Let me sit up," Jeremy said with more confidence. The hands holding eased their grip and he squirmed to a sitting position. His head spun. "I'm no Gestapo informer. You can see from the papers in my wallet that I'm an American. I used to live in the Bonner Platz. I was in the fight that night."

The two men exchanged glances. Jeremy could just make out the silvery outlines of their heads in the darkness.

"What's that to us?" the second man said harshly. He had a Hamburg accent.

"I'm a journalist. With the Allied International Press Service. I wrote the battle up for the world press as an eyewitness. I know it was used for Party propaganda. The apparat thought it was important."

"We don't know anything about that."

"You can check."

They were no longer holding him. Jeremy stood up and dusted himself off.

"So, then," the swarthy man said. "What's your game?"

"I've got another eyewitness account the Party will want. With pictures."

The Hamburg man gave a short, bitter laugh. "How do you know what the Party will want? Nobody else does. The great Kommunistische Partei Deutschlands, the hope of Europe, is just a lot of scared people hiding in rabbit holes, trying to make sense out of the inspirational nonsense that blows out of Moscow."

"Shut up," the swarthy man said.

"I've got to get in touch with someone with authority in the apparat," Jeremy went on evenly.

"Listen, this is dangerous," the Hamburg man said.

"Shut up," the swarthy man said. He turned the silver tracing of his head toward Jeremy. "Why don't you just peddle your lies to the capitalist press?"

"They're not lies, and the capitalist press won't print them. I'll settle for what I can get."

The outlined head nodded, as if satisfied. "What kind of pictures have you got?"

"They show what goes on at Dachau."

"We already know what goes on at Dachau," the other man said. "Our people there have ways of getting word out."

"I told you to keep your mouth shut," the swarthy man said without turning his head. "You want to run advertisements?"

Jeremy said, "I'm not talking about what you know among yourselves. I'm talking about influencing world opinion. Agitprop stuff."

The swarthy man pondered a moment, then said, "All right, come with us, but don't try anything funny." Rough hands hustled Jeremy through the alley and out the other side. There were more alleys and back streets, then a warehouse district and glimpses of the black mirrored surface of a canal between the rotting structures.

Jeremy found himself in a fish shed, with the door locked behind him. He heard departing footsteps. There was one dim overhead light, and nothing to sit on. He smoked all his cigarettes. Once he relieved himself in a bucket that had been used for that purpose before. He paced.

At daybreak the latch rattled and the door creaked open. An apple-cheeked gnome of a man, wearing a pea jacket and pinned-up trousers, came stumping into the shed.

"Hello, Jeremy," Tiny Ernst said.

"Congratulations, Sinclair," Walt Hanes said. "You've really out-done yourself this time."

He tossed copies of the Communist *Ce Soir* and *L'Humanité* on Jeremy's desk. The same picture of the piled corpses was splashed over both front pages. Jeremy recognized his own name. He knew enough French to translate the phrase: "The noted American journalist, Jeremy Sinclair."

"They just arrived in the pouch from Paris," Hanes went on savagely.

"I'm sorry, Mr. Hanes," Jeremy said miserably.

"Oh, don't apologize," Hanes said. "Allied International appreciates the publicity. I've already gotten two cables from New York asking me what the hell is going on. The *Daily Worker* version of your journalistic masterpiece kindly identified you as an employee of AIPS."

The British *Worker* lay spread out on Jeremy's desk. It had been the first to arrive that morning. In deference to their English readers' sensibilities, they, unlike the French, had airbrushed out the genitals of the corpses, but the photographs were just as horrifying.

"What got into you, Sinclair? I'd really like to try to understand."

The Party organ's rewrite man had filled the piece with the usual dreadful Communist jargon. The hell of Dachau had been trivialized into "the oppression of the proletariat by outworn capitalism in its ultimate manifestation of fascism." Instead of calling for human pity, the agitprop version exhorted its readers to "revolutionary vigilance."

And the Communists downplayed the systematic rounding up and extermination of Jews. To them it was the "class struggle." It was their own leaders and "heroic workers" who were heralded as the Nazis' targets, with the Jews being depicted as incidental victims.

The best that could be said for the result was that it did not give Jeremy an actual by-line, though it conceded that the article was based on his reporting—tainted though it was with bourgeois attitudes.

Tiny Ernst had played him for a sucker, all right. Of course Jeremy had expected to be played for a sucker. If that was the only way to get the story of Dachau into the open, he was prepared to pay the price. But he wished the propaganda hadn't been quite so strident.

At least he had managed to find out what had become of Elisabeth and the others—if he could trust Tiny Ernst to tell the truth. "Elisabeth?" the little man had said. "Oh, she's quite safe. No, she isn't in Russia. Where did you ever get that idea? She's working for the cause in another city, under an assumed name. No, don't ask me where. She doesn't want to see you in any case. You're too dangerous, Jeremy. You're a marked man from now on. I hope you realize that."

Klaus, it seemed, was alive and free. The SS had knocked him around a bit after his arrest, but he had managed to pass himself off as a nonpolitical tenant of the block, and he had been released a few days later along with the several hundred others for whom there was no room in the overcrowded cells. Tiny Ernst had been evasive about Willi, but when pressed had finally said, "I suppose you're entitled to know, Jeremy. Willi killed himself in the nursing home. I'm told he managed to get hold of a bottle of lye somehow, and conceal it in his bedclothes until after hours. Don't look like that, Jeremy. It was all for the best. Willi thought so, anyway. Cheer up. You've done a great service for the Party. Willi would have approved."

"I thought at least that you were smart, Sinclair," Hanes went on, shaking his head. "Why did you have to do a hatchet job on the little girl? I wouldn't want to be in your shoes when Himmler sees that."

One composite photo, marked by the blatant brushstrokes of the retouch man, showed Himmler's seven-year-old daughter playing with her paper dolls in front of a pile of corpses, while her father beamed fondly. Jeremy had been assured by the agitprop courier Tiny Ernst had sent to see him that they wouldn't exploit the child, and as a precaution Jeremy had held back the print of the picture in question, but they must have lifted it off the roll of original negatives they insisted they needed. "For technical reasons," the courier had said.

Jeremy glared defiantly at Hanes. "I don't care," he said. "At least the world has the evidence now. Nobody believed what was really going on in Germany."

"I'll give you the sad truth, Sinclair," Hanes said. "The world still won't believe it. In those rags it's just another helping of bolshie propaganda. You've lost your credibility as a journalist. You'll look like just another Communist hack."

The office boy called Hanes to the phone. He came back a few moments later, buttoning up his topcoat.

"I've just been ordered to the Ministry of Propaganda," he said. "They want an explanation. I'll be lucky if they don't revoke our credentials and expel the entire bureau."

He got his hat off the rack next to the door. He jammed it on his head and turned around. "Oh yeah, one more thing, Sinclair. You're fired."

A long black car was pulled up in front of the door of his rooming house. Jeremy saw it just in time. It was a long block, and the helmeted SS sentry they had left downstairs to watch the street happened to be glancing the other way when Jeremy rounded the corner.

Jeremy ducked into the nearest doorway, trying to look as if he belonged there. He didn't want to be too obvious about turning around and walking in the other direction.

He waited in the hallway, holding the brown paper bag containing the few personal things he'd bothered to take with him when he cleared out his desk. The onyx desk set that Millicent had given him when he first got the job, his notebooks, the paperweight with the little plaque from the Correspondent's Club. MacPherson had stood over him while he went through the drawers, and said: "Take my advice and get out of Germany fast."

A small, tidy man taking a Schnauzer for a walk came through the inner door and frowned officiously at Jeremy and his paper bag. "No loitering is allowed here," he said.

"I'm waiting for someone," Jeremy said.

"What is the name of the tenant you are waiting for?" the man said.

"He doesn't live in this building," Jeremy said, standing his ground.

The man opened his mouth, then thought better of it. He went out the door, pulling the Schnauzer after him. Jeremy watched him through the curtained entranceway. He saw the man spot the SS sentry down the block, glance back at the building entrance, and do a double take. The picture of civic responsibility, the man thrust out his chin and marched briskly toward the sentry, dragging his dog behind him.

Jeremy opened the door and walked with assumed nonchalance in the opposite direction, hoping he looked like someone on a mid-morning errand. He resisted the impulse to look over his shoulder.

As soon as he turned the corner, he quickened his pace and headed for the nearest side street. A few steps into it, he heard faintly, from around the corner, the shrill blast of a police whistle.

He walked past a cobbler's shop and a fish store, and stepped into a temperance restaurant that he knew had a rear exit; he had eaten there a few times to save money. A solitary customer in a clergyman's collar sat at one of the linoleum-topped tables, having an early lunch of mushroom cutlet washed down with mineral water. A stooped old waiter looked hopefully at Jeremy. Jeremy pretended he had changed his mind and went out the rear door. A trolley car was just opening its doors at the stop outside. Jeremy boarded it without bothering to see where it was going.

He spent the day moving around Berlin, mingling with the crowds along Kurfürstendamm, lingering over coffee in the vast restaurant at the zoo, sitting through a lecture at the planetarium. Once he called Frau Wurz and asked for himself in a disguised voice. She was flustered; a harsh male voice came on and asked who he was, and Jeremy hung up. Then he tried the office. MacPherson said: "Don't tell me where you are, lad, the phone's probably tapped." He told Jeremy that two Gestapo men had been to the bureau asking for him, and on being told that he wasn't there, had demanded a list of his friends, which Hanes had refused to give them.

"Mr. Hanes reported the matter to the American embassy," MacPherson told him, "but there's not much Ambassador Dodd can do except lodge an official complaint. The word is that Himmler's boiling mad. My advice is to stay out of sight until this blows over. If you get picked up, all they have to do is hold you at Columbia House and deny that they know where you are."

"It's not going to blow over, is it, Mac?"

"Don't say that," MacPherson protested. "They can't do anything to an American citizen."

"Thanks, Mac," Jeremy said, and hung up.

He had a dinner of sausages and beer at one of the Aschingers chain restaurants. At seven o'clock he went to a *Kino* and sat through two showings of a film about the life of Horst Wessel. It was controversial—it had been made by Putzi Hanfstaengl, who also had written the theme music, and Goebbels, jealous, had tried to have it suppressed—and so the crowd was large enough for Jeremy to lose himself in. After the nine o'clock show, he found himself on the sidewalk with no place to go; Berlin didn't go in for all-night movies. He spent the next hour in an obscure bar, nursing a drink.

The question of where to spend the night was growing critical. He couldn't register at a hotel. Even a fleabag would ask to see his papers. And as the streets of Berlin gradually emptied of their pleasure seekers, Jeremy would become more and more conspicuous.

The only thing that occurred to him was to find a Chausseestrasse whore who would let him spend the night with her. In recent months they had begun, cautiously, to reappear on the adjacent Friedrichstrasse—though without their former inventive costumes. No more imitation schoolgirls with book satchels, or circus performers with boots and whips. But Jeremy wasn't sure how much it would cost.

He got as far as the garish stretch past the Stettiner *Bahnhof* without losing his nerve. The premidnight crowds swept him along. Trains rumbled beneath his feet. Light and music spilled out of the bars and imitation French cafés. He saw a girl standing under a streetlamp. He was sure she was a prostitute. Her face was heavily powdered, and her mouth was a clown's red; she wore a tight skirt and ankle straps. He went up to her, cleared his throat, and said, *"Guten Abend, Fräulein. Warten Sie auf jemanden?"*

"Say, do you want to get your face smashed?" she said.

At that moment, a hulking SS officer in off-duty dress came out of the nearby comfort station, adjusting his trousers. "Is he annoying you?" he said.

"No, no, it's nothing," she said.

The officer scowled at Jeremy, took the girl by the arm, and walked off with her. Jeremy stood under the lamppost in a sudden cold sweat. After a moment he noticed that a leather-helmeted policeman across the street was looking at him. Jeremy turned on his heel and hurried down the steps of the corner underground station.

Ten minutes later he was knocking at Millicent Wickes's door.

"Well, love, you've got yourself in a proper mess this time, haven't you?" Millicent said.

She sat across from him in an overstuffed chair, wearing a tatty lavender chenille robe that had fallen open to show a triangle of bony chest. She looked older than Jeremy remembered. Her blond hair looked brassy in the lamplight, and her face seemed thin and drawn. But it may have been the hour. It was three in the morning.

"I'm sorry. I couldn't think of anyplace else to go."

"That's bloody flattering, isn't it?"

"I'm sorry. I mean—"

"How long has it been? Going on two years now. God, you were a mooncalf when I took you in! Grown up a bit since then, have you? Scattering yourself amongst the grateful Fräuleins? Then come crawling back to Mother when you're in trouble. You expect a lot, my lad."

"I didn't think—"

"No, you didn't, did you?" she said savagely. "Do you think Germany is schoolboy games? Or are you working for the Comintern?"

"It was the only way," he said.

"You certainly stirred them up. I'll say that. Goebbels has been firing off denunciations all day. I wore out a pair of shoes trotting down to the Propaganda Ministry to pick up each new mimeo. Sykes got off a long dispatch with the official Nazi denials."

"I'm a witness."

She looked at him oddly. "Yes, you are at that, aren't you?"

"I'll leave in the morning. Could you lend me enough money for a ticket to Paris? I'll wire it back as soon as I collect my back pay from Allied International through the bureau there."

"Oh, don't be a bloody fool! You'll be picked up as soon as you show your silly face at the ticket window." She bit her lip. "My cleaning lady comes Thursday. You can stay till then, I suppose. You'll have to stay quiet during the day, so that Mrs. Nosy downstairs doesn't hear someone moving around while I'm at work. I don't suppose I have much of a reputation left anyhow. You'll have to make do for tomorrow with what you find in the fridge."

"Thanks, Millicent."

"Oh, shut up." She looked at the paper bag he had brought with him. "What's in there? Nothing useful, like a toothbrush or a change of socks, I'm sure."

"No."

"You never learn, do you, chum? Well, don't expect to use my toothbrush this time. I'll pick you up one in the morning."

Jeremy said nothing. He was exhausted. The events of the day were beginning to catch up with him.

Millicent finished her coffee and stood up. "I'd better get back to bed. I'm a working girl, and I'm sure Sykes will have a full program for me."

She crossed to the bedroom door, and looked back at Jeremy, nodding in his chair. "Well, are you coming?" she said sharply.

It took him more than a week to contact the KPD. Tiny Ernst had told him that in an emergency he could leave a message buried in the sand of a certain potted palm at the Fatherland House, the enormous multichambered restaurant in Potsdamer Platz. It was a risk, though the three-thousand-customer nightly turnover at the place provided anonymity. Millicent wanted to go, but Jeremy wouldn't let her. He finally had to put it to her in practical terms. "If the Gestapo's discovered the drop and is watching it, it wouldn't make any difference anyway. They'd identify you and come back here and nab me. If they catch me, at least I can keep you out of it."

The Fatherland House was a maze of French bistros, Turkish cafés, Hungarian restaurants, Spanish bodegas, and Wild West saloons where the waiters dressed in ten-gallon hats and cowboy boots. Each had its own band; every time you turned a corner there was a blare of music in a different style. The potted palm in question was in the Bavarian room, with its diorama of the Alps and yodeling orchestra. Jeremy left his message at the height of the storm scene, while the diners were entranced by the wind machine and artificial lightning.

He went back every night for a week, but there was no answer. Millicent put off her cleaning lady once, then twice. In the end, the

KPD telephoned him. Someone had followed him back to Millicent's flat that first night, and they had been keeping him under observation to be sure he had no Gestapo tail. Jeremy shuddered to think of what might have happened if it had been the Gestapo keeping tabs on the potted palm.

They arranged a meeting in a park. His contact was not Tiny Ernst, but a turtle-faced man who looked like any pensioned clerk. "The Dachau exercise was extremely successful," he told Jeremy while they sat side by side on a bench. "That's the only reason the Party is bothering with you."

Jeremy nodded. He had no illusions. The Communists wanted to use him again, and had decided how.

"You're no longer connected with AIPS," Turtle-face went on, "but that doesn't matter. You're still a journalist, without any known involvement with us. We can get you credentials. That's no problem. We have friends among publishers and news organizations, people who think it's daring to do us a favor."

"What are you proposing, exactly?" Jeremy said.

Turtle-face tossed a peanut to the pigeons. "That you do another eyewitness article. A series of articles. We can arrange syndication in European newspapers. And a contract with an American publisher."

"On what subject?"

"Russia. The new Soviet experiment. An unprejudiced view by a neutral journalist."

Jeremy flared. "I won't write propaganda for you."

"You won't be asked to," the man said dryly. "Write what you like. What you see. We're prepared to take the risk. And don't think it was easy, persuading them on the other side that you're a friend of ours. Don't be suspicious. There isn't a Western journalist alive who wouldn't give one of his eyes for this opportunity."

Jeremy caught his breath. Turtle-face was right.

"How do I get a Russian visa?" he said. "They've only allowed a handful of reporters into the country."

"That's no problem. All we have to do is get you an official invitation from the Moscow Writers' Union."

"You can do that?"

"You've done a service to the Party. You told the truth about the insurrection at Bonner Platz, about the Party martyrs at Dachau."

"How will I get out of Germany? I need documents, a false passport—"

"We'll take care of all that."

"How long will this take?"

The man tossed another peanut to the pigeons. "A few weeks, a month."

Jeremy stood up. "All right, you've got a deal. I'll be waiting to hear from you."

"Sit down. You're staying with us. We're not letting you out of our sight until you leave."

"But Millicent . . . oh, damn, all right!"

He spent the next six weeks being shunted from hiding place to hiding place. He slept in barns, farmhouses, workman's flats, in the smelly holds of riverboats, in the servants' rooms of the houses of the aristocracy. In the end, they got him his visa, his false passport, the clothes and luggage he needed, and a cash advance of five thousand rubles from the Moscow Writers' Union against a book which he was supposedly going to write for Russian publication but which, it was confidentially explained to him, he needn't bother doing anything about.

At the end of the sixth week, he found himself standing in a field near Grodno, just inside the Russian border, waiting with the other passengers while Soviet customs inspectors went through their luggage. The train was being searched, compartment by compartment, by Soviet militia, even though the passengers would not be allowed to reboard it. They would be transferred to other cars that fit the Russian railway gauge. It was very cold. They had been waiting half a day. People warmed themselves at fires built in cut-open kerosene tins.

It wasn't much warmer inside the customs shack. A potbelly stove with a rickety pipe going through the ceiling wasn't doing much good. The officials wore overcoats, hats with earlaps, and mittens with holes cut for the fingers.

In front of Jeremy, the customs official was just finishing with a peasant. They had unpacked every single object the peasant possessed and held it up to the light. Now they were examining a large sausage that had been wrapped in a sheet of a Polish newspaper. The sausage was all right, but the newspaper wasn't. Solemnly, the official rewrapped the sausage in a sheet torn from a Soviet newspaper and handed it back to him.

"*Sledooyoosh-shee,*" the official said, motioning to Jeremy.

Jeremy stepped forward. He couldn't blame them for being careful. Not with enemies like the Germans all around them. He smiled to show that he didn't mind.

Russia! It was hard to believe that he was really here, in the mythical utopia they talked about at cocktail parties back home. He remained serene while the scowling official pawed through his possessions with grimy fingers. They'd only had nineteen years to build their new society so far. You couldn't expect things to be perfect. Give them time. He already had decided on the title for his series of articles: *Dispatches from the Promised Land.*

31

"Symbolic," the lobster-faced man with the English accent was saying. "Hitler's occupation of the Rhineland is purely symbolic."

He was seated diagonally across the table from Pamela, talking, as he was supposed to do, to the lady on his right, but his voice was so penetrating that it cut through the discreet scrapings of the hired orchestra and the rattle of antique silver.

"He said himself that Germany has no further territorial ambitions," the Englishman went on loudly. "I agree with Lord Lothian. After all, the Germans are only going into their own back garden."

Pamela became aware that her own dinner partner, a thirtyish, darkly handsome man whose name she had not caught when he had drawn the escort card with her name on it, was talking to her again.

"I beg your pardon?" she said guiltily.

"I said how long have you lived in Washington?"

"Three years. Or almost." She put down the forkful of salmon mousse she had been toying with and faced him with a dutiful smile. "But how do you know I don't come from here?"

"No one comes from Washington. Besides, I have an ear for accents. You've still got a touch of Midwest. Illinois?"

"Iowa."

"Impossible. No one comes from Iowa, either. It's just a place invented by Henry Wallace so he can keep talking about the heartland of America."

He looked very amused and superior. Pamela tried not to take a dislike to him. He was one of those people who got through life on looks, she decided. Looks and a little money from Daddy and some kind of a job in the State Department. Washington was full of empty-headed young bachelors like that.

"And what do you do in this town, Miss Sinclair?" he said with that cool complacency they all seemed to have. Conceited, she thought. She tried to remember his name. He had the advantage over her, with that damned little card he could peek at. Taffy didn't believe in place cards.

"Nothing very important," she said. "I'm just one of the clerical army that works under the Capitol dome. I'm with the Porteous committee."

"Oh?" He raised an overbred eyebrow.

"Why am I here, you mean?"

"I didn't say that."

"Mrs. McCandless asked me to fill in at the last minute. I've done it before for her. I guess I've got the minimum social credentials, and I'm reliable. She lost the Uruguayan ambassador's wife's sister tonight. The poor thing slipped on our icy sidewalks and broke her hip, and left her with an uneven number of men and women. You know Mrs. McCandless; she never lets a place go to waste."

Involuntarily they both looked across to where their hostess sat, lording it over a table of twelve, with the Vice-President at her left. Taffy McCandless, wife of G. Lathrop McCandless, the retired steel tycoon, had made herself one of the top Washington hostesses by virtue of determination and sheer money. She wasn't quite in the same league as Evalyn Walsh McLean, who had the Hope Diamond and the Star of the East to flaunt at *her* parties; she wasn't as amusing as Cissy Patterson, and she was no Mrs. J. Borden Harriman in social position and clout. But her Sunday night dinner parties were justly famous.

This one was for a mere sixty guests, seated at five tables of twelve. Looking around, Pamela recognized Bill Bullitt, back from Russia for consultation with the President; the French ambassador, looking very grim; Minority Leader Snell; Harold Ickes, being disloyal to Cissy Patterson for the evening; and a couple of the younger du Ponts. The tables were banked with great masses of flowers. Servants hovered at the diners' elbows. A huge glittering chandelier hung over each table like a benefaction made tangible. The imported orchestra, sawing away on their fiddles in the corner, contrived to make Cole Porter sound Viennese.

"Yes, Taffy's a bit rough around the edges," Pamela's dinner companion laughed. "Have you heard the latest? When the rumor started going around that Claude Swanson was going to be replaced as secretary of the navy, Taffy called up the wife of the leading contender for the job—we needn't mention his name—and said, 'I hear your husband is about to be appointed to a Cabinet post. If that's so, I'd like both of you to come for dinner Sunday night, and if it isn't so, would you drop by for coffee afterward?' "

Pamela laughed. She was starting to like him better.

"And what do *you* do?" she asked.

He seemed startled. "Oh, I'm just a newspaperman," he said.

That explained it. Taffy McCandless didn't invite minor diplomatic aides to her Sunday nights, no matter how good-looking they were. She even drew the line at the Lower House, except for important congressmen like Bertrand Snell. But influential columnists and gossip reporters were always an exception. Betty Beale, who wrote the "Top Hats and Tiaras" column for the *Post,* was considered a prize. The "Merry Whirl" reporters were fawned upon. And Drew Pearson, of course, had become a social force in his own right after marrying Cissy Patterson's daughter Felicia.

Pamela racked her brains to think of who her dinner companion might be. None of the Washington or Baltimore dailies, she decided, after running down the list in her mind. And he certainly didn't fit into the list of major syndicated columnists. Perhaps he had something to do with a paper in Wilmington or Richmond; Taffy McCandless's social warrant occasionally stretched that far.

A waiter was pouring more Château Climens into her glass. Across the table, the lobster-faced Englishman was still holding forth about the Rhineland crisis. The topic had been on everybody's lips since yesterday, when German troops had crossed into the demilitarized zone, and the French had let them get away with it.

"It's their own country, after all," the Englishman was saying. "How would you Yanks feel if, for example, you'd been kept out of Michigan for ten or fifteen years?"

Pamela's escort leaned in her direction. "That's Sir Benjamin Hewley, the British press lord. He and his pals, Lord Rothermere and Lord Beaverbrook, have been pushing that Michigan line in their papers. Only for the British public, it's Yorkshire. And the British public are swallowing it. Rothermere's out-and-out pro-Nazi. He's been encouraging the British Fascist movement under Sir Oswald Mosely. Lord Lothian and the Cliveden set, over at Lady Astor's country place, are a bit higher minded. But they've been taken in by that champagne salesman, Ribbentrop, who Hitler sent over to charm them. They think that a stable Germany under Hitler will be a bulwark against Russian bolshevism. And they don't trust the French."

"You seem to know a lot," Pamela said.

"Oh, I've seen the inside of Cliveden," he said airily.

On an expense account, I'll bet, Pamela thought. She gave him the adoring look that was required of women at Washington dinner parties, and said, "But why don't the French act on their own?"

"They've lost their nerve. They won't do anything unless they know they have the British behind them. But the British won't even give them moral support. The French ambassador asked Chamberlain if at least England would go along with an economic boycott against Germany, and Chamberlain told him, in that lofty way of his, that public opinion wouldn't support sanctions of any kind."

"But what's going to happen now?"

Her dinner partner shrugged. "Oh, the French will do what the Germans want. They'll put the whole matter before the League of Nations, and the politicians will talk it to death."

Pamela said brightly, "But I read in this morning's paper that Hitler's offered to sign a twenty-five-year nonaggression pact to replace the former treaties. And that he'll consider moving his troops out again if *both* sides of the frontier are demilitarized."

He smiled condescendingly. "Both sides? That's a joke. That would force France to scrap the Maginot Line, and she's not about to consider that. But it sounds good. It'll buy Hitler the time he needs."

"Time for what?" she said, wide-eyed.

"To build up his strength. Prepare for war."

"War? You don't mean that?" She pressed a hand to her chest, just above the dip of her gown's neckline. I'm overdoing it, she thought. Then: No, I'm not; you could never overdo it with men.

He leaned back with a self-satisfied expression. "No, not right away. Not over this issue. Not with Hitler making the noises of sweet reason now that he's got his way. But make no mistake. March seventh, nineteen thirty-six, was Hitler's Rubicon. And the democracies let him get away with it."

Pamela revised her estimate of him. No, not a society reporter. A political reporter of some kind. Not a heavyweight, like Walter Lippman or Raymond Clapper, but one of the up-and-coming young men.

"My brother Jeremy was in Germany last year," she said. "He said in his letters, the couple of times he bothered to write, that is, that he thought Hitler was a danger, too."

"Jeremy? Jeremy Sinclair? Is he your brother?"

"Yes." Pamela was surprised that Jeremy's name was familiar to him.

"Damn fine reporting he's doing from Russia." He leaned closer to her. "I wish—"

But the servants were serving the next course, and Mrs. McCandless was giving the signal for the tables to turn, and it was time for all the men to talk to the ladies on their left.

"Hi," the man on her right said. "I'm Billy Barrow. Who do you think the Republican candidate for President's gonna be this year?"

Pamela took a last look at her previous partner's back and wondered what he had been about to say to her. Then she put on her best smile for Billy Barrow.

"I don't know," she said. "It's awfully early, isn't it?"

Barrow chortled happily. He had a round, scrubbed face and a bald, baby-pink scalp surrounded by a fringe of very clean white hair. "Did you hear what Ed Wynn said on the Texaco *Fire Chief* program Tuesday? He said when he was in Egypt, he saw some fellows digging up the front yard of one of them pyramids, and he asked them if they were looking for King Tut's tomb. They said no, we're tryin' to dig up a Republican to run against Roosevelt."

Pamela laughed dutifully.

"Personally," Barrow went on, "I think it's gonna be Landon. That's what the Gallup Poll says. Of course you can't count out Hoover yet. And Senator Borah still has an outside chance."

Pamela tried to look properly amazed at the information. Evidently, Mr. Barrow, like so many other Washington dinner partners, had prepared a Topic in advance. It could have been worse. Once she had been seated next to a young, newly arrived Brazilian attaché who had spent thirty minutes lecturing her on coffee beans. After trying unsuccessfully several times to turn it into a two-way conversation, Pamela had realized that the Brazilian didn't speak a word of English; that he had memorized an encyclopedia article for the occasion.

"What do you do, Mr. Barrow?" she said.

"I'm just a plain businessman, honey," he said. He winked broadly at her.

"Are you a Democrat?" The Texas accent made it likely.

"Me? Not on your life. Not anymore. Even Al Smith can't stomach Mr. Franklin Karl Marx Rosenfeld anymore. I was at the Liberty League banquet at the Mayflower, and let me tell you, I like to have stood up and cheered when Al Smith let his old buddy have it. Him and his foreign-thinking Brain Trusters. There can only be one capital, Washington or Moscow, Al said. There can only be one atmosphere of government, the clean, pure, fresh air of free America, or the foul breath of communistic Russia."

Mr. Barrow was short of breath. Sweat had popped out all over his smooth, ruddy face. Pamela transferred her close attention to her dinner plate to give him a chance to recover. For the main course, Taffy's French chef had provided a magnificent beef Wellington with truffles taking the place of the mushrooms.

So Mr. Barrow was a Liberty Leaguer? If he was a "plain businessman," he must be a very rich one, then. The Mayflower banquet, according to a gleeful press, had included the greatest collection of millionaires ever assembled under one roof, including a dozen du Ponts. The guest list had become an embarrassment to the entire Republican party after the Democrats had got through with it. Joe Robinson, Al Smith's 1928 running mate, had sorrowfully compared the former Happy Warrior to "George Washington waving a cheery good-bye to the ragged and bleeding band at Valley Forge while he rode forth to dine in sumptuous luxury with the Tories." Roosevelt had immediately started to gain in the polls again.

"Say, have you heard the one about the psychiatrist who died and went to heaven?" Billy Barrow said. He took a long swig of his Beaune-Grèves. "Saint Peter took him aside and asked him to treat God for delusions of grandeur. It seems He thought He was Franklin D. Roosevelt."

That wasn't too bad. Living in Washington, Pamela was used to hearing the hateful things that were routinely said about Roosevelt at the tables of the wealthy. He was a giggling madman, a megalomaniac cripple, a syphilitic, he was having an affair with Frances Perkins.

Pamela smiled graciously. "So you're voting Republican this time, Mr. Barrow?"

"I'm afraid so, little lady." Barrow shook his head sadly. "For a while there, it looked like Huey Long might of took the nomination away from Roosevelt in thirty-six. But then they done gone and assassinated poor Huey. They say that doctor fellow who shot him acted alone, but if you ask me, it was a conspiracy."

"But I don't understand, Mr. Barrow. If you think the New Deal is socialistic, why would you want to vote for Huey Long? Wasn't he for a share-the-wealth program?"

Barrow smiled at her benignly. "Honey, once we would have got him elected, he sure as hell would of changed *that* idea in a hurry!"

He fell silent while he shoveled beef into his mouth, pushing aside the truffles and foie gras. Through the general hum, Pamela caught a few scraps of conversation from her handsome previous companion as he charmed the lady on his left, a Junoesque redhead with a plunging neckline.

"Eleanor knows how to fly, you know."

There was a peal of laughter from the lady. "Oh, Peter, you're too amusing!"

"No, no, I mean it literally. It's supposed to be a deep, dark secret, but she's been taking flying lessons from Amelia Earhart. The President made her quit."

"But how did you *ever* find out such a thing?"

"He told me himself. During a little weekend fishing trip aboard the *Potomac*. Over drinks with Pa Watson, Tommy the Cork, Sam Rosenman, and a few others. He said he had enough to worry about without the Missus flying around in the sky."

His first name was Peter, anyhow. She'd found out that much. And he was on intimate enough terms with FDR to be invited for weekend cruises aboard the presidential yacht. Pamela found herself becoming intrigued. Who *was* this fascinating man who seemed to know everybody important? Perhaps Brad could tell her.

But Billy Barrow had chewed and swallowed his mouthful of beef, and was returning to the fray. "Huey's followers are all split up now, though. That preacher fellow, Gerald Smith, claims to lead them. And he's trying to hook up with the Townsendites. There's an awful lot of votes in all them old people in the Townsend movement. Now, if the two of them can get Father Coughlin to hop aboard, I guess they'd have a third party. With maybe thirty million votes, Dr. Townsend says."

Pamela thought she might have a chance to exchange a few more words with Peter Whoever-he-was during the procession to the drawing room, but the Vice-President, coming up behind, seized him by the upper arm and said with boozy joviality, "Well, Pete, are you goin' to give us a hard time this November?" Garner was said to consume a bottle of bourbon a day, but he held it well.

"Not if you fellows buy me off," her mysterious escort laughed. "How about an ambassadorship? Court of St. James's would be nice."

"We're savin' that one for Joe Kennedy." The Vice-President chuckled. "But we're goin' to make him earn it."

The Vice-President kept a two-handed grip on the taller man's arm. With his thatch of white hair and his white tie and tails, Garner looked like a roly-poly penguin trying to wrestle. Still talking politics, the two of them disappeared with the other men for cigars and brandy.

Pamela found a seat in the outer orbit, with the young wives and the unattached women of lower rank, as she was expected to. Taffy McCandless, full-rigged in silk faille, tiara, and bib of pearls, enthroned herself on the focal sofa with the ranking ladies. Servants brought in the coffee and liqueurs. The room was filled with the chatter of thirty women talking about dressmakers, servants, the Washington climate, children, and Capital gossip.

"Whatever did the two of you talk about?" a breathless tall girl in an unfortunate peach chiffon gown asked Pamela.

"Who?" Pamela said.

"Who? Why just Washington's most eligible bachelor, that's all! How did you ever bribe Taffy to seat him next to you?"

She wasn't talking about Mr. Billy Barrow, that was for certain. Pamela wondered how she could coax Peter Who's last name out of the tall girl without admitting that she didn't know it.

"Oh, we talked about the Rhineland crisis," Pamela said.

"The *Rhine*land crisis? You're teasing me! Aren't you? Say you are! He talked *poli*tics with you? Him? Mister Playboy of the Potomac himself?"

"Why not the Rhineland? He probably spent all day writing about it. It *is* his line of work, isn't it? After all, he's a newspaperman."

She sat back and waited.

"A *news*paperman? Oh, you *are* a card! Come on, stop fooling and tell me what you *really* talked about. Did you get him to ask you out?"

The tall girl's eyes were aglitter. Two pink spots had appeared above her cheeks. Pamela was uncomfortable.

"No . . . I mean, we got along very well, but . . ."

The tall girl looked around to make sure that the other unmarrieds were busy with their own conversations. She leaned closer to Pamela. "I'll tell you what *I* would have done if *I'd* been sitting next to a prize catch like that. I'd have offered him my hot little body and anything else I could think of to hold his interest." She looked around again. "And you can *tell* him if you get him aside later. The name's Margie Kincaid."

She laughed as if it were a joke, but Pamela had the impression that she more than half meant it. Occupation for the evening, she thought: Peddle little Margie to Peter Who.

A servant stopped in front of them with a trayful of tiny cups, and a plump young matron sitting opposite leaned across to take one.

"Is Marjorie grilling you about Peter, dear?" she said.

Fine, Pamela thought. Everyone knows who he is except me.

"She wants to know what we talked about," she said.

The plump lady gave a tinkling laugh. "Don't tell her a thing," she said. "Marjorie is the worst gossip in Washington."

"Oh, Sylvia!" the tall girl said. She looked pleased.

"She'll tell *all* your secrets," the plump lady said. "She knows *everything* about *everybody,* don't you Margiekins?"

It was some kind of a joke between them.

Margiekins bared a mule's teeth, her small eyes glinting with malice. "I know all about Marcus Hale," she said.

Pamela felt faint. She managed to hold on to her coffee cup and not make a spectacle of herself.

"Oh yes, I know all about him and his *dear* secretary," Margie went on. "It'll be all over the newspapers tomorrow. He'll be finished in this town. And so will she."

Sylvia glanced at Pamela. "Well, don't keep me waiting," she said.

"He's had a succession of these cheap things working in his office," Margie said. "And he's always got away with it. But not this time. He had her on his *desk,* can you imagine that, with his back to the door, when a whole delegation from his home state walked in."

"No!" Sylvia gasped.

Pamela's face had gone stiff. The lacquered smile had stayed in place during the moment of faintness. She raised the tiny cup to her lips and took a sip.

"It was the ladies' sodality," Margie said, giggling. "And a Boy Scout troop."

"Oh, my dear!" Sylvia said, covering her smile.

"Even so, the senator's assistant might have managed to hush it up. He got rid of the girl, fast. But he couldn't find another job for her on such short notice, so he paid her off out of Senate funds. And since it's an election year, there were all sorts of seamy people waiting to *pounce* on Senate Document Number One. Some scandal reporter ferreted out the disbursement. I believe it was actually listed as a 'packing expense.' Of course he still had to get the silly girl to talk. He offered to pay for her story. Well, since he convinced her that it was all coming out anyway, she thought she might as well make some money out of it. So they got her to say that she couldn't type. That the senator hired her for you-know-what. And that tax money was paying for it."

"But you don't mean to tell me that the papers will actually *print* that kind of scandal? About a senator's private life?"

"They decided the gentleman's agreement doesn't apply, since public funds are involved. So there's going to be something in the 'Capitol Carousel' column tomorrow. And the Hearst papers. Only that stuffy Eugene Meyer who bought the *Post* isn't going to print it. But it will be all over Washington by morning anyway."

"How did you *ever* manage to find all this out?"

Margie smiled triumphantly. "At Henri's this afternoon. Mrs. Hale has her hair done there too. Henri swore me to secrecy."

"The poor thing!"

"Poor thing is right. She poured it all out to him. She had to talk to *somebody.* And you know Henri."

Sylvia laughed. "Oh, do I know Henri!"

"The reporters were after her for a statement," Margie said, licking her lips. "That's how she found out."

"I'm surprised she had the *nerve* to be seen in public."

"I think she, you know, wanted to look her best for tomorrow."

Sylvia's plump little mouth worked. "How long ago . . . I mean, when did it . . . in the office with the delegation walking in?"

"Oh, way last June, I think. The senator thought he'd gotten away with it."

Pamela's face felt as if it had been packed in ice. She wanted to put the cup down, but she was afraid her bloodless hand would make it rattle violently in the saucer, so she went on holding it, with the smile frozen in place.

Last June. Only a week or two after she had left, after Harvey Lucas had had that awful, awful talk with her. Who was the girl? Was it that overendowed peroxide blonde she'd seen sometimes in the Senate Office Building corridor, coming out of the Hale suite, or delivering papers to Harvey outside the Senate chamber? Marcus liked blond hair. And bosoms. She wondered if he had told the new girl she was his one and only, had wished her a young man to share her life, had hoped piteously that he would be a "good memory" for her when he was gone.

"We're shocking Miss Sinclair," Sylvia said. "Oh—I forgot, you're related somehow to Senator Hale." She contrived to sound both contrite and avid.

"Only very distantly." She put down the coffee cup successfully. She was surprised at how calm she felt.

"Oh, but you must think we're terrible!"

"No, no, really! I'm only connected to the Collier family through my brother's marriage, and the Colliers and Hales aren't that close kin anyway."

It had been forgotten that she had once worked for Marcus. In Washington, the social connections were more important.

Pamela had been working on the Porteous committee staff for nine months now, and the committee's chief clerk, a no-nonsense man of seventy who was a holdover from the previous chairman, had gradually increased her responsibilities, and had come to depend on her. She had been afraid, at first, of Senator Porteous's reputation, but at his age he was getting to be hors de combat. He had made a halfhearted pass at her when she first arrived, but she had easily fended him off. She was past that now. She was too valuable. Senator Porteous frequently slept through committee hearings, while the other members covered for him, and Mr. Theobald, the chief clerk, was no longer brimming with youthful energy either. Pamela now had the title of senior staff assistant and was given the responsibility of editing hearings and writing committee reports.

"Through the Talbots," Margiekins said.

"Pardon?"

"The Colliers and Hales are connected through the Talbots."

"Oh . . . yes . . . that's right," Pamela said.

"Marjorie manages to keep track of everybody," Sylvia said with a sudden wariness in her manner.

"So as you said, that doesn't make you and Senator Hale kissing cousins," Margie said.

"No."

"Senator Hale only kisses G-girls, it seems." Margie laughed gaily, with her eyes on Pamela's face.

"Marjorie, I don't think—" Sylvia started.

"Oh, but Miss Sinclair doesn't mind. She *said* so. My goodness, it isn't as if she and Senator Hale were close."

"It's all right," Pamela said.

"Some of these government girls are very nice," Sylvia said with desperate haste. "From the best families. Why, my own niece, Betsy, had a summer job with the Senate Foreign Relations Committee."

Three ladies on the angled divan nearest were listening to the conversation, their coffee cups poised. Pamela sat very straight with her hands motionless in her lap and her smile unchanged.

"Tell me," Margie said, watching Pamela's face closely, "didn't you—"

She was interrupted by the reappearance of the men. The women moved away from one another to make room for them. Pamela stood up. Peter, Washington's most eligible bachelor or the Playboy of the Potomac, depending on how you looked at it, came striding directly across the drawing room toward her.

"Hi," he said, ignoring Margie and Sylvia. He took Pamela's hand. "I've been finding out all about you from the Vice-President. 'Nothing important,' huh? You didn't tell me that you practically run the Porteous committee. As soon as the ranking lady leaves and breaks this bash up, let's you and I go someplace where we can talk."

With Margiekins's envious eyes burning holes in her bare back, Pamela gave the only answer she could.

"I'd love to," she said.

His name was Peter Aldrich Bainbridge III, and of course she had heard of him. She just hadn't connected the name with someone so young.

He was the scion of the Philadelphia, Pittsburgh, Baltimore, Wilmington, and Bar Harbor Bainbridges. The foundations of the family fortune had been laid by Peter's grandfather in the years after the Civil War. "Black Pete" was what they had called him, and he had slugged his way out of the Pennsylvania anthracite fields to become one of the region's coal and timber barons, fought the secret society known as the Molly Maguires with Pinkerton detectives, sawed-off shotguns, and the hangman's rope, and sent his sons to Yale and Princeton to learn how to be gentlemen. Peter's father had put his share of the family money into shipping, distilleries, steel, coke, and Pennsylvania oil. He was dead now, and the fortune was run by a family trust, headed by Peter's mother and uncles.

Before Peter's father had died, he had bought—almost absentmindedly—four run-down newspapers, all of them losing money. The family trust had wanted to liquidate the investiment. But Peter had persuaded his formidable mother to let him play with the struggling journalistic enterprise.

"Mother's given me five years to turn a profit," Peter said. "After that, as soon as I pay back the family trust, they're mine, all mine!"

He was as jubilant as a small boy. "But why have you decided to base yourself in Washington?" Pamela said. "Why not New York? Don't you have a paper in Trenton, New Jersey? The closest you are to Washington, you said, is that daily you have in West Virginia."

"Washington's the place to be," he said positively. "It's the center of everything. Those four dinky dailies—I've just bought a fifth in Indiana, by the way—are just the beginning. Have you heard of the Prince Feature Syndicate?"

"No," she admitted.

"You will. Right now, my own papers are its only subscribers. But I'm negotiating with more than a dozen dailies that're interested in my 'News from the Capital' column and the cartoon mat service that goes with it. I hired away one of Cissy Patterson's bright young reporters to write it. For now, the Prince Syndicate gives me a base of operations in Washington."

"It sounds very exciting," Pamela said.

"I tried to buy the *Washington Post* when it was up for auction, after Ned McLean ran it into the ground. Evalyn McLean tried to buy it back for her children, but she dropped out of the bidding at six hundred thousand dollars. Hearst went to eight hundred thousand. Eugene Meyer finally got it for a measly eight hundred and twenty-five thousand. A property that was worth three million just a few years ago!" He shook his head. "I could only scrape up seven hundred and fifty thousand."

"That's too bad," Pamela said.

"I'll have a Washington paper sooner or later," he said confidently. "It's just a matter of time. Meyer can't make a go of the *Post*. It'll never amount to anything. And Cissy isn't doing so well by Hearst, either. The *Star* is the only paper in Washington that's making any money. Sooner or later one of the others will drop out, and then I'll step in."

"You certainly seem to be ambitious," she said.

"Oh, newspapers are just the beginning," he said with total seriousness. "The coming thing is radio."

"Radio?"

"It's come of age. Already there are twenty-five million families with radios in this country. That's more than have automobiles or telephones. You can get a good table model for as little as twenty dollars now—that's going to encourage even more people to buy them. Eventually more people will be getting their news from radio than from newspapers."

"Do you really think so?" Pamela said doubtfully. "I like to listen to Lowell Thomas. And Winchell. But isn't radio for music? And stories?"

"Not anymore. The feud between radio and the press is simmering down. Before the Press Radio Bureau was formed, none of the newspapers or press associations would sell to radio. They even kept a stenographic record of news broadcasts to see if the radio boys had swiped anything. Even Lowell Thomas was hard up for news sources. Now that's changing. I intend to get in on the ground floor. I'm going to add a radio press service to Prince Syndicate—as soon as I can do it without losing print customers. And I'm on the lookout for radio stations that I can buy."

"It sounds very exciting."

His face was flushed. "Hearst owns newspapers *and* radio stations. *And* newsreels. Why not? It's all the same business essentially. The communications industry. I tell you, we're at the dawn of a new age."

"I never thought of it that way."

"Radio's already changing politics. A few people realize that. Look at Roosevelt. He's a master of the medium. Those fireside chats of his. Other politicians are going to have to take a leaf from his book. Why stump when you can reach a bigger audience over the air? From now on, candidates for public office will have to have good radio voices."

"That's a little scary, isn't it? I mean, you could have unscrupulous people who just happen to sound good over radio."

He nodded. "Power. That's what it's all about. Radio's been around a good many years, but until now the numbers just haven't been there."

His enthusiasm was contagious. "What about television?" she said, getting into the spirit of the game. "There was an article in last month's *Reader's Digest* about the newest experiments. You can actually see a clear picture on a sort of little mirror that's six or seven inches wide. Newsreels, football games, movie musicals—anything. They said it could be on the market in three or four years."

"Oh, television will never amount to anything," he said. "Don't believe everything you read. It'll never be much more than a rich man's novelty."

"But why not?"

"*Think* about it. You have to sit down and *watch* television. You can't just turn it on and then walk around doing your household chores, the way a woman can with a soap opera. It's no good for keeping people company on the job with background music—you'd have to have some kind of a dance number to go with it. You can't put television in a car. No, television could never be as popular as radio."

"I suppose you're right."

"Of course I am. And think of the economics. Where are you going to get the material to fill up all that air time? Hollywood doesn't produce enough pictures in the course of a year to do a tenth of the job. And as for football, by the time you developed your motion picture film and got it on the air, everyone would know the score anyway. From radio."

She laughed. "I give up. I'm no match for an analytical mind."

He was instantly apologetic. "I'm sorry. I didn't mean to be a bore. I tend to get carried away. Building this chain of mine is the biggest thing in my life right now."

"Your communications empire."

He smiled, pleased that she had remembered the phrase. "My communications empire." He leaned forward and tapped on the chauffeur's glass. "I promised to take you somewhere where we could talk, and I've been riding you around and chewing your ear off about business."

Pamela looked out of the limousine's window. They seemed to be in a dark and run-down part of town. "Where are we going?" she said. "I don't think we'll find too many places open at this hour."

"I know a place that's open all night."

He was being very mysterious. Pamela hoped she was not going to have to fight him off while the chauffeur stared discreetly ahead.

"I don't see any bright lights," she said.

The limousine was bumping over railroad tracks. Huge boxy shapes loomed out of the darkness—freight cars lined up on sidings.

It was a railroad switchyard, spooky and deserted at this hour. She glanced at Peter. He seemed to be very pleased with himself.

"There it is," he said.

The limousine stopped beside a dark green Pullman car standing by itself on a spur of track. By the flame of a sputtering arc light, she could make out gilt letters painted on its side. They spelled WAN-DERLUST.

The chauffeur was holding the door open for her. "Go on, get out," Peter said.

She hesitated. The chauffeur seemed to have a nice face; he was gray-haired and diffident, with a neat gray mustache. She gathered the skirts of her gown about her and stepped out into the grimy slush, holding the hem above her ankles. Her shoes and stockings were going to be ruined.

"It was my father's," he said. "The old boy liked to travel in style. There aren't too many of these old Pullman palace cars left today. It'd probably cost a couple of hundred thousand to duplicate it. The damn lawyers wanted to sell it, but I made a fuss, and Mother told them to debit it against my share of the trust. I'm going to hang on to it as long as I can."

He had lost the *Washington Post* for lack of a mere seventy-five thousand in ready cash. "It seems like an extravagance," she said.

He took it as a compliment. "Every self-respecting press baron needs a private railway car," he said. "Ned McLean had his *Ohio.* Cissy Patterson rolls around in her *Ranger,* and her butler telegraphs ahead for fresh flowers at every stop." He laughed with boyish delight. "Did you know that the toilet in the *Ranger* has a gold-plated flusher? Ray Moley tore it off during one of Cissy's rolling parties and lit into Cissy for flaunting her wealth while there was unrest in the land. Then poor Moley had to confess to FDR that he'd cost him Cissy's support in the election."

Pamela laughed, somewhat uneasily. Peter had her firmly by the arm and was urging her toward the steps of the *Wanderlust.* Washington's social taboos were fairly relaxed, but she didn't want to give him the wrong idea. What were the rules about a girl entering a private railway car parked on a siding after midnight? Were they the same as going to a bachelor's flat?

He sensed her hesitation. "It's all right, Miss Sinclair," he said dryly. "There's a chef aboard, a butler, and a private porter. That enough chaperones for you?"

"You make it impossible to resist," she said, feeling silly and trying not to show it.

A colored porter helped her up the steps and took her wrap from her. Inside, the car was lush and faded Victorian, with brocades, dull gilt, dark paneling. Tulip lamps cast a warm orangy glow. A bar had been set up at one end, with etched crystal and silver ice buckets. Pamela saw trays of artistically arranged shrimp, oysters in cracked ice, foie gras, toothpick-impaled morsels bubbling in chafing dishes. A smiling Negro in white apron and chef's hat presided.

"A glass of champagne?" Peter asked.

"My goodness, all this for me?" Pamela said in as flip a tone as she could manage.

"It should be," he said. "If only I'd known I was going to meet you at Taffy's party. I have guests coming aboard at Baltimore and Philadelphia. It's going to be a sleepless night for me, I'm afraid. Maybe I can catch a few winks in the master stateroom sometime before dawn and Albert's famous scrambled eggs."

"I don't understand," Pamela said.

Outside there was a grinding of metal. The car lurched and Peter grabbed at Pamela to keep her from losing her balance.

"That'll be the switch engine come to hook us up," he said.

"What are you talking about?" She freed herself from his arms. Albert was standing there, trying to hand her a glass of champagne.

Peter looked smug. "I'm kidnapping you," he said.

"Now wait a minute—"

"Do come along," he said. "It'll be fun. We'll have a party on the way. I couldn't resist showing off to some of my friends—we're celebrating the acquisition of the Indiana paper. That's why I'm due in New York tomorrow—to close the deal. Then I can take you to some shows."

"That's very nice." She looked around for her wrap. "But I'm a working girl. I've got to be at the office tomorrow."

"Take the day off."

"I can't."

There was the suggestion of a pout on his handsome face. "At least ride as far as Baltimore. I'll send you back from there."

She looked down at her bare shoulders and the flimsy evening shoes. "Like this? In the middle of the night? I'm sorry, but—"

"I'll send my chauffeur on ahead. He'll take you to your front door. In time for a catnap and a shower."

"Well, I—"

"It's settled, then." He snapped his fingers at the porter, who disappeared through the door.

Pamela laughed. "Do you always get your own way?"

"Almost always. I'm working on it. Come on, have a sip of champagne. Then I'll show you the rest of the car."

For the next half hour, while the car bumped and jerked and the voices of the yardmen outside punctuated the attaching of the *Wanderlust* to the train being made up for New York, Peter smothered Pamela with charm. He knew her in-laws; he had been a guest at Westbourne several times. "I have to hand it to Randolph," he said. "It looks as if his run for Congress this fall is going to succeed, in spite of the lack of help from Senator Hale. Now, of course, *because* of it." He knew all about the impending Hale scandal, of course, but his newspapers were going to downplay it. He thought that Brad would go far if he continued to stick to Harry Hopkins. "Everybody knows that Roosevelt is grooming Harry for the presidential run in 1940, so he can take over the New Deal when FDR's second term runs out. Is it true that Brad was the ghostwriter for Harry's book, *Spending to Save,* or did Brad plant that story himself?" He finished what he had been about to say at the dinner party before the tables turned: "I wish I could get Jeremy to work for my own news service. I don't know how he gets his stuff past the censors. My own man in Moscow—at least the one I share with a couple of other publishers—is a dud." He asked her about the Porteous committee investigation. It was rather disconcerting to talk to somebody who knew so much about her, and yet didn't know her at all.

With the train rolling smoothly through the Maryland countryside, he made the expected pass at her while showing her the master stateroom and the three guest compartments. Pamela twisted her face away without being too obvious about it and chattered brightly on about the ornamental fittings while backing out into the narrow corridor. Peter didn't pursue the matter; Baltimore was only a half hour away at that point anyway.

The friends who got on at the North Charles Street station in Baltimore all seemed to have names like Bucky and Ducky and Fluffs and Baby and Dicky-woo. They were all drunk and hilarious, the men in black tie from previous festivities, and the women gowned and disheveled. Dicky-woo, a frail patent-leather-haired fellow who convulsed the others with his imitation Leslie Howard accent, sat down at the Victorian parlor organ in the salon with Ducky in his lap, and tried to play it under the impression that it was a piano. "You have to pump, old fellow, or it won't make a sound," one of the others told him, and they all found this hilarious. In a minute, with Ducky crawling around under his legs to work the pedals, Dicky-woo managed a bagpipe-like caterwauling that sounded vaguely like "Penthouse Serenade."

Ducky's pumping was erratic because she kept having to use one hand to keep from falling out of her gown.

Peter took Pamela aside to apologize. "They're not always like this," he said. "Well at least not *quite* this bad. I know you think they're shallow. But I grew up with them. Suffered through first dance class together, and all that. Two of the fellows were frat brothers. We had some great times. But they never settled down to anything serious. Except Bucky. Believe it or not, he's a surgeon—daytimes, anyway. But for the others, life is just the party circuit. Newport to Saratoga. Will you put up with them?"

He looked so anxious for her approval that she felt sorry for him.

"Of course I will. You don't have to apologize for your friends. But how long are we going to be in Baltimore? I've got to . . . Peter, this train is moving!"

"Too late." He grinned triumphantly. "But don't worry. My chauffeur will be waiting at the next stop."

She gave in to the inevitable. When Peter's friends discovered that she knew how to work the parlor organ, they dragged Dicky-woo off the bench and installed Pamela. She remembered a lot of the standards from her stint in the music department at the five-and-ten in Beulah, and after Dicky-woo, they found this miraculous. They kept her supplied with champagne while she played requests—"Moonglow" and "Limehouse Blues" and "Body and Soul" and "Embraceable You"—and they sang raucously off-key. When the requests got tougher—college drinking songs and parodies she had never heard of—she discovered that all she had to do was play some kind of a vamp. They were too drunk to know the difference.

"Peter, thish girl knows *ev'rything!* Pam'la, y'r unbelievable! Where'd'ya learn to play like that?"

"At the five-and-ten," she said.

They shrieked with laughter.

"Peter, your girl's a *riot!*"

She rode as far as Wilmington. By that time, Baby, Ducky, and Dicky-woo had retired to one of the staterooms and Bucky the surgeon was pawing at her, and Pamela thought it was a good idea to leave.

A few middle-of-the-night people were getting on at Wilmington, but otherwise the long platform was deserted. The *Wanderlust* was sandwiched between baggage cars, for privacy and stability. Peter escorted her off. The chauffeur was waiting respectfully, hat in hand.

"You were wonderful with them," Peter said. "I know Bucky was getting out of hand."

"It wasn't anything. I was having fun."

He put his hands on her shoulders. "Pamela, listen, after New York

I have to go on to Indiana and put the fear of God into my new editor. Make a few changes in the plant. When I get back to Washington, I'll call you."

She shivered in the raw night air. Her dyed muskrat evening wrap wasn't all that warm. "All right, Peter."

The chauffeur turned his back. Peter's face loomed and blurred, and he kissed her. He didn't try to make too much of it, and she was grateful for that. Far down the platform she heard the conductor bawl, "All abo-ard!" and Peter released her.

"Give your phone number to Edwards," he called as he sprang for the Pullman car's steel step. The train was already moving. Peter hung acrobatically outward from the handgrip, waving back at her, a lithe trim figure in black tails.

Edwards replaced his cap and escorted her to the limousine. "You can try to sleep, miss, if you wish," he said. "I'll just pull that footrest out for you, shall I? I'll wake you up when we come into the city."

Daylight was breaking when the limousine deposited her at the door to her apartment building. Edwards pulled up behind a milk wagon waiting unattended at the curb.

"I'll see you inside, miss," he said. Pamela lived at the unfashionable end of Massachusetts Avenue, only a few blocks from a Negro slum, but her building itself, in a stretch of small apartment houses and tree-shaded residences, was respectable enough and was convenient to Capitol Hill.

No one was around to see the chauffeur help her out of the limousine. On the way inside she bumped into the milkman, rattling empty bottles in his metal basket. His eyes widened when he saw her in her evening gown.

"Oh, Miss Sinclair," he said, "your roommate left a note for a pint of cream. Would you mind taking it upstairs and saving me an extra climb?"

The bottle of cream in her hand, she let herself into the apartment. It was a big square sitting room fronting the avenue, a tiny bedroom which Pamela had won by paying five dollars over her half of the rent, a kitchenette, and a curtained sleeping alcove with a studio couch.

Her roommate, Willa, emerged yawning from behind the curtains, face creamed and hair in curlers. She wore pink flannel pajamas, drooping in the seat.

"Pammy, are you—" She stopped as she took in the fact of Pamela's gown. "Didn't you get home at all last night?"

Pamela was annoyed at the inference that she'd slept out. Willa spent weekends and an occasional weeknight with her boy friend Jack, an acned young lawyer with the Justice Department, and she was always urging Pamela to "break out of your shell, have some fun."

"I had a rather late night, yes," she said brusquely, heading for her bedroom door.

Willa followed her. "Wheredya go?"

"Baltimore for one place. And Wilmington."

"Yeah, yeah. Whodya go out with?"

"I took a ride in a private railroad car with Peter Aldrich Bainbridge the Third and some of his friends. They sent me back by limousine."

Willa's eyes narrowed. "You kidding me? A private railroad car? Come on, tell me all about it."

"You'd better get ready for work. And so had I."

She had time for a hot shower and some breakfast. She squeezed the oranges for juice and made the coffee, and found when she had finished her turn in the bathroom that Willa had laid out some cold cereal and prunes for her. Willa's mother in Ohio had always emphasized the importance of regularity.

She worked through Monday morning in a sleepless haze. The Porteous committee was gathering itself for a new round of hearings, and the staff was busy. She preferred that; if it had been a slow day, she wouldn't have been able to keep her eyes open.

When she returned to her apartment at the end of the day, she found flowers waiting for her—a lavish basket of four dozen long-stemmed roses. They had been wired from New York.

Peter returned from his business trip two weeks later. He called her at the office and said, "I just got into Union Station. Come on out and meet me. I'll take you to lunch at the Mayflower."

"Peter, that's very nice, but it's all the way across town."

"Edwards is waiting with the motor running, and one of my assistants is holding a table for us. I'll have you back in an hour. Promise."

Pamela glanced over at Mr. Theobald. He was tottering toward her with an armload of documents.

"We're really very busy here. I think I'd better just have a sandwich in the cafeteria."

There was a long silence at the other end.

"Peter? Are you there?" Pamela said at last.

When he came on again, his voice sounded sulky. Or did she imagine that? "Will you have dinner with me, then?"

"Yes, of course. That would be lovely."

He brightened immediately. "I'll pick you up at four-thirty. That's when the government quits for the day, isn't it?"

"Peter—wait!" She was amused and touched by his impatience. "Nobody has dinner at four-thirty, even in Washington."

"Then I'll take you for a drink first. At Chevy Chase."

Mr. Theobald was hovering with his documents, tapping his foot and frowning, but she pretended not to see him.

"That's very tempting. I've never seen the inside of Chevy Chase. But I'll be a mess after a day like this. I'll have to go home first. I'll need time to freshen up and change."

"How much time can a girl like you need? You're already perfect. I'll give you half an hour."

"You can pick me up at my apartment at seven," she said firmly.

There was that alarming silence again. Then he said, with the sulky note back in his voice, "That doesn't give us an awful lot of time to talk."

"All right," she laughed. "Make it six-thirty."

"Six-thirty it is," he said, his cheerfulness restored.

Pamela was vaguely disturbed. Had her little concession been that important? Peter acted as if they were having some sort of contest.

"Fine," she said. "You have my address?"

"I'll get it from Edwards."

"I've *got* to hang up. Bye."

"See you."

She turned toward Mr. Theobald with a persuasive start of surprise. "Oh, is that the new batch of depositions? I'll have them excerpted for the senator's opening statement by four."

She was expecting Edwards, but when Peter picked her up, he was driving himself, in a sporty little Cord roadster with aerodynamic fenders and recessed headlights that were concealed behind covers. Pamela had spent an hour picking up after Willa and frantically dusting and vacuuming, but Peter hardly seemed to notice the apartment. He took her to dinner at Harvey's, where they had seafood, and where Pamela saw a nattily dressed J. Edgar Hoover sitting at a table with another man. "He always has dinner here, usually with his assistant," Peter told her. He waved at Hoover, and Hoover waved back. "Jim Farley's trying to get him fired, but FDR isn't about to tangle with the national hero who nailed Dillinger, Pretty Boy Floyd, Baby Face Nelson, and Machine Gun Kelly." He lowered his voice. "I have it on good authority that Farley's phone is tapped."

She tried, over Maryland crab, to turn the subject toward Peter's interests. "Do you still think that radio's a growth industry?"

"Do I?" he said enthusiastically, his mouth full of crabmeat. "Joe Kennedy's drawing up a plan for RCA that'll convert their preferred shares entirely to common stock. They're paying him a hundred-thousand-dollar consultant's fee. When he finishes, they'll finally be free to move ahead. By next year, they'll be paying the first dividends in their history."

It was all very mysterious to Pamela, but she enjoyed Peter's excitement. He seemed appealingly boyish, not at all like the dull, careful men that Washington was full of. "Mr. Kennedy seems to have a lot of influence these days," she ventured. "My brother Brad says that the President's asked him to line up the support of his friends in business for the election."

Peter scowled. "He's been hanging around the White House too much lately. If the President doesn't watch out, Kennedy will talk him into recognizing the Vatican."

"Would that be so bad?"

He stared at her for a moment, then said grudgingly, "I guess not. Some of my best friends are Catholics. They're all right as long as they don't get too pushy."

"And you think Mr. Kennedy is pushy?"

"He managed to get himself and his wife invited to stay overnight with the Roosevelts on his way to Florida at Christmas. He helped set Jimmy Roosevelt up in the insurance business in Boston. And his liquor import firm sends complimentary cases of scotch to the White House."

Peter was too serious; he needed to be teased. "But you managed to get yourself invited to go fishing with the President," she said.

Peter threw back his head and laughed. "You're right—and I drank some of Joe Kennedy's scotch."

After dinner he took her for a spin in the Cord. Spring had not yet arrived in Washington, and after ten minutes of freezing the both of them, he was forced to get out and put the top up. They were parked on the motor drive encircling the Tidal Basin. The cherry trees were still bare, the flower beds had not yet bloomed, and a cold unpleasant drizzle had started. It was too dark to see anything anyway. Pamela hinted tactfully that they give up on the spin and try it again on some sunny day in a couple of weeks, when they could enjoy the scenery and perhaps have a picnic. But Peter, acting as if he hadn't heard her, headed the car with grim determination toward Hains Point. He didn't like being thwarted, evidently, not even by nature and the elements.

"Why don't we turn back?" she tried again. "There's nothing to see, and the teahouse at the Point will be closed at this hour anyway."

He didn't answer. Rain spattered on the windshield. The headlights carved tunnels in the darkness. There was hardly any other traffic, no people in sight, and only the hazy lights of Alexandria across the Potomac.

He seemed to be looking for something. At last he found it: a place to pull off the drive and park by the seawall. He switched off the headlights. "Cigarette?" he said. They smoked in silence, looking out across the gloomy water.

Halfway through his cigarette, he stubbed it out in the ashtray. Abruptly he seized her wrist, took her cigarette from her, and tossed it out through the open window. Then he was all over her, his mouth greedy on her lips, one hand crushing her breast, the other pulling at her gown.

Pamela had been expecting the obligatory move from him, but she wasn't prepared for this sudden all-out assault. Out of sheer surprise, she fought him off with a panicky violence that perhaps was unwarranted. When at last she had wrestled herself free, and sat, panting, as far from him as she could get, she was dismayed at the way she had overreacted. He was staring angrily through the windshield, his lower lip trembling. She had wanted him to kiss her, after all. She could have handled the situation better, she told herself.

And then he lunged again.

His hands crawled over her body, and he was forcing her down with neck-cracking insistence. His teeth bruised her lips. "No, Peter, no," she whispered, prying herself away.

Once more they were sitting upright, at opposite ends of the Cord's leather seat. She expected another bout of sullen rage from him, but after a moment he dug his crumpled pack of Camels out of his pocket and offered her one. She took a light from his cautiously, and he said, with no apology in his voice, "My mistake. I should have known you weren't that kind of girl."

What sort of girl, she wondered, liked to be pounced on like that? But she decided she had better keep that thought to herself. "Would you like to take me home?" she said.

"Not on your life. It's still too early."

He switched the headlights on and backed the Cord out onto the park drive. "Nifty car," he said. "This front-wheel drive is great on wet roads."

"Where are you taking me?"

"Oh, a place," he said vaguely.

He drove her to Georgetown, to an implausibly narrow house, barely eleven feet wide, that was squeezed between its neighbors. She felt a qualm when Peter led her by the arm to a basement entrance, but the place belonged to Drew Pearson, and a party was in progress.

"Glad you could make it after all, Peter," the columnist said. "Come on in. Things are starting to liven up."

"This is Pamela Sinclair, Brad Sinclair's sister," Peter said.

"Welcome, Miss Sinclair," Pearson said with courtly manners. His eyes took in her gown and Peter's dinner clothes. "It's just a little informal gathering, mostly working press. Nothing very grand. Neither is the house. It's what they call a spite house, built last century to cut off a neighbor's light."

But upstairs, skylights and an oriel window made for a dramatic interior, and the narrow width crowded the party together and made it work. Pamela walked into an explosion of warmth and noise. Everybody seemed to be trying to out-talk everybody else. There were a lot of men in rumpled business suits, and a few women, looking tough, competent, and assured, in daytime dresses. Peter's was the only dinner jacket except for Pearson's, and Pamela's was the only gown.

"I see you've snared Rex Tugwell," Peter said, looking across the room.

"He'll be out on his ear pretty soon," Pearson said. "It's an election year, and utopian professors make big fat targets. Hamilton Fish is after him, Barbour's trying to get another investigation going in the Senate, and Hearst and Bernarr Macfadden are calling him a bolshevik."

"He say anything about resigning?" Peter said.

"What are you going to do, Peter?" the columnist said. "Try to get him to write a column for your news service after he leaves, like Scripps did with Hugh Johnson?"

"It's not a bad idea," Peter said seriously. "The man certainly knows how to write."

"Forget it. The big boys will snap him up."

Peter didn't like that. "Let's go talk to him."

Peter walked off in Tugwell's direction. Pamela was furious. Peter had abandoned her without a backward glance—without even getting her a drink first—and left her on her own in a place where she knew nobody, and where she was conspicuous in an evening gown on top of everything else.

Pearson came to her rescue. "Let me get a drink in your hand, Miss Sinclair. What are you having?"

"Scotch and water. If it's not too much trouble."

He steered her over to the bar and mixed the drink for her himself. "Don't be mad at Peter," he said. "He's trying to pretend he doesn't have all that money and make himself one of the boys. He thinks that to be a real newsman, you have to be rude."

"Thank you," she said, taking the drink.

"Don't let these mugs intimidate you. They're not as hard-boiled as they like to make out. All you have to do is talk louder."

Pamela resolved to have a good time in spite of Peter's behavior. She took Pearson's advice. In a matter of minutes she was part of a noisy group arguing the merits of Roosevelt's Social Security bill. "It means that every workingman in America is sentenced to a one percent reduction in pay every week for the rest of his working life," complained a jowly fellow with a plaid bow tie. "And then, what if you don't live to sixty-five?" After that she talked to a fascinating man who had covered the fighting in Ethiopia. "The Italians are using mustard gas against those poor niggers," he said. "They're bombing Red Cross tents. They're using Caproni bombers and scooter tanks against a bunch of tribesmen who are still in the stone age." She even got a chance to talk to Professor Tugwell, a charming, urbane man who was as handsome as a movie actor.

It was fun, for a change, to talk to a lot of men who didn't automatically treat women like children or empty-headed ninnies. The newspapermen loved the sound of their own voices, but they listened to what she had to say without being male-smug or condescending, though of course there was a normal quota of eyes that wandered to her chest in the frivolous gown. Pamela didn't mind. She was holding her own in the conversations, and she was enjoying herself.

After a while she became aware that Peter was watching her from across the room. She caught him several times looking over at her, then pretending that he hadn't. She had the distinct impression that he was keeping tabs on her to see how she handled herself with his friends—or people he wanted to be his friends.

At three in the morning, with the party still going strong, he came over and said, "Come on, I'll take you home. Give these stiffs a break. They've all got to work tomorrow, and so do you."

"Am I the ranking lady here?" she joked. "I didn't think they stood on ceremony here."

"You're the *only* lady here," he said. "The others are just women."

At her apartment door he didn't attempt to get himself invited in, and he gave her a light, decorous, first-date kind of kiss, as though the manhandling incident in the car had never happened. "I'll call you tomorrow," he said, putting his hat back on and heading for the stairwell. It occurred to Pamela that she had just passed some kind of test.

32

Peter gave her the rush that spring. He bombarded her with flowers and invitations, and called her at work two or three times a day, to the annoyance of Mr. Theobald. Mr. Theobald was further annoyed by the fact that Pamela had begun to take her whole lunch hour—at least on the days she met Peter—and sometimes actually left work at quitting time. But he didn't say anything. Pamela did her work as efficiently as ever. Mr. Theobald was getting no younger; he wouldn't have been able to run the committee without Pamela, and he knew it.

There was no repetition of the frenzied assault of that first night in Peter's car. They progressed to long kisses and the allowable caresses, that was all. When Peter kissed her good-night, he cupped her breast with his hand without fondling her; it was a kind of impersonal possessiveness, as if he were claiming ownership.

Increasingly she felt herself stirred by him. And she was aware of his physical excitement. But by unspoken agreement, neither of them let it go too far. It was tacitly understood that Pamela should be the one to call a halt when necessary.

She was alive again—that was what counted. The wound that Marcus Hale had dealt her had healed, and now Pamela realized that it had almost been fatal. It had come too cruelly after Carl Fuller's betrayal, scar upon scar, and the twice-injured spirit had reached its limits of renewal. For a year she had spun a dusty cocoon around herself, and now, gloriously, she had burst through into the remembered world of color and sound and light.

The change in her was noticeable. She glowed. Willa said with chummy approval, "See, didn't I tell you?" after Peter started dropping by the apartment to take Pamela out. Peter, for his part, showed not the slightest sign that Willa existed, beyond the inescapable amenities, and Willa, who would have instantly detected condescension, took this as a sign that Peter was not "stuck up."

After reporters spotted Pamela coming out of a White House reception on Peter's arm, her name began to appear regularly in the gossip columns, which impressed Willa and annoyed Mr. Theobald. The Washington press, always eager to report on Peter's doings, regarded the conspicuous visibility of the reception—which actually had been a mass stampede that Peter had apologized for subjecting her to—as evidence that Pamela now was Peter's publicly acknowledged girl of the moment.

Peter did nothing to duck the conjecture. In fact he seemed to go out of his way to encourage it. When he had to cancel their usual Saturday night date to attend the Gridiron Club dinner in mid-April, he pulled strings to get Pamela an invitation to Mrs. Roosevelt's party for "Gridiron widows" at the White House, and he picked her up there afterward, to the clicking of the cameras at the east gate. Later he took her to Cissy Patterson's post-Gridiron party, where they had to run a gauntlet of photographers camped in front of Cissy's Dupont Circle mansion. Pamela ended up not only in the "Top Hats and Tiaras" column, but in that week's Movietone News newsreel.

"The guy's practically proposing to you in public," an awed Willa said to her.

"Don't be ridiculous," Pamela said.

But Willa's remark made her wonder.

"You're a fool, young lady," Aunt Cornelia said. "I warned you not to let Marcus Hale take advantage of you, and you paid no attention, and now you're making the same mistake with Peter Bainbridge."

Pamela set down her teacup and stared unflinchingly into the monkey-bright eyes. If you flinched with Aunt Cornelia, you were finished. "Peter and I are just friends," she said. "There's nothing serious between us."

"Nonsense!" Cornelia struck the floor a violent blow with one of her bamboo canes. "And I haven't time for nonsense at my age! When a Casanova like Peter gives up darting from flower to flower, and when my favorite adopted niece comes out of her self-constructed cloister after almost a whole year, then even these senile old eyes can tell that something's going on!"

Pamela smiled. Afternoon tea with Cornelia was never a restful experience, but paradoxically she always felt at ease here in the crumbling old mansion near Dupont Circle where Sally's aunt had lorded it over the Washington establishment for sixty of her ninety years. There were no pretenses here. When Cornelia, over a year ago, had guessed about her relationship with Marcus Hale, she hadn't bothered to deny it, though she wouldn't have dreamed of confiding in anyone else, even Brad. Especially Brad! "Don't you worry, Pamela my girl," Cornelia had said, "I've told Marcus that if he ever allows one single *word* to get out, he'll have *me* to answer to." Pamela dropped by for tea with Cornelia every three or four weeks. It had begun shortly after Brad's wedding, with a surprise summons by telephone. "Come keep a lonely old lady company," the voice at the other end had said. "It isn't often I acquire a relative I can stand." At first the visits had frequently been shared with Sally, but now, with Sally increasingly involved with her new baby, the duty had fallen to Pamela, though Peter's rush was making it more and more difficult for her to find the time.

"What have you got against Peter?" she said.

Cornelia drew her tiny, fragile frame erect in the straight-backed chair. "Peter is a charmer and a fashion plate," she said, "and he's handsome enough to make the juices flow even in a withered old thing like me, but he has all the regard for others that you'd find in a three-year-old. And a *spoiled* three-year-old at that!"

"You're being unfair."

"You know it yourself, my girl!" The eyes in the mummified face blazed a challenge.

Pamela kept silent. She tried to sort out her feelings about Peter. She had been attracted by his charm and vitality, by his quick intelligence. Anyone would have been. From the beginning she had seen the petulance that showed through the cracks, but she had ignored it. It simply wasn't important in a casual relationship. Having fun together was what counted. And now it was too late. The relationship wasn't casual anymore. It was Peter Bainbridge, after all, who had brought her alive again. It was Peter whose lips were on hers night after night, whose hand was shaped to her body, whose shared company was part of the fabric of her life, whose shared perceptions changed the focus of the world around them, and something had grown out of that. And Peter, for whatever reason, had bound himself to her in his own skittish way, and for that she owed him herself.

"People can change," she said. "I'll help him."

The old eyes closed as if in pain. "Silly women like to think that,"

Aunt Cornelia said. "I've heard that too often in my ninety years. I thought I could change the justice. I met him at Mr. Lincoln's reception for General Grant, did you know that? I was just a young girl. Perhaps it's lucky that he died when he did. Lucky for his reputation and my peace. Help me out of this chair, my dear, and take me up to bed. I'm suddenly very tired."

In May, Peter insisted on dragging Pamela off to Bradley Farms for the National Capital Horse Show, though as far as she knew, he had little interest in horses, and had no reason to believe that she was interested either. "Oh," he said vaguely. "My uncle Bertram usually has one or two of his jumpers entered."

She met Peter's uncle Bertram out by the paddocks between events. He was a stout man on stork legs, with a hard-drinking face crosshatched by little veins that were only slightly redder than his sunburn.

"So you're Peter's girl?" he said, inspecting her anatomy as if he were putting a price on her.

"Oh . . . well . . . we're friends," she said.

She appealed to Peter with a quick glance. He was staring off into space. Pamela looked at his face and saw that he was sweating.

"You're the girl who got her picture taken with Peter at that charity ball thing," Bertram said. "We don't follow the Washington papers much, but Peter's aunt is on the committee for that thing. Peter has a girl in his office send her the clippings on it."

"Oh, that's very interesting," she said. "I didn't know that."

"Yes indeed," he said, scrutinizing her hips and thighs, "you might say it was a family thing."

Pamela tried to catch Peter's eye again, but he was acting as if he were on another planet.

Peter's uncle turned back to the horse and resumed swabbing out its nostrils with a cloth.

"Have you spoken to your mother recently?" he said casually to Peter, without looking up.

"No, I planned to be in Pittsburgh next weekend."

Peter hadn't mentioned any such trip to Pamela. She had assumed he was taking her golfing. She willed him to look at her, but he was watching the horse as if it were the most fascinating object in the world.

"Well, I'll be seeing her before then," Bertram said. "We're having the quarterly meeting of the trust committee Wednesday. Bother all lawyers! I'll tell your mother that I saw you."

He paused with the grooming cloth in his hand to run his eyes over Pamela's flanks and brisket.

Peter was uncommunicative about his Pittsburgh trip during their drive back to Washington. "Can't a fellow go home for Mother's Day?" he said.

"I thought you were brought up in Philadelphia."

"Mother moved back to Pittsburgh after Father died," he said. "She never liked Philadelphia society. In Pittsburgh, she gets her due, even from the Mellons and Fricks."

An invitation from Brad and Sally kept Pamela from having to spend that weekend alone. She took a cab to the small brick house in Georgetown. Brad's new car was parked at the curb—a long-nosed Studebaker President or Dictator; she never could tell the difference except that one was more expensive. The colored maid let her in, with an impatient Sally crowding right behind her. Sally had become very domestic. She hardly gave Pamela time enough to take off her hat and gloves before dragging her upstairs to see the baby.

"Isn't she the cutest thing? Come on, Lissie, smile for your aunt Pamela."

"Let's see, how old is she now?" Pamela said.

"Five months," Sally said, her tone magnanimously forgiving Pamela's lapse. "Go on, you can hold her if you want. "

Pamela picked the baby up. She had been named Melissa, after Mrs. Collier's mother. She was a pretty little thing with Sally's golden coloring.

"She looks like you."

"That's what Brad says. But she has that stubborn Sinclair chin." Sally laughed indulgently. "He *spoils* her so, I declare!"

"Hello, little one," Pamela whispered. The baby looked at her suspiciously, refusing to coo.

"She's starting on strained vegetables now," Sally said. "I breast-fed her at the start. It drove Mama wild. She said I'd spoil my figure. She wanted me to get a wet nurse, like a proper southern lady."

The baby began to wriggle in Pamela's arms.

"I hardly left the house for the first three months," Sally said. "No one could believe it, especially Brad."

The baby let out a furious howl.

"She wants her bottle," Sally said. "No, no, sweetie pie, it's not time yet."

Pamela handed the struggling bundle over. The baby had worked itself into a kicking, purple-faced rage.

"Well, all right, sugah plum," Sally crooned, "I guess it won't hurt to go off your schedule this once."

"I think she's wet," Pamela said. "Shall I get your maid, or what?"

"No," Sally said. "I change her myself. Why don't you and Brad have a drink without me. Oh, would you tell Alvina to warm up a bottle and bring it upstairs?"

Pamela left. A parting shriek from the baby tore at her insides. Carl's baby would have been two years old now. She put the thought firmly from her mind.

At dinner, Brad talked entertainingly about his job with Harry Hopkins.

"With the conventions coming up, we shovel leaners are going to become more political. The President wants Harry to start hitting back. He says he expects the Republicans to make the WPA the big issue of the campaign, along with Social Security."

"I saw what Mr. Hoover said," Pamela said. "About the New Deal using the Russian alphabet to name its agencies."

"And that's just the start," Brad said. "It's going to get rougher."

"I'm not sure I *like* this new politicking that Mr. Hopkins is going to do," Sally complained. "It just means that Brad's going to be away more than ever this summer and fall."

"Sally's siding with Jim Farley," Brad said lightly. "He doesn't want Harry to hit the campaign trail either. He told the President that WPA is his greatest political liability."

"Isn't it?" Pamela said.

"Farley's uneasy about Harry's closeness to the President," Brad said. "Since Louis Howe died the night of the Gridiron dinner, Harry seems to have taken his place."

"He's even charmed old Mrs. Roosevelt and Eleanor," Sally put in. "In fact, the whole Hopkins family's been invited to spend their summer vacation at Campobello."

"The upshot is that the President is going to stick by Harry in this new appropriations fight. He intends to give him another billion and a half to spend, no strings attached, no matter what the opposition says. But Harry has to make the WPA look good before election day. And he's handed me one of the hottest of the hot potatoes."

"Federal Theater," Sally explained.

"It's all these un-American plays we've been putting on," Brad said. "Shakespeare, Shaw, Ibsen, Molière, Chekhov . . ."

"I've seen the criticism," Pamela said. "*Coriolanus* promotes communism, *Othello* encouraged miscegenation, *Julius Caesar* is an insult to Mussolini."

"What we need is a hit. A great big smash success that would open in WPA theaters all over the United States simultaneously."

Pamela thought a moment. What were some of the best sellers she had been reading before Peter Bainbridge started to monopolize her time?

"Why don't you get Sinclair Lewis to make a play out of *It Can't Happen Here?*" she said.

"Good idea. Lewis might go for it. Hollywood's afraid to touch it. I'll mention it to Hallie Flanagan at the next policy board conference."

The talk turned to Jeremy in Russia. "Have you heard from him?" Pamela said.

"Not since that first letter. Mailed in January, took over a month to get here, covered with censors' stamps and grimy fingerprints."

"He's having better luck in getting his stories out. Did you see the piece he wrote about the American workers' village on the Volga, where Ford is building a factory for the Russians?"

Brad grunted. "That's the kind of story the Russians *want* him to write. The glories of the new five-year plan. The workers' paradise. That writers' union, or whatever the hell it is that's sponsoring him, is shuttling him all over the place to admire all the hydroelectric dams and steel plants."

"At least he's getting to see more of the country than just Moscow, like all the other correspondents."

"They're using him," Brad said flatly.

"Oh, Brad, isn't that a little extreme? Jeremy's very bright."

"Too bright. And naive. He sneaks those little nuances past their censors and he thinks that means he's getting the better of them. But nuances don't count in Washington."

"Jeremy doesn't work for Washington."

Brad put down his fork and gave her a measured look. "I do."

"Oh, so that's it?"

"That's it."

Pamela was appalled. "Brad, that's ridiculous. No one can hold you accountable for what your brother says and thinks. Not in this country, for heaven's sake!"

"Not now, maybe. It's Roosevelt's turn. Martin Dies and Ham Fish notwithstanding. Red-baiting's only an esoteric art form for the time being. But political climates change."

"Well, I'm very proud of my little brother, and I'm not afraid to say so!"

Sally interposed hastily: "Who'd like another dumpling for their fricassee? Alvina let me make them myself this time."

"Uh, I'm stuffed," Brad said.

Pamela gritted her teeth and said, "I'd love one." The dumplings, served with an eloquent upward roll of the eyes by Alvina, had a jaw-tiring rubbery texture. Sally's newfound domesticity had not made her a better cook.

"Are you going to Gordon's June Week?" Pamela said after she succeeded in getting the mouthful down.

"I haven't been invited."

"Don't be silly. Of course you're invited. In Gordon's last letter to me he said that he's looking forward to seeing both of us at his graduation, and wants to know if he should make room reservations for us at the Thayer."

"I wouldn't know. He never writes me."

"What do you want me to tell him? I've arranged to take that Friday and Saturday off. Peter's offered to pick me up after work Thursday and drive me. He says he can get me there in eight hours." She added quickly, "Peter's staying with friends in Westchester."

Brad grinned lopsidedly. "I wouldn't miss baby brother's graduation for the world. Tell him Sally and I will be there with bells on. We'll take the sleeper."

"You go alone, Brad," Sally said. "The baby—"

"We're getting a nurse," Brad said firmly. "It's about time."

They fell silent while Alvina served dessert. She was a thin, quick-moving woman with a doleful umber face.

Ordinarily they avoided mention of Junie, but now Brad suddenly said: "You know, it'll be a year next month since I went to that migrant camp in Arizona."

"I know. Oh Brad, it seems so hopeless."

He chewed his lip. "Maybe not."

"What do you mean?"

"I had an idea. The Social Security system goes into effect the first of January. It's going to be vast. If any member of the Kinney family applies for a card, he'll have a number on file in Washington. The records are supposed to be confidential, but that doesn't mean anything to Hoover."

"I thought agricultural workers aren't covered."

Brad's mouth twisted cynically. "The depression's easing. Maybe one of the Kinneys will better himself."

"Maybe Junie doesn't want to be traced. You'd think she would have written us in all this time, care of Elroy."

"Yes, I don't understand that."

"Isn't there anything else you can do, Brad?"

Brad played with his coffee spoon. "Maybe. But you wouldn't like it."

"Brad!" Sally said. "It would just about *kill* your poor mother!"

"As you see, Sally and I have discussed it," Brad said with his crooked grin.

"What is it?" Pamela said impatiently.

"That picture of Junie with her baby. The one Leo Reisner took."

Pamela remembered the warm tears that had welled up when Brad had shown her the grainy photo. Junie had been so thin and drawn, the baby so pathetic looking.

Brad hadn't mentioned the photo or his Arizona trip to Gordon. There was no point in upsetting him, he'd said, and Pamela had agreed. Gordon and Junie had been especially close.

"What about the picture?" Pamela said.

Brad would not look at her. "I stole the negative out of the files. I suppose I *could* take it back to Roy Stryker and try to talk him into releasing it as one of the Farm Security Administration propaganda photos."

Pamela caught her breath.

Brad went on in a flat tone of voice. "The news agencies grab up the FSA pictures. It would get Junie's face splashed all over the newspapers and magazines. Somebody might recognize her. Some smart reporter might even follow it up."

"Do it," Pamela said.

Peter was in a strange mood when he returned from visiting his mother in Pittsburgh. Gloomy, subdued, and inclined to be quarrelsome. His conversation, when he took her out to dinner that night, was full of abrupt starts and stops.

"I wish . . ." he said.

"Wish what, Peter?" she said.

"I wish . . . oh, hell, never mind! Waiter, this isn't the brand of scotch I asked for!"

"The Chivas twelve-year-old, Mr. Bainbridge?" the waiter said in surprise. "Same as you always have."

"It's bar swill. Take it back."

"Yes sir, very good sir."

"And tell the bartender not to try that again."

Pamela tried to be bright for him. "How was your trip?" she asked, and for a while he was amusing about Pittsburgh.

"The holy soot still drifts down," he said, "a benediction which in due course turns green. The Pittsburgh grandees and we lesser tycoons are resigned to gray dinner shirts. Mr. Mellon employs three shifts of cleaning women to keep up with it."

"Did the flood do a lot of damage?"

"It's pretty well cleaned up by now, thanks to the WPA. Your brother's boss moved fast. But the Golden Triangle was completely underwater for a while. Sewickley Heights stayed dry, but Mother's still complaining about having to do without electricity so long and boiling her drinking water."

The waiter brought him another scotch and he gulped it down.

"It must have been frightening for her," Pamela said.

"Mother frightened?" He gave a harsh laugh. "She's made of steel. Some day I'm going to—" He broke off.

"Going to what?"

"Nothing. If only she didn't control the damn purse strings. Waiter, get me another drink. Put some more ice in it this time. What the hell happened to our steaks?"

"On the way, sir."

When he drained his third drink and ordered another, she said, "Peter, you shouldn't drink so much when you're in this mood."

"Don't you start giving me orders, too!" he flared.

"I'm not—"

"I've had enough of that over the weekend."

"Peter, please . . ."

His face was dark. "Mother's counterattacking, y'see. After her little talk with Uncle Bertie. I knew he'd get to her. I was counting on it."

"Peter, I don't understand what you're talking about."

"She's decided she'd better marry me off right away. All of a sudden she's pushing the Burrage sisters off on me, she doesn't care which one, the Schenley Park Burrages, after all the years she's been campaigning for me to marry into the Leeds or Frick families. Or the Morrisons or the Peacocks. Or the Moores or the Phippses. But now, all of a sudden, the Burrages are good enough, and God knows they're available, especially the younger one, with every fellow under thirty-five at the club having a pretty good idea of why she was packed off to Switzerland the year the golf pro and four of the caddies were fired. So somehow on less than a week's notice Mother managed to throw together a garden party so the sisters could display their wares to me, their well-known wares, if only Mother knew it."

Pamela was so angry she could barely speak. But she kept a dazzling smile in place as she said, "Is that what you brought me here to tell me? Well, I hope you'll be very happy with your Burrage sister. Whichever one."

He reached across the table for her wrist, knocking his glass over, and Pamela realized that he had been drinking before he picked her up.

"I don't want to marry a Burrage sister!" he blurted. "You're the one I want to marry. If only . . ."

Pamela worked her wrist free as gently as she could. Peter slumped morosely over his plate, his head drooping. The waiter hurried over and mopped up the spilled drink. Fortunately it had been down to the ice cubes.

It was not a proposal, and Pamela was not going to treat it as one. "That's very nice, Peter," she said briskly, "but your steak's getting cold." She picked up her knife and fork and sliced off a small, manageable piece of her own filet and chewed it with simulated appetite.

Peter's head snapped up. The dark, handsome face stared at her with the intensity of a Coptic portrait. "I'll work on it," he said. "You'll have to meet her, there's no getting around that, but not yet. Eventually she'll have to agree to see you, I promise you!"

All of a sudden Pamela realized that Peter was a coward.

He had been afraid to tell his mother about her. That had been the reason for the pictures in the papers, the gossip-column items he had encouraged, the provocative visit to Uncle Bertram. He had been waving a flag in front of his mother that she couldn't ignore.

"That's all right, Peter," she said gently. "No promises necessary."

Peter straightened in his seat, cheerful and charming again. "You'll see," he said. "The first thing I'm going to do is show her that I don't need her. She knows there's a nice little string of Missouri weeklies I want to buy, but I'm not going to crawl to her for the capital. I can raise enough of the missing cash by selling the *Wanderlust*. The damn thing's a white elephant anyway, in this day and age. Flying's the way to get places fast now!"

The next day he sent her a pair of diamond earrings. They arrived at her office by messenger, just after lunch. A card inside read: *For my patient Pamela . . . love, Peter*. It was as close to an engagement ring as he could manage. Pamela could not make herself commit the cruelty of sending them back. She wrapped them up again and put them away for later.

"All packed, Lieutenant?" Brad said, poking his head through the door.

The army officer with Gordon's face finished tying up the bedding roll and turned to face him. "Just about," he said.

Brad tried not to stare too obviously at this trim, fit stranger who stood there so smartly in the store-fresh uniform with the shiny new gold bars pinned to the tunic. Gordon had filled out nicely, with solid muscle and a boxer's shoulders. He was not quite as tall as Brad, but he held himself straighter. The cropped sandy hair was a bit darker than before, the pale blue eyes clear and steady and confident. It was hard to believe this was the same solemn kid he had left behind in

Beulah, still outgrowing that last despised pair of corduroy knickers.

"Pamela and Peter are waiting at the Thayer. Peter's going to take us all to dinner in New York to celebrate."

Gordon frowned. "I couldn't let—"

"Stow that, Gordie," Brad said. "You can unbend enough to accept Peter's hospitality. Give the poor guy a break. He feels a little out of place here among all—" Brad paused. "—us close-knit Sinclairs, and he wants to do something to impress his girl friend. Anyway, he's practically a relative."

"Okay, Brad," Gordon said. "You're right."

"Your hop date's invited, too, of course. Nellie, was that her name? We didn't have much of a chance to get acquainted last night. Sally said to tell you that she thinks Nellie's a knockout. She said you made a very handsome couple at the graduation ball."

"Nellie won't be coming," Gordon said stiffly.

"I thought she was your one-and-only. Your O.A.O.—isn't that what you call them here? I notice you're not wearing your class ring today."

Gordon glanced involuntarily at his hand, then put it behind his back. "No, Nellie and I don't have any sort of an understanding."

"Well, Peter will be disappointed, and I know Sally will. She lives here on the post with her father, doesn't she? Why don't you run over there and—"

"I said no."

Brad raised an eyebrow. "Oh, sorry. Well, we'd better get going."

"Just a minute, Brad."

Gordon went to his footlocker and took out a small, elaborately carved wooden box. It was an unusual little thing, no larger than a pencil case, but painstakingly decorated with whittled stars, hearts, and birds; Brad had never seen anything like it among Gordon's boyhood possessions. Gordon slid the lid open and took out some folded bills.

"Here's your three hundred dollars."

"What are you talking about?"

Gordon stood there, stubbornly holding out the money. "The three-hundred-dollar advance on uniforms and equipment. I couldn't get into the Point without it, remember? Judge Tanner said it came from you."

"It was a long time ago, Gordie. Forget it."

"No, Brad. Thanks, but no. I got through the Point on my own. I can't wipe out that anonymous letter that got Braithwaite kicked out, but I can wipe out a three-hundred-dollar debt."

"Oho, so that's it? You're still stewing after all this time. Christ, you're an elephant! What the hell makes you think I was the one who wrote that letter?"

"Who else could it have been?"

"Grow up, Gordie. You're still a clunkhead."

"Go on, Brad, deny it."

Brad studied the poised, controlled stranger in front of him and knew, with total certainty, that if he told Gordon that he had not sent the letter, Gordon would believe him, and that would be an end to the grudge. But he was angry.

"I'll be damned if I'll deny it!" he snapped, and took the money out of Gordon's hand. He stuffed it carelessly into his pocket. "Where the hell did you get three hundred bucks anyhow?"

"I saved it out of my cadet's pay. It's from my equipment fund. There's always a little left over after commutation of rations and the other deductions. They turn it over to us in cash when we get our commissions. It's supposed to defray the cost of the officer's uniforms and regulation gear we have to have."

Brad looked at Gordon's crisp new uniform and boots, and wondered how many changes were in the clothing roll. "How are you going to equip yourself now?"

"I'll get by. I won't need a winter overcoat or a lot of other stuff for a long time. I can pay for it little by little. A lot of fellows blow their whole equipment fund anyway in a big spending spree before they report to their first post." He suddenly grinned. "Why do you think so many army officers are in debt?"

Brad grinned too. "Gordon, you're a wonder."

"At least I chose infantry. The cavalry fellows have to buy a horse."

They faced one another, smiling. The tension between them had relaxed somewhat with Brad's acceptance of the money. Without putting anything into words, they arrived at a cautious truce now.

"Come on, Lieutenant. Let's not keep the others waiting."

"A bottle of your best Krug Private Cuvée," Peter said. The wine steward murmured assent and glided off to get it.

"I guess there's some money around again," Brad said, looking round the dance floor. "The last time I was at the Starlight Roof, the place was almost empty. And most of the few customers you *did* see were paid shills."

"Business is picking up," Peter agreed. "Don't expect me to give your man Roosevelt the credit, though."

On the bandstand, Wayne King's orchestra breezed smoothly through one of the week's popular hits, "You Started Me Dreaming."

A flow of people between the tables and dance floor kept the place lively.

"I didn't think they'd let me in without a full-dress uniform," Gordon said.

"Oh, they're still glad to get the business," Brad said. "See, there's a couple of fellows there without dinner jackets."

The wine waiter arrived with the champagne. They all made little festive appreciative noises while he popped the cork and poured a sample for Peter. Peter pronounced it all right and proposed a toast.

"Here's to Gordon and his new career. By God, the country's safe now!"

They clinked glasses and sipped. "Thank you, sir," Gordon said.

"I thought you didn't drink, Gordie," Brad said.

"I can drink now," Gordon said. "I'm not a cadet anymore."

Peter stared at Gordon in mild astonishment. "Do you mean to say that you never took a drink in all the time you were a cadet? Not even when you were off post on a weekend pass?"

"Gordon's very principled," Brad said dryly.

Pamela said quickly, "I'll never forget Gordon's first furlough. His *only* furlough, actually. That one summer they have off before graduation. Gordon was nearby, in Maryland, visiting the boy who had been his roommate. Hibbert. He had transferred to another school, isn't that right, Gordon? The Hibberts invited me out too, for the weekend, so I could spend some time with Gordon. Well, Mr. Hibbert poured a glass of wine for me and asked Gordon to pass it. And Gordon said he was sorry but he couldn't. Because he had given his word that when he was off the post he not only would abstain himself, but wouldn't even *handle* alcohol."

"Isn't that a little *too* scrupulous?" Peter said. "In a social situation?"

Gordon's gaze was steady. "When you make a bargain, you're supposed to stick to it."

Sally giggled. "Well, you're released from your vows now. Pour him another drink, Peter, and I'll pass it."

Peter was noticing the crossed rifles on Gordon's lapels. "How come you picked infantry, Gordon? You were in the top ten of your graduating class, weren't you? You could have picked the engineers. Isn't that supposed to be the big plum?"

"Infantry gave me my best chance at the assignment I wanted."

"Gordon's going to China," Pamela said.

"I've been assigned to the Fifteenth Infantry in Tientsin," Gordon said.

Sally waved an empty glass at Peter for more champagne. "Gordon actually speaks *Chinese!* Brad told me. Isn't that amazin'?" Her southern accent was starting to come out.

"A little," Gordon said. "Just the rudiments. My accent's no good. The army's going to send me to language school on the West Coast to brush up before I ship out."

"But how did you learn Chinese?" Peter said. "I thought that French and Spanish were the only languages taught at the Point."

"Oh, I had to study French and Spanish, too," Gordon said. "I read up on Chinese in my spare time. On my weekend passes I used to go over to Newburgh. I made friends with a Chinese laundryman and his family there. I used to practice with them. They were very nice to me."

"Spare time?" Peter said. "I thought you fellows didn't *have* any spare time at West Point."

"Gordon always was perseverant," Brad said, helping himself to another glass of champagne. "Not like the rest of us drones. Isn't that so, Gordie?"

"Well he *was!*" Pamela said. "When he was a small boy, he made his own telescope from directions in some boys' magazine. He spent *months* grinding the lens. Then he learned the names of all the stars."

"Say something in Chinese, Gordon," Sally coaxed.

Gordon hesitated. *"Wuh pu shih chung-gwuh-jen, wuh chung-wun shwe-duh,"* he said in a singsong tone. "That means, 'I'm not Chinese and I don't speak Chinese very well.' "

Sally clapped her hands in delight. "He sounds just like a real Chink!"

"I'm impressed," Peter said. "You've worked hard at it. What started you off?"

"I know someone in the Fifteenth Infantry," Gordon said. "Joe Stilwell. He was ahead of me at the Point. I might not have made it through plebe year if it hadn't been for something he did." Gordon looked down at his hands. They were calloused and competent looking, and Pamela noticed for the first time that there were scars across the knuckles. "His father, Colonel Stilwell, the one they call Vinegar Joe, is military attaché in Peiping. He just got appointed last year. Tientsin's only about eighty miles downriver from Peiping. I'm hoping to get a chance to meet the colonel. He sounds like a very unusual man."

"But why on earth would you want to bury yourself in a godforsaken place like China? Your career's just starting. The big things are happening in Europe. We'll have war there in five or six years, if Hitler and Mussolini keep on the way they're going."

"Sir," Gordon said respectfully, "big things are happening in China, too. Only we're not paying attention to them in this country. Japan wants China, all of it. They're not going to be satisfied with Manchuria and the northern provinces. When the war starts, it'll start there."

"And promotions for career officers will bloom," Brad murmured.

Gordon flushed. "I'm not thinking about that part of it."

"Let the Japs try to swallow China if they can," Peter said. "No one's ever been able to do it. American interests aren't involved. Less than one percent of our foreign investments are there."

"Sir, British interests are involved. Very much so. When war comes, we won't be able to keep from getting drawn into it."

"Since when have you become a global thinker, Gordie?" Brad said. He sounded amused.

Gordon stood his ground. "The Japanese are waking up a dragon," he said. "They went too far with their ultimatum to General Sung that the northern provinces declare their independence of Nanking and set up a phony 'autonomous' region—under Japanese control. That's what caused the student riots in Peiping last December. The Chinese are turning into patriots at long last."

Peter tapped the edge of his glass with a fingernail. "China is a complicated mess. No one understands her. Why don't we just sit back and let things sort themselves out? We can do business just as well with the Japs as with the British."

Gordon shook his head decisively. "The United States has to get on top of the situation in Asia." He leaned forward. "Look here, just take the Communists, for one example."

"What about the Communists? They're just a guerrilla rabble, aren't they? Eventually Chiang Kai-shek will stamp them out."

"People in this country just don't understand what's going on in China," Gordon said. "Do you know that one of the great events in military history took place in China last year?"

"Last year?" Peter frowned. "Just the usual skirmishes, I'd say."

Gordon shook his head. "The Communists call it the Long March. There hasn't been anything like it in military history since Xenophon led the defeated Greek army out of Persia over two thousand years ago. They taught us about Xenophon in our tactics class at the Point, but they didn't tell us anything about the Long March. Mao and Chu, the Communist generals, broke out of Chiang's blockade and led ninety thousand men, women, and children, bag and baggage, across six thousand miles of some of the roughest country in the world. It took them a year. They crossed mountains, rivers, deserts. They had to fight Chiang's forces every step of the way. Only twenty thousand of them made it. They're holed up in Yenan now. Other Communist forces are joining them. Chiang can't touch them there. Sooner or later they'll come on out of Yenan, and then we'd better watch out."

"American policy's based on support of Chiang," Peter said.

Gordon said flatly, "If we don't make friends with the Chinese Communists, someday we'll have to fight them."

Sally pounded her glass on the table. "How about more champagne, Peter?"

"This round's on me," Brad said.

"Not on your life," Peter said. "Waiter!"

"What were you saying, Gordon?" Pamela said.

"I was just trying to get across—"

"Speaking of China, the China Clipper flights start this month," Peter said. "San Francisco to Shanghai—with the first leg nonstop to Hawaii. Think of that! A three-decker flying boat that travels at over a hundred fifty miles an hour! I guess the Atlantic isn't the only ocean you can cross by air now!"

"Gordon, would you dance with me, please?" Pamela said, sliding back her chair.

Gordon was beside her before she could get up. He led her onto the dance floor. Wayne King's orchestra was playing "It's Been So Long."

"Where did you ever learn to dance like that, Gordon?" Pamela said.

"They taught us at the Point. Along with table manners and the other social graces. I even know when and what to tip the butler at a private home."

"You've grown up, Gordie. I can't believe it."

He gave her the old, winning, Gordon smile: reluctant, then total. "I'm just any ordinary shavetail in this man's army."

"I'm glad to see that you and Brad are getting along again."

"It's no use staying sore at Brad. He's just Brad, that's all. Anyway, Sally's very nice. I wish I could see my little niece."

"Do you want to tell me what it was all about?"

"No. It's not important."

The orchestra swung into a slow waltz. Pamela let herself be carried along by Gordon. He was very strong and smooth. "Are you going to be stopping in Beulah on your way to the West Coast?"

"Yes."

"Write and let me know how Mother is. I speak to her on the phone every once in a while, but it's hard to tell. She's very calm and dreamy and vague, and I can never seem to get any definite information out of her. I don't think she hears half of what I say."

"I will. Now that I'm getting a lieutenant's pay, I'll be able to contribute a little something. You and Brad have been carrying the whole burden too long."

"Save your money, Gordie. At least till you get your first promotion."

He grinned. "That'll be a long time in this army. We're down to two thirds of authorized peacetime strength, and we're top-heavy with officers. There aren't even enough funds to hold maneuvers this year."

"I hope it stays that way. Take care of yourself in China, little brother."

"Don't worry, Sis."

"I'm sorry Nellie couldn't join us tonight."

She felt his shoulder stiffen under her draped hand. "It doesn't matter," he said.

"Is she someone . . . special?"

"I . . ."

"You'd rather not talk about it?"

"No."

After another turn around the floor, Gordon said, "Are you and Peter serious?"

"Do you like him?"

"He seems like an all-right guy. He's used to having people listen to him, isn't he? He must be an important man."

She laughed. "Not very *very*. Not yet. But he will be, if I know Peter. Serious? I don't know. We'll just have to wait and see."

"Well, in case I'm stuck in China when the big day comes, best wishes, Sis."

"Thank you." She disengaged her arms. "We'd better go back to the table."

When they sat down, Peter was arguing with Brad. "Alf Landon's going to give your man a fight in November, and I'll give you fair warning, my papers are going to do all they can to help. 'Get off the rocks with Landon and Knox,' that's the line we're taking. Admit it, his acceptance speech in Topeka Thursday struck all the right notes."

"Struck them with a dull thud," Brad said. "He even stepped on his own applause. Ickes said, 'If that's the best Landon can do, the Democratic Campaign Committee ought to spend all the money it can raise to send him out to make speeches.'"

"Thank God you're back!" Sally said to Pamela. "They're talking politics again!"

"Let's order," Peter said. "Then we can take Gordon nightclubbing. How about taking in the Folies des Femmes, Gordon? It'll be your last chance to fill up on the sight of American girls this side of the Pacific."

They ended up in a small jazz club in Harlem, where Sally had insisted they hear a clarinet player named Mezz Mezzrow she had discovered on a new record she had just bought. "He's a white boy," she said, "but he blows colored." They were sitting in a dank, smoky cellar room, listening to the band and drinking watered whiskey, when a newsboy came in, making the rounds of the tables.

"Here, boy, I'll take one of those," Peter said. He turned to the others and said, "There might be something new on the Louis-Schmeling fight."

Sally was working on Gordon. "Now don't be an old silly! You don't have to report on the coast for thirty days, and you can't spend *all* that time in Iowa. From what I hear about your uncle Elroy, he'll begrudge you the crumbs on your plate. Why don't you come down to Washington and spend at least a few days with us? Get acquainted all over again."

"Well . . ." Gordon said, weakening.

"Then it's settled!"

"Is that the magazine section?" Pamela said to Peter.

"Yes, you want to have a look at it?" Peter said, passing it over. She was not quick enough to keep Gordon from seeing the cover. "Just a minute, Sis," he frowned.

He took the Sunday supplement from her. The cover page was a stark black-and-white photo of a huge-eyed young girl in a threadbare shift holding a tiny wrinkled infant wrapped in what looked like a piece of burlap sack. The caption read *Migrant Madonna*.

"It's Junie!" he said.

He leafed rapidly through the supplement, looking for the story. There were pictures of the dust storms, of fleeing Okies, of the wretched migrant camps.

"There's nothing about her," Gordon said. "It just says the cover photo is of an unknown mother and child in a cotton camp."

"Listen, Gordie . . ." Brad said.

"You can do something, Brad," Gordon appealed. "You're in the government. Trace the photo, find out where she is."

"He already tried," Pamela said.

"Tried?"

"Last summer. She's gone, no one knows where."

Gordon looked at Brad with dawning horror. "You knew about this last *summer,* and you didn't do anything about it?"

"The picture was already old when I found it in the files," Brad said wearily.

"He went all the way to Arizona trying to get more information, Gordon," Pamela said.

Gordon wasn't listening to her. "You could at least have kept the picture from being printed in the Sunday magazine!" he flung at Brad. "Do you know what it will do to Mother when she sees this?"

Everyone at the table was deathly quiet. On the bandstand, a clarinet tootled the blues.

"The *Weekly* has a circulation in the millions," Brad said steadily. "That was the idea. If someone happens to recognize Junie and the paper does a follow-up—"

"You'll never change, will you, Brad?" Gordon said. "You'll do any rotten thing."

Peter looked from one face to the other. "What's this?" he said. "What's going on?"

Pamela gathered up her evening bag. "You'd better take us back to the hotel, Peter," she said. "I think the evening is over."

33

The Iowa countryside fled by the train window. Gordon peered through dusty glass at neat geometric cornfields, still a tender green, clustered red farm buildings, the isolated clumps of trees that had been preserved here and there, the small tidy towns that rose briefly from the flatness. It all looked fresh and strange. The last time he had ridden by here, it had been in a boxcar going in the opposite direction.

"Next stop Waterloo, soldier," the conductor said, leaning over him. "You change there for a local."

"Thank you, sir," Gordon said.

He tried to get interested in his magazine again, a copy of *Astounding Stories* that he had bought at the station in Chicago. The cover story was something called "The Shadow out of Time," about gigantic cones that had lived on the planet Earth millions of years before man. Gordon found it hard to make any sense out of it. He wished he had bought a western instead. He sighed and put the magazine down. He turned stoically back to the scenery, but a sudden blurred aluminum curtain filled the window—one of the new streamliners to Chicago flashing by. The Rocket train. It made the run from Des Moines in only six hours.

"Say, excuse me, are you finished with that?" a goggled adolescent across the aisle asked.

"Sure. Take it." Gordon handed the garish magazine across. The aluminum curtain whipped past. The landscape returned. Gordon folded his hands and thought about the graduation hop.

Nellie had been an absolute stunner in a powder-blue gown that had a sort of huge lacy divided collar whose wings draped to give the effect of little sleeves. From its decorous frills, her neck rose swanlike to a small perfect head of strawberry-blond hair, bobbed and tightly waved. Her mouth was a carefully drawn Cupid's bow. Gordon thought she looked exactly like a Pond's glamour girl. He tried not to gawk at her as he helped her into her wrap.

"You be sure to have her back right after the last dance, mister," Captain Wilson said with cold dislike at the door.

"Oh Daddy!" Nellie said.

"Yes sir," Gordon said evenly.

He didn't have much choice anyway. He was still a cadet until tomorrow, and the rules said he had forty-five minutes to escort his guest home and return to barracks.

From the open door, Captain Wilson watched them with the stiff, tight stance of a greyhound. He was unpromoted and bitter, and his prospects, in the depression-stalled army of 1936, were zero. He was still the terror of the new cadets, but to Gordon, who had put on his final inches of height, he seemed a diminished figure.

Once out of sight of the married officers' quarters, on the slope that led down to the main path, Nellie stopped by a tree and said, "Wait a minute. Hold my wrap."

Perplexed, Gordon did as she asked, and watched as she carefully peeled the Dutch Masters collar off the gown. It had been held in place by only a few loose stitches. The transformation left her shoulders bare and more of her bosom showing than Gordon found comfortable.

"Gloria Littlejohn helped me with it," Nellie said. "She's good at sewing anyway, poor old thing. She found some lace that matched the color exactly, and made that—that *bib!*—look like part of the gown. Daddy would have *died* if he'd seen the gown the way it was when I tried it on in the shop. He would have made me take it back." She giggled.

Gordon was appalled. "You mean you did that to fool your father?"

She misunderstood his meaning. "Yes," she said, pleased with her cleverness. "But don't worry, he'll never know. I'll go to my room with my wrap on, and Old Glory can sew it back on for me before the next time I wear it."

"But Nellie, don't you think—"

"Here, fold it up and put it in your pocket for me."

After a moment's hesitation, he took the piece of lace from her and helped her back on with her wrap. They continued on toward Cullum Hall. Other couples were coming by foot down Thayer Road, and a steady, slow parade of taxicabs threaded its way through the pedestrian traffic. The grounds were full of strolling visitors, enjoying the fine summer evening and perhaps hoping to catch sight of a son, or a daughter's fiancé, in the glittering full dress uniform and white gloves that were obligatory for this climactic social event of June Week.

"Nellie, before we go in—"

"Not now, Gordon. Look, there's that stuck-up Barbara Hazlet *hanging* on Freddie Baylor's arm. She thinks she's snared him, while I happen to know that he's already proposed to his old sweetheart in Texas, who couldn't come east for the hop. Look at that old thing she's wearing! She wore it to the Christmas hop and got her mother to dye it and change the trim."

Gordon located Baylor, some distance ahead in the flow of people who were converging on Cullum Hall. He was the class football hero, one of the oversize A Company flankers, and a gold-star cadet. Baylor had driven him to despair earlier in the term, when Gordon had discovered that he was regularly escorting Nellie to the Saturday-evening hops. But he no longer felt any resentment. He could afford to be magnanimous now that Nellie was practically his own best girl.

Persistence had paid off. After winning Nellie as his drag at a couple of the tea hops at the Thayer, he had successfully monopolized her for every event since Easter, earning the enmity of Captain Wilson and the good-natured gibes of his classmates, who pretended to believe that wooing Nellie was the source of Gordon's high math honors. Tonight, he hoped to get Nellie to accept his class ring and come to some sort of formal understanding with him. Not, of course, to agree to wait for him during his tour of duty in China—you couldn't expect a high-spirited girl like Nellie to deprive herself of the social fling—but perhaps to think about resuming things seriously with him when he got back in two or three years.

"Nellie . . ." he began again, feeling in his pocket for the heavy gold ring.

"Oh, look, Gordon, is that someone waving to us from that *Rolls-Royce?*"

He turned his head and saw a long black limousine inching its way through the throng. A slender white feminine arm was thrust through a window, waving. The chauffeur skillfully maneuvered his way through the flow and docked at the curb next to them.

"How y'all, Gordon," squealed Brad's wife, Sally. "My goodness, aren't you tall! I never would have recongized you, but Pamela spotted you right away!"

Pamela smiled at him. "Well, we made it for your graduation, Gordie. Peter and I were here for the parade this afternoon, but we couldn't find you afterward in all that confusion, and then we had to leave to pick Sally and Brad up at Penn Station."

Brad, sitting beside the chauffeur, twisted round negligently. "Peter said he couldn't let us ride the rattler. Sally and I were supposed to take the sleeper last night, but Sally couldn't bring herself to trust Melissa's new nurse till today."

The dark, theatrically handsome man sitting between Sally and Pamela said, "Well, so you're Gordon."

Pamela said, "Excuse me, this is Peter Bainbridge."

"And who is that gorgeous girl?" Sally said.

Gordon peeled off a glove and acknowledged Peter with a handshake, then performed introductions all around. Nellie was fluttery and coy with Brad and Peter, wide-eyed and smiley and a bit inattentive with the women while she kept casting sidelong glances at Peter. Gordon found her performance entrancing. He couldn't help feeling smug about the way an important-looking older man like Peter responded to Nellie's allure.

"We'll see you tomorrow at the ceremonies, Gordie," Brad said. "I wish we'd gotten here soon enough to see you get your honor stars and the boxing and marksmanship trophies. It's going to be a proud moment for us to see you get your commission."

Gordon looked at Brad's face suspiciously, but he could see no sign of levity. "Thanks, Brad," he said stiffly.

"We'd better let you two go now," Peter Bainbridge said. "I think I hear the orchestra warming up in there."

"Have a good time, kids," Pamela said.

"Me, I'm for a cold martini and a hot bath after that train ride," Sally said. "Then bed for my aching bones."

"Not before I take you all to dinner," Peter said. "I know a nice inn near Tarrytown; we won't have to go all the way into the city."

They drove off with a flurry of waved good-byes. Nellie said: "Your sister's very pretty. Was that her boy friend?"

"I don't know. I guess so."

"He must be rich, riding around in a Rolls."

Gordon was uncomfortable. "I don't know. He owns some newspapers."

"You never talk about your brother."

"There's not much to say. He works in Washington."

"His wife looks like Society. Is she?"

Gordon said reluctantly, "I guess some people would say that."

He wished she would change the subject. As an army brat, Nellie was too keenly conscious of caste—on and off the post. From the time she had been a little girl, she had always been aware of which officer's wife was entitled to pour the tea at any given function and which to pour the coffee; and exactly when a reigning queen bee had been displaced by some newcomer whose husband, though he might have identical rank, held a commission that happened to be dated a few weeks—or days—earlier.

The trouble was that since her mother's death when Nellie had been only eight, Nellie had enjoyed a blurred status at the posts Captain Wilson had been assigned to. Her father—though he lived in married officers' quarters because of her—was accorded some of the free-floating social mobility of a few of the more presentable bachelor officers. He could fill in at bridge simply because he was good at bridge, or be used as a safe extra man to fill out a dinner party. Captain Wilson's little girl was no threat to any of the army wives, no matter how competitive. She could play with anyone, and with her finely tuned sense of precedence, she usually chose to play with children of the higher-ranking officers. Certainly no colonel's or brigadier's wife wanted to be unkind to the orphaned daughter of poor Captain Wilson, and have it commented on. But children themselves are cruel little snobs. More than once Nellie had been put in her place for presuming too much on a friendship. She recounted these childhood snubs to Gordon as if they had just happened, often with a malicious comment about how the girl in question had received her own comeuppance in the form of a father's stalled career or a mother's reputation for alcoholism. Or a flat chest. Or thick ankles. Or pimples.

"No, really, she is, isn't she, Gordon? I mean from a wealthy family?"

"That stuff isn't important. They just live on Brad's salary."

She squeezed Gordon's arm. "I didn't realize you came from such a prominent family."

"We're just ordinary." The warmth in her voice encouraged him. He fumbled in his pocket for the ring again. "Listen, Nellie, there's something I want to—"

Her eyes flew to the marbled entrance of Cullum Hall. "We'd better go in. We don't want to be the last."

He got his chance to talk to her seriously after the third dance. He had left her waiting under the brooding portrait of General Sheridan while he went to fetch her a glass of punch from the refreshment table. When he returned, she was in conversation with Freddie Baylor. The two of them were laughing about something together.

" 'Lo, Sinclair," Baylor said as he drew close. "You're looking spoony tonight."

"Only by comparison with you engineers, Baylor."

"All infantry are fungoids."

"Double for engineers."

Baylor scratched his handsome face. "I hear you've been assigned to China."

"That's right."

"Not for me. You poor sap. While you're scratching Chinese fleas, I'll be living the good life stateside at some cushy billet, building dams for the Public Works Administration. But don't worry, Sinclair. I'll keep the girls warm for you."

Gordon moved close to Nellie. "I think the orchestra's ready to start up again."

Baylor looked around. "Where's my drag? She spends half her time in the powder room, primping. She needs it." He laughed. "Not like you, Nellie. There she is now. I better go over and make her happy."

Baylor walked away. Gordon thought that at least Baylor had proved himself to be pretty much of a stinker to have made those remarks about his own drag, but when he looked at Nellie's face he could find nothing there to indicate that she shared his disapproval.

"What did he want?" he said.

"Oh, nothing. He just came over to say hello while he was waiting for Barbara."

The orchestra began a slow waltz. There was a rustling movement of gowns and white legs toward the dance floor. The lights began to dim and the colored spotlight up above began to play over the ballroom. Nellie put down her glass.

Gordon said quickly, before it was too late, "Let's sit this one out."

"All right. I could use a smoke."

Nellie didn't much like the waltzes. Gordon had noticed that. Perhaps it was because they darkened the hall then. You couldn't be seen very well on the floor. It changed the dance from a public event to several hundred separate, intimate universes.

Gordon and Nellie joined the trickle of other couples climbing the broad marble staircase leading to the balcony. You could get a romantic view of the Hudson from there, and smoking was allowed.

Gordon found a semiprivate spot around the corner by one of the antique stone mortars and felt in his pocket for the crumpled pack of Camels he carried to be sociable. He didn't smoke much himself. He lit one for Nellie, then himself.

She coughed. "These're stale."

"Sorry."

They listened to the waltz sounds coming from below and gazed side by side at the broad river at the foot of the granite cliffs. Nellie smoked in quick nervous puffs, keeping the cigarette displayed, and chattered about the June Week receptions she had been invited to. Gordon wished he had the nerve to try for a kiss. Others on the balcony, where screened by pillars or alcoves, were doing that. But Nellie had very definite ideas about the right time and place. Gordon knew that after the dance he would be allowed a half hour of kissing and light petting on Flirtation Walk if Nellie was in a good mood, and an all-out open-mouth good-night kiss on Captain Wilson's doorstep. But here on the balcony at Cullum Hall, he was expected to be sort of a dummy in dress whites, there to light her cigarettes, lend his arm, and generally to help her show off her new gown.

"Listen, Nellie, I've got something to ask you," he said.

She interrupted her account of the superintendent's tea to face him. Gordon felt a sudden pang at her beauty. Her hair glinted a red-gold from the muted light streaming through the tall doors. Her bare shoulders and the swelling hint of her bosom were a creamy expanse, mysterious in the shadows. The chinaware face gave him a baby pout.

"My goodness, don't you look serious."

"I don't know how long I'll be gone, Nellie. Quite a while, anyway. But—look here, would you wear my class ring?"

He blurted the last words just as he succeeded in working the ring from the recesses of his pocket. He held it out somewhat more brusquely than he had intended. Her eyes darted from the ring to his face.

"Oh, Gordon, that's very sweet of you."

"Will you?"

"I'd love to."

He took her hand awkwardly and started to draw it toward him. He felt a slight resistance.

"But not now. It's too big for my finger, and besides it wouldn't look right with this bracelet. I'll keep it for you."

She took the ring deftly from him and dropped it into her little beaded bag where it landed among the miscellany with a small clink.

"I'll write to you from Tientsin," Gordon said. "Will you answer?"

"Of course I will."

He broke into a relieved grin. "I'll send you something from China. A fan."

"Oh, Gordon, would you send me some Chinese lacquerware instead? Like those things Major Holbrook and his wife have displayed on their mantel from when they were stationed in Nanking?"

Gordon had no idea how much Chinese lacquerware cost, but he said, "You bet."

She cocked her head. "That sounds like the last waltz encore. We better go down."

For the fourth dance, Gordon was on Gloria Littlejohn's card. The cadet hostess knew that Gordon could always be depended on to do his share with the unpopular girls, and not humiliate them by disappearing into the men's room. For the fourth dance, Gordon had craftily arranged for his roommate, Pease, to stand guard over Nellie. "Be glad to, old son," Pease had said. "It's better than dancing with Old Glory."

The number was a slow fox-trot. Gloria clutched at Gordon and tried to lead him. "You're taller than me now, Gordon," she said. "You've turned into quite the handsome young man. I watched you grow up here."

"I was always taller than you," he lied gallantly. Gloria was five feet ten without heels, and Gordon had put on three inches at the Point, to top out at six feet one. He didn't want to guess how old she was. There couldn't be too many of these dances left for her.

"I still remember you at your first hop, Plebe Christmas. What an elephant you were! Your dancing's improved a lot."

She almost pulled him off balance. He recovered with an extra step and got back into the rhythm.

"You were under an awful cloud that fall," she went on. "All those demerits! Nobody expected you to make it past January. My father was awfully glad when you straightened out. He said you had the makings of a fine officer."

Gordon was surprised. He had thought that Major Littlejohn, the hanging judge who presided over the bat board, had it in for him.

Gloria gave him a toothy grimace. "You were stuck on Nellie even then, weren't you?"

He avoided a direct answer when Gloria steered them into a collision with another couple. Gordon apologized and by main force pulled Gloria back into step without making them look too bad.

"This is my last cadet hop," she said suddenly. "I'm getting too old and ridiculous. I know what they call me. Old Glory. This year the cadet hostess paired me up with a poor Filipino cadet who couldn't get a date, and he comes up to my chest and I'm embarrassing him. He spent the last dance in the men's room. Next year I'll offer myself as a chaperone and the hostess will be grateful."

Gordon was taken utterly by surprise. "Gloria, I think you're swell, really I do, and I've always enjoyed dancing with you," he said feebly.

She gave him a tired smile. "Don't worry about me, Gordon. I'll grow into my spinsterhood gracefully."

She was leading again, and he was tugged off balance and half turned around. But not before he had seen Nellie dancing with Freddie Baylor.

"You did that on purpose," he said.

"Well, you can't say I didn't try," she sighed.

"Why?"

"There was no point in your getting upset. Gordon, Nellie isn't worth it, really she isn't."

"But you're her friend."

"I suppose you could call it that. I do her favors. I sew for her and I tell fibs for her and I get her invited to the superintendent's teas. And I keep her boy friends from bumping into one another."

"I don't want to hear any more."

"Poor Gordon. Do you think I don't know how to dance properly? I've had enough practice."

"You don't know what you're talking about. Anyway, it doesn't matter. Baylor just got himself engaged to his girl friend in Texas."

"Yes, and didn't that make Nellie mad!" For a moment he thought he saw malice on her plain and uncombative face. "That was when she broke her date for the graduation hop with him. By the time she changed her mind again, Barbara Hazlet was glued to him."

"That's not true! Nellie promised more than two months ago to go to graduation hop with me!"

"Never mind, Gordon," she said tiredly. "Have it your own way."

They finished the fox-trot without further conversation. When the music stopped, he looked around for the Filipino. "I don't see your escort," he said.

"It doesn't matter, Gordon," she said. "Just take me back to the battle of Gettysburg."

He left her standing under the frieze. "I'll see if I can find your runt in the men's room," he said. "I'm going to burn his ears."

"Don't bother." She smiled wanly at him. "Thanks for the dance, Gordon. Good luck in China."

On his way to look for Nellie, he saw Pease, who was just taking his leave of a miffed-looking Barbara Hazlet at one of the portrait rendezvous spots. Before he could speak, Pease said, "Don't get sore at *me,* chum. There wasn't anything I could do."

He found Nellie at their meeting place under the Sheridan portrait, talking animatedly to a grinning Baylor. When they saw him coming, she said something to Baylor, who left hurriedly in the other direction. Gordon led Nellie grimly onto the dance floor when the music began.

They danced in silence for a few minutes, then Gordon said, "He wasn't on your hop card."

"I asked your lead-footed friend Pease if he'd trade with Freddie for one dance. Oh, Gordon, stop scowling! We just wanted to have one last dance for old times' sake. He's going to Oregon to build that dam, and I'll probably never see him again."

"I'm going to China."

"I know." Her manner softened. "Oh, Gordon, let's not spoil tonight."

He felt like a scoundrel. "I'm sorry."

The next dance was another waltz, and the hall went dark for the colored spotlight, and Nellie pressed him to lay her cheek along his. He could feel her young breasts against his chest, and their pelvises touching, and his mouth went dry, and it was very hard to remember to keep his hand from sliding down and to keep his feet moving in the steps of the waltz.

After the "Auld Lang Syne," with the floor clogged with scores of couples who had stopped dancing to stand holding hands under the dim blue lights, with the sideline chatter stopped and tears coursing down dozens of cheeks, Nellie turned to Gordon with her face aglow and said, "Oh, Gordon, this part is always so beautiful!"

It was over, Gordon realized with a sudden bittersweet sadness. Tomorrow noon he would no longer be a cadet. The West Point years and what they had turned him into would be behind him forever. He would walk out of this place as an officer in the United States Army. He and Pease and the other Firsts. And a new class of Mister Dumbjohns and Mister Ducrots would take their place.

But he didn't know how to express his feelings in words to Nellie, so he nodded gravely and said, "It's nice. Something to remember."

"Get my wrap, Gordon," Nellie said. "Let's get out of here before the crush." She seemed strangely excited.

On his way to the cloakroom, Gordon caught a glimpse through the dissolving crowd of Gloria Littlejohn with her Filipino cadet. His name was Aquilar or something like that, Gordon remembered, and inside of thirty days he would probably be reporting with his shiny new commission to General MacArthur's headquarters in Manila. He looked short and squat and uncomfortable standing next to Gloria, who was slouching as usual to try to disguise her gangling height. Gordon wondered if Aquilar had any inkling that he was ending a tradition at the Point—that he had the distinction of being the last senior cadet to escort Old Glory to a graduation hop.

As he helped Nellie on with her wrap, his hands shook. She noticed and whispered, "Come on."

The couples strolling along the path above the river avoided one another's eyes. Technically they weren't supposed to be here after dark. But on this special night the rules were stretched; an officer they passed strode by with clinking saber and tinkling spurs and pretended not to see them.

Nellie and Gordon found their special spot, the ruins of an old redoubt that contained the rusted remains of an old Revolutionary War cannon. It was overgrown with vegetation and partially screened from the walkway. Once Gordon had noticed a used condom lying in the grass and had quickly scuffed it into the ground with his heel, hoping Nellie hadn't seen it.

"Listen," she said, tilting her head. "You can hear music from the gymnasium. The Seconds' hop hasn't broken up yet. It must still be early."

"I still have to be back for lights out in—" He glanced at his watch. "—forty-one minutes."

"Oh, you're such a stick, Gordon!" she said impatiently. "This is the last night till graduation. What do you care if you get a couple of silly demerits?"

Gordon said nothing. He remembered a cadet named Jensen who, two years before, had been booted out of the Point only a week before graduation. Jensen lost his degree and his army commission for using "profane and improper language," a seven-demerit offense, to the Tac who put him on report for returning from a hop five minutes late, a five-demerit offense. Jensen had already been in trouble, and the twelve demerits had tipped the balance. The Tac he had sworn at had been Captain Wilson.

He reached for Nellie, but she twisted away and said, "My, what a warm night! Don't you think it's warm, Gordon?" in the high and artificial tone he thought of as her "party voice." Nellie would never let him kiss her until he had put in a few minutes of required small talk. She would gab on airily almost until the moment their lips made contact, and continue during their cigarette breaks, as though nothing were happening between them. Gordon had been trained well in this pretend game.

Afterward he could never remember what he had said that night. But presently her lips fastened greedily on his, and her mouth was open almost immediately instead of waiting until the later stages of the ritual. She put his hand impatiently on her breast and held it there; usually he was expected to slide his hand into place by imperceptible degrees. She was breathing hard.

"Nellie . . ." he began.

"Don't talk, Gordon," she whispered.

Her eyes were squeezed shut. She rubbed her body against his like a cat, brushing against his maleness. Gordon suppressed a groan.

And now she allowed him a further, undreamed of, liberty. She took his sweating hand and thrust it into the low neckline of her gown. It was the first time he had felt her bare flesh. His fingers began an exploration but she seized his wrist to keep his hand immobile.

The pressure of her lower body against his was growing unbearable. He stood a step backward to give himself a moment's relief, and his heel kicked her handbag where she had left it on the ground. There was a slight declivity there and the tinkling contents spilled out onto the grass.

Gordon broke free and stooped to retrieve them. Nellie's eyes flew open in annoyance. Gordon started an apology, and it stuck in his throat.

Two gold class rings glinted in the moonlight amidst a jumble of keys, lipstick, compact, hairpins, and small change.

"Leave that alone," Nellie said quickly. She bent, holding the neckline of her gown up with one hand, and stuffed the things into her bag.

"Whose is it, Nellie?" he said. "Baylor's?"

"Oh, Gordon," she said crossly, "I hope you're not going to make a fuss. It's just something to remember him by. It doesn't *mean* anything."

"What about my ring? Doesn't that mean anything either?"

"What do you expect?" she spat. "You all go away, halfway around the world, and I'm still stuck here in this prison of a place! My father's tour here's been extended another two years, and I'm twenty, and I've never been anyplace interesting!"

"It's supposed to mean something," he said stubbornly. "You even said you'd write."

"Oh Gordon, you're so serious. Of course it means something. They *all* mean something, but if it will make you feel any better, yours is more important than Freddie's because I'm still a little mad at him for getting engaged."

She smiled at him indulgently.

"All? What do you mean?"

"Don't be so *dense!* I've got one for every year. Except the year before last. I got two that year, too. Now come on and don't spoil my June Week."

She half closed her eyes and tilted up her chin, waiting. She was breathing hard again, like an engine put into gear.

Gordon picked his white dress cap up from the cannon mount and put it back on his head. "Come on," he said. "Your father's waiting."

*   *   *

"Waterloo!" the conductor called from the front of the car. Gordon glanced out the window. Grain elevators and livestock pens crowded the track. People started to fill up the aisle. Gordon stood up.

"Do you want this back?" the kid with the magazine said.

"No, you can keep it."

He got his bedroll and footlocker down from the overhead rack and joined the movement toward the door.

34

Uncle Elroy was doing well. There was a new clapboard addition to the house and a brand-new Hudson Eight in the driveway. Through the screen door, Gordon could see a gleaming white electric refrigerator that had taken the place of the old oak icebox that he remembered.

"You come too late for dinner," Elroy said, probing his teeth with a wooden toothpick. "We're just finishing up."

"That's all right," Gordon said. "I don't want anything."

He could hear the rattle of dishes from the dining room. It was only about twenty past noon. Gordon had eaten nothing since the soggy sandwich he had wolfed down at the station in Chicago the evening before, but he didn't feel like sitting down at the table and having Elroy watch him put food in his mouth.

"I suppose your aunt Ottilie could fix you a sandwich or something," Elroy said grudgingly.

"No, really, I'm not hungry," Gordon said. "I'll just go right on up to see my mother."

"Ain't fixing to stay long, are you?" Elroy said. "Ain't much room to spare in this old place, with Winthrop and Doris and the baby."

"I'll only be in Beulah a few days. I can stay at the cabin camp outside of town. It's not much of a walk."

Elroy's narrow features cautiously eased. "I guess you could sleep on the couch in the sunroom."

"The cabin camp'll be fine. Is she upstairs in her room?"

Elroy stood aside to let Gordon past. "Well, come on in and say hello to everybody first."

Gordon left his footlocker and bedroll on the porch and followed Elroy inside. A sallow girl in an apron was working at the kitchen sink. She gave Gordon a scared look and went back to her dishes. Elroy did not offer to introduce her. She would be the live-in maid that Pamela had mentioned. Pamela and Brad had recently started sending Elroy an extra six dollars a week to pay for the maid. Aunt Ottilie had insisted on it. With both of them making good money in Washington, she had said, they could well afford to hire someone to wait hand and foot on Mary Sinclair.

"Well, look at the soldier boy!" Winthrop said as he entered the dining room. "What are those things on your shoulders? Diaper pins?"

They were sitting around the remains of their noon dinner. Half a roast, a gravy boat, and a covered vegetable dish still sat on the table. Winthrop's plate hadn't been cleared away yet; he had just helped himself to another slice of roast beef.

"Through with that school, are you?" Aunt Ottilie sniffed.

"Yes," Gordon said.

"Can't be much of a living, being a soldier," she said.

The small puckered mouth and raisin eyes hadn't changed at all, but to Gordon she no longer seemed as formidable as she had when he was seventeen. "I get second lieutenant's pay," he said.

Behind him, he heard Elroy clear his throat and say, "We ain't putting him up. Says he wants to stay at the cabin camp."

Gordon's steady gaze brought a touch of color to Aunt Ottilie's pleated cheeks. "Since you're earning money, then, you can start contributing to your mother's upkeep," she snapped.

The maid came in with a tray and carried out the serving dishes and Winthrop's plate.

"That girl," Doris said. "Slow as molasses." She had put on weight since Gordon had last seen her. A puffy surrounding of flesh framed the remembered young face in the middle.

Winthrop nibbled with woodchuck aplomb at the last shreds of roast beef stuck in his teeth. "I don't have to get back right away. Slow day. My *Liberty* come this morning?"

"I didn't look for the mail," Doris said, not stirring.

"I'll get it," Elroy said. He rose hastily from the table. "You'd think that dang postman could get here before I leave for work. He was late last Thursday, too."

He hurried from the room. Elroy didn't like anyone to handle the mail before he had seen it, Gordon remembered.

The girl came in with apple pie and coffee, a glass of milk for Winthrop. She set out the plates, with a questioning sidelong look at Gordon standing by the sideboard. Aunt Ottilie did not ask him to sit down.

"Well, Landon's off and running," Winthrop said, helping himself to a large wedge of pie and a slice of cheese. "Looks like Brad won't be hanging on to that soft job in Washington much longer."

"Excuse me," Gordon said. "I think I'll go see my mother."

He ran into Elroy by the staircase, putting the mail on the hall table. Elroy jumped when he saw him, and put something in his coat pocket.

"Is that my mother's *Ladies' Home Journal?*" Gordon said. "I'll take it up to her."

He reached out for the magazine. The June issue had a white cover with a picture of a bride. Brad and Pamela had reinstated all of Mary Sinclair's subscriptions as soon as they started earning money, but after the first year, Gordon had taken over the renewal of the *Journal* each Christmas. It was only a dollar, and the corps treasurer had allowed him that out of his boodle money.

"Don't grab!" Elroy said. He recovered his composure and said, "Here, take it."

"Is there anything else for her?"

"No. And you can tell her that brother of yours is late with his check again."

Gordon looked his uncle over coldly and saw a skinny potbellied man who had never learned to stand up straight. The corps made you see people that way. He took the magazine from him and started up the stairs.

Elroy stared in fear at the departing back of the man in uniform. He was a big one, all right. And with that army way about him. As if he expected everybody to snap to attention. As if he thought the Lord had put him in charge.

Thank the Lord, he was only going to stay in town a few days. He'd be hanging around the house all day. Suppose the mail were late again, and he got to it first. Elroy broke out into a cold sweat.

Furtively he took the postcard out of his pocket. He thought the fool girl had finally given up and stopped writing them, but here, after a seven-month gap, was another one.

The postmark was someplace in California. The tinted scene on the front was an orange grove, with a movie starlet in shorts and a sinful top that uncovered her midriff. Elroy licked his dry lips and turned it over.

Dear Mother,
We are living in a real house now and have settled down for a
while. With all this war talk lately and jobs opening up, Floyd
hopes to get a good job at one of the shipyards or the aircraft fac-
tory. Little Leander is two years old this month, would you be-
lieve it? He is very active, but he is a boy. Maybelle is 8 months
old now and a joy. I wish I had a picture to send you. And also it
looks like you will have a third grandchild by Thanksgiving. I
don't know how long we'll be at this address, so please write
soon. I am fine.
             Love,
             June Alice

Elroy tore the card in two and tore it across again, then put the pieces in his pocket until he could get rid of them.

"Praise the Lord," he muttered. Temptation had been removed from him, and no one would find out. He thumbed through the pages in his mind and found what he wanted in James. "Every man is tempted, when he is drawn away of his own lust, and enticed." So it was not his fault.

He went back into the dining room for his pie. The girl gave him one of those sidelong looks as she served him. No one else noticed it, but she couldn't fool him. It was the itch of the flesh, that's what it was. And after he had taken the shameless thing in and paid her good wages, and given the girl her own room in the attic.

He shoveled a forkful of apple pie into his mouth. He would have to pray with her, that was all there was to it. It would be a test for him, too. "Blessed is the man that endureth temptation," he recited in his mind, "for when he is tried, he shall receive the crown of life."

It was like being in their old house on Elm Street for a moment. The shades were half drawn, and in the dim filtered light Gordon could see the remembered flowered drapes, the tall chiffonier in front of whose tilted mirror his father had stood putting in his studs, his mother's dressing table with the French mirror and all the lotions arranged in a row, the massive carved bed from which, when he was a small boy, his mother had sometimes fed him a honey-dipped morsel from her tray.

And then his eyes adjusted to the light, and he saw that it was just a room in Uncle Elroy's house after all, with cheap stock molding and wallpaper that had been painted over. Against one wall, on a chipped console, stood stacks and stacks of old magazines gathering dust. A breakfast tray with an uneaten slice of toast had not yet been taken away.

"Hello, Mamma," Gordon said.

Mary Sinclair turned her head in the nest of pillows that was propping her up and said, "Gordon, is that you? Why are you wearing that suit?"

"Didn't you get my telegram, Mamma? I said I'd be passing through."

"Telegram?" She looked vague. "Yes, I suppose so. Yes, I definitely remember. Come on over and let me look at you."

Gordon approached the bed. His mother was sitting up in a silk bed jacket with a magazine across her lap. In the submarine light, she was as pale and beautiful as carved marble. She had not bothered to pin her hair up that morning, and it spilled in raven profusion to her shoulders. As he came closer, Gordon could see that it was shot through with strands of gray. Over the fine structure of her cheeks lay a delicate cobweb of microscopic wrinkles that he had never noticed before.

He bent to kiss her. Her hand groped for his with a hummingbird flutter. It felt warm and fragile in his grasp.

"You've been a very naughty boy," she scolded.

"Mother?"

"My children never come to see me." She gave a Desdemona sigh.

"They don't give furloughs to cadets, just weekend passes. Except for the summer furloughs for Seconds, and I didn't have the fare to Iowa then. Don't you remember, I explained it all in my letter?"

She stroked his cheek playfully with the feathery end of her sleeve. "Nonsense. You could have insisted."

Gordon said nothing.

"At least there's an excuse for your brother Bradford. I suppose he's very busy with his law work."

"Mother, Brad isn't actually a lawyer. He's—"

"I know, I know. It has something to do with Mr. Roosevelt. The legal department. He explained it all to me when he was here."

"Brad was here? When was that?"

She looked confused, then annoyed. "I don't know. Not very long ago. After he got married."

"That was two years ago."

She gave him a blinding smile. "Sally's a lovely girl. I have her picture. She keeps asking me to come to Washington for a visit. Perhaps I will. But not right away. It's so far."

Gordon cleared his throat. "Pamela sends her love."

"Yes, I spoke to her . . ." She furrowed her brow. "When was it that I spoke to her? She wanted me to have my own telephone put in, can you imagine that? Your uncle Elroy made such a fuss! Even though Pamela said she'd pay for it herself. But one telephone in a house is enough, don't you think? It would be—oh—so *distracting* to have one in my room."

Gordon said carefully, "I think Pamela's right."

Mary Sinclair laughed gaily. "Pamela always had modern ideas. I do wish she wouldn't work. But I suppose times change. A lot of nice girls do nowadays. It gives them something to do until they marry, and nobody thinks anything of it. Have you met Pamela's young man?"

"Yes."

"She sent me his picture from the society page. So I suppose he comes from a nice enough family. For Washington, anyway. Not New England stock, of course, like the Everetts and the Bradfords on your grandmother Quincy's side." She added hastily, "Not that there's anything wrong with the Sinclairs. Your father came from a fine family, even though they did arrive later, and don't you forget it."

"No, ma'am."

She rambled on: "He worked too hard. That was what killed him. Overwork. I always told him not to work so hard, but of course he wanted to provide a good life for us all. I hope you'll always remember that."

Gordon could not look at her. "Yes, Mother."

"What was I saying? Oh yes, your father. He looked so handsome in his uniform, going off to France. The whole town gave him a parade when he came back. We were all so proud! Of course you wouldn't remember. You were just a little baby. But I held you up and you waved to your father." She looked in sudden alarm at Gordon's tight army tunic, as though seeing it for the first time. "You're not going to France, are you?"

"No. Don't worry, Mother."

She passed a hand over her eyes, then smiled at him, her face cool and serene again. "You were the youngest," she said fondly, "but you were never any trouble. You always kept your room picked up, not like Jeremy, and he was a year older."

Gordon realized that he was still holding the *Ladies' Home Journal*, rolled up in his hand. "I brought your magazine upstairs with me," he said.

"Oh?" she said vaguely. "Put it over there with the rest. I'll get to it sooner or later."

He glanced at the cover of the magazine she had been reading when he came in. It was an old *Vanity Fair,* dating from before the Crash, when his father had still been alive. The bright, glossy cover showed a cut-out caricature of a monocled gentleman in a straw hat and beach costume, sipping a tall drink.

"All right," he said.

"The magazines are so dull and drab lately," she said. "So full of depressing articles. I'd rather read the old ones over."

Gordon found the pile of *Journals* on the console and added the current issue to it. As he was about to turn away, a stack of Sunday supplements caught his eye.

The one on top was the latest copy of *National Weekly,* the one with Junie's picture on the cover.

Gordon's heart skipped. "I didn't know you got the Sunday magazine," he said slowly.

"Oh, yes—Winthrop saves them for me. It's so thoughtful of him."

The raw strength of the photo compelled his gaze—the shabby tent, the exhausted young woman with her wretched baby wrapped in sacking, still managing a proud, defiant stare for the photographer.

"Then you've already seen Junie's picture on the cover."

Too late he realized that she hadn't. His mother raised herself abruptly from the pillows, her drowned beautiful face coming to life.

"My June Alice? In the rotogravure? Let me see."

"Mother, I—"

"Why are you standing there like that? Bring it over here."

Wordlessly he walked over to the bed and put the magazine section into her peremptory hand. She looked at the picture without comprehension, then handed it back to him.

"That's not June Alice," she said with flat finality. "That's not my little girl."

It was a regular three-room house with plywood walls instead of paperboard partitions. It didn't have electric lights or an indoor toilet like some of the model FSA cabins the government was starting to put up for migrants, but it had running water and gas for heat and cooking, and a half-acre garden plot surrounding it. The enterprising rancher who had put it up on his property with the help of FSA money charged them fourteen dollars a month rent. She and Floyd had one of the plywood rooms all to themselves, and Sue Ellen and Purley had another. Wesley, being a bachelor, slept in the truck, except on rainy nights, when he brought his bedding inside to share the kitchen-dinette with Ma and Pa Kinney. But of course with five children making noise, even three rooms seemed crowded.

Junie stared past the flowered chintz curtains she had sewn, at the dirt road outside. "Do you think they got it?" she said.

Ma Kinney came and stood beside her at the window. "Ain't no use worryin' about it," she said. "They did or they didn't. They'll be back soon enough to tell us."

"Will . . . will we have to move out of here if they didn't?"

Ma Kinney set her lips in a firm line. "Now don't you fret. Of course we won't."

"I won't mind, truly I won't, if we have to. It's just that it would be so nice if the new baby could be born in a real house."

She looked down at herself. Nothing much showed yet through the billowing cotton Hoover. They were called Hoovers because they were so cheap, only fifty cents, but they were good for working around the house or for when you got big. Junie had three of them, and Sue Ellen had two.

Ma Kinney said quickly, "The guvmint says we qualify and they can't make us move as long as we can pay the rent. We're gettin' good steady day work, settled right here. The apricots and avocados right close by near Santa Ana. The oranges. The lemons up to Whittier. The tomato fields over to San Pedro. The bean fields over to Inglewood, no more'n an hour away. And there's the WPA work. Purley and Floyd got on it for nine days last month, and they'll get on it again."

Sue Ellen, sitting across the kitchen shelling the garden peas that Junie had picked that morning, spoke out wistfully. "It sure would be nice if they got it. Purley is set on us havin' a cottage of our own, and Miz Fallows 'cross the way tol' me their place'll likely be vacant the end of the month. They're givin' up and goin' back to Arkansas. It's only one room, but it's real nice. If Purley had a job at the airplane factory, we'd qualify. He says he'd paint it pink, like a real Californian."

The last place they lived had been a cardboard shack near Salinas. The men had made it as tight as they could, with railroad paper and flattened tin cans, but it got chilly nights. They had hoped for steady work there. The Oklahoma migrants had muscled the Mexicans and Japanese out of the lettuce picking business and taken it over for themselves. The settlement was nicknamed "Little Oklahoma City," and the trailers had started to sprout lean-to additions and even adjoining wooden shacks.

But the Oklahomans stuck together. They monopolized the fifty-cent-an-hour packing jobs, and snapped up the five-dollar-a-month lots as fast as the farmers put them up for sale. Ma Kinney had hoped to get the family into one of the model government cottages that had electricity and indoor plumbing, but there were never enough of them, and they always seemed to go to someone with an Oklahoma accent.

So the Kinneys had drifted south in the groaning Reo truck and the rattletrap Ford that Purley had somehow managed to keep going. There was another big Okie settlement near Bakersfield, a place of tents and trailers and converted cattle trucks and shacks made of packing boxes and oil cans. The men who found work contributed part of their earnings to a common pool that fed the others. Some of the younger children had started to go to school. The Okies dealt out their own brand of law, and kept the local sheriff out of the place. The Kinneys had stayed there one night, but they hadn't been made to feel very welcome. It was funny, Junie thought. To Californians, she and the Kinneys were just another bunch of Okies, but to the Oklahoma refugees, they were outsiders, too—just people from some other state.

The Kinneys had pulled up stakes the following morning, without bothering about breakfast. There were avocados to be picked in Orange County, Ma Kinney had heard, strange green-skinned fruits that the Californians liked to eat with their greens. They had crossed the coastal mountain ranges and found themselves in an outlandish sun-splashed world where tomatoes grew in fields next to forests of oil derricks and where roadside lunch stands were built to look like giant hats, shoes, bulldogs, teakettles, and other fantastic shapes. But there was plenty of work for those willing to do it. With the annual influx of Mexicans halted by the revolutionary government south of the border which was seizing the big estates and dividing the land among the peasants, the California farmers were starting to turn to the dust-bowl refugees as a new source of cheap labor.

It was while they were working the thriving belt between Los Angeles and San Diego, where everything from apricots to chili peppers was grown in the shadow of the oil derricks and power lines, that Ma Kinney had decided they would live in a real house. "We kin afford it," she said. "Long as we keep workin'." She had campaigned for one of the FSA-financed cabins with grim determination. Bungalows, the landlord called them.

Junie looked fondly round the place. It looked real homey, with the print curtains, and the massive domestic presence of the Kinneys' yellow oak dining table that they had hauled clear across the country, and the cheerful clutter of the cheap toys they had been able to buy the children. They were still mostly sitting on orange crates, but Floyd had promised to mend some broken chairs he and Purley had hauled from the dump.

Junie found it hard to believe that they were living less than a three hours' drive from Hollywood, where they made the moving pictures. She hoped that someday when they were picking fruit near Whittier or

Santa Ana she would be able to persuade Floyd to expend the gasoline on a side trip to see it. She still looked for movie stars whenever they crossed into Los Angeles County, even though Purley made fun of her. "Do you think you're goin' to see a *movie* star sittin' on a stool at one 'a these dinky ice cream parlors or tamale stands?" he said. "They're takin' their *ease* in their mansions in Beverly Hills, no dogs or fruit pickers 'llowed." Junie paid no attention to him. Hollywood was the dominating presence here in this lavish sun-yellowed landscape, even if the Kinneys weren't aware of it. Anything could happen in this magical place. Screen tests were given to carhops. Stars were discovered sitting at drugstore soda fountains. Junie knew that she wasn't pretty enough, but little Maybelle was every bit as cute as Shirley Temple. Junie spent hours putting up Maybelle's baby-fine hair in exactly fifty-six curls, the same number Shirley had, no matter how much she squirmed and cried.

There was a sudden scream behind her, and she whirled around in time to see Leander kick Sue Ellen's oldest, Cindy Lou. Leander was only two, but he was very active. "Gimme, gimme!" he shrieked, pulling at Cindy Lou's doll. Its head came off with a snapping of elastic, and Cindy Lou burst into tears.

Junie went to him and picked him up, looking apologetically at Sue Ellen. Leander kicked at her.

"Now it's not nice to do that to your mommy," she whispered to him. He howled and kicked at her again.

Sue Ellen gave her little girl a pat on the rear and said, "You go outside and play now. And take little Billie with you." Snuffling, the little girl took her brother by the hand and went out the door.

"I'm sorry," Junie said, looking at the doll. It had come from the five-and-ten last Christmas, after much agonizing.

"Don't matter," Sue Ellen said. "I expect Purley can fix it when he gets home."

The three women glanced involuntarily toward the window again. "I wish they'd get back," Junie said.

Ma Kinney busied herself at the stove. "A lot of fellows must have showed up for them jobs. They would 'a had to wait their turn."

"They were there five o'clock this morning, gone all day," Sue Ellen said.

"Thirty jobs were advertised," Ma Kinney said firmly. "Least one of them stood a good chance to get one."

She went on molding the pie crust. She had been planning a special dinner, with dessert, to celebrate in case one of the four men had succeeded in getting hired. Dinnertime had slipped by, and now the pie would have to be for supper.

"Maybe they're already working," Junie said. "All of them. Fifty cents an hour! Wouldn't that be something?"

They had all been picking beans near Inglewood when they had become aware that the big, noisy factory adjacent to the bean field made airplanes. At seven-thirty, when the gates opened, they had been amazed by the enormous flood of workers who flowed inside. There must have been thousands of them. "All them jobs," Purley had mused. He had resolved to find out more. With Ma Kinney's encouragement, he had drifted over to the gates after they were finished picking and talked to a guard. The family invested two cents in a newspaper to confirm what Purley had learned. It was true. The factory had landed a defense contract, and was putting on new men.

"Listen," Sue Ellen said.

Faintly they heard the cough and rattle of the antique Ford approaching. Outside, Sue Ellen's children stopped playing and lifted their heads. A moment later the Ford came into view, bouncing over the ruts.

"Here they come now."

The Ford pulled up in front of the bungalow and shook itself to death. Junie watched anxiously as the four of them climbed out. Purley had on his wedding suit, sponged and shapeless, over a collarless shirt. Pa Kinney was wearing a jacket too, over his best overalls. Wesley blinked at the setting sun, looking helpless and schoolteacherish in his new department-store eyeglasses. Floyd moved slowly, his shoulders slumped. Junie thought he looked tired, and even skinnier than he had looked when he had left at sunrise.

Purley walked by the children without stopping to pick them up. Junie thought that was a bad sign. They came into the house, Purley's narrow face dark and scowling, Wesley's blurred and fuzzy with its day's growth of light whiskers. Floyd and Pa Kinney crowded in behind them, not saying anything, just looking at the floor.

"A thousand men in front of the gates," Purley said. "A thousand men for those thirty jobs. Some of 'em 'd been waiting since the night before."

"Fights, too, over places in line," Pa Kinney said. "Till the guards opened up the gates at seven and a man came out and said anybody fighting wouldn't git in to apply."

"Did you get in?" Ma Kinney said. "Did you get to talk to anybody?"

"Floyd and me, we got in," Purley said. "They told Pa he was too old. They didn't want Wesley 'count of his eyeglasses."

Floyd cleared his throat. "That was 'bout noontime. Just in time, too. Little after that, they closed the gates and told everybody else to go away. Had to get the company police to chase them."

"Wesley and me, we went back to the car and waited," Pa Kinney said. "Cop came by, but I told him, and he let us stay, long as we weren't making no trouble."

Floyd cracked his big knuckles. "Then it took another two, three hours. We got to see a man at a desk. Big fat man with a cigar. Told him I could do welding and 'most any kind of electrical work. He looked like he smelled somethin' bad, and he said, 'Down-hand welding, boy?' I said, no sir, I can do overhead welding, too. Then he said, 'We mostly do riveting here, boy. Best you try the shipyards. They hire welders.'"

"They don't want Okies, that's all," Purley said.

"Now, that's not true," Ma Kinney said.

"Sign on the men's room door," Purley said. "It said, 'Okies and dogs not wanted. Dogs may use tree in yard.'"

"Now Purley, you stop that talk right now," Ma Kinney said.

Purley was flushed with anger. "I went inside anyway, darin' them. And somebody'd lettered a sign over the stand-up toilets. It said, 'Okie drinking fountains.'"

"You mind the way you talk in front of Junie and the children, and I mean it!" Ma Kinney said dangerously.

"They just want to keep us pickin' fruit, that's all!" Purley glowered.

"Well maybe that ain't such a bad idea," Ma Kinney said. "A factory job makes a fine dream, but meantime we got to keep body and soul together."

Pa Kinney gave a little nod. "I'll go over to Mr. Rawley's place first thing in the mornin' and ask if he'll put us on when the figs come due. Last time he paid ten cents a lug."

Ma Kinney wiped her hands on her apron and said, "That's fine. Now you all come over and set down. You ain't et all day. We're havin' berry pie for dessert."

Junie held her breath and listened to the house. Through the thin walls she could hear Purley mumbling in his sleep, the way he sometimes did. From the main kitchen area, where Ma and Pa Kinney had installed their bed in something called a dining nook, came muffled snores and nothing else. Outside, a million crickets chirped.

"Floyd," she whispered.

His body jerked. "Huh?"

"Are you awake?"

"What, yeah, I guess," he said muzzily.

"Shh, don't talk so loud."

He shifted around in the bed, bony and fleshless and hard, like a man made of wooden parts wired together. The faint honest smell of dried sweat clung to him, a man's smell, familiar and reassuring.

"Don't feel bad about the job," she said. "I don't care, truly I don't."

"Wish I could of got it, though," he said in his slow, deliberative voice.

"I know."

"Purley ain't the only one who wants a bungalow of his own."

"It's all *right,*" she said. She patted his shoulder and felt him stiffen. She took her hand away.

"Seems a man who's willin' to work hard ought to be able to do better by his wife and children," he said harshly.

"You've been a good husband," she said in a fervent whisper. "You've always done your best. You've taken good care of me. You just wait. There'll be other jobs. I know there will."

He fell into the brooding silence that she feared. But after a while he raised himself on one elbow and said, "You didn't say nothin' at supper. Nothin' in the mail from your ma today either?"

She was touched by his concern. "No. But I don't really expect anything anymore, really I don't."

"Seems as like after all them postcards you wrote her, she ought to answer *somethin'.*" He added hastily, "Not that I'm sayin' anythin' against your ma."

"She just doesn't want to have anything to do with me, I guess," Junie said, trying to keep her voice bright.

"Now that isn't true."

"I can't say I blame her. I know I've been a disappointment to her."

"Maybe she just didn't get around to it. Writin's hard for some folks."

"She just wants to forget all about me."

"Now don't say that," he said uncomfortably.

"I don't care. Anyway, I'm very happy here. I have my own family. You and Leander Bradford and Maybelle. And Ma and Pa. And Sue Ellen and Purley and their children. I'm a grown-up married woman, and I don't *need* a mother."

A tear splashed down her cheek. Floyd moved uneasily in the bed. She felt ashamed of making him feel bad.

"Floyd?" she said.

"What?" he said warily.

"I'm not going to write my mother any more postcards."

"You oughtn't to take on like that."

"I mean it. I'm not going to waste the money. There's a lot of things you can buy for a penny. I'd rather spend it on candy for the children."

He reached out with a large clumsy hand to comfort her and accidentally touched her breast. She heard him catch his breath, and then she was breathing faster, too.

She snuggled against him to let him know it was all right, and he diffidently lifted up her nightie. She tried to keep her breathing quiet, so as not to wake up the children.

The river teemed with sampans. They crowded the rusty flanks of the Japanese coastal steamer, jostling one another in competition. Half-naked boatmen, their knotted muscles shiny with sweat, shouted and waved from the bobbing craft, clamoring for the attention of the passengers gathered at the rail.

Gordon peered out across the brown waters, his nostrils filled with the stench of China. Sewage, vegetable decay, charcoal smoke, greasy cooking smells, hovering dust. Seagoing junks lined the flat ugly banks of the river, moored at rice warehouses and coal yards. The bare masts of fishing boats made inscriptions across the sky. Farther down the channel he could see a gray American gunboat riding at anchor, the Stars and Stripes drooping limply in the dead air.

"The mysterious East," a sardonic voice said at his shoulder. "The chief mystery at the moment being how we shall get to Tientsin."

Gordon turned his head and recognized the Englishman, Terrill, weedily immaculate in a well-tailored white suit. Gordon had played cards with him in the passenger lounge a couple of times during the two-day trip from Shanghai.

"I thought this was Tientsin," Gordon said. "That's what I paid passage for."

The oceangoing liner Gordon had taken from San Diego had deposited him in Shanghai. He had spent a few days sight-seeing before being overwhelmed by the frenetic pace of the huge city, with its Western-built skyscrapers and clanging trolleys, its noisy streets jammed with bicycles, rickshas, and taxis that seemed to be driven exclusively by White Russian refugees. Then he had been caught by the curfew that had been imposed at whimsical intervals since the Japanese bombing attack of four years earlier, and had been forced to spend the night sitting in a tawdry Russian nightclub filled with sailors from the U.S. Asiatic Fleet and cocky leathernecks from the Fourth Marines, who had finally goaded each other into a bottle-smashing, table-splintering free-for-all in the wee hours of the morning. Gordon had escaped down an alley before the arrival of the shore patrol, with no worse injuries than split knuckles and a bruised forehead. He had wired the Fifteenth Infantry in Tientsin that day, and found that he could get there by train in thirty hours or by ship in forty-eight. He still had over a week before he officially had to report, and he had decided it would be more romantic to go by coastal steamer.

Terrill looked surprised. "This is Tangku. The larger ships off-load here. The river becomes too silted for oceangoing craft, you see. Tientsin's farther up the river, and Peiping is farther still."

Gordon's mouth became hard. "That was dishonest of them."

Terrill laughed. "My dear chap, you're in the Orient now. Hang on to your wallet. I shouldn't bother complaining to Johnny Jap about it, if I were you. We shall just have to make our own arrangements." He surveyed the wickerwork fleet with distaste. "I don't fancy going ashore in one of those filthy things, though."

"How do we get upriver?"

"There's a train, very dirty. Or we could hire a river launch, if you want to share expenses. I'm stopping at Tientsin overnight. I have business in the British concession there. Then it's on to Peiping in the morning for me." He grimaced. "I don't envy you, Lieutenant, mired in a dreary place like Tientsin. Hot in summer, freezing cold in winter, and a bloody bore at all times. Peiping—there's the place for a white man. You can rent a hundred-room house with Chinese gardens for four pounds a month. That's about sixteen dollars, American. My number one boy costs me four dollars a month and my cook, five. The other servants are less. I even have my own private ricksha. And of course there are such delights as the golf club and the race club, and really marvelous pheasant and quail shoots."

"I go where I'm sent," Gordon said shortly.

"Yes, of course," Terrill said hastily. "Don't think we're not extremely grateful for an American military presence here. We white men have to stick together, eh what? Of course we've got our own garrison under the Boxer Protocol, and so do the French and the Italians. And your famous Horse Marines in the Legation Quarter are quite a comfort. But put us all together, and the Japanese outnumber us now."

Gordon pricked up his ears at that. "The Japanese are building up their forces in the area?"

"Oh my dear, yes. They've got ten thousand troops stationed between Peiping and Tientsin now. They're building permanent barracks for them. Their excuse was a railway explosion near Tientsin a couple of months ago. I shouldn't be surprised if they engineered it themselves, like the Mukden incident. But of course the real reason is Chiang Kai-shek's rejection of Hirota's latest outrageous demands."

Gordon squinted against the glaring sun. "I'd understood that Chiang's been very careful not to step on Japanese toes."

"Oh yes, he's gone to marvelous lengths to appease them. He sent six of his own divisions into Shansi to head off the Communist advance and keep them from clashing with the Japanese. And—you may not have heard this yet, since you're newly arrived—Chiang's taken extraordinary measures to squelch the anti-Japanese noises the rival government in Canton was making. Spent huge sums bribing all of Chen's aviators and leaders to the Kuomintang side, forced Chen to flee for his life to Hong Kong, and called a meeting of the Central Committee in Nanking this week to dissolve the Cantonese government. But of course the Japs don't want to be appeased. They simply want all of North China."

A loud dispute near the stern of the ship caught their attention. Gordon leaned out over the side and saw six or seven sampans jockeying for a favored position under one of the portholes. Gordon knew it was the location of the ship's galley, because he had seen garbage being flung out of the porthole during the voyage, but how the Chinese boatmen had figured it out, he had no idea. They shoved at one another's craft with poles, uttering insults. A Japanese head stuck itself out of the porthole and immediately the boat people stopped their quarreling and began shouting at him. The Japanese cook laughed and withdrew. A moment later a shower of garbage came out of the porthole. The Chinese scooped it up with long-handled nets and emptied it out on the decks of the sampans. Women and children scuttled out from under the basketwork vaults and began picking the garbage over.

"The beggars aren't very fussy, are they?" Terrill said.

"Maybe they can't afford to be," Gordon said.

Terrill was amused. "This is your first tour, isn't it, Lieutenant? Life is cheap in China. They breed like animals and die like flies. They always have and they always will. There's nothing to be done about it. You'll soon get used to it."

"I don't think so," Gordon said evenly.

"Oh, eventually you'll give in to the pampered life, like the rest of us. Even in Tientsin. Your regiment has coolies to do all the menial tasks. You'll never have to pitch a tent or polish a saber. It's no use fighting it. You'll find that the men in your command have their rifles cleaned by the company number one boy. Incidentally, where's your swagger stick?"

Gordon looked with distaste at the man. "I don't carry one."

"Oh, but you'll have to. It's Fifteenth Infantry policy. All officers must carry a swagger stick or riding crop." He swished his own rattan cane through the air. "Absolutely indispensable to the pukka image."

Gordon turned away and fixed his attention on the scene below, not caring if he seemed rude. On one of the scavenger sampans, a small naked child sat crying with a fishhook sticking out of a bloody finger. The Japanese cook evidently had hidden it in a piece of rotting meat that the little girl still held clutched in the other hand. A gaunt, drab woman matter-of-factly removed the hook, then gently pried the piece of meat loose. Both meat and hook were added to the little pile of treasures that the sampan's inhabitants had sorted from the garbage.

Farther along the deck of the ship, two of the other passengers, a Canadian missionary and his wife, were having an argument with one of the Japanese officers. "My good man, you *must* dock here," said the missionary, a crabbed elderly man in cheap clothes and broken shoes. "It's your obligation."

The officer, invincible in his lack of English, stood stolidly with his hands clasped behind his back.

"Tell him that you insist, Jock," the missionary's wife said.

"You must send us ashore in a launch, at least," the missionary said firmly.

After further haranguing, the officer acquired enough understanding to point a stubby finger at the portable gangway that was being roped into place by a small working party. The passengers would be lowered to water level to strike their own bargains with the Chinese boatmen, his gestures said.

"The sods don't want to pay a docking fee," Terrill said. "They're only off-loading some light cargo here. Then they're going on to Port Arthur."

The only other passenger, a blue-robed mandarin standing in the middle of a lot of carved teak chests and silk-wrapped bundles, waited, impassive and aloof. Gordon gathered that he was some kind of merchant. He had tried to talk to him in halting Chinese during the voyage, and had been politely snubbed.

"You can bet that *he'll* have his pick of the best of the water taxis," Terrill said spitefully. "They'll fall all over themselves to serve him, even though these rich Chinese treat the coolies worse than we do." He glanced over at the missionary couple. *"They're* no help to us. They're only going up the coast to Hangku. Missionaries never have any money, anyway. If we're going to hire a river launch to Tientsin, it's you and I, Lieutenant."

Their attention was distracted by shouts and motion on deck. One enterprising coolie had succeeded in hauling himself up by the cargo netting, had dodged the halfhearted kicks of the Japanese sailors, and flung himself abjectly at Gordon's and Terrill's feet.

"My takee you cross, master," he gibbered. "You likee, you see. Boat belong my plenty good. Takee you cross chop chop."

"Makee stop till by an' by," Terrill said with distaste. "My lookee plenty boat-Johnny before catchee one belong my."

The man crawled back, crablike, a few paces and looked up hopefully. He looked skeletal, with his cropped head and his ribs showing like exposed laths above the baggy short trousers that were his only garment. But Gordon could see the snaky muscles down his back and the work-calluses on his hands, and thought the man looked fit enough.

"To-te, shao-te ch'ien pi ch'uan ni-te?" he said in slow, careful Chinese. How much money for boat belong you?

The boatman stared stupidly at him. Evidently he was not used to hearing anything but pidgin from foreigners.

"I say, that's capital, Lieutenant," Terrill said. "But you mustn't stoop to their lingo. It only confuses them."

The boatman was not prepared to analyze their dialogue. He sprang up with great energy and began to gather Terrill's luggage.

"Get your filthy hands off my things!" Terrill roared. "No catchee thingee belong my!"

The rattan cane went up in the air and came whistling down on the boatman's bare back, once, twice, three times. Three magical red stripes materialized on the drum-tight flesh. The boatman put down the suitcases on the deck and backed off a couple of steps.

Gordon found that his fists were clenched. But the coolie was waiting, as patient and unresentful as an ox, and Terrill had already lowered the cane.

"I'm sorry, I must say it, Lieutenant," Terrill said, "but that was your fault. You don't do these animals any favor by treating them as human beings."

Before Gordon could speak, a head with a stiff-brimmed khaki hat on it popped over the rail.

"Excuse me, sir, is that Lieutenant Sinclair?"

"Yes, I am," Gordon said, surprised.

A large soldier in suntans that might have been crisp an hour earlier heaved himself over the rail. He wore infantry tabs and the stripes and rockers of a platoon sergeant. Evidently he had climbed the Jacob's ladder being used by the Japanese work party struggling with the still unsecured gangway, and would have had to have bulled his way past them. Two straw-hatted coolies followed him on deck.

"Sergeant Dobbs of the Fifteenth," he said, saluting smartly. He had a bluff red face that showed the effects of good living. "Captain Stilwell sends his regards. He thought it would be a good idea if I picked you up by launch when you wired you was coming by this tub." He looked disdainfully around the Japanese vessel.

Gordon returned the salute. "That was thoughtful of the captain." He walked over to the rail and saw a trim motor launch with a canvas canopy tied up at the foot of the ladder. An infantry private with a rifle stood in its stern, his presence warding off the surrounding sampans.

"Yes, sir, he thought you'd be more comfortable in this heat traveling by water. Train's crowded, and it gets pretty smelly, if you know what I mean. And since they blew up that section of track, it doesn't keep to its schedule. Just crawls along."

The gangway was finally in place. Gordon started to shoulder his footlocker.

"Don't do that, Lieutenant!" the sergeant cried. "You'll lose face if you carry your own luggage." He was as patient as if speaking to a child. "Here, just put it down, sir. I'll have the coolies carry it."

Terrill, a relieved expression on his face, was nodding to the newly arrived coolies, indicating which of the luggage piled on deck was his.

"Is this gentleman with you, sir?" the sergeant said.

"No," Gordon said. "Mr. Terrill is taking the train."

35

Jeremy slipped quickly round the brick wall and crouched in the factory rubble. He listened for the telltale crunch of footsteps in the cinders, and waited until they came to a stop. After a moment he risked a look through a broken place in the wall. Boris, his personal GPU shadow, was standing bewildered in the middle of the factory yard, squinting at the row of corrugated iron sheds on the other side. Finally the GPU man came to some sort of decision, and trudged wearily toward the sheds, a shabby figure in one of Jeremy's hand-me-down jackets and shapeless trousers stuffed into felt boots.

Jeremy grinned and came out of his hiding place. He glanced round to make sure that no more GPU men were skulking about, then, hands thrust deep into his pockets, set off with a springy stride in the direction of the special barracks that housed American and other foreign workers, a mile and a half away.

The clang of a bell made him jump, and he skipped across the tracks to avoid being hit by an arriving trolley. It was the number twenty-three from Gorky, crammed with late arrivals for the four o'clock shift. Passengers balanced precariously on the swaying roof, showered with sparks from the overhead wire, and clung in thick bunches to the side of the car. Some of them dropped off before the trolley stopped moving and made a dash for the factory gate. It was nearly five, but there was always the chance that the timekeeper was late, too.

Only a few passengers got on for the return trip to Gorky. The first shift was long gone. The Russians liked to knock off early whenever they could get away with it.

Jeremy found a piece of black bread in his pocket and munched it as he walked. He didn't want to arrive hungry and take the chance of abusing his host's generosity. Food was hard to come by, even for the privileged Detroit auto workers who lived in the American colony.

He stopped for a backward look at the Molotov auto and truck plant. It had been designed for the Russians by Ford, but after six years it was still unfinished—little more than a vast unheated barn whose roof leaked. Ford had only recently been able to bring itself to part with the obsolete dies for the Model A that it had promised. Today Jeremy had learned that the tractor department was secretly making military tanks. He was still trying to decide if it was worth-while trying to sneak the story past the censor in one of his dispatches.

The path skirted the Volga for about a half mile. The river was busy with traffic: dilapidated cargo steamers, antique-looking side-wheelers with strings of wooden barges in tow, huge log rafts drifting lazily south with lumber and firewood for the cities. A large excursion steamer sailed by, festooned with red banners and streamers bearing slogans. Passengers in their underwear lolled in deck chairs, soaking up what remained of the afternoon sun. Someone on board was play-ing a balalaika. A special vacation cruise for deserving workers, Jeremy guessed.

He was so engrossed in staring after it that he didn't realize he had stumbled onto the stretch of riverbank reserved for women workers from the Molotov plant. All of a sudden, there they were, hundreds of naked bathers splashing in the shallows and wandering around at the water's edge, in a stupefying agglomeration of pale, chunky flesh. A hundred yards upstream swarmed the men and boys, equally naked and unabashed, protected from embarrassment by the etiquette of the nominal separation. The entire Russian population thronged to the water at noon and after working hours, but the Five-Year Plan hadn't yet got around to producing bathing suits.

Some of the factory girls, recognizing the *amerikanets* by his clothes from the *valuta* shop reserved for foreigners and his unruly black hair, waved and jeered good-naturedly at him. Jeremy virtuously averted his eyes and followed the path inland. In a sea of ripening wheat, a lone girl with her head wrapped in a red kerchief sat atop a slowly crawling tractor.

He kept walking. The lump of black bread was gone, and he wished he had another. It hadn't taken the edge off his appetite. He'd eaten that noon in the factory dining hall and shared the usual skimpy lunch of black bread and watery cabbage soup.

Ahead, the tin onion domes of an old church rose out of the land, and Jeremy quickened his step. Dogs began to bark and soon the thatched roofs of a traditional Russian village came into view. Instead of walking around the village, Jeremy took a shortcut through it. He wished he had a camera with him, but the Russians never let you take a picture of anything old anyway. There was always some busybody to fetch a policeman or the uniformed GPU.

The low, tumbledown huts huddled behind rotted board fences. Each had its own vegetable plot, its own private haystack for whatever animals remained after the famine, but the rippling golden fields of the new collective stretched beyond. The young people had gone to live there, in new pine barracks, or had found jobs in the factory, but the old people preferred to stay in their hovels as long as they were allowed to. A toothless old man sat sharpening a scythe on his doorstep. When he saw Jeremy, he crossed himself.

Jeremy trudged through mud, between the board fences. A small retinue of ragged urchins and yapping starved dogs trailed at his heels.

"Hey, *amerikanets,* where's your automobile?" one of them yelled. He was about ten years old, scrawny as a chicken, with his feet wrapped in rags and a cigarette dangling from the corner of his mouth.

"Got a smoke, American?" another one demanded.

"Please, uncle, do you have any bread?" a barefoot little girl in a torn smock asked. She was frail and very pretty, with enormous eyes and corn-colored braids.

A little toddler, stumbling to keep up, could only cry, *"Eeda, eeda!"* Food, food!

The presence of the American compound nearby had taught them to beg. Mike, the man he was going to see, had told him that children often showed up at his door, asking for money or food.

Jeremy rummaged through his pockets and distributed his cigarettes and stray kopeks to the children. The boys grumbled when they saw that the cigarettes were the low-priced Sport brand, but Jeremy knew that they could sell them to the factory workers at five or six kopeks per individual smoke. He pressed a folded paper ruble into the hand of the little girl, hoping it wasn't noticed, but resigned to the probability that the boys would take it away from her.

An old woman came charging out of her dooryard, brandishing a stick and yelling, "Shame, shame!" and the children scattered, laughing. The old woman glared at Jeremy and went back to the baby she was tending for some daughter or granddaughter living in a factory barracks or, if lucky, with her husband in a single room shared with two or three other married couples.

He left the Russian village behind. The international colony was over a rise and past a stand of birch trees. It was a complex of rough, two-story wooden barracks that reminded Jeremy of an army post. The raw pine had begun to turn silver. It housed a medley of Italians, Finns, Britishers, refugee Communists from Germany. But Americans —most of them skilled auto workers and technicians from Detroit— predominated. The official name of the place was the Ruthenberg Commune, but the Russians in the neighborhood called it the American Village.

As he drew closer, Jeremy could smell garlic. The Italians were cooking tonight. They always managed a better feed than the Finns, whose ideas about food ran to smoked fish and potatoes, or the Americans, who relied heavily on imported canned goods bought at the closed *valuta* shops. Jeremy's mouth watered. His resolve faded. He hoped he was in time to get invited to supper.

Now he was close enough to see individual touches. The English had mounted window boxes against the bare sides of their units, and were growing geraniums. The Germans had somehow hacked flower beds out of the hard-baked earth bordering their barracks. And here and there he could see gay curtains fluttering in the yawning emptiness of the windows. Jeremy was touched. The Russians, numbed by their bare-bones existence, had given up on the amenities.

He found building number four and, following Mike's instructions, climbed the outside steps to the second floor. Down below, between the open treads, he could see an upturned Slavic face staring up at him. The owner of the face, realizing he had been noticed, quickly turned away and busied himself rolling a cigarette out of a square of newspaper. Jeremy smiled mirthlessly. More GPU. They were everywhere. Well, it didn't matter. They weren't very good at communicating with one another. As long as he hadn't been spotted by Boris or one of the other GPU men who knew him by sight, it never would be reported to GPU headquarters that the *amerikansky* correspondent had been seen visiting building number four. To the fellow down below, he was just another American face.

He grimaced, annoyed with himself. Why worry about it? The average Russian might be terrified of the "Gay Pay-Oo," but to an American they couldn't be much more than a petty annoyance. He just didn't want them to throw a monkey wrench into his plans, that was all. The moment Russian officialdom became aware that you wanted to do something, by reflex they invented some reason to prevent you.

The corridor interior was more rough carpentry, unpainted. The pine floor had been holystoned white. The third door on the right, Jeremy had been told. He knocked.

The door opened, and Mike Czernik stood there. He had a glass in his hand. He was a broad, hard-muscled, bald man, half a head shorter than Jeremy, with a flattened nose.

"Ah, you made it, Sinclair." He looked both ways down the corridor. "And without your tail. Come on in."

Czernik's "apartment" was one big, bare room whose starkness Mrs. Czernik had attempted to alleviate with vases of flowers, some small Caucasian rugs and wall hangings, and a few mementos from America. A party was in progress. Ten or twelve men in clean shirts and a few women in cotton dresses and jewelry stood around with glasses in their hands, talking at the top of their lungs or gorging themselves on heaping plates of food. A small German-made radio—a considerable luxury in this place—played thin, scratchy Chuvash folk music, evidently the only choice that the Gorky radio committee had graced the airways with this evening.

A tall, gangling fellow, built like a jointed lamppost, with a lantern-shaped head to match, lurched over. "Is this the American reporter? Listen, let me tell you about the way those factory bureaucrats—"

"Later, Horvathy, later! Give the man a chance to eat." He pushed the tall man away and led Jeremy toward the buffet. "Everybody wants to talk to the American correspondent. I didn't invite half of them, believe me." He gestured magnanimously at the crowded table-top. "Go on, Sinclair, help yourself."

Jeremy eyed the spread gingerly. The Czerniks had gone all out. On a white linen tablecloth that must have been one of their American treasures was an incoherent feast of canned sardines, deviled ham, canned Vienna sausage, salami, pickled mushrooms, hardboiled eggs, cheese, red caviar, canned peaches, raspberry compote. Supplementing the inevitable sliced cucumbers and raw tomatoes was a proud display of canned tomatoes from the U.S. The pièce de résistance was a saucepan of Heinz baked beans heating over a one-burner alcohol stove. Jeremy knew the brand was Heinz, because the empty cans had carefully been left in sight.

"You won't have to eat that wop junk in the communal hall tonight," Czernik said. "We can have a party right here."

Jeremy hid his disappointment. At any rate, he thought, after a diet of cabbage soup, black bread, and kasha, even a plate of American baked beans would be a treat. And he still wasn't tired of caviar. Before he could find a plate, Czernik spoke again.

"But I know you reporters! First you want a drink, eh?"

Czernik gave a jovial laugh and slapped him on the back.

The bar was an equal hodgepodge. Three kinds of vodka. French brandy. Georgian wine. Grain alcohol. Armenian cognac. Warm champagne. Jeremy let Czernik pour him some of the Georgian wine. It wasn't bad, he'd found out some time previously.

"This is the missus," Czernik was saying. There was a trace of eastern Europe in his voice, left over from childhood, but the cadence of his speech could have been heard in any industrial slum within smelling distance of the Great Lakes. "Helen, meet Jerry Sinclair, a heckuva good guy. He's gonna write an article that maybe will get some action for us from the big shots in Moscow."

Helen Czernik was a pleasant middle-aged woman with a comfortable figure and thick dark hair streaked with white. She cast Jeremy a despairing look.

"You'll have to excuse the way the place looks, Mr. Sinclair. Conditions here are just impossible. I can't even get decent material for curtains."

"Now, now, Helen," Czernik protested. "You mustn't complain. Mr. Sinclair here will get the wrong idea. The Russians are doing the best they can for us. Don't forget, they're making up for centuries of backwardness. They're trying to lift themselves out of the Middle Ages all at once. Look at the way they're living themselves. They don't have a lot left over to pamper foreigners with."

Helen Czernik gave Jeremy a tired smile. "Mike always makes excuses. He came here to help build socialism. Took out our life's savings, sold our house, and donated most of the proceeds to Amtorg and the international trade-union movement. I made him save out enough for fare home in case things didn't work out, but there's always some committee or something trying to get us to donate that, too."

"Well, it's . . . an interesting experiment here," Jeremy said cautiously.

"Experiment, hell!" Czernik boomed. "Listen, Jerry, maybe there are shortcomings, sure. But they'll be ironed out. This is the world's first true proletarian democracy."

"That's my Mike," Helen Czernik said, not without a certain pride behind the ruefulness. "Always for the cause of the workingman. He was just a boy when he came to America, a dumb bohunk kid, but he always remembered conditions in the old country. His father worked in the iron mines fourteen hours a day, and the family never had enough to eat. When the men went on strike, the owners called in a regiment of soldiers. They tied the strike leaders to the back of a cart and horsewhipped them in front of the whole village."

"That's when the old man decided to take the family to America,"

Czernik said. "God knows how he scraped together the money. He went first, then he sent for my mother and the rest of us. But he found out the bosses run things in America, too. He burned out his lungs at the furnace mouth in a steel mill in Ohio. When the bosses found out he was a socialist, they blacklisted him. I was only fourteen then, but I was doing a man's work in the mill for eleven cents an hour, and I was able to help my brothers support him. He lasted a year, coughing his lungs out."

"That's enough of that, Mike," Helen Czernik said. "Mr. Sinclair hasn't had any food yet."

"It's all right, Mrs. Czernik," Jeremy said. "This is interesting."

He wondered if he could work Mike Czernik's reminiscences into some sort of a biographical sidebar to go with his Gorky story, and, if so, if the Russian censors would pass it. Probably, if they thought it tended to show the oppression of the American worker.

"An American in Gorky," he could call it; "From the New World to the Newer." His fingers itched for a pencil.

"I made up my mind to learn a trade then," Czernik was saying, "so I wouldn't have to be under anybody's thumb. "I packed up, fifteen years old, before I even got my full growth, and worked wherever they were hiring. I was a miner, a steelworker. After the war, I went to night school and studied to become a machinist. Bill Foster was trying to organize the steel industry at the time. I was a charter member of the union. Got myself clubbed and arrested, picketing during the great steel strike of 1919. You're too young to remember. Twenty-two men killed, but we got the twelve-hour day abolished. I had to leave town. I finally wound up in Detroit. I heard from a hillbilly that they were paying good wages in the auto plants. You could make over a dollar an hour for skilled benchwork. Eventually I became a tool-and-die maker."

"And got himself kicked out of that job, too, after putting in all those years," Helen Czernik said with a trace of bitterness.

"I didn't get kicked out," Czernik said. "I quit on them."

"It was always the labor movement, never his family," Helen Czernik said. "We have two nice daughters, married, one in Chicago, and they never knew when their father was going to come home with a bloody head."

Czernik turned gruff. "To hear her talk, you'd think I was some kind of firebrand. I'm just an ordinary working stiff who happens to believe in worker solidarity. Sure, I joined the Young People's Socialist League when I was a kid. Who didn't? And I took out a card in the Communist Labor Party when it came along. So what? I'm proud of it. But I'm a worker, not an agitator."

"What made you decide to pull up stakes and come to the Soviet Union?" Jeremy said.

"I needed a job," Czernik said shortly.

"Suddenly he's tongue-tied," Helen Czernik said. "The pied piper of Detroit."

Czernik stared at the floor, beetle-browed and scowling, his feet planted apart.

"What do you mean?" Jeremy said.

"He even had a free preview first," she said. "The Michigan chapter of the Slavic Workers' Club sent Miklos to see the workers' paradise firsthand, all expenses paid. He was part of a trade-union delegation that the American Communist Party arranged to have invited to the Soviet Union, so they could observe the success of the first Five-Year Plan for themselves. And spread the word when they got back."

Mike Czernik chewed on his lip, his eyes kept fixed on the floor. It had the look of a long-standing family quarrel, and Jeremy was uncomfortable.

"You don't have to—" Jeremy began.

"Oh, how they wined them and dined them, and led them around by the nose, and showed them all the model workers' palaces and free clinics and state nurseries, and the Prophylactorium, that the tourists always ask to see so they can stare at all the ex-streetwalkers being taught to operate knitting machines. They didn't show them the starving peasants or the homeless children. Or the beggars. Or the factory girls who come around here to the American Village at night to prostitute themselves to the single men for a few slices of salami."

"Now Helen," Czernik said uneasily, "all these things will be corrected. It takes time."

She went on: "When Miklos came back to Detroit, he was a hero. Everybody was after him to speak at meetings, write articles for the *Syndicalist* and the Czech language newspaper. Oh, what a glowing picture he painted of life in a classless society! At the time, Amtorg had already started placing want ads in American newspapers for skilled workers to take jobs in the Soviet Union. When Miklos decided to submit his application, he persuaded a dozen people from the Slavic Workers' Club to go with him. Horvathy over there is one. He's one of those who stayed. Half of them turned right around and sailed back to the United States as soon as they saw what conditions were like here. But not my Miklos. He won't admit that he made a mistake."

Czernik was looking miserable but stubborn. Jeremy felt sorry for him. "Mr. Czernik . . ." he started.

"Mike."

"Mike, aside from your own group, are there many Americans who come to Gorky out of political conviction like yourself?"

Czernik seemed grateful for the chance to take charge of the conversation again. "Sure. Quite a few. Like Tom, the Irishman, over there." He pointed out a barrel-chested man whose front teeth were missing. "He's an old IWW organizer. But I guess a lot of them just needed jobs and couldn't get them at home. Those Amtorg ads sounded pretty good, you know. The Russians are desperate to industrialize. 'Fordization,' they call it." He cast a wary glance at his wife. "The Russians have a right to complain about being taken in, too. They brought over a lot of bums who don't know one end of a spindle lathe from the other, but persuaded Amtorg they were expert machinists."

Helen Czernik sighed. "What are you going to do with a man like this?" She turned a look of fond resignation on her husband. "That's enough propaganda, Miklos. Poor Mr. Sinclair hasn't had a chance to eat anything yet, and the food will be gone soon, the way this pack of wild beasts is wolfing it down." Her generous mouth widened in a sudden smile that showed two perfect rows of strong white teeth. "If you were visiting us in Detroit, Mr. Sinclair, I would make you roast goose and *knedliky* and red cabbage, but here in a Slavic country, the best I can do is that canned picnic. Here, hurry, while there's still some of the caviar and eggs left."

She thrust a fragile china plate, perhaps an heirloom, into his free hand. Jeremy balanced his wineglass on it and turned to the buffet. Before he could help himself to the food, Horvathy stumbled over and planted himself in front of him.

"Getting an earful, Mister Reporter?" he blurted, spraying Jeremy. "I'm the one you should talk to. Czernik's too lenient. But you'll tell them, won't you? Tell them about all the damaged castings they give us to work with. About the machines that burn out because no one oils them. About the lack of safety holes in the heavy dies. About the department chief's graft. About the speedup tactics of management— worse than the capitalists! We've got to get the ear of the Central Bureau and the Profintern. That's the way to make them jump. When they read it in the *Moscow Daily News,* they'll have to take action."

"Well, you see, I don't write for any of the Russian papers, Mr. Horvathy," Jeremy said. "That is, I did but I don't anymore. My articles are syndicated in Europe and America."

Horvathy paid no attention. "And the favoritism!" he wheezed. "The foreman's little *devooshka* is rated as an *udarnik,* even though she stands around doing nothing all day except wiggle her cute behind at him. And the best jobs go to the Party bootlickers, whether they know anything about machinery or not."

"Why don't you write a letter to the factory newspaper?" Jeremy suggested. He tried to lean past Horvathy to spear a hard-boiled egg, but Horvathy blocked him with a waving paw.

"That propagandist sheet? The editor is the biggest whoremaster of them all. He's got four of his chippies working under him as assistant writers, and I mean under him! Anyway I'm just a working slob. It'll take an article from someone like you to get their attention."

"Well . . ." Jeremy temporized, "once in a while Tass picks up one of my pieces abroad and relays it back here for *Izvestia* or *Trud*. But they always filter out anything that sounds like criticism."

During his first heady months in the Soviet Union, Jeremy, under the benign sponsorship of the Moscow Writers' Union, had turned out a number of articles for the Russian newspapers and literary gazettes, for which he had been paid in rubles. Mostly they had been innocuous travel pieces, or vignettes of the cultural scene. At first Jeremy had gone along with what the Press Board called "friendly suggestions," and had willingly changed the wording of his pieces if the changes didn't seem too important. But their demands became more insistent once he had given in, and Jeremy dug in his heels. In the end he was reprimanded for his "unfriendly" and "bourgeois" attitudes, and there were no more articles and no more rubles. Word got back to the Soviet publishing trust, and Jeremy's editor at Gosizdat, the giant Moscow publishing house, suddenly became very vague about the book he was supposed to write for them. Jeremy had taken the commission seriously, though other journalists in his position hadn't, and the book had actually been in the works. He was allowed to keep his five-thousand-ruble advance, but it was tacitly understood on both sides that there would be no book.

Jeremy didn't care. He was out of patience with the Russians and their exaggerated suspicion of foreigners—even friendly ones. It was much more satisfying to have a straightforward daily battle with the official censors, like all the other foreign reporters. The German Communists, at least, had lived up to their promises. Through the parlor socialists and Soviet sympathizers they knew how to exploit so skillfully, they had provided Jeremy with a European press-agency connection and American syndication. Jeremy was paid regularly in Belgian francs and American dollars—the *valuta*, or foreign currency, that the Russians prized so highly and that entitled him to spend his pay in the Metropole restaurant for an occasional halfway decent meal or the Torgsin luxury shops for a pair of shoes that didn't fall apart.

"That's the spirit, comrade! We're depending on you to get the truth of the matter out!"

Horvathy swayed over him like a flexible steam shovel, but Jeremy succeeded in ducking around him while he talked. The hard-boiled eggs were gone. Jeremy was just about to ladle himself a helping of baked beans when the man called Tom, the Wobbly organizer, laid a heavy hand on his shoulder.

"The truth, is it?" he said. "Don't listen to Horvy, chum. He thinks the truth is like foot powder. You sprinkle it over society and it stops the itch."

"Doesn't it?" Jeremy said.

"I'm still scratching." Insolent gray eyes stared at Jeremy from under a massive shelf of brow. "Aren't we all?"

"Uh . . . Mike says you're a Wobbly."

"Was, chum, was. They don't like labor organizers here in the land of the workingman. Strikes might interfere with the Five-Year Plan, y'see. The Gay Pay-Oo keeps closer tabs on me than it does on you apologists for the capitalist system."

"I'm not an apologist for anything!" Jeremy said angrily.

The craggy face registered amusement. "Oh, I beg your pardon. Was it the bolshevist system you were apologizin' for in your last article, then?"

"I only—"

"I read that particular fairy tale. About workers' rights under Mr. Stalin's marvelous new constitution. Of course the right to strike isn't included. Not necessary. The workers own the factories, y'see."

"All I did was quote—"

"Ah, man, what does it matter?" the big man said, suddenly morose. "Here they call the bosses commissars, that's about all there is to it. I'd go home if I could."

"Why don't you?"

The gray eyes flicked. "Jumped bail. They're waiting for me."

"After all this time?"

"The bastards never forget," the big man said vaguely. He spread out the fingers of one hairy hand and stared reflectively at them. "Those were the great days. Where the A.F. of L. made its mistake was in organizing the workers trade by trade. Like this." He waggled the fingers separately. "The IWW organized like this." He closed his fingers into a fist and shook it at an imaginary adversary. "One big union. That's what Big Bill Haywood used to tell them."

Tom's eyes were focused somewhere beyond Jeremy, and Jeremy suddenly realized the man was drunk. He started to edge away from him, but a huge hand shot out and took a handful of his sleeve.

"They broke Bill Haywood's heart, you know. They kept him on display like a tame bear, in a Moscow hotel room with a young Russian wife to take care of him and all the Russian booze he could drink, till he died. Political asylum, they called it, and they showed him to all the labor delegations to show what a friend of the workingman they were, and all the time Big Bill was eating himself away inside because he knew that Stalin was a bigger speedup king than Henry Ford, and he couldn't say anything about it. . . ."

"You've had him long enough, Tom."

The newcomer was a large woman in a low-cut peasant blouse and cascading ropes of colored beads. She pried Tom's grip loose and turned Jeremy around.

"I'm Gladys Cubberly. That's my husband, Dan, over there." She indicated a weedy man with thinning hair. "We're from Dearborn. Dan was a metal finisher. Do you sing?"

"Well, I—"

"We're trying to get up a group for a songfest. The radio's just going to play that awful Oriental music all night. Come with me."

She pulled him along after her. Jeremy cast a last despairing look at the buffet. Somebody was shoveling up the last of the sardines. His new friends shoved a fresh drink into his hand and made encouraging noises. One of them was under the impression that Jeremy was Upton Sinclair, visiting Russia to gather material for a new Socialist tract, and expressed surprise that he was so young. Somebody produced a guitar. Somebody else left the party and came back with an accordion. The radio with its Chuvash folk music was peremptorily silenced. Jeremy had expected labor songs, but they sang the old sentimental standards like "Beautiful Ohio" and "Alice Blue Gown." Several drinks and a lot of songs later, he found himself dancing the polka with Gladys Cubberly while a circle clapped in rhythm. Then there were square dances and reels. Somebody in an adjoining space pounded on the wall, and Mike Czernik pounded back.

By one in the morning, the vitality seemed to have drained out of the party. The participants were swaying on their feet, clutching drinks as though they were afraid they'd lose them. The vodka and wine were gone, and Jeremy at that point was nursing an inch of grain alcohol cut with mineral water. A few people hovered around the guitar player, trying vainly to breathe life into "Annie Rooney."

"The whistle blows at five-thirty, comrades," Mike Czernik said during a lull.

There were groans and reluctant sighs of acquiescence. The singers tried gamely to go on for a while, and there was a last furtive flurry at the bar, but twenty minutes later the last of them were saying good night at the door to Helen Czernik.

"I'd better be going," Jeremy said, buttoning his jacket.

"You can't go all the way back to Gorky tonight," Czernik said. "You better bunk here."

"I'll make up some cushions on the floor," Helen Czernik said.

Jeremy started to protest, but Czernik cut him short.

"You can get an early start. Stick with us all day and get the workers' point of view. Never mind the director and his guided tours. We'll help you give him the slip."

It was an attractive notion, and exactly what Jeremy had had in mind when he had fallen in with Mike's impulsive invitation earlier that day.

"All right, Mike. Thanks."

Helen Czernik was bustling around with bedding, and to Jeremy's dismay, it soon became apparent that it was the Czerniks who intended to sleep on cushions on the floor, while he was expected to use their bed. He protested again, but they were firm.

"We're used to roughing it. You'll need your sleep if you're going to keep your eyes open tomorrow."

On his way down to the latrine, Jeremy tripped over something soft. It moved and gave a moan of complaint. It was the GPU man, sleeping under the stairs like a dog.

The noise made him edgy. Around him was a merciless din of air hammers and pneumatic drills, clanging steel, the hiss of compressed air hoses. An insane whine of grinding metal cut through it all. You could go deaf here, Jeremy thought.

"What did you say?" he yelled.

"I said look at that automatic spindle lathe over there!" Mike shouted back. "The latest German machine. Wonderfully complicated. God knows how much of the Soviet Union's *valuta* had to be spent to buy it. And it'll be ruined in a week!"

They approached the machine. Jeremy could hear the tortured squeal of dry bearings. A bluish haze hung in the air. There was a smell of scorched metal.

"See that? No oil in the oil cups. They're full of metal chips. Some idiot took off the covers."

The lathe operators were looking at them curiously. They were an undershirted man who needed a shave and a haggard boy in the remains of what had once been an embroidered blouse.

"You're burning out the machine, comrades," Czernik told them, switching to Russian. "Why aren't you keeping it oiled?"

The undershirted man spat on the floor. "I don't know anything about taking care of foreign machines," he said. "I have a hard enough time keeping up with my quota. I only made eighteen rubles last week, and I had to pay two of those for my union dues and culture tax."

Czernik turned to Jeremy. "Piecework. We fought against that in the United States." He turned to the boy in the peasant blouse. "And what do you say?"

The boy removed his cap. "Please, *gaspadeen?*"

"Have you filled your quota?"

"N-no, *gaspadeen.*" The boy looked terrified.

"And who set the quota?"

The older man spat again. "Some Moscow bitch. Just out of school. She never saw the inside of a factory before. They made her the estimator."

Czernik pursed his lips. "I'll see what I can do, comrade."

As they walked away, Jeremy said, "Will you be able to do anything?"

"I'll bring it up at the next shop meeting. As a foreigner, I can get away with shooting my mouth off."

They left the machine area and walked out onto the main floor of the factory. It was an enormous, gloomy cave of a place, lit by thousands of random lamps, each shedding its own little circle of light. Overhead cranes cast complicated shadows. A long line of partially completed vehicles stretched down the center of the floor, in no particular order. Jeremy saw a sedan, an open-cab pickup on a Model A chassis, a closed van, a touring car.

"That's the Russian idea of an assembly line," Czernik said bitterly. "No conveyor. The line stands still and the workers move."

On the part of the line nearest Jeremy, a knot of about twenty workers had just finished some operation on a truck. They picked up their tools and moved on to the next vehicle in the line. But there was still a lone welder working on the chassis. The cluster of aproned men and women stood around, watching him and smoking cigarettes, chatting and calling out advice.

"They just don't get the idea." Czernik sighed. "Ford engineers laid out the line for mass production. Trucks one month. Passenger cars the next. Then maybe some army vehicle. But they've mixed all the jobs together. No standardization."

The welder finished his chore and moved on down the line. But the idle group was in no hurry to move in. They were having some kind of conference. Two men were gravely examining a socket wrench, while a circle of onlookers crowded close.

"Now they'll all wait around for a half hour while they delegate somebody to go to the tool room and sign out whatever they need for the next job," Czernik said in exasperation. "Then at the Party meeting they'll make speeches about Fordization."

They continued walking down the line. "Shouldn't you be getting back to your work brigade?" Jeremy said.

"Seen enough?"

"It's not that. I just thought . . . I didn't want to disrupt your work."

Jeremy had just noticed the shabby figure stalking them through the factory. Boris, the GPU informer assigned to him, had belatedly caught up with him. Jeremy didn't take Boris very seriously, but he didn't want to get Czernik in any trouble.

Czernik gave a harsh bark. "My brigade's not very busy this morning. Horvathy can handle things without me. We've been waiting over a week for the blueprints and castings we need to fulfill our part of the monthly program."

Jeremy tried to follow the progress of the prowling Boris without being too obvious about it. It was impolite to stare openly at your GPU chaperone, though some of his fellow correspondents in Moscow liked to tease them.

"Let's just take a look at the end of the line," Czernik was saying. "I think they've got a truck almost finished. Then we can have lunch."

They were passing a series of open bays where there wasn't much cover for Boris. As Jeremy watched out of the corner of his eye, Boris, like a character in a cheap spy movie, darted behind a palm tree.

Palm tree?

Jeremy looked again. No, he wasn't seeing things. A crazy grove of dusty and bedraggled artificial potted palms decorated the entrance to one of the work bays, as though it were a second-rate nightclub.

Czernik noticed the direction of Jeremy's gaze. "Oh, the palm trees?" he said with distaste. "The factory had a socialist competition to see which department could do the most to raise the cultural level of the workers. One department brought in a phonograph and played Tchaikovsky all day. At least they said it was Tchaikovsky, but you couldn't hear it in all this noise, and they only had the one record, and that was worn out pretty well after the first week. Our own group made spoons out of scrap metal, to improve the table manners in the cafeteria. It was the Reuther brothers' idea. They worked here then. But the forge department won. They sent a delegation to Moscow and got all those palm trees from some hotel. God knows what they bribed the manager with! Some say it was a car, diverted from the production line."

Boris peeked out from behind the cellophane bole of the tree, saw them looking in his direction, and popped back like a weasel.

"I thought you were supposed to be a booster of the Soviet Union," Jeremy said. "But all you've done all morning is knock the system."

"I'm not knocking the system," Czernik said, avoiding Jeremy's eyes, "just the managers. There's too much bureaucracy holding the workers back."

"It wasn't the managers who were running that machine back there. It was the lathe hands."

"It isn't easy to industrialize a whole society overnight. Most of those people are peasants. They never saw a machine until a few years ago."

"It's been eighteen years since the revolution."

Czernik said doggedly, "The people have a marvelous spirit. Give them time."

Jeremy saw movement at the edge of his vision and turned his head toward the production line. Work had slowed down or stopped all along the line. Men and women were deserting their posts and drifting toward the truck chassis that Czernik had pointed out before.

"What's going on?" Jeremy said.

"Come on over," Czernik said with evident relief. "I'll show you what I mean about spirit."

They forced their way into the crowd. A toothless old man turned to them, his face shining with joy. "It comes, comrades," he said. "Another truck out of pieces of metal. A miracle!" The verb he chose for "comes" was *raditsa,* to be born.

Czernik patted the old man on the shoulder. "It is indeed, comrade." He turned to Jeremy. "Can you imagine hearing anything like that in Detroit?"

A black-bearded giant, bare-chested and hairy in an open vest with no shirt under it, bellowed, "Make way for the *amerikanets.* Let him through so he can see."

The crowd opened up. *"Spaseeba,"* Jeremy said. Grinning Russian faces surrounded him on all sides.

"Tell the truth, *tovarish zhoornaleest,"* said a yellow-haired youth with a wide peasant face, "are we catching up to America?"

"Pachtee," Jeremy assured him gravely. "You're getting there."

His answer pleased them, despite his atrocious Russian grammar. Jeremy had found he could get along well enough by stringing words together without worrying about the complicated Russian declensions and verb tenses. He tried to learn a few new words every day from the dog-eared dictionary he carried around with him, and by now he had acquired a formidable vocabulary. This put him ahead of a lot of the American and English correspondents in Moscow, who relied on their Russian secretaries to interpret for them.

"Look at the way they're trying to lift that body shell," Czernik said in English to Jeremy. "Three hooks would do it if they had safety holes drilled where they could keep it in balance. They'll be lucky if it doesn't slip and smash someone flat. Or fall on the engine block and wreck it."

A gang of sweating, struggling women ran back and forth, tugging at twenty-pound iron hooks that hung on chains from a crane assembly overhead. The hooks kept slipping, and the women would jockey them back into place by sheer brute strength, wherever they could find a spot where they would hold. Their task was made more complicated by too many helping hands. As Jeremy watched, an eager little man in a burlap apron ran over to one of the straining women, and with a misplaced tug, dislodged her hook, which swung in a wide arc and almost brained a girl who was heaving with her shoulders under a fender.

"Why don't they use men for that job?" Jeremy shouted in English.

"The hook gang? Men and women are equal in Russia, except that women seem to be more equal when the heavy jobs are handed out." Czernik pulled a wry face. "The men are needed for precision work, you see, like turning the engine bolts with a ratchet wrench. Ever notice how on the rail crews the girl gets to swing the sledgehammer and the fellow holds the spike?"

"You're sounding cynical again, Mike."

Czernik gave a short laugh. "Don't worry about these girls. They're tough. They're proud of doing the heavy stuff. Call the men weaklings. If a man gets assigned to their brigade, they'll deliberately set out to make him look bad, so's he'll get bounced. They play rough, too. A while back, some Georgian lothario pulled strings to get himself assigned to the bonderizing booths. It's a poisonous job, but he thought he had it made. All women, and plenty of opportunities for hanky-panky behind those partitions. I guess the poor stupid bastard got himself a few free feels his first day. Told them all what a great lover he was, teased them that they'd have to take turns for the privilege. They took him behind one of the booths at the end of the shift, and said they'd have a look to see if he was exaggerating. They sat on him and pulled down his pants. Stuck a compressed air hose up his rear. Exploded him to shreds. They were just peasant girls having a joke, you see. They didn't realize what a high-pressure air hose could do to a man's insides. After that, the factory put up warning signs near the hose stations."

It was a horrifying story. Jeremy looked at the toiling women and shuddered.

"There she goes!"

The steel body shell swung precariously into the air. The hook gang scrambled to stay with it, guiding it over the waiting chassis. They seemed to have been poured from the identical mold—sturdy, bulging, chunky girls, bare-legged and bare-armed in short cotton dresses, with bright calico kerchiefs tied around their heads. All except one. One of the girls on the far side hardly seemed cut out for the job. All Jeremy could see of her was a pair of slender bare legs and the bottom of a shabby flowered cotton skirt that kept riding up to show smudged knees. The legs weren't bad, actually. Put silk stockings and high heels on them, Jeremy thought, and they wouldn't look out of place walking down Fifth Avenue, but it must have been hard for their owner to compete with her strapping workmates.

Then it happened. A girl stumbled and the hook she had been wedging in place slipped loose. The shell began tilting dangerously out of balance. In a moment, hooks on the raised side would slide free, and the shell would come crashing down.

"*Apasna!* Watch out!"

The shell spun round and the girls danced around with it. A collective gasp went up. The surrounding crowd backed away.

A beefy woman at a front corner deserted her own post and came charging round the side like a halfback. She retrieved her fallen teammate's hook and anchored it in a spot where it would hold. The only trouble was that her own hook had been none too secure either. In that frozen moment it was obvious to Jeremy that the deserted hook would escape the lip of metal it clung to, as soon as the tilt of the body shell increased by a few degrees more.

The girl with the slim legs saw that possibility too. Jeremy could see all of her now, as the pivoting of the shell brought her round. She was willowy and long-waisted in the cheap clinging dress, with the wide bony shoulders of a fashion model, and a lovely, starved face to go with them.

She dived for the abandoned hook and held on to it with all her strength, while keeping a skinny elbow crooked around the chain she had been tending before, so that the two chains were braced against one another. The sinew-stretching effort kept her on tiptoe, with her feet having only the sketchiest of contact with the floor. If the shell slipped, she would never be able to get out of the way. She could lose a foot, or be pinned to the floor and killed. Her head was lowered; she had lost her kerchief and her dark hair hung down, concealing her face, so that Jeremy could not see her expression. He wondered what thoughts were going through her head.

But there were no further disasters. The shell, with much strenuous heaving by the hook-and-chain girls, mated with the chassis beneath. A cheer went up from the crowd.

Beside him, Czernik said, "That was a close one. They don't realize it, though. Happens twenty times a day here. The bosses only make a fuss when someone gets hurt."

The crowd surged forward. Dozens of eager helping hands unfastened the chains. A couple of mechanics with big crescent wrenches stood by, looking smug. But they weren't going to begin the work of fastening the chassis bolts right away. They were going to make a ceremony of it.

It looked like an army truck now, even though there was still a lot of work to be done. People scrambled up on the engine hood and cab roof. The black-bearded giant posed astride the highest point of the barrel top, ready, it was all too obvious, to make a speech. The beefy woman who had deserted her hook to refasten the one that had come loose was suddenly a center of attention. People were pushing her forward, urging her to sit in the place of honor behind the wheel.

"You're a labor hero, Masha!"

"Da, da, vy prahvee! She saved the day!"

Blushing, the beefy woman allowed herself to be cajoled into the truck cab. Up on top, the bearded man was looking toward Jeremy and shouting something above the noise.

Czernik nudged Jeremy. "He wants a few words from the *amerikanets* on this great occasion."

But Jeremy had eyes only for the slender girl. She was standing modestly to one side. No one was paying any attention to her. To Jeremy, that seemed incredible. She was the most ravishing creature he had ever seen. She had a fine-drawn, translucent beauty that was made the more poignant by the shabby clothes she wore. Her face, with its spectacular cheekbones and high-bridged patrician nose, its startling eyes and long-winged upper lip, was framed by glossy brown hair that looked as if it had been freshly brushed. What was a splendid thoroughbred like her doing in this place of sweat and clamor?

"Go on," Czernik was saying. "You better say something or they'll never go back to work."

Reluctantly, Jeremy dragged his eyes from the girl. Everybody was grinning expectantly at him, and he tried to think of the Russian words for "well done." There was a familiar constriction in his chest, a clenched knot that was physically painful. He recognized it with a sense of dismay and disbelief. He had last felt it when he had thought himself in love with Naomi Weinbaum, but he had thought that he had grown too old and experienced ever to feel that particular adolescent ache of instant longing again. This is ridiculous, he thought, but he knew against all sense and logic that if he let her get away from him he would die.

The factory lunchroom, the *stalovaya,* was jammed with first-shift workers sitting hip to hip at the long trestle tables. Surly waiters in soiled aprons loped down the aisles, slamming down the fifty-kopek lunch of cabbage soup and sour-bread cutlets. The chipped walls were hung with colorful posters showing cartooned workers and capitalists, blaring such slogans as: *Shame on Drunkards, Carelessness Is Sabotage,* and *Those Who Are Not With Us Are Against Us.* The factory orchestra, a collection of bulge-eyed men scraping away on fiddles and cellos, serenaded the diners with selections from *The Merry Widow.* In the Red Corner adjoining the hall, workers who had already finished lunch loafed out the remainder of their hour playing chess or reading newspapers.

Jeremy lifted a wooden spoon to his mouth. "I thought you said your department made metal spoons so the lunchroom could be *kulturnee.*"

"We did," Czernik said, hunched gorillalike over his bowl. "We got a special commendation from the culture committee. Speeches, banners, and a brass band. And the next day all the spoons were gone. The workers took them home."

"So we made another batch," Horvathy said, slurping soup across the table from Jeremy. "And they disappeared, too. After that, a worker had to give up his identification to get a spoon. He'd get his papers back when he turned in the spoon. That worked for a while."

"Then the spoons started disappearing again," Czernik said. "Damned if I can figure out how they managed it. Somebody worked out a racket. So we gave up on the spoons."

Jeremy listened with half an ear. Two tables away, the slender girl from the hook gang sat among her teammates, grave and lovely and reserved in the midst of their camaraderie. The hook girls were having a noisy, convivial lunch. The beefy woman, Masha, was the reigning centerpiece of the table, deferred to by the others and getting all her jokes laughed at. Through all the heavy-handed hilarity, the slender girl ate her cabbage soup with quiet, unobtrusive manners that made the clumsy wooden spoon look almost dainty in her grasp.

"Do you know the name of that girl over there?" Jeremy said abruptly. "Third from the end of the table."

Horvathy craned forward. "Her? Her name's Valentina Petrovna. They say she's stuck up . . . nobody likes her. What do you want with a cold fish like her? You got an itch, get yourself a hot little *devooshka*. The factory's full of them."

Jeremy could have struck him. He got up and said, "I'm going to go over and introduce myself."

Czernik looked concerned. "I wouldn't do that, Jerry. You want to take her out walking, wait till the end of the shift and get her alone. You don't want to make it hard for her. Most of these girls'll fall over themselves to go with a foreigner, but they don't like to call attention to it."

But Jeremy was in no mood to listen. Stiffly he walked toward the other table. The women whispered among themselves and giggled as he approached. As he came within earshot, Jeremy heard them discussing him, making no attempt to lower their voices.

"Which one of us do you think, eh?"

"It must be you, Masha. He heard about your talents."

"You'll break his back, Masha!"

"*Kooi zheleza pakah garyacho.* Make hay while the sun shines, Marushka."

The women grew silent and hostile as they realized that he intended to ignore them. He planted himself in front of Valentina. She looked up at him with cool, composed hazel eyes, making him feel like a fool.

"*Dobraye ootra,*" he said inanely. "I mean . . . I should have said *dobree den.* How do you do?"

Alarm flashed briefly in her eyes, then was hidden away. "*Dobree den,*" she said seriously. "I am doing very well, thank you."

Her voice was contralto, with a rich, throaty quality.

"I . . . I saw you before, on the assembly." He cursed his oafishness. She must think him an idiot.

But her expression lost none of its gravity. "Yes?" she said, waiting.

"I'm Jeremy Sinclair. I'm an American reporter. *Ya zhoornaleest.*"

"I am very happy to meet you, Zheremee Seenclair. I am Valentina Petrovna Andreyeva."

She held out a formal hand, as if their surroundings were a drawing room instead of a factory lunchroom. Jeremy felt as if he was supposed to kiss it. He took hold of it hesitantly, and was immediately surprised by the strength and firmness of her grip. She shook his hand briskly, twice up and down, and dropped it.

He had intended to ask her, straight out, to go walking with him, but now he lost his nerve. "I'm . . . I'm writing a story about . . . about auto production in the Soviet Union," he floundered, "and I saw the way you grabbed that hook and braced it. Very quick thinking. It would make an interesting sidelight for my story. I wonder if . . . if I could talk to you sometime."

"You should discuss these questions with Marya Adamovna," she said quickly, nodding toward the woman the others called Masha. "She is our brigade leader."

"Yes . . . of course," he said, forcing a smile for the beefy woman and the rest of the women at the table. "Definitely, one must have the brigade leader's point of view." Masha preened, and he knew he was going to have to go through the motions of an interview. "Uh, perhaps tomorrow, in the Red Corner."

"It was Masha who saved the day, after all," one of the other girls said, looking with obvious hostility at Valentina, who appeared not to notice.

"*Da, da, savershenna verna!*" another girl said, nodding vehemently.

Valentina seemed a million miles away. A remote half-smile played on the long, gull-winged lips. In despair, Jeremy saw her slipping away from him forever.

"Miss Andreyeva," he blurted, "would you . . . that is . . . look, would you care to join me after work? Maybe we could have a bite together."

He waited without hope. She acted as if she had not heard him. The blatant mention of food had been thoughtless, most surely have offended her. The girl who was Masha's partisan was glaring at him. To top it off, he noticed, for the first time, Boris lurking near the bandstand, keeping an eye on him. I've muffed it, Jeremy thought.

Valentina lifted her face toward him. Her smile was measured and correct, the huge dark-fringed eyes tranquil. "I would be very pleased to join with you," she said.

She was waiting for him at the factory gate. She didn't see him at first. The day shift was surging out through the pretentious archway in a vast, jostling flood, and Valentina had to stand to one side, in a sheltered spot against the grimy cement wall.

Jeremy hurried toward her, bumping against the outgoing tide of people. Valentina looked tired and plain, as drab as any of them in her shabby short dress, the cheap summer sandals, the faded red kerchief wrapped around her head. Then she saw him and her face lit up in a dazzling smile. Before he reached her, she took off the kerchief and shook her dark, shoulder-length hair free in token of the social occasion that this was.

"*Zdrastvooite,*" he said.

"*Zdrastvooite,*" she replied. Her face shone with a cold-water, soapless scrubbing that was all the factory washroom could offer, and he saw and was touched by the fact that she had managed to wash the smudges off her knees.

She took his hand quite naturally. "So, where shall we walk?"

He looked around at the dingy factory street. It was a bedlam of colliding shifts; today was payday, a marvelous cure for absenteeism, in Russia as in the United States. The arriving trolley cars were almost hidden by the swarms of people who clung to their exteriors, and the departing trolleys were almost as crowded. Jeremy had entertained some vague intention of riding with Valentina to downtown Gorky, but fighting his way aboard one of those crammed boxes of sour human flesh with her was unthinkable.

"Let's get out of here first," he said.

They pushed through the currents of people. Valentina stayed very close to Jeremy, holding his hand tightly, like a child. Jeremy searched the perimeters of the crowd, and was thankful to see no sign of Boris.

The crowd thinned out as they walked. But ahead of them, blocking their path, stretched a long line of silent people. There must have been several hundred of them, reaching all the way back to a factory side entrance. Watching them, at intervals of fifty feet or so, were uniformed GPU militiamen, in blue caps and wearing the inevitable square dispatch case hanging from a shoulder strap.

Valentina's hand squeezed his, and she slowed down. "The Black Kassa has many visitors today," she said.

The line led to a black-painted shack on stilts. Perched on the roof of the shack, and almost as big as the shack itself, was a gigantic black bird, cut in profile out of plywood sheets, with shaved timbers for claws. A crow. Its yellow beak, open in a mocking laugh, pointed directly down at the poor unfortunates who had to go up a flight of plank steps to a pay window. Vicious cartoons labeled *Drunkard* and *Slacker* were painted on the sides of the high staircase.

Kassa—that was the Russian term for the cashier's window. There was another *kassa* inside the factory for workers who had kept out of trouble. The black pay booth had been put out on the street especially to humiliate unproductive workers. Every passerby could see who the pariahs were. It was a serious matter in a place like Russia, where everybody minded everybody else's business.

Valentina shuddered. "I would rather starve to death than to collect my pay at that place," she said.

A few spectators watched the entertainment stolidly. A ragged band of urchins jeered at the people in the line, unmolested by the militiamen. One little boy of seven or eight picked up a clod of mud and hurled it. It struck a man on the shoulder and splattered his shirt.

Jeremy waited for him to chase the boy, or at least shake a fist at him, but the man only looked down at the ground, shrinking his head between his shoulders. He had a whipped look.

Jeremy had seen the little burlap flags that were placed on the workbenches of workers who fell behind in their quotas. Nobody dared remove them. Sometimes whole departments were stigmatized with the "Order of the Camel"—a banner with a sleeping camel unfurled above their heads. The Soviet incentive system.

"That's a terrible thing to do to those people," he said.

Valentina shrugged. "They're slackers, after all."

She pulled him by the hand around the Black Kassa. Her gaiety returned as soon as they put some distance between themselves and it. "Let's not talk of unpleasant things," she said.

"What shall we talk about?"

"Tell me about America."

"It's a terrible place full of capitalist exploiters. The workers are chained to their machines and beaten every Monday. John D. Rockefeller runs everything."

"Now you are teasing me."

"The streets are paved with gold, everybody has an automobile, there are borscht fountains at every corner, no ration cards, and free cigarettes grow on trees."

She giggled. "You are still teasing me."

"I'm sorry. It was a joke."

"No ration cards! What an idea!"

"Well . . ." he said cautiously, "that part is true."

She looked at him severely. "Do you think I am a simple Russian girl, to be told such tales? I know all about America. The *proforg* has told us at department meetings. American workers have to live in dreadful places called Hoovervilles, because there are no barracks for them. And American trolley cars are not as crowded as ours. There are no passengers riding on the roof or hanging from the sides. Shall I tell you why that is so? It is because American workers are so poorly paid that they cannot afford the fare."

"Now you are teasing *me*."

She laughed. "You looked so serious."

"Did the *proforg* really tell you that?"

"Oh, yes, we are told many such things." Her tone indicated that she wanted to drop the subject.

It had taken them only a few minutes to reach open countryside. The automobile factory and the surrounding impromptu town had sprung up abruptly, by decree, as part of the first Five-Year Plan, and had not yet spawned outskirts, as had the older city of Gorky proper, across the river.

Band music floated toward them on the still summer air. Jeremy lifted his head.

"Shall we visit the culture park?" he said.

Valentina blushed and cast her eyes down across her old cotton dress. "I am not dressed," she said.

"Nonsense, you look beautiful. Anyway, we don't have to do anything grand. Maybe I'll rent a rowboat."

"And then what?" she said, her eyes flashing mischievously. "You will push me into the water and drown me, as the capitalist did to the poor working girl in *An American Tragedy?*"

The title was almost the same in Russian: *Amerikanskaya tragedeeya.*

"You've read Dreiser?" he said in surprise.

"And why not? We are not barbarians, you know. I have read your Jack London and your Sherwood Anderson and your Floyd Dell. And the one with the same name as you."

"Upton Sinclair?"

"Yes. *Myasa* is very popular in Russia. A terrible story of the exploitation of workers."

Myasa meant "Meat." Jeremy figured out that it was the name the Russian publishing trust had given to *The Jungle.*

"Yes," he agreed. "A very terrible story."

"He has not been suppressed in America, Oopton Seenclair?"

Jeremy laughed. "I wouldn't say so. He ran for governor of California two years ago. He might have won, too, if they hadn't ganged up on him."

"Everybody was against him because he is a socialist?"

"No, not exactly. He ran as a Democrat, but the Democratic organization wouldn't get behind him."

"Then he *was* suppressed?"

"No, you don't understand. That's not the way things work in America."

"Perhaps I don't understand," she said slowly.

Jeremy hesitated, then decided to give it a shot. "You see," he said carefully, "the Republicans invented a new method of campaigning. They put everything in the hands of a public relations company." He struggled for a Russian equivalent and finally came up with *spravachnaya kampaneeya,* literally, information business. "It's something like advertising. You know what advertising is, don't you?"

"I understand. It is like agitprop."

"Well . . . yes. Anyway, it was very effective. American politics will probably see a lot more of it in the future. The public relations firm combed through all of Sinclair's old utopian novels and quoted them out of context to make it look as if he was a nut who believed in atheism, vegetarianism, free love, and telepathy. They got Hollywood to make phony newsreels that showed bit players with beards and fake Russian accents supporting Sinclair. Documents were forged to prove him a traitor. They destroyed his reputation."

"Please, this is very sad. I don't want to hear any more."

Valentina was very upset. Jeremy tried to figure what he had said that was wrong. Her hand had gone dead in his, and he let go.

"I'm sorry," he said. "No more politics. I promise."

The gate to the Park of Culture and Rest loomed ahead, saving them from further awkwardness. It was a trellised arch with a huge photograph of the *udarnik* of the month mounted on top. He was a square-headed fellow named Aleksei G. Stakhanov. According to the painted inscription, he had mined 102 tons of coal in a day. A candy-striped ticket booth was beside the gate. Jeremy took off his necktie and walked up to the window. The girl inside looked him over and sold him a pair of fifty-kopek tickets. With a tie, they would have cost a ruble.

Inside the park, Valentina gave him a disapproving once-over. "You looked much more *kulturnee* with the necktie."

"I'm sorry. I'll put it back on."

"No, no, don't bother. It's not a free day, after all. You don't have to be formal."

They set off together down one of the winding paths toward the source of the band music. The park was not too crowded on a working day. Shirt-sleeved men snoozed under trees or sat in the grass with their wives while the children played nearby. Young couples strolled by, eating ice cream or little pies or slices of melon. Jeremy bought Valentina an ice cream at a little booth, and they stopped to watch a vaudeville show that was being put on within a three-sided canvas enclosure. When Jeremy offered to pay the admission that would get them inside the ropes, Valentina said, "But there is no need to spend money. We can watch from here."

Her frugality seemed to be shared by a majority of park patrons. Most of the folding seats were empty. Jeremy and Valentina stood outside the rope barrier with the rest of the crowd and watched a troupe of beefy acrobats in darned tights assemble themselves into a pyramid. Sometime during the performance, Valentina's hand crept back into Jeremy's and stayed there.

They went on to linger at the bandstand. A sweaty military band in crimson jackets and gold braid was playing a Meyerbeer march. There was desultory applause from the people sitting around in the grass. The bandmaster tapped his baton.

Next was some ballet music in a band arrangement. *Giselle*. Jeremy recognized it immediately. Pamela had played some of the pieces on the piano, and once had explained the story to him. It was about maidens who died before their wedding day and came out of their graves at night to dance in their bridal gowns. Jeremy, at age fourteen, had thought it corny.

Next to him, Valentina had a rapt expression on her face, as if she were hearing imaginary violins instead of the wheezy band instruments. She had stretched unconsciously on tiptoe, and was swaying in time to the music. Her eyes were half closed.

The music finished with a reedy flourish of clarinets. Valentina turned to him with a glowing face and said, "It was beautiful, don't you think?"

"Oh, yes, very."

"Even played by a band, it comes through."

"Yes, I agree."

"That was from *Giselle*."

"I know."

She sighed. "My mother told me many times of seeing Pavlova dance in this role. In Petrograd, at the Maryinsky, before I was born. By the time I was old enough to be taken to the children's matinee, Pavlova already had left Russia to dance in the West. When I was a little girl I used to dream that one day, somehow, I would see Pavlova dance, and now of course it is too late."

She squeezed his hand impulsively. Emboldened by the pressure, Jeremy said, "You look like a prima ballerina yourself."

She laughed. "What nonsense!" But she was clearly pleased.

"I mean it. You have beautiful bones in your face, a neck like a swan, marvelous shoulders, and—"

She slapped his wrist playfully. "You must not descend lower, or you will be too daring."

"I was about to say that you move with great grace."

She gave a lusty whoop of laughter, then said, quite seriously, "I could never be a ballerina. I am too tall, and my feet are too large."

"You can't see yourself. You'd look marvelous on stage."

"Please, it is silly to talk of such things."

Jeremy saw that he was skating on thin ice, and returned to safer ground. "Too bad you never got to see Pavlova before she died, but the Soviet Union still has the best ballet in the world. Perhaps another Pavlova will come along."

"Oh no, there will never be another Pavlova. But I would like someday to see the great Semionova dance."

"What's to stop you? Moscow's less than four hundred kilometers away. Surely you could get there on your annual holiday."

"Yes, that would be very nice," she said vaguely.

"Well then, why not?"

"You don't understand."

"No, I don't. Just get on a train and go. It's easy."

"Perhaps one does not like to call attention to oneself." Valentina traced a line in the grass with the toe of her sandal. "I would have to apply for a *propusk* to go to Moscow. Without *blat* it is difficult to get one. And then it would be stamped in my *legitimatsiya*."

Propusk, permit. *Legitimatsiya*, identity book. *Blat*, influence. The words that ruled every Russian's life. Jeremy lost his patience.

"You don't need a *propusk* to go to Moscow. It's the right of every Soviet citizen to travel freely. It's in the new constitution."

"Everything is easy for you foreigners!" she said with some spirit. "Even with a *propusk*, then what? Then I would have to apply for a *bronya*, an official priority for travel to Moscow. Then I would have to buy a ticket with it. That's not so easy either. There are others with more powerful *broni*. And what good is a ticket without a place card for the train? How do I get that? Can you tell me? Then where would I stay in Moscow? At the Grand Hotel with all the bigwigs and foreigners? I have an aunt in Moscow, it is true, but I haven't seen her for years. I don't even know if she's in a position to put me up. Even if her neighbors let her, she might not be willing to go to the police for a permit for a houseguest. That is asking a great deal, after all. And then, how would I get a ticket to the Bolshoi? Even if I could afford it. You must have plenty of *blat* to get a ticket on a night when Semionova dances, and I'm just an ordinary factory hand."

Jeremy was exhausted listening to her. "Excuses," he said. "Russian fatalism."

"What?"

"*Neetchevo.*"

She laughed good-humoredly, and patted his hand.

"Listen," Jeremy said impulsively. "I'm making you a promise. I'm a foreigner with a lot of *blat*. And I'm going to take you to the Bolshoi to see Semionova dance."

She refused to go to a *valuta* restaurant with him, saying she would be conspicuous in her old dress, but she allowed him to treat her to a snack at one of the culture park's dingy stands. They sat on low stools, facing one another across a small table, while an attendant with dirty fingernails brought them stuffed meat pastries and potato salad. Valentina, after a momentary hesitation, asked for carbonated sweet water, the cheapest of the beverages. Jeremy started to order a mug of the watery Pivo beer for himself, but a frown from Valentina told him it was not *kulturnee,* so he switched to a bottle of wine. Valentina picked fastidiously at the greasy *piroshki,* obviously restraining a hearty appetite.

He took her rowing, as he had promised. He had the foresight to take along a second bottle of wine and, against her protests, a couple of *bubliki* bought at a stand—huge crusty rings of dough that had first been boiled, then baked, and which if straightened out would have been as big as a French loaf.

They drifted lazily through a long summer night that would stay bright until a few hours before dawn. Midsummer eve had taken place not too long past, and even in Russia it was celebrated by lovers. From some of the other rented rowboats that floated by with no people visible in them except perhaps for a leg or an arm draped over the side, they could hear an occasional moan or cry. Valentina and Jeremy could feel the compulsion of that luminous sky pressing down on them, too, and they staved it off with chatter.

Valentina refused to take Jeremy's promise to get her to the Bolshoi to see Semionova seriously, and treated it as an allowable exaggeration —the sort of wild embroidery that a passionate and rather nice young man is likely to indulge in when he is trying to impress a girl.

"But no, that is enough foolishness, Zheremee. Tell me more about New York. Are American women as fashionable as the French? Have you been to Paris?"

It was like telling fairy stories to a child. Valentina's eyes glistened with pleasure. He could not supply enough details to satisfy her.

"Slow down! *Medlennee!* No, I haven't been to Paris yet. I was stationed in Berlin. I guess French women are still the most fashionable in the world. At least, American women follow the French fashions."

"Is it true that they change the length of their skirts every year?"

"Huh? I guess so."

"And how long are skirts in America this year?"

"I don't know. I guess maybe they're getting a little shorter."

"How short? Be more precise, *pazhalsta.* Ten inches from the floor? Twelve? Fourteen?"

"I don't know exactly. Sort of halfway between the knee and ankle."

"And the hats. I am told that in America, all the women wear hats. For an afternoon soirée, what kind of a hat is worn?"

"Oh, all different kinds, I guess. No special type."

"You don't know anything important," she said impatiently. "Tell me this, at least. Is it true that in America, all women have silk stockings?"

"Uh . . . not all. A lot of women, I guess. They're expensive."

She gave a small sigh of contentment at the information. "Ah, that is marvelous, Zheremee. *Choodnee!* Do you know what I wish? I wish that one day I would walk down the Fifth Avenue of New York wearing silk stockings and a hat and look into all the shopwindows."

The wine had got to Jeremy. "I'll take you back to New York with me," he said wildly, "and buy you all the silk stockings in Saks!"

She smiled ruefully. "Like you will take me someday to the Bolshoi. Ah, Zheremee, it makes a nice dream. Don't spoil it."

"I mean it!" he cried recklessly.

"Shh. Let us talk of other things. Tell me more about *le beau monde.*"

Jeremy obliged with more stories about the fashionable set in New York and the European capitals, embellishing shamelessly. Valentina drank it all in avidly. But when he pressed her to talk about herself, she was vague. He found out that she was twenty-three, a year older than he was. She would have been about five when the Bolsheviks took over, seven or eight when the bloody civil war had subsided. She had been born in Leningrad—which she still called by the old name of Petrograd—he knew that much, at least, but he could not pry any of her background out of her.

"*Tout s'en va, tout passe, l'eau coule, et le cœur oublie,*" she said wistfully at one point.

"Huh? French isn't my strong point. I flunked it in high school."

"It means, everything vanishes, everything passes, water runs away, and the heart forgets. It's from Flaubert. Don't you think *Madame Bovary* is a sad story?"

"Where did you get hold of a copy of *Madame Bovary?* I thought the state publishing trust banned Flaubert for being too bourgeois."

"I had an old copy in French. From the former days."

"Where did you learn to speak French so fluently?"

"At home."

"Was that in Petrograd?"

She grew moody. "It was a long time ago."

It was intolerable not to know more about this wonderful creature. Jeremy made another effort to draw her out. "Petrograd was where the revolution started. You must have been old enough to remember something of it."

"Please, let's not talk about it anymore."

"Valentina—"

"Shh. Let us be quiet now."

The boat rocked gently under the incandescent June sky. The moon hung in daylight. Their faces were only a foot apart. Valentina's carved features filled Jeremy's vision. He could not believe their beauty. Her eyes were huge, startling. She leaned forward the same instant he did, and their lips touched.

They did not embrace. He held both of Valentina's hands in his while they drank the long kiss. His pulse hammered and he could feel the answering throb of her blood through his fingertips. The moment passed. Neither of them wanted the tawdriness of the rowboat, and as a practical matter there was an inch of water in the bottom.

Their lips separated. They leaned against each other, foreheads touching, in regretful silence, then released each other's hands. Jeremy picked up the oars and started to row back to shore.

Jeremy tied up the boat at the dock and returned the wooden plaque to a pimple-faced attendant who smirked knowingly at Valentina. Jeremy turned a boiled red. Valentina waited with a detached expression for him to complete the transaction.

They were both subdued during the long walk back to the workers' barracks where she lived. Their conversation was guarded and polite. Neither alluded to what had happened in the boat, but they held each other's hands gingerly, as if they might explode. When they came within sight of the barracks, Valentina took her hand out of his and moved a few inches away from him.

The barracks were a row of narrow sagging buildings that reminded Jeremy of unused chicken houses in Iowa. Valentina would not let him come to the door with her. Jeremy guessed that she was ashamed of the place. He could smell kerosene and wet rot even at this distance. She said good night to him at a dilapidated stone gate that evidently had belonged to the estate that once must have stood on these grounds, judging by the charred foundations he could see within. Like other such ruins, most likely it had been burned down by a mob of peasants during the massacres of landowners that had marred the tenure of the provisional government.

Valentina turned to face him. She had put the red kerchief back around her head. The hollows of her features were filled with deep shadows by the dipping sun.

"Thank you for a charming evening," she said stiltedly, giving him a limp hand to shake. *"Je me suis très bien amusée."*

Jeremy did not have the nerve to try for another kiss. He could feel the pressure of invisible eyes from the mesh windows of the barracks.

"May I see you again?" he said.

Her eyes widened suddenly, making her look almost frightened. "If you wish," she said.

It was too late to go back to his hotel in downtown Gorky. He trudged the mile and a half to the American compound, hoping to find someone who could fix him up with a bunk for the night in the bachelors' quarters.

Czernik was still awake. He opened his door a crack and, with a quick, worried look over his shoulder, stepped out into the corridor with Jeremy.

"You still here? I thought you got your story. I figured you'd be on your way back to Moscow by now."

"I'm going to stay around here for a while," Jeremy said. "There are other stories in this region. I ought to cover the big collective farm over near Bogorodsk, and the new hydroelectric station that's going up. And the textile mill. I thought maybe I could arrange to use the American Village for my base while I'm here."

Czernik peered at him shrewdly. "It's the girl, isn't it?"

"Well, okay. Maybe. What if it is?"

"Forget it, Jerry. She's no good for you. And you're no good for her."

"What are you talking about? Anyway, it's none of your business."

Czernik hitched his bathrobe more closely about him. Under the twenty-five-watt bulb in the corridor, he looked old and bald. "I made some inquiries about her. She's a former person."

"What?"

"A former person. One of the *byvshiye*. Old Regime."

"You're crazy. She was about five years old when the Communists took over."

Czernik shrugged. "That's the way they think over here."

"Mike, look, she doesn't have anything to do with politics. She probably owns about two dresses, and she lives in that crummy barracks, and her biggest ambition is to get a ticket to the ballet."

"Her father was an aristocrat. A landowner. That puts her on the Gay Pay-Oo's books. She keeps her nose clean, walks a straight line, does her job, okay. The Gay Pay-Oo has bigger fish to fry."

Jeremy was stunned. He thought of Valentina's fine jawline, the way she walked with her head held high. The French would have come from a governess.

"What in God's name is someone like her doing killing herself on an assembly line in a truck factory?"

Czernik gave him an exasperated look. "Where else is she gonna work?"

A sleepy voice came through the partially open door to Czernik's quarters. "Miklos, what's happening? Are you all right?"

"Yeah, yeah. Go back to sleep. I'm coming right in." Czernik turned back to Jeremy. "Go back to Moscow, Jerry. And don't give the Gay Pay-Oo anything else to put in their dossiers."

"The GPU doesn't scare me."

"Maybe they ought to."

"Look, are you going to get me a bunk for the night or not?"

Czernik sighed. "You can have the Irishman's. He won't be using it anymore."

"Tom? The Wobbly organizer? What happened to him?"

"Didn't you hear? Why do you think everybody's still awake? The Gay Pay-Oo came a little after midnight and took him away."

36

Semionova floated across the stage, a gossamer vision. The swan maidens gathered round, and Semionova began improbably to spin like a top. She was a little thing, a blond sprite, and the colored spotlights had turned the stiff tutu and plumed bodice a mysterious twilight blue.

Valentina turned to Jeremy, her face suffused with awe, and whispered, "Thirty-two *fouettés!* I counted them."

People in the neighboring seats shushed her indignantly, and Valentina settled happily back in her chair to enjoy the rest of the third act. Jeremy hadn't been able to get tickets for *Giselle,* but *Swan Lake,* Valentina had assured him, was just as sad.

Jeremy tried to look attentive, but an evening of watching a lot of ballet dancers whirl and leap across the stage had almost put him to sleep. Jeremy's taste in dancing ran to Fred Astaire and Ginger Rogers. While Valentina was engrossed, he sneaked a look at the audience.

The Bolshoi Theater was packed. It always was when Semionova danced. Jeremy had moved heaven and earth to get front and center tickets. They had cost him about four and a half dollars apiece in American currency, but in unconverted rubles they would have added up to a fortune.

The audience was seedy, in spite of the glittering occasion. The dowdy daytime dresses, the unpressed suits and grubby collars, looked strange amidst the gilded nineteenth-century splendors of the Bolshoi. Even in the ornate royal box, where the imperial eagle had been replaced by a hammer and sickle emblem, Jeremy could see the flash of white shirt-sleeves against the red plush. Beside Jeremy, one unlaundered *udarnik,* sent to the ballet by his *organizatsiya,* sat with his arms aggressively folded and his cap still on.

Even the orchestra, sawing their way diligently through the Tchaikovsky score, looked threadbare. Jeremy, after studying a particular bassoonist through two acts, had just reached the startling conclusion that the man's black bow tie was painted on his shirtfront.

But all was magic on the stage. The costumes were dazzling, the backdrops and scenery opulent, and the dancers were clearly beings from a higher plane of existence than the drab Moscow that waited outside. Now the prince appeared with his little crossbow, a resplendent figure in gold braid and white tights.

Valentina turned to smile at Jeremy again. Her shiny brown hair had been waved for the occasion, and she had used the American lipstick that Jeremy had bought for her at a *valuta* shop. She wore a green velvet frock that her aunt had sewn and restyled out of an old dress that had remained in a trunk for thirty years. A few worn spots showed, but Valentina looked stunning in it. She wore a gay scrap of scarf at her throat. Valentina's superb carriage and natural loveliness made the brave attempt at style work; she was drawing envious glances from the woman at her right, some commissar's battle-axe wife with pudgy bejeweled fingers and a mask of powder and rouge that stopped at a ring of grime around her neck.

Jeremy had worn his good blue serge suit and a dark woolen tie to please Valentina, even though he knew he would swelter all evening. He had shown her the baggy summer seersucker he had bought in imitation of Kemble, the London man, and she had said, "But no, they look like pajamas!"

On stage, Semionova gracefully died. The music reached its throbbing climax. The curtain dropped. The audience stood on its feet and began the noisy coercion for curtain calls.

Jeremy itched to get away before they were trapped by the playing of the "Internationale," but he didn't have the heart to deprive Valentina of even one minute of her magical evening. He stood and applauded with the others until his hands were raw, then mouthed the words of the Communist anthem to the overblown orchestral rendition. *Arise, ye prisoners of starvation, arise ye wretched of the earth* . . . If Brad could see me now, Jeremy thought. Brad had sent him a cautiously worded letter; back in the United States, the presidential campaign was getting rough. The Republicans had charged that the New Deal was full of communists, and Roosevelt was on the defensive.

The houselights went on. The tiers of gilt balconies began to empty. Jeremy kept a firm grip on Valentina's arm so as not to lose her, and joined the crush.

"I will never forget this!" Valentina declared. "Never! Thank you, my dear."

"Don't thank me till I get you out alive," Jeremy said.

Ahead of them, in the struggling stampede doorward, Jeremy saw an astonishing vision of white tie and tails. It was Kemble, refusing to lower his standards, despite the proletarian stares he was attracting. The small woman beside him in evening gown and wrap was his wife. Kemble turned round and caught sight of him. "'Lo there, Sinclair, splendid performance, what?" he shouted before the crowd bore him along.

Outside, Jeremy found the Kembles again, standing under the tall columned portico that faced Sverdlov Square. Mrs. Kemble beamed at Valentina. She was a short, bosomy, quick woman who had always reminded Jeremy of a robin.

"We're just going to the National for a bite," Kemble said. "Care to join us?"

Jeremy's face fell. "Uh . . ."

Mrs. Kemble came to his rescue. "Can't you see these young people want to be alone?"

Jeremy made the obligatory protests. Valentina, whose English was limited, smiled graciously at the Kembles, having no idea what was going on.

"Just so," Kemble said, his eyes going politely glassy. "P'raps we'll see the two of you at Duranty's party. Try to make it if you can. Your embassy's Mr. Henderson will be there, I understand. He may drop a hint about why Bill Bullitt's been absent from Moscow for so long. I have a feeling a new American ambassador is imminent."

"Thanks for the tip," Jeremy said.

"Do come along, Herbert," his wife said, tugging at his arm. "You're off talking shop again." To Jeremy she said, "She's lovely." She turned with a warm smile to Valentina and said with careful articulation, *"Da novai fstrechee."*

"It is so pleased to having meet you," Valentina said. She sounded like royalty.

When the Kembles were gone, Valentina said, "Who was he? He is a very great man?"

"He's just a reporter, like me. I knew him in Germany."

"Oh no! He is so *vazhnee*. So *kulturnee*."

"How about me?" Jeremy said with mock indignation. "Aren't I *vazhnee* and *kulturnee,* too?"

She was immediately contrite. "But yes, of course. But you are not so old. And your hair has come uncombed again."

Jeremy smoothed back the stray tuft. "The Nazis kicked him out. He told the truth about them once too often. At the border they stripped his wife naked."

"Oh, but how terrible. The newspapers say we shall have to fight them one day."

"Come on, let's have a midnight supper."

Valentina hung back. "No, no, this evening was perfect. Supper is not necessary."

Jeremy laughed. "Don't be silly. Don't you want to see the capitalist excesses of the Metropole?"

She plucked nervously at the velvet dress. "I don't look well enough."

"Nonsense. You'll be the most beautiful girl there. Let's go."

He took her by the hand and dragged her across Sverdlov Square toward the Metropole. In front of the hotel, the Intourist fleet of limousines was parked two deep. They were all Lincolns. The lounging chauffeurs looked up with dull eyes as Jeremy and Valentina threaded their way between the cars. Jeremy hurried Valentina past the *valuta* girls who loitered in pairs at the entrance, but not before one of them, a dumpy blonde with thick makeup, had called out, "Get rid of her, *dooshka,* and we'll show you a thing or two!"

The Metropole was noisy and vulgar as usual, thronged with tourists, carousing members of the foreign colony, black marketeers with mouths full of gold teeth, and ordinary Russians braving the certain presence of GPU informers to have a once-in-a-lifetime splurge. A twenty-piece dance band played imitation American jazz, learned from phonograph records. The floor was crowded with dancing couples trying to do the fox-trot. In the center of the floor, a hazard to tipsy dancers, was a circular fish pool. In a dim Victorian grotto at the far end was the Metropole's crowning wonder—a genuine bar with leather stools and brass rail.

Valentina was subdued as the waiter seated them. When he was gone, she said, "This is like a restaurant in America?"

"Like a lot of them."

"There are many, then?"

"Well . . . uh . . . yes."

Valentina looked down at the tablecloth. "I remember a restaurant in Petrograd. It must have been before the October Revolution, and I must have been very well behaved to have been taken there at such an age. Perhaps we had been to the aquarium gardens. It was not noisy like this. It was very quiet. My mother spoke French to the waiters. I remember very well what I had. I had an omelette, and afterwards, ice cream."

"Perhaps it's still there."

"I don't think so."

"The building, I mean. Perhaps you could find the street."

"I don't wish to go back to Petrograd." She tossed her hair and gave him a determined smile. *"Tout est perdu,"* she said gaily. "All of that is lost. I am having a very good time tonight. This is my *jour gras*. My fat day."

Jeremy laughed. "Then we'd better order."

The waiter came over and sized Jeremy up after a heavy-lidded glance at Valentina. "Do you wish to see the dollar menu, sir?" he said.

"By all means," Jeremy said dryly. The ruble menu was artificially inflated to keep ordinary Russians out and attract foreign exchange. In rubles, a plate of soup would have cost a week's factory wages. Valentina's wages, Jeremy thought.

"Why don't I order a bottle of champagne to start?" Jeremy said.

"No," Valentina said. "I wish to have a Western drink."

Jeremy raised his eyebrows. "Are you sure?"

"Yes," she said firmly. "Wheesky soda."

Jeremy ordered drinks, with a portion of caviar and toast for an hors d'oeuvre. The waiter departed.

"He did not ask for a food ticket," Valentina said wonderingly.

"No, the rules are suspended," Jeremy said. "No ration cards, no *broni*, no *propuski*. Tonight you're in the West."

"It makes a nice pretend," Valentina said.

A gypsy chorus had joined the jazz band. At the Metropole, the outlawed music was winked at, in order to attract the *valuta* of decadent foreigners. The gypsies rattled castanets and began wailing something about *"kreezantema."*

"The chrysanthemums in the garden have faded!" Valentina exclaimed in delight. "One of the old songs!"

The drinks and caviar arrived. The caviar was served with grated eggs and onions, with thin slices of white toast. Valentina exclaimed again over the white toast.

"In America, a young lady would be more impressed by the caviar," Jeremy said.

Valentina tasted her highball and made a face.

"What's the matter, don't you like it?" Jeremy said.

"It's very tasty," she said without conviction.

"I'll order wine with dinner. You can get French wine here."

Valentina pitched into her dinner with gusto. She ate heartily but without greed. She was no longer constrained in Jeremy's presence now that they had become lovers. Despite the fine-drawn architecture of her features, it was obvious that she had a healthy appetite. She shoveled down the potted crabs, the sturgeon in champagne, the chicken *pokievski,* the strawberry ice with the inevitable biscuit standing straight up in it, as if she had them every day of her life. Jeremy found it hard to keep up with her. They finished up with a French brandy that cost half as much again as the meal.

They lingered, over brandy and cigarettes, until the restaurant closed at two in the morning. In the bar, a bunch of drunken American journalists were singing bawdy songs, while the bribed jazz band tried to keep up. Jeremy had been afraid that his colleagues would be horning in all night, but the *Chicago Daily News* man, after an admiring inspection of Valentina, had gone back to the bar and passed the word to the rest of them to leave Jeremy alone.

The waiters had hovered over Valentina, calling her *mademoiselle* and lighting her cigarettes, despite her Russianness, and Jeremy rewarded them with a large, illegal tip. The bill came to more than sixteen dollars. In rubles, it would have been thirty times that. More than Valentina earned in four months at the truck factory.

Outside, the Moscow night was a tremulous silvery haze. The streets had emptied out. Over the low rooftops you could make out the bulging onion domes of St. Basil's Cathedral, veiled and eternal. You could almost forget that now it was an antireligious museum. Over it hung a glowing red star—the crowning ornament of one of the shadowy Kremlin towers beyond.

Valentina sighed contentedly. "How do you say it, *paradis,* in English?"

"Paradise."

"It is almost the same."

"Come on, I'd better get you back to your aunt's flat."

"At two o'clock in the morning? Better not. We'll scare all the other tenants out of their wits. My aunt, too. At this hour they'll think it is the Gay Pay-Oo ringing the bell."

She laughed. She was a little drunk, or she never would have said such a thing. In Moscow and the other large cities, one couldn't avoid seeing the enormous closed vans that moved through the night after traffic had thinned, going from house to house to collect the people the GPU had marked for disappearance. But one didn't talk about it openly. The foreign correspondents avoided the subject by unspoken agreement. No one wanted to risk losing his credentials, or worse.

"Won't your aunt wonder where you are?" Jeremy said.

Valentina gave a charming little hiccough and put a hand in surprise to her mouth.

"One does not wonder about things nowadays," she said. *"Ne bespakoites,* don't worry about my aunt."

Valentina had not yet stayed the night in Jeremy's room during the four days they had been in Moscow together. They made love in the late afternoon, after he had filed his copy for the day. She would cook some sort of meal for the two of them on Jeremy's strictly illegal electric hot plate, out of the hoard of food stocks his foreigner's status entitled him to, and they would go on to a film or concert and a snack at the buffet before Jeremy deposited her at her aunt's. Mornings, Valentina went out on her own to see the Moscow sights, and arranged to meet Jeremy at the park, armed with a book for the wait. Jeremy fumed at the time he had to spend cooling his heels in the censor's office or waiting in line to transmit a cable. He knew he was skimping on his obligation to the press agency and the syndicate, but he thought he could get away with it for a while by using up his precious stock of "anytime" stories and backgrounders.

"All right, then," he said. "The hell with the hotel management! The hell with the chambermaid! The hell with the floor concierge! You're moving in with me."

"Oh, that will be *preevaskhodna,* my dear. Like our own little house." She laughed. "But so many in hell!"

Arm in arm they set off for the Savoy. It was only a few minutes' walk. Almost all of the hotels set aside for foreigners were in the vicinity of Red Square, in a small orbit that made it easier for the authorities to keep tabs on them.

The elevators were out of order again. They walked up six flights to Jeremy's room. On the way down the corridor, they passed Mr. Grenkov. He was on his way to the lavatory at the end of the hall, in an old dressing gown, with a teapot in his hand to bring back water. Jeremy felt guilty about Mr. Grenkov. He lived with his wife and three small children in a room that was smaller than Jeremy's, and had no bath of its own. He was some kind of functionary at the Foreign Office. Mr. Grenkov nodded politely at Jeremy, and did not look at Valentina at all.

Jeremy had been lucky. He had inherited his room from the AIPS correspondent, who had been reassigned just at the time Jeremy had arrived in Moscow, and who for old times' sake was willing to let Jeremy have it for a mere thousand rubles—needed, he said, to pay off his debts. Unfortunately, Jeremy had inherited the AIPS man's Russian girl friend with the room. He had barely moved in when the key turned in the lock and Irina walked through the door. Irina was broad-beamed, peroxided, and heavily powdered, and she took it for granted that Jeremy was to take over where AIPS had left off. In the end, Irina and her belongings had to be carried out bodily by two strong hall porters. She had returned several times over the next couple of months to bang at the door and scream at him.

Jeremy unlocked the door and let them in. As seedy as it was, the room was redolent of a past era. The ceiling was immensely high with florid carved cornices running around the shadowy upper reaches. The furniture was dark, towering, and weighed a ton. Some seamstress in czarist days had gone blind sewing the fringe on the moth-eaten green velvet curtains. There was a tall alcove with a canopied bed in it, and in the adjoining bath there was a marble sink with tarnished brass fixtures. The hot plate and Jeremy's few cooking utensils rested on a nine-foot sideboard that looked like a giant's coffin on clawed legs, and his typewriter monopolized the damask expanse of a huge round table. A scattering of spindly gilt chairs with threadbare silk upholstery stood around, looking uncomfortable. But the room was sunny in the daytime, and looked out on a fine spacious view of the broad boulevard below.

"Our little house," Valentina said, and came into his arms.

In the morning they went around to Valentina's aunt's to pick up her things. The aunt shared an apartment in what once had been a town house near Smolensk Square, and she had one tiny room to herself, with kitchen privileges. Valentina had slept across two stuffed chairs salvaged from her aunt's old home. There were bedbugs; Jeremy had seen the marks on Valentina's body.

The hall smelled of cabbage soup, centuries old. Tacked next to the bell was a list of names and directions on how to ring for each of them. For Valentina's aunt, it was two longs and a short. Jeremy pressed the bell, and there was an impression of suspended life inside the apartment, as each tenant waited to see who the bell would be for. Then there were quick nervous footsteps and the door opened.

Valentina's aunt was small and drab, a gray mouse of a woman in a rustling black dress and yellowed lace shawl. The planes of her face retained the traces of former beauty. She showed no surprise when Valentina said she was moving out. She held out a frail bony hand to Jeremy and said, *"Enchantée, monsieur."*

This was the Aunt Ludmilla with whom Valentina and her mother had lived during the years of chaos. Jeremy had pieced together a rough history, bit by bit, from isolated remarks made by Valentina during the past weeks in Gorky.

Valentina's family had lived a pleasant and comfortable existence before the revolution. In her first memories, they had divided their seasons between a town house in Petrograd—now Leningrad—and a modest country estate about fifty miles outside the city. There were always plenty of people about, and in her images of the past, aunts and uncles, nursemaids and footmen, were jumbled indiscriminately together. Her father had practiced the profession of engineer. Valentina's parents were of the type that had been known in those days as *intelligenty*—moderately progressive, enlightened people who believed in not very focused terms that perhaps some kind of social change was overdue in Russia . . . maybe some kind of land reforms by the czar.

After the February Revolution in 1917, Valentina's father had said that it was up to men of goodwill, of whatever class, to help the provisional government succeed. He had enthusiastically offered his services to the new Petrograd Soviet that had taken possession of the Smolny Palace, amid a litter of chicken bones and potato peels and urine stains on the rugs. He saw it as a manifestation of Narodnichestvo— the idea of a sort of peasant democracy derived from *"narod,"* the people, that well-meaning liberals in Petrograd circles liked to play with. The Bolsheviks, he thought, were just one of many factions in the popular uprising—a minority faction at that. They told him to go home. Perhaps he was lucky not to have been shot then and there.

Then the October Revolution came. The Bolsheviks had been a minority, it was true, but they had the best slogans. The mobs that stormed through the streets of Petrograd shouted, "Land, peace, and bread!" The rifles and machine guns used in the coup had been supplied, incredibly, by the Kerensky government itself.

Valentina had been six, and she dimly remembered the sound of gunfire from the direction of the Winter Palace, the ill-dressed men running in swarms through the streets with clubs and paving stones in their hands that she had seen from an upstairs window until her nursemaid had snatched her away and drawn the curtains. She wasn't allowed to play outside that winter, she remembered, because the truckloads of soldiers that were forever rumbling through the streets sometimes fired shots at random. The little boy next door had been killed that way, one day when his nurse was taking him with his sled to the park.

In the terrible famine year of 1920, Valentina's father moved the family out of the city and into a small cottage on what once had been their country estate. The main house, of course, was occupied. The local committee let them stay. Valentina's father had been popular with the peasants. Other landowners in the district had been killed, sometimes horribly.

They were better off in the country. There was food. The Reds had not yet got around to confiscating the grain and livestock here. Elsewhere in Russia, it was whispered, people were eating human flesh. The children were frightened by the tales. "The cannibals will catch you if you don't behave," the *babushki* warned. Valentina had nightmares.

Toward the end of the year, a detachment of Red Guards rode through. It was clear by then that the civil war was nearing a conclusion. Trotsky's armies had pushed back the White forces. In Siberia, Admiral Kolchak had collapsed. The joint American-British-French expeditionary force that had tried to intervene against the Bolsheviks had retreated in failure. The Red Guards took Valentina's father along as a reluctant but resigned recruit. "When this madness is over," he told Valentina's mother before he rode south with the unit that had drafted him, "it will be a mark in my favor."

Valentina never saw her father again. Whether he had been killed in the fighting farther south, or whether he had been executed by his new friends, or whether he was simply living elsewhere in Russia and unable to make his way home, she was never to know. One did not make inquiries about missing persons.

Things got worse after that. A new commissar from Moscow wanted the cottage, and Valentina, her mother, and her baby brother were moved into a cowshed. One night, the old man who had been their gardener before the revolution came secretly to the cowshed and told them, his voice shaking with nervousness, that for certain reasons it would be better if they left the district and went to live someplace where the Andreyev family was not known.

They went to Moscow to live with Aunt Ludmilla. The authorities were not very interested in her. Her husband had been an art historian, she an accomplished musician, but though they had been *intelligenty,* they had lived quietly. At the time, she had been allowed to retain two rooms of her former house, and Valentina and her mother moved into one of them. Her baby brother had not survived the journey to Moscow.

Valentina's mother died the following year, of a cold aggravated by malnutrition. Valentina was eleven. Her mother had harbored the fantastic notion that she must try out for the Bolshoi ballet school, for a guaranteed education and an assured future life in this strange new world the Soviets were creating. There had been a ballerina in the family fifty years before, still talked about. Aunt Ludmilla did her best to coach Valentina. Valentina learned the five positions of the feet and the seven basic movements quickly and easily, and went on to learn the simple dance sequences that her aunt was able to remember from the time she had been pianist at practice sessions. Valentina showed up at the Bolshoi competition with hundreds of other children, but she was already too old, and too tall.

"Well now we must find a life for you," her aunt had sighed. "Your poor mother was not very practical."

Valentina was permitted to attend a primary school, the one attached to the Amo automobile plant in Moscow. Russia's new rulers had determined that universal education was necessary to provide trained workers. After the fifth grade, a pupil spent two hours of the school day in the factory. A favored minority would be selected to go on to secondary school, a passport to something beyond unskilled labor, but it was made clear to Valentina that as Old Regime, she could not hope for this privilege. It was reserved for the children of the proletariat.

She was fifteen when the first Five-Year Plan was launched. The Piatiletka, Russia's frenzied new crusade, decreed by Stalin. The industrial miracle was to be achieved in four years. All over Russia appeared posters, billboards, electric signs, with the slogans *5 in 4* and *2 + 2 = 5*. Valentina was told that volunteers were needed for a new automobile plant in Gorky. It seemed that a new Detroit was being built on the banks of the Volga. The Amo factory had admitted that it could spare her. Living quarters would be found for her. She packed a bag and said good-bye to her aunt.

Valentina endured the rude living conditions with good spirit. She was with a lot of other teen-age girls, mostly sturdy peasant girls who thought themselves lucky to have escaped farm labor, and they were proud of doing their part to fulfill the Piatiletka. They giggled together, and talked about boys, and made fun of the men who came sneaking down their aisle in hopes of catching a girl getting dressed. Valentina made no close friends, but it was like being a part of a club. And it was only for a year.

The year stretched into two, and then came the 1930 decree that forbade workers to leave their jobs without permission, followed by a second decree that prohibited factories from hiring workers whose papers were not in order. Without a job and the right papers, there was no bread card. So Valentina stayed in Gorky.

"But," she shrugged, "at least I ate."

Jeremy understood what she was referring to. Famine had come again in 1932, after Stalin's disastrous attempt at forced collectivization had stripped the country of its grain and livestock. This time it couldn't be blamed on a civil war. Five or six million people had starved to death that winter. The true number would never be known. Foreign reporters were kept bottled up in Moscow to keep them from seeing the emaciated corpses heaped along the railroad tracks, the silent deserted villages whose inhabitants had fled to starve somewhere else.

But at Valentina's factory, the workers continued to receive rations. A pound and a half of bread a day. Cabbage soup, somewhat thinner. Stalin had determined to keep the industrial effort going, at least. Armed troops raided the countryside and took away the food needed for the cities. The peasants would be permitted to die. Valentina had almost daily seen the long double columns of gaunt, cowed peasants being herded through the streets by GPU guards with rifles and drawn revolvers, on the way to collection points.

"Many things were done so that the Piatiletka might be fulfilled," Valentina said. "Some must suffer so that all may be better off, they say. But such things are behind us. It is easier for us now. See, I am in Moscow now, after all."

She tossed her fine head and gave a resolute smile. "I had forgotten how beautiful Moscow is in summer."

They were sitting in one of the little parks, on a bench with a good view of the river. A fresh breeze riffled the leaves of the trees. The scent of roses came from a nearby flower cart heaped with bright blooms. A toddler clumsily chased an unconcerned squirrel while two old women watched fondly. On a bench opposite, a pair of youthful Red Army soldiers on leave sat with their collars loosened and their booted feet outstretched, making remarks at the girls who passed, and every once in a while one of them would sneak a look at Valentina.

Valentina had never looked lovelier. Three weeks in Moscow, away from the murky industrial caverns of Gorky, seemed to have taken the weight of an invisible troll off her back. The sunny afternoons in the parks and beaches had replaced the aristocratic pallor with a ruddy glow, a healthy brick-hued materiality that made you notice the long smooth muscles of calf and forearm, the admirable frame, and made you understand how she could stand on an assembly line all day and manhandle twenty-pound hooks. Now, as she chattered on happily about the gala athletic pageant they had just seen in Red Square, her eyes sparkled, her teeth flashed, and she was all animation.

"Those little children on the bathing float," she laughed. "So *lofkee*, so cute, do I have the right English word? One could really believe they were diving into the waves, that blue gauze looked almost like water! And the automobile workers' float with the fine new car filled with flowers! Did you see the athletes from the Gorky Sport Club marching behind? And the white doves, so beautiful!"

Jeremy watched her with fierce joy. It was intolerable to think that her annual leave was almost up, that he would have to put her aboard one of the overcrowded trains for Gorky, armed with the *broni* he had got for her at the Foreign Office, and perhaps not see her for months.

"Valentina," he said slowly, "wouldn't you like to live in Moscow? Move back, I mean, and have it as your official residence?"

She gave a throaty laugh, and patted his hand. "Yes, and I would like to live in the sugar palace in the children's story."

"No, I mean really. Have a job here, and a permit to stay, and you could use your aunt's address for your papers, but you could live with me at the hotel."

She turned and looked at him, her eyes getting very large. "But what are you saying? You know of the difficulties."

"I could help. Didn't I have the *blat* to get you to Moscow to spend your leave? Listen, I know you can't live in Moscow without a job. You could be my secretary. The one I have now was furnished by the Foreign Office press department. I never use her. I'm sure she's a spy for the GPU. I skim through the morning papers myself, and do my own translations. That's all the other correspondents use their secretaries for anyway, and they miss a lot of little items that their secretaries hold back. You could be a real help to me, another pair of eyes and legs. Of course I'd have to get permission. That might be a fight. But Mr. Kemble would be glad to help. I could ask Walter Duranty, the *New York Times* correspondent, to put in a word. He has a Russian wife."

"Please, my dear . . ." He was amazed to see a tear trickle down her cheek.

Jeremy's mind turned round and round in a frenzy of inspiration. All things seemed possible in the bright Moscow sunlight.

"Think about it," he said. "The pay will be better, you'll live an interesting life, and we can be together all the time."

She had gone rigidly, unnaturally still. She answered in something like terror: "No, no, you must not!"

He waited until she had stopped trembling. On the bench across the path, one of the Red Army soldiers was whispering to his companion, maybe to ask if they ought not to intervene for the girl against the foreigner who was upsetting her.

"It's all right," he said. "Don't worry. I won't do anything to get you into trouble."

They got up to go. He had a story to file about the pageant in Red Square. The professional part of his mind cast about for a theme. The children's float had carried a banner saying, *We thank Comrade Stalin for a happy childhood.* Nothing there. The automobile workers' placard had said: *Chauffeurs today, tank drivers tomorrow.* That was more promising. He could contrast that with the flight of white doves that had been released. One of them, to the crowd's delight, had symbolically alighted just above Stalin's head on the reviewing stand. Probably that had been staged, too.

Valentina had recovered. "You are too lazy," she said sternly. *"Leneevee.* You must not be late with your story again today. I will make you tea, and walk about on tiptoe, and not talk to you until you have finished."

He bought her some flowers at the little pushcart. It was just a tiny bouquet of violets, but it was ruinously expensive. The inhabitants of Moscow craved flowers as they craved the sun, and would sacrifice a couple of days' wages for a modest bunch. Valentina was overcome by the gift.

"I will put them in water at once," she said. "You must change the water every day after I am gone. You will see, they will live a long time."

He discussed the exit visa problem with Kemble.

"It's a crime to escape from the Soviet Union," Kemble said dryly. "That's the word they use. 'Escape.' Article Fifty-eight of the criminal code. The Soviets like to hang on to their citizens."

"I know that," Jeremy said.

"People get into trouble for even thinking about leaving," Kemble said, stuffing his pipe with Edgeworth. "Woman came to our consulate to inquire about a British visa. Just asking. Had relatives in London. GPU got wind of it somehow. Put her on the conveyor for forty days. The sweat room, the lice room, usual sort of thing. Tried to get her to confess to espionage, sabotage, currency violations, any damned thing. Saw her afterward. Teeth knocked out. Didn't write the story, of course. She begged me not to."

"Valentina wouldn't have to expose herself. I've thought it all out. We could get married at one of the churches. The Soviet government doesn't recognize church weddings, so there'd be no government record. But I'd have a marriage certificate. Father Braun would do it for us—he's an American. Then I could get it registered at the American embassy—that would make it legal in the United States, and I could apply for a U.S. visa for Valentina."

"Marriage doesn't affect the citizenship of either party, in the Soviet view," Kemble said, sucking at his pipe.

"No . . . but I thought . . . if I could get the embassy behind me, and if the fellows in the English-speaking press corps put on pressure for me . . ."

Kemble frowned. "There's no guarantee it would work, Sinclair. You know that as well as I do. We both know of any number of cases where some lonely American on a one- or two-year contract set up housekeeping with a Russian girl friend, married her at one of those wedding palaces for a two-ruble fee, then found that he had to leave her behind."

"It isn't like that," Jeremy said, turning hot. "This isn't one of those *zags* affairs. Some of those men even had wives back in the states."

Kemble peered at him with something resembling pity. "There's a possibility you *must* consider, Sinclair. Your young lady is very charming, very pretty, but we both know that in far too many of these romances, the girl is *byvshiye,* a former person. They're terribly vulnerable, you see. The GPU watch them, and when it's known that they've formed an attachment with a foreigner, they're forced to report on him, like it or not. They have no choice in the matter."

"God, that's a filthy thing to say!" Jeremy cried, getting up out of his chair.

Kemble had become icy and reserved. "I'm not saying that Valentina is a GPU spy," he said patiently. "I'm just pointing out that you may be placing her in an intolerable position."

Mrs. Kemble intervened. "Herbert, you do put things badly. Please sit down, Jeremy. I'm just making tea."

Jeremy sat down again, ashamed of his outburst.

Mrs. Kemble came back with the tray. Tea and tiny cucumber sandwiches. Russian cucumbers, but sliced so thin that they had taken on a British character. "I had no idea things had gone so far," she said. "These are terrible times we live in. That's what you've decided, then? To marry Valentina and take her back to America with you?"

"Yes." The realization struck home with startling force. Until this moment, he hadn't thought about it in those terms. Going home with a Russian wife. Introducing her to his mother, to Brad and Pamela and Gordon. To Junie, if he ever got to California; Brad had said she was living there. Settling down in—where?—in New York, where the best jobs were. Until Mrs. Kemble put it into those words, he had been thinking no further than a strategy for getting Valentina across the border.

"And what does Valentina think?"

"I . . ."

Mrs. Kemble looked at him shrewdly. "You haven't proposed yet?"

"I . . . no."

She sighed. "Never mind. You're wise not to raise her expectations yet. I know she loves you; I've seen the way she looks at you. And she certainly wouldn't do anything to hurt you, never mind Herbert's tactlessness. Poor frightened doe! I'm sure it will all work out in the end. Herbert will do anything he can to help."

Kemble's long reedy form stirred. "P'raps it's a good thing that she's leaving Moscow this week. Give things a chance to cool off a while. You have to wave things under the Gay Pay-Oo's nose for months before they notice. Don't do anything rash, Sinclair. And don't despair. I'll make some quiet inquiries and try to discover the mood of the passport office these days."

Mrs. Kemble beamed. "There, that's settled. Jeremy, your tea's getting cold."

Over the tea and cucumber sandwiches they discussed the current political situation. "Something's in the wind," Kemble said. "Did you notice that Molotov didn't appear on the reviewing stand with Stalin at the pageant yesterday?"

"He's on vacation."

Kemble brushed a crumb from his mustache. "They say he takes his vacations under GPU supervision these days."

"It probably doesn't mean anything."

Kemble went on imperturbably. "The last time he got Stalin mad at him was when he got wishy-washy about the death penalty during the Party purges three years back. All the old Bolsheviks lost their jobs, but no one got shot. Of course, Stalin's more powerful today. Did you notice his picture in Red Square yesterday? Just a little bigger than Lenin's."

"You think there's something going on behind the scenes, and Molotov's being wishy-washy again?"

Kemble looked thoughtfully into his teacup. "Something's afoot. There are all sorts of mysterious backstage rumblings. Last month something called a 'USSR People's Commissariat of Justice' was set up. Stage machinery, you see."

Jeremy tried not to show his chagrin. He'd missed that one. He'd been spending every spare moment with Valentina, neglecting his footwork. Of course it wouldn't have made much of a story—just a dull organizational change.

"What really interests me," Kemble said, "is the sudden increase in anti-Trotsky propaganda during the last few days. The Central Committee's whipping the provinces into a fever pitch. They're finding secret Trotskyists under every bed. One of them is Valentina's old boss, by the way. Smirnov. He was head of the Gorky auto works. They arrested him during the purge three years ago, but he wasn't shot. Now all of a sudden they've discovered that he's a worse villain than he was before."

"What's the point of denouncing Trotsky? He's in exile in Norway. He hasn't been a threat to Stalin since he was deported in 1929."

"Trotsky's a rallying point for communists who don't like what's going on in Russia. His influence is increasing among the faithful in the international movement. He's a pretty good propagandist himself, you know. If anything happens to Stalin, he's sitting up there in Norway, waiting to be invited back."

"That doesn't seem very likely."

Kemble stirred a second cup of tea. "Maybe Stalin thinks so. Our Oslo bureau says that the Russians are putting pressure on Norway to kick Trotsky out. They say that Mexico may take him in."

"You can't seriously believe that all these backstage rumblings, as you call them, are about a Trotskyite plot?"

Kemble raised an eyebrow. "I didn't say that. But Trotsky would make an awfully good excuse to get rid of some inconvenient fellows, wouldn't he?"

"The night of the long knives," Jeremy said suddenly.

"What?"

"The Roehm purge all over again. They always climb over the bodies of their friends. The ones that put them where they are."

"Oh, I wouldn't go that far. Trotsky got deported, that was all. And Smirnov, Zinoviev, Kamenev, and the rest of that lot never were shot. They only got jail sentences, and rather short ones at that. Just Stalin showing that he was boss. But if this story develops as I think it will, there ought to be a lot of fireworks. Keep us busy for a few weeks, at any rate." He paused and looked curiously at Jeremy. "Perhaps it's a good thing that you'll be separated from your Valentina for a bit. Keep your mind on your work, what?"

"Herbert!" Mrs. Kemble said.

"He's right, Mrs. Kemble," Jeremy said, his face burning. "I've been falling down in my work. All the fellows in the press section here know it. And if I don't buckle down soon, my bosses will know it, too."

Kemble laughed. "They're always the last to realize it. He's been doing the Sinclair thing brilliantly, my dear. Innumerable feuilletons on 'Gorky, Crossroads of the Volga,' and 'Gorky's Flivver Kings,' and 'A Walk through Old Gorky.' One can read them all the way through and never realize that there's not a scrap of news in them."

Jeremy grinned. Kemble had his number, all right. Well, he'd take Kemble's advice. He'd mend his fences here, then join Valentina in Gorky in two or three weeks. The brief separation wouldn't kill them. If he worked hard enough in Moscow and fired off enough really first-rate news material to his editors, he could afford to spend a couple of weeks a month in Gorky with Valentina, writing enough of those lightweight feature stories to earn his keep. At least till this visa thing was settled and he could persuade Valentina that there was a future in marrying him. His contract ran until the end of the year. There was plenty of time.

"At least I have seen Semionova dance," Valentina said. "I will always have that to remember."

Around them the railroad station seethed with humanity. Families of peasants sat on hampers and burlap bundles, companionably drinking tea they had brewed from the hot water spigot sticking out of the station wall. An unruly horde with teapots still crowded round the tap. Dissipated soldiers returning to their units slept in jumbled heaps, tangled together like puppies. A woman nursed a mummified baby at an enormous globular breast. Tourists with real suitcases stood in sheltered spots with their Intourist guides and the station officials who would guide them to their privileged compartments. A party of Uzbeks in Oriental dress huddled against the wall and looked around with wondering eyes. An old man with a shaggy beard and feet hugely swaddled in rags hugged a bundle shaped suspiciously like a ham and gave terrified answers to the gray-uniformed member of the station GPU who was questioning him.

"What do you mean, at least?" Jeremy said. "You talk as if you're never going to do anything again. You're going to see plenty of ballet dancers from now on. Next month I'm taking you to see Ulanova— the Leningrad ballet's stopping at Gorky on its fall tour. And one day you'll see Markova in London! And Toumanova in Paris! And Baronova in New York!"

She smiled wanly. "Ah, Zheremee, always the jokes, the beautiful dreams."

"Don't look so tragic. It isn't the end of the world. I'll see you in Gorky in two weeks—three at the most. I'm going to rent us our own dacha—one of those abandoned peasant cottages near the American Village. You can rent them from the old people, if you do it on the sly —*na levee*. How's that?"

She made a visible effort to perk up. The sensational cheekbones lifted in an all-out dazzler of a smile. Self-consciously she patted the faded bandanna wrapped round her hair.

"You will forget me as soon as the train is gone, and find a foreign lady at the Metropole," she said in an attempt at levity.

She was wearing her shabby old cotton dress again. She had left her "Moscow clothes" with her aunt, so they wouldn't get stolen at the barracks. It was this that encouraged Jeremy, despite the resigned melancholy that seemed to have overtaken Valentina last night when he had taken her to the Metropole for a farewell blowout. Somewhere inside her head, Russian fatalism was being held at bay by the plucky faith that she would return to Moscow to wear the velvet dress. From there, Jeremy told himself, it was only a step to believing in the possibility of what in Russia was only a daydream: travel abroad.

"No," he said. "No foreign ladies."

They leaned toward each other over Valentina's pile of baggage, not speaking. Jeremy longed to tear the inglorious kerchief from her head and kiss her. But people were pressing close around them. The peasants who would be Valentina's traveling companions were already eyeing his foreign clothing with curiosity. It wouldn't do to call further attention to Valentina. They had had their last kiss that morning in his hotel room.

A faint chugging could be heard down the track. The vast crush of people filling the platform began to stir. The peasants finished their tea hastily and stowed away their cups. The Red Army men unheaped themselves and began to gather their gear. Mothers shook their children awake and got them to their feet. The bearded old man had been made to unwrap his ham, and now, with eyes downcast, was being led away by the station GPU.

Jeremy helped Valentina organize her baggage: the rope-tied valise, the rolled blanket and pillow she would need for sleeping on the shelf her space ticket entitled her to, the little kettle for getting hot water for tea at the stations along the way, the straw basket filled with cheese, salami, bread, chocolate, and tinned food that Jeremy had packed for her over her protests.

"Do you have your ticket, and the travel permit?" Jeremy said.

"With the papers you have obtained, I could go to the moon," she said.

Their hands brushed amidst the baggage, scrabbled for each other, and clung. Valentina suddenly darted her head forward and kissed him quickly on the mouth.

The train filled the track, huffing and clanging and blowing great clouds of steam. The crowd surged toward the cars in a thick, battling mass.

Valentina picked up her bundles and battered her way expertly aboard. Jeremy had thought to help push and shove a path for her, but he lost her after a few yards as she plunged skillfully ahead, using her hips and shoulders like a quarterback.

He caught sight of her again as the train pulled out. Her face was surrealistically near the top of a window as she searched the platform for him from her upper shelf. He waved, but he didn't think she saw him.

Some of the crowd left behind on the platform was dispersing, but a sizable population remained amidst their heaps of belongings, waiting with dumb patience for a place on the next train. Or the next. The Uzbeks were still there, Jeremy noticed.

He turned to go, and saw his own jacket slipping away through the crowd.

It was Boris, his shadow. He thought he had left him behind in Gorky. The Moscow GPU had its own set of peeping Toms.

Jeremy hurried after the jacket. It was an old brown tweed with a torn pocket. He had given it to Boris one day when Boris had been obliged to stand for six hours in the rain waiting for Jeremy to come out of his hotel in Gorky. It was one of their open encounters. Boris hadn't been able to get out of Jeremy's sight fast enough, and he had pretended to be a metal worker at the auto factory, hanging around in the hope of buying black-market American goods. Jeremy had obliged him by selling him the jacket. He had felt sorry for Boris. It was an unrewarding task, being a GPU informer. Jeremy thought he ought to do his part to keep up the fiction.

Boris saw him coming, and tried to evade him. Jeremy caught up with him in a dozen swift strides and put a hand on his shoulder. He could feel Boris shrink at his touch.

"Well, if it isn't my old friend Boris," he said.

Boris brought his head around and up and looked at Jeremy over his shoulder with the expression of a trapped weasel. He managed a sick smile.

"Ah," he said with an air of surprise, "it is the Gaspadeen American. *Eezveeneete* . . . Gaspadeen . . . Gaspadeen . . ." He snapped his fingers in a show of impatience with his poor memory.

"Sinclair," Jeremy said. "I thought you'd have it engraved on your memory."

He ran his eyes over the tweed jacket. It had been falling apart when he'd given it to Boris, and it hadn't improved with wear. It was coming out at one of the elbows, and someone had darned a rent in the lapel for Boris with blue thread.

"Forgive me," Boris said.

"You're out of your territory, aren't you?" Jeremy said.

"I beg your pardon? *Ya ne paneemahyoo.*"

"What are you doing so far from Gorky?"

Boris smiled ingratiatingly. He had yellow teeth, very bad, and a bad complexion and scraggly day-old whiskers, and he looked as if his childhood growth had been stunted by malnutrition, and he wore the baggy pants of a tramp. All at once, Jeremy felt ashamed of harassing him.

"As you know, *gaspadeen,* I am a worker at the Gorky truck and auto factory, and my *organizatsiya* has sent me on a *komandirovka,* a business trip."

"That's very fine," Jeremy said gruffly, and turned to go. Before he could get away, Boris grabbed his sleeve.

"Excuse me, Gaspadeen Seenclair," Boris said diffidently. "Perhaps you have a pair of pants you would like to sell."

37

Peter was very nervous. "Don't mention Roosevelt," he said. "She gets upset if anybody mentions Roosevelt."

"All right," Pamela said. "But everybody's mentioning Roosevelt. We're in the middle of an election campaign."

"Don't bring it up," he said. "Christ, if she ever finds out that I'm going to have a brother-in-law in the WPA, I'm cooked."

They were speeding along a West Virginia highway in the red Cord sportster. They were three hours out of Washington. Peter was doing seventy. The top was down, and Pamela was holding on to her hat with one hand. A truck loomed ahead. Peter leaned on the horn and whipped around it, tires squealing.

"Peter!" she said. "Slow down!"

"Mustn't keep Mother waiting," he said with a mirthless grin.

Pamela clutched her hat with one hand, the door strap with the other. It was no good trying to get Peter to calm down. He had been on edge since he had picked her up that noon. His enormous, overbearing self-confidence had evaporated. The remark that had slipped out about Brad as a brother-in-law had been another of his indirect proposals. Just as if he hadn't really proposed, once and for all, the previous week.

Perhaps he hadn't, she thought. Not till his mother ratified it.

"The main thing is to keep from irritating her," he said.

"By all means," she said. "That's the main thing."

"It's going to be tough enough without irritating her."

He swung out again to pass another truck. Pamela grabbed at the door strap.

"I'd like to get to Pittsburgh alive," she said.

He only grunted, and looked annoyed. He didn't ease up on the pedal. The green countryside flashed by. In the folds and tucks of the hills she could see gray, grim shacks, leaning barns with daylight showing through. In the distance a blackened mine tower poked at the sky. Around it, patches of slag had erased the green of a valley slope. This was the land that Peter's family had torn their money from.

"What did they call your grandfather?" she said.

"Black Pete. A terrible old pirate. He started life as a breaker boy, picking slate out of the coal. At least that's what he used to like to tell people. I think my mother was relieved when he died. I was five."

He whizzed around a curve. Pamela was flung against the door. A quick snatch saved her hat.

"Peter!" she gasped. "I don't mind dying. Really I don't. But I care about what my hair's going to look like when we get there."

This time he did slow down. "Sorry. I should have put the top up. But it's too nice a day."

"Thanks, darling."

He forced a tense smile, a quick, meaningless flash of white teeth in his tanned face. He looked very debonair in his tropical worsteds and colored shirt, she thought, if only he weren't perspiring.

"It's hard to hold down those hundred and twenty-five horses under the hood," he said. "She's so smooth you don't realize how fast you're going."

He was careful for a while, but then he became preoccupied again, and the speed began to creep up past seventy, then seventy-five. She could see a knot of muscle working at the hinge of his jaw.

"You mustn't worry, Peter," she said. "It'll be all right."

"When she finds out I sold *Wanderlust*, there'll be hell to pay."

"Well, it was yours to sell, wasn't it?"

"I held title, yes. But you know, it was debited against my share of the family trust at less than market value. The lawyers didn't like that idea at all. But Mother told them to find a way."

"But it *was* yours to sell," she insisted.

"It isn't that simple, Pam."

No, she thought, it wasn't. His mother had given him an expensive toy for being a good boy. It had been his father's, and he was allowed to play with it. And here he had gone and acted as if it were his.

"Pullman stopped making those palace cars years ago," Peter said. "They can't be duplicated today. You could build a yacht for less. But the formula old Grimshaw finally worked out—Mr. Grimshaw, my mother's lawyer—was what my father paid for it back before the war, less depreciation."

"You were lucky to find a buyer."

"I have Brad to thank for that." He laughed. "The breakfast cereal king. How did Brad ever get to know him?"

"He met him at Saratoga at the races. He goes there with Harry Hopkins."

Peter grimaced at the mention of Harry Hopkins, then went on. "I didn't think there was anybody left since the Crash who could afford a private railroad car. I tried to sell it to Hearst, did you know that? But they say the old man is almost bankrupt. There's a story around that he tried to sell his magazines to Joe Kennedy. Even so, I bet I could have talked him into it. He's still spending millions on European relics for San Simeon. But he isn't in the market for a private railroad car. Cissy Patterson lets him have the use of *Ranger* whenever he wants to travel in style."

Peter had told her about Hearst several times. That was what had made her go to Brad. "All right, I'll sniff around," Brad had said. "I'm going to Saratoga next weekend with Harry. If there's any money around for private railroad cars, that's where it'll be. The Vanderbilts, the Whitneys, the Goelets. Glad to help out, Sis. If it'll get Peter off the dime."

He had been as good as his word. He wouldn't tell her any of the details. Brad liked to make everything seem easy. "Whitney already has a palace car," he said. "It was probably the last one made before the Crash. He rode up to Saratoga in it. And that was what made the cereal king jealous."

The speedometer trembled at eighty. The roadside markers were a blur. Pamela braced her feet against the floorboards, but she didn't say anything. This wasn't the time to criticize Peter. He was starting to get his self-confidence back.

"Well, you have the capital you said you needed, anyway."

He laughed with what sounded like guilty relief. "I closed the deal on those Missouri weeklies. Did I tell you?"

He had, but she said, "That's wonderful, Peter."

"And I'm negotiating for a thousand-watt radio station in Baltimore. My first."

"Congratulations."

"I wish I could buy up some of Hearst's radio stations before word gets around. Eugene Meyer knows he's strapped for money. I understand he offered him a half million for the *Washington Herald*. That's still too rich for me. Anyway, Hearst will never sell to Meyer. Cissy wouldn't let him. She's having too much fun running it for the old man. If it came to that, I bet she'd buy it from him herself."

He frowned.

Pamela patted his hand. She had to let go of the door strap and use that hand to keep her hat on, to do it. "Never mind, Peter. You'll have a Washington-based newspaper someday."

"I've got the feature syndicate, anyhow. I've already got twelve subscribers for the 'News from the Capital' column. A few more months and it ought to be self-supporting. Think Jeremy would like to work for me?"

"Isn't he too liberal for your papers?"

"It's a funny thing about correspondents in Russia," he said. "The longer they stay there, the less starry-eyed they get. I'm willing to forgive Jeremy his hot-eyed radical phase. The kind of stuff he's doing now is just what the readers want. 'Gorky's Flivver Kings.' Nice and colorful, and nothing controversial in it."

"I don't believe I heard that! Not from the publisher who just ran an editorial calling Roosevelt the Kerensky of the American revolutionary movement!"

Peter laughed. "Oh, Roosevelt isn't as bad as I say he is. Anyway, I was just quoting the Republican National Committee. But Pam, now that you bring it up—"

"Don't tell me. I'm not supposed to mention Russia, either."

"Well, the subject *does* upset her."

"Is there anything else I'm not supposed to mention?" she said angrily. "Tell me now! Harry Hopkins? Henry Wallace? Frances Perkins? That's a good one not to mention! A woman in the Cabinet. The CCC? The PWA? How about the NRA? Brad used to work for that, too."

"Now Pam—"

"It's not easy for me, either," she burst out, her frazzled nerves finally giving way. "I get upset, too. I don't know why I'm going along with this. I'm going to be looked over by a woman who hates me, and I'm not supposed to show any feelings, I'm supposed to take it all and keep smiling like the Oralgene girl!"

"Now Pam, she doesn't hate you. She's never even met you."

"She hates the idea of me. She didn't pick me out. I'm not a Burrage sister or a Mellon or a Morrison or a Frick. I don't have a Pittsburgh pedigree. What's worse, I don't *know* anything about Pittsburgh pedigrees. She can't awe me with Sewickley Heights any more than she could awe Philadelphia. That's why she moved back when your father died, wasn't it? She wanted to be in the center of the web. She wants to pull all the strings, especially the apron strings. She thinks I'm a threat to her control of you, and . . . and she may just be right!"

She was suddenly sorry she'd said so much. Peter's knuckles were white on the steering wheel, and his lips were pinched tightly together. Visibly he made an effort to control himself.

"Let's not quarrel, darling. We're in this together." His voice shook. "You're going to be Mrs. Peter Bainbridge the Third no matter what happens this weekend. But it will be easier all around if my mother gives the okay."

It wasn't Peter's fault. He had done his best. He couldn't help it if he was afraid of his mother. It couldn't have been easy for him to pick up the phone and tell her that he was bringing a prospective bride home. He had taken a couple of drinks to get up the courage to do it, and he must have drunk too much, because after he hung up the phone he had thrown up.

And, Pamela told herself firmly, it wasn't Mrs. Bainbridge's fault either. She couldn't help it if Peter had been too much of a jellyfish to assert himself all these months, if he had maneuvered her into the rotogravure and the gossip columns and even the Movietone News with him so that word would get back to his mother. You don't invite someone to tea just because somebody sends you her picture torn out of a newspaper. Once Peter had made that call, Mrs. Bainbridge had quickly done the correct thing and commanded their presence for the very next weekend.

"I'm sorry, Peter. You're right. I'll work hard on your mother. I'll *make* her like me."

He looked relieved. "That's fine. Give me a cigarette, will you? And see if you can find some music on the radio."

That was better. This was the Peter she liked, the one the world saw, the confident, take-charge person. She got a cigarette out of the glove compartment for him. He lit it one-handed, while the speedometer showed seventy, and the car didn't veer or wobble in the slightest. Pamela fiddled with the dial and got a hotel orchestra called Kennie Owens's Rhythm Caravan.

"That's Pittsburgh," he said. "We're getting within range."

"Who's going to be there?"

"What?"

"Who's going to be on the inspection committee?"

"Just the close family. My sister will be there. And Uncle Bertie. He's on our side. That's why I took you to meet him at the horse show. I knew you'd pass muster with him. And Uncle Ned will be there, I guess. My mother depends on him. My brother's in Europe.

You'll meet him later. Don't worry, it's all going to be very informal."

Kennie Owens's Rhythm Caravan was playing a swing arrangement of "When Did You Leave Heaven." Peter was humming the tune to himself, the cigarette dangling from his lip. Ashes and sparks flew along in their trail, despite the Cord's windscreen.

"Peter?"

"Huh?"

"Does your mother know I'm senior staff assistant for the Porteous committee?"

"What? Oh. Yes. She knows you have a job. Don't worry. It's all taken care of."

"What do you mean, taken care of?"

"I got Uncle Bertie to explain that it isn't like being a typist or something."

"It certainly isn't!"

"Don't get me wrong, Pam. *I* know you practically run that committee staff. The Hill knows it, too. You're doing old Theobald's job for him, and the committee couldn't function without you."

She settled back in the leather seat cushions as comfortably as she could, with the wind clawing at her face and dress from around the side of the glass. "Thank you, darling, it's nice to know I'm appreciated."

"Oh, I appreciate you. Didn't I tell you that when I met you?"

She was saving this for last. "The senator appreciates me, too."

"What?" He tossed the cigarette, still lit, over the side.

"I'm getting a raise and a title change starting with the next session. Administrative aide at *fifty* dollars a week! A woman's never had that job!"

"That's very nice, Pam." He didn't take his eyes off the road.

"You're going to be very proud of me," she said smugly. "It's one thing to run things behind the scenes. Every secretary does that. But it's something else to get the recognition."

It had dawned on him that this was important to her. "I am proud of you. It shows the stuff you're made of. I'm almost sorry that we'll probably have the wedding before the Seventy-fifth convenes." He laughed indulgently. "Unless you like *very* long engagements, that is. But the important thing is that the senator made the offer—you'll always have that feather in your cap."

"Feather in my cap?"

"I'll be the first to boast about it, you can count on that. It's too bad you'll have to quit before the raise takes effect—so you could say you actually got it. But of course your job is going to be being Mrs. Peter Bainbridge the Third."

He took a hand off the wheel and patted her knee.

Pamela held her tongue. She was *not* going to go into it with Peter now, she told herself. His self-esteem was too fragile. He'd need every bit of it for the coming battle with that dragon of a mother.

"We're getting close to Pittsburgh," Peter said. "You can almost feel the grit on your face. I always forget about that. It's a good thing I didn't put the top up. You can never scrub it out of the canvas."

No, Pamela thought, it's easier for your fiancée to scrub it off her face. She wished that Peter would take his hand off her knee. She wished that she would have a chance to wash her face before meeting Mrs. Bainbridge.

"So this is the girl from the rotogravure," Uncle Ned said heartily. He was a lean, expensively browned man with steel-blue eyes cupped by a pair of remarkable pouches.

"And this is my sister, Althea," Peter said, holding Pamela's elbow.

Althea was a tentative girl with a sallow complexion. She was long-boned and had Peter's fine brow and liquid brown eyes, and Pamela thought she could do something about herself if there were someone to tell her to square her shoulders and keep her chin high and make an effort with her hair.

Uncle Bertram was not there. Instead there was a bottle-shaped man in a pearl-gray suit, with plump talcumed cheeks, a pink circular bald spot, and parentheses around his mouth.

"And of course this is Mr. Grimshaw," Peter's mother said.

Why "of course"? Pamela wondered.

"Hhr, hhr, yes," Mr. Grimshaw said, clearing his throat. "How do you do?"

"You're just in time for tea," Mrs. Bainbridge said. "I suppose Peter drove too fast. I'm having it served in the garden. It's such a nice day."

She was about as Pamela had imagined; perhaps Peter had unconsciously sketched her with his body movements when he talked about her. Stiff and straight and iron gray, with an armored bosom that swept in one long starchy curve from clavicle to peplum. "As if they were smuggling bagpipes," Brad had once said of that generation.

"No, don't bother to change," Mrs. Bainbridge said before Pamela offered to. "Come along just as you are, there isn't time. Andrews will take your luggage up to your room."

Pamela recognized the move. It was to put her at a disadvantage after the long ride. She decided not to let Mrs. Bainbridge get away with it.

"Oh, I won't be a moment," she said. "I'll just—"

"Run along, Althea dear," Mrs. Bainbridge said, turning away. "You'll just be in the way. Miss Sinclair and I want to get acquainted. You too, Peter. Find something to do until dinner. Go with Althea."

Peter looked unhappy. He let go of Pamela's arm. Pamela had been counting on him. And on Althea's diluting presence.

Mrs. Bainbridge turned back to Pamela. "There."

In the interim, the butler had taken Pamela's traveling bag and cosmetics case. Pamela watched him start up the broad carpeted staircase with them. She couldn't very well run after him now.

"I'll see you at dinner," Peter said, and deserted her.

She was left standing with Mrs. Bainbridge, Uncle Ned, and Mr. Grimshaw. Evidently she was to get acquainted with the lawyer, if not Peter's sister.

A maid appeared and whispered something to Mrs. Bainbridge, and Pamela heard Mrs. Bainbridge say, "No, the *blue* room!" and the maid hurried off. Mrs. Bainbridge gave a martyr's smile and said, "You'd think they'd pay attention, with so many people out of work. Come this way. We'll have to go through the back."

Uncle Ned took Pamela's arm in a firm grip, and Mrs. Bainbridge leaned on Mr. Grimshaw, and they escorted Pamela through great, darkened, tall rooms whose upper moldings must have had to have been dusted from a stepladder. The main drawing room was too big for a cohesive decor, and had been divided into three quadrangles, each with its own furniture arrangement grouped around a Chinese rug. The furniture was dark and heavy and impersonal, with lots of scrolls and paws. On the three marble mantels and the draped surfaces of tables and consoles were a variety of weighty gilt objects in successive Victorian styles: clocks supported by human figures draped in togas, candlesticks held up by Greek nymphs, lyre vases, bowls, urns. The brocaded walls bore darkly varnished portraits and still lifes in massive gilt frames. It all must have cost a lot, once. Pamela knew that the money was newer than that of the Colliers', but also that there was a great deal more of it.

They passed through a corridor opening onto pantries and a kitchen area where people worked over long counters and did not look up. Opposite was a large square room filled with black, hewn furniture of a type that might have been found in a Teutonic hunting lodge, including a ponderous table that could seat twenty.

"The children's dining room," Mrs. Bainbridge said, pausing. "Actually, the servants' hall."

"Ah, yes," Uncle Ned said, smiling. "Many's the Sunday and holiday I spent fidgeting on a cushion at that table with all my little cousins, while the servants hurried by with great tureens and gave us mean looks."

"There's a little room off to the left," Mrs. Bainbridge said. "Perhaps you'd like to take a moment to freshen up. You can join us in the garden. One of the servants can show you the way."

Better and better, Pamela thought. Use the servants' washroom, be made to hurry like an inconvenient child, and then have to ask your way to the place where they'll already be sitting down, and walk over to them across yards and yards of garden tile. Mussolini, somebody in the State Department had told Brad, intimidated his visitors by making them approach him across sixty feet of open marble floor to where a single desk commanded all that yawning, gilded, Renaissance majesty. Mussolini could learn a thing or two from Mrs. Bainbridge.

It would be even worse to decline. "Thank you, I think I will," Pamela said.

She washed her face quickly and applied fresh lipstick. The rest of her makeup was upstairs where Andrews had deposited it. She patted her hair into place as best she could, and smoothed out her dress. She felt a lot better with the film of Pittsburgh grime gone. She remembered what Peter had said about Mr. Mellon employing three shifts of cleaning women.

They were waiting at a small table set in the middle of a rose arbor. A servant was busy at a large glass-topped wicker tea cart. Pamela noticed that the tea seemed to consist of a lot of sweet things.

Uncle Ned sprang jovially to his feet and helped her with her chair. Mr. Grimshaw rose halfway, holding his napkin, and plunked himself down again.

"You're not related to Sinclair Oil, are you?" Uncle Ned said.

"Now Ned, don't be so precipitous," Mrs. Bainbridge said.

"No, I'm not," Pamela said.

"Let's see, you live in Washington, don't you?"

"Yes, but originally I'm from Iowa."

"No oil in Iowa."

"We go in for corn there."

Mrs. Bainbridge signaled the servant. "Do you take sugar, Miss Sinclair?"

"No, never."

"You wouldn't prefer coffee, would you?"

"No, tea's fine." She looked around at the walled garden. To her right was a plinth with a bronze faun on it. A brick walk led through the arbor and divided itself around an oval pool with water lilies floating on it. The flower beds disposed about the pool and on either side of the walk were planted with mathematical symmetry. The hedges lining the beds were trimmed so severely that it was hard to believe that they were living things. "What a beautiful garden," she said.

"Thank you," Mrs. Bainbridge said. "One must keep after the gardener. Peter used to like to sail his boats in that pool when he was a child. The gardener complained, and of course I backed him up. Children are like little beasts. They must be controlled. Do you come from a large family, Miss Sinclair?"

"I have three brothers and a sister."

"Oh? Older or younger?"

"One brother is older. The youngest is my sister."

"Won't you try one of these jam tarts? They're delicious."

"Thank you." Pamela put the tart on her plate but did not touch it.

"Peter is my second child. There was quite a large gap between him and his sister, Althea. I'd guess that you and Althea are about the same age."

"I'm twenty-four."

"Oh, Althea is a year younger. Still not engaged, I'm afraid. She's not very good at attracting men, poor thing. Where did you and Peter meet, Miss Sinclair?"

"At one of those Washington parties. Given by Mrs. McCandless. Perhaps you've heard of her?"

Uncle Ned leaned forward. "We think a lot of old G.L. McCandless in this town. The steel industry hasn't been the same since he left. Took that job with Coolidge when he retired. Never got along with Hoover."

"Made a fool of himself when he married that woman," Mrs. Bainbridge said tartly. "Cheap thing; what was her father, something in insurance?"

"Machine parts," Uncle Ned said.

"Machine parts," Mrs. Bainbridge said impatiently. Her neck stretched turtlelike out of the vitrified shell of her dress. "Twenty years younger than him, and his wife hardly a year in her grave. What did they call her? Taffy, or some silly name?"

"She's one of the most important Washington hostesses," Pamela said.

Mrs. Bainbridge sniffed.

"Is old G.L. still alive?" Uncle Ned said.

"Yes, but he isn't well," Pamela said.

"Too senile to know how she's spending his money, you mean," Mrs. Bainbridge said. "The money that should go to his children when he dies."

Mr. Grimshaw put down his teacup and cleared his throat. "Hhr, hhr, I think the firm of Haslip, Grimshaw and Phelps may have something to say about that. The family is entirely prepared to contest the will."

"Oh, I wouldn't tangle with G.L.," Uncle Ned said. "Not while he's alive. They're not thinking of trying to have him declared incompetent, are they?"

The parentheses on either side of Mr. Grimshaw's mouth drew closer together, compressing his mouth to silence.

"I saw Mr. McCandless several weeks ago at a luncheon," Pamela volunteered. "He came in for just a few minutes. It's difficult for him to walk, but he's quite alert. He seems devoted to his wife."

"Wait till he's dead," Uncle Ned said to Grimshaw. "She's not spending the principal anyway. We don't want a scandal in this town about old G.L."

Mr. Grimshaw's parentheses enclosed his lips in a very tiny clause, and he sipped his tea prissily. Pamela looked quickly at Uncle Ned. His pouched blue eyes had darted expectantly toward Mrs. Bainbridge, as if giving a cue. He saw Pamela looking at him and gave her a genial smile.

"You know, of course, that Peter is heir to a very large amount of money," Mrs. Bainbridge said, as if they had been talking about it all along.

"Oh?" Pamela said politely.

"A great many young women have chased after Peter in the past without understanding that the money is thoroughly tied up. Peter's father arranged it that way to protect Peter and his brother and sister from impulsiveness . . . or predators, and Mr. Grimshaw and I have worked very hard to carry the safeguards still further."

Pamela had to sit with a smile fixed in place. She met Mrs. Bainbridge's ophidian gaze without blinking.

"Oh, yes, that must have been a problem with someone as attractive as Peter," she said.

"It was Mrs. Bainbridge's intent to see that the family trust was not weakened," Mr. Grimshaw purred. "Money in large blocks can do so much more than money broken up into smaller forces."

"Amen," Uncle Ned said.

"Fortunately we were able to take the necessary legal steps *nunc pro tunc* to see that the inheritance was tied up in joint investments and not easily torn loose. The children of course were *in statu pupillari,* but Peter's brother, as the eldest, was quite happy to go along with the arrangement when he reached his majority, and the other children followed suit."

Pamela remembered enough of the dusty Latin phrases that Brad had brought home from Yale Law School and tried out on the family to understand that Mr. Grimshaw was saying that he and Mrs. Bainbridge had fiddled with the terms of Peter's father's will while the children were too young to know better, and put Mrs. Bainbridge in charge of the purse strings.

"Of course Peter and I have never discussed his finances," Pamela said. She was amazed at how steady her voice was. "I know that Peter's making his mark in the newspaper business, and everybody seems to think that he has a bright future."

Mrs. Bainbridge laughed. "Oh, my dear Miss Sinclair! Peter likes to imagine himself a tycoon, but I have to keep bailing him out. I don't mind, of course. I like to see Peter happy, and feeling busy and useful. I think his latest brainstorm is wanting to acquire some failing newspapers in Missouri or some such unlikely place, but of course he could never raise the capital from his other enterprises. I think Mr. Grimshaw and I are going to have to say no to that particular idea."

Pamela checked her tongue before mentioning the sale of *Wanderlust*. Mrs. Bainbridge was going to have to find out about that from Peter.

"I'm afraid I spoiled Peter," Mrs. Bainbridge said. "Pony carts, circus clowns to amuse him when he was sick, I even let him keep a dreadful stray cur that he became attached to, until it dug up a flower bed. He got what he wanted by sulking. He played with dolls till he was five. Now Peter dreams of getting his hands on a large amount of capital so that he can pursue these fantastic schemes of his. And all because he admires those dreadful newspaper reporters with their cigarette ashes and wrinkled suits. Well of course I'll never permit any such thing while I'm alive."

Mr. Grimshaw coughed delicately. "Perhaps we might leave it there."

"Oh, don't be so tiresome! You're afraid I'll encourage Miss Sinclair, I suppose." She turned to Pamela. "What Mr. Grimshaw doesn't want me to mention is the provision of his father's will that Peter mistakenly believes will give him control of his inheritance in stages, with the births of successive children. I bring this up in case Peter has mentioned it. I think it's better to have things in the open so that we know where things stand. But I assure you, it isn't as simple as Peter may think it is. Peter's older brother has four children, but he has never exercised this provision. We have made him see that it is to his advantage to let his share remain in the family trust. Not that he could easily do anything to change things at this stage. Fortunately he married a wife who isn't greedy, and we have been able to avoid a lot of unpleasantness."

Now Pamela understood. Peter must have a wife who would not interfere. Mrs. Bainbridge wanted to be sure that Pamela was not a threat to the power she wielded. Money was what it was all about, not mother love.

Pamela's face burned with humiliation. She could hardly believe that such things had been said to her.

"Yes, I can see how you'd want to avoid unpleasantness," she said with her voice miraculously under control.

"This conversation's getting mighty dull," Uncle Ned said cheerily. "How did we ever get onto these legal subjects anyway? Comes from having a lawyer to tea. I thought we were here to get acquainted."

Mrs. Bainbridge was still smiling at Pamela over the teacups. "Oh dear, Miss Sinclair," she said, "you haven't touched your jam tart."

It was a relief, ten minutes later, when the men stood up and a servant came to show her to her room.

"We'll see you at seven-thirty, then," Mrs. Bainbridge said. "Oh, did Peter tell you we'll be dressing for dinner?"

I will not cry, she told herself. She was too furious to cry. You couldn't cry and be in a fury at the same time. Could you? She sat on the ugly carved bed, staring at the fussy blue wallpaper and puffing at a cigarette. People had no right to be so rude, she thought angrily, and then she began to cry.

They had looked her over, and put her on notice, and maybe she had passed. But did she want Peter on those terms?

That remark about Sinclair oil. Kindly old Uncle Ned. It had been deliberate, she was sure. He was just letting her know that *they* knew that she was a nobody.

The Sinclair inheritance, she thought harshly. That's what Brad had called it the day he packed a bag and went to Washington. Bankruptcy, disgrace, broken-off lives. The depression—that was part of the legacy, too, and a world that everybody said was drifting inexorably toward war.

For Brad, there wasn't even the law degree he had worked so hard to get. For Jeremy, there hadn't been even a full year in college—the education that was the due of his class and his good mind. And Gordon! Had Gordon wanted to be a soldier? What might he have chosen to do with his life if the choice had not been taken from him? And poor Junie. She had been robbed of a mother at the age when she most needed one. The mother had flown out of the body of Mary Sinclair that it used to inhabit and left behind a vague, beautiful, ghostly shell that stayed in its room all day rereading old magazines and forgetting what had happened.

But maybe spunk was part of the Sinclair inheritance, too. Brad had gone out into that raging storm, and with nothing but his brashness and glib tongue had risen high in the Roosevelt administration. And if Roosevelt licked Landon and won a second term, Brad would rise higher still. Jeremy was turning into a first-rate journalist instead of the poet and dreamer he had thought he was. Gordon had made his bargain and stuck to it without whining. She was proud of Gordon. And what about Junie? It had taken spunk, after all, to leave with that boy. Surely that terrible, terrible picture in the Sunday magazine, the Migrant Madonna photograph, couldn't be the end of the line for Junie and her poor baby. People lived, after all.

And what about you, Pamela my girl, she thought. Don't mope around feeling sorry for yourself. You were a helpless, useless object the day Brad walked away from the house on Elm Street forever. You didn't even know how to cook a lamb chop; you had no way to support yourself. And now look at you. Most valued employee of a Senate committee, making the unheard-of salary of forty dollars a week and soon to make more. Your own apartment. A whiz of a cook, if only for survival. Sending money home. And doing battle with a dragon for the most eligible bachelor in Washington society.

She got up off the bed and walked over to the window, holding her cigarette. She pulled aside the heavy drape and looked out. Down by the rose arbor, a girl in apron and cap was wheeling away the wicker cart.

There was a cough behind her, and she turned to see Althea standing in the open door.

"Am I bothering you?" she said.

"No, come in."

"The door was half open," the girl said. "I could see you from the hall." Her voice was breathy, and she had a tendency to talk too fast.

"That's all right, I wasn't doing anything." She smiled to put Althea at her ease. "Not enough time to take a nap."

"Pittsburgh must seem dull to you, after Washington."

"I haven't seen anything of Pittsburgh yet. This is my first trip."

"There's not much to do here," Althea said, depositing herself on the bench at the foot of the bed. "I play tennis and I swim, and I go to the country-club dances. I get to go to Philadelphia sometimes. Next summer Mummy says I can go to Europe with my Aunt Grace. That's Uncle Ned's wife. She's taking my two cousins, but they're so *young*."

"That sounds very nice," Pamela said. "I've never been to Europe."

"*You've* never been to Europe?" Althea said incredulously.

"No. Does that surprise you?"

"Golly, I thought you'd been everywhere."

"No. Not everywhere." Pamela smiled.

"Well, maybe not everywhere, but I thought you lived an exciting life, not like here in Pittsburgh, the Pitts, we used to call it at school, with all those society clippings."

"Clippings?"

"Mummy doesn't want me to see them, but I know where she keeps them. And anyway I clip out the Washington columns in the Pittsburgh papers and I see stories in the magazines sometimes, like the one where you were at that party with Mrs. Roosevelt where the lady jumped in the swimming pool with her pearls on."

"Cissy Patterson. It was her party, and the entire women's press corps was there. I was only included because Peter got me invited."

"But *you* were one of the ones who had your *picture* taken. You looked beautiful in that dress, with the big hat. And I saw your picture in *Today,* and the one in *Time,* where you were sort of behind the ambassador at that reception, but I could recognize your face."

"Then you've seen just about all of them," Pamela said. "I'm not that notorious. But where does your mother get the clippings from the Washington papers?"

"Aunt Addie started sending them to her. But now Mr. Grimshaw gets them for her. I think he hired a man in Washington to do it, a detective."

"That's very flattering," Pamela said grimly.

"He includes all the ones about your brother and his wife's family, the Colliers." She lowered her voice. "Wasn't that terrible about what happened to Senator Hale?"

"Yes, it was." Pamela was feeling a little weak in the knees. She sat down at the dressing table and lit another cigarette.

"I used to have a crush on Sally Collier," Althea confided. "A bunch of us at Miss Prout's School used to have a sort of club. We used to paste up movie stars and everything in a big scrapbook. Joan Crawford and Marion Davies and Janet Gaynor and everybody. But my favorites were the ones of Sally, where she waded in the pool with black pajamas and squirted seltzer at that playboy, and everything."

Pamela could see the little circle at Miss Prout's. There was one at every school. The unpopular girls, the graceless girls, the girls who were too tall or too fat or had bad skin or were myopic, the bookish ones, the ones whose fathers were common, the duty-dances. Sometimes it was only shyness or lack of self-esteem that put girls in those circles. She longed to tell Althea to straighten up, to stop slouching, to look people in the eye.

"Well, Sally's living a very quiet life now. She's bringing up a baby and expecting another one."

"I guess you never do anything interesting after you're married."

Pamela laughed. "I wouldn't say that." It was hard to remember that Althea was only a year younger than she was.

"I hope you and Peter get married!" Althea burst out.

"Well, Peter proposed and I accepted," Pamela said.

Althea fidgeted. "I know, but—"

"There's no but about it," Pamela said firmly.

"Mummy says—"

"It doesn't matter what Mummy says. It's what Peter says." Pamela spoke more sharply than she had intended.

Althea sat looking at the floor, cowed but obviously unconvinced. "It would be awfully nice to have you for a sister," she ventured. "I never really grew up with anyone my own age. Peter's nine years older, and Philip is two years older than *him,* and his wife's practically middle-aged."

"I'm sure we'll be great friends, Althea," Pamela said. "Now I think I'd better start getting ready for dinner."

Her eyes went to the bed, where the butler had laid out her things. The good navy linen, and the two-piece golf dress with the kick pleats in case they did anything outdoors on Sunday, and the very expensive dark printed silk chiffon that she had thought would be good enough for evening wear. There wasn't a floor-length dress among them.

Damn Peter anyhow, she thought.

What made it all the more exasperating was that she had just bought a stunning sapphire gown that she had worn only once, when Peter had taken her to one of Mrs. Roosevelt's Sunday-night scrambled-egg suppers at the White House. And she had been overdressed there! Maybe that's why she had been foolish enough to believe Peter when he had assured her that dinner Saturday night in Pittsburgh would be small and informal.

Althea's eyes had gone to the bed too. "You could wear one of my gowns," she said hesitantly. "I've got a violet faille that I bet would fit, and anyway the shoulders are draped with lots of tulle so you could get away with it."

Pamela looked Althea up and down. Peter's sister was about the same height as she was, if you took the poor posture into account, and really wasn't badly proportioned, with a length of waist that wouldn't be too far off, with a pin or two.

"I know you'd look beautiful in it!" Althea said eagerly. "Much better than I do!"

Pamela visualized herself coming downstairs in a borrowed gown, a gown that Mrs. Bainbridge had picked out for Althea, and sitting through dinner in it. It suddenly occurred to her that if Peter had told her the weekend would be informal, then he himself must have been

told that, and that if the butler had unpacked her things, it certainly
was within the realm of possibility that Mrs. Bainbridge knew full well
that she had not packed a gown.

All of a sudden she was burningly angry. Damn them all, who did
they think they were?

Althea was watching her warily. There was nothing in Pamela's
voice but the most cordial regret as she said: "Thank you, dear, but I
think that silk print will be good enough for dinner."

After the girl had left, Pamela tried on the printed silk dress. It was
really a nice dress, a cocktail-party sort of dress, with its hint of trans-
parency at the neckline and sleeves and its flowing lines. She smoothed
it down over her hips. She thought it looked very good on her.

The little gold clip she had bought herself wouldn't be too much
with it, she thought. Well, actually gold-filled, but no one could tell the
difference. All it needed now was a strand of pearls. They were cultured pearls, of course. She was sure that Mrs. Bainbridge's pearls
were not cultured.

Her eyes fell on the little box from the Washington jeweler's. She
didn't know what had made her take it along. It was the pair of diamond earrings that Peter had given her that time, in lieu of an engagement ring. To go with one of his almost-proposals. She had never
worn them. She had sworn not to take them out of the box till Peter
found some backbone. There still was no ring. There hadn't been time
before the weekend, Peter had said.

She looked at the willowy blond girl in the mirror. Diamond earrings with the pearls would be vulgar, the sort of thing that Mrs.
Bainbridge would notice.

Damn Peter, damn them all, she thought, and put on the damned
diamond earrings.

"A third of the nation," the man in the wing collar said with a
sweeping gesture that almost knocked over his water glass. "A third of
the nation's iron and steel is manufactured right here in Pennsylvania."

He was another uncle. Uncle Jay. He was a bulky white-haired man
with a parrot nose that turned red when the name John L. Lewis was
mentioned.

"Without us, Detroit would have to shut down," Uncle Jay went on.
"The major appliance manufacturers would be out of business. The
mines would be operating at one third under capacity. And that
Perkins woman and her lover, John L. Lewis, are trying to force us to
unionize. They're worried about eight million unemployed, are they?

Well, you can bet your grandmother's mittens that without us there'd be a lot less jobs!"

"And a lot less dividends," Uncle Ned said with a twinkle.

Pamela listened in fascination. She had heard the scurrilous stories about Frances Perkins being the mistress of Harry Bridges, of Franklin Roosevelt, of a colored handyman at the Department of Labor, but this was the first time she had heard that the secretary of labor was supposed to be having an affair with John L. Lewis.

"Don't spread it around," Uncle Jay said, "but big steel's second quarter earnings are going to be seventy percent higher."

"I'll hang on to my shares, and thank you," Ned said.

Pamela smiled at Peter across the table. He avoided her eye. He was probably feeling guilty about wearing a dinner jacket instead of showing solidarity with her. The women at the table were being very discreet. They hadn't said anything about her not wearing a gown. They had just looked.

"Well, this war boom should be good for business, anyway," Uncle Jay said. "We have Mussolini to thank for that. And this new war in Spain. This Franco fellow. More power to him if he can get rid of those communists."

"Wheat futures are up to a dollar forty-four," Ned said. "England's stockpiling it. So are Italy and Germany. Drives up the price."

"It's the defense spending that'll get this country on its feet," Jay said. "The Army Air Corps has those new Boeing bombers on order. And the navy's going to start work on a fleet of battleships as soon as the Washington Treaty runs out at the end of the year—of course the Japs and the Limeys will do the same. It'll sell a lot of steel. Even the Perkins woman ought to be happy. All those new jobs that are going to open up in California."

"If you can get those Okies to work," Uncle Ned cracked.

"Now Jay," said his wife, "you said you weren't going to talk about business." She was a colorless, blinking woman in a mauve gown.

"That's right," Ned said. "Save it for the cigars."

Uncle Bertram swirled the Burgundy in his glass. He had arrived with his wife from their farm in Maryland shortly after six. "You fellows," he said, "talk so much about money you forget there are other things in life."

"We're not all gentlemen of leisure like you, Bertie," Uncle Ned said.

"Stocks. Bonds. Profits. When there's a pretty girl in the room." He looked at Althea. "*Two* pretty girls."

"By George, yes." Uncle Jay remembered his manners. He smiled puffily at Pamela. "Peter's got himself a prize catch. Are you serious this time, Peter?"

Peter mumbled something and finished off his wine. He motioned to the serving girl to refill his glass.

"Now, don't go embarrassing Miss Sinclair," Mrs. Bainbridge said. "Peter is certainly welcome to bring his friends here any time he chooses." She let a steely gaze fall on Pamela.

Pamela waited for Peter to tell Uncle Jay that they were engaged, but he just sat there, looking into his wineglass.

Uncle Jay's wife took up the cue. "Do you read, Miss Sinclair?" she said dutifully.

"Yes, I've been known to read," Pamela said.

"I've been trying to get through the new Book-of-the-Month Club selection. It's an awfully thick one. Something called *Gone With the Wind*. Have you read it?"

"Not yet."

"Oh, you'll love it. It's all about the Civil War."

Uncle Jay broke in. It was only women talking. "How are you doing with your newspapers, Peter?" he said.

"Oh, they're doing all right," Peter said.

"You're supporting Landon, of course?"

"Of course." Peter took another swallow of wine.

"Good. The *Literary Digest* predicts a Landon landslide. Election day can't come too soon for me. Get that fellow Roosevelt and his bunch of communists out of there."

Don't look at me, Pamela thought, I'm not the one who brought up Roosevelt. But Peter wasn't looking at her.

Mrs. Bainbridge gave Pamela a long, deliberate stare, then turned to Peter and said, "Peter, Mr. Grimshaw and I have been talking it over, and we agreed that perhaps we can make a teeny-weeny exception for you just this one more time and *find* enough capital for you to buy those newspapers you're so anxious to have, though I can't for the life of me see why. Where did you say? Missouri?"

"Hey Peter, that's good news," Uncle Ned said jovially.

Pamela thought it had gone on long enough. "Peter's already bought those Missouri newspapers—and he's buying a *radio* station. In Baltimore. Isn't that wonderful? Didn't he tell you?"

Uncle Jay started a congratulatory smile, then stopped when he saw that something was wrong.

"How did you get the money?" Mrs. Bainbridge said sharply.

Peter stared gloomily into his glass. His face was very dark. Pamela was sure he was drunk. She could see him very clearly now, as if a projectionist in a movie house had suddenly put a blurred film into focus.

Was he worth having? She knew Peter's faults. He was weak and arrogant. But he needed her. She could mold him, help him. If he wouldn't stand up to his mother, then she'd stand up for him.

"He sold his private railroad car," she said with her most brilliant smile. "Wasn't that clever of him? It was just a white elephant. All the most important people are flying these days. You can fly coast to coast overnight in a Skyliner. And time is money for a businessman. Besides, Peter will save fifty thousand dollars a year in maintenance and salaries for his private car. That will give him more capital for expansion."

"Is this true, Peter?" Mrs. Bainbridge said. "You sold *Wanderlust?*"

Peter drained his glass and snapped his fingers at the maid for more.

"You've had enough," Mrs. Bainbridge said.

"My brother Bradford helped Peter find a buyer," Pamela said, forming the words distinctly. "As you can imagine, that wasn't easy in days like these. I asked Brad to see what he could do. I knew it was so very, very important for Peter to raise that capital. When you believe in a man like Peter, you ought to do everything you can to back him up in his ambitions, don't you agree?"

She smiled a challenge directly at Mrs. Bainbridge.

"Right . . . damn right," Peter said unsteadily. He *was* drunk, Pamela could see. He must have been drinking in his room before dinner.

Uncle Bertram cleared his throat for attention. He looked over at Peter and then at Pamela in the speculative manner which he must have used in looking over a prospective purchase at a horse auction.

"Every man has to have his chance," he said. "Peter's father had his, and old Black Pete certainly had *his*. Maybe Peter can make something of this newspaper business, maybe not. Peter, you're lucky this girl has faith in you."

Peter focused blearily on Pamela. "Thass right."

Mrs. Bainbridge did not like the way the geometry of the situation was shaping up. "Yes, Peter," she said quickly, "we all have faith in you. You should have come to me, dear. Made me understand. There was no need to sell your father's Pullman car."

Pamela wasn't finished. She wanted to make it very clear that she would not apologize, hide. If she couldn't have Peter on her own terms, then he wasn't worth having at all.

"Brad works for the WPA, did I mention that?" she said coolly. "Under Harry Hopkins. That's how he happened to find Peter's buyer. He went up to Saratoga Springs with Mr. Hopkins and met him at the races. Oh, and I have a brother in Russia, too. He's a journalist for a left-wing news service in Europe, though a lot of his material is syndicated here."

She paused to see the effect she was having. In her mind, she had fancied something like a scene from Dracula, where you hold up a crucifix and Bela Lugosi cowers and hides his face. But the uncles and their wives were just watching her with polite attention.

"How unusual," Mrs. Bainbridge said with an effort. "Well, Peter meets all sorts of interesting people in his business."

Peter rose shakily to his feet and made his way around the table to Pamela's side. He was drunk, and using being drunk, but Pamela thought he knew what he was doing. He smiled a crooked smile and kept his eyes on his mother's face as he said, "Yeah, Brad's all right for a New Dealer. I'm going to ask him to be best man at our wedding."

38

"These mad dogs," the prosecutor, Vishinsky, shouted, "tried to tear limb from limb the best of the best of our Soviet land!"

He paused to pat his forehead with a handkerchief. His violent words were at odds with his mild appearance: neatly combed gray hair and clipped mustache, horn-rimmed glasses, a nicely tailored dark suit, white shirt with carefully knotted necktie.

A murmur went up in the large, brightly lit hall. *"Rasstrelyat ikh!* Shoot them!"

Jeremy, sitting in the front row with the other reporters, scribbled as fast as he could, trying to get the words down. It was hot, with all the floodlights. Perspiration trickled down his ribs. He didn't understand how Vishinsky managed to look so cool.

"They killed our Kirov!" Vishinsky pounded his fist on the table for emphasis. "That bright and joyous man of the revolution, that admirable and wonderful man! They wounded us close to our heart! They thought they could sow confusion in our ranks!"

Jeremy glanced at his watch. Eleven-thirty. Getting close to lunchtime. Vishinsky had been going on with his closing speech all morning. It hardly seemed necessary. All of the defendants had confessed. Not only had they confessed, they had denounced themselves in the most abject terms, calling themselves "contemptible worms," "the dregs of the land," "fascist murderers."

Jeremy looked over at the prisoners' box. The sixteen men who sat behind the rails, surrounded by uniformed GPU guards with rifles and fixed bayonets, looked seedy and defeated. It was hard to believe that Zinoviev had been head of the Comintern, or that Kamenev had been one of the original members of the Politburo, or that the two men had formed, with Stalin, the triumvirate that had downgraded Trotsky after Lenin's death and brought Stalin to power. It seemed incredible that now they were accused of having been secret Trotskyites all along.

". . . Comrade Stalin foretold the possibility of the revival of Trotskyite counterrevolutionary groups. . . ." Vishinsky droned on.

Stalin saw Trot co-rev, Jeremy wrote automatically, and turned his attention to the courtroom.

The high-ceilinged room had been part of a fashionable Moscow club before the revolution. Now it was called "October Hall." There were still crystal chandeliers, marble columns, classical friezes of Greek dancing girls above the blue walls. But now red banners were draped everywhere, and red cloths covered the raised judges' dais and the prosecutor's table.

The judges were in uniform. The presiding judge, Ulrich, was a porky, red-faced man with a shaved head. He had let Kamenev and Zinoviev off with light sentences at their last trial. On the left was the butcher, Matulevich, who had ordered two hundred prisoners to be dragged out of their cells and shot after the Kirov murder in 1934. On the right was a colorless military judge named Nikitchenko. The court provost marshal wore the blue cap and insignia of the secret police.

"The murderer mourns over his victim!" Vishinsky was saying. "What words can one use to describe the loathsomeness of this?" He was talking about the eulogy for Kirov that Zinoviev had written for *Pravda.*

Indignant mutterings came from the crowd. They were handpicked delegations of workers from factories and other state enterprises. There was a new set for each session, escorted to their seats in awed, whispering groups by GPU guards. Foreign diplomats had their own section, across the aisle from the reporters. Ambassador Bullitt still was absent, Jeremy saw, and was being represented by Loy Henderson, the second secretary.

Now Vishinsky was attacking Smirnov, Valentina's old boss at the Gorky auto works. Smirnov had admitted receiving messages from Trotsky, but had denied plotting to kill Stalin or having anything to do with the Kirov assassination. He had finally come round like the others, but he had given Vishinsky a hard time.

The Danish correspondent leaned over and whispered to Jeremy. "This is very thin. Smirnov's friend, Holtzman, confessed to meeting Trotsky's son in the Hotel Bristol in Copenhagen. I happened to know that the Hotel Bristol was torn down in 1917."

"Thanks, Arne," Jeremy said, scribbling the information down. "I'll do you a favor someday."

"Glad to help, old boy," Arne said. "Especially as we're not in competition."

Vishinsky had got himself in hot water, Jeremy thought. The Hotel Bristol wasn't the only inconsistency. Smirnov was supposed to be the leader of the conspiracy. He had finally admitted it after hammering by Vishinsky, and a court recess to refresh his mind. But Smirnov had been in jail since January 1931.

As if reading Jeremy's mind, Vishinsky said, with elaborate sarcasm, "I know Smirnov will say, 'I didn't do anything, I was in prison.' A naive assertion! We know that while in prison, Smirnov communicated with the Trotskyites by means of a code. This proves that communication existed, and Smirnov cannot deny this."

Nothing about a code had been said all through the trial. Jeremy had the impression that Vishinsky was hurrying to finish his presentation, as if there were some sort of deadline.

He was whipping up his audience now, waving his arms and raising his voice. There was a restless stirring in the seats. Jeremy glanced at his watch again. Almost twelve.

Vishinsky leaned out across the table. The sixteen men in the dock waited with unnatural stillness. They had tired, grainy faces, already looking like old newspaper photographs.

"I demand that these dogs gone mad should be shot—every one of them!" Vishinsky said.

The crowd went wild. The reporters broke from their seats and ran out into the hallway toward the censors' room.

VISHINSKY FORENOON SUMUP TROTPLOT ASKS SHOOT-ALL STOP AFTERPLEA FORM STOP SELFACCUSED KA-MENEV ZINOVIEV OLDBOYS STOP SMIRNOV CRACKED DE-SPITE QUOTE WRIGGLINGS UNQUOTE

Jeremy sat back and looked at the cable he had just drafted. Depending on the creativity of the fellow on the other end, it would come out something like:

"Soviet prosecutor Andrei Y. Vishinsky, in a vehement and at times emotional summation that occupied the entire morning of today's session of the sensational Moscow treason trials, demanded death by shooting for all sixteen defendants. The final pleas of the accused will begin this afternoon, Moscow time, but are not expected to affect the outcome of the trial, since the defendants have, in effect, already accused themselves of the crimes with which they are charged. The two most notable defendants are the old Bolsheviks Lev B. Kamenev and Grigori O.G. Zinoviev, who once shared equal power with Stalin, as members of the ruling trio appointed after the death of Lenin. Only one of the sixteen, Ivan Smirnov, denied any part of the charges against him, and he too finally capitulated after being implicated by the testimony of Kamenev, Zinoviev, and the others. In the closing speech, prosecutor Vishinsky strongly decried the 'unseemly wrigglings' of Smirnov in resisting the evidence against him."

It would have to do, cable rates being what they were. There was about ten bucks' worth, right there. A more thoughtful and detailed report would have to wait for one of his mailed dispatches, or for an unguarded phone line like the one that the AIPS man had miraculously found before he was expelled. The important thing was to beat out the competition.

The real story was yet to come, Jeremy suspected. It was only to be expected that Vishinsky would call for the death penalty. It was the extraordinary self-abasement of the defendants that was the mystery. The correspondents had talked it over among themselves and decided that there were no signs of torture. A responsible journalist wouldn't suggest it, even if he had any chance of getting by the censor. True, once when Smirnov had been giving Vishinsky a particularly hard time, court had been recessed and Smirnov and the others led away. But it had been close to midday anyway. And when Smirnov had come back, there had been no marks on him.

"Shame on you, Sinclair, sitting there and daydreaming. I've got a cable allowance five times yours, and I'm already finished."

Jeremy looked up. It was one of the AP men, censored and stamped cable form in hand, grinning at him.

"You've also got an exclusive contract with Tass, you bastard," Jeremy said good-naturedly. "How do you expect the rest of us to compete with you?"

"Tass didn't have an advance handout on Vishinsky's speech," the AP man said. "They had to sweat it out the same as we did."

He hurried off on his way to the telegraph building, a mile-long dash through the streets of Moscow.

Jeremy lit a cigarette and pondered his cable. Should he even bother to try? It all depended on how alert the rewrite man in New York was, and even then it was a question as to whether he could sneak it past the censor.

He stubbed out his cigarette and resumed typing:

AFTERTHOUGHT DESPITE THREEYEAR PRISON SMIR-NOV CODED ORDERS STOP CONSPIRATORS MET HOTEL BRISTOL COPENHAGEN PRELEVELED

He took it out of the typewriter and carried it over to the censors' desks. The Russians had made a concession in setting up censorship facilities at the scene of the trial, in a room off the hall. Ordinarily, Jeremy had to go to the press department in the Foreign Office building on Vorovsky Street and wait until one of the censors was free. Or, if a news break came late at night, he had to track down a censor at home and camp in a kitchen smelling of stale cabbage soup while the censor's wife and children peeped at him from around the edges of the door. But the Russians wanted the news of the trial to get out to the world fast, without dangerous rumors, and they were doing their best to alleviate the usual logjam.

The censor he got was Popov. Popov was a moon-faced man with small steel-rimmed eyeglasses, a scraggly beard surrounding a mouth full of gold teeth, and a light snowfall of dandruff on the shoulders of his suit. He read the cable through, pursing his lips and forming words.

"Ho ho, Zheremee, you are trying to get away with something again!"

"I don't know what you mean," Jeremy said cautiously.

"You are inventing words to save money."

"It's an accepted practice."

"Ah, but 'shootall,' 'afterplea,' these are not recognized cable words. And 'Trotplot,' very clever, but too naughty."

He wagged a pudgy finger in Jeremy's face.

"Why do you care?" Jeremy said. "It's the telegraph office's concern. If I can get it past them, it's no skin off the press department's nose."

Popov's trapped eyes rolled. "Ha ha, you are so right. We are here to help you, not to cause difficulties. We are not like the censors in Spain and Italy. Our only job is to work with you to see that your facts are accurate, so that you do not step with your foot into it."

"Put your foot in it," Jeremy said.

"Ah, yes." Popov returned to the cable, blue pencil poised. He frowned. "Why do you say 'afterthought'?"

"Because Vishinsky obviously gave the problem of the code much thought."

"I do not think so. I think you are trying to put something over on poor Popov. In any case, the word is unnecessary." He drew a blue line through it and smiled up at Jeremy. "There, I have saved you some money."

Jeremy smiled back. Popov was right. The rewrite man ought to get the idea without a red flag.

Popov got out his official censor's stamp, then hesitated.

"What is it, this 'preleveled'?"

"It's American slang," Jeremy said. "To level with somebody means to talk turkey, to come across, to reach an understanding. Which is what the conspirators were doing in Copenhagen. But all of those other idioms take more than one word."

"Why 'pre'?" Popov said.

Jeremy gave him a tolerant look. "Because they agreed in advance. It *was* a conspiracy, wasn't it? *Konspiratsiya.*"

Popov nodded, and stamped the cable with the press department's official seal. The telegraph office wouldn't accept a correspondent's cable without it. He handed the cable back to Jeremy. "You had better hurry. There's twenty ahead of you."

Only one window at the telegraph office was authorized to send reporters' cables. There was still a crush of correspondents in front of it when Jeremy got there.

"You'll have to take hind teat, Sinclair," the *Herald Tribune* man said.

"I wish you wouldn't rhyme that with quit, Barney," Jeremy said.

"Would you rather have him rhyme it with sheet?" flung the *Manchester Guardian* reporter.

"Go ahead, you thieves. I'll wait."

When he finally got to the window, the clerk examined his cable to see if the censor's stamp was properly affixed, then scanned it with furrowed brow to make sure there were no problems.

" 'Shootall' is not a legitimate word," the clerk said.

"Sure it is. It's like 'shootout.' Haven't you ever heard of that?"

The clerk grumbled something under his breath, then looked up again.

"What is this 'Trotplot'? There is no such word in English."

"Very well, make it 'plotsky.' "

The clerk looked at him suspiciously. "What is that?"

"The genitive case of 'plot.' "

The clerk grumbled again, then tossed Jeremy's cable on top of the pile left by the other correspondents. It would be the first to be sent when the operator started transmitting.

Jeremy walked over to one of the other windows and picked up a blank for an internal telegram. You had to be a government or party

official to make a long-distance telephone call, and in any case, there
was no telephone in Valentina's barracks. And it was no use writing
letters, because letters took several weeks to travel to Gorky, and he
would be there himself before they arrived.

He lettered the Russian characters carefully with his fountain pen:
HELD UP ANOTHER WEEK. WILL SEE YOU SOON. LOVE,
JEREMY.

"No matter what my sentence will be," Kamenev said, "I consider
it in advance to be just."

He stood there irresolutely for a moment, a stocky man wearing
rimless pince-nez, with a walrus mustache and shaggy goatee which
once might have given him a jolly look, but which now merely looked
bedraggled.

There was utter silence in the courtroom for once. In a voice that
broke several times, Kamenev said: "To my children I say, don't look
back. Go forward. Together with the Soviet people, follow Stalin."

He sat down quickly and buried his face in his hands.

Jeremy wrote it all down. The final pleas had been extraordinary.
Holtzman, the one who was supposed to have met Trotsky's son in the
Hotel Bristol, had told the court that he was a murderer who was un-
deserving of mercy. Mrachkovsky had begged to be shot.

It was Zinoviev's turn. He looked pale and unwell. He had some
sort of liver ailment, Jeremy remembered, and he suffered from
asthma. He was a bushy-haired man with the thick, cursive features
seen in Assyrian carvings.

The audience leaned forward expectantly in their seats. Zinoviev
had never been well liked. In his heyday he had been known as a vain
and arrogant man who had attained power by fawning on Lenin. His
unpopularity had reached a peak when, as chief of Leningrad, he had
ordered all the opera houses closed, saying: "The proletariat doesn't
need opera houses."

When he spoke, it was in a rather unpleasant high-pitched voice, interrupted by fits of wheezing.

"To be loyal, to do every single thing that is demanded of us, is almost impossible," he said plaintively. "We are all obliged to lie. It is
impossible to manage otherwise."

Jeremy listened with new attention. Was Zinoviev giving some kind
of oblique signal to explain the crawling confessions?

". . . my defective bolshevism inevitably led to antibolshevism, and
through Trotskyism I inescapably arrived at fascism. Trotskyism is a
species of fascism, and Zinovievism is the same as Trotskyism. . . ."

No, the meandering presentation was a kind of psychological autobiography intended to show that the slightest deviation from the Party line led, through historical necessity, straight to treason. By this reasoning, Zinoviev said, any opposition whatsoever to Stalin was unthinkable.

The handpicked audience hissed and jeered as Zinoviev painfully dredged up examples from his past to paint himself in the worst possible colors. In contrast, there had been a sort of grudging admiration of Kamenev.

On the judges' dais, Ulrich's fat face was twisted in a sneer. He let each demonstration run its course before quelling it. Matulevich openly scowled. Only Nikitchenko maintained an expression resembling judicial neutrality.

Zinoviev, drained and exhausted, flogged himself on. "If in the Party's view I am a traitor, very well then, I am a traitor. To admit this is the last service I can do the Party."

It was late afternoon when the judges filed out of the courtroom and retired to chambers. Jeremy stayed in his seat, expecting that they would be back in no more than ten or fifteen minutes with the verdict. But at a command from the GPU officer who served as provost marshal, the guards cleared the courtroom.

Jeremy waited with the other reporters in the censors' room down the hall. A few of the reporters immediately got up card games. Most sat and smoked and talked. A very few took a chance on going out for a quick dinner. One, to the disapproval of the Russians, stretched out on three chairs and tried to nap.

"Strange business, what?" Kemble said.

"What made them do it?" Jeremy said.

"Oh, well, they've been in the GPU's hands for a long time."

"That doesn't explain it. Confessions obtained that way can be repudiated in open court, and these fellows had the whole Western press corps as their witnesses. But they jumped through hoops."

"It's not unheard of in human affairs," Kemble said, poking at the bowl of his pipe. "Think of the Inquisition—all that breast-beating and mea culpas at the stake. Or the witch trials in your country and mine. Men and women confessing to meeting Satan in a ploughed field. Only in this case it was Trotsky's son, and they met him in the Hotel Bristol. Confession is good for the soul."

"Communists don't have souls. At least they say they don't."

"They have a theology. It's central to their lives. They want to make their peace with the Party before they die."

"Are you going to say that in your story?"

"Heavens, no! Much too fanciful. Just report the dry facts, that's what my paper wants."

"The Hotel Bristol doesn't exist, by the way."

Kemble looked amused. "I know. Arne told me."

"The GPU doesn't have very good research."

"'What I tell you three times is true,'" Kemble quoted. "'The Hunting of the Snark.'"

Jeremy supplied another line. "'That alone should encourage the crew.'"

Kemble nodded. "Precisely. It's very Lewis Carroll, isn't it? But I'm afraid there's going to be a great deal more encouraging before they're through."

At the previous day's session, Vishinsky had announced that an entire new set of suspects was under investigation. The list of names included some of the most prominent of the old Bolsheviks—Tomsky, Bukharin, Rykov, Radek. On hearing the news, Tomsky had promptly committed suicide.

"More show trials, you mean?"

Kemble was trying to get his pipe going again. "I suspect that this trial is only the beginning," he said.

"Stalin can't shoot the entire old Bolshevist leadership."

Kemble raised his eyebrows. "Can't he?"

"You can't believe that Stalin would actually move against Bukharin," Jeremy said. "He's the darling of the entire Party—at least that's what Lenin called him in his last testament."

"And that's precisely why he's in danger. Mark my words, when Stalin finishes this grim charade, there won't be anybody left in the Politburo or the Central Committee except his toadies."

Jeremy squirmed in his seat. It was getting on toward midnight. "Wouldn't it be a coup to interview Stalin?"

Kemble laughed. "Every journalist's dream, my boy. I request an interview at least twice a month, and so does every other newsman in this city. But I've never been granted one."

"He gives interviews sometimes."

"They're very few and far between. And it helps if the writer is a visiting celebrity, like H.G. Wells."

"I'm going to put in a request tomorrow," Jeremy said stubbornly.

"My dear Sinclair, of all the English-speaking correspondents in Moscow, you're the least likely to receive a dispensation. You have a reputation for giving the censors entirely too much trouble."

"It's worth a try," Jeremy said.

"In any case, the question is academic," Kemble said. "Stalin's had the good sense to make himself inaccessible while the trial's going on. He's having a holiday at his Black Sea dacha. And most of the Politburo are out of town, too."

"He can't hide forever. When he comes back, I'll know that the purge is over."

"Hmmm, you may have a point there. It will be several more weeks, though, I'll wager. Have you heard from Valentina?"

"No."

"I wouldn't worry about it. You know what communications are."

"I sent her a telegram this noon telling her I've been held up."

Kemble pulled at his droopy mustache. "Do you think that was wise?"

"Why? It's not against Soviet law to get a telegram."

"Yes, of course," Kemble said hastily. "Quite so. You know, of course, that workers' meetings in support of the trial are being called at factories throughout the country? I don't imagine that the Gorky auto works are any exception. Duranty tells me that the same thing happened after the Kirov murder in thirty-four. Workers were asked to turn in lists of names of people they suspected of oppositionist sympathies. There was a positive frenzy of denunciations. People quite naturally took the opportunity to settle old scores, or have a try at their boss's job, and so forth. Some thousands of people lost their lives or got sent to the camps. Once these things start, I'm afraid, they tend to spread."

"Valentina's not important enough to have any enemies," Jeremy said gruffly.

"I'm sure you're right. Still, perhaps it's a blessing that your trip to Gorky's being held up. No point in having tongues there wag. Time enough to join Valentina after this madness blows over."

Jeremy was silent. He hadn't thought of that aspect of it.

"Don't look so glum, old chap," Kemble said heartily. "Things are bound to sort themselves out in the end. In the meantime I've made those inquiries that I promised about the visa. My contact agrees that it's best to lie low for a while."

Out in the corridor the sound of shuffling feet and intimidated murmurings were heard. Jeremy looked up hopefully. About a hundred people, women in kerchiefs and men in factory clothes, were being herded along by GPU guards.

"Ah, they're bringing in the mujiks for the final act," Kemble said. "First the audience, then the players."

But it was not until two-thirty in the morning that the court reconvened. The judges filed in and took their places on the dais. The accused men were prodded into the dock by their guards. Zinoviev was deathly pale, on the point of collapse. Kamenev sat with stolid dignity. All the fight seemed to have gone out of Smirnov; he watched the dais in a sort of daze.

Ulrich glowered at the prisoners' box. The expression of malicious satisfaction on his swollen face was undisguised. "The defendants are guilty on all counts," he said. "The verdict is death by shooting."

There was another stampede of reporters to the censors' room. It didn't take long this time. Jeremy had prepared in advance a cable blank with one word written on it: DEATH.

Twenty-four hours later, it was announced that all sixteen men had been shot. A telephone call from the Foreign Office woke Jeremy up at one in the morning. He assembled with fifty other reporters in Popov's flat. The correspondents crammed the two small rooms and spilled out into the corridor. Popov, disheveled and nervous in a faded bathrobe, told them there had been a short unavoidable delay, but that he would have something for them shortly. An hour later a messenger arrived from the Foreign Office with a stack of smudged mimeographed sheets. Popov distributed them. There was little information in them except for the bare fact that the defendants had been executed. Some of the correspondents were annoyed at having been roused from their sleep at such an hour. The telegraph office wouldn't open until morning anyway.

A week later, the rumor swept through the press corps that Stalin had ordered Yagoda, his secret police head, to pick out five thousand inmates from among the political prisoners being held in camps and shoot them. The rumor, of course, could not be confirmed.

At the end of the month, Molotov returned from vacation, thus ending whispers that he was in disfavor. His name, significantly, had been left out of Vishinsky's list of important government officials who were supposed to have been assassination targets of the Zinoviev conspirators. The word now was that in the next round of indictments, it would be charged that the assassins had planned to kill Molotov, too.

On September 10, the charges against Bukharin were dropped.

On September 22, Radek and Pyatakov were arrested. Stalin was still hiding out at his Black Sea dacha.

It had been over a month. Jeremy went to the telegraph office and wrote a message to Valentina that said, UNAVOIDABLY DETAINED. WILL LEAVE FOR GORKY AT EARLIEST OPPORTUNITY. LOVE, JEREMY. He read it over, and tore it up.

The hell with it, he thought. He went to the Foreign Office and got a *propusk* for travel to Gorky.

"What time is your train, Sinclair?" Murdock said. Murdock was the correspondent for Worldwide, a feisty little sandy-haired man with a broken nose.

"Russian time. Anytime between six in the morning and doomsday.

I'm planning to be at the station at dawn, and camp on the platform with my suitcase till it gets in."

"It's after eleven. You're not going to get much sleep."

"I'll catch up. There's nothing to do on a Russain train *except* sleep. You trying to kick me out of this party?"

"Hell, no. Have another drink."

The party was in Murdock's dusty two-room suite at the National. There was some kind of a gathering, impromptu or otherwise, almost every night of the week in one or the other of the rooms of the scattered press colony, and it was no trick to find it. This one was strictly stag, with a couple of poker games going on, and the serious drinkers clustered at one end near the bar.

"What the hell is going on in Gorky?" Murdock said. He squinted suspiciously at Jeremy. "You know something that the rest of us don't know?"

"I just wanted to get out of Moscow for a while," Jeremy said.

"You're making a mistake, Sinclair. There's gonna be another big break here. Stalin didn't get rid of the dwarf for nothing."

"The dwarf" was Yagoda, a revolting little man about five feet tall. People shivered when his name was mentioned. Today it had been announced that he had been replaced by Nikolai Yezhov, who had the reputation of being even more ruthless, if that were possible.

"I'll take my chances," Jeremy said.

Murdock squinted at him, one-eyed. "Maybe you're smart to get out of town, after the way you've been tweaking Stalin's mustache lately. That piece you did on the anti-Shostakovich campaign was the last straw. Laying it at Stalin's door—pointing out his interest in music and getting in the dig about him being fond of Wagner, like Hitler. I don't know how you got away with it."

The attack on Shostakovich had started with an unsigned editorial in *Pravda* called "Muddle Instead of Music." It had been prompted by the latest Shostakovich opera, *Lady Macbeth of Mtsensk District.* Stalin was supposed to have walked out of the performance in a rage. Now the Bolshoi had removed Shostakovich's ballet, *The Age of Gold,* from its repertoire, and another unsigned editorial had attacked the composer as "an enemy of the people," and a "formalist." Everybody was waiting to see when Shostakovich would disappear.

"I don't know what you're talking about," Jeremy said innocently. "All I did was admire Stalin as a music lover."

"Hey, Murdock!" a reporter at one of the tables called. "You going to play cards or you going to talk?"

Murdock went back to the poker game. Kemble came over.

"How did it go at the embassy?" he said quietly.

"I talked to Loy Henderson. He promised that the embassy would issue an American visa in Valentina's name within twenty-four hours after I showed him a piece of paper saying that she was married to an American national. He's got the form already filled out and he's keeping it locked in his desk till I get back."

"You're taking a chance."

"I've got to. Things are going to pieces in this country. And my time here is running out."

"Valentina may not want to risk it."

"Maybe." Jeremy took another swallow of Murdock's whiskey.

"You're drinking quite a lot," Kemble said.

"That's the general idea."

"Well . . . good luck, Sinclair."

"Thanks, Mr. Kemble."

Over in the corner, the telephone rang. A reporter picked it up. "What?" he said loudly. "Oh, sure, and I'm the Queen of Sheba. Come on, buddy, the gag isn't funny anymore. . . . What? Okay, okay, I'll put him on." He put his hand over the mouthpiece and called out, "Hey, Sinclair, it's for you. Some joker saying he's from Stalin's office."

Jeremy looked at his watch. It was eleven-thirty.

He took the phone, prepared to wisecrack to the prankster. It was an old one, but usually they tried it on newly arrived correspondents.

"Mr. Sinclair? This is Comrade Stalin's secretary."

"Sure."

"Please, you must believe me. Comrade Stalin wishes to see you in thirty minutes, in his office on the top floor of the Party Secretariat Building."

Jeremy was about to hang up, when he thought of something. He hadn't told anybody he was going to Murdock's party. He had been out for a walk, and decided on the spur of the moment to drop by and see if anything was going on.

"A limousine will pick you up at the door of the National in fifteen minutes," the voice went on smoothly. "Do you understand?"

Jeremy was aware of having had too much to drink. "I'll be waiting," he said.

Some of the reporters were looking at him. He saw a few expectant grins. "Well?" one of them said.

Jeremy said slowly, "I think it *was* Stalin's office."

"How did they know you were here?" somebody said, then paused. "Oh."

Conversation stopped over at the card tables.

"Oh, Kee-rist, it *would* be Sinclair!" somebody yelped in anguish.

"Sinclair, how do you feel?"

They were all watching him anxiously.

"I think he's half bagged."

Whoever said it was not too far wrong. The last drink had been a mistake, Jeremy thought. His motor control was not what it should have been, and he was conscious of a seductive, muzzy warmth. How many journalists had Stalin seen in the last eighteen years? Seven? Eight? The journalistic opportunity of the decade, he thought, and it had to come exactly when he had had one drink too many.

"Come on, get him in the shower!"

"Somebody get some coffee!"

They stripped off his clothes and pushed him into the shower. Murdock was very proud of his shower. It was the only one at the National. Helping hands held Jeremy down under the icy spray, then rubbed him dry. They helped him get back into his clothes, and forced a scalding cup of black coffee down him. Somebody tried to comb his hair, but Jeremy said, "Lay off, I can do it myself."

"Can you walk?"

"Sure." He could think, that was the main thing. He would have to be careful not to slur when he talked to Stalin.

"Get him down to the lobby. Sinclair, you lucky bastard, do it for all of us."

Kemble's face emerged from the confusion around him. He was holding out a tin of pipe tobacco. He pressed it into Jeremy's hand and closed Jeremy's fingers around it.

"Here, take this," Kemble said. "They say that Stalin likes Edgeworth. It's a new tin—I haven't opened it yet."

"Thanks, Mr. Kemble," Jeremy said, and put the tin in his pocket.

The limousine pulled up as he reached the curb. It must have been waiting in the darkness down the street for him to appear on the sidewalk. A door opened. Jeremy climbed into the back seat. A man sitting beside the driver reached back and closed the door. No one spoke. The car drove off.

Jeremy studied the backs of the two necks. They were large, solid men in GPU tunics and caps. He glanced out the window to see what direction they were taking, and found that he couldn't see very well. It was some sort of tinted glass. For a brief moment he played with a fantasy of being taken to the GPU cellars. Foreigners weren't necessarily sacrosanct. He remembered the Metro-Vickers case. The six Englishmen had been put on trial. Or a foreigner could just disappear. It had happened to Tom, the Wobbly organizer.

Jeremy told himself to stop thinking nonsense. He leaned forward, and in a friendly tone of voice said, *"Prayekhalee lee my oozhe ploshat?"*

There was no answer from the front seat. Jeremy told himself that the two men weren't authorized to talk to foreigners. The car hissed on through the Moscow streets.

When they got to the Old Square, an armed guard waved the car on through a narrow side gate. Inside the gate, the driver was questioned by another guard and allowed to proceed. The guard at the entrance opened the car door and let Jeremy out.

Jeremy was escorted to the top floor of the six-floor building and led into a large, sterile room that seemed to be an outer office. Jeremy's escort spoke to the woman at the desk, and she smiled and asked him to wait.

He took his place with the others on the benches. It was after midnight, but there were four or five people waiting, bleary-eyed, with some sort of business. A couple of them were bureaucratic types, in dark, badly pressed suits. There was a large brutal-looking man in peasant blouse and boots. And a woman from one of the Central Asian republics with embroidered headdress and sporting a large steel wristwatch.

A few minutes later, a square, pedantic-looking man in a business suit came walking quickly out of the inner office, nodding at the receptionist as he went out. Jeremy gulped. It was Molotov. Even if Jeremy never got to see Stalin, he had a story that any other reporter would have given his eyeteeth for—Molotov seen coming out of Stalin's office after midnight. Too bad he couldn't use it.

The receptionist gave the nod, and a clerk came to lead Jeremy into Stalin's presence. The entrance to Stalin's private office was through his secretary's office. The secretary was a coarse-looking man with a pitted face and curvature of the spine. He nodded unsmilingly at Jeremy, but did not get up. The clerk left. After a moment's hesitation, Jeremy stepped through the door.

Stalin got up from behind his desk to shake hands. Jeremy was surprised at how short he was. Seen from a distance, on the reviewing stand at the Red Square galas, he had always looked massive, bulky. His handshake was quite firm and dry. He wore a genial expression. *"Pazhalsta, sadeetees,"* he said, gesturing toward a chair.

Stalin's interpreter, a dark-haired young man, said, "Comrade Stalin wishes you to take a seat." But Jeremy had already sat down without waiting for the translation—his first mistake, he realized with chagrin. He needed all the breathing spaces he could get.

"P-please tell Comrade Stalin that I am grateful for the opportunity to interview him," Jeremy said. While the interpreter translated, he studied the Soviet leader, trying to fix an impression firmly in his mind.

Stalin was a squat, powerful figure with a controlled economy of movement and gesture that gave him an aura of intense personal force. His broad face was swarthy, pockmarked, a bit oily. The thick upswept eyebrows and the shape that the handlebar mustache gave to his mouth made Jeremy think of a great cat. The lower teeth were rotten, or perhaps tobacco-stained, Jeremy noticed. He wore an austere brown tunic and baggy trousers tucked into boots which, Jeremy had seen when Stalin was standing, were polished mirror-bright.

He was suddenly aware that Stalin had made some polite response to his statement, and that the interpreter had translated it, and that Stalin was waiting for him to begin. Jeremy's mind was a perfect blank. He couldn't think of a single question. It was a nightmare.

Stalin noted his confusion with an ironic tilt of one eyebrow, and offered Jeremy a cigarette from a box on his desk. Jeremy remembered the tin of Edgeworth in his pocket and managed to extricate it.

"Perhaps Comrade Stalin would enjoy some American tobacco for his pipe," he blurted.

Stalin made no move to take the tin from him, and Jeremy, feeling foolish, set it down on the desk.

"Ever since Mr. Walter Winchell wrote in the American newspapers that I am supposed to have a fondness for Edgeworth tobacco," Stalin said, looking straight at Jeremy and ignoring the interpreter, "everybody wants to send me gifts of Edgeworth. It should not be forgotten that the Soviet Union, also, grows tobacco." The interpreter hurried to keep up, adding: "However, Comrade Stalin wishes to thank you for the gift."

Stalin put the pipe tobacco in his desk drawer and reached for a cigarette. The interpreter took one, too, and they all lit up.

Jeremy's head was clearing rapidly. The whiskey was wearing off, or perhaps burning off. He still hadn't asked Stalin a single question. He had no idea how long Stalin had allotted for the interview. Five minutes? Perhaps ten, if he were lucky. That was all right. Five minutes with Stalin was headline news. He asked the first question that popped into his head, a rude one.

"Comrade Stalin, *Newsweek* magazine said this week that you were dying of heart disease, and that you had Zinoviev and the others shot because you want all Trotskyites to precede you to the grave. Is that so?"

Stalin chose to take the question in high good humor. He turned to his interpreter and said, "Tell me, am I dying of heart disease?"

The interpreter, with a smile, said, "As you can see, Comrade Stalin is in the best of health."

"What about the trials?"

Stalin spoke slowly and thoughtfully, all the while drawing doodles on a pad on his desk. "In the Soviet Union, we have a strict system of laws. Those who violate those laws are brought to justice."

"Are there going to be more trials?"

"It is up to the authorities. The People's Commissariat of Justice exercises constant revolutionary vigilance in its concern for law and order. If additional counterrevolutionary terrorists are uncovered, they will be arrested and tried."

"Pyatakov and Radek have already been arrested. Are they guilty?"

Stalin continued doodling. He picked up a red pencil and scratched it back and forth on the pad. "That is for the court to decide," he said.

Jeremy was astonished that he hadn't been thrown out of the office. He decided to push his luck.

"You've just removed Yagoda from his post as head of the secret police and replaced him with Yezhov. Does that indicate a get-tough policy?"

Stalin had lifted an eyebrow at the sound of the two names, but he went on drawing his pictures. The interpreter gave him a fearful look and hesitated.

Jeremy chose to pretend that the hesitation was a language problem. "For 'get tough' you can say 'krepkee.'"

The interpreter put the question. Stalin bore down so hard on the pencil that the point broke off. But he spoke calmly, with measured emphasis.

"In the first place, it is not in my area of responsibility to remove such and such a one to this and that job. That is the business of Molotov and the other members of the Political Bureau. Ask Molotov what this means in this case. In the second place, Yagoda was not *removed*, in your meaning of the word. He was, I believe, transferred to important new duties as people's commissar of communications." His brown eyes bored directly into Jeremy, and for a moment Jeremy saw a flash of sly malice in them.

"Wasn't that Molotov I just saw leaving?" Jeremy asked innocently.

There was a moment's silence, then Stalin burst out into harsh laughter. "Perhaps he should ask his questions of Yezhov," he said to the interpreter. "Only Yezhov doesn't answer questions, he asks them."

Jeremy spent the next ten or fifteen minutes asking innocuous questions about the new Five-Year Plan, the state of agriculture, the new Moscow subway which Stalin had just dedicated. Stalin gave terse, careful answers—enough for three or four interviews—and still showed no signs of ending the session. Finally he paused, folded his hands across his stomach, and said, "Don't you have anything else to ask me, Mr. Sinclair?"

"I don't understand," Jeremy said.

"About Soviet music, for example?"

All at once it was clear to Jeremy why he had been summoned for the interview. Stalin had read his Shostakovich piece, and somehow been piqued by it. Stalin took himself seriously as an arbiter of the arts.

"All right," Jeremy said. "Were you personally the author of the *Pravda* editorial 'Muddle Instead of Music'?"

"I'm not *Pravda*'s music critic," Stalin said, playing with him. "That's Zaslavsky's job."

"It wasn't in Zaslavsky's style. Isn't 'muddle' a favorite word of yours? In the same issue of *Pravda* there was a report on a speech you made attacking the new history textbooks. You used the word 'muddle' there, too."

"Oh, are you a literary critic, too?" Stalin said with heavy sarcasm.

Jeremy was aware that there had been men who had sat in the chair he occupied now who would have signed their death warrants if they had talked to Stalin the way he was talking to him now. But the late hour, the whiskey that had worn off, gave him a sense of unreality. He persisted.

"The article contained a warning, 'This is playing at abstruse things, which could end very badly.' It sounded like a direct threat. Many people are wondering if Shostakovich's life is in danger."

"You have strange ideas about the Soviet Union, Mr. Sinclair," Stalin said in his harsh, purring voice. "We don't do things that way."

"Is it?" Sweat was soaking his shirt.

Stalin looked at Jeremy with a gaze of peculiar intensity. The brown teeth were bared in a broad smile. "Don't worry, Mr. Sinclair. Nothing will happen to Shostakovich."

There was a silence in the room. Jeremy felt giddy. He had the sense that somehow he had saved a life. He could see the pad that Stalin had doodled on. It was covered with pictures of wolves, dozens of them, with the background filled in by the red pencil.

Jeremy stood up. "Thank you, Comrade Stalin."

The interpreter ushered him into the outer office. "Are you tired, perhaps, Mr. Sinclair?" he said solicitously.

"I don't think I could sleep now," Jeremy said honestly.

"Comrade Stalin is very anxious to see the piece you write. Could you perhaps write it here before you leave?"

"Can you find me an English typewriter?"

"Yes, that can be arranged."

They left him alone in a small room. Jeremy typed steadily for two and a half hours. Someone brought him tea and caviar sandwiches. He put it all down as accurately as he could. The quotes about the purge trials looked more bland on paper than they had been when they came out of Stalin's mouth—Stalin was a superb politican, and he knew what he was doing. It occurred to Jeremy that he was being used, to make Stalin sound like a reasonable statesman talking about the administration of Soviet justice. He didn't care. It was sensational material anyway. If they left even one tenth of it uncensored, he would be the envy of every newsman in the world. He could have any job he wanted.

He took special care with the part about Shostakovich. If that was allowed to pass, Stalin would have put himself on notice. It would be a sort of guarantee.

It was four in the morning when someone came to take away the pages. "Comrade Stalin has returned from dinner and a film showing," one of the women secretaries said. They brought him more tea. What kind of hours do they keep around this place? Jeremy thought.

The pages came back thirty minutes later. Only a few minor changes had been made—nothing like what the censors at the Foreign Office press department would have done to it. The part about Shostakovich had been left alone. Stalin had scrawled his name across the top page, and initialed the other pages with his red pencil.

Stalin's secretary, the one with the pitted face, took him downstairs to the waiting car. Dawn was streaking the sky. "Comrade Stalin says he's sorry if you've missed your train to Gorky," the secretary said. "He says he hopes it was worth it."

"I didn't say anything about going to Gorky," Jeremy said with a start.

There was no expression on the scarred face. "Comrade Stalin takes an interest in the smallest details."

He got Popov out of bed. The censor came to the door in pajama bottoms, his face puffy and mottled with sleep. "Are you crazy, to come here at such an hour?" he said angrily. "Go away. It can wait till the office opens."

Jeremy pushed past him and slapped the dispatch down on the kitchen table. "Read it."

Popov, looking annoyed, picked up the pages. His face went pale. "Is this a joke?" he said.

"Go ahead and check with the Kremlin if you want."

Popov waddled from the room, holding the pajama bottoms up with one hand. Jeremy heard him talking into a phone in the other room. When Popov came back, he had a dressing gown on. "It's true, then?" he said. "He signed it himself?"

"I still need a censor's stamp before the telegraph office will send it," Jeremy said. "You'd better get moving. You don't want to hold this up."

Popov turned the pages with a trembling hand. He seemed terrified of even touching them, with Stalin's initials scrawled in red on each one. Jeremy almost felt sorry for him, being handed a hot potato like this. Popov couldn't finish quickly enough. He stamped each page and handed the dispatch back to Jeremy. "Here," he said. He hadn't made a single alteration—not even corrected the typos.

Jeremy was at the telegraph building when it opened. He staggered back to his room and threw himself across the bed in his clothes and fell asleep.

The phone woke him a few hours later. The telegrams and calls poured in from then on. *Collier's* wanted him to do an article: "I Sat with Stalin." *The Saturday Evening Post* wanted an article on the life of an American correspondent in Moscow. *Liberty,* remembering his coverage of the Roehm massacre in Germany two years earlier, offered him an astronomical sum for a piece to be called: "Two Faces of Dictatorship." Henry Luce cabled him personally to inquire if Jeremy's present commitments would allow him to go on special assignment for a new ten-cent picture magazine to be called *Life* that he was starting up this fall. He got job offers from the major wire services, and AIPS offered him his old job back, with a substantial increase in pay—this time to cover the war in Spain. His own employers gave him a raise.

He could write his own ticket. But there was time to think about that later. He worked in a rush, hacking out the minimum necessary follow-up material for his own news organizations, and trying to fend off the bibulous congratulations of half the Moscow press corps. He was markedly unpopular with the other half. They were the ones who had been reprimanded by their home offices for having been scooped on the Stalin interview.

It was two days before he was able to board a train for Gorky. He consoled himself with the thought that his future with Valentina would be much more secure now. After all, he told himself, two days didn't matter that much, did it?

He found Czernik packing. The one-room apartment had been stripped almost bare. Even the bed was gone. Nothing remained except a broken chair and an old steamer trunk which had served the Czerniks as a dresser, but which now was being filled with clothes and dishes. Helen Czernik was wrapping her china in sheets from *Pravda,* and Czernik was kneeling in front of a worn leather suitcase, cramming it with folded garments.

"What's going on?" Jeremy said.

Czernik looked up at him. His rugged Slavic face was drawn. "We're leaving, Jerry. We've had enough. We're going back to America."

Jeremy found himself unaccountably disappointed in Czernik. "I thought that you, of all people, would stick it out, Mike."

Czernik resumed his packing. "It's getting too hot around here. I lost my best trim operator a week ago. They said he was a Zinovievist saboteur, for Christ's sake! Production's at a standstill. We spend all our time at meetings, listening to people getting denounced."

"It's terrible, Mr. Sinclair," Helen Czernik said. "You have no idea. Even here at the American Village, people are afraid. Nobody dares open their mouth after what happened to Horvathy."

"What happened to Horvathy?"

"He tried to go back to America," Czernik answered. "Can you believe it? Horvathy, the idealist! That shows how bad things are getting. He told them he was leaving, and they wouldn't let him. Poor Horvathy gave up his passport when he came here, and now he can't get it back. They say he's a Soviet citizen. His wife and the two little kids are stranded, too. The children were born in the U.S., but they're Soviet citizens, too."

"Miklos still has his passport," Helen Czernik said. "They tried many times to make him give it up, but I wouldn't let him, thank God. But we're afraid of what might happen if we stay."

"They fired Horvathy," Czernik said grimly. "They took away his bread card. He had to leave the American Village. They're sleeping under bridges. I don't know what's going to happen to them when it gets cold."

Helen Czernik's good-natured face had lines in it that Jeremy hadn't seen before. "His wife comes with the children sometimes to beg for food. They're all in rags by now. With us gone . . ." She shrugged.

"I've got our tickets and our exit pass," Czernik said, wiping his bald head with his forearm. "I had to go through hell and high water to get a legal discharge. They called two mass meetings to put the pressure on me to stay. It doesn't look good when people like me go back. I had to give up my ration card, but we'll be able to eat till we get on the boat. We sold our furniture, and the radio."

"Sorry it worked out for you this way, Mike," Jeremy said.

Czernik shrugged. He looked at Jeremy's suitcase. "You just get here, Jerry?"

"Yes. I thought I'd drop my things here first and arrange about getting a room for the night."

"You haven't been down to the factory yet, or the workers' barracks, then?" There was something reluctant in Czernik's manner, as though he hadn't wanted to ask the question.

"No," Jeremy said. "Why?"

Helen Czernik said, in a tumble of words, "I wanted Miklos to write you, but then we thought, better not to put anything in the mail."

"Write me about what?" Jeremy said.

"Valentina," Czernik said. He stood up and wiped his hands on his trousers. "She's gone."

"God damn you, what do you mean, gone?" Jeremy shouted, grabbing Czernik by the shoulders and shaking him.

"Take it easy, Jerry," Czernik said, freeing himself. "She's gone, that's all. She didn't show up at her job one day. I guess the Gay Pay-Oo came one night and took her away. Who can tell? No one will talk. You know how these things are."

"Sit down," Helen Czernik said. "You look pale."

"What happened?" Jeremy said in a whisper.

"She was denounced. It was one of the girls in her work brigade. Who knows, someone may have put her up to it."

"Valentina's not anybody important!" Jeremy cried hoarsely. "She's just small fry!"

"They're down to the small fry, Jerry," Czernik said. "Maybe four or five hundred at the factory so far, and it doesn't show any signs of stopping. It starts at the top and filters down."

"What kind of charges could they bring against somebody like Valentina?"

"No charges. Like I told you, just names. Oppositionist. Saboteur. Zinovievite. Old Regime. Trollop of a capitalist spy."

"Oh, God!" Jeremy buried his face in his hands.

"It's not your fault," Czernik said compassionately. "The grinder needed more victims, that's all. If it hadn't been that, it would have been something else."

"I'll find her!" Jeremy said.

"Now, Jerry, don't start thinking like that. You got to get over it, that's all."

"I'll find her."

"Only the Gay Pay-Oo knows where she is. Get hold of yourself."

"Then I'll go to the Gay Pay-Oo!"

"Are you crazy?"

Helen Czernik turned pale. "Please, Mr. Sinclair, don't stir up anything. They know we're friends of yours, too."

But Jeremy was already halfway through the door.

He stopped first at the workers' barracks. It was odd, he thought, he'd never been through the gate before. Valentina had never wanted him to come inside, or even near the place. She met him outside the factory or at a prearranged spot, and made him deposit her outside the moldering gateposts.

He hopscotched over a series of sagging planks that formed a sketchy pathway across the sea of mud surrounding the barracks. He headed toward the building that he had seen Valentina disappear into. Like the others, it was a long, narrow, slumping structure made of unpainted boards that had turned gray, with a tar paper roof out of which projected a random row of rickety stovepipes. A single outdoor water spigot stood in a little concrete island in front of each building, the bare pipe swathed in rags. In the back was a row of toilets or outhouses. Jeremy counted five of them.

He opened the flimsy door and stepped through. A wave of stale odors hit him: sweaty feet, kerosene, mildew, old cigarette smoke. Three men doing something illegal were huddled together just inside the entrance, their collars turned up. When they saw Jeremy they quickly passed things back and forth and stuffed them into their pockets; it might have been money or food tickets.

Two long rows of partitioned bays stretched on either side of a narrow aisle down to the far end of the building. Perhaps three or four hundred men and women lived there. Each cubicle was hardly wider than a horse stall, and contained nothing but a narrow cot and perhaps a chair or a box. The partitions, which Jeremy guessed were a recent addition, gave each occupant a sort of privacy from the people on either side, but left the cubicles open on the aisle side. At intervals down the aisle were small, low kerosene stoves which provided some heat in winter and allowed the inhabitants to boil water for tea and washing. Jeremy could see people sitting on their cots eating their evening meal, bread with a bit of sausage or herring and pale tea.

My poor Valentina, Jeremy thought. He tried to imagine her hurrying to get dressed for work in the morning, with her back to the aisle against the roving males she had made fun of, perhaps a blanket around her for modesty. He thought of her carrying water in a kettle from the pump outside and heating it on one of the little stoves so she could wash her face. He thought of her trying to stay warm on winter nights, huddled under one or two thin blankets, with all her sweaters on, while the tin stoves fought a losing battle against the wind coming through the cracks.

"*Eezveeneete*," Jeremy said to the three men, "*znahyete kavo nee-boot Valentina Petrovna Andreyeva?*"

"*Ya ne paneemahyoo*," one of them muttered, and the three of them melted away.

Helplessly, Jeremy scanned the barracks building on either side of the aisle. The women's section seemed to be at the other end. He started down the aisle, aware of all the eyes watching him. When he crossed into women's territory, he was followed by giggles and remarks. All he could think of was that Valentina had lived in one of these pigeonholes.

All of a sudden he saw a face he recognized. It was Valentina's brigade leader, the chunky blond woman named Masha.

"Masha," he said excitedly, "you remember me. Can you tell me what happened to Valentina Petrovna?"

She backed away from him. "What are you saying?" she said. "I don't know of any such person."

"But she's in your brigade."

"Please go away," she said. "You have no right to be here."

He was about to expostulate, when he saw the hopelessness of it. He turned to go. Frightened faces peered at him from the nearby cubicles. One of the girls was wearing a sweater he recognized as Valentina's. It was a tan cardigan he had bought for her in the *valuta* shop in Gorky. He took a step toward the girl and saw her eyes widen in alarm. There was no point in bullying her, no point at all. He walked past her, down the aisle to the nearest door, and stepped out into the fresh air.

The GPU's Gorky headquarters was a large ugly stone building on Vorobievka Street. The entrance hall was drab and harshly lit, with hard benches along one wall and a row of little windows covered with wooden hatches opposite. Every once in a while a hatch would pop open and one of the dispirited people waiting on the benches would hurry over, clutching a small piece of paper.

"But where is your ticket?" the GPU official behind the window said.

"I'm telling you for the fourth time," Jeremy said, "I don't have a ticket."

"But why would you come here without a ticket?" the official said.

"I told you. I have an inquiry. I want to see the man in charge."

The thought of someone voluntarily entering GPU headquarters without a summons was clearly beyond the comprehension of the man in the window. "You had better wait over there," he said, and the wooden hatch snapped shut.

Jeremy joined the unfortunates on the benches and waited. He must have represented an extraordinary problem, because someone came to get him in less than half an hour.

He found himself sitting opposite a tough-looking, shaven-skulled GPU colonel, with all his papers spread out across the colonel's desk.

"You are well connected, Meester Seenclair," the colonel said, "but we can tell you nothing of this person."

"Valentina Petrovna Andreyeva," Jeremy said. "You took her out of the workers' barracks at the Gorky truck and auto plant."

"This is none of your business," the officer said coldly. "I advise you to be on your way and not make difficulties here. We are very busy here these days."

"For God's sake, can't you tell me if she's dead or alive?" Jeremy cried out.

The colonel looked down at Jeremy's opened passport. "I see you have been in Germany before entering the Soviet Union. But your exit stamp has been forged."

"You can ask the apparat about that," Jeremy said. "I was smuggled across the border under the auspices of the KPD, in the interests of the Soviet Union. An invitation from the Moscow Writers' Union went with it. I'm sure there's a complete file at Moscow GPU."

A flicker of annoyance crossed the colonel's face. "You had better leave while you are still able." He gathered up the passport and other documents and handed them over to Jeremy.

Jeremy stuffed them in his pockets. "I promise you," he said, his voice shaking, "I'm going to make the biggest stink you ever saw."

The benches in the entrance hall were filling up, Jeremy noticed as he passed through. The little windows were doing a land-office business. Russia was a strange country, Jeremy thought. Needing a ticket to attend your own execution! Or maybe he was exaggerating. Maybe these people had been summoned to answer the Russian equivalent of traffic offenses.

A somewhat scrawny GPU officer with lieutenant's tabs hurried by. There was something familiar about him, and when he turned his head to say something to the porter, Jeremy had a look at his face. It was Boris.

The sullen red rage that had been building up in Jeremy spilled over. "You son of a bitch!" he yelled, and while the porter and the startled people on the benches looked on, he spun Boris around and began punching him around the head and shoulders.

"Please, Gaspadeen Seenclair!" Boris said, cowering and trying to protect himself. "I am only doing my job. I *like* you."

Jeremy got past Boris's guard and punched him solidly in the mouth, splitting his lip. Blood began to flow satisfyingly, and then the two GPU guards at the door reached the scene, and beat Jeremy to the floor with their rifle butts.

He woke up with a throbbing headache. He was lying on the bare springs of an iron cot. He probed with his tongue and found a loose tooth. His ribs hurt. There was blood down the front of his shirt.

He got himself slowly to a sitting position and put his feet on the floor. He couldn't have been unconscious very long, because there was still some daylight coming through the narrow barred window high up near the ceiling. Enough to see that the walls of the cell had been whitewashed many times, but that the person responsible had fallen down on the job the last time round, because there was still a splattering of bloodstains.

He rattled the door and yelled for a while, but there was no response and he gave up. The light began to fade, and he was left groping in pitch darkness. His documents were gone; they had been taken out of his pockets. He was conscious of being hungry, and he remembered that he had not eaten all day. There was nothing to do but go to sleep, so he rolled up his jacket for a pillow and lay down on the cot again.

Hours later, or so Jeremy thought, sounds in the corridor woke him up. It was still pitch dark. A man was whimpering, pleading, and there were sounds of scraping, dragging footsteps interspersed with the sounds of the boots of the men who were hurrying him along. Jeremy thought of yelling while someone was within earshot, and decided against it. The sounds faded down the corridor. Some time later, Jeremy thought he heard a faint shot, but he could not be sure. He might have imagined it, he told himself.

Gorky GPU was busy, the colonel had said. They would be working overtime, if the purge was down to ordinary workers at the auto plant.

A bugle call woke him up in the morning. He used the bucket in the corner, washed his face in the cracked sink that the cell contained. He sat on the bed and waited.

They came for him about a half hour later. Two men with shiny boots and large holstered revolvers. *"Prakhadeete,"* one of them said. "Come along." No breakfast, Jeremy thought.

They took him back to the colonel's office. He was not invited to sit down this time. He stood in front of the colonel's desk, the two guards close behind him.

"Meester Seenclair," the colonel said, the daylight glinting off his shaven skull, "you have assaulted a Gay Pay-Oo officer. That is a very serious offense. But we have instructions from Moscow about you. What they will do about you, I do not know. But you will be put on a train, and you will not return to Gorky district. You are Moscow's problem now."

39

"Russian balalaikas," Harry Hopkins said. "What are we doing sitting here on election eve listening to Russian balalaikas?"

Dorothy Thompson laughed. She was a sturdy, attractive woman with a flapper bob. "It's because you're going to give the country away to Russia," she said. "Colonel McCormack says that Stalin's issued orders to the American Communist Party to get Roosevelt reelected."

"Have you seen the latest?" Brad said. He reached around behind his chair and got the copy of the *Chicago Tribune* that he had bought earlier that evening in Times Square. He spread it out so the party at the table could see the headline. It read:

LAST DAY TO SAVE YOUR COUNTRY

Hopkins looked at the paper with disgust. "People are onto that kind of stuff. I hear a crowd turned over a *Tribune* delivery truck the other day and set fire to the papers."

Brad refolded the paper and tucked it away under the chair. "Anyway, they're the ones who are dancing to balalaika music," he said. "And they're all wearing sunflowers."

He looked out across the dance floor of the Iridium Room of the Hotel St. Regis. It was filled with dancing couples in evening clothes, who in the dim light were trying to do a fox-trot to the music of the Russian-costumed orchestra.

"I'm wearing a sunflower, too," Dorothy Thompson said.

"It doesn't suit you," Brad said. "Why don't you take it off?"

Hopkins leaned over, after a glance around at the Republican audience that surrounded them, and said in a lowered voice: "Did you hear what the chief said the other day—off the record. He said a neighbor told him that the sunflower was yellow, that it had a black heart, and that it was good only for parrot food. Then he added that it also was dead in November."

"Harry!" Barbara Hopkins said reprovingly. "Governor Landon is a nice man."

Hopkins wilted like a guilty schoolboy. "Yeah, but he's been saying some godawful stupid things lately."

Brad nodded sadly. Landon, as the campaign wore him down, had succumbed to the scare tactics of some of the people around him, and had begun to say things like: "We have a choice to make between the American system of government and one that is alien to everything this country ever before has known."

Barbara Hopkins smiled wanly. "Well, you've been pretty outspoken yourself during this campaign."

Brad admired her spirit. Few people knew it, but Barbara Hopkins had lost a breast to cancer less than a year ago. The operation, Brad gathered, had failed to halt the spread of the disease, but she remained determinedly cheerful. Harry was doing his best to fill her days with fun—trips to Saratoga Springs and other excursions. Eleanor Roosevelt knew about it, and conspired with Harry to see that Barbara was included in weekend outings on the presidential yacht. Strangely, one of the few Harry had confided in was his old archrival, Harold Ickes.

"I wasn't outspoken enough," Hopkins said glumly.

It was a sore point with Harry. He had been kept out of the latter part of the campaign. The WPA was too fat a target for the Republicans. Jim Farley had told him he was the President's greatest handicap. Still, he had managed to get in a few licks at Landon.

"The boss is plenty tough enough on his own, wheelchair or not," Colonel Westbrook said. "The wrap-up speech at Madison Square Garden Saturday night really laid it on the line."

Westbrook, now one of Hopkins's top aides, had been the man responsible for enlisting the help of the army engineers for flood control and other big WPA projects.

Hopkins brightened. " 'For twelve years this nation was afflicted with hear-nothing, see-nothing, do-nothing government,' " he quoted approvingly. " 'The nation looked to government but the government looked away. Nine mocking years with the golden calf and three long years of the scourge. Nine crazy years at the ticker and three long years in the breadlines.' "

Westbrook shook his head admiringly. "Powerful stuff!"

Hopkins inclined his head in Brad's direction. "Some of the credit goes to Brad," he said. "The President borrowed him from me to help write that speech."

"Along with Sam Rosenman, Tom Corcoran, and Stan High," Brad said quickly. "I didn't contribute much. They might have kept one or two phrases."

Hopkins turned to Dorothy Thompson. "Brad's also the one who's responsible for separating you from your husband this summer. It was his idea to turn *It Can't Happen Here* into a play for the Federal Theater."

Brad held up both hands. "The credit goes to Francis Bosworth. And Hallie Flanagan. And poor Jack Moffitt, who had to hole up at the Essex House for three weeks with Red Lewis to write the script. I'm afraid Mr. Lewis drove him crazy, with ideas for new scenes and revisions every five minutes. In the end, they weren't talking to one another. They passed notes back and forth through Hallie Flanagan."

"Well, it turned out to be a howling success," Dorothy Thompson said. "That's the important thing."

It Can't Happen Here had opened simultaneously the week before in twenty-one theaters in seventeen states, under WPA auspices. It was a sellout everywhere. It was also tremendously controversial. Critics charged that it was naked propaganda, that it would offend Hitler and Mussolini, and that its timing was a sinister ploy by Harry Hopkins to get Roosevelt reelected. Incredibly, it had been translated into German, but the Reich Theater production had been banned because Sinclair Lewis refused to supply evidence that he was of Aryan descent. Now he was working on a new play, about anti-Semitism.

"Look," Barbara Hopkins said. "I think they're going to flash some more returns."

The lights in the Iridium Room had dimmed a degree further. The hotel management had set up a magic lantern arrangement that projected election returns from a wire-service news ticker. The screen lit up and showed some tallies. The dancing couples stopped to applaud, though not as warmly as they had before.

"It's those same returns from that precinct in New Jersey," Colonel Westbrook chuckled. "This is the fourth time they've shown them."

"Trying to keep Republican morale up," Hopkins said. "That's probably the only county in the country that's going for Landon. I predict a Roosevelt landslide."

"This isn't the place for all of you tonight," Dorothy Thompson said. "You should be at Hyde Park, having cider and doughnuts with the rest of them, and waiting for the Landon telegram."

"We WPA types are keeping a low profile till this is over," Hopkins said with a forced smile.

"Is Harold Ickes there?" she said.

"Ow!" Colonel Westbrook said.

"He's home with an attack of lumbago today," Brad said soberly. "Steve Early let it slip. He'll be following the returns over the radio."

"I suppose he caught cold making all those campaign speeches," Dorothy Thompson said innocently.

"That's right, rub it in," Colonel Westbrook said.

"Well, I *am* a newspaper columnist," she said.

"Well, you're not going to get a quote from me tonight, Dorothy," Hopkins said, and everybody laughed.

The lights dimmed and the magic lantern screen lit up again. This time the returns were for the tenth congressional district in Texas. The Democratic candidate, Lyndon Johnson, had a two-to-one lead over his Republican opponent. There was no applause. The people on the floor didn't even bother to stop dancing.

"That boy will go far," Colonel Westbrook said.

"I'm almost sorry to see Lyndon elected to Congress," Hopkins said. "Aubrey says he's the best field director we have at NYA. It's a pity to lose him."

The young Texan, who had been Congressman Dick Kleberg's legislative secretary, had campaigned hard for the job. The same day that Roosevelt's executive order had created the National Youth Administration, Johnson had called up his fellow Texans, Tom Connally and Sam Rayburn, and asked them to push him as Texas NYA director. Aubrey Williams had bowed gracefully. At twenty-nine, Johnson had become the youngest NYA head in the country. He had pitched into the job with characteristic energy. Within six months he had signed up 350 sponsors and put 18,000 unemployed teen-agers to work, building parks, planting grass, laying bricks, and repairing school buses. When Congressman Buchanan in his district had died a few months ago, Johnson had immediately announced his own candidacy before Buchanan's widow could beat him to it, thus effectively freezing out most of the other possible competition as well.

"Lyndon won't be satisfied until he's President," Barbara Hopkins said.

"Well, he'll have to wait until 1944 to run," Hopkins said with a laugh. "He won't be old enough till then."

There was an uneasy silence at the table. Everybody was reminded that two of the people present had been touted as presidential material. Sinclair Lewis, on hearing that his wife was being discussed, first as a senator from Vermont, then as the first woman President, had snapped: "Fine. Then I can write my 'My Day.'" If he ever divorced her, Lewis said, he would name Hitler as corespondent.

Brad finished his drink. "I'd better get back to Sally. She'll be wondering what happened to me."

"I'm sorry you and Sally won't have dinner with us," Hopkins said. "Won't you stay for another drink?"

"I didn't want to tire her. It's been a long day. I'll just have something sent up by room service, and we'll follow the returns on the radio."

"When is the baby due?" Barbara Hopkins asked softly.

Brad kept his voice light. "Two months, the doctor says."

Hopkins reached across the table and poured a little champagne into Brad's empty glass. "Well, at least let's drink a toast before you go. Happy days."

The magic lantern screen winked on again. It was the same returns from the New Jersey precinct, the ones that showed Landon ahead.

"Happy days," Brad said.

Sally was in bed, reading *Gone With the Wind*. She'd been working on it for a week. "You rat," she said. "Leaving your pregnant wife alone."

"We had to make New York safe for Roosevelt. Did room service send up the radio?"

"Over there, sugah." She nodded toward the dressing table, where there was a new Atwater Kent five-tube table model, already plugged in. Brad walked over and turned it on. When it warmed up, he tuned in WJZ on the Blue Network. It was a musical interlude, but the election returns would be coming in sporadically.

He took off his dinner jacket and tossed it over a chair. "Hungry?" he said. "I'll call down for a bite."

"Later," she said. "Come on over here and have a seat."

He sat down beside her. She wrapped her arms around his neck and pulled him down for a kiss. Her lips were greedy.

"Ugh, you've been drinking cheap champagne."

"It wasn't cheap. I saw the bottle."

"Well, sweet, anyway."

"I'll wash out my mouth with honest gin, as soon as I can get the bellhop up here with some ice. Are you sure you don't want something to eat?"

She gave a tinkling laugh. "Poah Brad. Keeping little mother nourished. Don't worry, I'll have a club sandwich. And some potato chips."

"That's better." He held her at arm's length and looked at her. "Being seven months pregnant agrees with you."

"I'm not so *skinny*, you mean. Don't get used to it, darlin'. The doctor says it'll come off."

He gave her another kiss. "I'll call room service."

The radio sputtered an announcement. Connecticut, it appeared from the incomplete returns, would go Democratic, the first time it had happened since 1912.

Brad and Sally had finished their club sandwiches. Brad had just nibbled around the edges of his. He was too tense to eat. He poured more gin over his melting ice cubes. Sally, in deference to her condition, had diluted her gin with a little Canada Dry.

"Should you be drinking that stuff?" Brad said.

"Don't be an old worrier. It won't hurt Melissa's little brother to have a taste of gin. I had *my* first drink when I was three."

"You didn't."

She giggled. "Picked up Daddy's glass and drank it down. I got a spanking." She patted the bed beside her. "Don't stay out there like an old grouch. Come on in and cuddle."

He took off his clothes and got under the covers. They sipped their drinks and smoked, listening to the radio.

By nine-thirty, it was obvious that Roosevelt had swept every state except Maine and Vermont, with New Hampshire teetering on the edge. He had what looked like a ten million popular-vote lead over Landon. Lemke, the Union Party candidate supported by Father Coughlin, Dr. Townsend, and Gerald L. K. Smith, polled less than a million votes despite the lunatic fringe predictions that he would divert enough votes from Roosevelt to deprive him of a majority in the Electoral College and throw the election into the House of Representatives. Landon still hadn't conceded.

"It's a Roosevelt landslide," Brad said. "The biggest landslide since Teddy Roosevelt beat Taft. Poor Alf Landon is going to end up with exactly eight electoral votes. Maybe twelve, if New Hampshire comes across for him."

"Does that mean baby's papa will have a job?" Sally said.

"For the next four years, anyway."

"That's nice."

"The doctor said not to do that."

"No, but we can do *this*."

Landon conceded at about one-thirty. There was a gracious ex-

change of telegrams, read over the air by the WJZ announcer. Sally
was cuddled up against Brad, snoring. She yawned and stretched.

"Brad?" she said sleepily.

He stubbed out his cigarette in the ashtray on the night table. "Did I
wake you up?"

"What are we going to name Melissa's little brother?"

"I wouldn't mind another girl," he laughed.

"It's going to be a boy," she said firmly.

"How about Bradford Collier the Third?"

"Brad junior."

"No, the Third."

He would name his son, if it was a son, for his father, not himself.
It was time to start balancing the accounts.

"And I was supposed to be the millstone around the President's
neck!" Harry Hopkins said exuberantly. "What a day! I tell you, I'm
the happiest man in the world!"

Brad smiled with him, for the cameras. Reporters had swarmed
around them when they got off the train in Washington, and Hopkins,
his muzzle off, was giving vent to his feelings.

"And only yesterday the gloom boys were saying that if Roosevelt
lost the election, it would be the WPA's fault!" Hopkins went on.

"Does that mean that now the WPA's going to get the credit for
reelecting the President?" the *Washington Times* reporter said, smiling.

Hopkins's face clouded. "No," he said shortly.

Brad knew what was bothering him. That afternoon, Hopkins was
going to have to fire ten thousand people in the arts program. The
money had run out, had been used up by the drought emergency.
"They'll say we're doing it because we don't need their votes anymore," Hopkins had said to Brad bitterly.

"What about dog tags?" another reporter asked. "Is the administration going to start issuing dog tags January first?"

The Republican chairman had made a last, desperate election eve
attempt to discredit Social Security, saying that twenty-six million
workers would have to wear steel tags on chains around their necks,
like dogs.

"No," Hopkins shot back. "With Landon whipped, the country isn't
going to the dogs."

"One more question, Harry," a reporter said. "Are you going to be
made secretary of welfare?"

"Where'd you hear that?" Hopkins snapped. "There'll never be any
such Cabinet post."

* * *

"The President told me to bring you along," Hopkins said. "He's leaving on a fishing trip, and then he's going to sail on the U.S.S. *Indianapolis* to the Buenos Aires conference. He asked me to pop by before he leaves."

"Well, look what the cat dragged in!" the President cried jovially when they entered the Oval Room. "If it isn't Harry the Hop and Brad the Lad!"

The President had promoted him, Brad noted. From Bad to Lad. He didn't know if it meant anything.

It was a little after five. Some of the office staff were standing around, drinks in hand. Brad saw Missy Le Hand and the President's other secretary, Grace Tully, and Marvin McIntire, Steve Early, and Pa Watson. The President was mixing a pitcher of martinis. Brad winced when he saw how much vermouth the President was adding.

"Just in time for the Children's Hour," the President said.

The President, turning his wheelchair, handed Brad a martini, and beamed when Brad took a sip and praised it. Harry Hopkins asked apologetically for a whiskey sour, and just at that moment a valet came with a pitcher of them from the kitchen. So much for the pretense that we just dropped by, Brad thought.

" 'Twas a famous victory," Hopkins said. "Congratulations, Mr. President."

Roosevelt shook his massive head in mock sadness. "I knew I should have gone to Maine and Vermont," he said. "But Jim Farley wouldn't let me."

It was a tactless thing to say, and Roosevelt realized it as soon as he saw the stricken look on Hopkins's face.

"We've got our mandate," he added quickly, "and part of it is a vote of confidence in you and what you've been doing. There'll be no turning back, I promise you. You're going to have your work cut out for you."

Brad sipped his martini and discreetly studied the collection of junk on the President's desk. It had grown considerably; there was hardly any work space left. There were ceramic donkeys, bears, pigs, even a mechanical auto with Charlie McCarthy at the wheel. The white stuffed elephant had shrunk considerably since he had first seen it.

The President noticed him looking at the elephant. "He loses an inch or two every time Grace or Missy sends him out to the cleaners," he said. "He's just about down to GOP size now, don't you think?"

Brad laughed, and the President returned to Hopkins. "So I hope you won't pay any attention to what the Hearsts and the Colonel McCormacks have been saying. What's this I hear about your wanting to quit?"

"It's baloney, Mr. President," Hopkins said. "Those stories are cockeyed." A boyishly mischievous look transformed the long, hollowed face. "Not that there aren't a few industrialists who'd be willing to pay me a fancy salary to get me out of Washington."

"Good," the President laughed. "I'm losing Rex, you know. His letter of resignation came through this morning." He shook his head. "His position was made intolerable by a lot of little people. I'll have to find a new speechwriter, I'm afraid."

Brad tried not to show his interest. This was the first time he'd heard that the Tugwell resignation was definite. There were envious rumors that he had been offered a salary of $35,000 a year by the American Molasses Company.

The President held out the martini pitcher. "Have another sippy?" he said.

"Thank you, sir," Brad said.

The President poured. "Little dividend," he said.

"The Hearst dog-tag picture on election morning was the last straw," Hopkins said. "The guy with the bare chest and the caption that said 'You.'"

The presidential brow creased with annoyance. "He had the brass to call Hyde Park on election night, did I tell you that? John Boettiger took the call. It was Marion Davies. She said she just wanted to tell me that she knew that a steamroller had flattened them out, but that there were no hard feelings. Then Hearst came on the line, and repeated that he had been run over by a steamroller, but that there were no hard feelings at that end. Well, I can tell you that as far as this administration is concerned, Hearst is persona non grata."

The President extended a large thumb and turned it down, to show what he meant.

"Well, I'm with you there, Mr. President," Hopkins said.

Roosevelt looked refreshed, flushed, full of confidence. "There have been suggestions made," he said, "that I take it easy now, do a lot of fishing, run a lame duck administration. They're already jockeying for the 1940 convention. Well, we may give them a few surprises, eh, Harry?"

"I sincerely hope so, Mr. President."

Roosevelt's mood grew more somber. He screwed a cigarette into his holder and lit it. "No telling what those fellows Hitler and Mussolini are up to on the other side," he said. "We'll have to watch them closely, and old Joe Stalin, too. I don't like this thing in Spain. The Italians shouldn't have gotten themselves involved. Things like that tend to spread." He puffed thoughtfully on the holder. "And the Pacific. We'll have to do something about the balance of naval power in the Pacific. If we get anywhere on disarmament in Buenos Aires, we might try for something of the sort with Japan. But they may be on a collision course with us." He shook himself in the wheelchair, like somebody trying to shake off a bad dream. "But first we've got to set things right at home, don't we?"

"I'm with you there, Mr. President," Hopkins said.

"Oh, by the way, Harry," the President said casually, "may I borrow young Sinclair from you again? Just for a bit. Don't worry, you'll get him back in tip-top shape. There's a little chore he might help Judge Rosenman with. That all right with you, young Brad?"

Brad, dazed, said, "I'm honored, Mr. President."

40

"Fancy your going to work for British Overseas Press Service," Millicent Wickes said. "Considering what we pay. I should think that after your Stalin interview, you could name your own price."

"I need BOPS accreditization," Jeremy said. "I don't think I'd get very far into insurgent territory with my old Agence Soleil press card."

She curled her lip in disgust. "That scruffy little outfit! Really, love, you *were* a bit of a chump, weren't you?"

"Well they gave me the boot, anyway. I got a wire from Brussels. I think they got the word from the Comintern."

"Kicked out of Germany. Kicked out of Russia. You're collecting quite a few bruises on your backside, aren't you?"

She was sitting at a desk in a long row of desks in the news agency's rather run-down offices in Bloomsbury. Clacking typewriters sounded on all sides, and an unattended news ticker chattered to itself over by the wall. Millicent's desk was piled high with untidy stacks of teletype material and handouts, and her wastebasket was stuffed. She had something in the typewriter now, her bird claw hands poised over the keys, a cigarette sticking out of her mouth. It had taken Jeremy by surprise to see her sitting there, on his way through the outer office.

A sharp-featured kid in a shiny blue suit came over with a stack of folders and dumped them on Millicent's desk. "See if you can get anything out of this muck from the clipper pouch, Millie, that's a love." He gave Jeremy a curious glance and walked away quickly.

"Tell his nibs to sift through his own clipper pouch!" she yelled after him. "Bloody lazy sod!" she said to Jeremy.

"What about you?" Jeremy said. "What are you doing here in the London office?"

"I was rotated. Didn't you know we're rotated every so often, like tops. Actually, it was bloody Sykes! He went on one binge too many. The home office couldn't locate him for a week all during that dither about the Hitler-Ciano pact, and neither could I. I couldn't cover up for him this time. He got the sack. The new man didn't want me, so here I am."

"They should have put you in charge of the Berlin office. You were doing all the work anyway."

"A woman? *That* day will never come, love."

Somebody else came by and tossed Millicent a sheet torn from the teletype. "Do this one up, will you, Millie?"

She ignored it. "Well, you're bloody well out of Russia, anyhow. They've been going mad since you left. At the rate that Stalin is shooting people, he'll depopulate the country. Did I say something wrong, love?"

"No, no, I was just thinking."

"I don't understand why you didn't go back to Allied International. Their offer must have been better than ours, surely."

"They're sitting on the reports of Italian and German intervention on Franco's side. Too hot a potato for them. I want to report the war honestly."

"Still, all that lovely American money."

"I'll be doing some magazine work, too."

"When do you leave for Spain?"

"My ship sails tomorrow."

She looked down at her hands. "A lot of last-minute packing to do, I suppose?"

"No, I'm all packed."

Her bright, quick eyes darted to his face. "Then we can have dinner together, can't we?" She studied him anxiously. "There's no reason why not?"

"No," he said. "No reason at all."

"You can collect me here at five," she said. She picked up the teletype sheet that had been dropped on her desk. "Oh, here's news from America. You're installing your President again today."

* * *

"Why does it always rain on inauguration day?" Peter said, staring out the window. "It's coming down in sheets."

Pamela finished putting on her lipstick. "Think of all the ruined hairdos," she said. "All those fancy diplomatic uniforms with the soaked feathers. Are you going to wear rubbers?"

"Now, wouldn't I look goddamned silly wearing rubbers? Anyway, it's only a short dash from the curb to the door. Edwards will hold an umbrella over your head."

"It's my shoes I'm worried about. They'll get soaked."

He was pacing impatiently. "Almost ready?"

"Just another minute."

"The services start at ten."

"We have plenty of time, Peter."

"Can't be late when you're invited to go to church with the President, you know," he said, flashing her a quick smile.

"Only us and the Cabinet and half the department heads and their wives," she teased him.

He didn't like that. "St. John's doesn't hold that many people," he said. "It's still a feather in your cap to get an invitation. I guess I'm starting to get someplace in this town."

Pamela said nothing. The White House invitation to attend the special preinaugural service at St. John's Episcopal Church across Lafayette Square from the White House had come because of Brad. "I wangled a couple for you from Missy Le Hand," Brad had said, "but don't tell Peter. I don't want him to think he's getting any favors from his New Dealer brother-in-law."

Pamela went over to Peter and laced her fingers behind his neck. "It's nice to be married to an important man," she said.

"No regrets?" he said, nuzzling her.

"No regrets."

"You don't mind giving up that job with the Porteous committee?"

"I don't mind."

"I need you here, darling," he said.

It was almost a full-time job running the huge house Peter had bought for them on Massachusetts Avenue near Cissy Patterson's mansion, Pamela had found, with its staff of servants that she had to manage, and the dinner parties with their complicated Washington protocol, and the juggling of social obligations she had to do on Peter's behalf.

"I just wonder sometimes if we can afford all this," she said.

"Now, don't think about that," he said. "I'll worry about the money."

Pamela looked out into the rain and worried about her hair. It had to hold up through the services, the inaugural ceremony, the reception, the ball, and the late party at Cissy's. You ought to worry about something.

A bugle call ripped the air. Through the tall window came the shrill, furious voice of a Japanese officer screaming at his men. The drumming of horses' hooves mixed with the rumble and creak of caissons and the sound of marching feet.

Colonel Stilwell pulled back the bamboo blind and looked out. "Come look at this, Sinclair," he said in a voice taut with anger.

Gordon went over and stood beside the colonel. On the north field of the Legation Quarter, columns of brown-clad Japanese foot and horse soldiers, in full kit and helmet, paraded up and down while an officer, mounted on a horse that was too big for him, waved his sword at them. Howitzers and mortars were arrayed at the edges of the field. Machine gun crews raced back and forth, showing how fast they could set up.

"The bastards," Stilwell said. "They've been taking over as if they owned the place. Colonel Marston's ordered the marine guard to stay indoors today, to avoid incidents."

"It's the same downriver, sir," Gordon said. "The Japanese hold maneuvers near the bridges and rail junctions. Colonel Lynch has us training to come to the aid of the legations here in Peiping by forced march, in case it becomes necessary."

Stilwell let the blind drop. "It's a powder keg, that's for certain. Maybe the Peanut was right to insist that we transfer most of the legation to Nanking, and keep this one open as a consulate."

"Peanut" was what Stilwell called Chiang Kai-shek. It was about the most flattering thing he called him.

"Sir, do you think the Japanese will move?" Gordon said.

Stilwell took off his glasses and rubbed them on his sleeve. His spare, bony face looked tired. "I don't know, Lieutenant. All they need is an incident, and they're very good at manufacturing those. Now that Chiang and Mao have agreed to stop fighting one another for the time being, Japan has all the more incentive to move fast. One more shooting incident, like the one that gave them an excuse to take over the railway junction at Fengtai a few months ago, and we're going to have a full-scale war here."

He went over to his desk. "Well, the President's aware of the situation. I have it from the grapevine that he's hopping mad at the Japanese since Manchuria. Now that he's got the election campaign behind him, maybe he'll pay some more attention to what's going on here."

He looked at his desk calendar. "Today's the inauguration, isn't it? January twentieth. They moved the date up from March this year."

Outside a bugle blared. Gordon could hear the sound of horses breaking into a gallop. There was a sudden commotion: the neighing of horses, metallic clatter, and the shrieks of the officer. Gordon guessed that a caisson had overturned.

"I'd better be getting back to Tientsin, sir," he said. He picked up his dispatch case. "Do you have anything going back to Colonel Lynch?"

Stilwell didn't answer. "I need more eyes and ears," he said. "Washington has to be kept informed, and I've only got a handful of men to cover all of north China."

"Yes, sir," Gordon said.

Stilwell gave Gordon a piercing glance. "How'd you like to work for me, Lieutenant?"

Gordon was overwhelmed. "Sir, I still have ten months to go on my tour of duty with the Fifteenth."

Stilwell waved a sinewy hand. "I can fix it up," he said. "How about it? You can be one of my language officers—serve as an assistant attaché. You're a little young, and you're only a lieutenant, but you've got a good command of Chinese. That's rare around here."

"Sir, I'd like nothing better."

Stilwell's eyes narrowed. *"Ch'ing t'ing, chien cheng jen!"* he barked.

"Shir," Gordon said. *"Shir-shir shin-do."*

Stilwell had asked him if he was willing to be a spy—someone who listened and watched—and he had said yes, he'd try.

Stilwell laughed. "My son Joe tells me he gave you my old Chinese primer back at the Point. That's the best trade I ever made. An old book for a new attaché."

"It's gettin' on toward noon," Pa Kinney said. "They're goin' to miss the nauguration."

He was sitting in front of the radio in a kitchen chair, with a pillow in the small of his back. The pillow helped, he said. He hadn't been able to work for two weeks, ever since he picked up the crate of lettuce the wrong way.

"Maybe they're workin'," Sue Ellen said hopefully.

"Maybe they are and maybe they aren't," Ma Kinney said, stirring the pot on the stove. "Makes no sense to talk about it."

Junie rocked back and forth, cooing to the new baby. It was awfully cute. It was too bad that Leander was so jealous of it, but he'd get over that.

"You better turn the radio on," Pa Kinney said. "Get ready."

There was a lot of noise out on the stoop, and Purley came stumbling in. "Whoo-ee!" he whooped. "No more pickin' lettuce. We're in the what you call blue collar now!"

Floyd and Wesley followed him in. Both were a little unsteady. Wesley had a silly grin on his face. His glasses were fogged. Floyd looked guilty.

"Purley, you've been drinking," Ma Kinney said. "And you got them drunk, too."

"Just a little celebration. They got to put hair on their chest, too."

"Purley, did you spend that two dollars?" Sue Ellen said.

"Don't matter," Purley said. "We got a paycheck comin' the end of next week."

"You—you got the job at the shipyard?" Junie said.

Purley slapped his leg. "Start Monday," he said.

Floyd looked sheepish but proud.

"That's wonderful!" Junie said.

Sue Ellen was crying.

"You see, they've got the jobs now," Wesley said earnestly. "It's all just opening up. They say they're building ships over in Japan, so we got to build ships, too."

Junie smiled at Floyd to show that she was proud of him. They didn't have to say anything to each other. They could talk later, when they were alone. She knew that she could always trust Floyd. She and the three children.

"You going to have to wear one of them dog tags?" Pa Kinney said.

"No," Purley said in disgust. "I told you there's no dog tags. We just got to get a little card with a number on it, that's all."

Wesley had his ear to the radio. "Shh, I think it's coming through."

"Quiet, everybody, it's the nauguration," Pa Kinney said. "Turn that up, Wesley."

The Kinneys found seats and settled down. Roosevelt's voice came through the cheap speaker, muffled and scratchy, but you could hear the words and the passion with which they were uttered:

"When four years ago we met to inaugurate a President," the voice said, "the republic, single-minded in anxiety, stood in spirit here. We dedicated ourselves to the fulfillment of a vision—to speed the time when there would be for all the people that security and peace essential to the pursuit of happiness. We of the republic pledged ourselves to drive from the temple of our ancient faith those who had profaned it."

Floyd's hand crept into Junie's, big and calloused and warm. They clung to each other and listened to the rolling phrases of hope and comfort.

"We would not admit that we could not find a way to master economic epidemics just as, after centuries of fatalistic suffering, we had found a way to master epidemics of disease," the voice went on. "We refused to leave the problems of our common welfare to be solved by the winds of chance and the hurricanes of disaster."

"That's right," said Pa Kinney, nodding to himself. "That's right."

The rain whipped Brad's face. It was a driving rain that slanted under the roof of the shelter that had been constructed in front of the east portico of the Capitol. He was thoroughly drenched by now, as was everybody else who was anywhere near the edges of the platform.

He could see Harold Ickes standing with Henry Morgenthau a little in front of him. Their morning coats were sopping wet. The outline of a flask showed in Morgenthau's pocket, a damned good idea on a day like this. Ickes, he noticed, was wearing an old pair of patent leather shoes because of the rain, figuring, he supposed, that they wouldn't be visible to the people below. Brad's own shoes were decidedly squishy. He'd have to towel himself dry and change before going back to see Sally at the hospital.

Jimmy Roosevelt was standing tall behind his father and Vice-President Garner. The President had come in on Jimmy's arm, walking gamely on his braces down the long runner that led to the speaker's stand, one painful step at a time, an alternating swing of the dead legs in their steel supports, rather than a walk.

The President, his head bared, was taking the full force of the torrent with his chin up. Originally a glass shield had been set up around the stand for him, but he had ordered it taken down that morning. He wouldn't stay dry, he said, while people stood in the wet to hear him.

The Bible that Roosevelt had sworn the oath on, Brad saw, was wrapped in cellophane. It was a family treasure, an old Dutch Bible that he had used for all his oaths of office, as governor and President.

Brad edged a little farther into the platform. Water was cascading down his face from a bedraggled loop of bunting that hung just above him.

It was worse for the crowds out there. Spread out in front of the Capitol was a great sea of hats and umbrellas, pelted by the icy downpour. But they were applauding. By God, they were cheering and applauding.

"Have we reached the goal of our vision?" the President was saying. "Have we found our happy valley? I see a great nation, upon a great continent, blessed with a great wealth of natural resources. Its hundred and thirty million people are at peace among themselves. They are making their country a good neighbor among the nations. I see a United States which can demonstrate that, under democratic methods of government, national wealth can be translated into a spreading volume of human comforts hitherto unknown, and the lowest standard of living can be raised far above the level of mere subsistence."

Someone was edging toward Brad on the platform. It was Tom Corcoran. He was making slow progress. The platform was jam packed.

Corcoran reached Brad and put a meaty hand on his arm. "I just heard about the baby," he said. "Congratulations. When was it? This morning?"

"About five o'clock," Brad said.

"Boy or girl?"

"Boy."

"He picked some day to be born," Corcoran said. "There's going to be a meeting at four with the judge and Don Richberg. Can you be there?"

"Yes."

"We got to talk about this Supreme Court thing," Corcoran said, and moved off again.

"But here is the challenge to our democracy," Roosevelt was saying. "In this nation I see tens of millions of its citizens—a substantial part of its whole population—who at this very moment are denied the greater part of what the very lowest standards of today call the necessities of life. I see millions of families trying to live on incomes so meager that the pall of family disaster hangs over them day by day."

The bleak words struck a chill in Brad, though he had heard the President rehearsing them. He waited for the line he knew was coming.

"I see one third of a nation ill-housed, ill-clad, ill-nourished," the man in the steel braces went on. "It is not in despair that I paint you that picture. I paint it for you in hope—because the nation, seeing and understanding the injustice in it, proposes to paint it out."

Brad shivered in the rain. A hot bath, he thought. That's what I need. A hot bath and a rubdown and a drink before he went to the hospital. Then he thought, wonderingly, I have a son. He remembered Corcoran's words: "He picked some day to be born."

He began unobtrusively to inch toward the steps at the rear of the platform. There would be a mad dash in the rain for the autos as soon as the President wound up his address.

"The test of our progress," he heard, multiplied by all the loudspeakers, "is not whether we add more to the abundance of those who have too much. It is whether we provide enough for those who have too little."

He paused for a backward look at the big-shouldered, ruddy-faced man, standing straight and tall through willpower and borrowed steel so that he could face into the storm that slashed at him, and thought, maybe it isn't such a bad day to be born after all.

Victor Sondheim was two years old when Franklin Roosevelt was sworn in as President of the United States. He has lived through the historical events described in INHERITORS OF THE STORM—though at a distance of more than a decade and a half from the fictional lives of his characters, the Sinclairs.

"It's an odd sensation," he says, "to leaf through an old copy of *Life* or the *Saturday Evening Post,* acquired for research purposes, and realize that I once saw these same evocative pictures and headlines before, as a child, and that they were part of the fabric of growing up during a depression and a war." The 1930s and 1940s, Sondheim believes, are a part of a dream vision shared by all Americans, whether born during those seminal years or decades later. "It is reality and myth mixed together," he says, "the essence of our joined American soul, born of our own experience and the voices that surround us as we grow up."

Victor Sondheim is the pen name of a writer now living in a remote area of rural Maine, who over a period of more than twenty years has written nonfiction and fiction—ranging from spy stories and science fiction to men's adventure stories and historical romances—under a variety of pen names.

Born in New England, Sondheim left home as a teenager, "Determined," he says, "to see something of life and the world." In the ensuing years, Sondheim worked as an editor, reporter, public-relations man, political ghost writer, Washington lobbyist, industrial filmmaker —while writing fiction on and off in his spare hours. He had sold his first story, a gangster yarn, at the age of twenty-two, and went on to try westerns, science fiction, men's adventure stories, and eventually paperback novels. In 1972, Sondheim moved with his wife to Maine, where he had maintained a summer home for some years, to live and write fiction full time. It took Victor Sondheim four years to complete INHERITORS OF THE STORM. He is currently at work on a second volume in the saga of the Sinclair family.